This book is dedicated

to my dad:

Frank Cresswell

1928—2010

Crossings

A Palimpsest

By

Allie Cresswell

palimpsest

/ˈpalɪm(p)sɛst/

noun

1. a manuscript or piece of writing material on which later writing has been superimposed
2. something having usually diverse layers or aspects apparent beneath the surface

CONTENTS

BOOK 1

ACROSS THE BRIDGE

WET FOOTPRINTS ON the bridge. The whorls of the sole—intricate as a fingerprint—are swiftly drying in the brisk April breeze, but it is clear that wet trainers in a large size have crossed the wooden laths of the footbridge.

There are arcs and blotches of drying drips sprayed in carefree, wide-flung trails, dark brown on the lighter brown wood; an artwork of random splatterings.

Somebody has fallen in the river.

The man on the bridge places his own expensively-shod foot next to one of the drying imprints of wet trainer and finds his imagination unexpectedly captured by the circumstances that might have conspired to cause it. His interest has been piqued by the footprints, and caused him to venture onto the bridge. The vision of them—slowly fading, the sad reality of their inexorable evaporation—strikes him forcefully. The very existence of his interest is a surprise—nothing external has aroused even the slightest curiosity for weeks—and has turned him from his normal unvarying track. His feet and his mind experience, momentarily, the thrill of escape.

The bridge was a Millennium project whose doomed object was to unite the disparate communities on its two sides; the Fairways—the small, affluent development built on the peripheries of the golf course—on one side, and the Mere—the social housing clustering around what remains of the town's light industrial premises—on the other. Between the two an unremarkable river meanders, flanked by nettle-infested banks; an impassable, forbidding frontier between hostile territories.

Gingerly—casting a furtive glance around him because it seems a slightly shameful, invasive action—he places his feet onto the prints; walking in another's footsteps, wondering how life might be different from another point of view. From his new vantage point he surveys the landscape: frankly, it is not improved.

On its less salubrious side, the river is immediately bordered by a ragged recreation field; not well-heeled but very well-trodden by dog walkers and the occasional panting jogger and even sometimes by a gang of lads who will kick a disconsolate football around amongst the dog-mess, or perform acrobatics from the cross-bar of the dispirited, graffiti-scratched goal-posts. The dull grass is roughly mown by the council in summertime. The tractor macerates everything in its path, strewing shards of glass and splintered drinks cans and shredded litter across the park. Dangerous psychedelic flowers wink in the sunshine. In wintertime the uneven surface of the field collects pools of standing water that reflect the sorry, leaden skies.

Today the field is peppered with white paper. It drifts in flurries against the goal-posts, sheets gambolling gay as lambs in the spring breeze.

The bridge, now he has ventured onto it, has a pleasing but simple design. It is about six feet across; enough space for two to pass each other without touching. A slight arch makes a fairly graceful leap from one side of the river to the other. The walkway is wooden, boards about six inches wide with spaces between them big enough to trap a lady's high heel but not a dog's paw. The water, glimpsed through the gaps, flickers like a film run too slowly. The timber handrails are smooth and surprisingly warm to the touch, quite wide and sturdy, and below them is a series of narrower rails designed, of course, to prevent a child from falling into the river but in practice inviting them, like a ladder, to clamber up. At each end of the bridge an awkward chicane of narrowly placed stumps and a low barrier—designed to bar horse riders and make cyclists dismount—forces walkers to squeeze sideways or stoop down if they want to cross.

He removes his feet from the wet prints, relinquishing them. The swirls are overlaid now, distorted by the chunky track of his own tread, and the unlikely melding is growing fainter, almost dry. He is no nearer solving their mystery but, like an unexpected opening just discerned beneath overhanging foliage, or a tiny gap between two buildings, it calls to be pursued. The distraction from the obsessive preoccupation with his inner traitor is so refreshing, now he is aware of it—a view over open fields, a blast of sea air—and he is loath to let it go.

He steps up to the side of the bridge and looks up-river; the water is smooth and serene, sliding like innocent syrup towards the edge of the weir right below him. A fallen bough punctures the glossy surface of the flow but it looks as though it has been there for some time. Its forks are bearded with detritus from the winter's high water; leaves and weed and indeterminate mossy fibrous tendrils. There is no sign of disturbance; no discarded clothing, no flattened undergrowth to suggest entry or exit, no wet person drying, no drowned person dying. But when he turns to face downstream his attention is caught by yet more papers—letters?—dozens of sheets, littering the banks on both sides of the stream, caught in the thick undergrowth overhanging the sides of the weir that falls away in three shallow descending steps before plunging into a deep and swirling pool.

To his left the undergrowth is crushed and flattened; the site of entry and, presumably, of exit.

The papers are everywhere; snagged and torn, flapping listlessly, sodden and disintegrating, an abomination of wanton littering enough to make the blood boil, like toilet paper in trees and carrier bags in the hedgerow and supermarket trolleys that find their inexorable way into every watercourse in the land.

Even in his relief he manages to be indignant of the waste and vandalism but his rage is a shadow of its former stature; a pale, querulous bleating in place of incandescent, ranting ire. Outrage—even in its attenuated form—makes him breathe more quickly and his despot accelerates with an appreciable surge. He grips the handrail with both hands, struggling with the causes and the consequences of his annoyance. He surveys the limply flapping debris with helpless wrath and connects them, now, with the fluttering sheets on the playing field on his left.

Then a movement in the thick wall of thorny vegetation to his right catches his eye. Someone is struggling through the defensive planting behind the new houses of the Fairways. Somebody up to no good, doubtless, an opportunist burglar and wilful litterer. An explanation evolves itself in the man's mind. A burglar has gained access to one of the houses, rifled the drawers and brought away correspondence in the hope of finding—what?—Money? The raw material of identity theft? And here he is, lurking in the thicket rummaging through his ill-gotten gains, or preparing to force an entry into another property, and there is only one helpless old man on hand to prevent him.

A kind of blustering courage sweeps over him and, at the same time, the quailing voice of his inner demon beats it back with a bludgeoning cowardice. He wavers. It would be possible—oh, so easy—to walk calmly away off the bridge and up the snicket, shaking his head self-righteously about wilful vandalism, to go home to his quiet bungalow and to be re-entombed into the shrunken remnant of life he has salvaged for himself. He tells himself that he is a sick man, the victim of an attack, a post-operative patient. No one would expect *him* to tackle a violent criminal.

And yet his old persona has not, will not quite, die; he is John Pickering, the Chairman of Pickering's Light Engineering, an honourable life member of the Golf Club, an ex-Rotarian. These qualifications seem laughable in the light of recent revelations, but they remain, obstinately denying their obsolescence.

His heart is hammering, clamouring, like an angry captive, against the bars of his ribcage; he can hear the rush and suck of its tyrannical mechanism in his ears, strident and yet so fickle, while, on the bank, the manic undergrowth thrashes, branches snap and leaves lash against each other. The man lets out a shout, something between a yell and a cry, inarticulate and impotent, yet sudden, something, a remonstrance if a hopeless one, a token. Then from the clinging thorns and tortured branches a boy bursts into view.

The boy is tall, but has not yet started the broadening, thickening process that will change his youthful frame into wide-shouldered manhood; he is perhaps fifteen or sixteen years old. He has curly red hair that he no doubt hates and is teased about, and would have the milk-pale, freckle-spattered complexion that always seems to accompany it except that distress, heat and struggle have made it blush scarlet. On his forehead and one cheek are grazes; the one above his eyebrow is bleeding a little, red on red, and he is sweating. He drags his arm frequently across his eyes as the blood and sweat trickle down. In any case his eyes are red-rimmed. Not because of the blood, he is, or has been, crying. His lips are a bloodless white.

Alarmed by his initial emergence, John—the man—draws craven reassurance from the lad's appearance and demeanour. He displays no aggression and carries no weapon. He utters no obscenity or threat. He does not *look* like a thug. He is wearing, in fact, the uniform of a rather good school, not the local comprehensive, but it is wretched from its dip in the stream and its trip through the bushes. His jumper is soaked, torn and pulled almost off his shoulder, hooked on some grasping branch. He has to yank and haul to get himself free. His tie is badly askew. There is a green, slimy smear across the shoulder of his shirt, which is also dark with river water, and of course the blood and sweat from his forehead make a crusty, grubby smudge on his cuff. His trousers are black, sodden and clinging to his skinny legs. His trainers, inevitably, are oozing brown river water with every struggling step. He is hampered in his battle by the fact that one hand is clutching a sheaf of crumpled and dog-eared papers.

John's shout arrests the attention of the boy as he fights his way out of the undergrowth. He looks, just for a second, hopeful, as though John might prove to be a saviour. He blinks up at the bridge, rubs his cuff across his eyes again and refocuses, before recognition swamps his momentary hope. They regard each other across the gulf of yards and years that separates them. The boy's expression exactly reflects the man's: anger overlaid by fear in alternate layers; anger at the fear, and fear of the anger, the belligerent bewilderment of loss, a sense of livid disorientation. There is a flicker of recognition between them. They know each other, in fact, but the nature of their connection is a barrier rather than an opening, a cause of pain to each, too tender to be broached. The boy lowers his eyes, pushes aside the vegetation and jumps with a careless splash into the ankle-deep water of the fast-moving weir. He moves despondently along the bank, collecting up his ruined coursework. His hands, John notices, are shaking. His own hands, gripping the handrail of the bridge, are trembling too.

MATTHEW, THE BOY, surveys the scene around him with an utter, subterranean despair. Everything is wrong and calls insistently to be put right but he does not know where to begin. Some things are so wrong that they never can be put right and the intrinsic, fundamental wrongness of them is too much to bear.

Looming largest in his landscape of things out of place is himself, squashed here in this small house, constantly knocking into furniture designed for a bigger place, tripping over belongings with no home. Their outdoor boots and shoes—formerly swallowed easily by the hall closet—now clutter the tiny vestibule so that you can hardly open the door. Upstairs in his bedroom his prized computer and music system cannot both be accommodated. He can't open the wardrobe door without it hitting the side of the bed. He lies in bed sometimes and feels panicky and breathless, as though the ceiling and walls are closing in.

He hates coming home to it; it doesn't feel like home. He doesn't belong here. As the crow flies he has travelled perhaps a mile from the nice, quiet neighbourhood across the river. But it feels as though he has crossed continents and been washed up on a foreign, incomprehensible shore.

He has stripped off his sodden uniform and it lies like a drowned, decomposing body in a spreading pool of brown water on the worn kitchen linoleum. He shivers, standing in his underpants in the narrow doorway. His skin is clammy and cold and he thinks perhaps that he is in shock. The clothes need to be put in the washing machine; probably the shirt should be scrubbed with some stuff his mother keeps under the sink before going in the machine. He is sure that the shirt and trousers ought not to go in together but there won't be time for two loads. The jumper needs mending; its threads are unravelling around the tear. If, as in former days, money were no object they would simply buy another. But now the money cannot be spared; that's the whole point. It could not be spared for a new uniform for his horrible new school, for the sake of a term. He has had to continue to wear the uniform of his old school. He had said he did not mind but of course the different uniform has marked him out for unwelcome, aggressive attention. It identifies him as an alien, an enemy from across the bridge, a posh kid from a big house with rich parents. He has been unable to stop himself addressing the teachers deferentially as 'sir' and 'miss', or from involuntarily leaping to his feet every time one of them addresses him, to the amusement and merciless parodying of his classmates. No one wants him on their team for football and he has been repeatedly kicked and pushed around while the teacher's attention has been diverted.

He hauls his mind from the momentary, uncomfortable distraction of this memory. He must *do* something. The jumper still lies on the floor and it is still torn. He knows where his mother's sewing box is but cannot think how he might make the repair at all, let alone make it invisible. The trainers need to be washed and stuffed with newspaper and put on the boiler, he supposes, since they have no tumble drier now ... Then there is his bag; soaking wet. It, and the one dripping text book which, miraculously, remained inside it need somehow to be dried. The other books, pencil case, scientific calculator and his pen-drive are all lost and he can't even begin to think, just now, of what their loss might mean or how they can be replaced, or, even more pressingly, how their disappearance can be explained. And while his mind roves over the desolation before him this is the question that repeats itself most urgently. How is he going to explain it? Since he cannot deal with it, cannot hope to wipe away the multitudinous evidences, how will he explain it?

He had not explained it to the man who had helped him collect the scattered papers. By the time he had gathered what he could from the banks of the river—wading through the water, slipping on the slimy concrete of the weir—and hooked up his bag by its handle with a forked branch, the man had been waiting for him on the bridge with a loosely gathered armful of paper saved from the field. He had proffered them hesitantly, as though offering food to a ravenous tiger. Matt had taken them from him with equal timidity, expecting—knowing the man's reputation as he does—to receive a mauling, at the very least, for criminal damage. But it had not materialised. The man had not waited for the thanks which, belatedly perhaps, Matt had thought to mumble, but had stridden off the bridge with a purposeful step.

Matt wishes he could do the same, just walk away from it; it is, after all, what his father has done. The thought of his father adds a deeper layer of disaster to the mess in front of him and makes more urgent the need to *do* something. He stares helplessly at it all while it clamours to be dealt with. Whatever he tackles first will leave something in grisly evidence. He dithers helplessly between the washing machine and the sewing box and the boiler, knowing it is all hopeless. There isn't enough time and his mother will be home soon.

He turns his anxious attention to the coursework, pages and pages of it, which lies scattered now on the thin, cheap carpet of the pokey living room. Perhaps, after all, that is the thing that will distress her most and ought therefore to take priority. At worst, it is saturated beyond redemption, at best, it is crumpled and dirtied and torn beyond presentation, almost two years' worth of diligent study and careful collation at his previous school. He had taken it in to be looked over by his new subject teacher. It had—not surprisingly, considering the standards of the cloistered and academically brilliant private school—been declared 'exceptionally good'. It had been virtually ready to hand in, but now would all need reprinting, the diagrams would have to be redrawn, the sketches redone: hours of work, its prospect another insurmountable problem that he feels completely unequal to tackling alone. In the old days he and his father would sit in the study after supper and tap away at their computers side by side. His father would glance over now and again and say something encouraging. They would have some conducive music playing quietly in the background. But the sweet memory is bitter to him now, ruined, like the sodden, damaged uniform; contaminated, like the pool of dirty water on the floor and his own skin, pungent from the drying sweat of his distress.

He stands in the restricted doorway between the kitchen and the lounge, looking first one way and then the other. Then there is a crash from the party wall; a plate, probably, thrown in anger. It isn't the first time. Suddenly galvanised, he makes a lunge for the laundry, skids on the wet floor and stubs his bare toe on the kitchen chair. It doesn't hurt very much, but it is enough, and he begins to cry.

But presently he gathers himself. And when Rosie gets in from work the little table in the kitchen is set for tea, the washing machine is churning rhythmically and the kitchen floor has been swept and mopped. Matt's trainers, scrubbed, she supposes, after a muddy football match, are drying on the boiler. Matt himself is in the shower. Of the sodden coursework there is no sign at all.

EVERY TIME JOHN—the man on the bridge—gets back to the Close, he wonders, in those few moments before his house comes into view, whether, today, there will be a visitor: someone from work, a member of the golf club, come to see how he's getting along. He imagines seeing a car in the drive, a genial handshake, ushering his guest inside and making tea or pouring whisky.

But there never is.

Jack Perry, temporary MD of Pickering's Light Engineering, came once, to ask about moving a lad from the drawing office to the sales team. He refused a perfunctory invitation to go in, standing on the wide door step with nervous eyes, passing his car keys from one to the other of his restless hands. At the time John had thought nothing of it. It was the habitual demeanour of his employees, something he rather prided himself on—his unchallenged authority, their automatic deference. He had cultivated a capacity for fulmination.

Jack has been works manager for ten years, promoted from the shop floor. He has a thorough understanding of the production processes but John has always been exasperated by Jack's stumbling, halting way with words, and has frequently criticised his lack of authority over the men. He had criticised him *then*, loudly and in scathing language, for bothering a man only just home from hospital with such a pathetic question, and vocalised his doubt that Jack was up to the job. Indeed he would never have been John's first choice to step in as MD if Richard, sales manager, had still been with the company. But Richard had gone by then, sacked under an enormous, ugly cloud riven with disappointment and betrayal.

John pulls himself up short; he mustn't go there. The stress of it was too much at the time and the additional work it had necessitated had definitely been a contributory factor. Also, now, he feels a terrible disquiet over the way he handled the affair. Already there is heaviness in his chest, the flutter of fretful wings.

He rounds the corner and of course there is no car. In explanation, he can almost hear his voice reverberating round the Close haranguing poor Jack, see the shrinking embarrassment of the man, the slight tremor of the trouser leg. He shrivels with shame at the remembrance of it and the discomfort of the sensation—peevish ignominy—is so powerful that he is almost hounded by it along the pavement to his porch. He has his key in his hand. The cloistered serenity within is almost palpable to him; it calls, like a Siren.

John opens his door. A cooling billow of quietude meets him and envelops him in the safe amniotic air of home. He steps inside and shuts the door, shutting out the ghost of former iniquity. There is a welcome douse of utter silence that washes over his feverishness. He stands in the hall for a while rinsing himself in its balm. The stresses of the afternoon begin to subside; the boy, the papers, uncomfortable recollections. They cannot get him here.

He had not realised, until he returned from the cacophonous ward, how noisy an empty house can be. He had longed for silence; true, deadpan noiselessness that is not so much the absence of sound but has its own thick, soft, comforting presence. Like darkness you feel you could cut, or cold so brittle it cracks, real silence fills up a vacuum with itself and it is pervading and luxurious, like thick black velvet. He needed silence to concentrate on the valves, the spasms and rhythms, the expansions and contractions and regular cyclical renewals of his inner apparatus. He needed total concentration, pin-perfect poise to hear the smooth, liquid flow of blood through his heart and lungs and brain. He had turned every sense inwards; his eyes trained on the throb of blue cord at his wrist and the careful rise and fall of his chest, his ears tuned to the beat and surge of his pulse, his sense of touch monitoring the flop and lurch of his heart. Even his taste buds were on the alert for that metallic flavour of fear.

Distractions were everywhere; dripping taps and ticking clocks, creaking central heating pipes, the billow and breathe of curtains beside an open window, the sigh of air through the open window itself. The diatribe of the cleaning woman had been endless as she moaned about her health and her difficult daughters. When he had switched everything off and cancelled the cleaning woman, for the time being, there were outdoor noises that he couldn't control: birds, aeroplanes overhead, the susurration of breeze through grass and leaves, the plash of water in his own little pond and the hum of the electric pump.

He had found, at last, a place in an inner vestibule between the hall and the cloakroom and the kitchen, a windowless place where good timber doors excluded these exterior distractions. He had placed his chair and a low table there, with his blood pressure monitor and medications, and seated himself in his sanctum. Only by the sheer power of his will could he subjugate his wayward mechanics and live on. He found even the rasp of his slipper against the fibres of the carpet, the slight sigh as his sleeve shifted on the arm of the chair, the whispered friction of his very skin against itself a frustrating diversion. If he had to eat, he did it quickly, embarrassed and rather disgusted by the slurping and squishing, crunching and grinding in his mouth and the noisy gulp of his swallow. Hour after hour he sat completely still, balancing his breathing, controlling the rising tides of anxiety, and watched over his little traitor like a jealous gaoler.

Hour after hour. Day after day. Trying to regain the control he had always taken for granted. Struggling, the while, to come to terms with what it really means to have, finally, no power at all.

Hour after hour. Day after day. And nobody had come.

Now he slips off his outdoor shoes and places them neatly on the mat. He draws a heavy curtain across the door. He has already stuffed the letter box with newspaper and taped a sign, 'Invalid within, use box for post and news' on the door, with an arrow indicating a sturdy lidded box on the porch. His chair awaits him and he sinks into it, metaphorically pulling the peaceful blanket of silence around his shoulders. He closes his eyes and, gently taking one wrist between the fingers and thumb of the other hand, he begins to count.

ROSIE GIVES THE door of Matt's bedroom a courteous knock before pushing it open. Since he started bolting the bathroom door she has afforded him certain privacies. He has reached the age, she considers, at which he should not have to be subjected to the indignity of inspection or constant observation, and he clearly feels he can be trusted, now, to handle some things himself. At the same time she has felt uneasy, all too aware of troubled undercurrents that call for investigation but that she has left—in deference to him, and in the absence of her husband— unplumbed.

He looks up at her entrance, startled. His room is strewn with coursework but she doesn't, just then, pay attention to it. She has the telephone in her hand.

'Dad wants a word.' She holds the receiver out to him. He shakes his head and shrinks back from it. She extends her arm a little more, a pleading gesture, but he shakes his head more vehemently.

'No.'

She sighs and puts the telephone back to her ear. 'No, he doesn't want to, Richard. Yes, maybe.' She rings off without saying goodbye and mother and son regard each other across the tiny room.

'He's very unhappy that you won't speak to him, Matt.'

'He should have thought of that before.'

'If *I* can, why can't you?'

'I don't know how you can.'

'Because it isn't all about *me*.'

21

It is evening and Matt has closed the curtains across his small window. The breeze earlier has driven grey clouds across the sky bringing a brief, saturating downpour. A sagging gutter above the window is pouring water onto the sill and the heavy splash of it overlays the distant sound of a baby crying and the faint murmur of the neighbour's television, both of which would be far more intrusive if not for the rain. Rosie looks at her son as he squats uncomfortably on the small area of floor, and thinks again that she should have let him have the larger of the two rooms. His room smells of sweaty boy, a fetid hormonal aroma normal for a boy of his age, emanated irrespective of hygiene habits. There are socks and underpants and a pair of pyjama bottoms on the end of the bed, which is roughly made, and covered in paper. The paper, on close inspection, is in a sorry state.

'What's this?'

She knows her son too well to mistake the sudden duck of his head and evasive eyes. She takes another step into the room and leans over the bed, scanning the sheets. 'Geography coursework?'

'Yes.' Matt's voice is tight, like a closed door, almost challenging, a characteristic she is noticing frequently these days.

Rosie reaches out a hand and touches the nearest sheet. 'It's damp. What happened to it?'

Matt's head is right down, and beyond the belligerence Rosie sees a younger boy coming to her to confess that he has broken something or been told off at school. On each occasion he will have suffered agonies before actually coming to own up, heaping, probably, far more punishment on himself than she was ever likely to mete out. His biggest fear always was that she would tell his daddy, not because he was afraid of his father but only because he would die rather than disappoint him.

'Matt?'

'I was messing about by the river on my way home. I slipped and fell in. Everything in my bag got soaked. My clothes did too. And my jumper's torn.' It all spills out in a torrent and Matt experiences a kind of relief in expelling something bad that has been eating away at him all evening. It isn't the truth but in essentials the facts are the same.

'Oh Matthew, not again!' Rosie snaps, in spite of herself. There has been a succession of similar incidents since he changed schools. *'That's how you cut your face?'*

'Yes.'

'Not during Games.' It is a statement.

'No.'

'Mmm.' Rosie considers the issues. First, the immediate ones: the lie about the cuts on his face, the silly carelessness by the river, the damaged uniform, the ruined coursework. Then, the underlying ones: Matt's new friends and their irresponsible, thoughtless behaviour that he seems gradually to be adopting, this awful little house, their changed financial circumstances. And finally the most fundamental one of all: the precipitous fall of Matt's father from the lofty and impossible pedestal he had been placed upon, his shocking and irrecoverable fall from grace. She takes a deep breath and tackles the most apparent consequence of the escapade. 'Well it's in a fine mess isn't it?' she says, picking up one or two pages and turning them over.

'Yes. I'll have to reprint it. I've got it all on my computer.' Matt looks up at her now that he can focus on positives and solutions. His face in the dim light is so like his father's; large eyes thickly fringed with pale lashes, wide mouth, good, even teeth and the small crease between his brows suggesting earnestness and concern. The only feature recognisably hers is his dimple. 'I was just looking to see which maps I'd have to redo.' He indicates a pile of dog-eared papers at his side. 'There are quite a few,' he admits.

'Let me see.' He passes her the sheets and she leafs gingerly through them; maps, sketches, diagrams, all painstakingly drawn and labelled. Some are virtually illegible. 'You've given yourself a lot of work,' she observes.

'I know! You don't think I'm exactly happy about it, do you?' Matt asks sharply. His prickliness convinces Rosie that there is more to this than he is telling.

'*I'm* not very happy about the ream of paper and the new ink cartridge I'll have to buy, or the new school pullover.'

His head goes down again. 'No, I know. Don't go on, Mum. I've told you I'll re-do it.'

'Did you hurt yourself?'

Matt shakes his head.

'All right,' she sighs. 'Where's the pullover?'

'In the washer.'

Rosie takes hold of the door handle and edges from the room. 'I'll get the paper and ink tomorrow Matt,' she says.

'Thanks,' he mutters, barely audible, and adds, 'there were other things …'

She groans. 'You'd better make a list. I think you'd better stay home on Saturday and get started on all of this.'

'You're grounding me?' He looks up again, automatic outrage suffusing his face.

'I'm just suggesting, although I'd be interested to hear your reasons why I shouldn't,' Rosie says quickly. 'But Matt, keep away from the river from now on.'

'How do you suggest I get home?'

She does not like his tone, indicative, she knows, of a festering but deeply guarded anger, but she decides to ignore it. 'You know what I mean.'

Suddenly he relents. His hostility evaporates. 'Yes Mum.'

Later that night, in bed, Matt listens to the sounds of his mother locking up the house and going to bed. Security was always his father's job, as, indeed, was everything important and significant; decisions about holidays, choice of furniture and cars, all things financial. They had relied on him and he has betrayed their trust. The depths of their pecuniary crisis had come as a surprise to his mum. There was no money, she had explained to him, incredulously. The value of the house had gone down and the mortgage was large. Once the building society had been repaid there was hardly anything left. His father had lost his job at Pickering's and although he had found another it didn't pay so well. He gave them what he could but—and here she had struck the nub of it—he had two families to support now. School fees certainly couldn't be afforded. The car, too, would have to go. Thankfully she could increase her hours at Bridge House. But she spoke all these things with a kind of distance in her voice, as though speaking of somebody else, another woman's situation with which she was sympathetic but personally uninvolved.

Indeed, after that initial outpouring the day the news had broken, she has shown little emotion, but accommodated herself to their new situation with sad resignation; it is almost as though she had been expecting it.

He listens to her in the bathroom, the splash of water in the basin and the rasp of her toothbrush, the gentle flop of the laundry basket lid. At one time she had nightly luxuriated in a deep hot bath, with expensive oils and softly glowing candles. Now the hot water, the oils and the candles are unaffordable and in any case the tiny bathroom with its plain tiles and unreliable heater is no place to linger. He hears the bathroom door open and the light being switched off. Her bedroom door closes gently and he hears the creak of the bed. He wonders how she can face each day; the old people at the home, the long bus ride there and back, the careful, economical shopping, the table set only for two, the empty bed.

He hasn't told anyone what happened that day, but the memory of it haunts him. He had come home from school. It had been a good day; in fact it had been better than good. He had scored twice in football, it had been his favourite chicken curry for lunch and afterwards there had been a meeting about the skiing trip with a video of the hotel and the slopes. The maths teacher had told him that he should definitely consider taking maths at A level. Casey O'Brien had told him that the new girl, Jilly Shillingworth, liked him and wanted him to ask her to the end of year prom. Best of all the new season of Lost was starting on Sky that night. Matt and his dad had watched them all; it was one of the many things that they did together.

He had been surprised, as he had turned into their driveway, to see his dad's car. He didn't normally get home until well after seven or, lately, even later. Often he stayed away over-night, visiting new customers further and further afield, he had said. His mum, recently, had started a little job, working part time at an old folks' home. Matt had not enquired and nor had he been told the reason for this. He had assumed that his mum was bored at home on her own. Sometimes when he got home the house was empty, but he didn't mind that. There was always food, the TV, his computer. But that day both cars were on the wide drive and Matt had let himself in with his key, slung his bag down in the hall, kicked off his shoes and padded through to the kitchen.

His mum had been propped in the right-angle of the worktop, with her back to the glass display cabinets. It was close to the kettle and her radio, a place she often stood while she was making tea, or while she paused in some task to listen to a news item or the answer to a quiz question. But the radio was silent today and his mother's face, alone, made Matt skid to a halt on the polished floor. It was the face of someone who has been punched in the stomach; she looked winded, crumpled and folding in on herself. Her eyes were dull, exactly as though some inner light had been extinguished. She seemed literally to have shrunk in size and as he watched she sagged perceptibly like an inflatable whose stopper has been removed. Matt could see that her hands gripped the counter top as a means of supporting her; they were blue-white with the effort. For a second it was as if the earth literally trembled under his feet. Only a death, he thought, could have induced such a powerful reaction. Death, or cancer, perhaps. He had crossed the slate tiled floor to her and held her, as much to gain some shred of reassurance for himself as to assist her. It was clear that their family had been struck by a thunderbolt of enormous magnitude and he was afraid.

It wasn't until he had crossed the kitchen and wedged himself into the corner with his mother that he could really see his dad. He was seated at the round breakfast table behind the door. He, too, looked broken. He had his head in his hands and was crying, silent sobs that shook his shoulders. Matt had never seen his father cry before. It was the most shocking thing. He held his face in his hands but lifted it now and again in an effort to speak. His eyes begged and pleaded. His face was wet and smeared, his nose running, when he opened his mouth thick strings of saliva seemed to tie his tongue so that nothing comprehensible could be made of the sounds that came out. They were just moans and cries of abject misery caused by something so terrible, so earth-shatteringly catastrophic, that there were no words to describe it.

Matt was sure, then, that one of his parents was dying.

Afterwards, Matt asked himself what would have happened if he had seen his dad first that day instead of his mum. If, instead of going to her and trying to support her he had gone instead to his dad, and knelt down by his chair, and hugged him. Would he perhaps have been as moved by *his* obvious distress as he was by hers? Would *his* tears have melted his heart, as hers did? Would he have been more sympathetic, more likely to forgive, if, rather than his mother's choked voice sobbing into his shoulder whispering, 'Your dad is leaving us, Matthew. He's in love with someone else, and he's lost his job, and he's leaving', he had heard *first* what he was later to hear repeated a hundred times, 'I'm so sorry, son, please forgive me. I can't help it, I can't help it. I'm so sorry, please try to understand.'

The bonds between them had always been so strong. He had always been what his mother and father both had proudly declared to be 'a dad's lad', since the time, outside his remembering but gently and tearfully explained to him on its anniversary for a few years after it, that his baby sister had died, and it made his mummy feel very sad, and she

27

needed a little time alone, while Matthew and Daddy looked after each other. That had been the start of it, and Matt couldn't remember a time when he and his dad had not been best mates, going to the football together, building the model railway in the attic, having bike rides along the canal towpaths, watching their favourite TV programmes. Soon after they had moved into the big new house they had set up the study, wired up their computers and gaming consoles and surround sound system in there, and spent hours playing Age of Empires while his mother had sat alone in the lounge at the back of the house doing cross-stitch and what he and his dad laughingly decried as 'girl stuff.'

His mother, in fact, apart from the necessaries of food and transport and in times of illness, had been peripheral to their world, not just Matt's, but to his dad's as well. He realises it now, that distance between them. It makes him feel more responsible. She, in her separate world, might not have seen the signs, but surely Matt, as close to his dad as he was—or thought he had been—should have done. How could he have been so blind?

Perhaps his mother's charms had been for some time insufficient to hold his father. What had made him stay as long as he had? The obvious answer sits uncomfortably because it leads him inexorably to the conclusion that his own qualities as a son have become in some way inadequate, precipitating his father's defection. Where did he go wrong?

It makes him doubt everything; what he thought was so perfect has turned out to be catastrophically flawed. He includes himself in this. He has been blinkered and naive. Self-doubt is new and unpleasant.

It is this burning sense of having been a blind fool that eats Matt alive but it is not the most caustic source of his misery. His jealousy over the new boy in his dad's life is like acid. In comparison his father's other sins—his lack of adequate provision, imposing so many changes for the worse; his emergence as a sexual entity; even the various monetary scams—pale into insignificance.

Mr Pickering had not considered them insignificant of course. He had sacked dad for them. The man on the bridge. Matt had recognised him at once. Dad hadn't liked him, much. According to him, Mr Pickering is a bully.

Matt shifts in his bed. His room is eerily lit from outside by the caustic orange glow of a street light. The rain has stopped, now, and he can hear the distant sounds of traffic and—he almost convinces himself—the rush of the river.

JOHN PICKERING DREAMS of the river and the documents. The river is made of documents, a jostling inexorable surge like an advancing glacier, scouring the landscape. He is ankle-, and then knee-deep in the floe. Looking up into the grey sky it is thick with falling pages, like ash from an incinerator, they float against his face. Somehow he is transported upwards, as though as light and insubstantial, as translucent as a single page bearing a meagre life-story. He is carried on the air current up into the maelstrom, and is able to see through the swirling melee to the source of the papery blizzard. The wind is cruel and cold, and makes his eyes stream, and fills up his ears with its wildness. Across the landscape—the sports field, the untidy sprawl of the Mere, the scrubby woodland—he spies his factory unit. Sheets are spewing from its windows, disgorged like mechanical vomit by the lathes and presses, churned out in reams by the printers and the fax machine, flying from open filing cabinets in flapping volleys. Impossibly, the leaves foam forth in endless gouts, filling the skies, the land. He recognises his company logo and typestyle. Letters and faxes, memos and reminders, enquiries, delivery notes, invoices, estimates and job sheets, the paper-trail of his business, his life; impersonal and meaningless.

The levels are rising. Soon he is up to his armpits and he finds he cannot move his legs. The paper is damp, wet, sodden into mush, glutinous and disintegrating into thick grey fibrous glue. He is aware of pressure from behind, the flow of the river pressing him and he knows he will be swamped. He hasn't the strength to get out. Then he sees the boy leaning in from the bank, a forked stick held out to him. The boy is shouting but his voice is lost beneath the roar of the wind and the manic flap of the paper and a deeper, unearthly, subterranean creak of ancient ice-floe. The boy begins to wave the stick back and forth, and its rhythmic swish is the loudest noise in his ears, overlaying everything else. With every pass the branch comes nearer and John is stretching with all his might towards it. Then, with a start, he is awake, sitting upright in his darkened bedroom, his arms out stiffly in front of him, the sheets twisted around his lower body and damp with sweat, his heart leaping and listing like a wild thing in his chest and blood pumping in his ears. He lunges for his bedside cabinet, sending bottles of tablets flying, looking for his angina spray.

Later, he is calmer. He makes tea—weak, decaffeinated—and sips it as he stands by the large window of his lounge. It has been raining heavily; the patio is wet and shines dully in the late moonlight. Grey banks of cloud scurry across the sky. His garden is grey in the almost-dawn, kept neat by a firm of maintenance people, the spectral outlines of clipped conifers stand like sentries defending his isolation. The room behind him is a testimony to their efficacy. It is bland, empty and as impersonal as a hotel foyer in the half light. The furniture, now, seems chosen for its anonymity; plain, square leather suite, a low glass coffee table on a broad expanse of neutral carpet, massive marble fireplace where no fire has ever burned. On the long wall there is a modern cocktail cabinet and an expensive music system. A state-of-the-art home cinema takes up one corner. Everything is covered in a bloom of grey dust, the cleaning woman's absence making itself felt. Apart from the dust the room is pristine. There are no scratches or blemishes on the furniture to denote history, no old wine stain on the carpet to remind him of a jolly party or intimate dinner. In fact John has never entertained guests here. The corniced ceiling has never rung with the laughter of jocular company. He doubts the chairs have ever been sat upon more than three or four times and only then to serve the purpose of some business meeting or other. The room is cold; literally and metaphorically, it has a desolate and empty air and smells of vacancy. It is void of personal mementoes. There are no nick-knacks, no photographs of gap-toothed children or memorable vistas over blue, misty hills. There is no scattering of personal belongings; a book half-read, a discarded magazine, a pullover draped over the back of the

31

chair. It is in fact, he sighs, as he watches it draw into focus in the brightening dawn, a room that describes exactly his empty, unused life.

It is not, he considers, grimly, that he has had a boring life. On the contrary it has been full—too full at times—but of blinkered, self-absorbed busyness. He and his brother had taken on the workshop from their father. It had been just that, in those days, an unpretentious but nevertheless busy little foundry where they had fabricated or mended anything metal. The Pickerings had been blacksmiths for generations but the increasing mechanisation of everything—industry, farming, transport—had opened up new opportunities. Both lads had studied engineering at night-school and picked things up as they had gone along. Brian had always had more of a flair for the fabrication side of things while John had found that his no-nonsense style and meticulous eye for detail suited him to organisation and overseeing. Things had mushroomed and by the late 50s his father would not have recognised the business, had he lived. They were bringing in orders from the mining industry, ship-building and civil engineering projects. In the 60s they had moved to the Mere, into a purpose built industrial unit, and taken on more employees. The two brothers, from humble beginnings, suddenly had money. The company provided them with flashy executive cars and funded travel abroad; they ate out a great deal, 'entertaining', and put everything down to expenses. They began to socialise with professional types. Brian had joined the Masons, John the golf club. They both enjoyed being recognised by *maitres d'* and cutting a dash at high profile sporting events. The Pickering brothers. *That,* he recognises, was the beginning of it. A sense of personal importance had intoxicated him; a strong cocktail on an empty stomach, engorging his ego, breeding arrogance of the most insufferable kind and a disproportionately inflated sense of personal infallibility. He had revelled in it; *being* somebody.

Brian and Glynnis had moved house, to one of the exclusive villages outside town. In the 70s they had started taking skiing trips to St Moritz with their new friends, had bought a villa in Spain and a speed-boat. But by the late 70s and into the 80s the halcyon days had passed their zenith. Engineering parts could be mass-produced more cheaply—and more precisely, with computer technology—abroad. Pickering's retrenched and went back to its original niche, fabricating individual, specialist parts. Only the most skilled welders and machinists were kept on.

Brian did not live to see it. A road accident on a deserted stretch of highway in remote Spain killed him and Glynnis instantly. The trailer carrying the speed-boat had jack-knifed and sent them down a stony ravine. Soon afterwards their aged mother also died. John was left entirely alone.

It was not until Brian died that John realised how much he had relied upon his brother and his wife to supply a social perspective to his life. They had invited him regularly to their house and introduced him to single women with whom he had attempted but always, somehow, failed to establish a relationship that went beyond two or three evenings at restaurants and, if he was insistent enough, a night in bed. With Brian gone he found that his social interactions consisted solely of business lunches and golf, but even at the golf club his energies were invariably channelled into administration. Once he'd ousted most of the older officers he'd really shaken up the management committee and in a one-man war of attrition he'd been successful in up-rooting the bar steward who had become far too comfortably ensconced and almost certainly had his hand in the till. But despite being Treasurer and Chair he was never invited to be Captain, a role requiring personal qualities of easy good humour and careful tactfulness. He joined the Rotary and threw himself into a number of fund-raising events but found the crowd to be, on the whole, frivolous and infuriatingly cliquey. It transpired that on several occasions his invitation to a party had mysteriously gone missing or that a purported aberration on his answering machine had meant he had been left out of a weekend jaunt.

Work has occupied much of his time. It has been a ceaseless drive to grow the business, increase productivity, cut overheads and keep the workforce in check. He has had to be tenacious, hardnosed, brutal even, perhaps, at times, to get what he wanted. He has had little time and no patience at all for things of the heart. His heart, indeed, has remained touched.

His heart. His heart.

He places his hand over it now. It is meek, like a rapacious lion caught slumbering. Deceptively innocuous.

It is fully light now. It will be a pleasant day. The heavy cloud has dissipated leaving only a high, thin brush-stroke of transparent white. There is a breeze and the air is bright with spring. The hours yawn away interminably before him.

He has been ambitious and driven but the things desired have been material and psychological, not emotional. The only object of his heart has been himself which, he knows now, is no object at all. He has never been drawn, never yearned, never ached for another. His heart has remained cold, like a harvested organ in aspic. Untouched, like the chairs and table here in the lounge. Unused, like the crystal in the cocktail cabinet. Too little exercised, it had filled with the sludge of a rich diet and atrophied. It had never contracted at the sight of a face or the sound of a voice, never fluttered in nervous anticipation, never bloomed like a flower, with love.

This is the second fact that his heart attack has brought into unflattering review and with which he has had to come uncomfortably to terms. Not only can he not, ultimately, trust it to sustain his life but he has not, meantime, properly exercised its emotional capacity at all. He can only look back aghast at the years of cantankerous narcissism that have alienated anyone who might have been a friend. For the final truth that has emerged from the crucible of his heart attack and the many solitary hours since is that he is essentially friendless. He has received no cards or visits apart from that one from Jack Perry—a visit in all probability and for good reason, made with every reluctance. He isn't liked. He has had to recognise the unpalatable fact that while, in business, single-minded tenacity is an invaluable tool for success, in private life it is abrasive and repellent. A loud voice invites no confidences, bad temper no confessions. Too often he has achieved some distant goal over insuperable odds without pausing to look over his shoulder at the casualties strewn in his wake. Nobody could doubt his efficiency and success, even had they dared, (they had never dared), but the cost in personal relationships has been incalculable. He has been archly dismissive of the ideas of others, irascible, intolerant. He sees himself now—and the vision is every bit as distressing and hard to come to terms with as his mutinous heart—as an arrogant, cold-hearted, self-important bastard, and nothing brings it home to him with more clarity or causes him more remorse than his final dealings with Richard.

He had been able to tell, the moment he opened the door, that something was dreadfully wrong. The man was blanched; his red hair a lurid contrast to his bloodless face. He held his hands together in front of him, a gesture designed to prevent them from shaking but resulting in a semi-imploring attitude. The contrast to Richard's normal bearing could not have been more marked; usually he exuded confidence. Though not an especially tall man he held himself well, radiating energy, made, somehow, a presence. He had an open, attractive expression, lively eyes and a quick mind. He had been a valuable employee, prepared to travel far and wide to generate sales, good at identifying opportunities and heading off problems. Now he stepped into John's hallway like a whipped dog. He could barely speak. John had led him into the office and motioned him towards a chair.

For a while he had been unable to make any sense of it. Richard had spoken in halting sentences, stopping and starting, breathing in gasps as though his chest was being crushed, breaking down from time to time in hard, violent sobs, but he began after a time to piece things together.

There were debts; a huge mortgage, credit cards, school fees. Even though his wife had gone back to work part-time, the situation was getting worse every month. Like everyone, Richard had believed property to be solid. Property prices had escalated and he had always been confident that the value of his house would exceed any debts. But now there was recession and he was in negative equity.

In a panic he had done some shadowy deals with clients, doing some business on his own account for cash which, he knew, was dishonest as well as disloyal, and anyway could never have redressed the financial imbalances. It had all gone wrong. A client was very angry and threatening to blow the whistle. It would have repercussions for him but might also reflect on Pickering's.

He had even, he confessed, spitting the words out, as though bitter as gall, been cheating his expenses.

'I know you would have found out eventually,' he said, his voice tight and cracking, 'but even if not, *I* know about it, and I just can't live with it.'

But worse—more pressing at least—even than any of that, was his relationship with Jasmine, Pickering's telephonist and receptionist.

'Jasmine?' John had struggled to place her momentarily; he tended not to take much notice of the junior functionaries, but then he made the connection. She was a nice enough young woman, he supposed; not particularly well educated but very bright, a single mother with two small children. She had a past. Well, if Richard had been getting his leg over and things had turned awkward that was his own look out ...

Richard's face, now, from emotion, was scarlet. Suddenly he got up from the chair and paced restlessly across the room. 'She's ... just ...' he groped for the right word, '... just *amazing*. She, I mean, herself is, but also, the effect she's had on me, on my life. I mean ...'

'You mean she's good in bed?'

'It isn't just sex,' Richard almost shouted. It had taken John aback. He wasn't used to people raising their voices at him.

But Richard was too wrapped up in trying to explain. 'It's *so* much more ...' he stalled again. His hand moved back and forwards between his chest and a space an arm's length in front of him, denoting relation, connection. He sat down again abruptly, moving his head from side to side as though looking for some physical clue or image in the room that would help him to explain. Finding nothing, he sighed, gathering himself.

'She's just … we're just …' he said. He looked intently at John, trying to communicate what words were clearly inadequate to describe, but discerning also that he was using, anyway, a language which, to his boss, was unintelligible.

'I have never felt …' he tried again, speaking slowly, with enormous emphasis, his hand now clawing at his heart, 'never *felt* so *deeply*, so *strongly* …' His face creased into a grimace implying extreme emotion, before clearing suddenly. He held his hand open-palmed out to John, as though offering a gift. 'It's just love,' he said.

It is a word, for John, with no resonance at all.

MATTHEW ALSO DREAMS, or perhaps just remembers—through the anxious, disjointed filter of half-sleep—the incident by the river.

He waited until last to get off the bus. From the bus stop the route to the Mere led through the meandering pathways of the Fairways. He could not get to his new home without passing the old one; talk about rubbing it in! He dawdled while the crowd ahead of him surged along the pavement and into the Fairways. He always *tried* to put some distance between himself and them.

The pathways through the Fairways snaked between the high fences of the gardens with sudden twists and tortured turns awkwardly accommodated between the plots. Sometimes it was hard to orientate yourself especially while being pursued. In places the paths were overhung by foliage that could conceal a skulking school-boy. In the winter months, when it was dark early, the paths were inadequately lit; it was a favourite game with some of the Mere kids to throw stones at the ornate, pretentious street lamps. The high fences meant that whatever went on along the pathways was hidden from view and since starting at the new school after the February half term Matt had been ambushed and roughed up on a few occasions. His provenance, his accent, his red hair all marked him out as a target.

It had started with some high spirited pushing and shoving. On a couple of occasions his PE kit had been hurled over the fence into a garden; one trainer had lodged irretrievably high in an old tree. That had annoyed his mum. He had been 'happy slapped' and his shocked, start-eyed face had appeared on the internet. His iPod had been taken and only with difficulty recovered—disappointingly scratched—from a rockery. The householder had come to her front door and harangued him as he tried, with the minimum of damage, to find it amongst the alpines. This had made his tormentors laugh more than ever. He had tried to establish some kind of reciprocal relationship with the lads, returning their oafish banter, making out that it was all innocuous, laddish, behaviour that did not bother him, giving, as his dad would have advised him, as good as he got. But the fact was that the boys did intimidate him and something in the tone of his voice or the look on his face told them so.

There were four of them; two from his own year, one from the year below and the last a younger brother, rather an innocent hanger-on but whose shrill, boyish enjoyment of the high jinks seemed to egg on the older boys. All, of course, were Mere boys born and bred. Spencer, the ring-leader, was half a head taller than Matt and much broader shouldered. He had close cropped mousey hair and a stud through his eyebrow that the games master made him cover over with a plaster. His teeth were poor but apart from that he was attractive, with large, heavy-browed eyes balanced by a broad jaw. Spencer rarely engaged in contact himself but influenced and guided the others. He was an authoritative, charismatic character, laughed loudly, always had a plan and was confident in carrying it out. He considered himself unassailable, a confidence stemming from the possession of a notorious older brother, Maxwell, infamous on the Mere and beyond, who drove a noisy, much-modified, highly-tuned car that ought to have been way beyond his means. Maxwell was known for criminal involvement and a vicious temper. Spencer had soon learned that the mention of Maxwell's name, the suggestion that he might, 'Tell Maxwell' or that, 'Maxwell might have something to say,' would usually be enough to get him what he wanted.

Clark, Spencer's younger brother, was an appendage unwillingly taken on at the insistence of their redoubtable mother. Spencer must always 'watch' his brother, 'take' or 'collect' his brother and 'bring him home at a reasonable time'. Clark, her youngest, was her favourite, still having, at thirteen, the child-like charm and innocence that Maxwell and Spencer had long since left behind. She was a slave to all her boys, working long hours at the ice cream factory, hurrying home to cook food and keep house before, some nights, working again stacking supermarket shelves. She berated them for getting into trouble but loved them with all her heart. It was cruelly rumoured that she had named her sons for their various paternities. No fathers now were in evidence. Clark took a child-like thrill in the mischievous exploits of Spencer and his friends. He seemed to have no moral discernment or curiosity, did as he was told, accepted any explanation, questioning nothing.

The other two boys were comically un-like, as though Spencer had held auditions and chosen the two most ridiculous and anomalous side-kicks he could find. Mike Mole was rather a lumbering character, larger than life, much the biggest of all the boys in every way. He was perhaps a little slow, young for his years, more Clark's contemporary than Spencer's, but he was reliable, making up in physical presence what he lacked in mental capacity. He was easy-going, a ponderous follower of others, neither attractive nor ugly but with a round, bland, moon-like face. He was strong and biddable. His association with Spencer stemmed mainly from his willingness to oblige; he would affably crush or restrain anyone at Spencer's request. He was the only child of an older couple. His arrival had surprised them and they had continued to be astonished and rather awed by him since. Mrs Mole laundered his clothes with care—a herculean task, he was always spilling drinks and dropping food down himself—polished his shoes, cooked his meals and made his bed. Mr Mole, a taxi driver, spoiled him with too many sweets and often deferred to him in the matter of the remote control. They still thought of their son as being a child; according to them he 'played out' with Spencer and the others. They would have been shocked and dismayed at the suggestion that their son might be bullying a new boy in the neighbourhood. 'Not our Michael,' they would have said, 'he's only a baby!'

The other boy could not have been more different. His nickname— Skinner—was doubly apt. He was small and painfully emaciated, with a thin, narrow face, close-set eyes and a sharp nose so fleshless that in winter it was almost transparent. His complexion was poor, acned, made worse by his nervous habit of squeezing and picking; it was already badly scarred. He kept his hair very short, like a GI, revealing a persistent boil in the nape of his neck that alternately bled and wept on the collars of his grey, grimy clothing. He was quiet, but his sharp, darting eyes were everywhere while his small teeth gnawed at his filthy finger nails. He was moody and brooding and damaged almost beyond repair. A year older than Spencer, but very much in his thrall, he should already have finished school, but had been held back a year. Skinner shared one of the flats by the river with his father, his mother having fled the previous year. The two lived in very uneasy community. Skinner's dad didn't work, but drank. Food was intermittent, household hygiene very piecemeal.

That day the paths had been clear; only a few skittering crisp packets evidence of the recent transit of teenagers. Matt had kept his head down and walked as boldly as he could through the twisting by-ways.

It was two weeks into the new term and both had passed without incident. Perhaps they had lost interest in him, he thought. There were only another four or so weeks to go before study-leave began; then he would not need to go into school at all apart from for exams, at the end of May and in June. But even while buoying himself up with this encouragement he had clasped his bag closer to him. It was cumbersome, the geography coursework in its lever-arch file weighing heavy as doom.

They had been waiting by the bridge. Matt saw them from half way down the snicket and his step faltered. He did consider turning tail and running for it, but something kept him going; courage, or a resigned fatalism.

Clark and Mike were leaning over the parapet of the bridge looking into the water. Spencer sat astride one of the low barriers at the far end. Skinner lurked behind him. The field beyond was empty; the gaggle of Mere school kids had disappeared up the road past some lop-sided garages. A noisy breeze rifled the leaves on the trees and set the slender nettle fronds on the banks of the river swaying, pale green and deceptively soft.

Matt arrived at the bottom of the snicket, negotiated the chicane and stepped onto the bridge.

At the sound of his step, Clark turned towards him and as Matt approached the centre of the bridge remarked, 'We're playing Pooh-sticks. But they're all caught on the top of the weir, look.' He indicated the water below them, where the river spilled over the lip of the weir in a silky cascade.

Matt took a cursory look over, scarcely halting his step. A few sticks and twigs were indeed caught on the weir's brink. 'Oh yeah,' he said.

'We might dam it,' Mike said, his face alight with the plan. 'We could wedge a load of sticks and logs and things along there and dam it altogether. That log there,' he indicated the one up stream, covered in moss and weed, 'we could drag that one down, for a start.' He had put a hand out to Matt as he spoke, unconsciously, perhaps, including Matt in the plan, but effectively barring his way across the bridge.

Matt stopped reluctantly and pretended to consider the scheme. 'Oh yeah,' he said again, 'cool.'

Clark capered across the bridge to the other side. 'This waterfall would go dry!' he cried, 'and the pool! We'd be able to see how deep it is!'

'We might find that dog!' Mike said, following Clark across the bridge.

The pool had been artificially created by mechanical diggers as part of the Fairway's building work. It is deep and notorious and subject to strange eddies and weirdly boiling currents, the water protesting against the imposition of unnatural contours along its banks and the insertion of a submerged drain for run-off from the development. A dog is rumoured to have drowned in it.

'Yeah,' Matt nodded and smiled before carrying on his way, hoping that the boys were too caught up in their idea to bother with him today. But Mike and Clark fell into close step behind him, Clark calling out to his brother about the scheme for damming the stream. Matt was forced to stop again. Spencer, astride the barrier, made exit that way impossible and Skinner stood in the middle of the chicane. Matt found himself trapped between them.

'We were just thinking about putting a rope up in that tree,' Spencer commented, pointing to an old, dead tree standing right on the bank of the river some five yards downstream, half way between the bridge and the pool. Its branches, nude, high above, leaned over the weir. 'We could swing off the bridge and into the pool. In the summer, y' know.'

'Oh yeah,' Matt said, for the fourth time, but more doubtfully. He wouldn't fancy it.

'Not if we dam the stream!' Clark shouted. 'There won't be any water in there! You'll break your legs!'

'We're going to dam it with logs,' Mike clarified, the vision in his head now an almost accomplished fact.

'But we've no rope,' Spencer went on, ignoring completely the suggestions of Mike and Clark. 'Have *you*?' He asked the question directly of Matt. Matt hesitated to reply. Once more he pretended to make a serious assessment of the rope-swing idea while he considered the potential sub-text of the situation. Could it be that they had genuinely grown tired of tormenting him and were offering some kind of inclusion? He narrowed one eye as though estimating the distances involved, the length of rope required, trajectories and arcs. Then he shook his head and put on what he hoped would be read as an expression of regret. 'No.' He frowned, and tried to look as though he might be considering other sources of rope, keeping the idea, he hoped, in the forefront of their minds.

'I bet he *has*,' Skinner spoke for the first time, and nodded at Matt's bulging school bag, 'in *there*.' Skinner's voice, like the rest of him, was thin and reedy. If they had not been standing in such a tight huddle, around the chicane, Matt might not have heard him. Over his head, he glimpsed Spencer make an almost imperceptible nod.

'Oh *yes!*' Mike gushed, and took a firm hold of the shoulder strap of Matt's bag, 'let's look.'

Matt held onto it tightly, too tightly, the strength of his response belying his stretched, forced laughter. 'Don't be daft!' he spluttered, but his heart was sinking.

There was no room to manoeuvre. Clark unclipped one end of the shoulder strap from the bag and Mike easily pulled it clear. Matt made a lunge for it but Mike lobbed it over his head. Skinner caught it and began to open the zip. Matt tried to get through the chicane onto the tarmac path but was prevented by Spencer, who extended a casual leg that barred the way. Squeezing around the far side, he was stopped again by Mike, who caught him and pinioned him around his upper arms. The size and strength and weight of the boy were overwhelming; Matt could only struggle helplessly while Skinner and Clark rifled the contents of his bag, pulling out his pencil case, calculator and lever arch file. Clark began to lob the smaller items one by one into the river. Skinner rummaged in his trousers and began to urinate over the bag, grinning liplessly. Spencer sat on the barrier and laughed. Then Mike released Matt's arms and sent him, with an almighty cannoning shove, sprawling onto the tarmac of the pathway. Temporarily winded, his hands smarting and conscious of a warm trickle from his forehead, he registered the sudden spin of sky and smell of the earth as Mike used his feet to roll him like a log down the steep incline of grass and over the brambled bank of the river. He landed with a sharp smack on his back in the weir, its shallow waters creeping up his body—cold like a corpse's fingers—and filling his ears with a hollow guzzle. Strangely detached, he watched as, above his head, sheets of paper as innumerable as snowflakes flurried across the sky, caught on the gay breeze, as Clark tore them in handfuls from the file and flung them gleefully into the air. Presently his bag too flew overhead in an arc and caught in the branches of a bush.

When he had struggled to the bank and clawed his way through the brambles back onto the bridge, dripping, his trainers oozing, his coursework was everywhere but the boys had gone. A few seagulls wheeled and shrieked above the field, and they seemed to be laughing.

JOHN IS CAUGHT between two warring impulses. The rebellion of his heart has devastated him; the discovery that he is not, after all, in ultimate control. It must be nursed and placated. He doesn't want to die. He shrinks from any kind of encounter that might unbalance its equilibrium. To think that only the emergence of a boy from bushes had so unnerved him.

But oh that the boy should be *that* boy, of all others, seems like a sign, a life-line. He is compelled to pursue it.

He is responsible. Days of dialogue between his old arrogance and his new self-knowledge have brought him to the unalterable conviction; if he had been emotionally equipped to understand Richard's terrible dilemma, he would undoubtedly have acted differently. The outcome for Richard and his wife and for the boy might have been the same but it could have been managed with so much more gentleness.

But he had sacked Richard and the girl on the spot, and made no secret of the reason why, exposing them to gossip and censure. He had smoothed things over with the irate customer but only because it made good business sense. It had been the police, not him, who had considered the expenses fraud too negligible to be worthy of prosecution. He had wasted no opportunity, in the following weeks, while taking on the load of Richard's packed appointment calendar on top of all his other responsibilities, to heap bitter criticism and blame on him. Taking their cue from his high-handed denunciation of the his employees' affair, people in the office and on the factory floor had been vociferous in their condemnation of the pair. Wicked selfishness, they said. Wanton self-indulgence.

Most people had blamed Jasmine, a woman with a past; two children with two different fathers, herself the oldest of three girls brought up on the Mere by a single mother and a succession of short or medium term 'uncles'. The apple, everyone said darkly, doesn't fall far from the tree.

But now John sees what he had failed to notice at the time; that in fact she *had* broken the mould. In the face of the likelihood that she would repeat the pattern—her life restricted, like so many on the Mere, by a sort of pre-fabricated ceiling of sub-standard educational opportunities and narrow aspirations of which they were barely conscious—Jasmine had taken a course in word-processing, eschewed benefits and applied for a job. This was a considerable achievement but, at the time, had been lost on him. He remembers, now, her pleasant, self-effacing style, her efficiency, her smartness. Only now is he beginning to be able to appreciate the transforming effect the interest of a man like Richard might have on a young woman like Jasmine; brought up on the ragged edges of civilised society, passed over by life's material blessings and sidestepped by its opportunities. She had been a young woman repeatedly taken advantage of and abandoned by other men but the attention of a man like Richard might light her up. He understands at last the appeal of genuine, selfless and essentially honourable love.

Richard, they had said, must be in mid-life crisis; bewitched, entrapped. John's own bewilderment had been as extreme as it would have been had Richard come to him and declared his intention of taking holy orders or having a sex change operation. But now he sees and laments his blindness and its cause. His own heart has never drummed to love's beat.

The boy has given him a glimmer of hope, a chance for redemption. He wants to be different and here is a start. So, although he has no conception of how it might resolve, with a noose of anxiety tightening around his chest, John slips on his jacket at the appointed time and sets out on his habitual, circuitous route to the bridge. It is an effort of will, of mind over matter. It feels like running a sort of gauntlet. He girds himself.

He goes out of his wide and attractively block-paved drive, all unseeing of the massed display of tulips and the urns of winter pansies. A clockwork circuit of the cloistered Close of neat but substantial bungalows brings him automatically in two or three minutes out onto the Crescent. He passes the wrought iron gates of the sizeable houses, his head moving from left to right, seeming to admire the way the new estate is maturing. Cherry and apple trees are coming into blossom along the verges. Wisteria and Virginia creeper climb up the mock-Georgian facades. But his eyes scarcely take any of it in.

He registers only with the vaguest distraction that the houses on his right are all very large and set within enormous plots. Like his own bungalow they back onto the golf course with desirable open outlooks over fairways and greens.

Any crowing satisfaction he might once have had at this comfortable situation has evaporated. He is ashamed to think of the high-handed way he used his position as Treasurer of the Golf Club to broker the deal that sold off to the developer an area beyond the fourth fairway. He had thrown his weight around the clubhouse, pushing it all through bullishly dismissive of the protests of some of the members, then shamelessly reserved a premium plot for himself. That man is history; a man who lived another life, walked taller and wore larger shoes. He disintegrated in a chest-clutching spasm of panic. An involuntary, frenzied paroxysm withered and all-but annihilated him; he is a whisper of his former shout. Now he treads the pavement with humbler footsteps and looks frequently over his shoulder, before gathering himself, and moving on.

The Crescent takes him about eight or nine minutes to circumnavigate and brings him into the Avenue, which takes him a further seven or eight minutes to walk. At the top of the Avenue is the entrance to the golf club. As a member, he has unrestricted access, but of course ordinary members of the public are excluded.

He hasn't been to the club in weeks.

He always pauses here. It is the half-way point, and he is tempted to retrace his steps and go home.

But there is the boy. So he plunges on, scurrying along the periphery of the rough, past the backs of the houses on the Avenue and the Crescent and the Close, catching glimpses between the mature trees of the landscaped lawns, pools and pergolas, the orangeries and atriums. He passes the back of his own house, seeing the neat area of decking, the pleasant little water-feature—its pump, of course, switched off—the single sun-chair placed outside the French windows, viewing it dispassionately as though it is inhabited by a stranger.

He is conscious of curious fits and starts and feels overwhelmed at times by a sense of vulnerability—a mollusc deprived of its shell, or rather, perhaps, a shark without teeth—and his hand strays to rest on his chest, measuring and monitoring its mutinous vibe. Then he shakes himself and strides off once more, yanked by an invisible cord of determination.

Presently he arrives at the long, lush grass between indigenous trees, the woodland area at the extreme end of the golf course where the public footpath—much resented by members—skirts part of the course. To the left it leads to the echoic arches of the viaduct and out into a no-man's-land of amorphous green-belt. Eventually it connects up with the canal network. A fitter man would ramble that way with a packed lunch and make a day of it, getting the train home in the later afternoon. But he is not a healthy man and he never turns that way.

To the right the path borders the river for a short time, across from the playing field, before turning up through the estate at the point where they have built the bridge.

SINCE THE INCIDENT on the bridge Matthew gets up earlier than before and goes a different way to school; through the Mere and out onto the main road, catching the bus a few stops before the Fairways. Even in the brightness of the morning, after a night of rain, the Mere is dull and drear. Its pavements are broken and grimy with litter trapped in the gutters. Its sadness and desolation are far more than surface deep; hopelessness exudes from its foundations.

It is a longer walk but he has been going to and from school this way for a week now, avoiding the narrow pathways through the new estate and the bottleneck of the bridge. Certainly avoiding the river. There are three more weeks of school until study leave. He doesn't know how long his scheme will deter his tormentors.

But today a scheme offers itself to him. The games master asks him to stay behind and try out for the athletics team. The trials take a while and it is almost five o'clock when Matthew emerges from the snicket and starts out across the bridge. The field is occupied by a lady and her whippet, a man with a large Alsatian on a short lead and a solitary man over by the far hedge. There is no sign of his tormentors.

The sports field's official access point is down an unlit, pot-holed road lined with shabby lock-up garages. They lean conspiratorially together as though sharing furtive information. Their timbers are sagging and doors ill-fitting but secured by multiple padlocks, suggesting powerfully a sense of something predatory and sinister, the jealous concealment of something suspicious lurking within; ill-gotten goods, a mad dog.

Behind these garages are some kids. Somewhere, over in that direction, two dogs are barking manically.

Matt crosses the bridge with relief and sets out along the tarmac pathway, allowing himself—now danger seems past—to think about the athletics. He was easily the best javelin thrower and had come second in the 200 metre hurdles. After-school sports training would account for a few more missed buses home.

He wants, more than anything, to tell his father all about it.

He bets the *other* boy couldn't throw a javelin to save his life.

As he approaches the end of the pathway he passes, obliquely, the rubbish-strewn area behind the garages. Somebody has dumped a mattress and two broken kitchen chairs and there are heaps of builders' rubble and some roofing felt. The charred skeleton of a sofa is also in evidence and more ancient debris, alternately baked and soaked by the weather. It is scarcely recognisable as what it used to be; piles of amorphous mush and scree, angular elbows of rusted metal, intestinal twists of cabling. The grass is quite long—the council mower has not yet made its first cut of the season—and the tyre tracks of vehicles are clearly visible between the gate and the scrubby no-man's-land behind the garages. Rosebay willow-herb and cow parsley grow in profusion while a nearby elderflower gives off a pungent aroma of cat wee. The garages, like a row of terrible teeth, lean and jut in a ragged line up the jaw of the pot-holed road.

The kids are absorbed in something that is happening in the confined space between two of the garages. Matt recognises them as boys from the bus. They are not part of Spencer's crowd and as far as he knows they pose no threat. One is still wearing his school uniform but the other has changed into jeans and a sweatshirt. They have their backs to Matthew and don't see his approach. They are wedged into the small space between the garages, laughing and pointing at something out of Matthew's view. The noise of the dogs is much louder now, and sets the teeth on edge; a ferocious, frenzied cacophony of yelping and growling, barking and snarling: it sounds like a dog fight.

Matt hurries past the end garages, behind a row of hawthorn bushes and through the open gate. Now he is on the road and his way takes him past the front of the lock-ups, up the hill and into the body of the

Mere. But passing the tottering buildings to his right he becomes conscious of another sound interweaving the hysterical furore of the dogs; a high-pitched wail, human, denoting extreme anxiety, and the cries intensify with every renewed onslaught of canine fury. Matt slows down, although every instinct tells him to continue without delay up the hill. In front of the garages is a roughly gravelled area for parking some six or seven yards deep, although no car is ever left there. Between the garages weeds have been allowed to grow rank; thistle and nettle and bramble. Some owners have stacked timber in the narrow spaces, waste material sprouting with bent old nails, rotten window frames embedded with shards of glass. One person has pushed a roll of rusty barbed wire into the aperture between his garage and his neighbour's. For one reason or another passage between the garages is virtually impossible and anyone lured in from the back would be trapped.

Matt walks slowly past the garages, treading with care on the gravel, peering between the wooden buildings, trying to locate the source of the fracas.

Clark is trapped between the fourth and fifth lock-up. His exit is blocked by vicious weeds and stacks of cement bags that have been left to go hard in the rain. He is pressed up against the side of one of the garages, his hands alternately up above his head, then involuntarily reaching down to ward off the attack of two small, muscular dogs. Periodically he rolls on his shoulder against the wall to cower in a semi-upright curl, folding his vulnerable parts—face, chest and genitals—into a protective furl, but this only exposes his back and buttocks to assault. His face is puce and wet with perspiration, his mouth a square gash of fear. He is yelling remonstrance as well as begging for reprieve. He is very afraid. His voice—not yet fully broken—warbles between tenor and soprano.

The dogs are finding him wonderful sport. They bark and show their teeth and, although he poses no threat to them, his terrified reaction is fuelling their blood-lust. They jump up at him, scratching his legs with their claws. When he reaches down to fend them off they snap at his

51

hands. In fact his legs are fairly well protected by his jeans and the dogs' attack is mainly about feint and bluster. They are young and this is a game. Their owners, too young to be sent out to exercise such potentially dangerous animals, especially off the lead, are partly appalled by their pets' behaviour but partly thrilled by Clark's abject vulnerability. They jeer as Clark screams, but make occasional, half-hearted appeals to their dogs to desist.

Matt is walking back the way he has come before he knows it. He goes back through the gate and past the hawthorns. The man with the Alsatian has disappeared. The woman with the whippet is at the far end of the field. The solitary man is much closer; perhaps he has been attracted by the uproar and is curious to see what is going on. But Matt hardly glances at him. He is picking his way amongst the detritus in the long grass. On his way past the burned sofa he snaps off a charred strut. It feels surprisingly soft and light in his hand. The boys do not see or hear him and his sudden hands on their shoulders shock them. They abruptly cease their scoffing and pale as they turn towards him. They are both younger than him, but older than Clark.

'Don't you know who this is?' he says loudly, over the continuing tumult of the dogs and Clark. Realisation dawns on their faces as they appreciate for the first time the potential consequences of their cruelty. 'This is *Maxwell's* brother!' Matt says, unnecessarily now. He pushes them roughly to one side and steps into the space between the garages. Then he gives a piercing whistle through his teeth, the way his dad has taught him. The dogs cease their noise immediately and turn their heads to look at him. They are lathered in sweat, their mouths wet with foam. Matt waves the charred stick above his head, before turning and hurling it across the wasteland towards the river. Both dogs set off in pursuit as though released from a rifle, their stocky, brindled bodies jostling each other through the narrow gap and past Matt, past their useless owners, out onto the wider ground. Matt strides the few paces it takes to reach Clark. Stuff—rusty beer cans, and something wet and spongy—is under his feet, hidden in the grass. There is a strong smell of creosote coming off the wooden walls. Clark is crying quite openly, his nose is running, his legs, now the danger is past, unreliable. He smells of raw fear; the crotch of his jeans is dark.

'Come on, quick,' Matt urges, and Clark follows him unsteadily between the leaning buildings and across the rough, rubbish-strewn grass.

The man is by the gate and Matt recognises him now; it is Mr Pickering.

SOMETHING ABOUT THE boy has captured him—caught him up—and it is as refreshing as a new view from a previously undiscovered window in the cell of his self-absorption.

For the past week he hasn't clapped eyes on the lad. But every afternoon finds him here down by the bridge.

Today he has set out a little earlier and when he reaches the bridge from the path that connects it with the golf course, it is thronged with school children. They do not acknowledge him, but their riotous chatter ceases for a moment and they cast each other looks, and snigger. At the far side of the bridge he leaves the tarmac path and follows the river bank for a few yards, arriving at an old tree that leans out across the weir. He rests there, fussing with his shoelaces, while the crocodile of children ambles homewards, jostling each other, larking about, scattering litter asunder.

Covertly, he watches groups of older girls in conspiratorial, giggling conference and post-pubescent lads in twos and threes, walking in that loose-legged, shambling way that young men have these days, as though accommodating abnormally large reproductive equipment between their thighs. There are small girls, serious, with their school bags seeming too impossibly heavy for their little frames, and their hair, after a busy day, all awry. Younger boys run and weave between the other groups, their shoelaces undone and shirttails hanging out. They all flow in a continuous stream down from the Fairways and across the bridge, snaking along the tarmac path, filtering through the gate and up the steep hill home. It takes half an hour before the last, loitering one disappears.

There is no sign of the boy amongst them.

John wanders along the river bank for a distance, looking at the bright water on the pebbled bed, the rampant growth along the fringes. The day is fresh and pleasant; the sun is warm on his back. He walks down as far as the garages. The area behind them is a mess.

He considers walking on, behind the houses and along to the factory. There's a path that goes past the backs of the Mere houses and the burnt-out remains of the scout hut. The gap-toothed fences become substantial metal railings with saw-toothed tops looped by razor wire. Behind these are the compounds of small manufacturing units. You can glimpse stacked pallets and skips, drums and crates through the bars of the fence. One unit makes ice-cream, a cheerfully anomalous product from these gloomy precincts of social and economic depression. Another rattles and clatters all day with the thrum of litho presses and a third—his own concern, in the days of wellness and thoughtless authority, Pickering Light Engineering—manufactures a plethora of small engineering parts. They all emit the sound of mechanised activity; demonic robots devouring knives and razor blades. They emit also a sulphuric smell of caustic effluent and oily seepings. Between its steeply shelving banks, the river froths with rusty lather, its surface suddenly slick with filmy scum. Beyond these premises several others are vacant, their windows broken and partly boarded. Wind reverberates around the vast spaces and maddened, trapped birds flutter hopelessly high up amongst the rafters. There is a smell of stale dereliction; old oil, dirt, cat urine. Skirting their convolvulus-choked fences the pathway is oppressed by the shadows of the dark, deserted buildings; even on warm days there is a permeating chill from the rank vegetation and the black, polluted water.

He can't face it now. He feels stronger than he has in a while, but the idea of being seen by one of his employees skulking around behind the fence is intolerable.

He decides instead to walk around the field. The grass is reasonably dry, rather long, and he picks his way gingerly, with an eye to the dog walkers who are now beginning to emerge; a lean woman with a thin, pink whippet, a man with a German shepherd, his hair wild and wiry in the breeze, two boys with boisterous puppies. He finds himself smiling. How alike the dogs and their owners are! He pictures, wryly, his own dog-self; a wheezing, geriatric old collie, perhaps, or a clapped-out, pensioned-off greyhound.

The top end of the recreation field borders a neglected urban farm where emaciated, bad-tempered horses—likely to kick and bite—crop the churned turf. He considers the view; the kicked-up paddock, the river glimpsed in occasional bright-winking shafts through the greenery, the rise of the ground to the tailored turf of the golf course, the broad stretch of the viaduct across the horizon. It is pleasing, and he lingers, caught up in the extrinsic stimuli on his senses, the wide brilliance of the afternoon, the thrill of the air on his skin. He leans for a while on the trunk of a tree and closes his eyes, holding his face up to the April sunshine.

He is breathing easily, his anxiety levels low or even non-existent. His heart is docile. He sighs, and feels the dropping away of further tension. He feels, at last, as mellow as a warm crumpet, golden and oozing with butter.

He is half way along the far hedgerow when he sees the boy cross the bridge. The boy walks quickly and has covered the length of the tarmac pathway and left the field before John has traversed a third of it. They are too far apart for any kind of communication. It is a pity, he thinks, that the opportunity will be lost, although he is still unclear as to what, if anything, might be gained. His contentment of only moments before is clouded by nameless regret. But then the boy reappears and walks quickly to the back of the garages. The puppies have been making a dreadful racket over there; tied up and left, John has presumed, while their owners rummage around in the junk. He increases his step, within comfortable parameters, and by the time the boy emerges from behind the garages, another boy in tow, John has reached the gate. The boy's young companion is in something of a state and is occupying all his attention.

John says, 'Hello,' as they pass. They exchange a look, and the boy, *his* boy, nods politely before herding his companion through the gate and beginning the climb up the hill.

The draw of the boy is strong. John would like to know where he is living, to establish, if possible, some kind of rapport. These last days, with the boy on his mind, have been the best since the attack. But he has reservations. These days a man cannot afford to take any interest— no matter how innocent—in a young person, without opening himself to suspicions of the most vicious kind.

John dithers by the gate, neither advancing nor turning for home, watching the two lads as they progress past the garages and up the hill. The younger boy is distressed. The other reaches out an arm from time to time, and encourages him on.

They are met by three other boys. One is tall, another rather fat, the third thin and scrawny and almost hairless, like a shaved rat. Both parties halt and there is an exchange that John is unable to hear, but which clearly involves the state of the younger boy. Suddenly the fat boy flashes out a meaty hand and lands a punch. John's boy snaps backwards, as though shot, his hands to his face. The thin boy hits him in the stomach, or lower. John's boy doubles over. John is through the gate and almost past the garages. He does not know what reserves of courage propel him. He is walking quickly, shouting, angry imprecations pouring from his mouth, his old self suddenly back in possession. The boys see him, and there is a muttered conference. As he approaches, the three aggressors grab the youngest boy and hurry away, back into the Mere leaving John and Matt alone at the scene.

A LITTLE LATER, John is making his way home to the Fairways. The journey is fraught with trauma. He took too little notice of the route to Matt's house, busy pontificating in terms which, he realises—too late—were lost on the boy, and now he is unable to recall the way through the myriad by-ways and green-walks of the Mere. There are people everywhere. It is six o'clock, evening. Men arrive home from work. He is afraid that he might be recognised. Any one of them could be an aggrieved employee; heaven knows there have been enough of them, over the years. He feels the scrutinous eyes on him but keeps his gaze fixed fastidiously to the ground—another cause of his loss of bearings.

He passes for the second time a lady in an apron and bedroom slippers sweeping the pavement, and realises that he is going round in circles.

The sun is lowering, casting enormous shadows on one side of the road and golden pools of light on the other. He crosses the street frequently, not knowing which makes him feel more uncomfortable; the glare of the sun picking him out, or the gloom opposite that might conceal something untoward. The zigzagging itinerant route further disorientates him. Gusts of breeze reach him unexpectedly, funnelled down the dark passageways that dissect the tenements. They make him shiver with cold. The next moment he is overwhelmingly hot, his system in hyper-drive, pouring sweat. Every parked car along the road radiates vindictive heat at him and there is a foul, hot smell rising from the drains.

His throat is parched and his coat leaden. When he licks his lips he tastes salt. His heart is a tantrumming toddler beating pitilessly with its sharp little heels on his lungs. He berates himself for the opportunity with the boy that he has just wasted.

After what feels like hours—but which can, in fact, be only fifteen or twenty minutes—he comes across a row of shops; a hairdressing salon, a takeaway, a betting shop, a laundrette and a convenience store. In desperation he goes into the store, buys a cold drink and asks for directions. As he counts out some change his hands are shaking. There is a mirror above the counter and he can see himself—pale and glistening, cheeks sunken, chin unshaven, his hair untidy. The sight is shocking. Probably his own mother would not recognise him. For a moment he is distracted from the kindly, repetitive directions of the shopkeeper as he stares aghast at the impression he must be making, his waxy, deathlike complexion and shabby, unkempt dress.

'It's not far, not far,' the man is smiling. He indicates the shop doorway. 'Turn left at the door. Then right at the end of the road. Then first left.'

John drags his eyes from the mirror. 'First left?'

Suddenly the man shouts something in Punjabi and a diminutive sari-wearing lady emerges from the stockroom. She takes her husband's place behind the counter and John finds himself escorted from the shop and walked to the end of the road. 'There,' the shopkeeper points to a turning perhaps twenty yards from where they are standing. 'Down there.'

The far side of the field is in shadow, inky fingers creeping across the green. He hurries along the path towards the bridge, scenting home. His legs are like water and he knows that his footsteps are erratic.

He is on the bridge, his footsteps sounding hollow over the boards. The water below mocks him. It is bright in the evening sun and ebullient over the lip of the weir.

Up the snicket and around into the Close. His key fumbling for the lock. Indoors, he drops his coat onto the carpet, sheds also his pullover and shirt. His skin is clammy. His heart—un-muffled—shouts and shakes its angry fists against its cage. He sinks into his chair and reaches with an unsteady hand for a bottle of tablets.

Images are projected on the inside of his eyelids. He reprises the reckless way he has courted this encounter day after day, and the specious benignity of his walk on the field. The attack on the boy shocks him anew, as well as his impulsive, ill-advised response. He recalls the sad, drear little house where the boy and his mother are living, the confusing streets, the kindness of the shopkeeper. The images spin around him and at their centre is himself, a shrunken morsel of man, overwrought, overwhelmed, overcome.

MR PICKERING HAD insisted on walking him home.

'You know who I am?' he had asked anxiously. 'I'm not a stranger.' His eagerness to qualify himself as benign had made him put an earnest hand out to Matt's arm, but almost immediately he had snatched it back again, as though the gesture was in some way contradictory to his words, and might be misconstrued.

'I know who you are,' Matt had gasped. His stomach felt as though it was still impaled on Skinner's bony hand and things were rearranging themselves inside to accommodate it. His head was ringing. He had no idea it hurt so much to be punched. He had a brief, ridiculous image of a cartoon cat after a bludgeoning, birds twittering in circles round its head.

'And I know who you are. You're Richard's boy.' John had muttered these words almost to himself, as if needing reassurance that Matt was no threat.

'I'm Matt.'

'Yes. Matt. I remember now.'

They had walked together through the tightly packed cul-de-sacs and by-ways of the Mere, awkward in one another's company. Mr Pickering had ranted for a while about yobs and thugs and criminal injuries, but his tirade had soon dried up. The evaporation of his ire had coincided with a corresponding liquefaction in Matt; he had felt sick and loose-bowelled, his courage with the boys and the dogs and Clark had turned to water.

When they reached a small gateway and Matt had turned in, up a single width, unevenly flag-stoned pathway past the dustbins to the half glazed front door, Mr Pickering had hesitated. 'You're all right now?' he had asked, as Matt had fumbled with his key. He'd placed a slight emphasis on '*you're*' implying, perhaps that *he* was less than well, but, at the time, it had been lost on Matt.

Matt had nodded. 'Thanks,' he had said, an after-thought, when Mr Pickering had already begun to retrace his steps.

He had bluffed it out with his mother, refusing to explain himself in the face of her concern, submitting with bad grace to her ministrations with the medical box, avoiding her eyes. The ordeal was almost as bad as the fight. Worse, in some ways, with emotional substance the swift blows from Mike and Skinner had not contained. He is conscious of adopting, with his mother, a reserved, almost scornful air, sneering at her little concerns and fuss-making. It is purely defensive, an adamantine wall of belligerence behind which he is pulpy and undone.

She had questioned him closely, seeking out the circumstances that had led to his injuries, challenging his choice of friends, querying his actions and his new attitude that she described as 'closed'. He had shrugged and prevaricated and told her to 'leave it' in an angry voice he did not recognise.

She had called his father but Matt had refused to speak to him. Text messages from his father—already several a day—have redoubled, but Matt deletes them all.

The next day is Saturday and Matt is home alone, working on his Geography.

He has a black eye, and strict instructions to stay put.

He feels uncomfortable in the house on his own. There seems to be no security, no privacy. The neighbours and the outside world are divided from him by only the thinnest membrane that leaves him exposed and vulnerable. Nothing can be kept out. Next door's television and their arguments are an ever-present soundscape, infiltrating his meals, his thoughts, his sleep. The tiny square of garden between the house and the pavement is no barrier between the inhabitants and passers-by. Snatches of their conversation invade, disjointed and intrusive as people walk past the house, staring shamelessly into the window. There is a constant barrage of unsolicited mail coming through the door. A succession of people walk boldly through the gate and up the path bringing leaflets about pizza deliveries and new nail bars, car boot sales and church services, karaoke nights and the BNP. The gate of their garden has a self-closing spring and clangs closed with a sharp, resounding crash a dozen times a day. It still makes Matt jump. He doesn't know what he is afraid of, only that he doesn't feel safe. There is no sense of separation, nowhere to hide. Something about the Mere is invasive, almost infectious. Once it gets a grip on you, you are trapped.

The gate clashes and this time instead of the rattle and flap of the letter box there is a knock on the door. Matt approaches with caution and opens the door, the chain across the gap.

On the path is Spencer. His hands are deep in his pockets and his head is down. He scuffs the toe of his trainer against the base of the fence that divides Matt's house from the neighbours. Even as the door opens he doesn't look up. His usual over-bearing confidence has entirely gone. He is clearly present under penance, a deflated, shrunken Spencer. Behind him is Clark, fidgety, his habitual, easy cheerfulness replaced by an anxious, almost-manic hysteria. He grins and gurns idiotically, barely suppressing giggles, his whole body gyrating and twitching as though possessed. Behind them both stands the diminutive but all-powerful form of their mother. She is tiny. It seems barely possible that she produced the boys in front of her. Her hair— mousy and dull—hangs to her shoulders. She has broken veins on her cheeks and a mouth made slack by hardship. But her eyes are clear and bright and fiery. Her body is lithe, thin but strong. She has unusually large, hard hands, red and chapped by the work she does at the ice cream factory. She takes in Matt's empurpled eye and purses her lips into an angry slice.

Her voice, when she speaks, is as shrill as a saw-edge. 'Is your mam in?' She speaks past her sons. As it cuts past them, her voice makes both the boys duck and cringe, as though dodging arrows.

Matt shakes his head.

'Tell her I came,' the woman says with emphasis. 'Tell her I came m'self. And any more problems, she can come straight to me. Right? Right?' Her final words are addressed significantly to her boys.

'Right,' Spencer mutters.

'Right,' says Clark, smiling eagerly and nodding too hard.

'Right,' Matt echoes, not sure quite what he has just acknowledged.

She gives Clark a sharp shove from behind. He cannons into his older brother, who is in turn propelled closer to the front door. It is exactly what she had planned. She could not have exercised the manoeuvre with more skill if she had been a world-class snooker player. Spencer's head snaps up and he puts his hand out to stop himself hitting the doorframe. This brings him face to face, almost eye to eye with Matt, except their eyes slide away from each other with the stubborn resistance of similar magnetic poles.

'Go *on* then,' she says. Her high-pitched voice is as sharp as a shard of glass.

'Clark told me 'bout the dogs,' Spencer mumbles. He is blushing, looking anywhere but at Matt. ''bout what you did. Anyway ...'

'We've got a rope!' Clark blurts out, the excitement of it making him physically effervesce; he hops from foot to foot. The ordeal of the previous day seems entirely forgotten. 'For the tree. Maxwell's got it for us!'

'Yeah,' Spencer throws a frown over his shoulder at his brother before struggling on, 'So, Clark told us and we've come to say it's over. Right?'

'Right.' Matt is wary, but the significance of the presence of their mother reassures him. Spencer looks over his shoulder again, this time at his mother, to see if he has done and said enough. She cocks her head on one side and raises a wiry eyebrow. He sighs and turns back to Matt, to do further penance.

'Sorry.' The word is spoken quietly, and hardly enunciated.

'Sorry,' Clark echoes, too brightly to be sincere.

Their mother sniffs. 'And?'

'And thanks,' Clark gushes carelessly.

'And?'

'So, yeah. We've got this rope and we're meeting the others by the tree later. Y' know ...' the rest of the declaration of surrender sticks in Spencer's throat.

'Why don't you come?' Clark cries. There seems to be no contradiction, in his mind, between the war of attrition he has been part of against Matt, and this genial suggestion.

'I've got stuff to do,' Matt takes a step backwards, 'thanks.'

'There won't be any bother from them,' Spencer says, under his breath. He looks Matt in the eye for the first time. There is a sort of appeal in his look. Then, perhaps involuntarily, his eyes swivel upwards, indicating the domineering presence of his mother. Matt realises that Spencer needs him to co-operate in the process of his absolution before his mother will let him off the hook.

'Ok, well, I might do then,' Matt says at last, assuming a lightness of tone he hopes will convince. Nothing on earth would compel him to tell them that he has been grounded even though it would undoubtedly increase their mother's wrath. He is suddenly resentful of his own mother for her reaction, forgetting conveniently that though given every opportunity to tell her the truth he had persisted in the blustering assertion that it was none of her business.

It seems to satisfy Spencer's mother. She sniffs again and herds the boys back up the path. 'All right, all right, get along with you then,' she says. At the gate she turns again to Matt and gives him a significant look. 'Don't forget to tell your mam now,' she warns.

'I won't.'

'See you later!' Clark yells from a few yards down the pavement.

As he closes the door Matt can hear her voice sawing on in further terrible imprecations as she ushers her boys home.

As he enters the lounge the telephone rings and he snatches it up without thinking.

'Hello?'

'Matt.' It is his father. The voice causes an immediate noose of nervous anxiety, sadness and anger to constrict his throat. It is so strong Matt can scarcely breathe.

Eventually he manages to croak out, 'Yes.'

'Are you all right? Your mum says you've been in a fight.'

'And?' The vehemence of his response takes him by surprise, but is satisfying.

'Are you all right?'

The tension between them travels up and down the line in waves. It is weeks since they spoke. The mutual estrangement is enormous, as wide and salty as an ocean. Matt's throat tightens again and he feels that he will cry. The longing and equal loathing for his father is overwhelming. He wants to run to him and rain blows down on him and hold him and hurt him.

'*Are* you?'

'Yes.'

'She's worried about you. I am too.'

Matt's heart snaps shut. 'There's no need,' he says coldly.

'You've never been a fighter, Matt.'

His father's reproach infuriates him. 'I've never needed to be before. But life's like that here. Boys round here, they fight. Get used to it. *I* have to.' His bitterness is caustic and his father takes a breath before saying with studied control, 'But you're not like them, Matt. You know, it doesn't have to be like this.' His voice is taut but the underlying note of distress is evident.

'It *does* have to be like this!' Matt shouts, his voice breaking. 'It *does,* because of ...' he wants to say 'him', the other boy, the festering thorn in his side, but he can't bear even to acknowledge his existence. 'Because it does,' he concludes lamely.

'Why don't you let me come and get you? We could hang out up here for a while.'

The idea is appalling; the other boy squirming on his father's knee, calling him 'dad'. It makes Matt want to retch. 'No!'

'Matthew!' his father speaks his name sharply, in a tone he always used to use when something was important. Before, he would have placed both hands on Matt's shoulders and faced him squarely. When he was really small, his father would squat down to look him in the eye. The memory of it is so powerful it is almost as though his father is in the room. Matt finds that he is standing on his own foot, shrinking and cowering in the space from the pervading sense that his father is there. 'I know you're angry, and that's understandable, but you've got to get past it. Your mum agrees. You need you to be a bit more grown up about all this ...'

'No! No! No!' Matt crashes the telephone down and runs up the stairs to his room. He throws himself onto his bed. The pillow is rough on his bruised eye and through the paper-thin walls he can hear the music of the insipid, plasticised pop group favoured by the neighbour's nine year old daughter. It infuriates and nauseates him. There is no escape at all. Also, downstairs, the telephone is ringing and ringing. Everything is conspiring against him. It seems that even his mother, though he has sided with her, is now in league against him with his father, threatening to cast his jealous rage to the winds, wanting him to 'grow up' when all he wants is to be, again, the little boy, the *only* little boy in his father's life.

He is seized with anger. He leaps off the bed and picks up the wooden kitchen stool that has had to serve as his bedside table. The lamp and his clock radio and a glass of water all tumble onto the floor. He hurls the stool with all his might against the party wall, roaring, 'Shut up! Shut up! Shut up!' The stool bounces off the wall leaving a gash in the plaster. He hurls it again and again. One leg snaps off. The Sugadolls come to a strangulated and abrupt end. He bounds down the stairs and wrenches open the front door. The security chain, which he has forgotten to undo, snaps.

He is running, down to the field.

His mother, coming home at lunchtime to check on him after a quick trip to town for a patient, finds the house empty.

THE CAUSE OF John's severe reaction is soon apparent. He is ill with some virus, feverish at first and then shaking with cold. He mutters and raves in the night. The room swoons around him. There is a menacing black shadow in one corner that encroaches inch by inch towards the bed in the dark hours, but in the morning is only a chair with his clothes strewn across it. But even then he eyes it doubtfully; he doesn't trust it.

After a few days his temperature is normal, but he is weak and trembly. He returns with an effort to his sanctuary in the inner vestibule, cowering there, quelling rising tides of fretfulness with disciplined, steady breathing. He monitors his pulse rate and placates his capricious pulmonary apparatus with strict regimes of complete inaction.

He eats invalid food: tinned rice pudding and chicken soup.

He is wooed by the safety of his sanctum like a mammal in its burrow. His house becomes his world. He abandons his walks. He is shrinking into himself.

He cannot shut out the vivid recollections of past wrongdoing; the secretaries he has reduced to tears, the women he has bullied into bed, the public dressings down he has indiscriminately meted out on employees and golf partners and waiters. They are nameless and faceless and innumerable, but manifest themselves like a line of ghosts to parade before his cringing consciousness.

Days go by—perhaps a week—he loses track. His food stores are dwindling. He eats stale crackers and food from tins at the back of the cupboard and whatever he can get the milkman to leave.

He stops bothering with the curtains. His eyes become accustomed to the cool gloom within and are in any case focussed on his inner mechanics. He only continues to clear the post and papers to prevent the meddling intrusion of their deliverers. He is scared witless one day by the insistent hammering of a determined neighbour who has noticed the closed curtains. She defends her interference by claiming to be the local Neighbourhood Watch representative and perhaps he should feel grateful for her concern, but it all he can do to keep his nerves in check as he assures her he is perfectly well.

He sleeps, either in the chair under a tartan travel blanket, or in his bed. His tiredness is characterised by a gradual weakening of his will. He finds even the process of getting washed and dressed unbelievably debilitating, likely to bring on an attack of palpitations. In any case his pallid image in the mirror is too painful. Some days—increasingly—he doesn't bother, remaining in his pyjamas and dressing gown. But the mental effort of monitoring his rhythms is more wearing than any physical exertion, tuning in to each twinge and inner burble, imagining ugly yellow coagulates of cholesterol choking up the ruby channels of his heart or the spongy grey by-ways of his brain.

He is religious in his tablet-taking.

Even post-fever, the dreams continue and on occasion the division between dream and reality is blurred. He feels sure that the plunge and throb of his heart is a thundering die-cutter in a far room, that he must keep the doors closed against an outsized glutinous ball of yellow matter that threatens to ooze in and swamp him in his chair.

In rational moments he believes that he is going mad. It is a growing certainty that in addition to his failing heart there is *something else* seriously amiss.

His most distressing and recurrent dream is of the boy, who is drowning. Emotionally he thrashes violently to act, mustering every ounce of strength and determination, but his best efforts are infuriatingly impotent. His leaden body is obdurate, his feet firmly soldered to the floor.

He thinks a great deal about the boy. The situation goes round and round in his head, his only point of reference beyond the walls of his insularity. As inconclusive as their encounter turned out to be he cannot help retaining a keen sense of affiliation. He thinks of Matt and of himself in the same heartbeat. He *feels* for the lad. His empathy is an unaccustomed emotion, employing muscles unused to the exercise. The boy's image—struggling out of the undergrowth, beaten by bullies, drowning—haunts him. Haunts and inspires him.

The thought of the boy lifts his heart.

After many days, these two things—the fear of madness and the image of the boy—trigger the release of some final, emergency supply of determination. He *must* fashion something better from what remains. He drags himself into the shower, draws a razor across his face, pours his watery limbs into clothing. He opens the door and goes out.

MATT IS LIVING a double life. It is a way of dealing with things—effectively *not* dealing with them. He slips from one life to another, sliding awkwardly on the glassy, treacherous surface of each. He goes down to the river when the oppression of the house and of his rage becomes unbearable, then clings to the mast of routines and parental expectations when the narrow, skewed world of Spencer threatens to suck him under.

He watches his two selves with a strange detachment, trying to discern which is the real and which the reflected Matt and coming to the bitter conclusion that neither is. The real Matt still lives across the bridge. But there, too, he is a barely remembered shadow. He has not seen or heard from his old friends in weeks. He is at home nowhere but goes through the motions, acting the parts he has written for himself: one-man show, one-man audience.

He goes out while his mother is at work, wallowing in the guilty freedom wrought by his duplicity. He and the boys play with the rope or range through the woods. They explore the derelict factory units and spy on golfers from the long grass under the trees. At other times he sits at the kitchen table and does his work—innocent as milk—while Rosie reads or crochets in the lounge under a dim light, the television switched off in deference to his studies. For a time the deception has been satisfying and he has nurtured the thrill of calculated deceit as one might a secret hoard of dynamite, wilfully disregarding the fact that it might one day grow unstable and explode in his face. He tells himself that his mother assumes *anyway* that he is mixing with Mere boys. She has put his missing kit, damaged uniform and ruined coursework—not to mention his changed attitude and his fight—down to their bad influence. If she thinks so little of him ... He luxuriates in despising her and, in a small-minded nose-cutting exercise, spends a fortnight or so squeezing himself into her narrow view.

And of course *he*—the other boy—is a Mere boy, though so much younger. Presumably he was used to free rein amongst the dilapidated tenements, a grubby-faced boy who hung around outside the shop or kicked a punctured football around the street before he was transplanted to wherever Matt's father now lives. The other boy was an embryonic Spencer or Skinner but is now miraculously saved from the hopeless fate of perpetual limitation.

The cessation of hostilities from Spencer and the crew has only partially resolved matters. At least now there are no injuries or missing equipment to explain away. He is, nominally at least, a member of Spencer's gang. His anxiety has lessened, he is sleeping better; there is almost no sense of personal threat—although Skinner is still a profoundly disturbing unknown quantity. But in truth there is no affinity. He does not know them, doesn't understand them, or even much like them. They live on a harder plane than he does, even now. Their experiences of life are narrow—none of them has ever flown on an aeroplane, for instance—and their expectations of it are narrower still. The highest pinnacle of achievement they can conceive is occupied by Maxwell. They aspire to be and do what he is. Spencer talks of nothing else. He has no ambition at all beyond joining Maxwell in his enterprises. Whatever Maxwell does or says is revered. He is the last word.

Matt, who has his sights set on college and then an internship with a firm of engineering draughtsmen, or even architects, is amazed by the smallness of their vision. The galvanising effect on them of even such a small thing as a length of rope—it is suspiciously good quality rope, of the calibre Matt has seen used at outdoor pursuit centres and on the tall ships—puts everything in perspective. The joy and interest it engenders can only reflect the rest of their lives in lack-lustre hues.

They have spent hours down at the river experimenting with different heights and positions for the rope, testing its weight and trajectory.

Directed by Spencer, Skinner has repeatedly scrambled up the tree, clambering amongst the dry, leafless branches like a monkey. Mike has hauled down on the rope to test its strength. Clark has capered and clapped his hands and clamoured, with each new configuration, to be allowed to have the first go.

Matt's contribution has been to come up with a method of creating a foot-loop on the bottom of the rope using a knot he had learned from his dad, back-woodsing with the Cubs. You can step into it, like a stirrup, and swing almost without effort from bank to bank without having to support your weight on your hands. They have evolved a technique. You run down the grassy slope behind the tree, rope in hand, leaping and stepping into the loop as the bank falls away and you are over the weir. The rope creaks above you and the air rushes past your ears. There's the drop and rise of the arc, a whisper of leaves and sudden coolness as you enter the shade on the other side. Then, at the top of its swing, your belly lingers while the rest of you drops back down the arc, back into the sunshine, up, over the bank, where you make an easy dismount.

None of them has yet attempted Spencer's original plan for the rope. It will reach to the bridge and it would be possible to swing from there right over the pool. Clark has urged Spencer to try it but he has refused. 'Not today,' he says. The water levels are unseasonably low. The water in the pool is turgid and cloudy, subject to unpredictable gouts and spurts, a mystery he is not ready to fathom.

Their activity over the past few weeks has stamped and flattened the undergrowth around the tree, defining a sort of territory comprising the tree and the steep, grassy bank around and under it, the river and the weir, and—because of its proximity—the bridge. Mike and Clark—neither of whom, of course, will finish school for another ten weeks—make endless plans for the summer holidays that all centre on this spot; they will camp here, build fires, fish, and snare rabbits on the common land beyond the viaduct. The others, with a long vacation after the exams and—for Spencer and Skinner anyway—no very specific plans beyond, build no such castles. But they tend to loiter in the spot, leaning against the bole of the tree, or sitting right on the bank with their legs swinging down over the man-made sides of the weir. It has become their meeting place, after school and at weekends, the place where they gather in a desultory way, with no particular plan or purpose, drawn perhaps by the rope itself, and their achievement in getting it and fixing it. It is theirs, jealously guarded.

There is room to breathe by the river and the rope swing project has been a welcome focus for Matt's attention. But, perhaps accidentally, perhaps inevitably, it concludes in him being soaked once more.

IT IS LATE afternoon. A lively breeze puckers the surface of the river above the weir. The weeds on its steps are emerald green against the grey of the concrete construction. They yearn towards the pool, reaching longing, feathery fingers. The pool is shadowy, shaded by trees in full leathery leaf above and overhung by verdant bramble sprinked with white flowers. Beneath the overhang the restless current scours the bank away, loosening soil, staining the waters silty brown. There is a line of white foam, a perpetually frothing lip where the water cascades off the weir and joins the maelstrom in the deep pool. Whatever lies beneath its surface causes crazy eddies and whirling currents to jostle and boil in volatile surges.

Mike has brought food—he is usually amply supplied by his mother—crisps and chocolate and bottles of lurid orange fizzy pop. He sits beneath the tree sharing with Clark. Skinner is up the tree, perched on the branch they have chosen to anchor the rope. Spencer swings lazily on the rope itself—his habitual position—gliding proprietarily over his domain. Matt squats nearby, pulling long, wide blades of grass from the ground exposing their sweet, white roots and stretching them between his thumbs to make a reedy whistle. He takes only a desultory interest in the other boys.

Also today there is a girl. She has come with Spencer although he has resolutely ignored her. She is the palest wisp of a thing, with ash-blond hair and milk-white skin and eyes so light blue that they meld into the whites with scarcely an edge, and looking at her is like looking into the eyes of someone who is blind. Their dark pupils seem like empty, fathomless hollows. She is skinny, hardly developed. Her dress, in contrast, tells another story; short skirt, tight cropped top revealing flat white tummy and a pierced belly button, a jangling collection of bracelets at her wrist, much blue eye-shadow and stiff, doll-like lashes. She sits on the grass a little apart from the others and moves her thumbs dexterously over the pad of her mobile phone. Her fringe, straight as a die, hangs down over her eyes, its silken ribbons lifted and shifted by the breeze. From underneath it she casts the occasional glance at Spencer.

Above her, Skinner, on his branch, is watching her, and rubbing his groin furtively.

There is a sense of anxious anticipation: Maxwell has promised to come and view the rope. It seems very important that he approves.

Spencer leans back on the rope, causing it to increase its momentum. In two swings he is back on the bank.

'Let's see,' he says loudly, in that rousing way he has, 'how many of us this rope can carry.' He holds the rope out to Matt. 'You get on first.' It seems never to occur to any of them to refuse co-operation in Spencer's schemes. Matt hoists himself to his feet; they are numb, from squatting. He shakes and wriggles them before taking the rope from Spencer. He inserts his foot into the loop.

'Hang on. I've got a better idea,' Spencer says. He walks a little way along the bank and comes back with a dry stick about eighteen inches long and of girth equivalent to Matt's wrist. He pushes the stick through the loop. 'There. Sit on it. It'll make more room above you.' Matt guides the stick between his thighs so that it is behind his legs, underneath his bottom, and braces himself. Spencer motions Mike forward. Mike hauls himself to his feet and brushes orange crisp crumbs from his hands. He has an orange tide mark around his mouth and as he comes close to Matt his breath smells of cheese and artificial bacon. Mike slips his foot into the small gap of the loop. Because of the stick it is a tight fit. He places the other foot on the stick where it protrudes from beneath Matt's thigh. Suddenly Matt is taking Mike's weight. His knees sag and he sits on the stick, letting the rope take the strain, but bracing them both with his legs to prevent them taking off. He struggles to get a hand hold on the rope, reaching between Mike's ample thighs with one arm, the other has no choice but to grasp a handful of Mike's tracksuit trousers. The effect is to bring his face uncomfortably close to Mike's saggy crotch. Spencer is laughing. Above them, there is a catarrhal snort from Skinner. Clark is hopping round the tree. 'Shall I get on next? Where shall I go? Spence? Spence!'

'Let her go!' Spencer shouts. Matt releases his heels from where they are dug into the soft dry ground and the rope lurches out over the water. It sways wildly while Matt and Mike try to accommodate each other. The stick is digging into Matt's thighs. The rope and Mike's foot are dangerously close to his genitals. Mike's other foot, shifting for position, keeps stepping on Matt's flesh. Every time one of them moves the rope oscillates perilously, and the branch above creaks. Matt clings to the rope as the centre of gravity even though it means pressing his head into the underside of Mike's soft belly.

On the bank, Clark is beside himself. He has one of those infectious, bubbling geysers of a giggle that undoes everyone. Mike and Matt cannot help but laugh, but there is an edge of hysteria to it. They know they look ridiculous but it has occurred to them both that this adventure can hardly avoid a wet ending. Mike is shaking and his eyes are streaming, partly in laughter, partly panic. He lets go a fetid, noisy fart.

They have just about reached some kind of equilibrium when the rope veers in another direction. Skinner has dropped from his branch and is sliding down the rope. His feet are on Mike's shoulders and then he is sitting on them. Mike's amusement quickly turns to outrage.

'Your bum stinks!' he protests.

On the bank the girl has stood up and is taking pictures with the camera on her phone. Spencer is urging them to swing near enough to the bank for him to climb on board but it is proving impossible to control its trajectory. Clark's helpless laughter has changed key and become impotent hysteria. He has realised that he isn't part of the scheme. The rope continues to thrash and twist as the three boys lean and jockey their weight. The branch it is anchored to gives an ominous groan.

Mike starts to wriggle his feet around. The foot in the loop has been taking most of the weight and now Skinner is on his shoulders the pressure has become too much. 'Just a minute,' he says, trying to readjust his balance. He eases his foot out of the loop and gropes for a purchase on the stick, bracing himself, one foot on either side of Matt, whose thighs are clamped around the rope. Again, Matt's thigh is tweezed and he yelps. Mike tries to steer the rope back towards the bank but only succeeds in causing it to veer in the other direction, over the darkly churning pool. Their shouts and whoops become loaded with anxious sub-text.

Then the stick snaps.

Matt is plunged downwards. One jagged end of the stick digs into his testicles before falling away. He lets out an expletive in a high-pitched squeal. Only his hands support him, one on the coarse rope, the other grasping a handful of Mike's trousers. The hand on the rope begins to slide and burn so that most of his purchase can only be on the soft, oft-washed cotton of Mike's trousers, which also begin a rapid descent. Matt begins to move inexorably down towards the water. For a moment Mike is carrying his own, Skinner's and more than half of Matt's weight by his hands alone; his feet kick to regain the rope's loop. Skinner, saving himself, shimmies back up the rope relieving something of the pressure and Mike manages, with a supreme effort, to get his foot into the stirrup.

But Matt inches inevitably towards the water until his feet are in the pool. It feels as though cold scaly hands are pulling at his ankles. The drag of the water downstream is sufficient to prevent the rope swinging back to the vertical. Matt thrashes and kicks, suddenly powerfully afraid of whatever mysteries the deeps of the pool might hide, swivelling his head from side to side. Sheer walls or loose-soiled overhang give little hope for escape. The pool extends for about fifteen yards between high banks before rounding a bend and bottoming out. It is an easy swim except for the unknown quantities beneath its surface and the fickle suck of the currents.

Mike's sweatpants are around his ankles now, stretching and offering no support, the hand that held the rope is raw and on fire and Matt knows that he is going in. Mike's face, looking down at him, is bright red apart from the lurid O of the stain around his mouth as Matt releases the rope and drops into the pool. A strong rush of water bombards him, the white foam fizzing and breaking over his head. The roar of the water is loud. The foamy taste of it is bitter and brackish. Beneath his feet he can feel nothing at all; no river bed, no pebbled slope, no metallic struts of construction or reinforcement. The surge of water down the weir is pushing him into the swallowing throat of the pool.

JOHN HAS SEEN it all and it seems to him that his dream has been an iniquitous prophecy. Indeed, looked at from a long perspective, it feels as though all of his hard-hearted life has been leading to this doomed epiphany—a lost opportunity for a truly selfless, altruistic act, the instinctive urge of one person to aid another. It is an empathetic impulse in which the heart leads, the body follows and reason is left far behind. The newspapers are full of such heroic acts: neighbour enters burning house to rescue baby; mother donates kidney to save son. But John's heart, unpractised in love, fails him. The boy slips from the end of the rope and disappears into the pool. The cry of John's heart to act is feeble and his limbs easily ignore it. His feet are rooted to the bridge. He will fail the boy as he failed Richard. His failure to engage will be terminal for this boy. His stony heart is unable to make a compassionate leap; choked up and atrophied, it will kill them both.

It is beating now with brutal, self-serving determination; me me me.

Then there is a flash of red visible on the bottom lip of the weir. From John's angle it is like fire seen through water. A white hand and a skinny arm grapple for a purchase. Gradually the boy struggles to safety, grasping at overhanging shrubbery.

A car horn attracts the attention of the lads on the bank and they instantly abandon the scene and run towards it. Their departure releases John. Too late he thinks about their descriptions, clothing— the police will surely want to know. He is too far away to discern accurately the make and model of the car. Blue, he thinks, low-slung and gleaming with chrome modifications. It pulsates with the outrageous basal thrum of some primal beat.

He makes his tentative way across the bridge, through the chicane and down the bank to the tree in time to hold out a hand to Matt. Matt grasps it and hauls himself out onto the dry bank. The strength and water-logged weight of the lad almost overwhelms John and they both collapse, breathing hard. Matt is shivering. The breeze is chill on his saturated skin.

The sudden reversal bewilders John. From a precipice of fateful failure it seems that he has stepped onto a plateau of renewed opportunity. He begins to think frantically of what action he can take to redeem himself. Emergency services, hot food, sweet tea. John hasn't brought his mobile phone with him and the thought of entering the Mere once more is too much for him even though he despises himself for this feebleness, this craven habit of putting *himself* first. He must *offer* something. Make a gesture—more than a gesture—a sacrifice.

'We can go to my house and call an ambulance,' he blurts out. 'Do you need one? It isn't far.'

To his surprise Matt laughs. 'No!' He is wet and cold and his gonads ache, but he is unhurt. Mr Pickering, on the other hand, looks white and is gasping for breath. 'Do *you* need one?'

'Ah. No.' John manages what he hopes is a self-deprecating, heroic smile. 'I do have some tablets at home ...' he shakes his head. 'But never mind about that. If not an ambulance, then we ought to call the police. This is the second time ...'

'This was different. It was just an accident.'

'But surely ...'

'No, really. Just a prank that went wrong. I'm fine. Just wet.'

Matt's determination to make light of the incident frustrates John who has, for the first time, within his grasp, a possibility for atonement. It frightens him and yet he sees it more and more clearly. It makes such sense.

'Oh, well ...' John is struggling to find a hook that will land the boy. At the same time a gutless habit of self-preservation causes him to be wary of the ways that anything he says might be misconstrued.

In the end it is Matt who makes the leap. 'But you've got a shower, right? And a washing machine?'

'Oh yes, of course.'

'Great!' Matt is on his feet. He holds his hand out to John, helps him to rise. 'I'll get skinned alive if I go home wet again. Which way is it?'

They are crossing the bridge, man and boy.

JOHN'S HOUSE IS as cold and cloistered as a grave. Because of the sign, 'Invalid within' Matt keeps his voice low and treads carefully, imagining a bed-ridden elderly relative or a wheel-chair bound wife. The air is old and there is an eerie, echoey, deserted feel about the place as though no one lives there at all. As though someone has died. He strips off his clothes in the bathroom and showers. Even he can see the signs that no one cares for this house. There is nothing to indicate a woman; no face creams or make-up or perfumed soaps. Neither are there any signs of invalidity; no sturdy handles or hoists or special non-slip mats like the ones he has seen at Bridge House on his occasional visits there.

But he recognises the bathroom fittings from home—his old home on the Fairways—with a nostalgic lurch.

In the shower cubicle he is overcome with nervous reaction. He is not afraid, but wary, as though treading on ice that may crack. This is the furthest he has ever forayed into independence. Always, in the past, he has had a parent or teacher with him, has been told what to do or expect, how to behave. What would his parents say if they knew where he was, who he was with? Is *this* what they mean when they talk about being more 'grown-up'? The freedoms—and the uncertainties—of self-determination make him dizzy. He is a free-climber on an impressively high but dangerously narrow ledge.

He keeps the towel wrapped around his waist and puts a bathrobe on top of it that he finds hanging on the back of the door, hoping it is Mr Pickering's and not the aged incapacitated relative's. Even so, it feels very weird—too starkly personal—to be wearing the intimate apparel of a man he hardly knows.

In the kitchen Mr Pickering is making cocoa. He has an idea that it is the right thing for shock, and milk is the one thing he has plenty of.

Stepping through the vestibule Matt eyes the oddly placed easy chair, the table with its packets of pills, the grey arm cuff and white monitor, but makes no comment. The kitchen, like the bathroom, is like looking at something familiar through a bent lens, recognisable objects rearranged.

John busies himself around the kitchen, stacking the dishwasher, clearing the cluttered worktop, trying up the bags of rubbish that have accumulated by the bin, suddenly ashamed of the detritus of his debilitated, bachelor life.

'How was the shower? Not too hot?' he asks ridiculously. He has no idea, he realises, how to engage in conversation on an equal footing.

'No, fine.'

They look at each other briefly. Matt gives a nervous laugh. It comes out too loudly in the silent house and he puts his hand swiftly to his mouth and ducks his head. 'Sorry,' he whispers. He indicates the dressing gown. 'Was it all right to ...'

'Oh yes. Fine. I should have thought you'd need something. Your clothes?'

Matt cocks his head. 'Still in there. I put them in the bath. I didn't want to drip on the carpet.'

'Right.' John dithers momentarily before opening the door of the utility room and fetching out a bucket. 'Put them in here then and bring them through and we'll wash them.'

Matt pads back to the bathroom, squeezing past the chair. Through doors ajar he spies an office, a bedroom. There is no sign of anyone else in the house.

'This is very kind of you,' he says in a low voice, proffering the bucket.

'Not at all,' John replies, absurdly pleased.

They put the machine on. John regards the oozing trainers, lost.

'If you have some newspaper we can stuff them, and put them in the drier,' Matt offers.

'Really?'

'Oh yes, that's what I do ... did when we had a drier. We don't have one now.'

It is a golden opportunity. 'Your new house, it's ...' John pauses. What on earth can he say about it? Nothing that would not seem insufferably patronising. '... very different. I mean, you must feel ... it must be hard.'

Matt shrugs. 'It is what it is.'

'Of course. And your dad's new place? How's that?'

The mention of Richard shuts a fierce door. John sees it clearly. 'I wouldn't know.'

'Ah. You haven't ..?'

'No. I don't see him now.'

They are worse than John thought—the consequences of his heartlessness.

They screw newspaper into balls and stuff it into the trainers, and then put them in the drier. Now both machines are whirring and whining. The trainers thump and rumble. The microwave is also droning, the jug of milk within rotating in stately circles. Then it pings. John jumps and without thinking puts his hand on his chest.

'Did you have one of your tablets?' Matt motions with his head to the collection in the vestibule.

'Oh no. Not yet. I'm ok.'

John makes the cocoa, pouring the milk into two mugs. His hand is shaking with the sudden realisation of his hopes: the boy, *here* in his house. But the house is in such a state. He sees it through his visitor's eyes. The boy must think he's a lunatic, living here like this. What chance is there that he can win the lad's confidence?

The unknown third occupant of the house is on Matt's mind. Only two mugs. 'Is there anything you need to do? I don't want to be a nuisance. Is there someone you need to check on?'

For a wild moment John wonders if Matt has somehow seen him in his lair, placating his wilful, querulous heart-patient.

'No,' he says too quickly, a defensive note in his voice.

'Oh. Ok.' The kitchen floor is cold on Matt's feet. 'Where shall we drink this?' he asks.

John considers the lounge—funereal, with its drawn curtains and accumulated dust—and rejects it. 'Let's go into the office,' he says. It will hardly be an improvement, but the blinds can be quickly opened and there is a small electric fan heater in there. They edge awkwardly past his chair, which, John can see now, is hopelessly in the way and looks completely bizarre.

The office—on a number of different levels—has poignant resonance for them both. It is very similar in size and shape and furnishings to the one Matt occupied with his father in their previous house and calls back instantly to mind echoes of their shared hours there. It was their space. Dad called it their 'man cave'. His mother rarely entered except to deliver snacks or clear debris. During the day, when not on the road, Richard would work from home. The paraphernalia from Pickerings that Matt sees now stacked in piles and bursting from files is achingly familiar. There is a box of samples—machined widgets, angular fixings, lengths of extruded pipings—that he knows well.

John fusses with the blinds and takes a stack of unopened post and accumulated junk mail off the leather chair. He bends down to plug the heater in and there is instantly an acrid smell of hot, singeing dust. When he stands up the view he has of Matt, hovering diffidently in the room, is powerfully evocative of Richard six months earlier. John reviews again, in his mind, the interview they'd had right here.

'If only I had known,' he murmurs.

Now the blinds are open Matt can see the dereliction in the room; the blooms of grey fuzz—like ashes—the unopened mail, cobwebs, the bone-cold chill of unoccupied space.

He sips his cocoa and it is gritty, as though contaminated by the debris of the room.

They have not spoken for some moments. Matt decides to keep to safe ground. 'How are things at the factory?' he asks.

It is John's turn to close a door. 'I wouldn't know,' he says, unconsciously repeating Matt's own words. Then he takes a deep breath. 'I haven't been well. I had a coronary in March. A heart attack. I've been off work since then.'

'Ah.' Things fall into place in Matt's mind. He takes another sip of his drink. There is a shiny, trembling skin of fatty milk on its surface, buoyed up by the thick sludgy cocoa. He stifles a shudder and places the mug down by his feet.

But a hidden lock has been opened in John. Words tumble out like ill-disciplined puppies. 'That's why you've seen me around, walking. Ordinarily I'd be at work in the afternoons. It comes as a terrible shock, you know, something like that. You never see things in the same light again. It isn't just all that you'd lose—how unreliable it all is. It's all the things you didn't get right ...' John knows that he is speaking too soon, too earnestly, of things unsuitably personal.

'Yes.' Matt looks around the room, at the ceiling and the bookshelves of engineering manuals, anywhere but at the man in front of him. John follows his gaze and remembers how Richard had sought inspiration from the room to explain his terrible dilemma, and found none.

'He came here, you know, your dad.'

'Did he?' The subject grates on Matt, like the grainy cocoa powder between his teeth, and sets him on edge.

'Yes, in November. He was ... I've never seen a man so tortured.'

The idea is almost more than Matt can bear, here in this evocative room. He shifts in his seat.

'Yes, and you know, I've been thinking about it all a lot since I first saw you that day by the river. And it occurs to me that I really didn't understand then what I understand now. His unhappiness ...'

Matt is wringing his hands, toying restlessly with the belt of the bathrobe. He doesn't want to hear it, but with his clothes in the washing machine and his shoes in the drier he has no option but to remain.

'He sat in that very chair ...'

Matt leaps to his feet as though the chair has suddenly caught fire around him. His foot knocks over the cocoa and they both watch as the brown liquid soaks into the pale beige carpet.

THEY HAD SPOKEN no more of personal things, busying themselves with cloths and carpet shampoo on the cocoa stain, transferring his clothes from the washer to the dryer and discussing safe, neutral topics like sport and music. John had opened the door to the lounge and switched on the enormous television set. He had Sky, innumerable sports channels which, he admitted, he never watched.

In Matt's eyes the whole house was like a mortuary, cold and bleak. It was as if Mr Pickering had died from his heart attack, not survived it. Amongst the impersonal furniture and neutral decor, Matt felt strangely at home, his dislocation at one with the anonymous rooms.

Afterwards, walking home through the dusk, unable to face, just yet, the empty house on the Mere, Matt takes the long way home along the Crescent and up the Avenue, probing the wound of his misery.

The Fairways is a picture of self-satisfied smugness. The inhabitants are cosily immured from life's unpleasantness by their double glazing and insulation, their security systems and determinedly insular eyes. Within their spacious homes they are safe and separate. Everything on the Fairways is so civilised and agreeable, a world away from the Mere. Separated by merely a mile, an insignificant river, a local bridge, the two are worlds apart.

Matt feeds his anger by lingering long outside his old house. The curtains are the same, the decor, from what he can see, unchanged. He can almost, by half closing his eyes and squinting into the gloaming, imagine them inside. His dad and him tinkering with their bikes in the garage or playing pool on the table they had—much to his mother's dismay—installed in the conservatory. His mother, quietly cooking or reading, or absent altogether, working at Bridge House.

Why can he not just walk up the drive and put his key in the lock and find everything as it was?

But there is a new boy in his bedroom. He and the new boy in his father's life meld in Matt's head and he experiences, there on the pavement in the gathering gloom, an over-powering deluge of sickening jealousy. Their appropriation of his perfect life is a violation, almost physical in its impact, tearing the delicate tissue of his blithe, unthinking happiness.

His parents' reasonableness in the face of this desecration is unbelievable. They are too quick to minimise the shocking repercussions their failures are having on his life, far too keen to rationalise the whole thing. They are waiting to talk in an adult way about when things started to go wrong; perhaps it was the death of his little sister, perhaps the debts, or something else. And then they want to talk up the positives of their new situation—as though there *are* any—as though it is the latest, improved version of some inanimate object that has become obsolete and can simply be scrapped.

Nobody at all seems to be able to appreciate the particular sticking point of the other boy, the little boy, who has usurped Matt's place. Can't they *see* what a betrayal that is? How impossible to adjust to? The possibility that he might be better, faster, cleverer, more beloved, preferred.

This insecurity is newly-sprung, a direct result of his father's defection, a vulnerable, hollow place so palpable he can almost point to it in its nest beneath his heart. It must be guarded with vigilance from further hurt. As long as he has a stronghold from which to shore up his defences he will be saved the daunting task of reconstruction—of wresting, from the carnage, something entirely new.

THE ENCOUNTER WITH Mr Pickering brings home to Matt that he will not be able to keep his two lives separate forever. His secret Spencer's-gang-rope-swing-world cannot run neatly parallel to his façade of diligently completed homework and early nights. There are cross-overs and intersections. Not just the appearance of Mr Pickering on the bridge. It transpires that Mike's mother works at Bridge House too. And, in a spiteful irony of melding worlds, another convoluted connection concerning Spencer's girlfriend is brought to Matt's startled attention.

She is almost always with Spencer these days, saying nothing; a pale ghost-like presence on the periphery of their awkward, odd collective. Sometimes he ignores her completely and she is left to her own devices as they pursue their pointless projects—setting fire to piles of grass-cuttings, throwing stones, whittling sticks—but occasionally he will pull her roughly into an embrace and it makes her melt. She becomes liquid in his arms, more translucent than ever, pouring herself against him. It makes Clark and Mike grin and giggle but the effect on Skinner is electrifying; he goes rigid and stares, his eyes ravenous, his snake-like tongue repeatedly wetting his thin lips. Spencer—one eye on Skinner while his mouth moves over hers—slowly and deliberately lifts a hand and squeezes her tiny breast before releasing her and pushing her abruptly away with the air of someone who, having slaked his thirst, has no further interest in the water. Often, after these episodes, Skinner will skulk away while the others carry on, the girl forgotten.

Matt is surprised when, one evening as he sits idly on the grass beneath the tree waiting for the others, she joins him, silent as a whisper.

'You're Richard's boy,' she announces. Her voice is soft and breathy. Her hair, today, is pulled back into a ponytail but her fringe, as ever, drapes a veil over her eyes. She glances up at him from under it. She knows his father? The collision of his lives is violent and Matt is thrown off balance momentarily. He manages only to look a question.

'I babysat for them last night,' the girl says. 'I'm Jasmine's little sister.'

'I didn't know.'

'I only just put two and two together. I can't think why. You look just like him. Weird, isn't it?'

'Yeah.'

'He's nice, your dad.'

'Did you ..?'

'No. I didn't tell them I know you.'

The myriad sub-strata of interweavings and cross-connections deepen daily. His mother is becoming a regular customer at the local convenience store where Spencer's mother stacks shelves in the evenings and where Skinner's dad buys his booze. Matt knows that Mr Pickering disapproves of his association with Spencer and the others and while he does not *think* he will interfere by informing his parents, it is quite likely that some other meddlesome dog-walking ex Fairways neighbour will do so. Carmel—the girl—will, in all likelihood, say something to her sister.

Nothing, it seems, happens in isolation. In a way the inevitable emergence of the truth will be a relief. The dynamite is becoming difficult to handle.

One day the lads just turn up. Matt is at the kitchen table devising a revision schedule. The table has been given over entirely to him. It is the only surface in the house that can accommodate his books and laptop and provide space to write. Matt and his mother have been eating off trays in the lounge, a temporary measure, Rosie warns; it is— by their lights—a slovenly practice. The door is open to the evening and Rosie is in the tiny front garden preparing the soil for summer bedding. It is a thankless task. The ground is hard and packed down and full of stones.

The arrival of the four boys in the limited space seriously restricts her industry.

'Hello,' she says, looking from one to the other. 'Can I help you?'

'We've come for Matt,' Clark explains.

Rosie regards them doubtfully. Skinner looks particularly awful; his face a rash of pustules and his clothes unspeakably grim. Spencer—more presentable as a rule—has had his hair cut very short and is wearing camouflaged combat gear that has been newly acquired. Like most of the family's belongings it has come from some mysterious source accessed by Maxwell. He looks like a guerrilla fighter fresh from manoeuvres. Mike, as usual, has his mouth full and the evidence of previous consumption—crumbs, smears and stains—lards his sweatshirt. Of them all, only Clark looks reasonably fit to be seen; his comparative youth and habitually cheery, gregarious expression masking his malleable, unthinking amorality.

Rosie looks at them aghast. She calls in through the door.

'Matt. You have visitors.'

Caught in the claws of his deceit, Matt shrugs on his jacket and swaggers down the path without looking her in the eye, casting his lot.

Even as he walks with them down the pavement he wonders why he does it. He knows that his participation is manufactured and specious. He watches himself sometimes as though from a distance, going through the charade of exchanging high fives and whooping with satisfaction with the others. It is the first time in his life he has deliberately rebelled. It makes him feel heady and powerful, yet also small and vulnerable.

On his return his mother's dissatisfaction is forcefully expressed. The following day his father too makes his feelings known in the form of a long and strongly-worded email. These are not boys, they both tell him, with whom he has anything in common. They remind him about the importance of his exams and his opportunity to go to sixth form college, about not allowing himself to be restricted by the narrow view of others. Unsuitable distractions at this stage, they warn—with laughable hypocrisy—could be dire. Again and again he is entreated to go round to his father's new home and to meet his new 'partner'. Even his mother urges it. He doesn't, she implies, *need* these new, disreputable friends. According to her there is no reason why his previous hobbies and activities—the things he shared with his father—should not continue. 'Your father misses you dreadfully,' she concludes, as though Matt is somehow to blame.

After a while, with study leave and examinations looming, the subject is left to pend. When he goes out his mother looks reproachful and he looks defiant. But neither says a word.

IT IS LATE MAY, and for Matt and others in his year group, school is out. They have two or three weeks of home study leave before the examinations commence. They have been armed with advice and pastpapers and exhorted to return to school with any queries or difficulties if they arise. At their last Assembly they are told severely, but hopelessly, that this is *not* a holiday. There is work to be done and their success in the examinations will stand or fall on the use they make of it.

The rest of the day is pandemonium. School-leavers exchange, remove and deface each other's uniform—the outward and most resented symbol of their enforced conformity. A few get silly on cider, smuggled in and swigged in the toilets. Most celebrate with sweets and cakes, signing year books and lounging across the desks, savouring the commencement of a new era of autonomy. A small but significant faction of boys—who might struggle with the spelling of a word like 'autonomy'—range around the school corridors defiantly, half-dressed, shouting inappropriate words because they are now beyond retribution. They bid glad goodbyes to hated history rooms and science labs that might have been the scenes of prolonged and torturous abuse. The fire alarm is repeatedly set off, there is a food fight in the cafeteria, water bombs are dropped from the roof of the Technology block and an unpopular teaching assistant is locked in a stationery cupboard. The inmates have temporarily gained the upper hand in the penal institution and although little real damage is done the attitude of disrespect and ingratitude does nothing to recompense the teaching staff which has done its best to instil discipline and knowledge into the thankless pupils for five years.

But when news arrives that a cohort from a neighbouring Academy is on its way to wage battle on the playing field the students are suddenly voluble in their outrage and prepare loyally for a blood bath in defence of their school. None of them seem aware of any contradiction, and indeed there is some disappointment when the rumour turns out to be a ruse.

Matt has handed in all of his coursework files—something neither Spencer nor Skinner can say—although admittedly the geography work had been considerably below its original standard. He holds himself somewhat aloof from the end-of-year uproar; not because he does not appreciate the significance of the occasion—perhaps, back at his old school, he might have entered with more enthusiasm into the traditional (less anarchic) frivolities—but just because he feels so personally disconnected from it all. He *has* no axe to grind, no special slow-burning resentment, no notable relationship at all—negative or positive—with the place. He has been unhappy here, but his unhappiness has not been caused by the school. The school, like the cramped little house, is just another feature in his landscape of discontent. His predominant emotion, as he trails at a distance behind his rampaging classmates, is jealous disappointment that he will miss the end of year prom at his old school, and a burning desire to know who will be accompanying Jilly Shillingworth.

In a day or so he will find out; the photographs will be all over Facebook and he will pore over them, feeling like a voyeur. His posts on friends' walls are rarely even acknowledged, cursorily dismissed, as though he is an insubstantial shadow from the distant past, irrelevant to their world. But he stalks it, like a ghost haunting familiar places.

It all adds to Matt's sense of disconnection within his bleak vista of accidental associations and painful, partial detachments. Who is he? Where does he belong? He has no clue.

MATT AND SKINNER idle by the bridge. Spencer is elsewhere; it is possible—but not very likely—that he is revising. Matt himself has diligently pored over his books all morning but the airless house and constant distractions—a cold-calling double glazing salesman, an unemployed immigrant selling dusters, and a pair of sweating, black-suited Mormons—have made him restless and cross.

Now, just after two, it is quiet. The field is deserted apart from a stray dog trailing a length of tether, snuffling and burrowing in the far hedgerow. The sunshine illuminates everything in slightly augmented brilliancy. The mown swathe of field looks almost lush. The hedge is a riot of white and pink blossoms disguising the tangled shreds of plastic bag caught amongst the thorns. The water cascading down the weir is bright with glitz and even the whipped surface of the pool glows with a kind of milky effervescence.

Skinner lobs careless stones into the far bank of the river on the far side of the bridge. Low water has revealed an oozing area of greenish mud. The stones, prised from the drier upper layers of the opposite bank, make a satisfying splat as they land in the viscous sludge. The log, which has lain partly submerged since winter, is now almost fully exposed. The growth of weedy beard has shrivelled and fallen away. Its underside is emerald green with algae, and spongy. When a stray stone hits it, it bounces off with a rubbery rebound.

Apart from a grunted greeting Matt and Skinner have exchanged no words. Skinner is taciturn by nature anyway and Matt's acceptance into Spencer's crowd has put his knife-like nose out of joint. He tends to glower at Matt and appraise his clothing with sneering disdain. His own wardrobe comprises a selection of saggy tee shirts in indeterminate, faded hues worn in rotation—not always via the laundry—and jeans.

He wears old, cracked trainers, often without socks. There is always, around Skinner, an animalish aroma, a pheromone of neglect. The sun is drying his acne somewhat. His spots appear crusty, his skin perhaps a little less livid, but perched on the parapet of the bridge close to him now, Matt can see a peppering of blackheads around his eyebrows and in his ears. His dirt is more than deeply ingrained.

Suddenly Skinner grins, revealing pointed, slimy teeth.

'My dad fancies your mum,' he announces. 'Saw her in her uniform in the shop. Says he'd like to do her. He likes nurses.'

Matt frowns. He has never seen Skinner's father but the idea is repellent. Before he can think of a suitable reply, footsteps on the bridge make both boys swivel on their narrow perches. Mr Pickering makes a hesitant approach.

'Afternoon,' he nods.

'Afternoon,' Matt nods back. Skinner's head pivots on his scrawny, tide-marked neck from one to the other. His eyes are beady, ferreting.

'All right?' It is ten or so days since Matt was at Mr Pickering's house. Overall Matt's remembrance of the encounter is positive; the man was kind in spite of apparent frailties. He looks, today, less harried, with a slightly better colour than formerly. Matt would be happy to converse but Skinner's rapacious curiosity spells warning.

'Yup,' Matt flicks his eyes in Skinner's direction.

Mr Pickering seems to catch the inference. He nods, 'Good,' and walks on.

'Who's that?' Mr Pickering is barely out of earshot.

Matt shrugs. 'Just a bloke I know.'

'Where's he live?'

Matt jerks his head in the direction of the Fairways. 'Somewhere up there.'

'Thought so.' Skinner gnaws his fingernail. 'One of the big houses I bet. Got plenty of gear, I bet.'

Matt thinks: about the music system, the home cinema, the computer. There are other items no doubt—cameras, power tools, credit cards, cash. 'Not really. Just an old bloke lives on his own.'

'*Does* he?'

Matt is conscious of a curdled uneasiness in his stomach.

Suddenly Skinner slips down from the bridge's balustrade. He walks to the tree and takes hold of the rope. Grasping the noose at the bottom he drags it onto the bridge and climbs the first two rails. The rope is taut, drawn to its furthest extent. Matt sees now that it will be a real feat to climb onto the handrail and counter-balance the weight of the rope effectively while you steady yourself enough to make the jump. Making the leap and risking the pool would take nerve.

'Are you going to do it?' he asks Skinner.

'I *could* do.' Matt doesn't doubt it. Skinner is easily the most athletic of the lads and is without a sense of personal danger. 'But Spencer has to do it first.'

'Why?'

'He has to be first at *everything*, doesn't he?' It is the first time Skinner has intimated any question of Spencer's self-appointed leadership.

'*I* don't fancy it,' Matt admits.

'You're scared.'

'I've been in that pool once, remember? The current's strong. It pulls you under.'

'*He's* scared as well. But I'm not. I'll show him, one day.' Skinner drops the rope. It swings in a perfect semi-circular sweep down over the weir and rises over the pool. He glances at his watch and, 'Got somewhere to be,' he says. 'Come, if you want.'

Skinner leads him behind the garages and onto the overgrown path between the river and the flats. Tenacious brambles grasp their clothes as they pass. A dog hurls himself against the fence, making Matt jump. Skinner sniggers; he had expected it. On the left, past the wonky fence panels and through chain-link, Matt sees a series of ragged gardens, rain-washed, sun-bleached collections of neglected toys and rusting tools, lines of washing hanging in the windless air. A grubby toddler digs in the soil with a stick. A man squats on the back step, smoking. A baby in a pram thrashes and cries. It seems as though they pass him in a sequence of still photographs; the briefest glimpse before flickering on.

They turn up by the charred remains of the scout hut. The once neat grassy apron is rank with weeds. A poster on the gate announces an upcoming jumble sale. A group of local women is trying to raise funds to rebuild the hut. Skinner tears the postert down as he passes.

They arrive at the parade of shops. A series of scents envelops them as they walk its length. Sweet grease of cheap meat melds with thick, stale tobacco. Hot wet hair, acrid perm solution and sticky lacquer fuses with Persil and cooking cotton. Then there's a tumultuous cacophony of earthy vegetables, pungent cheese, yeast, toffee, coffee and spice. Opposite the shops is a primary school; a shrill buzz of childish chatter exudes from its open windows. On the school playing field little children are playing rounders. From deep within, the halting strains of 'What shall we do with the drunken sailor?' stumble from the reeds and valves of the infantile orchestra.

Skinner perches on one of the concrete bollards that line the area in front of the shops, and picks at the boil on his neck. He is waiting.

Mothers with buggies arrive and begin to gather around the school gate. It is almost three o'clock.

Presently a dull roar, increasing in volume and proximity, can be heard. A sleek blue car turns smartly into the road with a slight squeal of tyres. In spite of the heat, all its darkened windows are closed. Even so, the thud of the sub-woofer permeates the air and makes the glass of the shop windows vibrate. The car cruises to a standstill on the yellow hatched area outside the school gates. Its engine trembles like a thoroughbred horse. The conversation of the women by the gate is drowned out. The buggy occupants crane their tousled heads to see. Skinner slips off his perch and saunters over to the driver's window, which is lowered no more than four inches. Matt glimpses a pair of dark glasses and nothing more.

Skinner leans towards the window but is careful not to touch the car. He keeps his voice low when he speaks but in the main he listens, nodding eagerly now and again. It is a wonder, given the volume of the music, that he can hear whatever is being said. At one point he glances over his shoulder at Matt, who has remained in the shade underneath the canopy that protects the shop windows. The dark glasses turn momentarily in his direction before dismissing him.

Skinner steps away from the car, the window is raised and the car slides away. He is clearly pleased by the result of his encounter. He has a spring in his step and his eyes are lively.

'Going to do a job for Maxwell,' he says as the boys make their way along the pavement.

'Really? That's great,' Matt's voice is hollow. 'What kind of job? What does Maxwell do?' He can hardly imagine that it is anything very savoury, much less legal. Skinner throws him a look that both sneers at Matt's pathetic naivety and gloats in his own superior knowing. Matt is wrong-footed. 'When will you start?' he asks, feeling lame.

'One night next week, maybe.'

Matt thinks that Skinner will say no more but after a while Skinner is unable to stop himself from boasting, 'Says he needs someone just like me. Small. Good climber.'

'You *are* a good climber,' Matt agrees.

'Yeah. Maxwell saw what I'd done with the rope.'

Unexpectedly, Skinner leads Matt to the tenement where he lives with his father. They climb a gloomy stair to a small landing. Two doors face each other in equally poor states of repair. Skinner grapples a key from his jeans pocket.

'Keep it down, just in case,' he says, before opening the door.

There is a gust of foul air; old cigarette smoke and alcohol, sweat and something feral. The passageway is dark, with threadbare carpet, tattered wallpaper. Three doors, two to the right and one to the left, are closed. The first one on the right has a hasp that is padlocked.

Skinner creeps along the corridor and peeps into the room at the end.

''t's ok,' he says. 'He's out.' The living room is a shambles. The door is off its hinges and leans against the wall. The curtains are only partly opened. Piles of newspaper, beer cans and take-away food cartons cover the carpet. The settee is sagging and torn, yellow foam innards poke through the cushions. There is a burn on one arm. A filthy green candlewick bedspread is thrown over the chair. Skinner leads the way into the kitchen, a tiny space where there is barely room for two people. The sink is full of dirty dishes. The food debris on the plates is dry and crusted, plainly days old. A burned pan is on the stove. The worktop is sticky with things spilled. There is an empty bread bag in the open-mouthed bread bin and the yawning cupboards reveal no food of any practical kind; half a jar of piccalilli, some curry powder, vinegar, ketchup.

'Drink of water?' Skinner fills a glass from the tap and drinks.

'No thanks,' Matt says. He is working hard not to betray any mark of his revulsion. 'Nice view,' he comments, nodding at the kitchen window, which looks out over the river. It is the only positive thing he can think of to say about the flat.

Skinner nods. 'Show you my room,' he says.

They return to the padlocked door and Skinner opens it with a key. The room is small, similar, in fact, to Matt's own. A single bed along one wall sits close to the floor, its legs absent. The bottom sheet is untucked, rucked, revealing a stained pale blue mattress. A tangle of sheets and blankets in the corner create what can only be described as a nest. There is a blue striped pillow with no slip. Next to the bed, under the window, is a book shelf with some children's books that Matt recognises from his own childhood—*The Very Hungry Caterpillar, Peace at Last, Can't you sleep Little Bear*—and a jumble of school books and folders. On the top, placed centrally, on its own, is a framed photograph of a smiling woman holding a chubby toddler.

'Your mum?' Matt ventures.

Skinner nods.

'Do you see her?'

'Nah. She can't come back here,' Skinner cocks his head in the direction of the rest of the flat, referring, Matt understands, to its other occupant, rather than to its virtually uninhabitable state.

'Do you mind?' Matt, of course, is thinking of his own dad. With all their other incompatibilities, perhaps the desertion of a parent might prove common ground. To Matt's surprise though, Skinner shakes his head. He turns slightly away, towards the window. His eyes, for a moment, in the light, shine. 'She's safe,' he says, as though that is all that matters.

'Why don't you visit her?'

'I *would*. But he'd find out where. Too risky. She writes, sometimes.'

In the corner of the room are two cages, stacked one on top of the other. They are the source, Matt realises, of the feral smell. 'Seen my rats?' Skinner asks proudly, and squats in front of the cages. Each holds a white-furred, pink-eyed rat. The cages are clean, strewn with fresh wood shavings. The water bottles are topped up and there is dried food. The rats' whiskers quiver as Skinner peers in, a sign, Matt detects, of pleasure. 'Want to hold one?'

Matt shakes his head, 'No thanks.'

'All right,' Skinner stands up. 'Better go. He might be back.'

They wander back down to the field. Soon the children from school will emerge from the snicket, including Mike and Clark, and the girl, Carmel. There is still no sign of Spencer. The heat is intense. Matt's fair skin is feeling tight. The river glares, hard as a mirror. They walk on, by common, unspoken consent, over the bridge and turn right, up the path that skirts the golf course through cool, native trees.

'Might find some golf balls,' Skinner remarks, making towards the course.

'We aren't really allowed,' Matt demurs. Skinner throws him a look; what is 'allowed' or 'not allowed' is clearly irrelevant. They skirt the fairway, keeping to the rough and the shade from the ancient trees that were spared by the developer. Skinner keeps his eyes down. They dart like mice in the undergrowth, searching. He does, in fact, find two lost balls. He pockets them with a grin. 'Sell these,' he says.

'Are you sure you want to get mixed up with Maxwell?' Matt asks. 'I mean, you know, it isn't a *long term* arrangement, is it?'

'It could be.'

'You could do better.'

Skinner turns to him, his face a picture of incredulity. 'Better than Maxwell?' It is impossible for him to conceive of such a thing.

The Fairways gardens are neat. Canopied swing seats and lazy hammocks sit on vast areas of decking. A lone woman strokes easily through the blue waters of her pool. A few doors up a lady hosts her friends to afternoon tea. China cups clink against their saucers. There is a waft of warm scones.

'Where's your friend live, then?' Skinner's question seems casual, innocuous. The afternoon has progressed their relationship by a mighty bound. Matt wonders whether Skinner's decision to include him in the news about Maxwell and to take him home might have been some kind of trade-off. The glimpse behind the grimy façade into Skinner's sad, hungry deprivation has startled and moved him.

'Oh, I don't know. Over there somewhere.'

Skinner sniffs. 'You must know,' he mutters darkly, almost sulking.

Matt *does* know, of course. They have already passed Mr Pickering's brooding, shuttered bungalow. 'I've only been once.'

'You've been *in?*'

'Only once.'

'What was it like?'

'I've told you. Empty, really. He's just a bloke on his own.'

'What was it like?' Skinner asks again, more insistently. 'Was there, like, security?'

Matt is uncomfortable with Skinner's thread of thought. It is perfectly clear what is on his mind. He casts his mind back. He does not recall any warning trill of an alarm console as they entered the house. 'Oh yes,' he says solidly. 'They *all* have, these houses. Built in.'

Skinner shrugs and stretches his mouth down at the corners. 'No problem, that.'

They have stopped walking now. They have reached the entrance to the golf club; brick pillars and wrought-iron gates. Skinner faces Matt squarely. Behind him a sign with bold red lettering declares NO TRESPASSERS.

'It's the kind of thing Maxwell likes to know,' Skinner says and adds, significantly, 'It does to keep in with Maxwell.' Skinner's tinny voice grates on Matt. His breath is sour; they are standing close enough for Matt to be able to smell it. There is a new spot erupting on his scalp, a red weal with a yellow pin-prick at its centre. Matt says nothing, staring at the spot to avoid Skinner's eyes. 'I offered to let you hold my rat,' Skinner whines. He is suddenly pathetic.

Matt laughs and takes a step back. It is a ridiculously unequal exchange. But Skinner's pitiful camouflage is threadbare. His eyes become steely and narrow, like flints. He shrugs. 'I'll just tell my dad where you live,' he says. 'He likes nurses.'

JOHN IS RESTLESS and discontented in the house, seeing its oddness from another point of view. The boy had said nothing during his visit, but his eyes had spoken volumes; flickering over the spartan furnishings, taking in the uncared-for air.

'Must have thought I was some kind of recluse,' he thinks.

He removes the chair from the vestibule, attempts some cleaning, contacts the garden maintenance company and asks them to recommence their visits. He shops, braving Tesco, keeping his head down and mechanically filling his trolley. He fears meeting an acquaintance. He has no idea what effect an enquiry after his health might have. The very idea of anyone being kind to him makes him want to cry. He doesn't deserve it. Work remains un-faceable; his employees' frightened eyes and clipped, nervous laughter. He won't go back to being the man he was, but until he knows what kind of man he might become, he is no man at all. His whole life, his very sense of self, is in flux.

In the meantime he continues doggedly with his walks, sometimes overcoming debilitating anxiety to force himself to step out of doors. It is an exercise in self-discipline. He consciously tries to vary the routes and distances, the times, exposing himself to the possibility of the unexpected. He is, at times, frankly terrified, at other times he is deluged by a kind of marrow-sapping sorrow. Venturing under the viaduct one day he finds himself in a small, choked copse where a massive, rotten-hearted elm has collapsed, crushing the hopeful growth of neighbouring ash and alder. The waste and ruin brings tears to his eyes. A guilty lament for the cowed, tortured branches of the struggling saplings mingles with mourning for the diseased, decaying giant under whose oppressive limbs they are bowed.

His sulky heart continues to exercise vindictive control, subjecting him to quakings and bowel-loosening qualms. He doesn't trust it. The idea that it might usurp power again before he has had a chance to make good horrifies him.

He exercises himself over the boy; his estrangement from his father, his undesirable new alliances. It sustains him, to think of somebody other than himself.

MATT HAS NEVER given much thought to the daytime hours that pass outside of school except to know that weekend and holiday hours pass more quickly than classroom ones. Now he is out of school he is surprised how they drag by. He sits at the kitchen table and tries to revise. His mum potters about, cleaning and ironing, trying to make tasty meals from cheap ingredients. Hours seem to pass but when he looks up it is only mid-morning.

He stays home more now, especially when his mum is home. The desire to challenge her has evaporated since his walk with Skinner. Clark, when asked about Skinner's dad, had frowned and said, 'I'd keep away from *him* if I were you.' So he volunteers to go to the shop for her, and accompanies her to the bus. At night he is alert for her key in the door and if she is late he sets out to meet her.

The weeks of heat wave have made everything dull and dry; Matt himself feels the same way. The vitality of his angst is ebbing away, leaving only a limp, shrugging carelessness. He still does not reply to his father's daily text and email messages but now he finds that he just can't be bothered to delete them. The flowers in the garden gasp for water despite nightly doses. The paint on the door and window frames is cracking. Even with the doors and windows thrown wide there is no through breeze. The only thing that enters is a smell from the bins—where things turn putrid days before the bin men come—and fat bluebottles, which buzz and dive in clouds for any patch of moisture, and frowse round salty, sweaty brows. They circle mercilessly, driving Matt insane. At night he kicks his bedding off and lies sleepless in the heat, bathed in the amber glow from the street light outside his window.

Down by the river the air is cooler, moving across the field in little wafts and winnows that caress hot skin. But the ground is hard and parched, the grass browning daily and turning crisp. Under their tree the grass has gone altogether, leaving fine, silty soil. Vegetation is limp and papery, the vibrancy of various greens reduced to a desiccated sage along the river bank and a drowsy muted olive above. The boys swing on the rope, enjoying the rush of air on their bodies, or laze on the ground, their energy sapped. They cool their feet in the river. The river is like a casket, its bed of golden sandstone glitters with the mica of glass jewels and winking aluminium. Its water is liquid bronze coloured, mineral-rich, tempered in the heat, refined and sliding like silken ore between the armoured banks.

Mike submerges himself in the waist-deep wallow before the lip of the weir, his flesh magnified and shockingly white, sending a wash of extra water down the steps. He looks like a subterranean slug. Clark, plunging in to join him, steps on a piece of glass and cuts his foot quite deeply, causing recriminations. Spencer has to take him home. He and Mike support the howling Clark between them leaving Skinner and Matt and the girl behind.

Skinner lounges close to Carmel—much closer than he would have done had Spencer still been present—and looks at her through slitted eyes. She is wearing shorts and a skinny tee shirt. Her legs are turning the colour of peaches in the sun. Skinner's eyes loiter on the place where her thighs meet in the crease of her shorts. His Adam's apple bobs relentlessly. She is trying to make daisy chains but the stalks of the daisies are dry and hard. She uses her thumb nail to make a slit along their length but only succeeds in shredding the stalks. There is a gathering pile of ruined daisies on the bald, sandy earth at her side.

Presently she gets up to gather more daisies and when she returns she sits closer to Matt. Skinner remains where he is for a full minute before leaping to his feet. He gathers up the discarded daisies and flings them over Carmel. Flowers and fine dry silt from the ground catch in her white blonde hair, stick to her shoulders and slither down her top inside her bra. She blushes rose.

'Skinner!' Matt protests.

Skinner shins up the tree and dangles from a high branch, laughing and shrieking like a monkey, 'How's your mum? How's your mum?'

'What does he mean?' Carmel asks under her breath.

THE WAITING ROOM is crowded with emphysemic old people and hot, tired toddlers. As John enters the consulting room the doctor—a young woman—is busy reviewing his notes on the computer screen. She offers him a seat while she scans the screen and then swivels her chair around to face him. She smiles encouragingly.

'How are you?' she asks, and before he can answer she comments, with a satisfied nod, 'you look a bit better.'

'I am ... a bit,' he admits, not wanting to make too much of it. 'But I'm not great!' he adds snappily. The truth is: he is just not sure any more.

She smiles again and begins to unroll the blood pressure cuff. 'Roll your sleeve up, please,' she says. 'I'll just check your blood pressure. Then you can tell me about it.'

John struggles out of his jacket and wrestles with the button on his shirt cuff. 'I can't ...' he begins. There is so much to say that he doesn't know where to begin with it. The doctor misinterprets his words and leans forwards to help him with the button. As she does so, her skirt rides up her thighs, exposing, just for the briefest second, the frill of an underskirt and the thrill of a stocking-top.

'Have you been taking some exercise, as we discussed?'

'Yes, yes. I go out walking. I *am* trying ... but I'm afraid it's too much, sometimes.' It comes out more sharply than he had intended. *Everything* seems too much. On the other hand, everything seems not enough.

She seems impervious. 'Good,' she says smoothly, 'very good.' She wraps the grey blood pressure cuff around his arm and touches the button that begins to inflate it. The display is frustratingly out of John's sightline. He tries to count, anticipating the result.

'Hmm.' She makes a note on the keyboard.

'It's high, isn't it?'

'No, pretty good.'

He wants to ask her to take it again, but she has picked up their conversation. 'Why is it too much?'

'Recently, I had ...' he wants to say an attack, but knows that this would be over-stating things, 'a funny turn,' (that sounds pathetic) 'an *episode*.' That sounds better, more serious. 'I had an encounter with some young people. They were fighting. I tried to intervene. *That* was too much for me. I didn't go out for a fortnight after that.'

She nods and types a few words onto his notes. 'A gym might be a better plan. It's a controlled, carefully monitored environment. Nothing unexpected would happen there.'

'A gym?' he almost shouts. Physical jerks on that scale are way out of his competency at the moment. He's on the point of making a scathing jibe to that effect but bites it back and admits instead, 'I think maybe I'd picked up a virus.'

'Ah. How is your wound?' John quails. The tiny incision in his groin where the stent was inserted has completely healed, but he doesn't want to show it to her; the glimpse of lace and stocking top has resulted in an inappropriate and long dormant response in the vicinity.

'Fine.'

'Good. And you're taking your medication regularly? The blood pressure tablets are clearly working a treat. I'll take some blood and we'll see how much the statin has brought your cholesterol down. Tell me about your symptoms.'

'Chest pain, shortness of breath, rapid heart rate, a feeling of panic, cold sweats, hot sweats, trembling, anxiety, lethargy ...' He reels them off. These are the easy ones. She is typing rapidly, trying to keep up.

'Goodness,' she says. Suddenly she stands up and adjusts her stethoscope into her ears. 'May I listen?'

He opens his shirt and she presses the chrome disk to his chest at various locations. She asks him to breathe in and out. She listens to his back. 'Hmm. Tell me, when do you suffer from these symptoms?'

'All the time,' he says quickly, 'Well, whenever I ...' He tries to rationalise. 'First thing in the morning. Sometimes I wake up with them in the night. Before I go out. Like I said, situations outdoors—like the boys—and once, I thought I had surprised a burglar ...'

'So, stressful situations bring them on. But that's normal, to a degree. Potential danger stimulates the flow of cortisol that arms you to deal with it; typically fight or flight.'

'Just stepping outdoors shouldn't be stressful!'

'I agree. Would you say your susceptibility to stress has increased?'

'Definitely. That's what I'm telling you. I'm afraid my heart can't take it.'

'It can. Are you very conscious of your anxiety levels?'

'Oh yes. And my heart rate.' He is almost boasting. 'I've bought a machine.'

He thinks she suppresses a smile. 'Would you mind stepping onto the scales for me?'

He obliges her, wondering how he is going to get around to the psychological symptoms. How do you confess to feelings of self-loathing and hopelessness? But as she adjusts the scales, he realises that she has changed her terms of reference, from 'stress', an external stimulus, to 'anxiety', an internal response; a sort of cue.

She makes a note of his weight. 'Very good. You've lost nearly two stones. Excellent. That brings you well out of the obese percentile. Let me just take that blood and then you can get dressed.'

'I was obese?' This news shocks him.

'Clinically, yes. All these things add to the potential for heart attack.' She reels them off, 'Obesity. Too much stress resulting in high blood pressure. Lack of exercise. A poor diet high in cholesterol. Especially for a man of—how old are you?'

'Ninety four,' he says wryly. In truth it is the age he feels.

She smiles, 'Really?'

'Fifty two, but ...' he takes the plunge, 'I have *feelings* ...'

She is gathering the blood-letting equipment. 'Oh?'

He kneads his hands. 'When I look back at things—my life—I feel, well, I *know* that ... I don't want to carry on in the same way,' he trails off lamely. He has no vocabulary for self-doubt and insecurity.

She frowns. 'Is that when you get anxious—when you think about it?'

He nods. 'And, sometimes, overpoweringly emotional ...'

'Tell me, Mr Pickering, generally, on a scale of one to ten, how anxious do you usually feel?'

He considers. 'About five or six.'

She looks up sharply. 'Just at work or at home, on a normal day, you feel as anxious as that?'

'I haven't gone back to work yet.'

'Haven't you? Why not? Sharp scratch now.'

'I don't feel well enough. And,' he avoids her eyes, 'I feel embarrassed—for the way I was.' Finally, he gets it out. 'I can't face them, the people at work. I think I was an absolute ... absolutely horrible. And also ...' He points to his swimming eyes. How can he go back to work when *this* can overtake him without warning?

As he dresses she talks to him about how normal it is for victims of a serious health scare, or a physical attack, or even a divorce, to find themselves re-evaluating their lives. 'It concentrates the mind like nothing else,' she says. 'Lots of people take the opportunity to make a completely new start; they go travelling, for example. Sometimes they go back and make recompense for some incident in the past. One patient of mine aged 65 enrolled at University and took a degree! It was something she'd always regretted not doing. It's a normal process and a very positive one, I think. But the other side of the coin is that it's all a terrible shock. It's terribly undermining. Post-traumatic stress syndrome and depression aren't uncommon. That's what I think you have. It's perfectly understandable; you're all out of coping. Who wouldn't be, in your situation? All your symptoms point to it. But I can help you.'

She shows him his pre- and post-operative X-rays. In the first he can see the labyrinthine byways of his chest, ghostly interwoven circuits looping and coiling, branching and splicing, filled with ink. The one spot where the aneurism has caused a blockage and caused the heart attack is cloudy and blurred, unnaturally distended, but the rest is perfectly clear. In the second he can see the stent sturdily holding open the place. Blood flows freely, like orderly traffic, through the junctions.

'You're an engineer,' the doctor says. 'You understand the mechanics of things. This is a healthy, efficient heart.' She places her small hand on his breast. 'These aren't *heart* attack symptoms you've been describing, they're *panic* attack symptoms. When your brain thinks there's a threat, the heart speeds up, increasing the blood flow to your limbs and organs, getting ready for action. The strength of its response only shows us how healthy it is. What we need to do is re-educate your brain so that it stops crying wolf.'

He returns home via the chemists. A packet of anti-depressants now joins his other tablets. In his pocket is a note with the telephone number of a coronary support group. He is to see a counsellor. He has promised to continue his walks and also to look into joining a gym.

He is weak with relief. To have seen for himself the healthy open byways of his interior geography, and to be told that his experiences are not only normal but positive. He can be well *and* different.

For the first time this year he opens the patio doors and takes a seat on the lone chair, enjoying the sun and the gentle burble of the fountain.

THERE ARE FISSURES appearing in the relationships between the boys. Cracks of disquiet and annoyance flare up increasingly.

Perhaps it is the heat. It has a way of enlarging small matters, allowing them to get out of hand; minor niggles mushroom into serious altercations. The boys chafe; the damp skin of their relationship rubbed raw through lack of air and too frequent contact.

Spencer is livid that Skinner has been recruited to help Maxwell in his doubtful schemes. Maxwell is *his* brother and represents, to Spencer, everything a Mere boy can and should become. Being passed over in favour of Skinner has wounded him. Skinner does nothing to salve the wound, making smugly veiled but repeated references to their upcoming excursion.

This event has its own corollary for Matt. He is eaten up with anxiety over the house on the Fairways.

The girl is a further cause of conflict. Skinner is completely unable to conceal his lustful cravings for her and Spencer is cavalier about flaunting his possession of her, mauling Carmel with exaggerated lewdness in front of Skinner's starved, rapacious eyes.

For no reason that Matt can identify the sight of the girl's tender, translucent skin—the small mounds of her breasts, the hand-sized rounds of her buttocks—under Spencer's rough handling makes him seethe. She subjects herself absolutely to him, as though programmed. It isn't that Matt desires her himself. It's just that she deserves better. Her helpless vulnerability moves him.

117

The exams are only a week away. A chance conversation in the shop between Rosie and Spencer's mum ratchets tensions between the lads a notch higher. Spencer is hauled over the coals for his lack of preparation. Suddenly he is under orders to stay in and revise, 'like Matthew.'

'Wish your mum'd keep her mouth shut,' he snaps.

Matt, Spencer and Skinner have walked all the way down the river to the derelict warehouses. The compound behind the ice cream factory is full of refrigerated trucks; business is brisk. The air is laced with a nauseously sweet, greasy aroma. Employees swathed in overalls and hairnets mill about smoking surreptitiously. Naturally, out of her view, Spencer is swaggeringly careless of his mother's edicts, but he would not like to be caught red-handed. He hurries them past. The printing factory and the engineering works emit the jibber and rattle of machinery; metallic demons demented by the heat. Beyond these there is a heavy, unnatural silence, haunted by all that is absent.

The river smells dank and sour; it is turgid between the gasping banks, and covered in blobs of brown foam. Shade from overhanging trees gives some respite from the sun, but is alive with insects that whir and whine around them.

The mention of his mum makes Matt glance involuntarily at Skinner, who sniggers, and winks a lashless eye.

'Leave her out of this,' Matt says darkly. 'Anyway, I presume you do *want* to pass the exams.'

They squeeze through a loose section of fence and saunter across the open yard of a deserted unit, its surface ravaged by ragged weeds that burst through fissures in the concrete.

'You *presume* that I give a flying fuck,' Spencer spits. 'We haven't *all* got places at college.' He picks up a half brick and hurls it at a rusted oil drum. It clatters off with a resounding gong. Skinner bends back a piece of corrugated metal across a doorway and slides himself into the gap, disappearing into the gloom of the interior.

'You *could* have,' Matt says defensively. His own plans for the autumn have been continually sneered at.

Spencer barks out a bitter shout of laughter. He indicates the dilapidated building, the choking vegetation and the frowning, relentless sky, implying the pointlessness of Matt's suggestion. He follows Skinner into the warehouse.

Matt looks around him. The desolate premises and the decay of the yard do have a flavour of the post-apocalyptic and the Mere itself is almost the last stop on the road to brutish, lawless anarchy, but Spencer's narrow vision is incomprehensible to him. As drastically as his personal circumstances have been altered Matt has never considered they will impinge on his potential in the long term; *that* is within himself and his own volition. Spencer seems to look at the Mere as a kind of Alcatraz.

Matt follows the others inside. After the searing brightness the gloom is disorientating. Matt can hear the other boys somewhere in the empty space, the echoes of their movements reverberating around the lofty shell of the building. As his eyes become accustomed to the murk he sees Spencer scouring the ground in search of missiles to throw at the windows. Skinner is half way up a vertical metal ladder heading to a gantry that spans the width of the structure. Matt makes his way towards Spencer, collecting chunks of rubble as he goes. He holds one out to Spencer.

'There *is* life outside the Mere you know, Spencer,' he says quietly, but in the hollow of the empty building his voice carries up to Skinner, who is stepping out onto the narrow gantry twenty feet above them.

'Yeah,' Skinner says. His thin voice is almost disembodied but carries an unmistakable note of triumphalism. 'Look at Maxwell.' He stands above them, balancing on the framework, his arms akimbo. His body language, if not his voice, adds, 'Look at *me*.'

With a mighty heave Spencer hurls one of his missiles at Skinner. It is a poor shot taken in haste. The lump of rubble falls well short but

Skinner's instinctive duck unbalances him and he lurches dangerously to one side. For a moment he is on one leg, the other flailing in a desperate attempt to attain equilibrium, his arms helicoptering wildly. Then he drops, heavily, down onto his knee. The metalwork vibrates and Skinner, on all fours, clings with both hands onto the beam. Matt looks at his hand, held out to Spencer, frozen. It is empty, the piece of rough masonry it had contained now lies split into smithereens on the floor.

Skinner looks down at them and Matt imagines the tableau he and Spencer must make in Skinner's eyes; Spencer breathing heavily, his arm still swinging, Matt with empty palm up, having supplied the ammunition, equally culpable. No wonder Skinner's eyes narrow.

Spencer checks his watch. 'Time to meet Carmel,' he says pointedly.

Matt follows him through the gap in the corrugated metal and across the baking yard. Spencer walks quickly and Matt finds himself breathless trying to keep up. Spencer's shoulders are hunched over, his hands thrust deeply into his pockets.

Matt recognises the posture and the feelings. The pain of being let down by someone you thought you could trust, the hollow jealous hole of finding that someone else is preferred above you.

THE NEXT AFTERNOON Skinner is absent.

The field is a furnace, without a vestige of relief from breeze or shade. Beneath the trees clouds of gnats make infuriating, itching towers. Even as the sun sinks and releases the air from its fiery fist the ground seems to exude stored heat into it. Underfoot the grass is brittle and exhausted. The river is reduced to a sluggish, syrupy flow.

Clark and Mike take turns swinging on the rope, Clark holding his injured foot out at a melodramatic angle and wincing when he lands. It is the first time he has been out since he cut it. He has shown them the stitches that are beginning to dissolve; a longish gash on the ball of his foot is sewn closed like a pursed mouth. He wears a thick sock and his trainer loosely laced and he limps exaggeratedly, when he remembers to. He has been garrulous about the ambulance, the hospital, the injections, the blood, as though it was all the most exciting thing that has ever happened to him.

'You squealed like a baby,' Spencer sneers. It is the first time Matt has heard Spencer criticise his brother. Brotherly vexation is spreading, like gangrene.

Spencer is restless, pacing, a coiled spring. Now climbing the bridge rails and perching on the balustrade, now swinging from the barrier. Carmel leans against the chicane, texting. She wears a little skirt and a strappy top. Her hair is as soft and light as feathers.

Matt lies under the tree with his back against the trunk and his hands folded on his stomach. Up through the grey empty branches he can see the white hot, wide sky.

Time goes on and it is obvious that Skinner is not going to make an appearance. Spencer boils with jealous rage, knowing where he must be, who he is with. He flings stones of temper at the indifferent river, thrashes the wilting undergrowth with a stick. Gradually the shadows of the far hedgerow reach across the tired grass, there is a gasp and the sun slips below the horizon of trees, roofs and chimney pots. The field takes on an ultra-violet hue of gloaming—neither night nor day—and the clenched hand of heat relaxes. The dusk gathers around them but its cloaking does nothing to comfort Spencer. The onset of night brings closer and makes more inevitable his brother's treachery and Skinner's ascendance.

For Matt, watching Spencer's sufferings is like looking at himself in a mirror. But his sympathy is tempered with scorn. Maxwell, after all, is no hero; only a small pawn in a larger game, the tool of some older, more hardened, intimidating player. As glamorous as he might seem— gliding around in his car, coming and going, making deals and getting gear—he is surely only dancing to the beat of a fiercer drum. Whatever rewards he reaps will be meted out in careful measure to keep him hungry. Skinner's only achievement—what Maxwell has, in fact, spared Spencer—is the dubious honour of joining him on the very lowest level of a vicious and ensnaring hierarchy characterised by fear and dependency. Skinner is therefore to be pitied rather than envied. But Spencer is in no position to see things in their real light. Maxwell has dealt him a dreadful blow of disappointment. It is bitter gall to him and he wrestles with its caustic burn as it eviscerates his emotional innards. But it is towards Skinner that his anger burns most brightly; it is Skinner who has usurped him, somehow inveigling himself into Maxwell's confidence, taking the thing Spencer has desired above all others.

His instinct is to hurt back, to hurt Skinner by inflicting an equal wound.

Suddenly he grasps Carmel by the arm and begins to drag her across the bridge. He manhandles her roughly through the chicane and sets off up the path towards the golf course, where the grass is long and the on-coming night is made heavier by the coppice of trees beyond the fourth green. Carmel—usually so compliant—balks slightly at his ferocity. Matt watches them disappear into the thickening dusk, Spencer stalking ahead, Carmel behind, resisting the pull of his arm, leaning her insubstantial weight at a reluctant angle.

Later, when they return, Spencer's angst has ebbed. He flops down onto the ground next to Matt. Carmel lowers herself gingerly a little distance behind him. Her eyes are dark and smudged. The sky is orange-dark, the amber aura of city lights casting a tint across it like a raging inferno burning at a distance. The field is a deep black mass of impenetrable shadow. The lamps along the tarmac path have been broken for weeks. Here, by the river, under the tree by the bridge, only the faintest gleam of light from the sky reflects up from the quietly sliding water. The boys are mere moving shadows, black against the blackness, but Carmel is wraith-like, a miasmic glow, exuding an inner luminosity.

'Tomorrow night I think we'll have a party,' Spencer announces. His habitual good humour has been restored. 'Maxwell will get us some booze.'

Clark and Mike take the idea up with enthusiasm. Matt says he isn't sure he's free.

'Course you are,' Spencer says. He lies back and puts his head on Carmel's lap. She winces.

MATT REALLY HAS no intention of going. He knows all too well what the combination of alcohol, heightened hormones and aggressive resentment will come to. He walks his mum to the bus stop just before eight o'clock; she is working a night shift. On the way home he calls at the shop to buy a big bottle of Coke and some chocolate. She'd pressed the money into his hand as she stepped onto the bus.

'It'll help the maths along,' she had smiled.

Maths is his first exam, Monday morning.

Before him at the check-out is a wizened, dehydrated version of Skinner, swaying slightly and painstakingly counting out change for a pack of beers and half a bottle of whisky. The smell is a fermented version of Skinner; distilled dirt. The features are the same: the sharp, fleshless nose and beady eyes. But whereas Skinner's complexion is slick with weeping furuncles, Skinner's dad has leathery skin, gnarled and shrivelled as though kiln-dried. He has none of Skinner's easy elasticity. He is stiff, stooped and shrunken. The effect is to concentrate the unappealing Skinner qualities rather than to diminish them. This man has a brooding, scaly menace. His hand, as he laboriously moves coins across the counter towards the lady shopkeeper, is reptilian. The idea of it on his mother's soft flesh makes Matt literally step backwards in revulsion. He puts the Coke and chocolate back onto the shelves and leaves the shop.

He wanders for a while around the streets, debating with himself. It is Saturday night, traditionally an occasion for unleashed tempers and released tensions on the Mere. House doors stand open to catch the evening coolness. There is a melee of crying babies, shrieking women letting their weekend hair down and children running wild—out much too late. Televisions with their volumes turned too high yell like angry, incoherent men. They all meld to make the characteristic soundtrack of the Mere. Tonight this is augmented by the caterwaul of Karaoke from the Social Club. He smells barbecues, baking bins, the hot metal of cars, tobacco and the occasional sweet anachronistic scent of roses on the night air. The street lights flicker on above them, cherryade red in the dusk; it must be almost nine o'clock. Matt arrives at his house. It is dark, apart from one lamp dully glowing behind the drawn curtains of the front room. The leaves of plants in his mother's garden are yellow, their petals brown and papery. She hasn't managed to keep them alive.

They don't belong here, ill-equipped for the hardness, the raw, un-tempered atmosphere, the kick-and-trample of survival.

He takes the path behind the tenements. Skinner's flat is lit up like a beacon, bare light bulbs blazing through dusty windows. Only the light in Skinner's room is off. It is the only flat with all its windows closed. Matt imagines the shrivelled, lizard-like form of Skinner's dad basking on the filthy sofa—a fug of cigarette smoke, the acrid tang of whisky.

The river is a muted whisper of moving liquid, an indistinct splash and hiss of water expiring on gasping dry stones.

From the shadow of the garages Matt looks across the field. Clark and Mike have spent most of the day gathering firewood and heaping it on the grass, running off other kids who want to join in with the task and, later, with the bonfire. What started off as a modest camp-fire has now assumed enormous proportions, a ceremonial pyre, the tinder-dry wood eager for the lick of flame. The boys are desperate to light the fire. Matt can hear the shrill whine of Clark's imploring voice across the field. But Spencer won't let them. He is waiting for something.

Matt begins to walk across the field. There is music from a ghetto-blaster, and, on a large, thick blanket, set at a little distance from the fire, sits the girl, looking small and fragile amongst the debris of a picnic.

Matt is looking for Skinner.

Spencer sees him immediately and approaches with an expansive smile. He enfolds Matt in a welcoming arm and draws him into the party.

'There you are,' he says with affected, slightly slurred joviality. 'Been waiting for you. Wouldn't let them light the fire before *you* came.' He knocks the top off a bottle and hands it to Matt. 'Here y'are, mate.' While the fire has had to wait, clearly the drinking has not. A number of discarded bottles litter the site. Clark and Mike are as merry as puppies, gambolling and giggling in excitement now that Spencer has told them they can light the fire. There is a moment of dismay when they realise that neither of them has any matches but then, from behind the tree, Skinner steps forward with some.

Spencer's brow contracts at the sight of him. 'Are you still here?'

Matt looks at Skinner and Skinner looks back, savouring the power of his threat, which is alive in the air between them, made all the more vital by his encounter with Skinner's dad in the shop.

Then, 'I helped Maxwell get the stuff,' Skinner retorts bullishly, indicating the booze.

'So?'

'Maxwell said it was for *all* of us.' While Skinner's tone retains a trace of his customary wheedling note, there is also a new essay towards confidence, a trial of challenge in it. It is blustering, experimental, but very apparent. He speaks Maxwell's name with a hint of possession, a dilute version of the way Spencer uses it. Spencer's Maxwell is a guardian angel, blazing in glory, an undisputed champion. Skinner's Maxwell is a secret weapon, the power of whose possession he has yet to fully unleash.

Spencer hesitates before nodding towards the collection of bottles behind Carmel and simultaneously snatching the book of matches from Skinner's outstretched hand. 'All right.'

Skinner enjoys his victory. He swaggers up to the rug and reaches unnecessarily over the girl to get one of the bottles from the stash behind her. She ducks to avoid his touch, the reek of his armpit, spilling her own drink in the process. He stands on the rug right in front of her, one foot planted between her knees, while she wipes ineffectually at the stain on her dress. He prises the top off the bottle, downs the contents, then he lobs the bottle over the river before snatching another and walking away.

Matt sips his drink and indicates the fire. 'Cool' he says.

While Spencer supervises the ignition of the fire Matt saunters over to the rug and sits down next to the girl. 'Are you OK?' he asks.

'This is Jade's. She'll kill me,' Carmel complains. Her voice has a tinkling wobble of inebriation in it.

'That's not what I meant. Last night ...'

She drops her head. Her fringe shields her eyes. He knows she is blushing. She nods almost imperceptibly. 'Oh. Yes.'

They watch while the other boys argue about which way to light the fire.

'Who's Jade?'

'My sister. My other sister.'

They finish their drinks and open new ones.

'Going up to see *them* tomorrow,' she says, her voice low. 'Why don't you come? On the bus. I know which one. Just you and me.'

He knows who she means, of course. He is filled with an overwhelming yearning to see his dad, to sit next to him playing F1 on the PlayStation, to compare playlists on their iPods, to smell his familiar scent. He shakes his head sadly.

'Why? It's nice.' The girl sighs wistfully. 'He's so nice. The children love him.'

'I bet they do,' Matt croaks.

Carmel's tongue has been loosened by the alcohol. 'They've never had a daddy.' A hot knife of jealousy slips between Matt's ribs. 'None of us has. I didn't know it could be so nice.'

'Skinner has! Mike has!' Matt barks defensively.

'But not like Richard. Nothing like *him*. You're so lucky.' She looks up, through her heavy, black lashes and the screen of her fringe. Her pale eyes reflect empty, bleak space.

The fire leaps into life with a sudden roar and crackle. Spencer, Clark and Mike are thrown backwards by the intensity of heat and flame. Skinner steps out from behind the tree, his eyes eager. Matt jumps to his feet. The wood consumes the fire like a ravenous beast, sucking it into its thirsty, dehydrated heart, spitting showers of red saliva in glowing arcs. The flames leap high, threatening the overarching branches of the blasted oak above like wild caged things suddenly given the opportunity to escape.

Matt has been to bonfires—dozens of them. Jolly family occasions with soup and treacle toffee and excited children in wellingtons and bobble hats. There is careful supervision of sparklers, writing your name with the glowing tip, hot face and cold feet. He knows there ought to be an army of dads milling around with garden rakes pressing the fire back within its confines, keeping it all central, taming rogue brands and pushing the embers back into its midst.

'But of course,' he thinks, scornfully, 'these boys have no dads.'

Neither do they have any control over the ravening inferno they have created. There is a moment when they look at each other, foreseeing a forest fire, homes ablaze, charred remains. In the searing light of the flames their faces are white, eyes round. But all at once the loosely piled branches sag with a creak and sigh of ancient bones. The fire diminishes, in size at least. The tree above is out of reach. The windless night carries no sparks. They rise a little powered by the volition of their own exploding molecules and then expire in the cooler air.

With a triumphant hoot the boys burst into action and sound, their radiant, exhilarated faces exuding unalloyed rapture. Even Skinner is drawn out of the shadow to bask in the joy of it, his skin a shining, greasy mask in the heat. Matt is amongst them, his hair a tongue of flame. Someone turns up the volume of the music. The fire and the raw, aggressive beat thundering from the speakers have unleashed something primal in them. They are electrified by it, circling and whooping like savages. One moment they are alight, brightly illumined as though by stage lights. The next they are dark silhouettes against the white blue orange pyramid. They leap and stamp around the fire's circumference, shouting and bellowing up through the sparks to the black dome of sky. Clark—his legs plaiting, overcome by helpless laughter, eyes glazed. Mike—sweating freely, the stains on his shirt looking like the splatter from the day's kill. Spencer and Skinner—all enmity forgotten in the heady abandon of the moment. And Matt, for the first time in so long, feeling as though he belongs.

In its light, Carmel is transformed to pure gold. Her pale skin glows golden and her hair shines with burnished filaments. The shadows of the men flicker across her and extinguish her brilliance before she sparkles into glorious light again. They dance on, as evening turns into night.

Later, the fire has burned off the worst of its rage and settled to a mound of molten incandescence. The boys lie exhausted on the ground, basking in its heat while slaking their thirst with the bottles of sweet, potent drink. Clark and Mike are having a disjointed conversation about some computer game they have both played. Their words are slurred and jumbled up and it makes them laugh. Presently they both fall silent. Clark is asleep. Mike gets up and goes back to the fire, poking it with a long stave.

Matt lies with his hands folded behind his head, gazing up at the sky. He feels uncoiled, his limbs flaccid and aching, and there is a delicious warm glow in the pit of his stomach spreading outwards. He is conscious of weeks of tension ebbing away into the cool grass and in its place a surge of goodwill towards Spencer and the others, even Skinner. He turns his head slightly to where Spencer lies, across the corner of the blanket. He is smoking. Carmel is on the other side of him, curled up in the crook of his arm. A little way off, in the shadows, Skinner is stretched out like a strew of clothes on the ground.

'This is great, Spencer,' Matt says.

Spencer nods and takes a pull of his cigarette. He holds it out. 'Try this,' he says.

'You know I don't smoke.'

'I know, I know. But try it.'

'*I will*,' Skinner says, his voice seeming to come from nowhere, propelled on the wings of its own eagerness. Spencer ignores him. Matt knows exactly what Spencer is smoking and that he ought to refuse. But he's sick of being different. The sensation of homecoming is too strong. It is too hard being a Fairways boy on the Mere. It's time he decided to be one or the other. He reaches out a hand and takes hold of the fat, loosely packed joint. The end of it is ragged with shreds of stuff. They, and the paper, are damp with the moisture from Spencer's lips, and from hers. The idea of Carmel's lips stirs him. He sucks the joint and inhales the fragrant smoke. It sears as it goes down but then extends caressing fingers of comfort and well-being into every cell.

'Wow,' he breathes. He is conscious of a spreading pool of peace. It feels at once to be coming from within him and yet also flowing from the fire, the night sky, Spencer and the others. It is up-lifting, quasi-spiritual, an enlargement of the heart. He draws again at the joint, letting the euphoria carry him away.

Minutes—or hours—later, Skinner is standing over him.

'Give me some,' he says thickly. Matt glances over at Spencer. He has turned his back and now lies on his side, towards Carmel. His head is over hers, he is kissing her. His arm is moving, his hand down between her legs. He is stroking her in quick, rhythmic sweeps. She makes a low, sighing noise in her throat.

'*Give* me some. *He's* not bothered,' Skinner says bitterly. Matt stands up and hands over the joint. They move to the other side of the fire and sit down again. Matt's legs feel weak and unreliable and his head strangely swimmy. Skinner sits next to him and produces two bottles of drink. He sucks greedily at the joint but when he offers it back Matt waves his hand; the idea of *Skinner's* mouth is somehow untenable. The enfolding aura of goodwill is already dissipating. Skinner curls his lip.

'Suit yourself.' Matt tips the bottle and drinks, thirsting to recapture the elation of a few moments ago.

The joint doesn't raise Skinner's mood but carries him further down the spiral of his obsession.

'He says ... he *says* ...'

Matt knows exactly what Spencer will have said, at the earliest opportunity, crowing about his conquest of the girl without any respect for her feelings or delicacy about her reputation. It was cruel and unnecessary; she is Spencer's girl. It's not as though Skinner is any threat.

'Saw your dad in the shop earlier.' He doesn't know why he says it. It is the last subject that he and Skinner can discuss equitably, or almost the last. He stares at the sentence with disbelief as though it has physical presence on the grass.

'Did you? Were you with your mum?'

'No.'

'We should fix them up.' Skinner isn't serious but Matt doesn't find it funny.

A knee-jerk reaction. 'I don't think so!'

'No, I know,' Skinner shakes his head slowly. 'Who'd want a bloke like him?' He stares past the fire into the darkness, towards the girl on the rug with Spencer.

Matt finds that he is thinking of the woman in the photograph in Skinner's bedroom, and the cherubic baby that the Mere and hardship and cruelty have turned into Skinner.

'He's like Sméagol,' he thinks, wanting to tell his dad.

The thought brings with it a tide of sympathy for Skinner, but on a kind of time-delay, a tardy emotional response to the thought.

'Your mum did, once. Before he changed, I mean,' he says.

'He didn't change. He's always been like he is now.'

'Then, why did she ..?'

Skinner shrugs. 'I dunno. Why do they ever?' Now they are both thinking of Carmel, a hapless, helpless puppet in Spencer's hands. 'All men are bastards,' Skinner pronounces solemnly.

The suggestion filters through the gathering fog in Matt's brain. 'No. No they aren't ...' he remonstrates, but his words are thick and without conviction. 'My dad ...' he says lamely, and trails off. 'And that man you saw the other day,' he tries again. 'He isn't a bastard.' Again, Mr Pickering is the last person Matt had wanted to mention. He gapes at his liquid verbosity.

Skinner laughs soundlessly and shakes his head. 'You're too soft. You'll never be one of us.'

Matt doesn't know whether he feels glad, or sad.

Mike is busy feeding the fire, dragging brushwood across the bridge. 'Someone's been doing their hedges,' he says, dumping an armful of clippings onto the fire.

'They'll be too green,' Matt says distractedly, through woollen lips. Sure enough, a plume of thick acrid smoke begins to rise like a signal, into the sky.

'All men are bastards,' Skinner repeats. 'And we're just boys learning to be bastards. Once you get that, everything's easy. That's why *he,*' a nod towards Spencer, 'can do what he's doing now. That's why I can do what I did last night.'

'It isn't right.'

'What's right? What's wrong? There's only me and what I want. It's easy.'

'It's *selfish*. What *did* you do last night?' Matt asks, in spite of himself. 'Did you tell Maxwell about that house?' Skinner doesn't reply.

Spencer walks around the fire to join them. He drops more bottles into the grass. His approach produces, from Skinner, an electric current of angry resentment.

'How many *are* there of these?' Matt gasps. There is something wrong with his voice. His tongue is too big.

'Loads. *My brother* looks after me and my friends.' Spencer's possessive reference to Maxwell is designed to rile Skinner. He is swollen up with something, grinning and swaggering. 'Carmel's wasted,' he cocks his head in the direction of the blanket. 'I just made her come.'

Skinner, next to Matt, makes a strangled groan. He grips the neck of his bottle so tightly it breaks. Blood oozes from his finger. He wipes it on the grass. His head is right down between his knees.

'We're just talking about dads,' Matt says quickly.

'Oh.' Spencer drops onto the grass beside them. 'What?'

'That they're bastards. Do you think yours is?'

Spencer shrugs. 'I don't know anything about him. I never met him.'

'Do you ever think about him?' Matt's voice is low.

'No,' Spencer smiles. 'I don't need a dad. I've got Maxwell.'

They drink for a while. The fire burns through the green wood and begins to snap and spark again. It echoes a crackling fizz in Matt's head. Mike is flicking from track to track on the CD player. Disembodied phrases float across the fire, ghostly cries from another universe. Each track lasts only a few seconds. It makes it seem like time has been accelerated. Matt looks up at the sky as though to see the Milky Way streaming past in nano-quick time, but of course the stars are invisible, outshone by the lights of the city. He knows the notion is ridiculous, and that he is drunk.

'Dads can be great,' he says, maudlin nostalgia swamping him. 'They play with you when you're little, and take you places. You can make things together. Watch telly, play computer games ... stuff you can't do with a mum ...' His voice sounds as though it is coming from somebody else. Matt listens almost wonderingly, to see what it will say next. The words, when they come, are wrenched from a deeply hidden inner place where they have been locked and buried for too long. 'But they *are* only human.' He nods slowly, sadly, acknowledging the truth of it.

Skinner snorts. His smouldering charge of emotion unleashes itself and finds, not its true target but a more accessible one. 'I don't know what fucking planet you've been living on!' he spits. 'Dads are drunken, lazy bastards. They wake you up in the night and send you out for fags. They call you names and break your stuff. They laugh at your school-work. They laugh at *you!* They beat your mum up and then they beat *you* up ... and they beat *you* up ...' A sluice gate seems to have opened in Skinner. His eyes are pouring tears; they plough through the grime on his face. He looks as though he's wearing war-paint. He scrabbles to his feet and stands in front of them. 'This ... *this* is what dads do.' He pulls off his t shirt and turns his back so that it is lit by the glow of the fire. His back is livid with acne but laced across his bony shoulders, down his starkly prominent ribcage and nobbled spine is a network of recent, infected weals and fresh welts.

The sight is sobering. Matt and Spencer take it in. Mike switches off the music.

'But now ...' Skinner sniffs and wipes his nose with his arm. He holds his head up. 'Now Maxwell ...' He speaks the name in a reverent whisper as though Maxwell is an avenging seraph, a messiah come to save him.

'Maxwell?' Spencer sneers. 'What do you think he's going to do? Buy you a little place of your own? Adopt you? Oh! I know: take you under his wing?'

Skinner blanches, for all the heat of the fire. These are exactly the words Maxwell has used.

'He just needs a little runt who can squeeze through windows and shimmy up drainpipes! He *told* me. Those are the *only* plans he has for you.'

Spencer gets to his feet, steps right up to Skinner and yells. 'He's MY brother.' His words resonate round the field. Far away, a dog barks. Spit sprinks Skinner's face. Skinner is visibly eviscerated. As they watch, the small shred of self-respect he has gathered to himself—the most infinitesimal thread of hope—is stripped away as clearly as if his flesh had been flayed from his bones. He bleeds before them and Matt is moved to say, quietly reproachful, 'He'll always be your brother, Spencer. Skinner can't change *that.*'

'Man.' It is Clark, groggy from sleep and booze. He is staring at Skinner's back. He struggles to his feet and then bends over and vomits on the grass.

Spencer and Mike take him home. Matt and Skinner are left alone. The girl still sleeps on the rug. Skinner is shirtless, his agonised, tearstained face and scarred, skeletal body eerily lit by the lurid light of the dying flames. He looks like a tortured soul in hell. Suddenly he is struggling back into his shirt, ashamed. He turns and walks into the night.

MATT DOESN'T KNOW how long he has been asleep. He wakes up frozen and wet. He opens his eyes but cannot move; his body, on the hard ground, is stiff. The fire has died to a dull red smoulder. Beyond it, the field and the river are otherworldly, swamped in mist. It pours off the water like steam from a kettle, rising in ghostly whorls. The ground breathes it out of earthy pores. The sky is greyish brown but lightening to pewter over the roofs of the Fairways. The trees stand like spectres in the stillness. He swivels his eyes. There is pressure in his head. Every bone aches.

The smallest sound and a tiny movement catch his attention. He moves his head fractionally. He can see the blanket where Carmel is sleeping. She had been insensible with drink and the marihuana. He had wrapped her in the blanket and carried her closer to the fire—he remembers it now, the featherish unresisting weight of her in his arms—while waiting for the others to return. In the murk she is an insubstantial bundle, a chrysalis, her hair visible at the top like sprouting strands of silk. There is a movement in the mist, little more than an eddy in the hazy tendrils. A phantom figure kneels at the side of the blanket. He is so grey and flimsy that he is barely distinguishable from the rising vapour around him. He moves with incredible slowness. One thin hand holds up the edge of the blanket. The other, fingers like gossamer, undoes the buttons down the front of Carmel's dress with the infinite gentleness of angels.

In his disorientation it seems to Matt that the ghost of his own desire is enacting his fantasy. He holds his breath. The wraith lays the edge of the blanket aside and spreads the front panels of the girl's dress wide. She stirs but does not wake.

She is white and lean, her pelvis and ribcage finely chiselled like marble. Her pubescent breasts are no more than a soft swell of flesh. Her aureoles, dark red and soft as velvet, pucker in the chill air.

A breath of air moves the spectre across the blanket. He kneels between the girl's legs and extends a careful finger towards her groin, to lift aside the flimsy material of her underwear. Matt's throat is dry. He cannot think. He is inflamed and consumed. He tears his eyes away. The sky is lightening; pewter has become platinum. The trees are emerging as solid forms. The first bird chirps an experimental morning song. He can see, just, through the unreal air, the outline of the bridge.

He is on his feet, his bones shattering like ice. He staggers, his leg is numb. His voice, when it comes, is hardly recognisable from his parched throat.

'Skinner!'

Skinner is already upright, backing away. Matt's movement had been enough to divert his purpose. He cowers at the sound of his name, loud in the still, vacant air. He is cringing, bent over, kneading his hands together with restless friction. They both look at the girl between them. She is moving blindly, searching for the covering of the blanket.

Skinner speaks. His face contracts into frowns and furrows. He looks aged, a reflection of his father. His voice is pitiful, pleading. 'I just wanted ...' he says haltingly, 'I only wanted a little ...' he swallows. His Adam's apple bounces in his throat, '... just a tiny bit of what *he* has. Is it too much to ask? He has it *all*! He's always had it *all*!' He holds his hands out in front of him, appealing to what he presumes Matt will see as the justice of it.

Matt draws himself upright. Feeling is returning to his foot. Red hot needles shoot into it.

'You wanted it too,' Skinner goes on, an accusing note. 'I saw you watching. You want her too.' He takes a step forwards, his face clearing a little, lit by an idea. He glances down at the girl and then back at Matt. 'We could both ...'

At the suggestion, Matt covers the few yards between them and raises his hand. Skinner recoils a pace. He looks Matt up and down. 'You're no better than us,' he states coldly. He nods at Matt's raised hand. 'You *are* turning into one of us after all.'

Matt looks up at his hand. It holds the bottle Skinner broke earlier, like a weapon.

Skinner steps up close. The smell of him is rank, a decaying animal. 'I *did* tell Maxwell. He was interested. Very interested.'

FRENZIED KNOCKING ON the door. John sits bolt upright in bed, his anxiety levels soaring skyward like Red Arrows.

The boy on the doorstep is in a dreadful state, barely articulate, shivering with cold in the chill mist of dawn. He can hardly hold his mug steady; even with two hands wrapped around it tea slops over its rim. John's own hands are scarcely less agitated, but he resists the urge to dispense tablets.

Matt's story is disjointed, stops and starts, travels forward and back as though at the mercy of a mischievous hand on the remote control. John can't piece it together. A bonfire, drink, a girl, drugs, somebody's brother, a broken bottle. It tumbles out in a rambling shambles. The boy smells of drink. He looks a wreck, as pale as death, hollow-eyed with sleeplessness. They are in the kitchen, the bluish glow of the fluorescent tube casting as bleak a light as possible on them both, white with shock. John catches sight of his own reflection in the kitchen window. His hair is sticking up in tufts, his chin dark with stubble. His pyjamas aren't buttoned up right.

Finally, something graspable. The main point. A tip-off: a potential burglary. John looks instinctively to his windows and doors and pictures masked hoodlums with baseball bats. His heart is a percussion concerto but he tries to be rational.

'When? Today?' His voice is a squeak.

'No, I don't think so,' the boy shakes his head, 'but maybe, yes. I don't know. I don't *know*.' He is emphatic, then it seeps away. He groans and rubs his eyes.

John doesn't know what to think. He wants the boy to go away. He wants to drag his chair back into the vestibule, his safe place.

He has been doing so well, this past couple of weeks.

Matt paces nervously around the kitchen. He doesn't take his eyes off John, expecting, now that he has laid it all out to a grown-up, that the solution will appear, magically, like a rabbit.

'I don't know,' John echoes the boy's words. 'I don't know what *I* can do.'

Matt catches an exasperated breath. 'I need you to help me.'

'You need *me* to help *you*?' John retorts. '*I'm* the one who's under threat here.' He's instantly sorry. 'But I *will* help you.'

'No, no, no,' Matt wails, as frustrated as a school-master whose pupil repeatedly fails to get the point. He steadies himself and tries again, speaking slowly, using simple words.

'I did tell Skinner that you lived on your own. I didn't know *then* what he was up to. But when he asked me to show him your house, I didn't. I showed him another house. I wouldn't have shown him any house but he threatened my mum.'

'Whose house did you show him?'

'Mine. The one I used to live in. It's on the Crescent.'

John relaxes slightly. Every self-serving instinct tells him to push this away; it has nothing to do with him, after all. But he resists it. 'What do you want me to do?'

Disconcertingly, Matt begins to cry. 'I don't know!' he sobs. 'You're the grown-up, a man, a businessman. People listen to you.'

Matt doesn't want the family to be robbed but if Maxwell is foiled he would know exactly who was to blame. His own position, his mum's, both are so precarious. He feels, all at once, that rather than skirting its edges he is knee deep in the sucking, stinking mud of the Mere. Skinner was right. He *is* one of them. He doesn't like it.

'Why don't we ask your father?' John asks, his tone gentle, discerning, in Matt's extremity, an opportunity for reconciliation.

Matt sits heavily on the kitchen chair and puts his head in his hands. '*He* won't care.' The words are deeply coloured by lonely despair.

John draws another chair up and perches on it.

'Why on earth not?' he asks gently.

Matt struggles with it for a while. When he speaks it is as though he has torn his heart out by the roots, its severed arteries waving like tentacles, spraying bitter blood in arcs. 'Why would he, now? When he has *him*?' His voice is an agonised wail. He knows he sounds like a child. He is crying like a child. In his heart he knows he is behaving like a child; obstinate and mean-spirited.

'Him?'

'The other boy.'

'Ah,' John sighs, understanding at last.

MONDAY MORNING. THE corridor outside the hall is crowded with anxious candidates, pale, beneath their tans; they all look as if they have been on holiday.

Matt pushes a way through to Spencer who is leaning against a pillar uselessly scanning his text book.

'Where's Skinner?' He has decided he must get Skinner to promise that he and Maxwell won't burgle the house. He doesn't know how; what he might have to offer, or risk. But he has been thinking about nothing else. He is eaten up with guilty liability over it, overlaid by anxiety for the new family in his old home.

Spencer shrugs, blinking at formulae it is too late for him to commit to memory. 'Done a runner.'

'What?'

'No one's seen him since Saturday night.' He holds out the book. 'Do *you* know anything about this stuff?'

Matt pushes the book away. 'What do you mean? Nobody? Not his dad?'

'Nobody. I told you.'

Matt thinks of the last time he saw Skinner, fading into the mist early on Sunday morning. He had been stripped to nothing, the violent welts of his reality all too lividly revealed, his dreams of a future association with Maxwell in shreds, his desire for Carmel thwarted and hopeless. He thinks of Skinner's room—the bare, comfortless bed, the rats, the photograph.

'Hasn't Maxwell seen him?'

'Why should he? What's Skinner to him?'

'I need to ask him ... I want to know ...' Impossible to explain. 'Skinner told Maxwell things, gave him information ... has he ... will he ..?'

'Course he will, if it's sound.' Spencer closes the book, his interest piqued. 'What was it?'

The bell shrills and the hall doors are opened. The students file in.

In the midst of the exam, Matt has a vivid, shocking picture of Skinner floating face down in water.

After the exam he hurries to the field. It is another blistering day. Everything is wilting for want of water. He races to the tree. The rope hangs limp and still. The river itself is reduced to hardly a trickle, the merest film of moisture sliding like mucus over the slimy lip of the weir and seeping along the gasping, grasping fronds of algae-choked weed.

The pool shows no evidence of occupation but Matt is suddenly certain that Skinner has made the leap from the bridge into its milk-green, turgid flow. He narrows his eyes against the glaring sun and thinks he sees signs of snapped, overhanging foliage, evidence of grasping hands. An occasional bilious breath breaks through with a noise like a wet fart. Matt expects to see the bloated body of Skinner rise to the surface at any moment, emitting gaseous odour. He feels the responsibility like a heavy cape, weighing him down. Poor Skinner.

But obviously if Skinner had drowned they would have found his body by now. So of course he hadn't drowned! He has survived the jump and the swim through the pool, the only one of them who could have achieved such a thing. Matt is suffused with relief. It all makes sense. It was the only thing left to Skinner. Propelled by desperation, determined to best Spencer in this one thing, he had leapt off the bridge and into the pool and conquered the currents.

Presently he finds a sign, notched crudely into the downstream handrail of the bridge. The word, 'Skinner.'

Matt sits down on the patch of grass more flattened than the rest, the place where Spencer had lain on the rug with Carmel under Skinner's agonised eyes. He is relieved, and experiences a soaring admiration for Skinner, to have done such a thing, in the dark of dawn, all alone.

The field is brown and desiccated, panting for rain. The circle of their fire is a deep sable scar, kicked about with ash and charred remains. In the blinding day it looks nothing like a site of ceremonial passage. He can scarcely credit now that they had leapt and hollered like savages, that he had danced on the very threshold of the tribe and even believed that he might want to be one of them. Ugly debris is carelessly scattered; bottles and ash, the crusty remains of Clark's vomit. Other unresolved issues are more widely spread and call, like the litter, to be dealt with; the craven way he sold out the new family in the Crescent to Skinner's threats; the very real possibility that they might now, because of him, be at risk; the part he has played in breaking Skinner, doing nothing—simply standing by—while Spencer destroyed him piece by piece.

He is ashamed. The Mere has leached into him.

And overarching it all, as intense and blinding as the day, is his loneliness—high as the aching sky—for his father.

WHEN MATT GETS home on Tuesday afternoon, after his English exam, Rosie is waiting for him. She holds a Neighbourhood Watch poster and a hand-drawn leaflet.

'Mr Pickering was here,' she says wonderingly. 'He says you're going to help him design some fliers and deliver them.'

Matt looks at the pamphlet. It is poorly drawn: a silhouette of a burglar complete with swag bag and underneath the lettering 'THIS AREA TO BE TARGETTED BY THEIVES. YOUR HOME IS AT RISK.' A number of wavy lines indicate further text.

'What's this all about, Matt?'

Matt fusses with his bag, gets a drink of water. 'I met him on the bridge. We got talking ... You know.'

'That's what *he* said,' Rosie frowns. 'There must be more to it.'

Matt shrugs and sticks his bottom lip out, playing innocent.

'Anyway, he says he'll pick you up at seven.'

'Oh? Where are we going?'

'That's what I'd like to know.'

The subject is dropped. Rosie prepares supper. Matt looks through his revision notes for the following day's exam: Graphic Design. He can see Mr Pickering's plan, his scheme for dealing with the potential threat posed by Maxwell to the residents of the Fairways and especially the occupants of Matt's old house. It is a good plan. A general campaign that will heighten awareness and urge people to address any specific security issues without being explicit about where the information has come from. No one—neither Maxwell nor the house-holders— will think that Matt is behind it.

When Rosie speaks, from the kitchen, there is something in her voice—a bubble, rising through gelatinous fluid. 'I was surprised … from what your father has told me … but no. He was ever so nice.'

PICKERING'S LIGHT ENGINEERING is deserted, shut up for the night. John—Matt has been told to call him John—parks in the spot marked 'Chairman' and opens the doors into the lobby with a key. He takes a deep breath before crossing the threshold.

The reception desk is tidy. The computer is switched off. A visitors' book and pen are neatly arranged. There is a box of flowery tissues and an artificial plant. On the wall, behind the desk, is a studio shot of John in a smart suit holding a beautifully milled bevelled gear. He looks steely and hard, unlike the diffident actuality hovering in the foyer.

To the right, large double doors give access to the production floor. John holds them open and Matt looks in. The floor is neatly taped to show work zones, storage areas, walk-ways. Signs remind workers to wear protective clothing. There are calendars with naked women on the walls, an FA cup wall-chart filled in with all the games and the results except for the last; the up-coming final is a local derby and excitement is at fever-pitch. There is a pungent smell—of men, hot metal and oil—but it is eerily quiet; only the soft clash of metal chains high aloft, and a sense of echoes floating beyond hearing. A variety of machines are placed in the space. John names them—lathes, presses, die cutters, pillar drills and milling machines—and describes the men who operate them as though introducing Matt to a line-up of celebrities.

'Clive works this press; he's been with us longer than anyone. He lost his grandson in Iraq. Omar is very skilled; the best welder in the company.'

It feels to Matt as though he is being introduced to John's family, from whom John himself has been somehow estranged. Each machine has a

147

job in hand holes to bore, brackets to bend. There is an accumulation of half-formed grommets and widgets in the process of production at every station. Heavy lifting gear hanging from a gantry makes Matt think of Skinner, somewhere. Metal rods are in transit from the stores to a machine at the far end of the workshop; they dangle, suspended. A forklift is stopped mid-lift with a pallet on its forks. It reminds Matt of an enchanted castle, asleep under a spell.

John takes him to the drawing office and switches on a computer at one of the desks. He walks around the space, touching the chairs and the filing cabinets with a proprietary hand.

'This room used to be full of proper angled drawing boards and high stools and slide rules. We used to work with pencil on graph paper, but it's all computerised now.'

It seems to Matt that John is more familiar with things here than he is with his own furniture.

The office smells of stale breath and coffee. It has tall windows all down one side of it. Venetian blinds deflect the sun. Their disarray— higgledy-piggledy heights and varieties of slant—is testimony to frantic efforts to keep the room cool during the day. There are fans, too, on several desks. Matt imagines men in shirt-sleeves and women in summer dresses busy here designing sprockets and gismos that will come to life on the factory floor. Rows of thick files line the window ledges, along with a hundred dead bluebottles. John ushers Matt into a chair. Some of the workstations have personal belongings—a picture of a baby, a cardigan left on the chair—but this one is bare. Even so, Matt asks, 'Won't he mind? The person who sits here?'

John shakes his head. 'Ryan's moved into sales. No one sits here now.' He indicates the desktop publishing program. 'You know how to use this?'

'Yes.'

John explains his agreement with the woman from Neighbourhood Watch; a leaflet like the sketch with home security advice and the logo lifted from the poster. 'I said that Pickering's would produce them free of charge. You and I will deliver them. I think it's the best we can do to solve your problem, don't you?'

Matt begins to stammer thanks. John holds his hands up. 'Think of it as a job interview,' he says. 'If you make a decent job of it you can come and work for me when your exams are over. Your dad convinced me you're a decent draughtsman. Ryan's chair needs filling.'

'You spoke to my dad?'

John nods.

'I don't understand.' Is this all, then, his dad's doing?

'He's very proud of you.'

Matt gets to work on the pamphlet. In moments he is lost in the task, his hands now moving over the keyboard, now nudging the mouse, drawing boxes, typing text, copying and pasting images off the internet. He experiments with different layouts and typestyles.

John moves quietly around the office, his hands straightening the blinds and touching the files. In his mind he peoples the office; Bruce, who loyally wears pullovers not very ably knitted by his wife; Geraldine, who has unfortunate teeth; Roger, who stands outside in all weathers to smoke. They have worked for him for years yet he knows only these most cursory details about them. Do they have children? How do they spend their spare time? He has no clue. He sits in each chair in turn, trying to feel what it might be like to be them. Geraldine's chair is seriously wonky: she must have a new one. After a while he leaves the room and wanders down the silent corridors, putting his head around the doors of the accounts office, marketing, sales, picturing the people who work there. Marcus, the bald-headed buyer who sits in the corner; how long it is since he had a holiday? Pauline, in accounts; didn't her daughter have a baby? He yearns to know. He wants to buy gifts, throw a party. 'I will do,' he says to himself.

He lingers outside the sales office, where Richard used to sit when he wasn't on the road, exchanging banter with customers over the phone, always remembering the names of their wives and which football team they supported. Kenny has rearranged things in the office, acquired a big leather swivel chair and a tooled brass name-plate: 'Kenny Roach, Sales Manager.' He has fixed a blind to the glass pane in the door so that people can't see in. He is a hard, self-interested individual, over-fond of expense-account lunches. His tenure as Sales Manager will not be long-lived, John decides. He invites uncomfortable comparisons.

Finally he pushes open the door of his own office. Nothing has changed. His name is on one side of the door, his jacket and golf umbrella are hanging from the hooks on the other. On the wall is a picture of him and Brian and their father, standing in front of the old premises. He doesn't know quite what he was expecting, but there is nothing. His desk is tidy. His deputy, Jack Perry, has not even been using it. His telephone is placed as he likes it, his rotor-file of contacts to hand. One file is placed for his perusal—a copy of all correspondence received and sent since the day of his attack; an orderly record of business ably carried on. If he has not been missed at least he has not been deserted. The place on the floor where the heart attack struck is only that—a patch of carpet like every other. It is all just waiting for him to come back. His absence has been a hiatus, an opportunity to regroup. Nothing is set in stone and there is the potential for something new, a different approach, if they will give him the chance and if he has the courage to take it.

The window looks out over the yard where deliveries come in and finished goods are despatched. He had always liked to see the cycle of it; metal arriving as one thing and leaving as something else, the alchemy of engineering transforming the useless into the useful. From here he had felt at the heart of it, could hear the pulse and thrum of it, the hammering machines beating a constant, creative, sustaining rhythm. The steady measure of his life.

He sits in the waiting chair and listens. In the silence, he can hear it still.

THEY GO FOR pizza at an exclusive *trattoria* in town. John is known at the restaurant and is instantly ushered to a quiet table on the terrace. Two bottles of expensive beer, ice cold, are produced along with the menus. Matt orders pizza, John a salad Niçoise.

John is different. Matt had been aware of it as they printed and counted the fliers together, the self-assured way he helped himself to new packs of paper and a box from the stores. John moved with ever-increasing ease through the building, pointing things out with a confident wave of the arm. His voice became louder, firmer. Even the way he drove the car—with a light-handed poise—through the thronged evening streets of the town was a world away from the tentative way he had negotiated the car-lined roads of the Mere just a couple of hours before.

Matt feels as though he too has undergone a pantomime transformation. The problem on the Fairways is solved, and his inclusion in the solution assuages something of the guilt. Then there's the job; a way to live in the Mere without succumbing to its seedier denominators.

'You're like a fairy god-father!' he blurts out at last. 'You've solved all my problems in one swoop!' Even as he speaks, Matt remembers his father's mysterious role in it all, and the thought brings tears near.

'*All* your problems?' John raises an eyebrow.

The question is left in the air as John goes on, 'Anyway, we're quits. I'm experimenting on you; seeing how it feels to be nice.'

Matt laughs. 'You *are* nice!' he says, but he is aware that certainly his father never thought Mr Pickering was nice.

151

'It's good of you to say so. But the truth is that if the heart attack had killed me nobody would have been sorry. No sad loss.' He holds his hand up as Matt commences a rebuttal. 'No, really. I know it's true, because nobody came. And really, when I think about it, why should they, the way I had behaved? But I hope they'll give me another chance.'

'I think you're very brave,' Matt says sincerely, appreciating the fearfulness of allowing those who have hurt you a further opportunity, of putting yourself forward knowing that, given the choice, they might choose another.

'Everyone deserves a second chance Matt, don't you think?'

Their food arrives. It is delicious.

'And how *does* it feel?' Matt asks, through pepperoni.

'Good.'

'And ... will you go back to work now?'

'Yes. I think so. Next week perhaps, or the week after.'

'And can I really come and work for you?'

'In the holidays, yes. Your dad came over and showed me some of your work on disk. Your exam portfolio, I think.'

'Oh, yes.' He had forgotten that they had made a back-up disk of it. Now he thinks of it, they had scanned *all* his coursework and stored it on disk, even—he remembers ruefully—his geography.

The mention of Richard all but conjures him into being, a third diner at their table. Seeing things suddenly from a new perspective, Matt wonders if that is how *he* feels: 'unforgivable', 'no sad loss'. In Matt's desire to protect himself from hurt he has hardly thought what message his refusal to see his father might have conveyed. It is unspeakably bleak.

Eventually Matt asks, 'How is he?'

John lays his fork down and wipes his mouth with his napkin. Richard had responded quickly to his call. He had come and they had spent many hours talking. Richard had talked while John listened. He has no idea how to describe Richard: the happiest, most wretched man alive. As foreign as the language of love is to John's tongue, he is at least able now to comprehend the wanton unpredictability, the sheer pre-eminent power of the human heart. It is clear to him that Richard has undergone a catastrophic emotional eruption—unsought, much fought, but in the end absolutely irresistible. Like his own coronary, Richard's 'heart attack' has usurped and unmanned him. It has shaken utterly everything he took for granted. But for him, for Richard, the new-turned soil of the wasteland is flowering, producing outrageous, extravagant blooms with intoxicating scents in myriad rainbow colours. His relationship with Jasmine is daily more fulfilling, as satisfying and necessary as food and yet bleakly, fundamentally tainted by the enduring shadow of what has been lost. Richard will never, John thinks, be able to reconcile his extra-ordinary chance for happiness with the distress that taking hold of it has caused those he loves.

'He misses his son,' he says.

On the way home John comments casually, 'Your mother is a lovely woman.'

'Oh God,' Matt groans.

THE CONSEQUENCES OF the heat wave begin to be felt. Hospital emergency departments are crammed with people suffering from heat-stroke, dehydration and sun-burn. Fire crews are constantly called to attend incidents caused by carelessness or spontaneous combustion. A National Forestry Commission site is devastated by a raging inferno that kills a pair of osprey chicks. Transport is disrupted by cars overheating. Hose pipes are banned country-wide. Some areas have water only at selected times of the day; stand-pipes and tankers are the only other source. The price of fresh food escalates. Water treatment works struggle to cope; the air is heavy with the stench of stagnant, untreated sewage and thick with flies. There is a vociferous but short-lived protest amongst GCSE candidates about the stultifying heat of examination rooms. Several girls and one invigilator faint. A dog that ingests stagnant water from a murky, fetid pond dies of a virulent bacterial infection.

Beneath the overt repercussions of the heat are the more insidious, less tangible effects. People are on edge, their tempers and tolerances unusually short. It is common to hear raised voices in shops as customers squabble over unappealing vegetables or berate the owners for profiteering. Sometimes the outbursts result in fights, smashed windows and serious wounds. Neighbours harangue each other over fences. Too-frequently-filled paddling pools and suspiciously vibrant bedding plants fetch bitter accusations from formerly affable fellow residents. Everyone is drawn out as thin and sharp as needles, brittle and likely to snap. There is a sense of weary, burdensome pressure that distresses and exhausts. Sleep is a stranger. People move slowly, as though dazed, their thought processes muddled. For some, the load is intolerable. It presses them down into the bottomless chasm of depression. Suicide is prevalent.

Matt struggles doggedly on through the next few days. He and John deliver the leaflets one evening, hoping it will be cooler, but the tarmac exudes heat in waves and the air swarms with insects. All the houses, he is distressed to note, have their doors and windows flung invitation-wide. Garages gape, displaying bikes and power tools like shop windows.

John insists that Matt delivers to his old house personally. As he approaches the door a man steps out with a bag of rubbish for the bin. Matt hands over the leaflet.

'Read it carefully,' he urges, feeling like an evangelist. 'A burglary would be so ... upsetting for the family.'

The man nods, and takes the paper from Matt's hand. The two walk down the drive together, Matt regurgitating the advice from the handout as though his life depends upon it. 'Lock all doors and windows. Do not omit to set the alarm. Ask for all callers' ID ...'

'All right, all right, laddie ...' the man says tetchily. He manoeuvres the bin from its enclosure behind the fence and out through the gates. As Matt walks away he sees the leaflet pushed down into the bin with the rest of the rubbish. He almost weeps.

'Some people you just can't help,' John says.

The exams crowd, one after another, day after day, without respite. The pressure is intense: the airless rooms and pacing invigilators, frayed nerves, dry mouths, hot, itchy eyes. Matt's arm and hand begin to ache. Sometimes his hand is so sweaty that he cannot grip the pen. His mind goes blank and then is fervid with inconsequential information that clamours and crowds out the very word or formula or date that he needs.

His mother is exhausted, working extra shifts in preparation for some big shindig at the old folks' home. The harridan in charge is putting them all on edge and upsetting the residents to boot. One evening Matt breaks a glass and Rosie almost bites his head off, and then runs upstairs in tears. After a little while he carries up a cup of tea. She is sitting on her bed looking wan and she smiles and says she is sorry, but the atmosphere is thick with things unsaid between them. They are in a kind of holding pattern. These incidents will recur, awaiting a resolution between Matt and his father. Until then, they cannot move forward and forge anything new.

But he has his exams, and she has her work, and it is so hot. And so they do not press it now.

The weekend brings no relief. A uniformed policeman disturbs Matt's revision. He is looking for a missing boy, Stuart Scanlon.

'No. I don't know him,' Matt says.

The policeman shows a picture—Skinner's latest school portrait.

'Oh. Yes. I know him.'

There is so much it would be unwise to mention. Skinner's association with Maxwell and the rift it had caused with Spencer. Skinner's envy of Spencer's relationship with Carmel; the nature of that relationship— Matt doesn't even know if she is sixteen. The party on the field; the drink and the marihuana, not to mention its source. He picks up the most convincing and least controversial thread he can think of—that Skinner had missed his mum and had a very difficult time coping with his father. He waxes lyrical on the evidence of physical abuse.

'I expect he's gone to find her,' he says.

'Was he especially disturbed on Saturday evening?'

'We're *all* disturbed here,' Matt says bullishly, indicating the neighbourhood.

The policeman nods.

THE DAYS, THE exams, drag interminably on: science, geography, IT, German. The heat is a relentless, sapping burden.

He sees nothing of Spencer; he is never at the field. His exam timetable differs from Matt's and their visits to school do not seem to coincide. Matt scans the crowds of younger pupils, looking for Clark or Mike or even Carmel but they are lost in the multitude, and it is like looking for ghosts. Sometimes, in the night, waking from a fevered dream, he wonders if the past few weeks have been some kind of delusion. But the charred circle where the fire burned is still there. The rope still hangs over the weir. He can only infer that their tumultuous celebrations that night had been the zenith of their association, a riotous but natural parting of their mismatched ways.

He finishes his last exam.

The field, on his way home, is silent and entirely empty. The sun is a fireball. Birds drowse on the branches, unable to summon up the energy for a song. Vegetation is limp and papery to the touch. The air is thick and almost visibly striated with layers of stagnant particles, pollen, pollution. There is no oxygen in it; breathing is like drowning. The pressure, like a strap around his head, makes his eyes ache. He shakes his head and watches his distorted reflection in the silver surface of the river as he leans over the bridge. He is twisted all out of shape. Overlying his image is the shadow of another boy—mocking, mimicking his movements a fraction of a second behind—and the sensation of another person leaning over his shoulder and staring down into the water is so strong that Matt turns around with a gasp. The bridge is empty, of course. The other boy is only in his head, a menacing adversary separating him from his father. He will always be there, a shadowy foe constituting perpetual competition for his father's affection, a weighty burden of inadequacy to dog his days. He realises with a start that the prospect of it is intolerable and that there is only one person who can rid him of it.

He takes out his phone and texts his dad. *I'll meet you on Saturday, 4pm, on the bridge.* Almost immediately the reply comes back: *Great.*

He goes home, over the spongy, sticky tarmac, past the exhausted garages and through the broiled streets of the Mere. He closes his curtains and lies on his bed. He sleeps deeply, dreamlessly, for the first time in weeks, and when he is awoken a full twenty four hours later it is by thunder. It tears the sky in two and through the gash there is an explosion of lightning. The sky lights up indigo and violet. The clouds unleash pent-up rain, pellets rattle the roofs. In a few moments water is spouting out of drainpipes and gouting along gutters. It is filthy grey with weeks of dust and dryness. The broken gutter above his room is a pouring tap. The grids of the Mere are choked with litter and silt, the sewage system crusted and sluggish. Gardens are baked and impermeable and quickly awash. There is nowhere for the water to go. It deluges the roads and makes them rivers. The noise, the unspeakable refreshment of water, the sudden release of pressure, has Mere residents out in the streets, children laughing and splashing in pools of oily dark water, women holding their tired hot faces up to the rain, men in vests paddling out to their cars to close the sunroof and windows for the first time in weeks.

It rains and rains all night. Water streams from the hills and off the parched fields. It gushes along streets and pavements. It swirls and guzzles through underground channels and torrents along ditches and drains, embankments and gullies. It falls unendingly in cascading sheets from the sky.

The rivers swell.

MATT ARRIVES AT the field early. He feels—like it, like the river, the landscape, the whole world—transformed.

The field is almost completely submerged in a plashy film of water; wide glassy expanses have turned the sorry grass into glossy seaweed. Occasional shafts of sunlight through the heavy, racing clouds silver the surface with bright reflections. The brisk wind shivers the surface. The tarmac path is only just above the water level, a black silk ribbon through the mercury water meadow. He walks along it as excited and delighted as an explorer in a new-found, magical land.

Children are running and wading in wellingtons. At each step a plume of disturbed dust blooms up through the shallow water like a strange anemone. A dog frolics around his owner, barking at his shadow in the mirrored ground. Grasses and trees, bushes and weeds are revived, quivering with life, their leaves glistening with moisture.

The river is in spate. It is bursting and leaping in exuberant brown gouts against the palings of the bridge. A cascade of whipped, frothing water surges under it, submerging the lip of the weir entirely and crashing in a torrent over the shallow steps in a series of boiling, furious rip tides and counter-currents. It has spilled over the concrete walls and the depression where their tree sits is a sliding milk-brown flood of river water, eroding the sandy ground, undermining the dry roots of the old dead tree, before pouring back into the roiling, leaping geyser of the pool. The site of their bonfire is submerged, washed away. The place where the blanket lay, the spot where he raised the broken bottle over Skinner, both are erased, scooped up in the churning maelstrom of tannin-coloured floodwater. On the far side of

159

the river the thick plantings are partly under water; the gardens of the houses beyond the fences will be waterlogged.

The end of the rope is submerged in the water, the flow of it pulling as surely as a tugging, insistent hand, downstream.

He steps through the chicane, onto the bridge. Between the scouring river and the standing pools on the field only the path is above water. The effervescent river is visible through the gaps of the boards. Occasional spurts jet between them and slap like wet hands on the wood. Up-stream the old, bearded log has disappeared. The river carries a flotilla of debris jostling on its agitated surface.

In the horse field the animals are cantering, bucking and whinnying, stirred by the rush of fast-moving water. Now and again a shower will hurl itself from the skies, pattering on the leaves, pimpling the surface of the water on the field with noisy wet splashes and spattering loudly on the impervious surface of Matt's waxed jacket. The sound of the rushing river is almost deafening, a scourging roar, a many-voiced bellow of surging, frenzied, swollen waters.

Only the quiver of it in his pocket alerts Matt to the fact that his phone is ringing. He glances at the time before answering the call. His father is a little late.

His father's voice comes from far away. It is stretched tight and anguished. He too is near a river, a much bigger one. He is shouting above its furious, terrifying rush.

'Oh God Matt, I'm sorry. I know you're waiting, but I can't come. It's the boy. We can't find him. We think he's fallen in the river.'

The alteration of Matt's emotions is as violent and shocking as a Christmas tree suddenly consumed by fire, the assassination of a bride. From the brightest of expectation he is confronted with the black menace of his worst fear. He thinks he will explode; his anger is volcanic. He hurls his telephone into the frothing river, watching it disappear with an impotent splash. Propelled by fury he rampages over the bridge, kicking helplessly at the railings. From his gut rises an animal, incoherent cry but it is lost in the roaring river.

'The *one* thing ... the *ONE* thing ...'

Everything goes dark. A frowning cloud—laden with rain—blocks out the limpid sun and the dilute sky. A deluge is coming. The children hurry home, squealing. The dog owner drags his reluctant mutt briskly over the bridge.

'It's going to pour son,' he says as he passes, 'and the second half will have kicked off.'

Matt is drowning. He swallows and gulps but the tears keep on coming and he can't breathe for the voluminous swell of emotion that is bursting his heart. Salt water torrents down his face. His nose pours liquid. He opens his mouth to inhale but it fills with water and his voice is lost in the onslaught of storm. He is subsumed, gasping under a bucketing, torrential downpour and swept away on a tsunami of overwhelming suffering. The volume of water makes vision dim. The field is blurred, the trees are dark shadows in the unnatural night. His ears are filled with the rush and push of oceans. He stands and lets wave after wave flood over him. Wave after wave after wave.

A boy in the water. A boy in the water. It is his nemesis.

He gropes his way blindly to the end of the bridge. His face is assaulted by piercing spears of rain. His feet feel the path, its edge, then they are under water—ankle- then knee- then thigh-deep. He can feel the powerful pull of it. It is chill and it smells of cold caverns; forgotten, underground places. There are burrowing fingers working under his shoes, digging away the ground. Then his toes find the exposed roots of the tree, hugely undermined. The water presses him against the trunk; the force is relentless. The dividing waters swell and wash around him. He inches further and further until his toes find the concrete edge of the weir. His arms are flailing and his hand meets harsh, hairy hemp. He hauls the rope in, feeling the drag of the current weigh heavy on its end. Then he turns and scrambles back up the treacherous slope to the path, back onto the bridge.

Mr Pickering is waiting for him. His hair is plastered to his head. He is without a jacket. His pullover literally pours water from its hem.

'Your dad called me. He told me to come,' he shouts. His voice, like everything, is torn away by the river.

'*I* can be the boy in the water,' Matt cries, 'if that's what it takes.' But the arrow of his father's concern for him, even amid the crisis, nicks his agony. A little of it ebbs.

John puts his hand on the rope. 'Nobody *wants* a boy in the water Matt. But there is one. And one is enough. Look at it! Just *look* at it!'

They look down at the water. The flood is inexorable, crushing, a stampede. Nothing could survive it; not a strapping teenage lad, not a little boy. He knows it. The merciless torrent is tugging at his jealousy; he knows he ought to let it go, but his grasp on it is stubborn.

'He's MY father!' The clogged saliva in his mouth sprays out with his words. On the wings of the storm they seem not to come from him, but from Spencer, cruelly screeched echoes eddying around him in manic falls, stripping Skinner of the little vestige of comfort he has gathered. In a sucking whirlpool of unspeakable sadness, he hears Carmel repeating, 'They've never had a daddy; *you're* so lucky. They've never had a daddy; *you're* so lucky,' and then, from far, far away, dimly lit by watery flames, Skinner himself, 'I only wanted a little bit of what he has. He has everything. Is it too much to ask?'

'He'll always be *your* father Matt, nothing can change that.' He knows it's true. John's voice turns the tide, and they are all gone, drowned out by a heart-snapping wrench of ancient wood. The ground, the bridge, trembles. The old tree quivers and teeters away from them. A yawning chasm opens up at its base revealing, for a moment, the rotten empty heart of it before the eager waters rush in and occupy the space. In their hands, they feel the rope tauten. They let it go. It rests for a moment on the saturated handrail and strokes across the carved letters of Skinner's name before falling into the raging waters and being carried away.

Matt is crying still. But he cries now for the things that are gone and will never come back, and in gladness for what will remain.

JOHN DRIVES HIM across town. Everywhere there is water. Several roads in town are closed and it takes John a while to negotiate an alternative route. On the radio news they hear that homes nearest the river are being evacuated. Emergency services are stretched; a bridge has collapsed; a policeman is feared drowned; a car has been swept away; a small boy is missing. The streets are eerily quiet; everyone is glued to the match.

The lane outside his father's house is almost blocked with vehicles parked tight against the hedgerow. Their nearside wheels have crushed the wild flowers and waving grasses of the verge. John edges past them to find a spot in a muddy yard by some farm buildings. They walk back together. Matt's legs are trembling. They pass an ambulance. Two men in the cab are crouched over the radio. A commentator is in full spate. One of them turns as they pass.

'Still one-all,' he says. 'Five minutes left of extra time.'

'For God's sake!' John barks. 'A boy might be dead!'

A grim team is almost assembled—police, press, friends and family come to search. They stand in anxious knots in the front garden. Their boots have turned it into a quagmire. Carmel is there, her waif-like arms around a stocky, wailing girl. She smiles at Matt sadly.

Richard sees Matt and John and detaches himself from a group of uniformed officers by the door. He walks down the short drive and meets them at the gate. He is grey with fatigue and Matt finds that he needs nothing from his father at all, except to be allowed to hold him and feel the weight of him resting against his shoulder.

Richard sobs, 'My beautiful boy. My son, my boy,' and Matt doesn't care who he means.

BOOK 2

THE LAST CROSSING

THE FIRST THING that hits her is the heat; a boiling wall of it, hanging like a thick, musty curtain, just inside the door. The wheelchair—which she doesn't need or want; it makes her feel powerless and stupid, but Jennifer *will* insist upon it—is pushed through the suffocating veil, and it is like a filthy fabric dragging across her face. The chair—like her—is unwilling.

The quarry-tiled porch gives way to thick carpet in the foyer, and the wheels are suddenly bemired in the pile. The grunt of her daughter as she is taken by surprise at the sudden resistance is like someone giving the final massive push of birth. But she is not giving birth, only death. Jennifer has brought her here to die.

The chair travels through the death-canal of overwhelming heat, the door behind them swings closed, and she is trapped. The heat sears her nostrils and catches in her throat and makes her scalp prickle. It smells of cloying lavender, sickly-sweet and nauseous, like old women. And, not quite masked by the lavender, she can smell the old women themselves; fusty and stale, sugary and acrid; biscuits and wee.

Her daughter, Jennifer, takes a deep breath and opens her mouth. A flow of tense and determinedly cheerful verbiage pours out.

'Well now! This is nice, isn't it? Very spacious! Look at the view of the garden, Mum! You'll enjoy sitting here in the mornings, I should think. Oh! And look at that! All the newspapers are laid ready! You'll enjoy those, won't you? That must be the dining room. We'll just pop our heads in, shall we? Yes. All laid for lunch. One or two eager beavers are already waiting. Rather early. It's only half past eleven. But still, I expect it takes a while to get everyone assembled.'

The woman in the wheelchair says nothing. She doesn't even look at the decrepit old bodies slumped in the dining chairs.

'Hello! Good morning!' Jennifer shrills. 'Are you waiting for your lunch?'

The would-be diners continue to stare emptily at nothing.

'I don't think they can hear me,' Jennifer mutters. She reverses the chair and points it down a corridor. 'Now what's down here? Looks like a TV lounge. Nice big screen, with subtitles, look, Mum. That'll be handy for you won't it?'

Her mother bridles in the chair. She is not deaf.

'Although the volume's high enough,' Jennifer adds. 'I can hardly hear myself think. There are lots of comfy chairs, though. I must say everyone looks very relaxed.'

'Relaxed? They look comatose,' her mother thinks. But she says nothing.

Her daughter ploughs on. 'It's nicely decorated, too, isn't it? Very cheerful, I think, don't you? Here's another lounge, quieter, smaller. A bit more private. I expect this is where we'll sit when I come to visit. Oh look!' Peering through some French doors. 'There's a little terrace for when the weather's fine, and a bird table. That's nice. Quite a home-from-home, don't you think? Mum? Don't you think?'

A silence opens up but the older woman does not fill it.

Jennifer sighs, and then, all the artificial buoyancy gone from her voice, says, 'We ought to find the matron. I'll leave you in here while I go and find her. Then we can bring your case in and get you settled. I won't be a moment.'

The woman watches Jennifer march off down the corridor with that quick, no-nonsense stride she has had since she learned to put one foot in front of another on Whitby beach. Her lips quiver a little at memory of it. One moment there was a baby on her bottom behind the wind-break and the next there was a tyrant on a mission, half-way to the sea, with a bucket gripped in one hand and a gritty meat paste sandwich squashed in the other. Jennifer was always such a little busy-body; stubborn little madam. The woman's lips press back into a hard line and her forehead furrows. Stubborn little madam: always did get her own way in the end.

The quiet lounge is mercifully cooler. The quarter lights are open and the putrid fug of over-heated, decomposing flesh streams out into the air, replaced by the merest hint of fresh green freedom. A blackbird, on the terrace, cocks an eye at her; she can see it through the French doors before it flies away, but its trill is inaudible over the booming volume of the television that yells uselessly at the collection of old bones and sack-like flesh slumped in the chairs, snoring and dribbling.

She feels sick with frustration and fear. She hates her helplessness. But she would rather die than admit it, even to Jennifer. Especially to Jennifer.

Jennifer returns with the matron in tow. The matron is middle-aged, short and stocky, with small, beady eyes and tightly permed, wiry-grey hair reminiscent of a dog's coat. She wears lipstick a rather shocking shade of vermillion on a small pursed mouth the size and shape of a dog's arse. She has bandy legs with a number of varicose veins like purple worms trapped between her skin and her tights, and an upside down watch pinned to the yoke of her tunic. Numerous pens bristle importantly from the pocket.

She perches gingerly right on the edge of one of the comfortable chairs, as though its surface might contaminate her, and leans in towards the woman in the wheelchair, enunciating carefully with obscene bright red lips over narrow, wet, yellow teeth. 'Well here we are then, Mrs Fairlie. The fresh air has done us good, hasn't it? We have roses in our cheeks! I'm Mrs Terry, the matron here. Welcome to Bridge House! We're feeling a little uncertain just now I know, but I'm sure we'll feel right at home in no time.'

Mrs Fairlie remains silent in the moment or two of pause which inserts itself into the room. She feels that to make any kind of coherent response would be a disappointment to Mrs Terry, who has clearly assumed that she is deaf, or daft, or both, and has rendered speech unnecessary in any event by presuming to articulate every thought and feeling on their joint behalves. In any case Mrs Fairlie fears that she cannot trust herself to not address Matron as 'Mrs Terrier.' She stares past the perching woman at the place on the terrace where the blackbird was only moments before. The empty terrace makes her think of her deserted house, her vacant chair, her empty teacup—the one with the chip in it the shape of South Africa—her unoccupied bed, and she is filled with longing for familiar things.

Over her head Jennifer and Mrs Terry are talking practicalities with tense enthusiasm. Jennifer will go and get the suitcase out of the car. Mrs Terry will 'just take us through a few details while we wait,' Jennifer will provide contact details and the doctor's address, and a list of medication. It all sounds to Mrs Fairlie as though she is to be neatly packaged and tagged with a label on her toe, filed and forgotten. Mrs Terry will 'take us up to our room, and introduce us to key staff members'. Mrs Fairlie's face darkens at the mention of keys. There it is: she is to be locked in, a prisoner, watched and restrained until she dies. Perhaps she will be starved slowly. Perhaps she will be despatched more swiftly—a night visit from a wide-shouldered orderly, a pillow pressed down over her face.

Jennifer hurries off down the corridor towards the foyer and Mrs Terry mentions meal-times and recreational opportunities, which days the hair-dresser and the podiatrist visit. She enthuses about the opportunity to take communion with the local curate once a month. Mrs Fairlie stares resolutely out of the window and makes no response. She doesn't wish to be rude but she refuses to co-operate in any way that might indicate her complicity.

Jennifer arrives back with the suitcase. It really isn't very heavy but in that overly dramatic way that Jennifer has she manages to make it look like a herculean task, puffing her cheeks in and out and shifting the handle from hand to hand. She proffers a type-written sheet of information for Mrs Fairlie's file. Then they all move back up the corridor into the sunny foyer and Mrs Terry presses the button for the lift.

The smell in the upper corridor is far worse; musty old bodies and stale night-breathed air and un-emptied commodes. And floating on top of it all, like scum on water, the astringent tang of disinfectant and bitter medications denoting sickness and death. There are no windows and the fluorescent tube lighting is more honest than the elaborate charade below; this is an institution, not a home. The corridor is wide but more practically covered with a short-pile, utilitarian carpet. The chair travels along without difficulty past doors on either side. Most of them are open and Mrs Fairlie imagines damp, dishevelled beds containing incontinent, toothless old women and old men abandoned in various stages of being dressed; propped up in chairs, helpless in their vests and pants. But she keeps her eyes resolutely on the carpet. There are breakfast trays outside some of the rooms, and heaps of soiled linen waiting to be loaded into a big-wheeled trolley. Orderlies wearing polythene aprons bustle in and out. They are bright and smiling and brisk. Mrs Terry mentions their names: Rosie, Olga, Selene.

They all behave as though they are delighted to see her. 'Here she is!' they cry, as though their whole morning has been brightened by her arrival. 'How lovely to see you!'

Mrs Fairlie's room is in the middle of a corridor towards the end of which, she will find out later, there is a stairwell and a communal bathroom (no doubt filled with ugly metallic contraptions for undignified hoisting and sluicing) and a further doorway with a sign proclaiming 'staff only', restricting access to auxiliary areas where she imagines vats of disinfectant, oxygen cylinders, and containers of misappropriated dentures.

The bedroom has a window opposite to the door with a high sill so that, from her chair, she can see only the lofty April sky. The bed is narrow, with a grey metal headboard and foot with curious fixings for mysterious attachments—restraints, she speculates, which can be brought into play in the later stages of senility or for patients who are unmanageably truculent. The walls are painted a cool green. There is a white chest of drawers, bedside locker and single wardrobe, an easy chair and a wheeled tray-table. A door leads into the much-vaunted 'private facilities'. Jennifer has waxed lyrical in their praise; their convenience, their luxury, their expense. In the midst of these pieces of furniture there is barely room for Mrs Fairlie's chair, the matron, Jennifer and the suitcase. Matron tweaks the bedspread unnecessarily into place and adjusts the curtain before 'leaving us to settle in, and assuring us that our door is always open at any time for anything that might arise to worry or concern us.'

Mrs Fairlie has taken it all in. It is reasonably commodious she muses, bitterly, as coffins go.

Jennifer hauls the suitcase onto the bed and proceeds to unpack. Mrs Fairlie observes her from beneath stubbornly lowered lids. There are a dozen pairs of white knickers, three bras and some tights, three or four vests, a couple of crisp cotton night dresses, a floral dressing gown and a pair of slippers, none of which Mrs Fairlie recognises; all new. The underwear makes her gulp. She hasn't worn a bra—its fixings too tortuous for her arthritic joints—or, for similar reasons, tights for months. All these items are briskly arranged in the top drawer of the chest except for the slippers, which are placed by the bed. Then there are a number of more familiar—but scarcely worn—clothes that Jennifer carried away for laundering about a week ago, declaring them 'just about fit to be seen'. They have come back smelling of Persil and bearing neatly-printed name labels, I. FAIRLIE, inside their collars. Jennifer lifts out cardigans and blouses, refolding them with deft, business-like hands and lays them in the drawers. Mrs Fairlie eyes the tiny buttons with dread. Her Christmas and Easter dresses, her funeral skirt and three other conservative skirts not worn for years—she doubts they will even fit—are hung in the wardrobe. She abandoned all these clothes long ago in favour of easy, elastic-waisted trousers like the ones she is now wearing, loose jumpers and the warm woollen socks of Frederick's she has kept all these years, comfortable old flat shoes.

Jennifer places some framed snap-shots of herself and Kenny, one of the dogs, and the black and white studio shot of Michael as a boy on the chest of drawers, along with a hair brush and a pot of Pond's face cream. An unfamiliar toilet bag is spirited into the bathroom. Finally a puzzle book, her spectacles and a box of tissues are placed on the bedside table and a bag of Werther's Originals slipped into the top drawer.

While she has been unpacking Jennifer has maintained a flow of observations, a running commentary on her actions, but now as she zips the case up and puts it by the door it seems that the stream of narrative, like the case's contents, has been exhausted. In silence they look around the room—at the window, the photographs, the hairbrush—anywhere but at each other. The paltry collection of belongings is a miserably small legacy of a life almost lived-out.

This is what she is reduced to, this is what Jennifer has reduced her to; a few photographs, a puzzle book and a packet of boiled sweets.

The enormity of what she has done hits Jennifer at last. 'I am certain,' she says, with less certainty in her voice than she has had before, 'that you can have more personal belongings here, if you want. We only brought today what, you know, I could carry easily. I could bring a few of your pot-plants next time, or your patchwork quilt off your bed, or anything else that you wanted to make the place more homely.'

There *are* things that she wants, of course. Her two dogs and the cat, all sent to be re-homed. The dogs had stared mournfully at her from the back of Jennifer's hatch-back and the cat had yowled and scratched her when she'd put him into the carry-box. The sewing box she has had since she was a little girl, with her mother's pearl-headed pins and her grandma's knitting needles. The things out of her bottom drawer; the children's Christening gown, their school reports and the Altoid's Mints tin with their milk teeth inside. She wants her marriage lines and Frederick's death certificate. And yes, the patchwork quilt that she made in her honeymoon year and which has been on her bed ever since. And her wireless. She does not know how she will be able to sleep without the BBC World Service whispering into the darkness. But to mention any of these things would make her complicit in the procedure. It would indicate agreement, acceptance. So she says nothing and keeps her eyes on her lap, where her hands—swollen and purple like misshapen plums—conceal a balled handkerchief. Out of the corner of her eye she sees that Jennifer has sunk onto the armchair. Now their heads are level and Jennifer reaches out her slim, cool, white hand and places it on top of hers. The juxtaposition of their flesh is quite astonishing and Mrs Fairlie stares down at it.

'It all seems very strange and perhaps you think me cruel,' Jennifer says quietly. 'But really, Mum, this will be better for you. The house was too big for you, the dogs were too much. You couldn't manage the stairs or the bath and now that Annie ... isn't there to help you, how are you going to cope? You were struggling to make it upstairs to the toilet. You know you were. Well *that's* no good, is it? Here there will be nice meals three times a day, company, things going on, kind people trained to help ...' She trails off. Her mother says nothing, and makes no response to the squeeze of her hand.

Jennifer sighs. 'You're making this very difficult for me, you know,' she says more loudly, removing her hand and standing up. She smooths the tight-fitting skirt down over her slim hips. 'I'm sure I didn't punish you this much when you left me at school for the first time. I didn't really want to go there either but it had to be done. It's only the same, really.'

Jennifer turns her back and stares out of the window, drumming her painted fingernails gently on the window ledge.

Mrs Fairlie finds that her memory, unreliable at other times, takes her straight back to that day like an arrow. Jennifer's first day at school. The brightly lit classroom. Mrs Livsey, the teacher, all bosomy and pink. The low tables set out with crayons and building blocks and beads to thread onto thick green cords. The children solemn in their name-labelled uniforms—the irony of this does not escape her—the row of clearly named pegs for their coats and plimsoll-bags. Jennifer had settled immediately to the beads, threading them with furious concentration onto a long cord as requested by Mrs Livsey. Mrs Fairlie had hovered for some moments by the classroom door, waiting for Jennifer to look up, to wave, to smile, but the child had been so completely absorbed in her task that in the end she had walked down the polished corridor and across the playground, scarcely making it to the corner before the tears had overwhelmed her. The memory, or perhaps the current ordeal, causes a large tear to slide down her cheek. It drips off her chin and lies quivering and pink on her chapped hand. She dabs it quickly with her handkerchief.

'Oh, I don't know,' she thinks.

Jennifer turns from the window. It's possible that she does so in time to see the tear and its swift removal. Her voice softens again. 'I'll go and get your sticks out of the car,' she says, 'and then we can get you out of that wretched chair.'

As she makes to leave the room, Mrs Fairlie speaks at last. She is looking at the bed.

'Do you think,' she says, 'that the last occupant of this room died in that bed?'

JENNIFER ROAMS AROUND the house, feeling like an interloper, which is ridiculous. She has been born and brought up in this house, eaten and slept, been ill and well, played and raged and hidden in it. At various times she has run around, to and away from it. But she can hardly ever remember being alone in it. Because of the shop, which had, for a long time, occupied the downstairs portion of the house, there had always been somebody in attendance; her mother, predominantly, behind the counter or toiling in the dairy at the back, hauling sacks of produce in the yard, cooking, ironing, mending.

Now that Jennifer has possession at last, now that she has off-loaded the responsibility of her mother, she feels like the giant holding the carcass of the golden egg-laying goose. The house is lifeless without her mother at the centre of it—as impenetrable and inscrutable as she had been, at times—and the realisation brings home to Jennifer how flayed and raw her mother must feel in her removed state. The empty rooms are crowded suddenly with accusations. The late afternoon sun slopes in through the dirty windows and paints everything with a blush.

The house remains as her mother left it. Since she left it so unwillingly she made no preparations for departure, believing until the very last moment that she would be able to stay. There is no finality, no closure. It is as if she has merely gone out for the day with every expectation of returning as the dusk draws in. The covers on her bed are thrown back and yesterday's clothes are over the back of the chair. The weekend papers are spread over the gate-leg table, their careful perusal always drawn out to last until the next edition drops onto the mat. And indeed the next editions will make their weekly appearance since, doubtless, she has not cancelled them. There is milk in the fridge and more will arrive in due course on the step. There is food in the cupboards including the remains of a particularly nice, moist fruit cake in the cake tin; the last that Annie brought round before she died. Jennifer throws it in the bin.

Her mother would weep if she knew: it is all she has left of Annie and, somehow, she has not been able to bring herself to finish it.

There are dishes in the sink that need washing and plants on the window ledge that need watering. Her armchair, drawn up close to the fireside, still shows the imprint of her body; the cushion more depressed at one side than the other, where she tended to lean to relieve the pressure on her bad hip. There is an unfinished cup of tea on the small side table; she was drinking it when Jennifer's car drew up outside. The cup is badly chipped. Very unhygienic. Beside the cup is a scattering of letters and bills. There are personal papers stuffed in drawers that need sorting through and dealing with. There are items of glass and porcelain that might be valuable but mainly the ornaments are worthless and ugly. There is untold rubbish that needs throwing out. The house is dirty; thick cobwebs loop between the light fitting and the curtain rail, there is a coat of dust over everything and dog-hairs lie in mats on the settee and the hearth rug and the window seat. The window above the seat is smeared and slimy with dog-nose. The walls are grimy at dog-height and the inside of the door marked and scratched by their paws and claws over the years. The place smells of dog; of dog-breath and dog-fur and lately of dog-wee because her mother couldn't get to the back door fast enough to let them out. There is still, too, the lingering smell of burning plastic from the microwave meal ill-advisedly heated under the grill. The kitchen curtains are greyed by the acrid smoke that billowed and gusted through the window, and there is a greasy film on the window ledge. The smell of dog and carbon is under-girded by the musty wet rottenness of the ceiling, like soggy newspaper, saturated by the water that spilled over the bath when her mother forgot she had left the taps on.

This is Jennifer's legacy—the house itself and the money it must release, and the guilt and the work—the unlooked-for consequences of removing her mother into care. Now Jennifer stands in the middle of it all and doesn't know where to begin. It is all so untidy; not just practically—the house is in the shabby and slightly chaotic disarray that her mother seemed happy to exist amidst—but emotionally. Placing Mum at Bridge House against her will has generated tendrils of resentment and remorse like pernicious weeds; they threaten to strangle what small, flat, functional accord exists between them. And legally, Jennifer supposes, casting a doubtful eye at the documents poking out of the half-closed drawers, there will be the bank, solicitors, accountants all to be convinced that things are ready to be wound to a close.

While Annie was alive and living next door it had all seemed manageable, and Jennifer's gentle suggestions that her mother 'sort through a few things' and 'rationalise' and 'consider down-sizing' had been without real urgency. Annie did the shopping and the washing and kept on top of the dirt. Annie took the dogs around the block twice a day and carried in the coal and laid the fire. A telephone call or even a good strong shout could bring Annie around in moments whereas it took Jennifer a good hour to negotiate the cross-town traffic, always assuming she could get away from work, which wasn't always possible, then, at the drop of a hat. Ironically, now, when it is too late, Jennifer has a new job, right in town, not ten minutes away. Annie was such a good and long-standing friend that she had even been happy to help with the personal care that her mother had increasingly needed as arthritis and forgetfulness took hold. Annie had always included Mrs Fairlie at Christmas—a kindly meant gesture, although Jennifer cannot imagine that it was a particularly enjoyable occasion, with Annie's prolific family squashed into the tiny house. But it had meant that she—Jennifer—and Kenny could go skiing for Christmas and not feel guilty about it.

Jennifer's visits had been rare, then, a testimony to how uncomfortable they were for both parties; her mother's tight-lipped pride and disapproval equal only to her own careful reticence.

But then Annie had died and Jennifer had to step in. And it had seemed from the beginning that all her efforts were to be sabotaged. Her mother had resolutely refused to get the hang of the system of frozen meals that Jennifer had organised—and paid for—to be delivered. Either she forgot to put them in the freezer when they arrived at the beginning of the week, or she forgot to get them out in time to defrost. Or she tried to heat them up in the oven (and once, disastrously, in the grill) instead of the shiny new microwave bought for the purpose. She sent a number of cleaners packing and refused even to admit the carers who were supposed to help her in and out of the bath. She declined a stair-lift and a privately funded hip-replacement. Stubborn, proud, independent old woman!

The fire and the flood had been the last straw. Even *she* had had to admit that!

So now Jennifer has finally got her mother into a home, she has returned to assess what needs to be done. A firm of house-clearance people. A skip—or several skips. A roaring bonfire. Really every single thing needs ripping from the house. Every piece of furniture, every old and worn out sheet and blanket and threadbare towel, the faded pictures, the chipped crockery and bent, tarnished cutlery. The tatty ornaments, the keepsakes—the sake of whose keeping is now long forgotten—the smelly settee and grimy carpet, the dusty curtains, the old clothes not fit even for a charity shop. The old fashioned kitchen and bathroom, the peeling wallpaper, the soggy trusses between the lounge ceiling and the bathroom floor, the rotten windows, the sagging roof, the crumbling mortar between the weathered, frost-damaged bricks. A bulldozer, Jennifer thinks, would be the best solution, except that the house must be sold to pay for Bridge House. Surely, as an empty shell, stripped and sanitised with gleaming new paintwork and double glazed windows and a garden rescued from the frenzied digging and circling of under-exercised dogs with smooth green turf and some decking ... Surely, even in this rather down-at-heel area, it would be worth *something*, and, God knew, the fees at Bridge House were not small.

At the same time, passing now from room to room, trying to picture it all neatly packed into bin bags for the dump or the charity shop, her eye falls upon some things of evocative value, memories, icons of childhood. That quilt on her mother's bed had been a hiding place, a tent, a den, a magical cave of wonders. It had been her hospital bed in times of fevered delirium. A comforter when friends had been fickle. A safe retreat on stormy nights and a picnic blanket on summer days. It was soft with much washing, smelling of Mum and home. In spite of everything it is powerfully nostalgic, although it is hard to equate her feelings for her mother *then* with those she has now. She stoops and lifts the corner of the quilt. The stitching is tiny, all done by hand, the squares of floral cotton, paisley print, gingham and seersucker all faded now but still strongly reminiscent. There is one square, a paisley square, that once, when she had a raging temperature, she had been convinced was a lion's face peering through jungle foliage. But since then she has been unable to identify it. She looks for it now, a hopeless quest for the lost things of childhood.

She catches sight of herself in the blemished mirror, peering narrowly at the old quilt. On the dressing table, below the mirror, there is a set of flowery china dishes and trays where her mother used to keep her brooches and hairpins and costume jewellery. It was one of Jennifer's favourite things, at one time, to transport the dishes across the room and place them like holy objects onto the quilt, to sit cross-legged next to them and lift the lids on the little pots and pill-boxes and rummage through the beads and dangly earrings. She would stand up on the bed so that she could see herself in the dressing table mirror, all draped in her mother's finery. That, she recalls, is how one of the lids got broken. She sees the line of clumsy glue, now, and feels her mother's reproach. Of course the jewellery had been all tasteless paste and glass, but it had seemed, in those days, to be riches beyond price, carefully treasured, valued and valuable. Not that her mother had ever worn these trinkets. They were anomalous to the daily grind of the grocer. They had come down from Mum's own mother and her deceased sister, and Jennifer presumed they had on occasion been bought by her dad, much appreciated no doubt but carefully stored away. As far as she could recall Jennifer herself had taken more practical pleasure in them than her mother ever had. And now—because of those associations—they seem too precious to throw away, because those hours were happy and won't come again.

She picks up each piece in turn, and lifts the lids. From within, the gilt and the glass gleam dully, evoking early enticements. For a moment she is transported back into childhood. And with a foot, as it were, in each era, she tries to place her mother into the scene; sitting alongside her on the bed fingering the jewellery, standing in the doorway looking on with an indulgent smile. Something, *anything*, which would justify the sense she has that there was once a warmer relation between them. But she can conjure up only a vague impression of a burdened back disappearing into the darkened yard, deft, practical hands serving food or folding linen, a distracted smile, the smell of clean earth and sour milk. It had seemed, she admits, at the time, to be enough. Her mother had necessarily been busy and burdened by the responsibilities of the business and was by nature anyway of a reserved and realistic cast of character. But while there had not been the effusive, demonstrative affection that some mothers and daughters enjoy, there had been— hadn't there?—a kind of comfortable confidence between them. They had quite simply not ever been the kind of family that talked about feelings. In the past it had been a merciful relief not to have to articulate emotions she hardly understood. At other times, when she had given way to angry outbursts, they had been met with silent shock and bafflement that had served, if anything, to intensify her rage. There was no escaping from the fact that right now, a frank exchange of views would have been a welcome relief to the palpable tension between them. On the other hand, recently, Jennifer has had additional cause to keep her tongue on a tight rein, and she resents that, too; the necessity of it.

She replaces the dishes carefully onto the dressing table, onto the lacy doilies, made, she presumes, by her mother or by some more ancient female relative. As she replaces the china, the doilies move fractionally and she can see that the wood beneath them is lighter, protected over the years by the coverings.

She is beginning to understand, a little, the permanence of what she is seeking to disassemble.

As she looks around the room she realises that everything has made its indelible mark; is fixed in time and space and routine and expectation. The chair in the bedroom has always been where it is now, and has always been used for discarded clothing between the wardrobe and the wash; the carpet is faded around its shadow. The rug by the bed is the same one and is in the same place with the same stain from some ancient spill. That little watercolour on the wall above the bed, the brass dish for keys on the whatnot, the nasty glazed squirrel and improbable log on the shelf—as individual things they are so much rubbish, but together they form a structure of home and history. To deconstruct it will be a kind of butchery.

Abruptly she puts a stop to this dangerous train of thought. If she goes on like that she won't be able to get rid of anything and Kenny will go spare if she lands home with boxes of her mother's tat. Not quite as spare, she considers, as he had gone when she had made the tentative suggestion that she might, one day, be forced to arrive back with the woman herself, but spare enough.

Jennifer takes a mental grip on herself. She goes downstairs and takes off her jacket, hanging it gingerly on the back of one of the dining chairs. She props the fridge door open and pulls the plug out of its socket. She pours the milk down the sink and writes a note to leave in the bottle on the step. 'No more milk thanks. Leave bill'. She takes all the perishable food and puts it in the bin, with the cake. She empties the bin and scrubs it out. She washes the dishes in the sink and dries them and puts them away in the cupboards. She checks the windows are all shut and then leaves the house, pulling the door quickly closed and locking it firmly. There is a sigh as the dust lifts and settles.

AFTER JENNIFER HAS gone, Mrs Fairlie sits on the chair in her room and listens. One by one the other inmates have been manoeuvred down the corridor to the lift and taken down to lunch. She has watched from under lowered eyelids their painful progress past her door and down the corridor, supported by Zimmers or sticks or nurses, or wheeled in chairs. They all look like broken furniture; awkwardly angular and tortured out of shape, or so pale and flimsy that the least breath of wind would carry them weightlessly into the air. Every time the lift door slides open there is a metallic 'bing bong' noise. Cooking smells gust up from below.

Mrs Fairlie thinks about the slice of toast she might have had for lunch at home.

Now the corridor seems to be deserted. The inconsequential chatter of the nurses has ceased, the rattle of the trolley collecting the breakfast trays and morning coffee cups has disappeared. Although her door is open she feels relatively safe in the silence and allows her eyelids to droop closed for a few seconds. Sleep is the only privacy she can hope for now and she sinks tentatively into it. Very distantly she can hear the timid scrape of cutlery across crockery and the TV announcer on the lunch time news shouting the headlines.

When she wakes up she does so with a start. She is disorientated and stretches a hand out to where Clarry's soft head would normally be, pressed against her knee, her warmth a comfort on the aching joint, her eyes soulful and reassuring. But of course there is only the tray-table by her side, empty and impersonal in the unfamiliar room. But she isn't alone. There is a woman sitting on her bed—*the* bed, it will never be hers—with a tray on her lap. Mrs Fairlie's hip hurts where it has been

181

pressed against the hard side of the chair and she has a crick in her neck.

The woman, noting that she is awake, nods in her direction but goes on eating. The food on the plate looks something like shepherd's pie; greyish brown mince and whitish grey mashed potato and pulverised carrots and turnip and translucent, flaccid white cabbage that looks as though it has been floating in lukewarm bath water for about four days. The woman eats it with a spoon, her arm rising and falling and her jaws filtering—it hardly needs chewing—the food in a mechanical rhythm which, once got underway, she is reluctant to interrupt with any niceties of introduction or conversation. She is round and fat, like a lady blackbird, with a head thrust unnaturally far forward in an eager, bird-like way. Her hands and feet are tiny, out of all proportion to the rest of her, but very fleshy. She is small. Mrs Fairlie, who is tall, wonders how the woman managed to get onto the bed at all without a considerable and undignified struggle. Her feet stick out from the edge, like a child on a grown-up seat. Her face is remarkably unlined, her skin rather delicate and fine, and she has surprisingly big eyes with straight lashes that are still dark. Her hair, too, is mouse-brown, fine, cut straight with a side parting and held in place with an Alice band. She looks like an aged child. She is wearing a floral skirt and an embroidered white pullover and pop-socks and slippers with pom-poms. The pullover has a stain down the front. All this Mrs Fairlie has time to take in while the woman clears the plate with industrious attention and, without pause, once it is clean, commences work on the fruit sponge and custard, using the same spoon.

Finally, when all the food has gone and the spoon has been thoroughly licked, she slides the tray onto the bedspread at her side and folds her pudgy little hands in her capacious lap. Then she takes a deep breath and begins to talk. She speaks quickly, as though fearing that time, or her breath, might give out before she has said all she needs to say. She half closes her eyes, perhaps to shut out any facial expressions or non-verbal signals which might try to interrupt the flow, or perhaps to aid her memory as she recites the oft-repeated narrative.

'Of course when I moved back in with Mummy and Daddy people said that it isn't right for grown-up children to live with their parents. They said I couldn't go home and be Mummy and Daddy's little girl again when I'd been a married woman with my own house and had a baby. They said that my baby would become like Mummy's baby. They said that *I* would always be Mummy's baby and never get a chance to be an independent grown-up.'

She pauses. This is a big question, like a pot-hole in the road that has to be got around.

Then, with a rush, she hurries past it. 'But it was never like that because Mummy and Daddy gave up the small sitting room for William and me and he had his own room and Mummy never got up to him in the night or fed him or anything; it was always me. But we often sat in the big sitting room together in the evenings because I was lonely by myself after William had gone to bed. Of course, when I went to work as Daddy's secretary Mummy looked after William *then* until he started school. After that she just took him and collected him again, and looked after him until Daddy and I came home, which was sometimes rather late. People said that William spent too much time with grown-ups; they said he'd be old before his time. But it was just his nature to be quiet and sensible. He's a quiet and sensible boy, my William, and Daddy always said what a good thing it was; there is so much silliness in the world. William played with other children at school but we didn't invite them to come to the house; there were appearances to be kept up. Surely that's understandable?'

Another pause for thought, before a dash onwards. 'Daddy was the local solicitor and I was his secretary and we had a certain standing in the town. We had to be the soul of discretion, you know; people needed to be able to trust us. We couldn't have just *any* boy coming to the house! There were appearances to be kept up: Daddy was the local solicitor and I was ... certain standing ... couldn't have any boy ...' She falters, conscious of being somehow stuck on a loop. Under her breath she repeats 'appearances to be kept up' a couple of times, searching for the right exit before lunging on with, 'Mummy washed all our smalls through at night and left them on the maiden by the fire to dry overnight. She *never* put smalls on the line; that wouldn't have done at all. And I never did either, when I looked after Daddy after Mummy died. The local doctor, the clergy of course, perhaps even one or two of the gentlemen farmers. They were all of a similar social standing. Perhaps, one of their sons ... but then again they were all clients as well, so we couldn't mix with them socially. We handled all their legal business and Daddy always thought it was best that business and pleasure be kept strictly separate. So William didn't have boys round to play. Perhaps he was lonely? I don't know if he was lonely. He never said he was lonely ... He never *said* he was lonely ... We all kept each other company and we didn't need anyone else, and Mummy said that we were 'once bitten twice shy' when it came to mixing socially, even with people you ought to be able to rely on to behave properly. We'd tried it once and it had been a disaster, she said, and if it wasn't for William I'd have agreed with her about that too. But if it hadn't been for Reverend Baker there would have been no William and I wouldn't want that. And I thought it was a bit harsh of Mummy really. Reverend Baker was a very kind man, and Mummy and Daddy had seemed very keen that I should marry him when they found out. They certainly arranged it all in a towering hurry and it wasn't his fault that he died and I had to move out of the vicarage.'

A nurse bustles into the room and the woman's story falters. She looks like a child caught out in a misdeed. Her hand goes to her mouth.

'Now Pearl, I hope you're not tiring poor Mrs Fairlie out. She's only just arrived and you know how tiring it is coming to a new place and trying to find your feet.' The nurse addresses the woman as though she were a child.

'I know where my feet are,' Mrs Fairlie thinks to herself, mulishly, but she says nothing.

'Oh no,' Pearl wriggles her bottom towards the edge of the bed and slides off onto her tiny feet. 'I just came to say hello.' Once she is upright Mrs Fairlie can see that the little woman carries an enormous widow's hump. It bends her over into a curl so that it is only really when seated and leaning quite far back that she can look properly ahead of her. She scuttles from the room and the nurse busies herself with medical activities, taking Mrs Fairlie's blood pressure and temperature, helping her onto some scales to be weighed, making notes in an orange file. Mrs Fairlie makes monosyllabic replies to her questions: does she have her own teeth? Hearing-aid? Spectacles? Is she allergic to anything? Any food intolerance? How often does she move her bowels?

'I'm not answering that!' Mrs Fairlie snaps.

'Suit yourself,' the nurse says calmly. 'But if you need anything to help you go, or something to soften the stools, let me know. These pain-killers you're on can cause problems.'

Mrs Fairlie regrets her short temper. This young woman isn't to blame, after all—she's only doing her job. She is filling in a chart with a busy ballpoint and Mrs Fairlie steals a good look at her while her attention is distracted. Beneath her calm efficiency the woman has a troubled face and fraught eyes, as though there are things she is worried about. Her eyes are dull; perhaps she hasn't slept well, or has cried a lot, recently.

'I can't remember your name,' Mrs Fairlie says in a quiet voice.

The nurse seems to accept Mrs Fairlie's confession as an apology. She smiles. She has a lovely smile; kind, brown eyes, a delicious dimple on one cheek. 'It's Rosie. Look, it's written on this name badge here. We all wear one, to help you. But you'll soon know everyone here. Can I call you ...' she checks the file, 'Iris?' Mrs Fairlie's eyes widen. No one ever calls her by her Christian name. Even Annie never did. It was a mark of respect amongst the customers, recognition of her status in the neighbourhood. Rosie lets the question go unanswered. 'This is a small place,' she says. 'There are only twenty residents and eight staff. When you've been here a while ...'

'I don't want to stay here,' Mrs Fairlie's words jerk out of her. She had not known she was going to say them. Rosie's niceness is suddenly the most threatening thing she has so far encountered. She cannot afford to let go of her anger, to cave in. It will be in just such a moment of inattention that they will get her. Her hands are gripping the arms of her chair; it makes them hurt. Her hip is still hurting; the chair is uncomfortable for her. She wants to stand up, as if she could walk away and leave the pain behind her in the chair. In a moment of ridiculous distraction she wonders what it would look like—her pain in the chair—it is dry and coarse like rubble, like a stone permanently in a shoe or grit always in the eye, grating and grinding and aggravating. She pictures her pain in the chair and it looks like pumice. She looks past the nurse—Rosie—and realises that Jennifer has left her sticks completely out of reach. She feels trapped and helpless—stranded in the chair, in the room, in the building—as isolated as she would have been on any desert island. 'I want to go home. I don't like it here. I need to go home, in case he comes.'

Panic rises in her chest. If she isn't there, how will he know where to find her?

Rosie follows her eyes and passes her the sticks, helping Mrs Fairlie to rise from the chair. Her knees are stiff; they creak as she straightens them. But it isn't the pain which make tears well into her eyes.

'I know,' Rosie says kindly. 'Everyone feels the same when they get here. Generally people are used to living on their own and they find the close proximity of other people unsettling. People don't like accepting help; they want to stay independent for as long as possible. We understand all that.' Gently, Rosie takes one of Mrs Fairlie's swollen hands and smooths her cool fingers over the reddened joints. 'Just take things slowly. There's nothing to worry about. I've been here a little while and I've seen it happen.' They look at each other for a moment. Rosie sees her fear. 'I could massage your hands with some oil if you like. Very gently. Roman Chamomile and Lavender.'

At the mention of lavender Mrs Fairlie snatches her hand away. Lavender is for old women. She hobbles painfully to the window and looks out. There is a pleasant garden below her, bordered by a thick hedge, and she can just see the drive to the far left. Beyond the hedge is a busy road. She can't remember now which direction Jennifer's car arrived from this morning. It took them a good thirty minutes to get here, across town. She has no idea which way she would go to get home. It is years since she travelled independently around the town and lately Annie has not been up to driving too far; the local co-op has been her limit. She is hopeful for a second that Annie might, anyway, make the journey and come for her, until she remembers that Annie has gone. 'Has anyone ever escaped?' she asks hopelessly.

Behind her, Rosie is packing up her medical paraphernalia. She laughs. 'I don't think anyone ever tried it!' Mrs Fairlie turns and they exchange a look. 'It isn't so bad. This isn't an institution, you know, it's a home. We want you to feel at home here. You'll see, in a little while.' Rosie collects the tray from the bed. 'You don't have to, if you don't want to, but this hour or so, after lunch and before tea, is a quiet hour. Most people have a snooze before their visitors come, so there's no one about. Why don't you have a walk up and down the corridor while it's quiet? You mustn't let those joints seize.' She indicates the clean plates on the tray. 'I'm pleased to see that there's nothing wrong with your appetite, anyway! I'll bring you a cup of tea up shortly, shall I? And it'll be time for your pain-killers by then.'

IT IS NIGHT-TIME and Mrs Fairlie stands stiffly by the narrow bed. She pulls the covers back warily, looking for something to find fault with; a stain, hair, a tear from an untended toe-nail. But there is nothing; the sheets are white and clean and crisp and smell pleasantly of cotton. The pillow, too, under its slip and protector, is perfectly clean. She knows she is being hypercritical. At home her bed is never made and, even when Annie was alive, was not religiously laundered either; it was a job they always intended to do but, when it came to it, often decided that 'one more night could not hurt.' The cat had taken to curling up on the sheet during the day, in an envelope of sunshine that came in through the window and sidled across the room as the day progressed. His tortoiseshell hairs made a smear across the sheet's softly napped surface. During stormy nights or on Guy Fawkes's both the dogs would creep onto the bed, their ears laid flat against their dome-like skulls, burrowing under the quilt and pressing against her. Her bed smelt of friendly animal comforts. This bed smells strange and anonymous. It looks cold. Experimentally she presses the mattress with her knuckles. It crackles; there is a plastic covering below the layers of sheet and lambswool fleece. Mrs Fairlie smiles, cynically; they expect her to be incontinent like the rest of the dribbling inmates.

She has closed her door to get undressed and to use the bathroom. There is no lock on the door and she feels vulnerable. Sure enough there is a perfunctory knock and one of the nurses pops her head into the room. It isn't Rosie. Rosie went home after delivering the supper tray. She had eaten it—despising herself—with her fingers because it hurts to curl her hands around cutlery and, at her solitary mealtimes, Mrs Fairlie has not used it for some time. The quiche had been rather nice, still warm, the pastry very light. The salad had been fresh. But the lid of the yoghurt pot had defeated her and Pearl Baker, passing by soon after, had taken it away in her pocket.

This nurse is Indian, with a narrow face and long hair tied back tightly. 'Are you all right?' she asks, with a raised eyebrow. 'You don't need any help at all? With washing or anything? Can you manage to get into the bed on your own?'

'Of course I can manage to get into bed on my own. I've been doing it for eighty years,' Mrs Fairlie replies with a scowl. 'And I won't be needing the plastic sheet. I haven't wet the bed since I was three.'

These people seem impervious to offense. 'That's all right then. We like you to be as independent as possible for as long as possible, here. Here are your night-time tablets and a glass of water. I'll put them by the bed for you. Now you see this red button on the locker beside the lamp? That's for you to press if you need anything. All right? Press the button and I'll come. Good night now, Mrs Fairlie.'

She is wearing one of the nightdresses Jennifer has bought. It is stiff and unfamiliar and smells of nothing at all. Just putting it on made her feel defeated. She looks down at it in the muted light from the bedside table. It has a white background with a riot of tumbling flowers all over it, flowers cast over snow, and some pretty lace at the neck and edging the sleeves, and some satin ribbon in a bow on the yoke. It is fresh and bright and brings to mind the countryside, the promise of early summer, skylarks and swifts and late sunsets that she recalls vividly from her girlhood on the farm. The recollection takes her for a moment, as they do these days, descending like swift hooks out of a white sky and transporting her in an instant to former times. Anything can do it; a smell, a certain colour, or just the random thoughts that come on the periphery of a doze or are dredged from a dream. Suddenly she is lifted bodily out of the small alien room and is back on the farm, the smell of the hay and the cows in her nostrils, the yard under her booted feet, pocked by hooves in winter rain and baked hard by spring sunshine. She can almost feel the cold metal of the bucket handles in her calloused hands, their weight as she crosses the yard to the dairy, the wind in her eyes and her body vibrant and reliable. Then, with a jolt, she is back.

Against the fresh material of the nightdress Mrs Fairlie's legs, visible from the shin down, are an abomination; swollen, discoloured, mottled purple and blue, the skin flaking and another ulcer breaking out on the calf. Her feet are misshapen by arthritis, her toes awry and calloused, with brown, horny nails. It is the sight of them that gives her the final impetus to get into the bed. She lies stiffly between the sheets, her arms straight by her sides, and wonders at the surprising treachery of her body, which has disgraced her. Her body, always so strong, as strong as many men, has proved so much weaker than her will and given the lie to the twenty-odd year old she still feels inside. It has surrendered without a fight to the enemy, which surges inexorably on, pushing her helplessly ahead of it like driftwood on the tide towards the beach of bones.

And she isn't ready, yet. There is something she needs to know.

She lies the whole night long, missing the night-time whisper of the World Service, alarmed by the occasional buzz of a distant bell and the footsteps passing outside her door. She drifts in and out of sleep, and thinks of Frederick.

Her Frederick was the 'son' of Frederick Fairlie & Son, Grocers. When she married him he had already taken over the family business, a thriving little shop in the maze of terraced houses and cobbled back alleys in the busy mill town. They sold fruit and vegetables and tins and packets and sweets and tobacco and, once she had settled in, cheese and butter and home-baked ham. Her father had been a farmer, one of Frederick's best suppliers. She was a robust, hard-working no-nonsense girl who could carry a hundredweight of spuds and churn butter in a freezing dairy without complaining. She neither expected nor wanted the sentimental frills of breathless romance. Frederick suited her; he was a man of few words, but a deep man. Some called him taciturn but she had known he was just shy. A nod of the head, a squeeze of the hand could say as much as a love poem. It had had to suffice, anyway. Ever tender, kind, considerate, but incapable of expressing affection, he had made swift and wordless love to her in the dark on Sunday nights, and, in spite of the dark, she had respected his privacy and kept her eyes tightly shut. He read extensively, in the evenings, in the little parlour above the shop. History especially, had fascinated him, and when the children came he told them the stories of Bonnie Prince Charlie and Joan of Arc in a quiet, intense voice that had them round-eyed over their bedtime cocoa. With Michael's arrival, a Son for Fairlie, their life had seemed complete. They had felt settled and secure; their definition of happiness.

Their shop had been the centre of the little community; they had always been the first to know if a couple was walking out, or if there was to be a new baby, or if a man had been laid off. Before the National Health came she was often asked to lay out the dead because she was strong and gentle and could be sympathetic without being sentimental. She was fearless, big-boned and strong-armed; she intervened in many a post-pub brawl. She took mouthy husbands to task on behalf of their frightened wives and cuffed more than one young whippersnapper who showed disrespect to an elder. She was known as a woman who knew her own mind and spoke it, had no time for daft notions, no sufferer of fools. To her surprise her rather abrasive manner did not deter confidences; on quiet afternoons while Frederick pored over the ledgers upstairs, the counter became a kind of confessional. People came to her for advice and sympathy. That's how Annie, a neighbour newly arrived in the area, had come to work for them. Annie had confided one day that they were short of money and another baby was on the way. The next day she was helping out in the shop and baking scones and tea cakes for them to sell.

Frederick had died suddenly in the mid-sixties, carried away by a massive seizure in the brain, and she had soldiered on alone, bringing up the children and running the shop, going to the market to collect the fruit and veg, making cheese and butter, baking, home-roasting hams and topsides. Annie had helped as far as she was able, with her own brood of children and unreliable husband to manage. Then, in the 1970s, Pakistani shops and supermarkets and the ridiculous red tape of the EEC had rendered them obsolete, and Fairlie & Son had closed its doors. By that time there had been no Fairlie nor, to all intents and purposes, any Son. She had reclaimed the shop as a front room, and enjoyed sitting on the window seat in the old shop window, watching the neighbours go by. For a long time they had continued to bring their worries to her, she and Annie were in and out of one another's houses, she was busy and active in her little community. The two of them had organised the street party for the Queen's Silver Jubilee; it had been a splendid success, with a magnificent tea and bunting and balloons, the best in the district, the newspaper had said.

The children had left home. That had been the beginning of the end of it. Gradually the old people died or were carted off to homes, their houses passing into the hands of young couples who drove off every day to work, who didn't want to get together to celebrate the Royal Wedding in '82. The streets were busy with cars and unpredictable, unruly youngsters whose violence and language cowed even her. The community died away, and then Annie died, and there was only her, a crumbling relic of a time passed by.

She has lived forty years without Frederick, and can hardly recall his face or the tone of his voice, now. He is like a dream to her, a comforting dream of something once real, but his realness is harder to recapture here in this place. She has nothing of his to orientate herself by; their home, their furniture, his writing on a document, his books on the shelf, his brown grocer's overall, hanging, still, behind the door, their children. She realises, with a gasp that makes her drowsy eyes fly open, that she will never be able to visit his grave again, visit it as she has every year on the anniversary of his death, with fresh flowers and a trowel to scrape away the moss from the stone. No. She will not be able to go there until she is taken to visit it one last time, a visit from which she will not return.

It ought to comfort her but it doesn't; she's afraid of it, fiercely resistant to it. The thought of it makes her clench her fists even though her finger-joints creak and complain. She isn't ready, yet. She determines again to fight with every fibre the gradual sink into semi-comatose oblivion, the diminishing of her mental faculties, the pressure to become a senile bag of bones in an over-heated television lounge. She mustn't, she *mustn't* let go. Not until he comes.

In the morning, early, she gets up and goes into the bathroom. She washes herself with the soap and flannel she finds in the sponge bag, and, with infinite difficulty, gets dressed. She opens the curtains and watches the grey dawn melt from the garden below. When the nurse brings tea she is dressed and sitting in the chair.

'I'd like a wireless and a newspaper,' Mrs Fairlie says.

JENNIFER'S HUSBAND KENNY is away for the weekend *again,* playing golf. His recent promotion to sales manager necessitates it, he claims. There is, apparently, much ground to make up, after his predecessor's fall from grace, and the sudden heart attack of the MD has left Kenny alone in the field. Flesh must be pressed, the wheels oiled. He works for a small engineering company but the way he talks of it you'd think it was NASA. Jennifer's new job, as editor of the local weekly paper, is *nothing* in comparison, according to him.

With him off the scene Jennifer is at liberty to continue her work sorting out her mother's things. She sits on the floor of the old house and sifts through the contents of the dresser drawers. She feels awkward, like a trespasser, trampling on the private territory of another, and yet she knows that it has to be done. She treads carefully, lifting out documents with her fingertips, opening the papers with caution against tearing or spoiling, trying, almost, to make no noise, as though her mother is present and must not be alerted to the intrusion. But that makes her feel furtive, which is ridiculous; who else will do this if she doesn't? It is a self-conscious process. She is scrupulous, in case her actions today might, later, come under critical scrutiny.

There is a whole history here. Old electricity bills and hand-written receipts for pieces of furniture she cannot identify, the ink of them brown with age, like old blood. There are price lists from long-defunct grocery wholesalers and circulars from some historical society that her father must have been a member of. Here is a bundle of newspaper cuttings about some street party or other: the Queen's Coronation, perhaps? There are ancient Christmas cards from people whose names she does not recognise and a letter of condolence from the president of the local Chamber of Commerce on her father's death. Here is the invoice for his funeral costs; a hearse, flowers, a burial plot, a headstone. She has hardly any recollection of her father at all; a spectacled man sitting in a corner reading, a figure in a brown overall moving crates of vegetables. Jennifer wasn't taken to the funeral—she was, perhaps, about six at the time—but has a vague memory of being left with a neighbour and her spiteful daughter for the afternoon. Her brother Michael, being older, *was* taken, in his school uniform and highly polished shoes, his hair carefully combed. That is all she remembers. Some years later Michael had confided to her that his enduring memory from that grey afternoon was not the ceremony or the people or even any sadness, but the thought of the weight of sticky cold clay bearing down on the lid of the coffin, its dampness eating through the wood, slimy soil falling into their father's mouth and worms burrowing into his ears. That was why, he had said, she must be sure that he was cremated, when the time came. He had specified, in fact, an open-air pyre of the type he has seen in India, but that was just proof of how far gone he was.

There is a bundle of postcards from Michael, sent from his various travels to these far-flung places. Some of them bear only his signature and are undated. Some have brief references to the views on the card: 'The Kalahari at sunset', 'Hong Kong—the view as the boat approaches the harbour'. A very few have a more personal message: 'Hope you are well. Crossed the border with Nepal yesterday, travelling with Ghurkhas cross-country. All well.' Most, the ones with more recent post-dates, bear only the address, their left hand sides full of words that cannot be said. Their stamps are exotic and much post-marked. They smell, weirdly, of spices and home, and the many postal hands that have passed them across the world. She imagines her mother turning them over curiously, and propping them on the mantelpiece for a few weeks before slipping them into the drawer. She must be utterly unable to conceive of the world outside this small mill town. The clamour of foreign voices, for instance, or the collage of foreign features; flat noses, narrow eyes, skin tones from coffee to cream. The riotous colour of ethnic costumes would daze her. The pungent smell of indigenous foods would make her sneeze. She has no words to describe it, no imagination to encompass it. No wonder she is silent. Michael had stepped into the world and never returned.

He might as well, Jennifer supposes, from her mother's point of view, have stepped off the edge of the planet.

Also in the drawer are some of the letters Jennifer herself wrote, from university. They are carefully bundled with a perished rubber band. She re-reads them. Her handwriting starts off well rounded and reasonably neat, but becomes markedly worse as the years progress. Nowadays it is virtually illegible; the years of extended essays and time-pressured exams covering reams of paper with literary criticism means that she *can* only write in a hurry these days, a frantic scrawl. But then the advent of the computer means that she rarely has to hand-write anything at all. Her letters describe the friends she made in Freshers' week (and then spent three years trying to shake off) and her unsuccessful campaign for the SU Presidency. There are details concerning her struggles with her dissertation. *The Conflict of Duty and Desire in the novels of Henry James* must have seemed an absurd irrelevance to her mother, who rarely read anything and certainly not any Henry James. One letter described the discomfort of her leaky digs in Moseley and the creepy landlord who turned up at inappropriate hours to inspect them. There is a postcard bearing the news that she would not be returning for the Christmas holidays because she had the chance of a spare place on the faculty skiing trip. That was the Christmas Jennifer had started going out with Kenny. She does not know, now, what she hoped to achieve with the letters, or why she wrote them, other than the fact that communication was expected and letters were easier than the telephone. They, like Michael's postcards, must have meant nothing to her mother. It must have seemed completely alien to her, almost like a foreign language, the world of Birmingham University and the Arts Faculty as remote as Rwanda. Certainly her mother's punctilious replies, as far as she can recall, never referred to any of the detail. They never asked, for example, what mark she had received for the essay she had stayed up all night to write, or whether the party she had been on her way out to as she signed off had been fun, or whether the landlord had fixed the leak. The only information they might acknowledge would be references to health: 'I hope your cold is better, Annie's chilblain is much improved, Rex's paw is not healing well.'

And yet she has kept them, all these years, and they show signs of much re-reading.

There are packets of photographs, of herself and Michael squinting into the lens wearing shorts and t-shirts on some beach somewhere. Some show Annie and Annie's children, others various dogs and cats. There are shots of her mother, dressed for some occasion, uncomfortable in a smart dress and her best shoes. There is a grainy, black and white wedding photograph. It is the only one with her mother and father together. Jennifer is surprised to see that her mother is some half-head taller than her father. In the picture she is wearing a light coloured suit, smart but unadorned, and holding a small bouquet. She is not a beautiful bride and her expression is solemn. He, too, looks tense, standing almost to attention at her side. They are not touching each other at all. They seem to be outside a country church. On the back of the photograph is written the date; May 12th 1951. She checks again the date of the funeral: November 21st 1966. Fifteen years. That's all they had. She and Kenny have had more, already.

In another drawer she finds ancient insurance policies, a quantity of post office savings books in her mother's name, a sheaf of bank statements and, in an opened foolscap envelope, her father's will. A companion envelope, still sealed, contains her mother's. There are savings bonds and a number of premium bonds and, at the bottom of the drawer, the carefully kept accounts ledgers for the grocery business, filled with columns of figures in a succession of handwriting; her father's presumably, at first, or maybe even his father's, and finally mother's. The paper of the ledgers is yellowed, and occasionally smeared with finger marks where it has been touched with hands made dirty by potatoes or greasy with home-roasted hams. On the corner of one of the pages is a doodle. She remembers doing it, idly, one quiet, hot summer afternoon, and being slapped for it once it was discovered. The injustice of it smarted more than the slap.

She has been putting this job off, knowing how difficult it would be to decide what to do with all this stuff. While she avoided it she has cleared the kitchen and a lot of the lounge. The kitchen cupboards are all empty now; every pot and pan and plate and fork washed and dried and packed into cardboard boxes and taken to a collection point for transportation to the area of a recent earthquake. The fridge and cooker and nearly new microwave have been collected by a church organisation which helps battered women set themselves up in flats. Jennifer has packed the ornaments that she thinks might be worth something into a separate crate and will take them to the local auction house for valuation. This dresser, the oak gate-leg table and the four spindle-backed chairs will go there too. All the rest will go to a charity shop. The curtains, the suite, the nasty pictures and the carpet will be put into a skip that is due to be delivered on Monday. Then she will tackle the upstairs.

The papers are scattered around her now, on the faded, threadbare carpet. She has vacuumed it countless times but it still smells of dog and there are still dog hairs on it. She begins to organise the documents. She makes a heap on her left of things to be recycled; the circulars and price lists and meaningless receipts and old bills. On her right she makes a pile of things to be investigated; the insurance policies and savings accounts, the bonds and the bank statements and the envelope with her mother's will. This leaves her with the personal documents; the postcards and the letters and the photographs. They sit in front of her, pending. She cannot throw them away but then she has no desire to keep them, either. They belong to her mother but to hand them over would be to make apparent that her home is being dismantled, which is sure to unsettle her even more. It is a delicate time, Mrs Terry has said—the first few weeks—a transition period, and the staff at Bridge House have instructions to tread very softly with new residents while they acclimatise. For many, their short term memories being unreliable, only a very few weeks would seem like many, and their relatively recent past become very indistinct. There will come a point, she has said, when Bridge House is pretty much all the residents know apart from their vividly real childhood memories. They will turn to their neighbour at lunch and be as ready to see their paternal grandmother from Gorton as Mrs Bailey from room 12. That's why Mrs Terry has suggested that Jennifer does not visit frequently at first. 'Let her settle and adjust,' she has said, 'and come to terms. There comes a point when death ceases to be the enemy and becomes a friend.'

'Do you mean you make life so miserable for them that they only want to die?' Jennifer had barked.

Mrs Terry had smiled. 'Not at all. We try to make it as enjoyable as possible. But they come to see that it's all so pointless and that they're ready to move on.'

Jennifer does not want her mother to die but she can see with a pragmatism that some might think cold that her life is, to all intents and purposes, lived out. Bridge House is the ideal place for her. There is creature comfort and medical care, companionship and a cocooning from all sources of anxiety; a safe and enjoyable place to wait for the inevitable. Her husband and dearest friend have gone. All the old neighbours and familiar faces have disappeared, replaced by strangers. She is unable to live independently with any degree of safety to herself or others. This is the liturgy Jennifer has rehearsed over and over, reciting it like a bulldozer over her mother's objections. She cannot understand the older woman's reluctance; where has this sudden attack of silly sentimentality come from? She has always been such a practical woman, with no time at all for fuss-makers or sulkers. 'Be sensible,' she used to say, in a brisk, business-like voice, shaking her head and making a frown at anyone who threatened an exhibition of emotion. 'Don't make a to-do, now.'

The last of the evening sunshine streams into the room and illuminates a dull grey carpet of dust and a stray brass button underneath the dresser. Jennifer shifts her position and reaches for a box behind her, tearing two large polythene zip'n'seal bags from a roll. She has no idea whether these letters will aid or interfere with the process the matron seems so confident about. Perhaps they will raise more questions than they answer, but then again, what harm can a few more unanswered questions do? Her mother is so proud and stubborn, a hard, impervious shell. Jennifer herself has given up any hope of reaching her or being reached by her. There is an impenetrable wall between them. She doesn't know why, but it has always been so. They never talk about things. They never, for example, talk about Michael. There *are* things to say. But she has promised.

AFTER A WEEK—or longer—perhaps *much* longer—Mrs Fairlie isn't quite sure—Rosie comes into Mrs Fairlie's room and sits on the edge of the bed, opening her orange file and poising her pen. Morning coffee has been served and soon, with indecent haste, lunch will appear. Life at Bridge House seems to be a relentless bombardment of meals and snacks.

'Murder by Marie-biscuit,' she thinks, wryly.

'Did you sleep all right?' Rosie asks. Mrs Fairlie nods. She surmises that Rosie is perhaps in her early forties. Her curly brown hair has the occasional silver thread. Today it is caught back in a pony-tail but a few tendrils have escaped and she tucks them impatiently behind one ear. 'And how is your pain?'

'The same.' In fact the ulcer on her leg is very sore, and Mrs Fairlie wonders about mentioning it. There is another one coming on her hip. It began to weep in the night and this morning she has tried to wash the yellow stain from her knickers in the sink. Rosie turns the pages back, leafing through the notes made by other nurses on previous days. She frowns; she can't find what she is looking for. She looks at Mrs Fairlie for a moment, taking in her clothes. Her eyes narrow. Then her face clears and when she speaks it is as though it is on an entirely different subject.

'I was wondering,' Rosie says, in her measured, quiet voice—she is one of the few people who have gathered that Mrs Fairlie isn't deaf— 'whether, this afternoon, while it's quiet, you might enjoy a shower.'

Involuntarily Mrs Fairlie folds her arms across her chest. The picture that this suggestion conjures up in her mind is informed by images from the holocaust; emaciated naked bodies, white as bleached bones and pressed together in a cold concrete bunker, vicious hoses directed by sneering uniformed men for maximum discomfort, heaps of skeletal cadavers piled high in the snow.

'I'm managing, thanks,' she says, staring hard at her knees.

'It doesn't look to me as though you've been given much choice,' Rosie says drily. 'Anyway, you're doing very well. But it might be nice to have your hair washed and,' she hesitates, 'to wear some clean clothes.'

Mrs Fairlie's clothes are a subject of some embarrassment. She has been wearing virtually the same clothes since she arrived; the skirts—and especially the tights—have utterly defeated her. She has tried and rejected the fussy blouses and ludicrous cardigans that Jennifer thinks old women ought to wear. In any case she cannot do the buttons. She has been washing her smalls through at night and drying them on the radiator. Mrs Mole, the cleaning lady, has tried to take them down to the laundry but Mrs Fairlie knows better than to let a woman like that make off with her underwear. Subconsciously she throws an anxious glance at the wardrobe. Rosie follows her thought and gets up. She opens the wardrobe door and they survey the contents together.

Understanding dawns. 'Ah! You didn't do your own packing, then.' It isn't a question.

'No.'

Rosie stands close enough for Mrs Fairlie to smell the clean, soapiness of her. She is as fresh as washing on a line in the country, and her body radiates a pleasant glow of warmth. Mrs Fairlie wants to reach out and touch her, to press her face against the pristine cotton of Rosie's uniformed body, to know human contact, but she quells it. She is suddenly acutely conscious that in spite of her efforts at the wash basin night and morning she probably smells ripe from sitting here, in this hot room, day after day after day. The thought makes her squirm.

Rosie gives her head a little shake and the strand of hair comes loose from her ear and falls across her cheek. 'I see. All right then. Leave that with me.'

Rosie closes the wardrobe and the subject. She sits back down on the bed. Mrs Fairlie feels so ashamed she can barely look her in the eye, but when she does so at last she knows that the girl barely sees her. Her eyes—so transparent, she could never tell a lie—are clouded with troubles. Her skin is dull and tired and there is something very determined and brave about her smile, a tension around the jaw. Every so often she sighs, as though trying to relieve an emotional pressure. She makes an extended note in her file, underlining some of the words heavily. Then she looks up. Perhaps, in spite of her own troubles, she is as aware of Mrs Fairlie's discomfort. In the air between them there are invisible filaments of sympathy. Mrs Fairlie wrestles with them, desiring and denying the connection. But sheer human kindness, and the sudden realisation that she is not, in fact, able to manage entirely on her own, dislodges a brick from her defences.

'When I had the shop, people used to tell me things,' Mrs Fairlie mentions, carefully casual. 'I never asked. I'm not one to pry. But for some reason they did, and it seemed to help.'

'I didn't know you had a shop,' Rosie says, but her voice breaks in the middle of the word 'shop'. Her eyes become glassy, their whites suddenly mapped with red. She bites her lip and small pools of silver-blue teardrop gather on her lower lashes. She shakes her head and the drops tremble, but do not fall. She is holding back a torrent of emotion. She gropes in her uniform pocket for a handkerchief. It is a proper linen one, Mrs Fairlie notes, not a tissue. She approves of this.

'Don't be nice to me,' Rosie whispers, frowning. 'I can just about cope as long as people aren't nice.' She looks over Mrs Fairlie's head, at the window, and then down at the floor, the handkerchief clenched in a ball. Presently she takes a deep breath and blows it out again as though inflating a balloon. Then she wipes her eyes and puts the handkerchief away. She closes Mrs Fairlie's file and puts the lid on her biro, stands up and makes as though to leave the room, but at the last moment she turns and smiles. 'Thank you.' No sound comes from her mouth; it is merely the motion of her lips which speaks the words.

Now she is gone, Mrs Fairlie reaches a tentative hand up and touches her hair. It is stiff and dirty. She never did have nice hair; a brownish dung colour, coarse textured, she tended to keep it short and never bothered much with styling. It has turned a grimy grey with time, like dirty wire. Latterly Annie had trimmed it for her, and washed it too, using the showerhead from over the bath while Mrs Fairlie bent over the bathroom sink with a flannel pressed to her face. Annie, who was little and dumpy, had had to stand on an old orange box to reach. It had made them laugh, these antics they got up to in Mrs Fairlie's bathroom. The first time Annie had helped her have a bath they had done it at night, in the dark. Annie had dropped the soap on the floor, slipped on it and banged her head on the sink. The tension and the ludicrousness had made them helpless with giggles. Mrs Fairlie had laughed so hard she had weed in the bath.

Now she thinks about it, she can't remember laughing, really laughing, since then.

Mrs Fairlie thinks about Rosie's suggestion. She would like to have a shower and have her hair washed. It would be nice to have warm water on her skin. She has contemplated it more than once over the last few days. At one end of her private facilities is a curtained-off area with non-slip tiles and a plastic drop-down seat fixed to the wall, and grab-rails. But the shower controls are unfamiliar and there is no telling how the texture of the floor may change once wet. The thought of being stranded, naked and vulnerable, scalded or frozen by the incorrectly adjusted shower, of slipping and being discovered legs akimbo, of breaking a hip—the beginning of the end for a woman her age, as everyone knows—is just too terrible. At the same time it would be insufferable to be helped by hard, impersonal hands, manhandled, steered and intimately soaped, looked upon and apprised in her gnarled and discoloured curvature.

God knows, she shrinks from herself; she is not something she can impose on others.

The day wears interminably on. She is beginning to know Bridge House by its sounds. The bing-bong of the lift doors is incessant, also the swish-swish of the fire door at the end of the corridor as the staff come and go. The rattle of the trolley and the clinking of the cups and saucers at coffee and tea time brings a bright and cheerful note to which the insistent yelling of the TV set in the day-room is a manic accompaniment. The phone in Matron's office rings and rings. Why doesn't somebody answer it? Less intrusive are the sounds of cutlery on crockery at meal times and the banter of the nurses as they go in and out of the rooms. She is learning to know them. Rosie is her favourite. Olga, the Polish auxiliary, constantly urges her to join in with domino drives and bingo, or to come and hear some kindly local spinster who plays 'all the old favourites' on the piano. Selene, the Indian nurse, is brisk and clipped, with hard, cold hands. Mrs Mole, the cleaning lady, makes jokes and laughs at them herself like a donkey braying, and is continually showing residents snap-shots of her 'little boy', Michael. The name of course conjured a frisson of instant resentment in Mrs Fairlie, envy and despair, until she saw the dog-eared photo. 'Little' Michael is a wobbling, overweight pudding of a boy, with small round eyes devoid of intelligence. He is nothing like *her* Michael, with his angel-eyes and fine, silky hair.

As much as she resists it, she is coming to know the residents too, by the laboured shuffle of their feet, the static of their nylon slippers on the utilitarian nylon carpet, the fizz of their chair-wheels. She is attuned to their muffled cries and wheezing breathing in the night, their catarrhal coughing, their inconsequential conversation as they pass her door. A few pass her regularly, the others she glimpses only occasionally, as they go to the bathroom at the end of the landing. Some of them she is beginning to know by sight as well as sound. She catches only the briefest glimpses of them, keeping her glance down to avoid eye contact; she doesn't want to know them or to be known by them. She fears that if they see her, or speak to her, or acknowledge her presence by other means, she will be as fixed and indelible—as trapped—as they are.

There is a wisp of a woman who always wears pink; pink in any and every connotation; rose, cerise, coral, bubble-gum, peach, salmon, flesh. And indeed she is so lacking in flesh that the hue of her clothes bulks out her bones in its stead. She is so thin and frail she is scarcely solid, barely tangible. At first Mrs Fairlie had thought that the nurse was using the chair to transport a strew of clothes from one place to another. The woman is swamped by her garments. They—rather than skin and flesh—seem to define her torso. Her pop-socks wrinkle round her translucent, bird-like ankles in gathers, like saggy skin, providing a grip for gravity to cling to; without them she would surely float away. She must feel the tenuousness of her grasp on the earth. Her hands, with blue veins like ropes, clutch like claws onto the arms of her chair.

There is a man, stooped and bandy and always accompanied by a brown leather shopping bag. He is a creature of habit, emerging at the same time every day as though setting off, with his bag, for some regular and important appointment, and returning in the evening, his bag bulging with booty from his foray. Mrs Fairlie cannot imagine that he actually goes out anywhere; the residents of Bridge House are not allowed out, unless under close supervision. The purpose and apparent contents of his bag are mysterious until they turn out to be only newspapers, collected from the foyer and stacked in strict chronological order around his room. She finds this out from Mrs Mole, who complains about them to Mrs Terry and to anyone else who will listen. He won't have them removed, however, shooing Mrs Mole and Mrs Terry from his room with incoherent cries of remonstrance. He walks unaided, but comically, like Charlie Chaplain, his feet at awkward angles, his clothes shabby and loose-fitting, as though made for a larger man; a suit that at one time must have been very smart. He regains his room in time for *The Archers* at seven o'clock, the theme tune and the jolly rural banter is audible to Mrs Fairlie from his room a couple of doors along. It does not bother her. The sound of voices from the outside world is comforting and evocative, like a scent of childhood or an old flavour tasted anew. The shopping bag man mutters to himself as he goes along the corridor, his words disappearing into his beard, their sense stranded and lost in its forest. Their gist, like his purposeful stride and busy preparedness, is meaningless and wasted inside these cloistered walls.

And there is Pearl Baker, unwanted visitor and purloiner of food, reciter of interminable ancient anecdote, moon-faced, unnaturally fat, her capacious clothes stretched and strained and stained with dribbles and drips and splashes of spilled food. She totters in uninvited every few days, curled under her hump and over her abdomen, and hoists it all onto Mrs Fairlie's bed with an ungainly scramble and a flash of fat, folded thigh. Pearl smells of food, her clothes impregnated with the aroma of their splodges, her breath sweet with stolen biscuits, her skin sticky and sugary like a baby. Today she arrives with the afternoon tea tray and helps herself to the square of Battenberg cake. She eats the yellow marzipan icing first, then the yellow squares and finally the pink. Then she licks her fingers with an eager and competent tongue before folding her small fleshy hands in her lap and taking the deep breath which signals the commencement of her narrative.

But before she can start Rosie arrives with two carrier bags. She looks flushed and harried and can't suppress a groan at the sight of Pearl perched on the counterpane. Beneath the hot skin of Rosie's face Mrs Fairlie discerns bloodless white concern, anxious eyes. Rosie dumps the carrier bags on the floor and slips off her jacket. Pearl slides off the bed and disappears. Rosie closes the door.

'Look what I got,' she says, opening the bags and letting their contents slither to the ground. She herself, however, does not look at them. Her eyes are focussed on her troubles. Everything she does is with an air of distraction. Whatever was troubling her earlier has intensified now. She picks up the clothing and lays it on the bed where Pearl was seated only moments before. There are three pairs of soft jersey trousers with elasticated waists, some cotton socks, three or four practical, light, unfussy sweaters. 'Aren't these more your kind of thing?'

Mrs Fairlie nods and smiles uneasily, trying to read Rosie.

Her smile, loaded as it is, pulls Rosie back into the room. 'I thought so. Easy to put on and get off, comfortable, plain, practical. They're just what I'd choose to wear if I were you.'

A thought occurs to Mrs Fairlie. 'Oh, but I can't pay you, dear. I haven't any money. I mean I *have* money, but I can't get at it.' It is the first time she has thought about money and she wonders how things are being paid for. She makes a mental note to ask Jennifer to bring her cheque book, but she doesn't know when that will be. Jennifer has not visited once.

Rosie shrugs. 'Don't worry about that now. There's a system. We often have to shop for people. Some of the residents don't have relatives to get them things, so we go out for sweets or birthday cards or, well, you'd be amazed how many bottles of sherry we have to buy.' As she speaks, Rosie is busy, removing the labels from the clothes, folding them up and putting them into Mrs Fairlie's drawers.

'I didn't know we were allowed sherry,' Mrs Fairlie says. She has never been much of a drinker but a glass of sherry, from time to time, might be nice.

'You're allowed whatever you want, so long as it doesn't do you any harm,' Rosie says. She folds the carrier bags up neatly. 'I'm afraid I haven't got time now, because I got back late and Matron is on the war path, but after supper I'll come back and help you get showered, shall I? And then in the morning you can put some of your new clothes on and I can get these ones laundered for you.' Rosie must see the anxious shadow that crosses over Mrs Fairlie's pleasure at the new clothes. She reads it clearly, through the fog of her own preoccupations. She bends down through it and looks into Mrs Fairlie's eyes. 'Don't you worry now. It'll just be me. I'm going to look after you.'

When she has gone, Mrs Fairlie does not know if it is Rosie's sheer selfless kindness that disarms her—Rosie's willingness to add a crotchety old woman to her already unwieldy cargo of burdens—or the idea of being looked after, when, for forty odd years, she has had to be self-reliant. Whatever it is, she is unable to control herself and, in the loneliness of her little cell, behind the closed door, she gives way to tears.

IN THE DARKNESS of her room Mrs Fairlie lies in the narrow bed. Her skin feels soft and refreshed, and her hair smells of something pleasantly herbal.

The shower turned out to be less of an ordeal than she had feared. Rosie had brought her a towelling gown and left her to undress and put it on while she got things ready in the bathroom. Then she had walked, with Rosie's help, into the shower area and lowered herself onto the seat, which felt firm and secure under her unreliable body. With a practiced arm Rosie had swept the robe from under her bottom as she sat, so that, when the time came, it was easy to take off. The room was already warm and steamy. The shower was running against the tiled wall. Rosie had pulled the curtain across, enclosing her in its vinyl seclusion, reached in for the gown and then flicked the shower head around so that the water played deliciously on her mottled, desiccated skin. Rosie had handed in soap and a flannel. Presently she had reached in and adjusted the shower head again before stepping around the curtain to massage shampoo into her hair. The room was filled with steam and Mrs Fairlie had kept her eyes tightly closed, one arm against her empty breasts, the other across the vee of her groin.

Throughout, Rosie had remained distant. Had it not been for her distraction earlier Mrs Fairlie might have put this down to professional detachment, but her anxiety was so apparent as to be virtually palpable; restless eyes, shallow breathing, a furrowed brow. Whatever the trouble was, it was getting bigger with time.

Suddenly, while the water coursed down the tiles and her expert hands massaged in the shampoo, Rosie had asked about the shop; what kind was it? Whereabouts? How long had she had it? Mrs Fairlie had answered briefly, through the suds, knowing that detail was not required really, just an introduction, and a kind of orientation for Rosie, who wished to step through the metaphorical door into the gloomy interior, smell the earthy vegetables and the pungent cheeses, approach the long counter and unburden herself in the confidential silence.

She waited until the shampoo was rinsed off and Mrs Fairlie was back in the soft robe. They walked together out of the bathroom and into the bedroom, her gnarled feet leaving wet prints like a pre-historic three-toed reptile on the carpet. After the splash and spray of the shower the room was very quiet. Rosie's hands pressed the robe gently onto Mrs Fairlie's skin, blotting up the water without rubbing.

'I can't understand why he wasn't at home,' Rosie said, almost to herself, kneeling down and drying Mrs Fairlie's legs with deft hands. 'He *promised* me, after the other day's fiasco, that he'd stay home.'

'At home?'

'At lunchtime, before I went to the shop for you, I called in at home. He should have been there.'

'Your husband?' Mrs Fairlie ventured.

'My son.'

Mrs Fairlie winced; a son not at home. Rosie inspected the ulcer on her calf. 'That looks sore. I'll have to tell the doctor about that. Are there any others?'

'On my hip. How old is your son? You must be worried about him.'

'Sixteen. I'm not worried, exactly. He can take care of himself, I should think. But he promised me he'd stay at home and do his coursework. Can I see?'

'All right.' Mrs Fairlie leaned to one side and drew the robe away from her body, revealing the red and yellow sore on her bony blue hip. 'Maybe there was a good reason. You'll get to the bottom of it when you get home. Sixteen year old boys become a law unto themselves, especially when there's no man about the house.'

'Hmm. You've got that right. This needs dressing. They both do. Can I?'

'What are they?'

'Just ulcers. You might have had a scratch that didn't heal. Lack of exercise results in poor circulation; toxins build up that need expelling. They can indicate problems in the digestive tract, liver or kidneys. I'll clean them up with tea tree oil and then we'll see.'

'I'll go out for a brisk walk tomorrow. Climb a mountain or two.'

'That might be a bit ambitious. But you should try going downstairs. You're vegetating up here.'

'Tell me about your son.'

'Oh,' Rosie stood up and began to rummage in a bag of medical bits and bobs. 'He's at that age, you know? And we've had other things to deal with recently. My husband left us, we've had to move and where we live now isn't very … Well, the neighbours aren't the same. He's mixing with a new crowd of boys who aren't … Let's just say they're a bit dubious. But he's reached that age when he has to be allowed to have secrets. He's gone sort of … *closed.* I miss him. Now then hold still while I put this on. It might smart.'

'Yes. I know.'

Now, in the night, Mrs Fairlie thinks about Michael before he became what Rosie describes as *closed.* In the early days he was anything but closed and there were no clouds between them, no skies or seas. He was intensely, vibrantly open—to her, anyway. She could read him. The look in his eye, the cast of his smile, the way one eyebrow would contract when he didn't understand something. She knew when he was excited from the brightness in his eyes, saw his anger in the pursed line of his mouth. She could sense his feelings, read his silences, see past his words. For a woman who eschewed sentimental silliness he had provoked in her a heady, thin-blooded faintness of heart-stopping adoration. He was her son, made in her womb, carried by her and delivered from her, yelling loudly and shockingly hot. He had fed from

211

her, his greedy mouth pulling at her breast, cried for her, run to her, slept in her arms. His silky hair had made her weak, the smoothness of his skin, giddy. The smell of his flesh … The taste of him could make her mouth water. Miraculously, he was so much more than the sum of his awkward and unattractive parents. Michael had inherited none of his mother's angular ugliness, none of his father's shyness. He had been beautiful, bright and glowing, ravenous with hunger and curiosity, raucous with laughter, racing with energy; a mystifying, magical, marvellous boy. She pictures him running across a field towing a kite, his fair hair streaming back from his forehead, his arm aloft tugging urgently at the string, the sound of his laughter echoing across the landscape making the ruminating cows turn their heads. Or lying on his stomach on a riverbank staring intently at the newts in the shallows, his brows furrowed in concentration, one hand cupped over his nose and mouth so that his breathing might not ripple the surface of the silver water. Or in his bed at night, the covers tucked under his armpit and his hands pressed together beneath his cheek, his face smooth and untroubled by dreams, his night-breath sweet in the curtained room.

The recollection of Michael makes a weight press down on her chest, she is breathless with it, the missing him.

'PEOPLE SAID THAT Fenwick's was much too far for William to go to school every day,' Pearl says. She is sitting on Mrs Fairlie's bed, having scuttled in and scrambled up onto it, and helped herself to the two digestive biscuits from the morning coffee tray. 'But Daddy wanted him to go to a good school and he was prepared to pay, so that was that, and he said it didn't matter if it wasn't near where we lived at the time. In fact it would be better, he said, for us to widen our horizons. And, he said, much as he liked having his 'small ones' at home—that's what he called William and me, his 'small ones'—he couldn't expect to keep us there forever. William sat the exams for Fenwick's and Mason's and St. John's and Beddlington when he was ten. You'll have heard of all those, I expect. They're all good schools.'

Mrs Fairlie neither confirms nor denies this. She has discovered that it is fruitless to interrupt Pearl Baker's soliloquies. Her conversation is not interactive. The narrative goes on and on, round and round, whether there is an audience or not. Mrs Fairlie has watched Mrs Baker scuttling along the corridor, bent over her slippers, talking absolutely to herself. Her story is on a continuous loop, like a hamster on a wheel. She speaks it with furious determination and energy, but no matter how hard she tries she doesn't seem able to get to the end. It is as though there is a way out somewhere, an exit, but she cannot see it. It is like a maze and she is stuck inside it, wandering its interminable avenues without hope of explanation or escape.

Pearl pauses only to collect a stray digestive crumb that has become lodged on her nylon blouse, before continuing. 'I went with William for the examinations. We had to go by bus, it was such a long way, and Daddy said we must stay over-night as well. He said we mustn't worry about Mummy and him, they'd be all right for a night or two. So we stayed at Mrs Hetherington's and Mrs Finchley's and Miss Banburgh's and The Crown Inn. Mrs Hetherington was a kind lady with a twin bedded room and she cooked us a good breakfast, but I wouldn't go near Mrs Finchley's again; nothing matched, the sheets were flannelette and there was a spider in the bath and in fact that's why we decided that William wouldn't go to Mason's School even though he did pass the exam and was offered a place and was very excited by the music department. He was already very keen on music but that isn't surprising when you think how proficient Reverend Baker was. I didn't like The Crown. There was a bar with men in it and the language was not choice. In the morning the breakfast waiter gave me a look I didn't like, so that was St John's out too, which was a shame, in a way, as it was the nearest. I took him to the schools and waited in the foyer while he did the tests. It was Easter time. Easter was early that year and there was snow on the ground. The walk up the hill to Fenwick's from the bus was quite tricky; the pavement was very icy and there's a cruel wind that blows from the east coast, you know. After each exam we had tea in a tea shop while we waited for the bus. I liked a custard tart and William would have a doughnut or sometimes an Eccles cake. I didn't think William would like it at Beddlington; he's a sensitive boy, my William and they had a lot of rough sport there. So in the end he went to Fenwick's. Fenwick's was quite a journey and more than one person said it was too far to send him, every day, on the bus by himself. And Daddy said that much as he liked having his 'small ones' at home— that's what he called William and me, his 'small ones'—he couldn't expect to keep us there forever. Of course we wouldn't hear of it, William and me, not after everything they'd done for us. William didn't seem to mind the journey too much. Except in winter, that slippery hill *was* a trial, and he would come home with his little bare knees red raw and chapped, and I wonder if perhaps it wasn't a *bit* awkward with his trombone.'

Jennifer enters the room and is pulled up short by the presence of Pearl.

'Oh! Hello!' she says brightly, 'that's nice, Mum! You have a visitor! Please don't leave on my account.' But Pearl is off the bed and out of the room, her head and shoulders bent under their weight of remembrances, and already, before she is out of earshot, the diatribe is recommenced with, 'People say it's very bad for a boy to attend his local university ...'

'That's a shame,' Jennifer says, lifting a holdall onto the bed. She hesitates before leaning over and kissing her mother's cheek. It makes them both feel uncomfortable. 'You look nice,' she says, filling in the hiatus. 'I don't recognise those clothes.'

'Don't you?' Mrs Fairlie is tight-lipped on that subject.

'I'm glad you've made a friend,' Jennifer says, moving on. 'How are you? How are you sleeping? I looked for you downstairs in the day room but they said you haven't been down there yet! Is that right, Mum? You don't stay up here all day every day?!'

'What have you brought?' Mrs Fairlie looks hopefully at the holdall, imagining outdoor shoes, a coat, travelling clothes.

'Well I got your message. I'm sorry it's taken me a while. I was in London last week and then, you know, there is quite a bit to sort out at the house, and we were away at the weekend.' She leaves a gap here for her mother to make an enquiry. Where did they go to? Who with? Did they have a good time? But Mrs Fairlie remains stubbornly silent.

'Well anyway, here I am.' She lifts out Mrs Fairlie's old wireless with a triumphant flourish. 'Is this what you wanted? This old thing? And I brought a few other things I thought you might like.' She produces the brass key dish from the whatnot and the shiny glazed squirrel with his slotted log, and two of the china dishes from her dressing table and then, finally, from the bottom of the holdall, the patchwork quilt. She has consulted Matron about their introduction and they have been given the all-clear. The letters and photographs are lodged in Matron's filing cabinet; Jennifer has absolved herself of responsibility for them. Seeing her mother's face now, she is glad. Mrs Fairlie feels herself pale at the sight of her things, removed from their proper environment, as anomalous here in this soulless waiting room as butchered body-parts.

Jennifer is nonplussed. 'Well I hoped you'd be pleased. Never mind. I'll leave them anyway. I can always take them away again next time.' She arranges the ornaments on the window ledge and begins to spread the quilt over the bed.

'No,' her mother says sharply. 'Not on the bed. I'm dying with heat as it is. Put it on the chair, here. It might cushion it a bit.' She struggles to her feet and Jennifer spreads the quilt on the chair, tucking it in down the sides.

'Isn't the chair comfortable?'

'No. It's made my hip sore. I wish I could have my own from home.'

Jennifer looks shifty. 'Oh. I see. Well, I'm afraid you can't have that one.' Mrs Fairlie watches her daughter construct a lie. It is the way she looks up and right with her eyes, and chews her inner cheek with her eye-tooth. 'It's to do with the fire regulations, Mum. All the upholstery has to be fire-proofed. It's the law.'

'Humph!' Mrs Fairlie ejaculates.

'I don't suppose these chairs are made for sitting in all day, anyway. The ones in the day room look much more comfortable. And remember there is that nice big television in there.'

Mrs Fairlie picks up on something Jennifer said earlier. 'What do you mean about things in the house to sort out? I don't want you poking around in there. There are private things.'

Jennifer brushes her fringe out of her eyes. 'You left bills to pay and things,' she says evasively. 'Now then, tell me about how you've been getting on. How's the food? Mrs Terry says you're eating very well.'

'Does she now?' Mrs Fairlie's original intention, to refuse all nourishment, has been unwittingly abetted by the voracious Pearl, but she has to admit that on a few occasions recently Pearl has been disappointed. As far as she can, though, she holds resolutely to her independence, keeps herself contained in her room by day, reads the paper from cover to cover and keeps her brain in gear. She gives monosyllabic answers to enquiries and leaves her room only in the quiet hour between lunch and tea, when the corridors are silent and the shouting television downstairs is briefly silenced. She thinks of it as 'splendid isolation'. Rosie is the only exception. Her fears of immediate, forcible termination have faded with time; she does not, now, expect to be bundled away in the night. No one has been cruel to her and Rosie has been positively kind. The food is adequate and regular. Only at night-time, in the narrow, crackling bed, cocooned in the privacy of darkness and quiet, does she allow her guard to drop and acknowledge 'splendid isolation' as 'incredible loneliness'.

No amount of kindness or cake can hide the truth that Bridge House is the final staging post to death, a waiting room where the decrepit linger, awaiting the final degeneration of their vital forces. They are pending, side-lined, now that every experience and phase of their lives bar one has been travelled. She knows there are only two ways to leave Bridge House and both offer one way tickets—via ambulance or hearse—to the same destination; the final, short crossing that has to be made. Either it will be sudden—a cataclysmic seizure, a violent ceasing, staring eyes, scrabbling fingers, choking and terrible—or it will be slow—a gradual fading, dawdling diminution, a measured retreat down narrowing passages of awareness, the sense that somewhere, someone is dimming the lights. Nothing here can possibly be of any lasting worth. It is a siding of waiting, the end of the line. Because the future is a blank she comforts herself by travelling at a leisurely pace through her memories, lingering over the treasured moments, replaying the everyday scenes, picturing the familiar faces. And on some nights her dreams are illuminated by a shaft of yellow light from the corridor and she senses the cool and calming presence of Rosie in the room, on night-shift now, and feels her smooth hands stroking the roughened skin of her ancient gnarled hand, and Rosie's being there does not feel like an intrusion in her dreams.

JENNIFER FLOUNCES OUT of the post office and returns to her car. The surly woman behind the counter has been infuriating in her refusal to co-operate. She wouldn't even enter the account numbers to verify the balances. In fact she held the books at arm's length and commented to her colleague in a voice quite loud enough to carry to the back of the inevitable queue, 'Gosh, Dorothy, I haven't seen one of these in a good few years, have you?'

'What do you mean?' Jennifer asked, in a voice shrill with indignation and embarrassment. 'This is the Post Office isn't it? And those are Post Office Savings books aren't they?'

'Oh yes,' the woman agreed. 'But ever so old. We have swipe cards now and PIN numbers. We do everything electronically, you see dear.' She pushed the books back under the window towards Jennifer with a sickly, patronising smile.

'But the money's still in there? You could tell me how much there is, with interest and so on?'

The woman sighed and pulled the books back towards her, flicking through their pages. 'There haven't been any deposits or withdrawals for *years*,' she said, shaking her head. 'The accounts might have been suspended.'

'What?' Jennifer squeaked.

'But in any event, I couldn't give that information to anyone except the account holder or their legal representative.'

Behind her, the queue was getting restive. It was pension day, a bad day, Jennifer realised, to have embarked on this enquiry.

'How do you know I'm not the account holder or her legal representative?' she said imperiously. The woman smiled coldly and cast a glance at Dorothy, beside her.

'You'd have been a very little girl indeed when these accounts were opened, and if you were ...' she consulted the front page of one of the books, '... Mrs Fairlie's legal representative, you'd have told me by now and you'd have a legal document to prove it. Power of Attorney, they call it.' She pushed the books back under the glass.

'I'm her daughter,' Jennifer said defensively.

She was aware of a hiss from behind her. 'Trying to get her hands on her poor mother's savings,' an old woman said loudly, to the person next to her in the queue.

'Shocking.'

'Next!' the woman behind the counter shouted.

Clearly, the interview was over.

Jennifer sits in the car and smokes a cigarette. It is something she doesn't often do but having wasted her lunch hour on a long wait and a virtual slap in the face at the Post Office she feels desperate. There won't be time to get a sandwich now, nor to collect Kenny's dinner suit from the dry cleaners. He's cross enough at the amount of time she's been spending at her mother's house recently and won't be pleased if she arrives home without the suit that he needs tonight for a Sportsman's Dinner at the Rugby Club. She can only hope and pray that there's time later to dash out and get it before the dry cleaners close. It won't be long before he finds out that clearing a house isn't cheap. The skip hire, the man-and-a-van to take the stuff to the auction and the charity shop, the two labourers who ripped out the bathroom and the kitchen and took up the carpets for her all had to be paid out of the joint account. This is not to mention the outstanding gas and electric bills. There is money—clearly, her mother has money—but the bank and now the Post Office have been uncooperative. The insurance companies, too, while confirming the existence of the paid-up policies in her mother's name, won't tell her the surrender value without her mother's written permission. The estate agent won't put the house on the market without her mother's say-so. Jennifer is not used to not getting her own way. It seems that she can manage everything in life except for her mother.

Jennifer blows smoke crossly from her pursed lips and throws the last third of the cigarette, un-smoked, out of the window. She had been softening toward her mother. The gradual exploration of the recesses of the house had revealed a sentimental side to the old woman that she hadn't suspected. In addition to the letters and postcards from Michael and herself she has found, boxed in the loft, their old school books, every Christmas and birthday card they have ever sent her, and their earliest ham-fisted attempts at drawing and sewing and pottery. In the drawer at the bottom of the wardrobe there were more treasures; a box of faded photographs and a red and white tin of milk teeth and a yellowed lace gown that she presumes was worn at a christening. There were tiny shoes—their first pairs, she supposes—and a balding, much-cuddled Teddy Bear with a red gingham bow tie and one eye missing. It must have been Michael's. As a child she never had much time for cuddly toys. On the top of the wardrobe there were Christmas gifts going back several years, their shiny wrapping paper crisped and fragile with age, soft with dust. The Sellotape was set hard and gluey on the seals like yellow scabs, except for at one end, where they had been opened, briefly peeked into and then carefully resealed. Standing on the bedroom chair making this discovery, Jennifer had not known how to feel about it. It made her fume to think of the hours spent trailing around the shops in search of something acceptable. Not clothes—her mother didn't like new clothes and anyway never went out. Not perfume or make up or toiletries—such things were silly fripperies. Not books or CDs or videos. Not an electronic gadget of some kind. Not alcohol or food or chocolates. And then again, the trip to drop off the gifts before they set out for their skiing had always been so inconvenient, through the Christmas traffic and the grisly weather, a journey that had to be fitted in around office parties and drinks with neighbours and getting the last minute essentials for their holiday. It could never be done so early that it seemed pre-seasonal, but never left so late that it would appear like a last-minute after-thought. After all that angst, had the gifts been so despised that they had not even warranted proper opening? Then Jennifer herself had peered into the packages. Slippers, a warm scarf, a recipe book, a photograph frame. They *were* uninspiring, she supposed.

But then the thought occurred to her; had they, on the contrary, been saved and protected because they were so cherished, *too* cherished to use?

The thought had swamped her, standing there, on the chair in the deserted house, and she had been quite conscious of a melting sensation in the region of her heart, and a feeling that perhaps she might cry. Her poor mother, left year after year at Christmas to the charity of friends, spending week after week in this house of memories and ghosts, watching the seasons turn interminably from one to the other, seeing the world progress while she was left further and further behind. And before that, coping alone with the shop and the two children, and with the dawning realisation that Michael would never take the shop over.

She must have felt tired and lonely at times.

As she had climbed down and let the Christmas parcels tumble into a box Jennifer had felt softened, discerning a chink in her mother's armour, a weakness in the facade. It had disorientated her, standing albeit briefly, in her mother's shoes.

But now the obstreperous woman in the Post Office has hardened her again. Her mother and her finances are locked up tight, too proud and haughty to accept the inevitable, making Jennifer feel bad, as though she is desecrating something sacred when all she is doing is trying to get things straight. The money in those accounts isn't for herself, for God's sake! It will pay for the work on the house, and *that* will pay for her mother's care at Bridge House. It's the only thing worth having in the entire place, and she can say that with some authority having trawled through every last drawer and cupboard of useless tat and dross. All that rubbish! Worthless and bygone! Isn't it just typical that the only useful thing should be withheld from her? For an instant she allows herself to be angry with Michael. Why is she always left to deal with the crap? It isn't fair.

Well, it doesn't make any difference now, Jennifer thinks to herself as she starts the engine and pulls out into the traffic. It has all gone. Every shred of it. Gone to be burned or buried or to sit on the shelves of the charity shop. The house is empty. The walls are stark and nude, the floors stripped to their boards, the windows naked, the light bulbs bare. There is nowhere left in that house to hide.

And yet, she thinks, as she turns into the car-park, somehow, Michael is still managing to do it.

MRS TERRY BUSTLES in to Mrs Fairlie's bedroom. It is mid-morning, almost coffee time. Mrs Fairlie is listening to the Woman's Hour serial, the memoires of the wife of an Archbishop, now deceased. She likes the voices, the human stories. They connect her. She is buoyed up on the radio waves that swell out through the atmosphere to break on far-slung shores. It is why she wanted her little radio. It reminds her that, outside, life continues. There are scandals and wars and governmental faux pas that make up for the remoteness and vacuity of Bridge House. Melvin Bragg is still as incomprehensible and pompous, John Humphreys as provocative, Humphrey Lyttelton as mischievous as ever. At night-time the idea is so strong that she can almost feel the surge of the static water-waves lifting her bunk and carrying her out across the deeps. She likes the idea of people across the world listening in as she is doing, keeping abreast of the cricket scores in Cape Town and the election results in Estonia, having a vague picture of them crouched in grass-roofed huts and perched on cratered mountainsides while the clipped accents of the announcers embrace the globe. It takes her out into the world and brings the world home to her. The world is a foreign concept to her; she has never been abroad, and is informed only by television programmes and the occasional post card. The world seems wide and impossibly vast; incomprehensible, unpredictable, uncomfortable, unsafe, but somehow brought to heel by the BBC.

Michael is out there somewhere, in the world, trudging across sand dunes or thrashing through a jungle. He is pushing through jostling hordes of some diminutive almond-eyed populace or squatting in a hide-covered tepee eating doubtful indigenous foodstuffs with painted, punctured tribesmen. Her pride in him—and her love for him—is not quite suffocated by her enormous anger at him, or the pain of the wound he has so cruelly inflicted. It burns like a constant flame.

Mrs Terry is accompanied by a wheel chair.

'Ah *there* we are!' Mrs Terry says, as though she has been looking for Mrs Fairlie for some time in a variety of places before discovering her here. 'Hop aboard, then. We have a visitor.'

Mrs Fairlie frowns. She has been enjoying this serial and today is the last episode. Also, she does not want to go in the chair and neither does she want a visitor.

'A visitor? Who?'

'Ah ha! Wouldn't *we* like to know? Well, there's nothing for it. We'll have to go down and *see.*' Mrs Terry nudges the wheel chair closer.

'Why can't they come up here?' Mrs Fairlie shrinks back into her chair. Rosie has had a new one brought into her room from somewhere else in the place. It is wider, much easier on her hip, and the seat is higher, with a lever at the side that tips the chair forward a little and makes it easier to get in and out. Rosie has tucked the old quilt onto the chair for her and it feels homely and safe. They have rearranged the furniture a little so that the chair can be close to the window, and the window is left open so that she can hear the birds and smell the fresh air. They have turned the thermostat on the radiator right down. She has the tray table on one side of her. Rosie has shown her how to tilt the table part to make reading the newspaper easier. The bedside table is on the other side, where the radio and her spectacles are always to hand, and where she can put her coffee cup. Her sticks are propped against the wardrobe, within easy reach.

'Goodness me! We couldn't allow that!' Matron responds as though Mrs Fairlie had suggested that they run naked together across the lawn. 'We don't receive gentlemen in our bedrooms, do we?'

'A gentleman?'

Matron claps her hand to her mouth in mock alarm. 'Oh! Now look what we've done! We nearly let the surprise slip then, didn't we?'

Mrs Fairlie's mouth goes dry and she is conscious of her heart leaping and hammering in her chest like a caged bird. Her hands begin to shake.

He has come.

She pushes the tray table away from her and reaches for her sticks. 'I don't need the chair,' she says, 'I can walk.' She will not meet him in a wheel chair.

'Not at all! Let's travel in style. Now, do we need the little girl's room before we go?'

'Well *I* don't,' Mrs Fairlie rejoins, 'and I'm *not* going in that chair.' She fixes Matron with a glare that has withered others in the past, but she is aware of a note of hysteria in her voice. Like an over-taut violin string, it belies her imperiousness.

Matron sighs. 'Very well, then. If we insist.' Mrs Fairlie grasps her sticks in one hand and operates the lever at the side of the chair with the other. She rises majestically to her feet. Matron pulls a lever at the back of the wheelchair and it collapses down the middle, defeated. Mrs Fairlie gives a triumphant snort and walks from the room. Although she has walked up and down the landing almost every day, today her legs seem less reliable than usual, and the landing longer than ever. She is trembling. It is like a dream, she thinks, when you're in a hurry to get somewhere and you can't get your knickers on and you don't want to arrive without them. She is frantic to get downstairs and yet frightened to think what might greet her there. She can barely dare to believe that it might be him. She has dreamt of it and longed for it. But now that it is here she dreads it too.

The walls of her defences are crumbling. She cannot shore them up, will not be able to keep him out, to protect herself from the hurt he may inflict on her. The joy of his coming can never assuage the jealousy of his going. All that effort all these years will be undone the moment she sees him, her little boy, home again. The hard shell of her accusation—where has he been? What has he been doing? Why hasn't he sent her word?—is weak and fissured by old wounds of love. None of it matters now. She will hand over the ring and the richly embroidered coat without a murmur, and kill the fatted calf. This is what she has been waiting for.

Each step is agony.

Mrs Terry walks tetchily at her side, like a small dog anxious to get to the park and to be let off its leash. She tuts and mutters and consults her upside-down watch. She darts to the end of the corridor and presses the lift call. Close to, its 'bing bong' sounds quite different, Mrs Fairlie notes distractedly. They step into the lift together.

There are amber tinted mirrors inside the lift. Mrs Fairlie is appalled at the sight of herself, tall and gangling. Her face is thin and her forehead furrowed. Her eyebrows beetle over her eyes, her periwinkle blue eyes, the only nice thing about her, she has always thought. Her body is hunched over her sticks. One shoulder is higher than the other. One hip juts out at an awkward angle. Her clothes—baggy and commodious, their colours leached by the amber glass—make her look like a shapeless sack. She turns away from herself. At least her hair is reasonably clean.

The lift descends, then judders slightly. Bing bong. The doors open. She begins to wish she had visited 'the little girl's room' after all. The anticipation is overwhelming, the passion of motherhood courses and races through her like rich wine.

She steps out of the lift. The heat is beyond endurance and the hot sharp brine smell of Friday lunch makes her feel nauseous.

'This way,' Matron says brightly, indicating the corridor down past the dining room. David Dickinson is booming from the television room, his voice reverberating up the corridor and bouncing off the walls.

Mrs Fairlie's hands are sweaty. Her palms keep slipping on the handles of her sticks and it hurts her tender finger joints to grip more tightly. The shake in her legs is almost uncontrollable. She can hardly breathe. The smell of smoked haddock is rank and she baulks at inhaling it, like someone clearing up someone else's sick. When she does breathe it is as though there is no air; she is drowning in hot salty sea-moss, thick and heavy and saturated with moist fishiness and she cannot get it into her lungs. They proceed down the corridor, Matron breathing heavily at her heels.

'Our visitors are in the small drawing room,' Matron says, pointing at the door of the small lounge. There is the merest trace of freshness emanating from the room; perhaps the window is open.

'Just a minute.' Mrs Fairlie stops. She leans against the wall and reaches into her pocket for a handkerchief, wiping her palms one at a time, and then her mouth; she can feel a prickle of sweat on her lip. She is almost panting for breath.

'We should have used the chair,' Matron says nastily.

'Oh shut up,' Mrs Fairlie snaps. Then she steps into the little lounge.

There are two people in the room. Jennifer, dressed in a sharp suit and more make-up than usual, perches on one of the chairs. A man in a dark suit and holding a briefcase has his back to the room. He is looking out of the French windows at the terrace. The man is quite tall, slim. It is impossible to tell what age he might be. His hair is neatly cut above his collar. At her entrance Jennifer stands up and smoothes her skirt down over her hips.

'Hello, Mum,' she says. There is something in her voice Mrs Fairlie doesn't like, an underlying note of brittle anxiety, like breaking glass. She smiles but the smile does not reach her eyes. At the sound of her voice the man turns from the window, very slowly. He has his back to the main source of light in the room. Mrs Fairlie cannot see him clearly. She takes a step towards him. She hasn't seen Michael in years. She has lost count of how many, perhaps five, or more. He would be almost fifty now. Perhaps she would not recognise him. This man is about the right age and size and shape; for all she knows it could be him.

Last time she had seen him she had thought Michael looked thin and ill, and certainly this man is sparely built. Then, Michael's skin was tanned but sallow and his hair was lank. He had needed a shave and good wash. His beautiful eyes—blue like hers—had been milky and dull, and sunken into their sockets. His hands had been restless and he had paced about like a caged lion, unused to the confinement of buildings, she had presumed. He had drunk cup after cup of tea but refused food.

But this man, as she steps closer to him, inch by agonising inch across the carpet, is healthy, clean-shaven, smart and respectable. He is self-possessed. Hope almost chokes her. She gasps. Because she is leaning on her sticks she cannot raise her hand to cover her gaping mouth. He steps out across the space to meet her and as he does so he smiles at her and extends a hand. Then she knows that this is not Michael and her heart deflates with a tiny whimper like a vulnerable animal run over by a car. The sound gets as far as the back of her throat. Her insides fold up. The sound of her disappointment is drowned by Matron from the doorway.

'Isn't this nice? We'll organise some coffee, shall we?' she gushes.

'Come and sit down Mum,' Jennifer says. Mrs Fairlie is ready to fall down. 'Let me introduce Mr Bowyer. He's going to help us sort things out. He's a solicitor.'

An hour—perhaps more, or less—Mrs Fairlie isn't sure—passes. The others speak in carefully measured voices; Mr Bowyer and Jennifer and occasionally the matron, whose presence is unexplained and intrusive and yet resolute. Mrs Fairlie says little. They use easy words and short sentences and are calm and assured; it is as though they have rehearsed their parts. There is talk of unpaid bills and financial complexities which must be addressed, many letters to be written and replied to, deeds and policies and statements. Vaguely, Mrs Fairlie wonders if she is in some kind of trouble. Why else would she need a solicitor? Interspersed with these weighty matters are seemingly irrelevant enquiries; would she happen to know what day it is, and who is Prime Minister just now? She responds dully, but accurately. But mainly she lets them talk over and across her and she nurses her disappointment like an abjectly unhappy child in her arms. She had so wanted it to be

Michael, to hold his hand in hers and tell him that all she wanted was to know that he was happy; nothing, absolutely *nothing* more.

Presently a small table is pulled out and Mr Bowyer lays a document on it. She realises that he is speaking to her.

'I need to be sure that you're perfectly happy for us to go ahead with this, on your behalf,' he says, laying his pen on the document. 'And that you fully understand everything we've said.' Mrs Fairlie looks at them in turn. Matron is wriggling with self-importance. Mr Bowyer looks carefully neutral. Jennifer is biting the inside of her lip in that way she has when she's worried. Mrs Fairlie wishes they would go away, that she could get back to her room, that she could rewind time and go back to the Archbishop's wife. But a response is clearly needed at this juncture. She casts around for one that might placate them.

'Bills need to be paid,' she hazards, picking up on something they had mentioned. 'My late husband and I were very strict about it.'

Jennifer nods. 'Yes, I know you were.'

'We used to do the accounts every day, in the shop. It was always the last thing we did. Count out the float from the till and then add up the takings. Then we'd use the money to pay the suppliers. We always did that before we took any money for ourselves.'

Everybody nods sagely. She seems to have pleased them.

'So you'd be happy for me to see to those things for you, Mum?' Jennifer says.

She frowns. Has Jennifer, in her absence, re-opened the shop? 'Count the takings?'

'No, of course not. But pay the people that you owe?'

She thinks of Rosie. She certainly wants Rosie to be reimbursed for the clothes. It is this recollection which makes her say with some emphasis, 'Oh *yes*. If you don't mind.'

'Of course I don't mind. I'd be happy to.'

The word sounds a note that rings through the fug. She grasps it. 'If it makes *you* happy. That's what I want.'

Mr Bowyer slides the document towards her. 'Excellent,' he says. 'That's entirely satisfactory. If you'll sign here, and Matron will witness your signature, and then we're done.'

Mrs Fairlie picks up the pen. It is difficult to get it right in her fingers and the lines on the form begin to swim. She draws the pen across the paper as best she can, and immediately Matron signs underneath with one of her many pens. The tension in the air seems to ease and there is some trivial talk of the weather while Mr Bowyer puts the form in his briefcase. Underneath their words, underneath their notice, now that the deed is done, Mrs Fairlie repeats, 'That's all I ever wanted for either of you,' and begins to cry.

'WHY IS THIS place called Bridge House?' Mrs Fairlie asks.

Rosie gasps. 'Don't you know?' Rosie hasn't been at work for a few days and she seems brighter, now. Mrs Fairlie has missed her but the break seems to have done her good. Presumably things with her son have resolved but Mrs Fairlie doesn't trust herself to mention it. The subject of sons is still too raw for her. It is a week or so since Jennifer brought the solicitor. Since then she has been aware of a heaviness around her heart. She has found it harder to concentrate on the wireless. She has been going over and over things in her head. She hasn't slept well. She shakes her head.

'Come with me.' Rosie passes her the thing that they call the zither, a word which comes more easily to Mrs Fairlie's recollection and pride than zimmer. It has chunky rubber wheels and a padded shelf for a handbag or library book. The shelf can also be used as a perch if she needs a rest. It has brakes that Rosie says, with a smile, will keep it from running away with her. It is more stable than the sticks and more dignified than the wheelchair. It is a compromise they have come to.

They saunter together down the landing. Rosie places her hand on the side of the zither, and it reminds Mrs Fairlie of pushing Jennifer in her pram, with Michael holding on at the side like a good boy. Lunch is over and it is the quiet time. The man in room 4 has gone to sleep with the radio on. His snoring is strangely complementary to the classic concert which flutes and trills around his dreams.

'Mr Swindell, our oldest resident,' Rosie says. 'He's a hundred and two.'

'Poor bugger,' Mrs Fairlie mutters.

The lift bing-bongs and takes them downstairs. The man with the shopping bag is sitting in the foyer, perusing the papers. He seems to be reading them aloud to himself.

'Hello Mr Goldstein,' Rosie calls.

He breaks off his reading and looks up at her, blinking through his huge spectacles. 'They'll be here soon!' he shouts. 'Won't be long now!'

'I'm sure you're right,' Rosie says loudly, adding in a confidential tone, 'Poor thing. He waits every day for visitors who don't come.'

The dining room is empty apart from Mrs Mole who is setting tables ready for supper. They pass the small lounge. It is May now, and very warm. Indeed, the country is basking in the heat wave. The French window is propped open and a party of ladies is sitting on the terrace. Three women in summer dresses and a fourth, with a rug over her knees, are distributed around a table playing cards. In the cool interior of the room, a trolley is laid ready for afternoon tea.

'That's nice. They must have come from the Bridge Club. Miss Hill misses her bridge,' Rosie comments.

They approach the large, bright room where the shrieking TV is. Mrs Fairlie hesitates on the threshold. She doesn't want to go in. 'Is this where you're taking me?'

'No. Come on,' Rosie says. She smiles and encourages Mrs Fairlie to keep going.

In the TV room the set is on but the sound is turned down to a muted yell. There are chairs arranged around two sides of the room and bodies in various stages of decomposition are slumped in them. Rosie names them quietly as they pass: Mrs Bayliss, Mrs Quirk, Miss Thompson, Dr Fellowes. They are all shrivelled and brown like wizened fruit. One has hairs sprouting from her chin, another hair so sparse that her scalp shows pink through it. They all wear clothes that look as though they were bought for larger, more substantial people. And there is that earthy, vegetable smell, of oldness decaying into death.

'Death's waiting room,' Mrs Fairlie frowns. She forgets the names as soon as Rosie speaks them. She has no desire to begin to think of these relics as people, like her, or, indeed, of herself as a relic, like them.

The pink woman is parked up in her wheelchair by the wide window that looks out over the formal gardens at the side of the building. She raises a feeble, translucent hand to Rosie. Her lips move but no sound comes out, then her hand drops, exhausted by the effort of movement. 'Pinkie Pritchard, she's our longest-standing resident,' Rosie smiles.

'She isn't standing now,' Mrs Fairlie thinks to herself. Aloud she says, 'Is she really called Pinkie?'

Rosie smiles and shakes her head. 'She has a flowery name, like us. Petunia. But we all call her Pinkie.'

A couple sits a little apart from everyone else. They are both asleep but they are holding hands.

'Mr and Mrs Irons. They're devoted to one another.' Rosie leads her through the room and out of a door in the corner into a glazed corridor. There are wicker chairs and many frondy pot-plants arranged along its length, magazine racks and deep squashy sofas with scatter cushions, and ethnic rugs.

'It's a shame,' Rosie says. 'No one ever sits here.'

'I'm not surprised,' Mrs Fairlie laughs. 'You'd need a hoist to get me out of those chairs.'

Rosie laughs. 'You're right. They aren't very practical, are they? But this corridor features on all the brochures. It's called an Atrium, apparently. We're almost there.'

They turn the corner. The glazed porch wraps round the corner of the building and opens out into a sunny conservatory. It is pleasantly furnished but it is the view that Rosie has brought her to see. On this far side of the building the gardens slope down a short, easy incline and border a wide silver-blue river.

'There's the bridge,' Rosie points to the left, where an old stone bridge arches over the water. It is solid and strong, its dark stones leaping light and graceful and taut as a ballet dancer over the moving water and reaching down below its flow on either side. 'That's why this is Bridge House. Isn't it lovely?'

Mrs Fairlie makes no reply. It is not the bridge that has caught her eye but a grey stone house across the river, squatting amid neat gardens a-riot with colour. There is a child's swing in the garden and a trampoline. Beyond the house there are farm buildings. Apart from the house there is only open farmland on the other side of the river, spreading up to the horizon. Mrs Fairlie catches her breath. It is many years since she saw fields and crops like this. There is wheat and barley and close-cropped meadows where the silage has been cut, but mainly the land is laid to pasture and grazed by Friesians. Nostalgia swamps her. She takes in the details of the farm with hungry memory.

'That's a tidy farm,' Mrs Fairlie says. 'It reminds me of where I grew up.' Indeed it is like looking back in time. If she narrows her eyes she can picture herself walking across the yard to the dairy, following the cows across the field, their lazy, angular rumps swaying from side to side.

'I try not to look at the farm,' Rosie says sadly. The unaccustomed melancholy of her tone makes Mrs Fairlie twist round to look at her. 'It's where my husband lives now, with his new ...' she seems unable to speak the next word, as though it is stuck in her throat, '... partner,' she gulps out at last. 'It is a nice view though. Shame about the motorway. Can you see it, there, on the horizon?' Just discernible on the grey line between land and sky ants crawl from right to left.

'Is that where the road goes? To the motorway?'

'It's just a service road to the motorway services they built up there. A few locals use it but all the main traffic goes by the motorway.'

Mrs Fairlie's eye is drawn back to the farm. Selfishly—because she knows it is uncomfortable for Rosie—and yet helplessly—the memory it has evoked is so strong—she says, 'Is he a farmer then, your husband?'

Rosie barks a laugh. 'No! He's a salesman. He sells mechanical parts, or he did do. I think it's office supplies now. They only rent the house. I don't know who farms the land.'

Mrs Fairlie is not really interested. She only wants to talk about the farm, *her* farm. 'I grew up on the farm and I used to take the children there for holidays until Frederick died. They liked it. He could never come with us, of course. He had to mind the shop.'

Rosie brings her a chair and helps her ease down into it. 'The children? So your daughter isn't an only one?'

Mrs Fairlie shakes her head but doesn't reply.

'I thought you'd like it here. I know you like your own company,' Rosie says, 'and no one else ever comes. I can't think why. Some people can see this view from their bedrooms, of course. Shall I leave you to sit a while? I'll bring your tea in a bit, shall I?' Mrs Fairlie nods and gazes out across the river, at the farm.

She sits alone, looking out. The colours dazzle her; intense, fresh squeaky-green grass, green-gold ripening barley, hot reds and oranges in the flower tubs and borders of the farm garden, velvet black and silk white of the cows, bright mirror river, eye-blue sky. It takes her breath away, like a drench of cold water. Nothing has seemed this vivid, this real, since Michael began to go away. Her girlhood, early married life, the shop, the children, and Frederick's death—sharp as a knife wound, not mortal but shocking—soldiering on with Annie ... She sees all *that* in Technicolor. It is as solid and real as a good firm King Edward's in her calloused hand. But then, as the shop began to fail and Michael began to drift away from her, the hues are muted and bland, washed out, dilute. It is as though between then and now her life has been lived in shades of grey. A thin film of dust and dirt has coated over the colours of the days, tainting everything in disappointment and bewilderment. Just like the soil which used to float from the potatoes and come clinging to the carrots, and lodge in the lettuce leaves, it has spread and settled across the whole stock, dulling the flavours and leaving a gritty residue between the teeth. The years between have been restless and zestless. She knows they have made her dour and resentful. The loneliness and disappointment of it all has soured her.

She considers for a moment the poor old bones strewn around in the lounge, whose names she has already forgotten, apart from Pinkie, who is so personally insubstantial that her blush of colour—all she has to define her—is so much more vivid an identification than a name. Perhaps they think her proud and cold, refusing to join them for meals, baulking at bingo and the piano-playing spinster, declining dominoes. It may be that somewhere—deeply buried inside the brown parchment of their skin, beneath the wizened, wasted musculature and cowering inside the chalky disintegrating bones—flutters the residue of life eager for friendship. Perhaps they yearn for companionable chats, to establish, even at this late stage, relationships which will assuage the yawning boredom of the last futile hours. It is just conceivable to her that if she were to rummage amongst the remnants there on the chairs she might find a solid and graspable kernel of empathy, something quick and warm and responsive. But there isn't time and she hasn't the inclination to invest any of herself here. The temporariness of it all makes it so useless. They and she are disintegrating; stretched out thinner and thinner, ground down to dust by every interminable day. She will not number herself amongst them lest it accelerate the decline towards death, like the blue bloom of mould passing from one fruit to another in a box.

She closes her eyes and withdraws into a doze. The sun is warm on her aching body although blinds across the glazed roof deflect its glare. It is like bathing in honey. Her limbs are sticky with the sweet heaviness of its warmth, an easing balm oozing into her joints. She feels as delicious as a drunken bee. Presently she is roused by the gentle placement of a cup on a small table by her side, smiles a thank you from behind closed lids, recognising Rosie's soapy smell. They have arrived at a place, the two of them, where the formality of words is unnecessary. She rests for a while in the blessed blanket of warmth, in a comfortable place between rest and tea. Then the allure of hot tea calls her and she opens her eyes.

Her eye is caught immediately by a blue car that travels across the stone bridge and turns into the gate of the farm. Even without the Rosie connection the scene sparks her interest. A woman and two children spill out. The woman busies herself with shopping bags but the children run round the outside of the house. The woman is young—perhaps ten years younger than Rosie, it is hard to see clearly—with long fair hair. She wears tight dark trousers and an oversized red t-shirt. She carries the shopping into the house. The children are in the garden pulling off their shoes and hurling themselves onto the trampoline. A boy who is perhaps seven or eight years old and his sister, who is smaller, blonde and sturdily built. They both wear uniform and have evidently just been fetched from school. Everything about the boy is awry; his tie is askew and his shirttail hangs out. One grey sock is almost off. As he bounces he flings his arms and legs wide, his body arching in mid-air as though he aches to fly. Even across the river and the lawns, and through the double glazing, Mrs Fairlie can hear his exuberant yells, and she smiles and bites into the slice of gingerbread which has accompanied the tea. The girl is neat, all buttoned up, her hair in tidy braids, white socks to the knee. She jumps with her knees, holding her arms rigidly to her sides and her hands clenched. There is a weightiness about her, a resistance to the lift of the trampoline. While her brother flings himself higher and higher above her, she is restrained by invisible cords to the earth. After a while they tire of the trampoline and dismount. The boy thrusts his feet into his shoes and careers around the garden, kicking a football. The girl sits on the ground and does up her shoes with patience and care before perching on the swing. Then their mother appears at the back door of the house and motions them inside, indicating her watch with the impatient stab of a finger. The boy abandons his game immediately and rushes past her into the house. The girl continues to swing, gently, ignoring her mother who remains at the door gesturing urgently. She swings; five, ten, twenty times. Then, when the mother has given up and gone inside, she hops neatly from the swing and goes into the house.

'Stubborn little madam,' Mrs Fairlie thinks to herself. 'Just like Jennifer.'

Jennifer was such a difficult baby; difficult to conceive and carry and an absolute fiend to produce. It had taken her hours of grunting and straining to get the hot, red, angry body out of her own and onto the bed. Then she had screamed and yelled her way through infancy, eschewed the breast, gagged on the bottle, vomited constantly. She had refused to sleep, roaring and arching her back in her cot with little fists so tightly balled they had gone white. She had hated being carried, disliked being cuddled, but complained vociferously when put down.

'Nothing pleases that one,' Annie had said.

Lactose intolerance was unheard of, in those days.

Toddlerhood had brought a ravening desire to be independent and fierce flashes of uncontrollable anger. She was stubborn, wilful, and— once speech came—embarrassingly argumentative. Jennifer disrupted the quiet order of the Fairlie household and blotted the respectability of Fairlie & Sons.

'You'll have to be firm or she'll rule this roost,' Annie had warned. Frederick had looked up from his history book and regarded his wife over his horn-rimmed spectacles when she had reported this to him. Without him saying a word it was understood that discipline was not his field. Mrs Fairlie had threatened and administered smacks, disliking the task but acknowledging the necessity. While Jennifer would often cry in sheer frustration she never cried when smacked, but would regard her mother through shocked, angry eyes. After a while the necessity had lessened. Jennifer learned self-control. Mrs Fairlie never knew whether the memory of the smacks rankled or even existed; they never talked about it. Their relationship, never demonstratively affectionate, settled into one of wary mutual respect. Jennifer's anger was absorbed into herself and metamorphosed, manifesting itself in an obsessive desire for neatness and order and an extreme pickiness over food, as disruptive, in some ways, as the temper tantrums and belligerency had been. But you can't discipline a child for insisting on a tidy bedroom or for knowing what she likes.

Once Jennifer had started school she was fanatical about the work, the first in her class to read, top in maths. It channelled her energies away from her other fixations somewhat and a stray pea amongst the carrots on her plate might be overlooked. In spite of missing quite a lot of school—she had been prey to every ailment; lurid rashes, foetid throats, gastric upsets and glandular disorders—Jennifer continued to succeed academically, and it was sad that, by then, her father was not there to foster and enjoy it. In that, and in other ways, she had been completely on her own, an anomaly in the Fairlie family; articulate, intelligent and ambitious. Both her children, when she thinks about it, had been like changelings, seeming not to belong. She does not know how she and Frederick could have produced either of them. And it occurs to her that they, too, might have felt their strangeness. She wonders whether all that initial angst had just been Jennifer's sheer outrage at finding herself somehow in the wrong household, the result of a sense that somewhere there was a well-heeled professional family that would have cared for her, understood her so much better than her bewildered parents had seemed to.

'Finished your tea?' Rosie asks, materialising at her side in the conservatory.

Mrs Fairlie turns her head and says, aloud, as though all the foregoing thoughts and memories have been projected on a screen for Rosie to see, 'They couldn't have been prouder of her than me, though.'

'Of course not,' Rosie says. She lets her words sink and soothe. Then, bringing the zither forwards, she says, 'It will be dinner time soon. When the sun goes off this room it turns chilly quite quickly. You won't stay downstairs?'

'Oh no, dear. I'll go back up.'

SHE IS BEGINNING, in spite of herself, to feel familiar with the Bridge House routine. The menu rotates and she knows now that on Wednesdays a tuna sandwich supper will inevitably follow a lamb risotto lunch. On Sundays a creditable lunchtime roast will try to atone in advance for some paltry tinned offering in the evening; macaroni cheese, perhaps, which can be left to the staff to serve while the cook has an afternoon off. She is disgusted with herself one Thursday to find that she is actually looking forward to rice pudding and the buttery shortbread biscuit that will accompany it if she can get hold of it before Pearl does. The daily schedule is well-known to her now and she feels comfortable with the comings and goings of the staff, can anticipate the days when her bed will be changed, when her hair will be washed and her medications assessed. She knows the ropes. Her sense of anxiety and distress has been dulled as the days and weeks go by without atrocity or affront.

There are glorious days when nothing at all disturbs the succession of meals and hot drinks, but the home is all-too-frequently besieged by local organisations that disrupt the peaceful tedium. The local primary school visits every month to caterwaul inharmoniously or gabble out incomprehensible little plays. Various churches turn up to sing psalms and press dry palms and administer earnest prayers. The WI and Townswomen's Guild send cohorts to run craft workshops at which residents can wrestle with raffia or make unrecognisable things out of blobs of salt dough. These group visitations are eagerly anticipated, especially by Pearl, because the kitchen makes an extra effort and there will be homemade cake served from the trolley in the overwhelming heat of the day room. Its limpness and glistening, sweaty icing deters the visitors, who demur and murmur about their waistlines, but it is fallen upon by the residents as a welcome change from the usual bought-in Battenberg and Garibaldi.

Other visitors cause less of a stir. The podiatrist gravitates grimly from room to room, paring corns and filing nails as thick and yellow and horny as teeth. The piano-playing spinster's repertoire of wartime favourites is only a cruel reminder of loved ones lost and youth mislaid but she turns up relentlessly every few weeks to pound the keys and encourage the residents in thin, reedy choruses. The curate, as promised, serves Communion in the small lounge and stays behind afterwards to perch on the edge of a succession of seats and whisper what comfort he can into deaf, elongated, bristling ears.

Other clandestine visitations are made via some rear access. Mrs Terry guards the secret by-ways of the back stairs and a larger, stretcher-sized lift in the nether regions of Bridge House. They are forbidden to residents until their allotted time should come; reserved for one-way traffic. Twice Mrs Fairlie has been woken in the night by the flash of a blue strobing emergency light raking her room, and the surreptitious tread of ambulance tyres on the gravelled drive leading around to the service yards behind the main building. And once she saw black-suited funeral directors in an unmarked black van disappearing in the same direction. These visitors are unheralded and unremarked and certainly there is no cake. What they remove from Bridge House hardly warrants the efforts of two or three paramedics or a funereal posse, let alone a long wheel based vehicle. Really, a small shoe box or, in some cases, an envelope would suffice. The residents fade and dematerialise day by day until their wisp-like auras are scarcely discernible on the vinyl seats. Left to themselves, one day their miasmic remains will just blow away in the breeze, a smudge of fine, powder-grey dust dispersing amongst the motes in a shaft of sunlight.

At the weekends relatives call by bringing gifts; bags of sweets, magazines, a pot plant. Perhaps, if they are very thoughtful, a bottle of whisky to stiffen up the night-time beverage. They gather the chairs into circles in the lounges and the staff fetch tea while the hapless residents are interrogated. 'How are you feeling?' 'Are you sleeping well?' 'Where are your teeth?' They proffer photographs and deliver news, trying to reawaken their relation's interest in the family and the outside world. 'Our Michelle has had her baby. You know: your grand-daughter? Rupert's eldest. You're a great-grandma again! How many does that make now? She says she'll bring him in to see you one day. That will be nice, won't it? He has the family nose!' The residents, bewildered, nod and smile and wonder who these people are or sometimes make querulous accusations that are ignored, glossed over, with sugary pleasantries.

All of this washes past Mrs Fairlie. She plays no part in it even when importuned by Olga, the most persistent evangelist, gushing enthusiastically about the importance of mental stimulation and social interaction. She cajoles and inveigles in her broken English, making the words seem too large and unwieldy for her mouth, as though they are large glutinous toffees stuck to her teeth. Meanwhile she wheels chairs into the day room deaf to the protestations of the occupants. But Mrs Fairlie has her zither and will not be herded anywhere and deters Olga with a scowl.

She stays in her room for much of the day, with her newspaper and her radio, but in the afternoons finds herself drawn down to the conservatory to look at the farm and to watch the children. She has discovered that even on days when the day room is crowded by school children or tambourine-wielding charismatic Christians, she can access the conservatory by taking a short cut through the dining room. She can make her way there perfectly well on her own with the zither. Rosie's suggestion that she takes a little exercise each day has strengthened her limbs and her confidence. Her sense of hunted anxiety is lessened. She remains wary, but is not so fearful of being subsumed into the leathery ranks of insentients, firmly, sometimes rudely rebuffing any advances. She wakes less often in the night disorientated by the strange surroundings. She thinks about Frederick and the dogs, and Michael of course. Annie is often in her thoughts. But they have been joined by Rosie now, and Mrs Terrier, and she is aware of a surprising stab of sadness on seeing poor Mr Goldstein shuffle past her room each day, smartly dressed for his long over-due visitors. Even the shrimp-like shape of Pearl scuttling into view to babble another—or repeated—episode of her never-ending story is, if not welcome, then at least endurable.

PEARL CORNERS HER outside the lift and launches without preamble into her diatribe. 'People say it's very bad for a boy to attend his local university and Daddy agreed, so when William went to University Daddy and I went too, to look after him. Mummy had died long before that. Of course I couldn't leave Daddy to look after himself.' Bent over like a banana, she addresses her pom-pom slippers, earnestly regurgitating her flow of memories into their gaudy nylon plush. 'We rented a nice house in a suburb and William went off every day to the campus while Daddy and I visited the art galleries and the museums and of course I joined the local Mothers' Union. What a lovely time we had! Daddy's pension was quite sufficient to support us and in those days, you know, students got grants. Here's the lift. I'm going down. There's going to be a meeting. About the open day. We're having an Open Day. A whole day, when we'll be open and anyone can come. And they *will* come. They will. It's all very important and Mrs Terry wants to tell us all about it and afterwards there will be cake.' Pearl scuttles into the lift and Mrs Fairlie pushes her zither in after her. The doors close slowly. For some reason, in the cloistered lift, Pearl's voice drops to a conspiratorial whisper. 'One day William brought a girl home with him but I could see at once that she wasn't suitable; she couldn't manage a cake fork. William saw it too. She never came again. William didn't need a friend like that—or any friend. We had each other, just like always. And then Daddy got poorly. And William joined an orchestra. They toured to ever so many places and of course William wanted me to go too but poor Daddy was so frail and he couldn't manage the travelling. Here we are. Bing bong! Doors are opening!' They exit the lift and Mrs Fairlie expects Pearl to hurry off down the corridor towards the day room, still parroting her endless story, but instead she stops dead in her tracks and stares intently at her feet. 'And then ... and *then* ... One day William came home and said that he had found a new place to live. Somewhere different. And when I said that of course Daddy and I would go too he said ... he said, 'No.' He said ...' Pearl takes a deep breath as though about to make a momentous pronouncement. Her rounded back lifts perceptibly. 'William said that it isn't right for grown-up children to live with their parents.'

Pearl shakes her head sadly. She is rooted to the thick carpet outside the lift. There has only just been space for Mrs Fairlie to manoeuvre her zither out of the lift before the doors closed behind her. They are wedged, the two of them, behind some invisible and insurmountable obstacle in Pearl's reminiscence and Mrs Fairlie wonders if at last she has arrived at the terminus of her tale. Then there is a beat and she has skipped over the impediment. 'Of course when I moved back in with Mummy and Daddy people said that it isn't right for grown-up children to live with their parents. They said I couldn't go home and be Mummy and Daddy's little girl again when I'd been a married woman with my own house and had a baby. They said that my baby would become like Mummy's baby. They said that I would always be Mummy's baby and never get a chance to be an independent grown-up.' Suddenly back on solid ground Pearl moves off down the corridor towards the day room.

A cruel retort rises in Mrs Fairlie's throat. 'Will we ever get to see this son of yours?' she calls. Of course poor Pearl's obsession with her son is no less than Mrs Fairlie's and in truth the question is asked as much of herself. 'When will we ever,' she is asking, 'get to see these precious sons of ours?' She does not expect a response but Pearl is arrested in her tracks. She turns round and, as well as she is able, lifts her eyes. 'Oh yes,' she says, 'I told you. At the Open Day. Everyone must come. William will come.'

JENNIFER ARRIVES HOME early. This week's edition has fallen together perfectly and she has signed it off with a flourish. The new reporter is settling in a treat. Things are going well. She is looking forward to peeling off her business suit and getting the sun lounger out of the shed. There is a sheltered corner in the garden where the afternoon sun is trapped at this time of year, and it is not over-looked so she will be able to sunbathe topless if she wants to. The weather is so warm; remarkable, even for late May. It will be bliss to lie quietly and feel the heat on her skin.

As she opens the door there is some resistance from the pile of post wedged behind it. She gathers it up and shuffles through it quickly before depositing it on their hall table. The Power of Attorney has opened all the doors for Jennifer and it has been pleasing to make those who had been obstreperous back down and do her bidding once the document was produced. There is post for her two or three times a week now addressing her mother's affairs. The insurance companies have confirmed the details of the various policies. The post office has up-dated the savings accounts and the—quite considerable—amounts of interest accrued. The house is on the market and is attracting interest from property developers. Following a meeting with her mother's bank manager she has reimbursed the joint account for the various expenses incurred and set up a direct debit payment for Bridge House. All this has eased considerably the tension between her and Kenny. There had, as predicted, been a row following Kenny's discovery of the debits that she had been making in order to clear her mother's house. A row and then a sudden and protracted sales trip that had extended to more days than seemed strictly reasonable, given that his new assistant, brought over from the drawing office, was supposed to have lightened his load.

But then the letters had begun to arrive revealing her mother's financial abundance. She had intimated as much in an email and he had come home, looking jaded and smelling of stale Scotch but proffering flowers. She had responded to his gesture by donning the black lace underwear ensemble he had given her for Christmas and thus, in their customary way, the crisis had been averted, with a weekend of sex that seemed at times more combative than consensual but that had burned away the last of their mutual anger. And if, during that period, she had the objectivity while spread-eagled across the bed or bent over the banister, to wonder if her mother had *any idea* what sacrifices she was being called on to make on the old woman's behalf, she did not voice it.

What she did voice was a question as to whether Michael ought to be sought. She has all the correspondence in a folder upstairs in the study, all in order in case anyone should need to see. She feels that she must have things in readiness. Kenny's response had been brusque; let sleeping dogs lie. She can see his point. Unearthing Michael at this stage will bring to light all manner of unanswered questions and unpleasant truths and will in fact be in direct opposition to his expressed wish that she should behave as though he were dead. Jennifer suspects, in an uncharitable corner of her mind, that Kenny's motivation might not in fact stem from the desire to save her the stress and anxiety that attends Michael, but from the hope that, with her brother effectively deceased, she might appear to all intents and purposes as sole beneficiary.

She leaves the post for now and walks up the stairs to their bedroom. The neatness of their house gives Jennifer pleasure every time she enters it. It occupies a corner plot on a modern estate on the rural periphery of the suburbs. Their garden is prick-neat with tidy shrubs and biddable perennials. The interior is cool and clean, painted in shades of cream and taupe; there is white leather furniture and glass and chrome that would show every speck and smear of dirt, if there were any. Her tiled bathroom gleams, her kitchen is immaculate, the bed is dressed with a heavy white embroidered throw and scattered with cushions and looks like it belongs in a window display for Harrods. Her mother has never been invited to this house. It is not that Jennifer would not like to have her mother here; there would be a certain pride in displaying this outward manifestation of her success. At the same time there could only be the harshest comparisons drawn between this house and her mother's. This house would cast a hard and critical light on the old house, which would be pointless and cruel. And she has always known that her mother could never be comfortable here. She cannot picture the old bird perched on the leather two-seater sipping Earl Grey tea from Denbyware with any kind of pleasure. What is more she knows that she herself would be uncomfortable with it. Knowing, as she does, the state of her mother's house, the grime and soot, dog hair and stale air that seemed to impregnate her clothes and skin, she just did not want it in her home; it would be like a contamination. She is ashamed of herself for feeling this way, but there it is. In addition she knows that her mother would not have been able to swallow back some retort or other about the house's suitability 'for a family' before sighing 'but of course if *you* like it, Jennifer, that's all that matters.' And then she would be forced to wonder if she really did like it because of what it was, or because of what it wasn't; homely, familiar, comfortable, forgiving, a *home*, as opposed to merely a *house*. As nice as it is, it is not even the best that they can aspire to now, what with their new jobs. Kenny's promotion and increased salary, she presumes, is permanent. No one seems to know when the MD will return from his prolonged recuperation, if, in fact, he ever will. His stand-in is close to retirement and Kenny is perfectly placed, now, to take over the whole shebang. They speculate about it endlessly, she and Kenny. Less exciting—to Kenny, anyway—is her own potential for promotion, up into the umbrella organisation of which the *Weaver Weekly* is a dim satellite.

Jennifer removes her suit and blouse and fishes one of her bikinis from her holiday drawer, pulling on a beach shift over the top. Downstairs she slides open the patio doors and steps onto the decking into the heat.

The weather has surprised all the commentators these past few weeks; day after day of blue sky and warm sun. The news has been full of lobster-red bodies frying on beaches and hospital corridors crammed with heat-stroke victims. There is concern already over the levels in the reservoirs and a hose-pipe ban is imminent. This remembrance brings her attention to their numerous patio containers, which she notes with a frown, are looking dry and parched. She makes a mental note to turn on the sprinkler for an hour when the evening cools. The wall flowers are looking ragged and need removing and the spaces they vacate will need filling with annuals. She considers, just for a moment, getting dressed and driving to the garden centre, but the lure of the sun-lounger is too strong. She pulls it from the shed and places it in the sunny corner, and then goes indoors to fix herself a cool drink and to get the post.

She has not been to see her mother for some time, although, in the home, she has to say that she finds the older woman more palatable. She is regularly washed, at least, and her clothes are laundered, although the clothes she has got from somewhere—cheap and shoddy, if, she supposes, practical—are something of an embarrassment. These last weeks have been busy at work, not to mention dealing with her mother's affairs, and the weekends have been filled with golf events and various work-related social engagements that Kenny has been keen on and which, therefore, she has not liked to pass up. But now, examining the post, it is clear that a visit will be necessary. 'Bridge House is delighted to announce its forthcoming Open Day, to which all residents' relatives are most warmly invited and strongly encouraged to attend,' she reads. 'Raffle prizes are sought, along with contributions to the tombola and home produce stalls. Relatives are requested to consider donating their time to run one of the many popular stalls for a short period during the day. The Open Day is an annual event, much enjoyed by residents and staff alike, which is an opportunity to say thank you to the local community organisations that support the home throughout the year, providing social and occupational therapy, entertainment, care and companionship to the residents. Bridge House is delighted to confirm that His Worship the Mayor and the Lady Mayoress and a number of leading local Councillors, Social Services and Healthcare executives have already accepted invitations. Our Open Day is always kindly covered by the local press.'

'Is it really now? I wonder which hat I shall wear,' Jennifer muses, putting the letter to one side and leaning her head back against the lounger's pillow. Although the reporters work on Saturdays, Jennifer never does, but the invitation sounds like a three-line whip. Saturday is such an inconvenient day to hold these events; they interfere with the sporting calendar and she is almost certain that that particular Saturday afternoon is some football final or other. Kenny will not be pleased.

THE CHILDREN ARE having such fun in the garden. It is Mrs Fairlie's daily treat now to sit in the conservatory and watch them play. The door through to the cool interior of the dining room is open admitting faint wafts of vegetable air underlain by the smell of the vegetating residents who recently consumed lunch there. The clash and clatter of saucepans can occasionally be heard from the kitchen. All the windows, the roof-lights and the two French doors are open and a pleasant breeze blows through, rustling the leaves of the plants and bringing with it the exuberant songs of the birds and the quiet plash of the river.

The curious juxtaposition of smells and sounds from indoors and out swirl around Mrs Fairlie's comfortable chair; foetid interlacing with fresh, the wheeze of the earth-bound against the whistle of the air-borne. She is in a vortex of outside and in, the present and the ever-present past. The sun is so intense it casts an almost artificial brightness on everything, putting the world into unnaturally sharp focus. Memory is like a Technicolor film projected at times too slowly and at others much too fast. At times she is unsure whether what she sees is real or only really remembered. Here in her chair she finds she is less and less conscious of her body. It sinks into the cushion and is content to be left while her mind is occupied and engaged by sight and remembrance; her inner life is daily more vital than the corporeal. Perhaps it is because she is better cared for now—she must, if reluctantly, admit that this is so—better fed and rested, medicated regularly, her mind relieved of the practical diurnal worries of survival and subsistence. What if death, she considers, is just this process; the enlargement of the mind, the domination of the mental over the physical until the point when the mechanics of living, the breathing and the pulsing, are unnecessary, in fact a hindrance, and there is suddenly available an opportunity to get up and leave the body behind, to step unfettered by it into a bright Arcadian scene?

The river is very low but a mallard has hatched her brood of chicks and they waddle behind her on Bridge House lawn and down to the water, little balls of cheeping fluff on matchstick legs. Mrs Fairlie counts them daily. On the farm, when a broody hen managed to hatch a clutch of eggs or when they allowed the geese to hatch young to fatten for Christmas, they were always so vulnerable to predators especially in the early days; stoats and later mink, crows, even the farm cat. But every day this mother duck leads her nine babies down to the river and back again and Mrs Fairlie is glad. She does not like to think of the chicks savaged and mauled, or of the distress of the bereft duck.

The children at the farm share her daily joy. They watch the ducks from their side of the river, and sometimes run inside for bread to throw into the shallows. The little girl wants to name the ducklings but they will not stay still long enough for her to be sure she has not named the same one twice. She wants to capture and keep them and raise them as pets, but her brother shakes his head sagely and tells her that you can't keep wild things captive.

Their garden has become a holiday camp, the glorious weather bathing it in light and warmth. A large paddling pool has joined the trampoline and the swing. Every afternoon the children hurry around the house from the car, peeling off their uniforms and plunging into the cool water in their underwear. Mrs Fairlie chuckles to herself as they squeal and splash, and remembers sea-bathing at Whitby, the cold water numbing her knees that even then were beginning to creak and complain with arthritis. She would stand between the two children as they leapt over the waves, holding Michael's bucket while he dug around in the sand for shells and molluscs, lifting Jennifer clear of the odd strand of leathery seaweed she was sure would kill her. Her feet used to turn white and bloodless in the water, like strange marine curiosities not belonging to her. Her skin would go goose-fleshed long before the children began to feel the least bit cold. They were too busy paddling, absorbed in the shining water and the shells as opaque and tiny as babies' finger nails, and in the bright perfect pebble-gems which, when laboriously carried home and dried, would become dull and ordinary.

These children paddle too, in the river, cautiously, the boy poking the bed with a long stick, unearthing pebbles to throw with a satisfying plop into the deeper places where the water eddies round fallen boughs and banked up shingle. The girl floats flotillas of daisy heads down stream, and makes rafts from laurel leaves plucked from the garden, but she does not like the feel of the oozy mud between her toes and soon retreats to the grassy bank. The mother comes to them and smears white cream onto their milky skin and pops hats on their heads against the sun, and brings them ice-pops in lurid colours to keep them hydrated in the desiccating heat. Day by day their blemishless skin—all smoothness and perfection—turns apricot then golden, and their hair bleaches in the sun. They have two tents, a splendid Hiawatha tepee in bright red and a homemade one constructed from a clothes maiden and a travel rug. The girl has taken possession of the tepee and filled it with cushions and dollies, leaving the boy to squirm into the tunnel of the other tent. He stacks likely-looking branches and sticks outside against attack by enemies. He climbs a tree—a pear tree she thinks—and surveys the landscape. She can hear his voice shouting orders to his men; that they should barricade the fort and mount a guard. He fires imaginary arrows across the river making 'peeow' noises to denote their flight through the still air. The little girl plays inside the tent, arranging her dollies neatly in rows, tidying the cushions, making forays out into the garden to 'shop', buying little twigs, stones and leaves and taking them back into the tent to prepare meals. They play independently but sometimes their two worlds meld. The soldier is enticed inside the tent for 'tea', and the girl is a captured Indian squaw, and tied to a tree with a skipping rope, screaming blue murder. They are so like her own children that Mrs Fairlie is halfway out of her chair to intervene before their real mother emerges from the house to mediate a truce.

There is a round table and four chairs, and most afternoons the mother serves tea outdoors. Often they are joined by a man who Mrs Fairlie presumes to be Rosie's husband. If *she* sees him, when she brings Mrs Fairlie's cup of tea, she does not say anything. The man is older than the woman, but he plays with the children on the lawn, teaching the boy badminton and pushing the girl on the swing. In spite of the sun he retains his shirt; he is red-haired and his skin too fair to be exposed. The woman wears a bathing costume and shorts and is soon deeply tanned. They behave in normal ways, she watering the garden and deadheading the flowers, he pushing the lawn-mower and trimming the edges. But whenever they are near each other they cannot resist touching as they pass. He holds out his arm and gathers her to him by the waist. She pushes her cool hands under the lose flap of his shirt, making him jump and her laugh. They stand on the riverbank behind the children pointing at the ducklings and holding hands.

Whoever is farming the land is taking advantage of the weather to take his first cut of hay. An enormous machine crawls up and down the fields scything the fragrant grass and leaving it in dark green ridges on the pale green shorn ground. Presently another vehicle whisks and turns it so that it will dry, before a third scoops it up and blows it into a trailer. In adjacent fields cows are producing calves, miniature black and white versions of their dams. It makes Mrs Fairlie sad to think that all the bull calves will be disposed of. Why, she wonders, must all the sons be lost?

In the Bridge House garden there is activity, too. A large gazebo has been erected on the lawn outside the day room with a covered walkway to it from the French windows. Residents are wheeled or walked into its shade every day to watch the river and feel the warm breeze on their cold, dry flesh. Pinkie is anchored into her chair with a heavy blanket, lest she blow away. The place is swarming with bustle and there is plenty to watch from the shade under the canopy. Maintenance men climb into the trees to check on the lights festooned amongst the branches and to string bunting between the trees. In the gardens an army of gardeners snip and dig and prune and plant out banks of geraniums and lobelia, impatiens and alyssum, marigolds and petunias in riotous floods of colour. They weed the gravel walkways in the formal garden and scrub down the wooden benches placed in sheltered arbours. At the front of the building an enormous banner is stretched between two trees declaring 'OPEN DAY' and the date. One day a low-loader arrives with a cherry-picker on the back and a team of men erect a May-pole in the centre of the lawn. Its coloured ribbons dangle limply in the breathless air. Mrs Terry, bustling around with a clipboard under her arm, fears for the turf, but the ground is so hard and baked that the wheels of the lorry leave no imprint. Another lorry delivers trestle tables and folding chairs and they are stacked in an outhouse. Indoors, contributions for the raffle and the tombola and the other stalls are beginning to arrive. Local businesses have donated plants, hampers, boxes of chocolates and toiletries, vouchers for meals for two at nearby restaurants, a selection of gardening implements, an enormous teddy bear, an exercise machine, innumerable bottles of wine.

'What would we do with any of this if we won it?' Mrs Fairlie asks Rosie as they survey the collection building up in the foyer.

Rosie slips her arm through Mrs Fairlie's. 'If you won a bottle of wine you could share it with your favourite nurse,' she smiles.

'Pearl seems to think her son will come.'

'He probably will. Most of the relatives make the effort for Open Day. They come from far and wide, actually.'

'Even Mr Goldstein's?'

Rosie shakes her head. 'Ah no. Sadly, he doesn't have any relations left. His brother used to come but he passed away a couple of years ago and unfortunately his son died last year. He hasn't anyone left at all.'

Mrs Fairlie's step falters. 'Hasn't anyone told him?'

'Oh yes, but, you know, these things don't always sink in. Now I drew the curtains in your room but it will be very hot in there still. You're sure you won't stay downstairs for supper? It's only sandwiches today. No cutlery required ...' she smiles encouragingly and Mrs Fairlie is almost tempted to agree, just to please her. She looks past her at the residents being brought in from outside and taken into the dining room. They shuffle and creak on the arms of the nurses, groping in the sudden darkness after the bright outdoors like blinded, subterranean creatures. They are shrivelled, hairless, toothless husks.

'Oh no, no thank you,' she says, shrinking from their fate

IN THE MORNINGS Mrs Fairlie's room is cool but as midday comes the sun slants in and by late afternoon it is stifling. At night the room is still almost unbearably hot. The nights are still and sultry. The open window admits scarcely any coolness but only all the traffic noise from the road, which is as disturbing as the heat. Mrs Fairlie, in the snatched moments of almost-slumber, has been dreaming—or thinking about— the distinction is hazy—hay-making on the farm, the periods of dry weather two or perhaps even three times in the summer, when the grass would be cut and stored for winter feed. It was a window in the forecast eagerly looked for by the farmers, when every worker and vehicle would be thrown into the effort to cut, dry, collect and store the fragrant meadow grass. Women and girls were no exception; they would be put behind the wheels of ancient tractors and sent into the fields alongside the men from first light until sunset, and even sometimes beyond, working by moonlight until the dew fell. All the workers became green with grass-juice, their hair full of seeds and stalks, their nostrils overdosed by the sweet pungency of mown grass. Michael had revelled in it, if silage time fell in with school holidays, riding on the backs of the tractors, standing on the flat-beds forking hay. He would rest in the shade at lunchtime with the men, swigging lemonade and wolfing sandwiches, his hand on his hip in imitation of them, wagging his head up and down like they did, gazing at the sky and reading the clouds. His lithe little body turned amber from the sun and green from the grass so that from a distance, with her eyes narrowed against the glare of the sun, he was a green-gold elf man.

Jennifer had had to stay indoors, her eyes and nose streaming with hay-fever.

A car screeches past and jolts her back into the present. She realises that she needs the toilet—their drinks have been supplemented with elderflower cordial and homemade lemonade because of the heat, another evocative reminder of hay-making. She pushes off the sheet and gets up. Sitting on the toilet she considers that perhaps opening her bedroom door will allow a through-draught. Out on the landing everything is quiet, but surprisingly light. There is a sliver of yellow light from under the door of a small room that serves as a nurse station but the main source of light is the moon, which pours like milk in through the end landing window and bathes the utilitarian ash-coloured carpet in a pearlised sheen. The colour of everything is bleached out like an old photograph into monochrome tones; ghostly greys and wraith-like whites, and as she pads in her bare feet along the corridor she feels barely more than a spectre moving through the pale, surreal air. She has no consciousness at all of her usual stiffness and puts the slight ache and heaviness in her limbs down to the long day on the bone-shaking tractor hauling hay along the narrow lanes to the barn. The bing bong of the lift, when it comes, is like the distant chime of the church clock carried across the silent fields.

In the evenings, after work, and full of supper and cider, they would have music. One of the men might play the guitar or the violin and one year there was an itinerant worker who played the accordion. That was when Michael got the bug for it, unwieldy instrument as it was and far from being as cool as the guitars and keyboards his friends at school were taking up for nascent, discordant pop groups. But its leathery bellows and intriguing keys and buttons had him spell-bound as he watched the man play; the easy motion of his arms opening and closing and the deft dancing of his green fingers over the pearly keys. His whole body rocked and swayed as though the instrument was an extension of it, an external organ, the bellows an addendum to his lungs. The keys and buttons were like supplementary fingers, the gleaming chrome reflected his silver tooth and the wire of his spectacles. And the reedy vibrato of the notes melded with his voice and rose like incense up to the stars.

The ground floor is deserted and silent. Even the television is quiet for once. It is gloomier along the corridor to the day room but that and the Atrium are both flooded with silver moonlight as bright as day but leached of colour, lending them a fantastical, timeless, dream-like aura. The key turns in the French window and the scent of mown grass floods sweetly into her nostrils from the fields across the river. The heat of the ground is condensing the moisture in the air and there is a plume of rising white mist across the lawn, eerily spectral, but the concrete slab is solid under her foot when she steps out into the night. So too is the silver tower of the May-pole that rises from the mist, its ribbons in shades of grey; miasmic white, steely platinum, pearlescent silver, like strands of ancient angels' hair reaching down into the vaporous haze. The huge plate of the moon out-shines everything, even the dully glowing stars in the sky and the feebly glittering fairy-lights that loop between the trees. But there is music, drifting from across the river. Not accordion music but something soulful, and across the knee-deep sea of mist, illuminated by the silvery moon, she can see two people dancing. They sway and circle, ghostly lovers rising from the gauzy white. And although she is suddenly very sad for poor Rosie and her boy, she is happy for the children in the farmhouse, safely tucked up in bed without a care to distress them, glad that they will have this security and these memories to ground them. She hopes that when life comes and snatches them away and flings them over far horizons that this will call to them, the voice of this time and this place, and guide them home.

Does Michael ever think of it? Does the smell of new-mown hay carry him back to those summers on the farm? Does the lilting song of his accordion remind him of that man with the silver tooth? Does he think of his mother at all? Of her soothing hands on his fevered head? Of her smile in the morning? Of her comforting breast and capable arms? Though shrouded now in grizzled age and empurpled, arthritic motley, can he not still read her faithful heart? Where in the world could he be that would be too far for him to come back? What obstacle prevents him?

The idea that he might, like Mr Goldstein's son, be dead, assaults her momentarily, like a body blow, and she realises that she is unsteady, trembling, and that her face is wet. The mist is cold, eddying around her like a kind of sea, and permeating her nightdress with chill dampness. Was she told of it perhaps and has wiped it from her mind? Or has the devastating news been kept from her as an intended kindness? Would the supposed purposefulness of his desertion be easier to come to terms with than the permanence of his death? The idea of his perfect flesh and silken hair corrupted by the sucking clay of the grave is too much to endure.

Almost in answer to her questions a small figure appears from the back door of the house across the river. He is bleary with sleep, his hair tousled and his pyjamas baggy and askew. Seeing him, the man and the woman hold out an arm apiece. Mrs Fairlie also reaches out her arms to him, and Michael's name is on her lips. She takes a step forward into the opaque air and her foot fails to find solid ground. But as the child is embraced into the dance, so Mrs Fairlie finds herself caught and tightly wrapped by warm woollen arms, enfolded in a blanket.

'There you are!' Rosie scolds quietly. 'What a fright you gave me!'

MRS FAIRLIE'S NIGHT-TIME perambulations have had serious repercussions. Mrs Terrier has been in and given her a severe talking-to, threatening a cot attachment to the bed that will prevent her from getting out of it in the night or even in the morning without assistance.

'We cannot be permitted to wander around in the night,' she yaps, quite literally shaking her finger. 'I am surprised we would wish to give the nurses so much *more* trouble. It is bad enough that we insist on having our meals in our room.'

Mrs Fairlie pleads against the cot, and as a compromise is provided with a special bed-side rug that will ring an alarm if stepped on in the hours of darkness. She says nothing about the slight tightness in her chest or the heavy, heady feeling that presages a cold, and when Selene brings her lunch in on a tray, she is more voluble than usual with her thanks. In spite of the heat she is unable to leave her room in the afternoon. Her legs are trembly and weak. She lies on her bed and tries to sleep. Selene brings her a whirring white fan to cool the room. She cannot get out of her head the idea that Michael is dead and that no one has told her. She grapples with it until beads of sweat break out on her forehead. She wishes that Jennifer would come.

THE NEXT TIME Mrs Fairlie gets downstairs preparations for the Open Day have reached fever-pitch. Trestle tables have been erected and placed on the gravelled walkways under blue and white striped awnings. The folding chairs have been arranged in a ranked semi-circle around the May-pole and a class of school children have come to practice their dances, clutching the ends of the ribbons, skipping and weaving in intricate patterns to the tinny music from a portable cassette player. One girl is determined to be very silly and is eventually sent to sit alone on one of the chairs while the teacher, a capaciously girthed woman in her sixties, takes her place. She looks ridiculous as she capers and leaps in time to the music, and crouches to get under the arms of her diminutive class. Extra staff has been hired and they scurry around with stacks of plates and rolls of cutlery wrapped in napkins, pot plants and superfluous flower arrangements. There are other strangers, deliverymen, coming and going all day long with additional consignments of food. Every available space has been occupied with boxes and bags of donations. Mrs Quirk stumbles and almost falls over a fruit basket ill-advisedly left in the hallway. The kitchen is under pressure and meals are not served on time. Furniture has been moved around and there are signs pointing 'to the Tombola' and announcing 'Cream Teas' and indicating the nearest lavatories. The disruption has caused a few of the residents to look bewildered and distressed. Some are frustrated; they think today is the day. Pearl sits for an hour and a half in the Cream Tea room. Dr Fellowes wanders around waving a £20 note wanting to buy raffle tickets.

It is remarkable how, more and more, an episode or echo will trigger off a memory-journey, transporting Mrs Fairlie back in time into remembrances that are more vivid than the trigger. She sinks into them—like lying back in a comfortable, familiar bed—and lets them play across her mind; a cinematic treat. The Open Day preparations sweep her back thirty years to the Jubilee street party she and Annie organised; weeks in the planning, a list on the counter where people could sign up to provide a table or some chairs and the food ... But wait. *Was* the shop still open then? Maybe they went door to door ... For the Coronation street party they definitely had a list but she had only been married a few months then and Frederick's mother had done most of the organisation ... There had been a hoo-ha with the police and the council over sealing off the road to traffic; contingency plans had to be made for emergency vehicles. The men had put up the bunting between the lamp-posts, striding about and shouting directions, showing off, shouldering their ladders, looking gung-ho as men do when called upon to play a part in anything women have organised. She and Annie had carefully calculated the number of people in the street and decided how to deal with interlopers from neighbouring streets without the enterprise to organise their own party. They had gone into the pub on the corner to discuss things with the landlady—before this a person with whom they had had nothing whatever to do—so that she would be ready for additional off-sales of beer for the men and pop for the children. And through it all they had had an eye constantly on the weather, that could put a dampener on everything, or even cause a complete wash-out. It had been a source of constant anxiety because they had no contingency plan; no church hall where they could remove if the weather was poor. She recalls getting up early on the day, standing in the yard and smiling at the cloudless blue sky, and setting-to making the sandwiches and the sausage rolls, fairy cakes and pies. Later, they watched the Queen on television on walk-about in the capital, and she and Annie raised a glass to each other as neighbours emerged, manhandling tables through narrow front doors, fetching out table cloths and covering the tables with food and drink. Everyone had dressed in red white and blue. Even Jennifer, a sullen seventeen, enjoyed herself and got tiddly on cider from the pub, mischievously supplied to her by Annie's wayward youngest. And in the evening, Michael, arriving at the last minute from goodness knew where, played his accordion for them all as they danced on the cobbled street.

Her memories soften the disruption and intrusion of the Open Day so that she begins to feel even a frisson of excitement over the preparations and the bustle. It is like the same event but seen from a new angle and she finds herself juggling juxtapositions—the arrival of ghosts from her past parading through the doors of Bridge House—neighbours long-dead bearing plates of sandwiches and bottles of beer, children long-grown grasping the May-pole ribbons and dancing on the lawns, Jennifer and Pearl's William dancing in the mist on a moonlit night and Michael, arriving travel-stained and sun-browned, smelling of exotic foreign grasses, a silver tooth glinting in his mouth and his accordion swinging from its shoulder strap.

THE LITTLE BOY is building something against the sandy bank of the river. He must have been hard at it for a day or so. At first she thinks it is a bonfire; a tangle of sticks and brushwood—perhaps hedge trimmings or lopped off tree branches, stacked at an angle. But then she notices that he periodically disappears into some opening at the side and she discerns careful planning and design in his actions. Stakes are driven into the mud at an angle and he has woven branches between them to make a wattle wall that slopes towards the bank making a sort of lean-to.

She watches him as he labours. He wears shorts and trainers and his sun-hat, and a pair of what look like oversized gardening gauntlets—the branches must be rough or even prickly—she cannot quite see, at this distance. Her long distance vision is good but it is perhaps forty or fifty yards from where she sits, down the short slope of lawn, across the river to the bank where he is beavering away. She imagines red scratches and welts on his skinny arms. Sometimes he has difficulty dragging the branches from where they have been down at the far end of the garden under the fruit trees. The grass there is long—the man has not cut it—and the branches snag and tangle as the boy tugs at them. They still have leaves clinging to them. He pulls them between the flower beds, past the paddling pool, behind the trampoline and around the tepee. The other tent has been dismantled, she thinks, until she sees that it has been moved down to the flat river bank and incorporated into the den, the plaid of the rug is just visible in the shadow of the overhanging trees and bushes on the bank.

The boy works with quiet determination, overcoming obstacles with patience and ingenuity, and entirely alone. His sister swings, or bounces on the trampoline, or lies in the paddling pool. She talks to her dollies and passes in and out of the house from time to time, returning to the garden with biscuits or drinks or more toys to add to the collection inside her tepee. Every so often she wanders over to the den and casts an appraising eye over it. She must ask questions because the boy stops and points things out to her; the den's various facilities. It is an ambitious project and he works at it all afternoon. As a final touch he brings several wheel-barrow loads of grass cuttings and spreads them inside the den to make a soft floor. Mrs Fairlie smiles as she thinks how smelly and slimy they will turn in a few days' time. But perhaps by that time the den will have lost its appeal, or the weather will have broken.

The boy makes a flag pole from a bamboo cane and a tea towel, and plants it proprietarily in the soft sand of the exposed river bed. He makes several trips indoors and carries out a number of den accessories; a pair of binoculars, a notebook and pencil. Perhaps, she surmises, this is to be a hide, from where he can observe the ducklings and other wildlife. A large torch, a hearth rug and a sleeping bag all disappear inside the gloomy interior of the den, and a camping stove is carefully placed on a flat stone near the entrance together with a small metal saucepan and four brightly coloured plastic mugs. At this point the girl arrives with an armful of dollies and attempts to gain access but she is sent away with an imperious wave of the boy's grubby, scratched arm and she retreats in tears to the tepee.

The man arrives home and there is a flurry of activity. First of all the den is admired from every angle, inside and out. He puts an approving arm on the shoulder of the boy and nods and smiles, and the boy beams up at him from under the peak of his baseball cap. The man supervises the lighting of the camping stove, using his large hands to shield the match from the slight breeze as the boy strikes it and places it against the gas burner. Water is brought in a container and poured into the saucepan. The mother brings a tray with milk and cakes and the grown-ups perch on a fallen log while the boy makes cocoa, stirring the powder into the water.

'It will be lumpy,' Mrs Fairlie thinks to herself but of course she doesn't say anything and the two other grown-ups exchange a look but also keep quiet. The girl is eventually fetched from her sulk in the tepee and joins them with bad grace for their picnic. When the cocoa boils the woman makes as though to pour it but the man restrains her and the boy does it, very carefully, brown sludge sliding into the cups, adding sugar and milk and proudly handing them round. The girl pulls a face and shakes her head at the first sip, but the others bravely swallow the drink.

Her own afternoon drink is placed on a small table at her side.

'Look,' Mrs Fairlie says, turning her head slightly, 'Michael has made a den by the river.'

THE WEATHER BREAKS the evening before the Open Day. The whole day is as still and hot and tense as a balled fist. There isn't so much as a breath of breeze to lift the listless May-pole ribbons or rouse the sweltering leaves. It is crushing weather, the harsh sun making everything garish and painful to look upon; bright colours like knives.

The residents languish in the shade of the gazebo, oppressed by the heavy air, their chests rising and falling with difficulty. They swat ineffectually at the swarms of tiny black thunder flies that gather in towers in the shade, scratching at their pink, crawling scalps and repeatedly wiping their sweaty upper lips. They whimper and complain. Those who cannot bear it and who are sufficiently mobile attempt to gain access to the cool shade of the small lounge but it is all disarranged for the Open Day; the Mayor and Mayoress and a few select guests will enjoy their afternoon tea in privacy here. Mr Goldstein, perched in the foyer amongst the raffle prizes, fruit baskets, hampers and wine, like a booby prize in the draw, is the only one to feel relatively cool. Other inmates loiter around him looking for a seat, but they have all been rendered inaccessible by Open Day paraphernalia.

By late afternoon the sky has banked up a tower of purple-grey clouds and the crackle of electricity is almost palpable in the charged air. Then, like a breath held over-long the sky emits a long warm sigh, a gust of hot wind that shakes the blue and white awnings over the trestles with a snap and rattle, unnerving everyone. The scalloped edges of the gazebo quiver and tremble and the sheets of Mr Swindell's newspaper are sent fluttering like fledgling, birdless wings across the lawn. A plastic tumbler falls from a table and skitters across the gravel. There is a collective gasp and moan of anxiety from the dry-throated crones marooned like castaways on the wickerwork chairs. The wind boils the purple cloud over the sky and as the nurses scurry backwards and forwards assisting residents indoors it begins to go supernaturally dark. The garden is bathed in indigo and there is a sense of Armageddon. They can hear the thunder approaching like an enraged animal stalking over the land. The wind is portentous, warm, as though straight from hell, whipping the tops of the trees. The awnings flap like maddened, trapped creatures trying to tear themselves loose before the beast arrives to devour them. Then, with an ear-splitting crack the thunder breaks the sky apart and the rain descends in a deluge from heaven.

MRS FAIRLIE IS in her room, lying on the bed under the whirring breath of the electric fan. She has a slight fever but has managed to pass off her sweats and poor appetite as simply down to the heat. She will not for worlds cause the nurses more work after Mrs Terrier's jibe and in all the bustle of the Jubilee preparations her weekly medical check-up has somehow gone undone. She is thinking about Michael, letting images of him pass before her inner eye like a series of slides on a screen: the soft, peachy beauty of his baby skin, his funny single-toothed smile as he sat for the first time unaided on the patchwork quilt, the intensity of his eyes, his gossamer hair. She sees how smart he was in his school uniform on the day of his father's funeral, and feels his little hand holding tightly on to hers as they followed the coffin down to the graveside. She observes anew his frown of concentration and the physical effort required to wrestle his first accordion; it had been like an unwieldy prehistoric reptile writhing and wriggling in his inadequate arms. And then, as a teenager, his hair growing long and unkempt, his preference for shabby, frayed clothes, the strange, sweet, herby smell about him that she did not place until years later as the smell of marihuana. He had begun to go off for days, to 'gigs' and festivals, with his accordion and insufficient clean underwear. Then he had announced that he would 'busk' his way around Europe. She had watched him go, with his long-legged, loping stride, off down the cobbles of the street, a bulging back-pack over one shoulder and his accordion over the other. He had waved, once, from the corner, and she had experienced a sudden, inner sinking feeling, as though her heart had slipped out of her chest and landed with a soft, wet plop at her feet.

The soft thud is transformed into the noise of a falling dustbin and it makes her eyes fly open. She is amazed to see that her room is plunged into an unearthly purple darkness. There is rain like a shower of pebbles against her window pane and she identifies the crash as thunder. Immediately she is taken back to the last time she saw Michael.

A thunder storm—just like this one—but on a wintery night. The dogs had gone frantic at the sound, maddened by the sheets of blue-white lightning that had torn across the sky like the flicker of a demented celestial fluorescent tube. They had yelped and torn around in circles and cowered under the gate-leg table. Clarry had made a puddle. The sound of the rain against the window had been like a percussion instrument then, too, and she had been hurrying around the house to close the curtains when a sheet of lightning had illuminated the silhouette of Michael standing like a spectre out in the yard. She had thought for a moment that he was a ghost until he had smiled and lifted his hand in greeting.

How easy it is, from a distance, on the hundredth re-run of a scene, to see what a difference other words would have made. What if, while finding the back door key and wrenching it around in its un-oiled lock, and struggling with the bolts, she had used that few minutes to fight off the proud shield of hurt feelings so that when she opened the door to him, instead of barking out a gruff and unwelcoming retort like, 'Hello stranger,' or, 'About time too,' or even, (she grimaces) 'I'd almost given you up for dead' she had opened her arms to him and gathered him in, drenched as he was, and spoken the words her heart was crying out, 'My lovely boy. It's so wonderful to see you!' What if, instead of frowning, 'You're dripping on the carpet,' she had said, 'Take off your wet things son and come by the fire.' Why hadn't she offered to cook him food rather than baldly stating, 'I've had my supper,'? How had, 'You don't look well Michael. Are you all right?' turned into, 'Well! You look a state and no mistake.'? How could she not have interpreted his restless pacing and fidgeting hands as a sign of some inner turmoil, his several attempts to begin a sentence, his anxious, loaded eyes as evidence of some heavy, difficult pronouncement? But instead she had wittered on about Annie, making much—too much—of how good her children were to her, what regular visitors and generous benefactors, what good lives they had all made for themselves, that even the youngest, who had been in all kinds of bother, had settled at last. She had bemoaned the new neighbours and complained about her arthritis as he had roamed around the room, touching ornaments and gazing at pictures, stroking the material of his father's brown grocer's overall on the hook behind the door. In her head she had noted his sallow skin and fleshless bones, the yellow hue of his eyes, his filthy clothes, the grey in his hair and matted beard, but all her mouth had been able to utter was a sharp reprimand, 'Sit down lad, for God's sake, and keep still; you give me the jitters wandering about like that!'

In the morning the storm had gone, and so had Michael, and she weeps now, to think of all the things she could have said, as the rain lashes down and bruises all the summer petals.

IT POURS IN sheets all night long; a deluge of biblical proportions, and in the morning, although the worst of the downpour seems to be over, there is still a steady drenching drizzle. The lawn oozes with wetness, the gazebo and awnings flap and drip, and in the occasional gusts of wet wind fling sheets of water from their pooling roofs over everything adjacent. The seats of the folding chairs are all saturated and the ribbons of the May-pole have become impossibly tangled. The beautiful floral displays in the gardens are battered and flattened. Water stands in pools on the baked ground. In the night one end of the banner must have become detached; now it droops dejectedly across a bed of ravaged roses. Mrs Terry is beside herself, barking at the staff and residents alike, making hasty alternative plans for the Tombola and produce stalls. The nurses hurry everyone through the morning routine, and although Mrs Fairlie eyes the dresses in her wardrobe she pulls on the trousers and jumper she knows she can manage herself rather than put anyone to any trouble.

She has been harbouring the promise that the Open Day will produce relatives. Rosie's prediction and Pearl's confidence that her William will come has exhumed hope, and the arrival of last night's thunder has breathed into it an almost overwhelming sense of expectation; that once more the storm will bring her son. It makes her breathless with a choking, tight-chested anxiety that she will not, again, make the same mistakes. In spite of the rain and the cooler temperature the anticipation makes her hot and distracted, and she allows herself, after lunch, to be led down to the chair reserved for her in the day room and seated with the other residents ready for what she thinks about, in her heightened and confused state, as the Queen's walkabout.

On her slow walk through the ground floor and from her seat in the day room she can see that there is organised chaos. Stalls have been set up in the foyer and along the corridor, manned by relatives and cheery volunteers from the various church and women's organisations who regularly support the home. They are loaded down with jars of jam and pickle, cakes and pies and bottles of home-brewed wine. The tombola is crowded with a bizarre assortment of goods: toiletries and toys, plants and car accessories, a toilet brush, some crocheted place mats, an enormous stuffed Orang-utan, packets of sweets, satin-covered clothes hangers and sachets of pot-pourri. The curate is selling raffle tickets from a small card table stationed by the entrance. There is a hubbub of conversation as stall-holders make the best of the new arrangements and bemoan the change in the weather. The carpet is dark with moisture from wet footprints and dripping umbrellas and Mrs Mole is trying to lay strips of clear plastic matting to protect the main thoroughfares, getting in everyone's way.

The school children have been corralled in the conservatory; it seems that the wet grass and driving rain will not deter them from exhibiting. They are shrill with excitement, squealing; their voices set the residents' dentures on edge. Outside the stout little teacher is struggling to untangle the ribbons from around the pole, her light suit growing quickly dark with damp across the shoulders and under the arms, her hair—especially permed for the occasion—looking frizzled.

Everything outdoors is disconsolate, greyish brown and dejected. The bunting flaps like wet, psychedelic fish fillets from its string. The river has doubled in size, brown turgid water rushes past the banks now in a soupy flow. The mallard keeps her ducklings close to her; they crouch on the grass away from the bank, the brown fluff of their feathers black and matted by the rain.

The residents sit around the walls of the day room blinking dazedly at one another. Dr Fellowes complains querulously that she has not had her daily nap. Mr and Mrs Irons cling together as though about to be riven asunder by some judgement of doom. Pearl, uncomfortably seated, her little legs protruding from the chair, not able to raise her head very well, is desperately twisting and turning this way and that, spying through the crowds, gabbling her narrative at double quick time as though her life depends on her getting to the end of it before the ribbon is cut. 'It was Easter time. Easter was early ... and there was snow ... The walk up the ... quite tricky; the pavement was very icy ... a cruel wind ... After each exam we had tea ... a custard tart ... doughnut ... Eccles cake.'

Someone comes and takes a picture; an unpleasant, unctuous man who addresses them as his darling and his beauty. Mrs Fairlie never takes her eyes from the doorway.

The ribbon has been strung across the day room; a good idea when the event was to be held in the gardens but somewhat mystifying now that it is spread around indoors, mainly before the ribbon can be arrived at. Mrs Terry wanted it moved to the foyer but somebody had suggested that the residents would not, in that case, be able to witness the ceremony.

'Damn the residents!' she had been heard to yell, but the ribbon remains in the day room.

The space is becoming more crowded as relatives and visitors assemble. There is an overpowering smell of damp wool and overheated bodies as more and more people cram into the downstairs rooms. There are dignitaries from various organisations, local business people, neighbours and well-wishers, relatives, of course, bringing with them children—just this once, to make Granny's day—sullen and under sufferance. Also present against their wills are prospective future residents, brought along under the guise of a pleasant afternoon out, but really as a subliminal introduction to the idea of residential care. They are not fooled. They scowl and find fault, thinking of their own arm chairs and their independence. A number of reporters and press photographers mingle with the rest probing for a story that will make the gig worth missing the kick-off of the cup-final. From rival local papers, they greet each other with resigned smiles. 'Nothing doing here,' they agree in undertones, 'unless one of the old folks decides to croak.'

Before long the foyer and corridor is packed, with people spilling-over into the dining room and the small lounge; the sign declaring 'VIP Guests ONLY' has been knocked aside and is now underfoot. People are restive, wanting to begin the activities, eyeing the tombola stall and the produce, enquiring about teas. But the Mayoral party is late and Mrs Terry will not countenance a commencement until the protocol has been fully observed.

The unaccustomed noise and activity and disrupted routine are beginning to have a detrimental effect on the old people. The nurses disperse themselves around the patients, perching on the arms of their chairs or stationing themselves behind, stroking anxious hands and giving reassurance. There is an unmistakable and pungent aroma of urine in the day room. The nurses throw each other significant glances, but it is far too late to identify the culprit now and so the lavatorial lapse goes politely unmentioned.

Finally there is a rustle of excitement and the news permeates around the room that the Mayoral car has arrived. Mrs Terry is like a dog with two bones, quivering with self-importance and wagging her metaphorical tail. Even the school children are silenced at the prospect of the august arrival. The kitchen staff are ushered in, hastily tying fresh white aprons, and a waft of hot scones adds itself to the medley of scents already at large; wet clothes, hot-house flowers, distressed old people. The press take photographs of the arrival with eye-dazzling flash bulbs. Later, reviewing the press coverage, Mrs Terry will be dismayed to see that in every single picture her eyes are closed.

Mrs Fairlie finds herself placed next to Pinkie. Close to she is even more insubstantial; a mere gossamer of existence. Her skin is the finest translucent tissue over a tracery of blue veins and grey, bird-like bones. Her eyes, milky with cataracts, are sunk deeply into her fragile skull, the contours of her sockets as visible as smooth porcelain under their opaque membrane. Her hair is a diaphanous white wisp of down on the pink shell of her crown. Her hands are skeletal, claw-like, the twin twigs of her wrist bones disappearing into the sleeves of a candyfloss pink woollen cardigan that lies on her chair occupying the space where her body ought to be. The empty cardigan and some brushed cotton trousers in strawberry milk-shake pink, and a rose-pink cellular blanket take up the seat of a substantial wheeled reclining chair that can now be seen to house beneath it a discreet oxygen cylinder and a pouch of some clear fluid with a tube that disappears underneath Pinkie's clothes. It looks as though Pinkie's essence is being decanted into the pouch drip by drip.

Mrs Fairlie's attention is distracted by Mrs Terrier's voice, yapping at the guests to step to one side, and there is some good-humoured pushing and squashing as they make way for the party of dignitaries. Then the Mayor is in the room. It is not, of course, the Mayor with whom Mrs Fairlie has had dealings in the past, when Frederick was involved with the Chamber of Commerce. This is a disappointingly diminutive man, dapper but thin to the point of emaciation; his heavy official chains seem to weigh him down almost beyond his endurance. Before cutting the ribbon he passes around the room stooping to greet one or two of the residents with a kindly word. Arriving at Pinkie's chair he reaches out and grasps her hand-bones with all the grim determination of a medical student commencing his first post-mortem.

She smiles up at him sweetly, before asking, in a voice surprisingly loud and clear, 'And who the fuck are you?'

AFTER THE FURORE of the ribbon-cutting, events move quickly. Visitors surge, first towards the stalls and tea tables and then towards their relatives, overwhelming them with extravagant—and unusual—gestures of affection. There is wholesale scoffing of cream teas; the inmates don't stand a chance in the crush around the tables and look on in dismay as the heaps of scones, pastries and savouries disappear before their eyes.

Out in the rain the school children skip and caper around the May-pole on the sodden grass. With the doors and windows closed against the rain their music is inaudible and the glass, steamy on the inside and beaded with rain on the outside, makes them all but invisible. But anyway, nobody is taking any notice of them apart from three or four parents, who shrink from the wind and drizzle under inadequate umbrellas.

Jennifer makes her way eventually to her mother. Kenny loiters two steps behind her, alternately rolling his eyes and glancing at his watch. An enormous Orang-utan is squashed under his arm and it is difficult to tell which of the two of them is most unhappy with the unlikely pairing.

'Hello Mum!' Jennifer gushes. 'It's so nice to see you in here with your friends, instead of skulking in your room.' Mrs Fairlie cranes her neck, but there is no Michael.

'I can't stay very long today, I'm afraid, there's a …' Jennifer is saying but Mrs Fairlie interrupts her.

'Where is your brother?' she asks clearly.

Jennifer is visibly taken aback. 'Michael?' she prevaricates.

Mrs Fairlie nods patiently, as though, of the two of them, Jennifer is the more likely to exhibit signs of forgetfulness. 'Yes. Where is your brother Michael?'

Jennifer looks around her. There is no available seat and she has been squatting in front of her mother. Now she stands up. 'Gosh! It's such a crush in here. What a crowd!' She looks across at Kenny who has been pushed back towards the day room door, but he offers her no assistance other than to shift the Orang-utan bad-temperedly from one arm to the other.

'Jennifer!' Mrs Fairlie calls her attention back.

'Oh Mum, I don't think we can talk about that now,' she says nervously.

'I *want* to talk about it. I want to *know*,' Mrs Fairlie says. Her eyes, eyes the colour of her name, are earnest.

'Michael is ... oh Mum ... were you hoping he'd come?' Jennifer suddenly cottons on. She sees her mother's iris-blue eyes fill up with liquid. She has dreaded this. She looks over her shoulder again at Kenny, who slowly holds up his wrist and points at his watch. 'Kick-off in half an hour,' he mouths.

'He couldn't come, Mum. Michael couldn't have come,' she says vaguely.

'Why?' She takes a deep breath, ready to push it, the possibility of it, out into the open, giving it birth. 'Is he dead?'

Jennifer starts. How can she explain it, here, *now?* Her eyes rove around the room, anywhere but at her mother's anxious but determined face. Eventually she leans forward and speaks.

'He's gone, Mum. Michael has gone.'

'Gone?'

'Yes. The Michael we remember has gone.'

Suddenly Mrs Fairlie crumbles back into her chair. 'I don't understand,' she sobs, wringing her swollen, painful hands. 'I don't understand.'

Jennifer feels a hand on her elbow. 'Jennifer.' It is Kenny.

'I'm sorry Mum, but we have to go.' Jennifer puts her cool white hand over her mother's and then is gone into the crowd.

Close by Mr and Mrs Irons have been joined by their family; three sons, their wives and numerous children. They nod and blink at the small crowd that surrounds them. They can hardly believe that their atrophied flesh can have been the source of such abundant life. Pinkie is accompanied by a lady and a gentleman who cradle her between them. The gentleman administers sips of tea from a spouted beaker gently placed between her parched lips. 'There you are, Mum,' he says tenderly. Across the room, Pearl bends over the hand of a tall, upright man, smartly—if a little flamboyantly—dressed in a cream suit, colourful paisley cravat and a rakish boater. He allows her to hold his hand. She is talking to it earnestly. Mrs Fairlie can make out the words, 'Doughnut, custard tart, Eccles cake,' repeated several times. Pearl has got stuck like a needle on a record. The round curl of the woman and the tall, thin erectness of the man make them look like a question mark and an exclamation mark next to each other on a page. He looks over the heads of the crowd towards the exit where his companion waits, languidly inspecting his nail varnish.

Alone in a corner Mr Goldstein weeps unobserved, clutching a toilet brush.

From her seat Mrs Fairlie can see only the hips and bottoms of the visitors who stand in garrulous groups around the day room exchanging pleasantries. The aspect makes them all seem too tall and intimidating and rather rude; they tower over her and make her feel small. The noise of bright conversation is too much for her. The humid air is making it difficult for her to breathe and the overwhelming smell of hot, damp bodies is making her feel nauseous. She reaches for her zither and the crowds part and let her through.

The Atrium is empty of people but there is in evidence the sticky detritus of cream teas; jam- and cream-smeared plates are stacked on the low tables and also on the floor; someone has left their sandwich crusts on the soil around a yucca plant, a lump of pork pie has been dropped on the carpet and trodden on. But at least it is a little cooler in here. The predominant noise is of water on glass, rain drops like a million tiny beads being dropped onto the glass roof. The windows are not as steamy although they still run with water on the outside; it looks as though the rain has intensified.

The garden is empty. The school children have been taken away by their teacher, leaving a brown muddy circle of trodden grass around the May-pole; a filthy fairy ring. Mrs Fairlie takes a few deep breaths and makes her way into the conservatory. As she enters, a small party exits through the doors into the dining room and she is alone.

From the dining room she hears shushing and a distant male voice begins to make a speech. The voice drones on interminably, rising and falling. At intervals there is a polite ripple of laughter and someone says, 'Hear hear'. Mrs Fairlie makes no attempt to listen; she leans on her zither and rests her hot forehead against the cool glass of the French doors. Her breath steams up the window. That, and the runnels of water on the outside of the glass, and the pouring rain, and the strange dull yellow light outdoors all mean that she is not able to see clearly at first. It is like trying to see underwater, and when the time comes for her to move that too comes with a dream-like, underwater slowness.

Through the driving rain, under the leaden sky, across the thick brown viscous waters of the river a small child is struggling. The water level has risen dramatically, swollen by rain and surface-water that has poured off the sun-baked fields and from drains under roads. The surface of the river now slides almost level with the grassy embankment. It roils and boils, its surface a churning, coffee coloured scum. Gouts of yellow foam ride its waves and cling to overhanging foliage. It carries fallen trees on its surf as well as detritus washed off the banks upstream and sluiced from the drainage system; plastic bags, a punctured football, a solitary shoe and other flotsam not clearly identifiable beneath the agitated surface. The water flows swiftly, like

281

boiling milky gravy gushing from some spout, deep and dangerous. The silty beach and the sandy bank are entirely covered. The fallen log where the adults sat and drank cocoa has been submerged or, more likely, carried away in the irresistible surge of rain-engorged waters.

The boy is pulling and tugging at something trapped in a tangle of branches against the water's edge. It is badly snagged up, a drenched reddish brown blanket. The boy leans all his weight against it and finally yanks it free and drags it onto the grass; the tartan travel rug. Then he kneels on the bank and plunges his arm down amongst the sticks and wattle of his den, groping around up to his shoulder in turgid water and grasping twigs. His actions are destabilising the den and gradually its outer layers are loosened and carried away on the water. With a cry he pulls out the binoculars and flings them behind him onto the blanket. Then, as she watches, he reaches with a tentative foot down into the water, testing to see how deep it is, his body prone on the wet grass of the bank-top as his foot reaches deeper and deeper. Alarm bells begin to ring in Mrs Fairlie's head. Her hand is on the door handle. She must tell him to stop; it's too dangerous.

His foot finds the bed of the river and he stands up. He is almost waist deep in the cold, fast-flowing water. He holds his arms up and begins to plunge them into the den, searching for its opening, pressing himself against it and at the same time pulling away more outer and uppermost branches. The water eddies around his insubstantial form, churning chocolate and thick with choking silt and perilous debris.

The door is locked. Mrs Fairlie's swollen fingers struggle with the tiny key. Her hands are shaking.

The boy ventures a little way from the bank, his arms and one leg is deeply enmeshed in the fabric of the den. She knows what he is looking for; the torch. Away from the bank the water flows more quickly and she can see that he is struggling to keep himself upright. Almost as though she can read his mind she sees him decide that it's too risky. His little body stiffens with encroaching panic and he begins to flounder as he tries to make his way back to the bank where there are overhanging grasses and shrubs he can cling on to.

Finally she gets the key to turn and she opens the French door. If the crowd in the dining room is aware of a gust of cold air or the sudden sound of wildly rushing water, no one turns to look. The Mayor is still speaking, at length, propounding some political dogma with evangelical zeal.

The boy's machinations have fatally undermined the den's construction and suddenly it breaks free and is carried swiftly downstream, a nest of sticks and foliage undulating on the current. With nothing to hold on to the boy's predicament is suddenly much worse. With his whole body he tries to resist the push and surge of the tide. He is chest-deep now. The water against his back rises up in a bow-wave and reaches the hair at the back of his neck. He is an arm's length from the bank but he knows that if he raises one foot off the river bed to take the necessary step he will be swept away.

From the French window Mrs Fairlie shouts a warning; to the boy, to the people in the dining room. The boy hears her and turns his small white face to her, but just at that moment the Mayor's droning speech comes to a close and there is a burst of grateful applause that drowns out her voice.

The boy holds out a hand to Mrs Fairlie and she lifts the zither over the threshold and steps out behind it to begin the short descent down the sloping lawn to her side of the river. Of course it is quite hopeless; they both know it. She is a helpless old lady marooned in debilitating age and arthritis and he is a helpless little boy stranded in a river in spate. Before she has covered ten yards her zither wheel catches on a tussock and comes to an abrupt halt. Unable to stop the impetus of her motion she is sent headlong over it and as she lands across its metal frame she hears a dull crack from her right hip. Prone across the frame, she raises her head and stretches out her arm to her son. With a brave, hopeless smile, he is swept away.

SHE IS BEING dragged by the leg. The pain is intense and she struggles against them, her attackers. So at last they have come; those brisk, faceless, rubber-handed orderlies. They will drag her down to the river and fling her by the leg across its tumultuous surface. She will drown in its brown foaming waters, with the Queen looking on in polite interest.

The more she struggles the worse it hurts but she is not ready to be taken yet. Her boy needs her and she tries to tell them that he is drowning but they have taken away her teeth and incoherence is all she can manage as her tongue flaps uselessly against her shrivelled gums.

Faces loom in and out of her vision. Some she recognises; Mrs Terrier, snarling through her bottom-shaped mouth, Rosie, a cool, reassuring hand snatched away as her body is thrown around, first on the grass and then on a gurney, jolted over rough terrain towards the river. But as she is lifted and braces herself she is aware of the smooth white ceiling of some vehicle, the sharp restraint of straps and being smothered by a plastic mask that magnifies the sound of her own breathing in her ears; the wheeze of constriction in deep chambers, the laboured breath of an enormous, wounded beast. She wonders again if she is already under the water, but when she opens her eyes she is in a repository for the dead, a cold place with cold white lights, wrapped in a cold white shroud.

*

Why must they drag her by the leg?

*

Somebody is moaning and complaining, a ceaseless whine of misery that echoes around the white empty space and grates on her nerves. Her leg has gone; she has no feeling in it at all. She is decomposing from the feet; her limbs will fall away like withered leaves until only her head will rest on the pillow. How could she not have recognised it in Pinkie? Her strew of pink clothing where her body had once been.

She thinks again of the boy in the river, of her boy on the seas, her son on the tractor in an ocean of waving grass. He is sinking under the water and needs rescue and she tries again to get her rebellious tongue to form the warning. At the same time another voice, vaguely familiar, begins to rabbit about dining furniture and compost. The whimpering becomes more urgent but the other voice redoubles her efforts, as though on purpose to drown it out.

She wishes she could turn her head to see the bodies stacked against the walls, waiting for the final guttering breath, the last flickering flame of consciousness to be extinguished. She knows they are there; tens, perhaps hundreds of them in a holding pattern in the anteroom, being readied for their descent, for the final crossing, the last bridge of all. But she is restricted by tubes and a band around her chest; they are squeezing the life from her, draining her away.

*

She is hot, so hot. Is it the fires? Then cold, drenched in ice cold sweat.

A green-masked official leans over her. She has dark eyes, not unkind. When she speaks her mask quivers and billows.

'Shush now. Shhhhhhh,' she says.

*

At some point—at several points, perhaps—there is Jennifer, and also Rosie. She sees them pass the periphery of her vision, or senses them sitting nearby. Or perhaps she only thinks she senses them. Minutes, hours, days. She has no idea. The only clue to time passing is the change in her view of the ceiling. She is moved from one side-room to another, then to a windy corridor, then a warm chamber, finally to a noisy intersection. She takes no notice of it. She has withdrawn to the innermost chamber of herself to guard her treasure, her last bastion, to make her final stand. But when she un-cups her hands to glimpse the precious thing they are empty, and the misery is overwhelming because it is gone and she can't remember what it was. In the extremes of her distress there is comfort from someone, but it does not permeate the hard shell of her loss.

THE FIRST AVAILABLE off-peak train is as packed as it can be with evening travellers going north from London. There are business people—self—important with their laptop computers—and holiday-makers who tow wheeled cases. Day-trippers struggle with shopping bags alongside back-packers, students and squaddies on leave. They all cram the carriages. Those who have reserved seating locate and sink into it gratefully. The others range up and down the narrow aisles looking for a seat. In carriage F, the quiet carriage at the back of the train, every seat is reserved and all but two are occupied. The two spare seats are eyed by hopeful passengers who are not looking forward to standing between Euston and Watford, or even beyond. There is jostle as people struggle to accommodate their luggage, get out their books and spectacles and crosswords for the journey. They strategically occupy space on the tables, establishing boundaries.

The doors close. On the platform the guard raises his baton and puts his whistle to his lips. There is a collective sigh amongst the passengers as they bring themselves to terms with their agonising journey to the station by tube or in taxis ensnared by traffic and their frantic search for the right platform. They put behind them their dithering over whether they had time to buy an over-priced sandwich on the station concourse before boarding. Once the whistle is blown there will be a sense of no-return to the whole day. The passengers wait for the blessed finality of it, and for the jolt of movement, ready to accept the consequences of whatever, now, cannot be undone: the meeting that cannot be revisited, the purchases that can't be returned, the decisions which must now remain.

But at the last possible moment there is a cry from down the platform and a final passenger runs for the train. The guard makes an urgent signal with his baton and presses the open-door mechanism to admit him. The occupants of carriage F eye him with alarm as he makes his burdened way along the platform and there is a communal in-drawing of breath as they make the connection between him and the two unoccupied seats in their midst. The standing passengers in the vestibule between carriages let go of all hope as he struggles past them.

Like them he is harassed. He has had a difficult day. He carries, like them, awkward, unwieldy luggage that must be borne, stowed and watched with a jealous eye. He has a duffel bag and a cumbersome boxy thing that some identify as an accordion although it seems odd that a man like *him* should possess such a beautiful instrument. It is encased in iridescent mother-of-pearl with bright chrome facings and creamy ivory keys. Additionally, like them, he has emotional burdens that encumber him. But he is not like them. They know it, and their reaction is to ignore him with grim-faced determination.

He is a traveller, an itinerant. A man you might see squatting in a doorway or on a park bench, and pass by quickly. He does not conform to the settled mores of traditional social patterns; he has rendered himself outcast. Perhaps at first by choice he took the road to wild and unfrequented places, enjoying the freedom of a careless day-to-day existence, falling in with bands of like-minded wanderers for a while before drifting off alone in his own direction. In his youth it was romantic and enviable, a heady cocktail of experiences, free-roving, transported and sustained by music. He was a lone figure amid exotic landscapes, a partaker, a taster of all that came his way. A figure of legend—in his own mind at least—questing, borne along towards some inner place of truth by a plethora of hallucinogenic stimulants, their magic coursing through his veins with a deadly potency.

But later he found he was so far off the beaten track that a return to normality was a journey too far. He was out on a limb, way, *way* beyond the pale. Too many boundless, empty desert distances separated him from the ordinary. He is indelibly stained by travel and non-conformity, out of step with the world as it has become while his back was turned; a perpetual outsider who can never be readmitted. He has the look of a lost one—will always be the subject of glances cast askance—and is socially ill-equipped, with no money, profession, friends or home, no history, no laurels on which to rest. Physically and socially exiled, his mind is also expatriated to a distant twilight periphery; addled by addictions and by loneliness, subject to a chemical experiment of counter-active intoxicants that have loosened connections and dulled receptors. He is subject now to bizarre volitions, fantastical notions and sudden incongruous impulses barely kept at bay by the medications dispensed by philanthropic doctors during his occasional sojourns at hostels and shelters.

He is unwashed. His clothes are travel-stained and grimy. His hair is matted and his beard unkempt. In his eyes there is that distant, disconnected look that makes him unpredictable and frightening, unlikely to behave or react in any expected way. He is the kind of travelling companion nobody wants, involuntarily shrunk from. Those seated closest to him re-address their boundaries, pulling bags and packages a little closer to their feet, refolding jackets, keeping their eyes resolutely away from him, wanting to avoid at all costs any inadvertent contact. They know, from shuddering, memorable past experiences on tubes and at bus stops late at night, he is the type of person with whom a polite and meaningless pleasantry, a mere smile, will signal an opening to endless, relentless, rambling talk.

But in fact in this assumption they are only partly justified. The man brings with him his own companion and conversational repository; a medium sized black dog of indeterminate but predominantly terrier breed attached to the man via a piece of string and also via connections of a deeper, emotional fabric. The dog follows where he leads, sits where he is put, does as he is told and regards the man at all times with a steadfast, unclouded trust and affection. The man addresses the dog as Snowy, perhaps in an ironic reference to his colour or, more likely, in literary tribute to the companion of Hergé's adventurer. The allusion spreads its allure, perhaps, from the dog to the man; he would be a hero. From the moment he steps on board, as the train finally shudders and pulls away, and for almost the entire duration of the journey, the man addresses his comments and observations at inappropriate volume to Snowy, who absorbs the meandering diatribe with gentle equanimity.

The traveller is immediately voluble at the fare for a man and his dog, as the platform and the broad fan of Euston's rails slide past the carriage windows. As he rants, he settles Snowy in the foot well in front of their seats, rummaging in his duffel bag for a bowl and pouring water from a plastic bottle. His language is vitriolic and causes one or two passengers to frown; someone even tuts, but regrets it and stares with deeper concentration at her paperback.

'A hundred and sixty fucking quid for the two of us, to get crammed in here like fucking sardines! Can you believe it, Snowy? And then they weren't going to wait for us!'

He is not unaware of the inappropriateness of his words, that he is too loud, that in the restrained silence of the 'quiet' carriage his voice is causing uneasiness. His next words to the dog reveal his consciousness and his carelessness of the reaction he provokes.

'There you are, Snowy, lad,' he says, placing the water down. 'Don't you worry; you've a right to be here, same as these fuckers.'

He strokes the dog fondly for a moment before bursting out again, 'A hundred and sixty fucking quid! I couldn't believe it! We'll be writing to Richard Branson!'

He is still standing, divesting himself of his heavy coat, the kind that used, in the days when it was fashionable, to be called an Afghan. It is old, heavy, much stained pale leather with a shabby, flea-bitten fur trim and exotic embroidery now rendered indistinct. For the heat of the City in June it is unsuitable garb and as he takes it off there is a tangible escape of body heat and odour from the man and the coat alike, from which those nearby cower.

From his elevated position he casts his eye around the carriage but nobody meets it. 'A hundred and sixty!' he repeats, defiantly. 'I'll be telling Richard fucking Branson what we think about that; don't you worry. It's highway fucking robbery! That's what it is!'

There is a pause while he manoeuvres his coat and duffel into a tight space on the overhead rack next to somebody's laptop case. The case's owner tenses but says nothing. Those around the vagrant allow their gaze to travel surreptitiously along the carriage floor to his feet. They are encased in substantial leather sandals; large feet, thickly tendoned, thin and very dirty. Jesus feet. He wears pale blue jeans, frayed around the bottoms. Beyond that they do not dare, at this stage, to look.

He begins to hold forth again. 'See how *he* likes paying that kind of money to get crammed into a tin can with the great unwashed, eh?'

It is impossible to tell whether he is conscious of the irony or of the insult he has just uttered. He places the accordion carefully onto the seat next to his, in front of Snowy. It is a beautiful thing, speaking of history and quality and craftsmanship, probably a very valuable and precious artefact. Against this man it seems an anachronism and yet he is clearly very attached to it. He alternates his touch between the lustred surfaces of the instrument and the soft head of the dog, stroking both at intervals, seeming to derive comfort equally from both.

'I wouldn't put a dog in these conditions if I didn't have to,' he sallies again, at the top of his spleen. But suddenly his anger dissipates. 'But it's all right, Snowy,' he says reassuringly, more quietly, 'it'll be worth it when we get there. Yes it will.'

Presently the man sits down. Like the other passengers he is now ready to let the history of his day go; the money is paid, the train is *en route*.

'And where we're going, Snowy, is home,' he says, reaching out a long-fingered hand to the dog's head and caressing it. 'Yes, we're going home.' At the word, there is a strange catch in the man's voice. If anyone had dared to look at his eyes, they would have been glassy.

He spots the unseated passengers loitering in the vestibule. 'Need a seat?' he cries, indicating the one next to him, its cushion encumbered by accordion, its foot-well by Snowy. The unhappy seat-less avoid his eyes. 'Suit yourselves!' he shouts, triumphantly.

'This is a 'quiet' carriage,' says a lone, disembodied voice from much further down the carriage, impossible to identify.

'Shut the fuck up then!' the man reposts.

There is a squeal and the public address system leaps into life. The announcer begins to list the scheduled stops of the train, but his message is rendered incomprehensible by the squeak and crackle of the defective tannoy, tooth-shattering feedback undergirded by a far-galactic whisper of fuzzy static. Place names are distorted beyond recognition.

'He's speaking binary!' the man shouts, uproariously. 'Better remind me, Snowy: *note to self,* Snowy, *note to self:* when we write to that bastard Branson, we'll tell him that he oughtn't to be employing bloody *aliens* on his trains. Bloody *aliens!* Can't understand a fucking word, can we Snowy?'

His language causes a frisson down the carriage and disaffects still further—if possible—the other travellers. He continues in this vein for some time, before absent-mindedly lifting the accordion onto his lap and running his long, grimy fingers along its immaculate keys. The action seems to soothe him and he lapses into a partial silence with only the occasional expletive or ejaculated comment bursting from his lips, as though escaping from some inner soliloquy.

Then, abruptly the man gets up and walks unsteadily to the end of the carriage. From the doorway he looks back at Snowy, whose anxious eyes peer round the edge of the seat.

'You stay there, lad. I'll be back,' the man says.

In his absence, one or two passengers exchange sympathetic looks. More than one of the people closest to his seat contemplates getting up and searching for alternative accommodation further along the train, but the knot of travellers without seats convinces them that other seats are not to be had.

He returns from the buffet with a packet of beef flavour crisps, two miniatures of vodka and an empty plastic tumbler. He opens the crisps and places them on the floor for Snowy before pouring both bottles of vodka into the glass for himself. They are swiftly gone.

The next time he stands up it is to pull a much folded newspaper cutting from his back pocket. The empty cup falls unnoticed to the floor. He re-reads the report, which concerns an Open Day held at a nursing home at which an elderly resident suffered a fall. The resident's name is circled and at the top of the cutting the words, 'You had better come,' have been written almost illegibly in a black biro scrawl. The cutting and £200 were waiting for him in an envelope at St Boltoph's crypt, a place where he occasionally goes for food or medical attention.

He shakes his head wonderingly. 'I just can't believe it, Snowy,' he says. 'My mum in a *home*. They've put my *mum* in a *home!* Whatever for? She could eat a social worker for breakfast could my mum!' He chuckles for a while at this idea, before sobering again and hissing, 'Without telling me. Without even *asking* me. Like she has no one to look after her. And ...' he chokes for a moment, at the nub of it, '... she will have wondered, Snowy, why I didn't *come!*

The outrage and bewilderment that brims through his voice register with his listeners. They all have mothers. He looks up abruptly, as though sensing their awakening sympathy, but alienates them all at a stroke with his next words, pent up with anger and distress, which both, generally, require someone to blame.

'No one,' he bawls down the carriage, 'puts *my* mother in a home, Snowy! Not while there's breath in my body!'

The tannoy crackles once more into life and the announcer tries to alert passengers to their imminent arrival at Watford. A few grateful travellers begin to gather their belongings. The man strides off down the carriage once more towards the buffet, haranguing Richard Branson at the top of his voice.

Later, after more vodka, he opens up the accordion, nestling it onto his lap like a small child. It is dusk now and the electric light inside the carriage illuminates the sheen of the mother-of-pearl and glints off the bright chrome. The passengers are reflected in the windows against the pinkish blue gloaming light, mirror images of themselves rushing through the evening like holograms suspended above the embankments. Slowly he unclips the various straps and fastenings that release the bellows and the accordion inhales, a new-born breath. Then, with a motion as smooth and unconscious as breathing, he begins to play. The instrument is so integral that it seems as though the music exudes from him, from the breath of an extrinsic lung playing over the delicate reeds of his bones. A personal essence of beautiful sound escapes in harmonious, glistening streams from the very flesh of him. The music swells and freshens the stale carriage atmosphere with bitter-sweet poignancy. It leaps over personal barriers and the borders of accepted commuting conduct in a bound.

There is a collective shudder as the sound assails the travellers, speaking to them too suddenly of things too naked; a streaker between the seats. It is his expression, speaking his travelogue, painting the colour of exotic air and the splendour of astonishing vistas. In the stuffy confines of the railway carriage it is an anachronism. It has voices, this aria, and pictures; its tinnitus of images flows into the inner ear and whispers. The notes reach joyous peaks and plunder deepest darkness, and linger in lonely hours of solitary flight across featureless landscapes; the indescribable loss of being lost; a lilt of lunacy. The music speaks the words he cannot say and the feelings he cannot express; the bitter depths of the man's heart, the extraordinary breadth of his living, the heights of his impossible dreams, his isolation—a barren expanse. The song seeks his resting; a safe, sheltered harbour, the firm handhold in the cacophony of his life that seems perpetually to evade his grasp.

The response from the other passengers is typically British; they remain unmoved as the reeds sing like plucked heart-strings, the music swelling and filling the space in wave-like crescendos, washing around them with heavenly cadences, weaving the rhythm of the wheels over the tracks into its fabric, a song which needs no words, speaking of home.

SOMEWHERE AT AN impossible distance there is noise and activity: people walking and talking, bells ringing, the swish of doors and the squeak of feet on polished floors. There are bells and alarms and the regular rhythmic bing of some electric thing.

The lift doors must be stuck. The shop bell is pinging. There is someone in the shop. She must go through. There is a customer.

But she cannot move. Her leg is trapped and the pain of it makes her cry out. Somebody comes and there is a sudden flood of warmth, a sense of everything draining away, the pain goes with it, slithering off the table in a viscous coagulated flow like the stuff that comes with a lamb or a baby or in an egg. It has a name but she cannot think of it. She is annoyed by this but soon her annoyance too begins to drain away. She is releasing it all, feeling at last that the time for fighting is over. She cannot remember, exactly, now, what she has been fighting for. Why has she been clinging on so hard? Better to just let it go.

In her head, the shallow wheeze of her breath falters. The bing of the lift is slowing, slowing ...

... In the hiatus she thinks of Frederick waiting for her in the good grey suit he was buried in, looking dapper, his spectacles polished and a clean white handkerchief in his breast pocket. Waiting for her patiently at the far side of the bridge with the book he has been reading to pass the time. There was always a book, with Frederick. There will be Annie, too, and all the dogs they have lost over the years. In her mind they are joined by a shadowy, lean, insubstantial figure ...

No no no.

She rallies herself. There is a catch and a huge in-breath, as though she has surfaced from under water. The lift door recovers itself. Bing. Bing. Bing.

*

Amniotic fluid.

*

Then he is there. A hue and cry announces him. Nurses protest. A dog barks somewhere; not Clarry. He leans over her and she can see his eyes— iris-blue, like hers—over the mask. She can feel his hand rummaging under the shroud and taking hers. It is warm and strong. Her words spill in water from her eyes and she experiences at last a drenching out-pouring of everything. She releases it—every last pent up drop—although what it is she cannot remember now amid the joy that floods in.

Her beautiful boy.

They do not speak. There is nothing, nothing at all that needs to be said. His coming, his being here, the flesh and blood of him is all.

From the golden centre of the overwhelming peace she is aware of one final ounce of something that prevents its completion; a last, tiny, tenuous thread clinging, making a hazy shadow on the periphery of the bright illumination. He sees it too. They always had it; that ability to see the same thing at the same time, to know without saying. It is the smallest thing, a glimmer of gossamer. Quite deliberately she plucks it loose.

She smiles and closes her eyes with a sigh. A long, long, contented sigh.

She can rest, now.

BOOK 3

THROUGH TROUBLED WATERS

SKINNER'S MOTHER HAS almost stopped looking for him now, in the faces of the breakfast-eating crowds. She is beginning to believe that she might be free.

Free at least within this removed, unreal world, suspended between the roaring tarmac and the yawning sky. It is a bridge from nowhere to nowhere else, set within an artificial landscape of spurious hills and counterfeit woodland.

He would never think of looking for her here; the indigenous population never gives this place a second thought. They have no need of its facilities and behave as though there is something slightly shameful about it, its blatant commercialism as reprehensible as a pollution-spewing chemical plant or a vivisection laboratory. It is held firmly below their collective radar.

No one at all intends to go there but every day thousands are inexorably drawn. They are crumpled and often short tempered, but not because of this; it has no bearing on their mood. It hardly features as more than a necessary hiatus as they hurry from A to B. There is no excitement of departure, no relief of arrival, only the interim of the incomplete journey. And while they frown at the prices and grumble at the queues, in half an hour they will be back *en route* and their brief diversion will be insubstantial in their memories. The food they ate, the woman clearing plates in the all-day-breakfast café, will be forgotten.

She sometimes thinks of it as just a mirage; that she herself is nothing more than a hologram, hazily projected as part of its space-age architecture. It has twin domes—many-faceted in mirrored glass—with a skeletal cladding of bone-white joints. Arching steel girders and sloping windows form a bridge from one to the other across the deep gorge of the motorway. It all shimmers in the pearlescent haze of pollution. It is surreal, plonked here onto the bucolic topography like a pair of umbilically connected, glowing meteors. It is some dew-eyed designer's idea of a contemporary oasis from the rigors of travel; a sanctuary of terraces, fountains and piped music. But the terraces are always deserted, their furniture slick with grime and slime, the fountains choked with litter, the pan-pipes inaudible above the roar of traffic. She stands there sometimes, on the south-bound site, waiting for the bus, and imagines the outside spaces peopled by ghostly motorists impervious to the smell and noise, calmly drinking lattes and eating perpetual breakfasts. Like the café customers, like her, they are arrested in time; always breakfast and never, ever, lunch.

SHE—MEGAN—QUITE likes the early shift, especially on cool clear mornings like this one. Such a relief, before the oppression of heat-wave overwhelms them all. She likes the sleepy calm of the town as she quietly closes and locks her door and steps through the gloom of the archway and out onto the empty street. It is at rest, released for the time being from that fretful angst that is eating at them all with parched ferocity.

At just after five o'clock the light has a blue-green, almost aqueous hue, and the grey buildings reflect back only a dull chill. The rosy tints on the perimeter of the sky, which would quicken them, are invisible from street-level; the horizon jostled out by the tall facades of former mills and weaving sheds. The shuttered shop windows, the deserted restaurants—everything slumbers. And although the pavements are strewn with litter—discarded take away food containers and spilled chips—it is possible to imagine, because of the quiet and the emptiness and the twilight, that a sort of enchantment has overlaid the town. As she walks up the hill to the bus station she is empowered, as one is in dreams. She could walk, even fly if she wanted, up the centre of the road, and be perfectly safe.

The magic ebbs though, at the bus station. The drivers drinking tea from steaming polystyrene cups are all too prosaic. An inspector, spruce with clip-board, hurries them along. Bleary-eyed passengers—scarcely awake—suck on cigarettes as though for oxygen, and eat slices of toast hastily scraped with margarine and wrapped in kitchen towel. They wear light summer clothing that—later—will seem almost too much in the record-breaking temperatures, but which—at the moment—is insufficient. They shiver in the dawn shadows. Two or three buses have their engines running. The noise drowns out the squabbles of the starlings on the roof.

There is a service bus that trundles between here and work, fetching and carrying employees to and from their shifts. The bus is just a little one, sixteen seats or so, and is, like everything on the site in these belt-tightened times—jobs, the ground-floor franchises, cleaning supplies, the entire 'customer offer'—up for stringent review. But lately—in spite of the dark threats of 'use it or lose it'—she has let the service bus go without her, preferring, even though she has to pay, the regular 457 service that takes her out of town and drops her opposite the old people's home. From there she can use the old grey bridge to cross the quietly sliding river, pass the farm and walk the mile and a half along the beautiful sequestered country lane to the little-used service entrance of the south-bound site. But for an early shift the timing is a bit tight, so today she climbs on board the service bus and promises herself that she'll come home via the lane when her shift ends at two.

She walks past the book-shop girl and chooses a seat a few rows back, in front of Paul the cleaner, who is panting and damp, puffed from his hike up the hill. He is enormous and needs a double seat to himself. In the beginning the book-shop girl had smiled encouragingly and indicated by a flick of her eyes that she would like Megan to take the seat next to her. But Megan had ignored her, propelled by a fierce and urgent need for solitude, swathing herself in it like a nettle shroud, and now hurt pride makes the girl keep her eyes averted. Megan slides across to the window and places her bag on the seat at her side so that when the matey maintenance man arrives—late as usual—he will have to sit across the aisle from her. Given the chance he would slide in too close and press his bony hip into hers. Now, Megan realises, that was what the stationery girl had wanted to avoid, and to save Megan from, but it is too late to repair the damage of her snub and in any case Megan is still– even after all these months— inclined to shrink from contact, clasping her privacy to her like a protective mantle.

The bus sets off with a shudder and lurches out of the bus station. It passes the Refuge's charity shop. There is a heap of donated clothing in its doorway, but as the bus passes its noise disturbs the clothes and a woolly-hatted head emerges from amongst them. The vision gives Megan an involuntary shiver of reminiscence; the deadly cold of the night-time ground; the way it sucks at the body's reserves of heat.

The shop windows are like blind eyes, unlit and glassily reflective, like corpses'.

They plunge down the hill, past a bar with elaborate outdoor arrangements for smokers and a bathroom showroom—its displays unreally bright and gleaming—to the traffic lights. The Registry Office is on the corner. A strew of yesterday's confetti peppers the steps.

She can hear Paul breathing through his nose, the breaths laboured and whistling as though the passageway is constricted. He needs a handkerchief; every so often he gives a wet sniff. The maintenance man smells of stale alcohol. It is a distinctive, sickly-sweet smell that rises from the skin. It is uncomfortably evocative and Megan gathers herself away from it, shrinking like a mollusc inside its shell. From its depths she is conscious of a telephone chirrup and the stationery girl's low voiced inquisition as she leaches the second-hand flavour of somebody else's drama into her own eventless life. 'What happened ..? Did she ..? Oh my God ..! What time was that ..? Oh my God..! What did she tell him ..?'

The traffic lights turn green and the bus proceeds. They swing round a mini roundabout, pass a DIY store and a long wall of terraced houses, like a rhythm—door-window-door-window-door—their curtains all closed. Behind them, row upon row of other identical houses; streets separated by narrow alleys, a labyrinth of separately boxed lives.

Just now the bus is the only vehicle in sight. The road, which later will thunder with ceaseless traffic, is empty and benign. A loose dog lopes along the pavement.

They pass a little parade of shops, the college campus, more traffic lights, more houses—bigger ones, with little gardens at the front and cars on the drives. A jogger or two and a few dog-walkers glance at the bus as it passes. There are a few people at the bus stop waiting for the

301

457. She was right, she thinks, to have taken the service bus today. If she'd waited for the regular bus she would have been late.

A long stretch of road takes them out into the country. Here are large houses with their bedroom windows open. Dew sparkles on the gardens; a white-wet drenching coats the thirsty plants. But now the sun is fully up in the perfect blue sky it will snatch the moisture back into the air before it can satisfy the dry roots.

They are on the main road out of town, passing the old people's home and the narrow lane entrance. There is more traffic now, but not much. It is still early. Fields stretch to right and left, parallel lines of mown grass, dark green on a lighter green-yellow ground. Rabbits, befuddled by their suddenly changed environment, their abrupt exposure, sit bewildered amongst the stalks, their ears up. Above them, buzzards wheel silently in the still air.

A police car sits like a spider in a web at the centre of the roundabout watching motorists enter and exit the motorway. An unmarked van straddles the pavement on the fly-over, a surreptitious camera spying on travellers. The bus swings hard right, plunges down the slip way and is on the motorway. Suddenly they are part of a coursing surge, joining a flow of shrieking rubber on hot macadam, a tide of endeavour to attain some distant objective. Cars race past the bus, past each other. Motorbikes weave dangerously across the lanes. Lorries strain up inclines and hurtle down hills. Flat grassland and crops slide by the windows as though on screens. Then, on the horizon, there is the enticing gleam and glimmer of sun on glass. The futuristic architecture of the twin domes of south- and north-bound sites is coy behind mechanically made slopes and contours. Between the two, the opaque plume of the bridge spans the carriageways, a frozen fountain gouting from one side to the other. Unexpected, it distracts drivers from their fixed determination to *arrive* enough to allow the idea of food, respite and the lavatory to filter in. Large lettering etched into the glass of the bridge draws them: The Bridge Café.

The bus slows a little and edges left, taking the slip road off. It passes through the switchback of a little chicane that is unnecessary for any practical purposes other than to suggest the mysterious entrance to Arcadia. Then the view opens to gleaming glass and elegant white infrastructure, leaping fountains, the sultry whisper of woodwind.

GUY WAKES EARLY and, in those few seconds of returning consciousness, there is still the urge—in-bred since early childhood— to leap out of bed and stand to attention, awaiting inspection by the immaculately-uniformed dorm sergeant. He would keep them waiting there, sometimes for a long time, checking beds for urine and humiliating the boy who had wet the sheets. In later years he would make them stand with their hands by their sides, their juvenile morning erections poking their pyjamas, allowing them no dignity. After washing and dressing there would be bed-making; sheets and blankets stripped and folded to precise measurements, and stacked in prescribed order on a specific spot on the bed. Any boy even half an inch out would have his whole mattress tipped off its base and have to do the whole thing again, missing breakfast.

But by this stage in remembrance he is fully awake and reason can suppress the instinct. He will stretch his full length with a sort of luxuriant defiance, and rake his fingers through his mop of hair, where, for so long, only close-cropped bristles were permitted. Presently he will get up and shrug on a dressing gown, and pad down to the little kitchen, where bright with slats of sunshine filter through the venetian blind and fall like luminescent rulers across a riotous collection of exotically painted crockery. Many pots of fresh herbs and a ludicrously loaded fruit bowl crowd gregariously and with joyful excess onto the limited work surface. No place for anything and nothing in its place. He will stab his finger onto the radio and Weaver FM will fill the air with something mindless and cheerful while he makes coffee. The cupboards groan with food—more than a single person can eat; the kind of plenty that only somebody who has known hunger can need. He will consider an extravagant array of children's breakfast cereals, highly sweetened and conspicuously unhealthy—there isn't a whole grain between them—before opting for toast with far too much butter. In the sitting room he will throw himself onto the sofa, the largest, squashiest, and most prolifically cushioned he could find, on which it is physiologically impossible to sit up straight. Guy will eat his breakfast with no regard for scattered crumbs and devour the morning papers.

Occasionally his eye will stray with satisfaction to his bookshelves. Some books are stacked sideways, others vertically, in neither size nor subject order; James Herriot rubs shoulders with Stephen Hawking, The Tenant of Wildfell Hall and Lemony Snicket nestle in perfect accord. Glorious bibliographic disorganisation reigns, a deliberate snub to Dewey. The walls are crowded with photographs, variously framed in wood and metal of different styles, hung randomly, some at angles. Quirky shots—two dozen pairs of psychedelic wellington boots, a selection of buckets in bright colours balanced and stacked. There are landscapes with waterfalls, the water like smoke over brown boulders. A shot of a robin taking flight from a bird table is his current favourite, its wings out-stretched, the contour and texture of every tiny feather and the brightness of its beady eye perfectly captured. There are no faces.

The room is filled with rainbow light, reflected through the French windows from the plethora of pots jumbled onto the diminutive patio—plain terracotta, blue glazed earthenware, old Belfast sinks, wooden troughs, even an old porcelain toilet. They burgeon with an exuberance of red geraniums and pink petunias and orange nasturtiums. A tiny table and single chair are squeezed amongst them. He will open the door and potter amongst them—shameless in his dressing gown and slippers—sloshing in water from a can and nipping off faded flowers. He will revel in this; his very own space, his own choices, his own, anarchic rules.

Upstairs again, in the shower, he will sing as the warm water courses over him and he will perhaps linger a little over-long in it, appreciating it; that it is warm and not cold.

All this he will do presently. But it is still early. Guy is his own man, and need dance to no tune other than his own.

CARLOS HAS A strop on. Megan can hear him through the swing doors crashing pans and cutlery around and swearing in ripe, wet, lisping Spanish. He is always touchy on an early shift anyway, arriving late, unwashed, the sleep still in his eyes, and looking daggers at everyone. Megan has made fresh coffee and poured Carlos a cup—placing it diffidently on the stainless steel work surface just inside the kitchen door, avoiding eye contact—but it doesn't seem to have placated his ire. As she polishes cutlery and tidies the cups and checks the condiment baskets, she follows the cadences of his one-sided argument with her highly-tuned anger-antenna.

Sylvie, her night-shift counterpart, has left things nice and straight, today. By the look of the till they'd had a quiet night of it. The tables, a mixture of rounds and squares, are arranged down the length of the bridge, up against the thick, sloping windows so that customers can watch the endless streams of traffic, a perpetual exchange, north and south, and rue their resting; all those people getting *there*—wherever *there* is—before them. All the tables are wiped, the chairs pushed trimly under, cruet and napkins neatly centred. At the west end are the toilets. A yellow plastic A board warns of wet floors within. Megan smiles; Sylvie has even managed to swab the loos before the end of her shift.

They had passed each other almost without a word, Sylvie hurrying to catch the departing service bus. There was hardly time for speech but there was, as always, a special smile, and today, a brief squeeze of soft hands. There is recognition. It adds just a suggestion of perspective to this artificially foreshortened present, assuaging the sense Megan has that she is less than real because she lacks the normal associations that identify and anchor. She and Sylvie are connected by their enforced anonymity. They share an invisible web of secret understanding and shared experience. They see each other's scars.

It is early—a little after half past six—but even so there are customers. Two lone lorry drivers read the sports pages and a businessman puts the finishing touches to a sales presentation on his laptop. A couple—very tanned and wearing garish holiday clothes—arrive *en route* from the airport, which is three or four junctions north. Megan takes their orders and their money, pours their complimentary beverages and gives them a numbered disc on a precarious metal stand to place on their table so that she knows where to deliver their breakfast when Carlos has assembled its component parts. Bacon, eggs, sausage, black pudding and beans for him, bacon, eggs, tomato and mushroom for her. She pushes open the kitchen door and flaps the print-out just enough to get Carlos' attention before placing it on one of the nails that sprout from a batten on the wall. The kitchen is tiny and Carlos' irritation seems to be enormous within it. He flails his arms at her and indicates the sink full of washing-up, the mushrooms still in their box, the empty griddle. His mop of woolly black curls quivers. A stream of Andalusian expletives pours forth. She gives him an apologetic smile and lets the door close on his wrath, knowing that in seven or eight minutes the bell will ping and he will have prepared two perfect breakfasts.

One of the lorry drivers leaves and Megan goes to clear his table. He has left nothing on his plate except four closely-nibbled crusts. The vagaries of human nature displayed in the café continue to surprise her: such a big beefy man but finicky about crusts. There is a 50p hidden under the rim of his plate, which she slips into her apron pocket. She cleans the table, re-centres the cruet.

It is yet another glorious day. The sun slants in from over the south-bound embankment and the wet smears from her cloth are dry almost instantly. She is above the south-bound carriageway. Cars and buses, lorries and coaches, vans, trucks, motorcycles—she can see them bearing down on the road, their radiator grilles snarling, their tyres devouring the tarmac like ravening locusts. They grow larger the closer they come and there is the merest instant when she can see the drivers' faces through the rectangle of their windscreens. She gets just the briefest impression of hair colour and clothing before they are snatched under her feet and swallowed down towards their destinations. And she is caught up again in wondering if they are journeying away from or towards. Are they running? If so, who from? Or are they drawn? What to? And what is the urgency? She sighs, and laments the little-appreciated joys of transit; the beauty of being neither here nor there; the freedom of the crossing.

The kitchen bell pings and breaks her reverie. Carlos nods at the two plates of food on the counter. They are beautiful, the white of the eggs pristine, their yolks golden and liquid, the bacon a rich rusty brown with a crisp, inviting curl of fat, plump sausages holding back an eager sea of beans. His bad temper has expiated itself in the process of cooking, as she knew it would, and in a moment she will go into the kitchen and help him with the washing-up without fear of being caught up in his anger. She delivers the breakfasts to the couple with a smile.

The woman puts her cup back onto its saucer. 'There is nothing,' she says, 'like an *English* cup of tea.'

THE NEWSPAPER OFFICE is a shambles, as though vandalised. It is approached via an unprepossessing door that is wedged between a newsagent's and a frozen food shop on the main pedestrianised thoroughfare of the town. Visitors and staff pass through a small vestibule with a tiny table and a bell, up a steep and filthy staircase to the grandly-named 'news room'. Unflatteringly illuminated by the light that filters through a row of large, grimy windows, its flaws are amply displayed. It is badly in need of decoration, the utilitarian carpet is worn, the furniture scarred. Five desks are invisible beneath spreading avalanches of detritus. Filing cabinets gape open, archives erupting from their drawers; they teeter, perilously close to toppling. Shelves bow under the weight of lever-arch files akimbo. Somewhere a telephone is ringing but it is impossible to source the noise beneath layers of old and breaking news.

Guy's desk is as bad as the rest. Worse. In fact it has been noted that the shambolic state of the office has increased since his arrival, out of the blue, some few weeks before. It is evidence of his carefree lawlessness, a mischievous tendency to do the unexpected. He takes delight in it. Yesterday he brought ice-lollies in—a bunch of them clutched in his hand like a spiky bouquet—and gallantly presented to each in turn. His desk is adjacent to the window ledge and he has appropriated its surface for further stacks of paper, books, magazines, junk, a chilli pepper plant. Yesterday's papers are strewn in a circle on the floor around his chair. His chair has two jackets dangling from the back, which he has worn, shrugged off and forgotten about. His monitor is feathered with yellow post-its to the point that the screen is virtually obscured. The keyboard is hidden by a strew of pink lead-sheets; information about potentially news-worthy events that he ought to follow up; dog dead after ingesting pond water, warning of possible burglary spate on exclusive golf-links development, neighbours suspect foul play re: hosepipe ban, seventeen year old boy missing. There are numerous cups from the machine in the corner and from proprietary coffee shops, their rims shredded, sticky with brown residue, and a brown bag of something that might have started life as fruit but is now a still-life of decomposition. He is shockingly, almost self-indulgently disorganised and yet produces snappy, incisive reports that throw refreshing new light on tired local issues.

He swings into the office and in half a dozen strides his long legs have carried him to his desk. He is tall, with a well-tooled profile and a shock of brown wavy hair. He dresses in a style that reflects his character— determinedly careless, a joyously haphazard mix of busy shirts and ties not always happily chosen to complement them. His jackets are dilapidated, misshapen as though left out in the rain. His neglected appearance is, however, more than amply compensated for by his Home Counties accent and an occasional assured use of the indefinite third person pronoun. It is a voice that would command authority here in this northern mill town. It automatically conjures associations with an illustrious blue-blooded lineage and echoes of powerful corridors. Except that he is far too nice to use it in that way. Instead, it is part of his arsenal of charm. He opens doors and gains confidence not with the bark of a brigadier but with the smooth assurance of a Royal equerry. He ought to be at a national newspaper or at the BBC. But, unaccountably, he is here, a hack on a local rag.

His mobile is sandwiched between his ear and his shoulder. There's a cup of Costa coffee in one hand, a bunch of keys and his sunglasses in the other. Listening, he allows his eyes to sweep the office. The chair immediately adjacent to his is, as always, empty. Monica, 'culture and leisure' rarely puts in an appearance before lunch time and only then to deliver her expenses claim and pick up any messages before drifting off on a cloud of Madame Rochas to critically assess a new menu. She is mystery-dining her way around the county and in the evenings devours art at theatres and galleries for her 'Cultural Corner'. Gerry, sports reporter, acknowledges Guy from across the room with the raise of a woolly eyebrow. He is unshaven. There is a smear of egg yolk on his polo shirt. An unlit cigarette dangles from a bottom lip that is abnormally, almost comically large, and gives his grey, pallid face a perpetual comic-book sulk. In the corner Ahmed, cold-calling his way through the yellow pages to drum up advertising, ignores Guy altogether, intent on charming. He is the shiest, most self-effacing young man but, on the telephone, exudes a velvety, sexy charisma. He is single-handedly keeping the paper afloat on advertising revenue. Shirley, who covers everything not 'news', 'sport' or 'culture and leisure' (she refers to it as 'community news') regards the coffee with a covetous gaze. She is bosomy and maternal and occasionally insipidly self-righteous. Her loud floral blouses—voluminous with flounces or eye-smartingly crazed with elasticated ruching—are booty from the many jumble sales she covers.

Only in one corner of the room is there order and it seems as though an invisible barrier holds back the chaos generated by the rest of the office; a distinct line, separating the clutter from the calm. The desk is neatly arranged with computer screen and keyboard perfectly aligned. A sturdy plastic pot of pens—all working—is ready to hand alongside a telephone. A notepad with a clean top sheet sits ready. There is a stack of trays clearly marked 'in' 'action' and 'out'. Chairs on both sides of the desk signify that the desk's owner anticipates enquirers, seekers after advice and guidance, and mark her out as something above the others. In confirmation, a tooled brass name plate boldly announces *Jennifer Roach, Editor*, and, as though conjured, she enters the room, smart in a linen suit.

'All right everyone,' she says, stepping carefully over the cascades of paper and into her own pristine domain. Guy murmurs a farewell to his caller and slides his mobile closed. He moves to the window and yanks on the beaded blind pulley. A pile of papers slides to the floor and he kicks them under his desk with his foot. The room subsides into gloom. Gerry removes the cigarette from his mouth, places it behind his ear and stands up. Like the filing cabinets, he is dangerously front-heavy, with a hard, round, beer-drinker's belly projecting over the low-slung waistband of his disreputable trousers. He moves across to the chair opposite Jennifer's, settling his distended gut onto his thighs. Shirley hits 'save' on the document she is working on and swivels her chair to face the wall behind Jennifer's sleek blonde head. Ahmed draws a line in pink highlighter to mark his place in the Yellow Pages before crossing the room to perch, like Guy, on Monica's desk.

'Putting to bed tomorrow afternoon.' Jennifer taps a few keys on her computer and above their heads a projector begins to whir. Presently the front and back page spread of the weekly paper appears on the white wall behind her. 'Looking fairly good, considering,' Jennifer comments. 'At the moment we're going with the students' protest against exam conditions for the front page. Any success in getting an interview with the fainting invigilator, Guy?'

'I'm seeing her later, at the school. They're preparing a press release. Hopefully it will give us something definite re the actual temperature in the hall.'

'Good. And get some pictures of her injuries.'

Guy frowns. 'Only superficial bruising. Not great in black and white.'

'Shame. Talk to the students while you're there. See if you can find an eye-witness.'

'I will.' He sighs. 'But I must say it's getting rather tedious. There are only so many words one can use to describe a heat wave. It's been with us weeks. It's scarcely *news* ...'

'Exactly!' Gerry humphs quietly.

Jennifer ignores him. 'I know. Stick at it. It can't last. If there isn't enough substance in the story we'll go with the suicide instead. Has that been confirmed?'

'What about the cup final? Doesn't that constitute front page news?' Gerry barks.

'Next week it will do, of course Gerry.' Jennifer placates him with barely-concealed irritation. 'But this week all we have is speculation. We just can't know what's going to happen. But I liked the piece you

313

did very much. A really deep analysis, nicely even-handed. Do you really think Johnson will start off on the bench? And you did a good write-up on Saturday's division four relegation battle, too. It's on the back page, look.' She motions towards the image on the wall where *Weavermen Keep it Up* is the back page headline. 'I managed to squeeze the under 16's hockey in there as well. The Ladies' Crown Green had to go inside, though. So, Guy. News on the suicide?'

'Actually yes. I've just heard from my contact at the Coroner's. The post mortem confirms suicide; she threw herself off some scaffolding. But of course it's unofficial until the inquest.'

'That won't be until next week; there's a backlog. More deaths than usual for the time of year. The hospitals are packed: heat-stroke, dehydration, sun-burn. I suppose you wouldn't like to pursue *that* as a story?'

Guy groans. 'More hot weather hyperbole ...'

'All right. Perhaps we'll save it until next week then.' Jennifer makes a note on her pad. She alters the display to show inside pages of the newspaper. 'A nice, up-beat piece on the Council meeting Guy, thank you. You make it sound like it was almost fun! *You've* been kept busy, Shirley. More summer fetes and church bazaars than you can shake a stick at. Not to mention the Scout Jamboree. I don't know how you manage to cover them all.'

Shirley simpers and picks an imaginary thread from her blouse. 'I feel I owe it to the volunteers. *They* put so much in.'

The meeting continues. 'Cultural Corner' is worryingly empty. 'No news from Monica, I suppose?' Jennifer sighs. 'I wish she were here. You,' she indicates Shirley, 'and she need to decide who's going to cover *Pirates of Penzance* at the Girls' Catholic Grammar next week. I don't know if it's culture or community.'

'Hardly high culture, I suspect. A lot of school girls cavorting around in hose and false moustaches,' Gerry's guffaw is slightly dubious. Shirley and Jennifer exchange looks and then Jennifer refers to her notes.

'While I think about it Shirley, there's an Open Day at Bridge House on Saturday. Are you covering it?'

Shirley checks her diary. 'The Mayor's going to be there, isn't he? What time does it start? I'll struggle to get there before two. It's the Beaver Olympics; they always run over, and I promised I'd drop in on Talented Pets at the Animal Shelter as well.'

'I'll go,' Guy volunteers. 'The whole town will be at Wembley or at home in front of the television. There won't be much else happening I shouldn't think.'

They skim over *readers' letters, lost and found, births deaths and marriages*. Ahmed is praised for his successes in generating advertising in the teeth of the recession. He gives a shy smile. They are short of a story for page 5. 'There are leads on your desk about a dead dog, a spate of burglaries and a missing boy, Guy.'

'A missing boy sounds like front page news to me,' Shirley says under her breath, 'poor lamb.'

'Oh yes.' Guy gropes across to his desk for the lead-sheet. The bag of decomposing fruit falls to the flood with a wettish thud. 'Oops. Oh dear. He lives somewhere called the Mere. Where's that?' Guy scans the information.

Shirley's sympathy shrivels. 'Oh, well ...'

'We'll just break the story this week,' Jennifer says, 'if you can get anything Guy. If he's still missing next week we'll do something bigger. He'll probably turn up. They usually do. It's just sheer thoughtlessness, generally.'

Downstairs, someone is pounding on the bell in reception. Business at the paper is subject to constant interruption by members of the public delivering their small-ads and drumming up coverage for their fund-raisers, but Jennifer insists that for this daily meeting there are to be no distractions. Accordingly she has placed a sign declaring MEETING IN PROGRESS on the tiny desk down in the vestibule and secured the door at the bottom of the stairs. They ignore the bell whilst previewing stories for the following week but presently the door resounds with frenzied knocking and handle-rattling and Jennifer at last concludes the meeting with an exasperated sigh. Guy opens the blinds and Ahmed goes downstairs to open the door. He returns with Monica, flushed and frustrated, her rigidly set hair crackling with static. There is the unmistakable cloying scent of lacquer.

'I've been *literally scrabbling* for admittance for the past half an hour!' she says bitterly.

'The key-code hasn't changed,' Gerry snaps defensively. As the senior male staff member he takes responsibility for security.

'I can never remember it,' Monica says archly. Such mundanities are below her cultural ken.

'The meeting always starts at ten,' Jennifer says, a curt edge to her voice. 'Have you brought your copy?'

'Of course!' Monica proffers a memory stick. 'A new French restaurant in the market place and a local history exhibition of photographs upstairs at The Loom, plus all the latest on their summer holiday events.' She places the stick with rather a heavy hand on Jennifer's desk.

'It sounds a bit sparse. You didn't pick up anything culturally newsworthy at the hairdressers?' Jennifer enquires with caustic.

'Oh!' Monica's hand involuntarily travels to the back of her head, patting her stiff curls. 'I had to do *something* with myself. I was up all night finishing a book. I'm meeting its author for lunch. *That* will pad things out a bit.'

'Isn't a *local* author a community story?' Shirley growls from behind her monitor. Her responsibilities never seem to include taking anyone out for lunch.

'Only if she isn't any good darling. And this one is—remarkably good.'

Guy, Gerry and Ahmed exchange looks. Monica perches at her desk and makes a moue.

'This place really is the pits,' she says, sweeping papers to the floor. 'I wonder you can bear it.' She gets to work on her expenses claim, unfurling receipts and dockets from her purse. Jennifer casts a smug glance at the area around her own desk. Shirley reaches into her handbag for her low-calorie organic fair-trade mid-morning cereal bar.

Guy looks at his watch and drains his coffee. 'Time I wasn't here,' he says. He gathers up the pink lead sheets. Gerry and Ahmed, rather enviously, watch him leave.

AT TEN-THIRTY REINFORCEMENTS arrive at the café in the shape of a wheezing, pendulously-breasted woman whose hair has been so abused over the years with peroxide and perming solution that what little of it remains is wiry and grizzled; her head is as bristly as a balding Brillo. She is one of the casual staff, brought in to cover for the café's supervisor, who is on holiday in Florida. She waddles amongst the tables with asthmatic effort collecting plates while Megan slips away for a break, gliding down the escalator to the ground floor. It feels—as it always does—like a slow immersion into a flowing river. The people are a constant current of movement in and through and away again. Regular as waves they lap against the counters and gush down to the lavatories, eddying around the tables leaving deposits of litter before surging out and away. The flood of bodies is so tangible to her that she is almost tempted, as she descends, to hold her breath.

Food franchises are arranged at intervals around the circumference of the dome, scaled-down facsimiles of their high-street relatives, offering burgers, fried chicken, pizza slices, frothing coffee, pastries and unnaturally vivid fruit and vegetable smoothies. Each little unit is autonomous, with dedicated storage and food preparation areas. Their serveries are all gleaming with stainless steel, brightly lit as operating theatres, and as high-tech; the staff, smartly uniformed in corporate colours, are as brisk as nurses operating an impressive array of dials and triggers, nozzles and valves. They dispense caffeinated fluids from coils of tubing like life-supporting elixir, and milk-shake pink as antiseptic balm. The food that emerges from behind the servery—hygienically sealed in squeaky polystyrene trays—is so uniform in shape and colour and texture that it seems to be the product of some precisely calibrated machine, untouched, an immaculate conception. Certainly, Megan smiles as she wanders anonymously amongst the crowd, not constructed by a line of acned teenagers who work from laminated picture templates that illustrate each stage of assembly down to the exact positioning of every slice of gherkin.

In the centre, under the wide crystal roof, tables are arranged. Some are in alcoves, some elevated on plinths. Some are tall, with precarious stools, some sequestered in arbours of artificial ivy. The number and size and arrangement of tables have been precisely calculated following extensive market research, customer profiling and an ergonomic survey of the space. Couples, families and boisterous parties are all accommodated. There are sofas too, clustered in clans, close to the coffee concession, and a row of tiny booths with internet access for businessmen. The booths are swathed in greenery; they look like bowers designed for clandestine encounters. Everywhere, in fact, there is prolific growth of synthetic creeper, smothering trellises and swarming along pergolas; the Eden Project meets The Day of the Triffids. The fibrous trunks of bogus tropical trees erupt from containers. High aloft, the rustle and sway of reproduction rain forest forms a cooling canopy from the sun, and dapples the diners below. The designer planned to have the wide glass doors to the terrace standing open, admitting the burble of water and the sound of natural birdsong, blurring the lines between indoors and out. But the noise and grime from the motorway, and the scavenging pigeons, meant that the idea had to be abandoned. Now, amongst the tree-tops, concealed speakers squawk and whistle, suggesting fantastical, bright-feathered birds. Megan stands close to the glass wall, completely immobile, her utter stillness melds her into the infrastructure and people brush past her as though she were invisible. The splash of the fountains outdoors does not permeate the thick plate. She can hear only the metamorphosed hubbub of conversation, the shriek of steam heating milk at the coffee concession, the clash of coffee cups and cash tills ringing.

Right under the apex an open space is reserved for special sales promotions, occupied week by week by organisations exploitative and altruistic; luxury car dealers, the Salvation Army, double glazing companies, blood and organ donor drives, time-share salesmen, disaster relief charities. Well-groomed salesmen, well-endowed promotions girls and well-meaning, earnest evangelists work an ever-changing crowd of potential punters, exhorting and enticing, and paying well for the platform. Today, as every day this week, a lady is demonstrating some new kitchen gadget. Megan has heard her patter a dozen times; *a miracle new utensil that grates and grinds and shreds and peels, chops and dices, mashes and splices* ... Behind the façade of her kitchen units a bin overflows with fruit and vegetable fragments, uselessly ground and shredded.

The main entrance projects from the dome towards the car-park. Here is the stationery shop selling cut-price paperbacks and exorbitantly-priced sandwiches as well as emergency essentials—sanitary requisites, nappies, wiper blades, screen-wash, batteries, maps. There is also a gift shop selling a ludicrous and eclectic array of souvenirs; accessories in Tartan, models of London buses and Beefeaters, dolls in Welsh National costume, tea-towels of the counties, Wedgewood and Waterford crystal.

Opposite the entrance and across the food court, escalators carry customers up to the Bridge Café and down to the cavernous lavatories. Down there, the corridors of cubicles are artificially lit, every surface tiled in unappealing beige. Customers, reflected in the mirrors, look wan and bloodless. Beyond these, beneath the dome, is a warren of plant-rooms where engineers supervise heat and water and the disposal of effluent. There are storage facilities and the administration offices where pale, sun-starved employees toil on forecasts and cash-flows and the minutiae of lease agreements. They juggle the hoops of health and safety legislation and oversee personnel. The decor is hard, the lighting harsh, the relentless air conditioning causes dry eyes and slightly hectic activity. Whatever Arcadian chimera is being generated above, here there is no illusion about the matter in hand; the weight of commercial responsibility bears down on them—a hard, practical reality—as palpably as the dome itself.

Deeply buried, the metal and concrete of the dome's foundations anchor it in the earth. Sometimes, the creak of expanding or contracting metal makes ghostly, hollow echoes and the ground is said to shudder.

Megan, her forehead pressed against the cool glass, can almost feel it quivering, resounding with the noise and movement, like a bell. Her own body rumbles in sympathy; a tremor in her legs and a low-range tremble in the pit of her stomach. Everything inside the dome is somehow magnified. Movements, like on a stage, are inflated. Sometimes they seem like involuntary spasms. The number of drinks spilled and trays dropped every day is astonishing; Paul is constantly removing slip-hazards. Perhaps the air is in some way thinner, less resistant, its sparseness heightening emotion and removing natural inhibitors. Energetic people become more hectic, arriving in a whirlwind of disgruntled need for toilets and sustenance, barging into cubicles ahead of the patient queues. Conversely the lethargic are more lugubrious, indecisive at the counters, dawdling over their trays and lingering in the gift shop. They all bring their issues with them— itineraries almost visible, like thought-bubbles overhead. Tides of feeling flood across the space and bounce off the walls, rebounding back and re-drenching. And even when the people have gone—folding themselves back amongst the sticky toffee papers and stale, too-breathed air of their vehicles—echoes remain behind, reverberating high up in the dome.

THE PRESS CONFERENCE at the school is less than electric. The Head and two deputies plus the chief invigilator and three reliable members of the student council have gathered to fend off questions from the assembled press. A spirited attempt by students to claim a breach of their human rights and a less strident but still notable representation from parents has caused the governors to fear more negative publicity. The staff has rallied accordingly with a printed statement and an unspoken but unanimous determination that no consideration will persuade them to show the press the site of the incident. In any case the gymnasium has now been abandoned as an examination room in favour of the—air conditioned—sixth-form common room. The invigilator who fainted is to be present, but enjoined to remain silent.

There are only two other reporters in addition to Guy so the press conference is over in ten minutes. The other reporters shamble off in search of better drama, or off for a pub lunch, clutching the press release in their sweaty, disappointed hands. But Guy lingers in reception for a while, amongst candidates now waiting anxiously for the afternoon's exam. Presently he spies the invigilator and follows her at a distance along the corridors and down a flight of steps. He is still wearing his 'visitor' badge but classes have now resumed and there is no one to question him. The woman is perhaps in her early sixties, small but rather fat. Her grey hair is curly, dark with sweat against her neck. She wears a cotton skirt across capacious hips and a loose polyester blouse, flat, open-toed sandals and tights in American tan. He can hear the nylon rasp of her thighs as she walks. From classrooms to right and left Guy can hear the murmur of teachers, occasionally a child's response, sometimes a buzz of general activity and debate. Outside one classroom a boy is seated on the floor against the wall, chewing gum and staring blankly ahead of him. He is huge, moon-faced.

'Not *again* Michael,' the woman comments as she comes level with him. She peers in at the square window that is set into the classroom door. There is some mouthed conference between her and the teacher within. Then she says, 'Stand up and tuck your shirt in, lad, and come with me.' The boy lumbers to his feet and ambles after her. They make a strung-out procession now, the three of them, which passes through a quadrangle and past the library and eventually out of a set of double doors that are propped open to admit any breeze. They proceed up a slope to a fenced-off plot with a large greenhouse, a small shed and an allotment about the size of a tennis court.

The ground is being worked by about a dozen students in sun hats and shirt-sleeves. Some are weeding rows of carrots, others working around a row of strongly-staked tomato plants, pinching out the growth between the stalk and the trusses. Two others are filling a watering can from a stand-pipe and carefully sprinkling the soil at the base of a wigwam of runner beans. At the woman's approach however, they hurry to greet her.

'Are you all right, Miss?'

'We heard you fainted yesterday.'

'Did you have to go to hospital Miss?'

'Was it your heart again?'

She ignores all their questions but her brisk, to-business directions cannot hide her gratification at their concern. 'Thank you so much for making a start everyone. I'm sorry I'm late. Remember we decided to pot-up those sunflower seedlings today. Shall we get on with that?' As she speaks she opens the padlock of the shed and begins to distribute tools. The fat boy has joined the others.

Guy sidles alongside and the woman eyes him.

'You were at the press conference,' she observes narrowly.

'I *was*,' Guy agrees, giving her his most charming smile. 'A fuss about nothing, wasn't it? But *this* looks *much* more interesting ...' Soon the children are clamouring to show him around and the teacher, pleased by their enthusiasm, softens.

'All right,' she says, casting her eye over the eager faces. 'Clark, if you put your shirt back on, you can show Mr ...'

'Crouchback.'

'Mr Crouchback around.'

Clark is a mine of information, not only about seed-beds and compost and the best ways to kill slugs—some rather grisly—but also about Mrs Hetherington, the teacher.

'She's one of the nicest,' he says. 'She's going to retire at the end of term but she says she'll keep on helping out with the garden. She had a heart attack at Christmas. She's only supposed to be back part-time. This isn't really a lesson, you know. It's just for the trouble-makers. It gets us out of the classrooms so the others can learn. It was her idea, all this. We're allowed to take some of the stuff home, if we want. I don't though. My mum makes us eat enough green stuff already. I'd rather have chips, wouldn't you?'

'Oh yes, every time. Life's too short for greens,' Guy says.

'Do you want to see in the greenhouse? We've grown flowers and some of the older ones are making baskets and things to sell at the fair. And there's peppers and things in there too. And there's big purple things. They look like a cow's bollocks! That's what we call them. But not when Mrs Hetherington's there of course.'

'Cows don't have bollocks, you goon,' the fat boy says, passing by.

Out on the playing field a group of girls is jogging without enthusiasm around the athletics track. In the brightness they are like flowers, their hair glinting sunbeams, their brightly coloured sports kit as vivid as petals. One, with white-blonde hair, waves to Clark as she passes.

'Is that your girl-friend?' Guy asks with a wink.

'My brother's,' Clark tells him.

He leads Guy into the oppressive humidity of the greenhouse, continuing to chatter, a medley of anecdotes and information randomly collated. Guy interposes the occasional question, gradually garnering useful information. A group of students surrounds a workbench, transferring sunflower seedlings to pots. Mrs Hetherington carries in a tray of plastic cups, brimming with lemonade. She distributes them around to a chorus of, 'Thank you Miss.'

'It's warm.' She smiles apologetically. 'But at least it's wet. We mustn't get dehydrated.'

There is a little hiatus while the students drink. They natter amongst themselves. Then Guy's ear catches mention of the Mere. 'Do you know the boy who has gone missing?' he asks casually, reaching for a seedling.

'Skinner?' Clark says. 'Oh yes. Mike and me ...'

The fat boy pokes Clark sharply.

'But no, not really,' Clark mumbles, his eyes suddenly evasive.

IT IS A brisk day at the café and Megan's shift passes quickly. Plate after plate of breakfast is ordered and consumed. She serves and clears with efficient cheer and enjoys the sense—in the supervisor's absence—of being in charge. The wire-wool casual is slow amongst the tables and Megan steps up her own productivity to compensate.

Today's Megan is not the one who arrived for her first day at the café a few months ago. Then, she had moved through the day like an automaton, her body mechanical whilst her mind tried to find a fix within the maelstrom of its confusion. Back at the refuge she had sat in her room staring at nothing, conscious of nothing except a gnawing anxiety and a non-specific ache like the pain of an amputated limb. It had all seemed so unreal, the abrupt disconnection from everything familiar. Welcome in some ways, in others, terrifying. The sensation of being entirely lost had, for a time, whirled her around in a vortex that had threatened to consume. She couldn't bear to think of it, what she had done. It was too dreadful. Her appetite had been poor; the kindly women at the refuge had almost despaired of her, and at work the sight of yolk-smears and the bits of greyish-white gristle from the sausages— spat out and left on the side of the plate—used to make her stomach turn.

But the nausea has gone now, along with the hunted insecurity—she had expected him any minute. She has emerged from the interim-state of zombie-like bewilderment and can work in relative contentment. The food is good—for what it is—and there are few complaints. The bridge is bright, cheery, always ambient regardless of the weather outside, with panoramic views of the countryside and sky. The road below is an ever-moving conveyor, carrying the world away north and south beneath her feet while she floats, an aproned angel, above them.

Her colleagues are agreeable, even Carlos, when his early morning ire has evaporated, and Megan finds their professional interaction quite satisfactory. She likes the fact that it *is* merely professional, without the complications that overlapping lives inevitably cause. Some days they hardly speak at all. At the end of their shifts they all disappear into the landscape, going their separate ways.

She is like someone who, after the trauma of ship-wreck, discovers that in fact the island is quite tenable, and escape is by no means imperative.

Later, after her shift, she walks back along the dusty, deserted lane, feeling a million miles from anywhere and from anyone. It is one of the unlooked-for joys of her new, disconnected state; the opportunity to be entirely alone. Two bus rides and a leap across the town have brought her from the pilchard-packed humanity of the Mere tenements to this; a complete and glorious absence of human angst. She enjoys the wide, unthreatening solitude. She has become good at this, a fixed concentration on the here and now, looking neither right nor left, but just at each current moment as it unfurls. It is a blessing; the ability to leave the wound alone. Beneath the crust are layers of damaged tissue calling to be excised, but exploring them would be too painful and so she hasn't done it. While she is not ready to look into the future she has largely switched the light off on the past. She looks neither forward nor back but just at *this*, maintaining a precarious equilibrium over the chasm.

Alone today, under the bright glinting sky, her ears are free of indictment, hearing only the muted rush and roar from the motorway subsumed into the rural soundscape. Tall grasses gently clash, their blades like soft metal meeting in desultory combat. She can hear the distant thrum of a tractor on a far field. She tunes her ear to the busy burrowings of small creatures amongst the hedgerows. The verges on either side of the narrow lane are a tangle of wild flowers; pink campion, fluffy, fragrant meadowsweet, dancing hordes of large-headed daisies. Elder trees are weighed down with blossom and alive with birds tending their nests. She stops for a time and leans against a gate, contemplating a public footpath sign that points the way across the field towards a copse, beyond which, she imagines, will be the river. The sky above her is white and shimmering with heat, the sun a fireball. The road before her is grey and warm, a highway for hopping rabbits and furry, inching caterpillars. She breathes in and smells mown grass and the musky, unmistakable scent of her own hot skin. She closes her eyes for a moment and concentrates on the peace.

Towards the end of the lane is the farmhouse. Old stone is fuzzy with lichen. It has a frowning roofline and a cluster of farm buildings set back at a little distance from it. They look dilapidated and unused.

The bridge arches sturdily over the low river. Behind the old folk's home a striped awning shades recumbent, insubstantial figures while men tend the gardens in the glare of the sun. At the bus stop a brown-haired woman with a dimple in her cheek is waiting. They stand side by side but do not speak.

She sits on the bus and watches the view from the window. At the bus station she gets off and walks towards the supermarket, where she buys a few things; salad, a small loaf, a pint of milk. The shop is crowded with people buying sociable food; meat to barbecue, beer and ice cream. Teenagers harass the woman at the check-out, trying to buy alcohol with fake ID. In the end the manager is summoned but before she can arrive the teenagers have left. Megan avoids the 'teenagers today' conversation the woman would like to have with her, pays for her purchases and walks home. Her road, the erstwhile High Street, is, since the construction of the new pedestrianised concourse, a sad collection of demoralized little businesses struggling to survive. They have grimy windows and despondent, dusty displays. Cars crawl along the narrow streets but yellow lines prevent people from parking and patronising the shops. At the end of the row an archway gives entrance to a rear yard that stretches behind the shops allowing service access. The windows are all barred. Often there are cardboard boxes and untidy heaps of polystyrene strewn around. At night the back door of the Chinese take-away is open, the sweet smells of garlic and ginger and the sound of oil cracking in a hot wok make her mouth water. The bewildering, high-pitched, barely enunciated flow of verbiage from within conjures echoes of exotic places. The take-away closes at midnight and then the yard is a quiet pool of deserted shadow. In the upper storeys the windows are lightless, the rooms just musty storage. Megan's is the only residence.

The dog has gone. It had been a poor, ill-kempt creature, tied up behind the pawn shop, presumably for security. A derelict construction of pallets and old carpet had been its only shelter from the rain and cold. It had howled at night, keeping Megan awake, until she had taken to untying it and bringing it indoors under cover of darkness. She had fed it and washed it and liked the heavy warmth of it on her feet, its grateful, beating heart her only company. She would return it reluctantly each dawn, avoiding its doleful eyes, and creep back to her lonely, cooling bed. Then one day she had been woken by the sound of it yelping, a pitiful, hopeless remonstrance as the pawnbroker rained blows on it with a stick. He had been burgled in the night, while Megan and the dog lay oblivious. Megan had cowered in her doorway, feeling each lash, unable to intervene, wishing the dog would turn on its attacker with avenging teeth. But the bleak acceptance she recognised in its eyes—as though it deserved no less—had later caused her, in broad daylight, to untie the dog and walk away with it. She had delivered it to an animal shelter. She missed it in the night. But she knew she had done the right thing.

Her little flat is stuffy but she dare not leave a window open. Now she props open the door with one of the pots of geraniums she has grown from seed and that stand in a defiant line of colour, one on each of the half dozen grim iron steps that lead up to her door. At this time of day the sun shines directly in, a hard yellow envelope of light on the dull brown linoleum. Her flat has been awkwardly accommodated into some redundant space at the back of a denture repair shop. A bed-sitting room with a single window, it has an alcove with a fridge and a small sink and an old card table holding a microwave, toaster and kettle. Above, two shelves support a small assortment of cups and plates and Pyrex, some tins and packets. A single bed, pushed against the wall and spread with a bright, crocheted blanket, doubles as a settee. Under the window are a small table and a single chair. A chest of drawers beside the bed contains her clothes. On the chest is a chrome-framed photograph of a younger Megan and a laughing, fat-faced baby boy, and a stack of library books. In the corner, one door gives access to a dark, narrow stairway leading to a former basement scullery, now Megan's tiny bathroom. Another, securely bolted on Megan's side, is the way through to the shop. Sometimes, through the door, she can hear the mechanical processes of palates being extruded from sheets of pink plastic, the grind of wheels perfecting pearly smiles.

She quickly unpacks her shopping and makes tea, which she takes out onto the little iron landing to sip in the sun. Later, when the sun has sunk out of sight below the parapet of wall that divides the yard from a car-park, she goes in and carefully locks her door. She showers and sets her little table and eats her meal; salad, a little tinned tuna, a slice of bread. Hidden away like a hermit who has renounced the world, safe and unknown, hardly registering on the corner of the world's eye, she opens *Lady Audley's Secret* and reads until the light has gone.

IN A QUIET suburb beyond the college campus a large house stands a little way back from its neighbours, screened by laurels from the road and partly shadowed by an enormous monkey puzzle tree that is planted in the centre of its lawn. Two wrought iron gates give access to a semi-circular sweep of drive but the macadam of the drive, especially at the edges, is furred by thick spongy moss; cars come rarely. The house itself is somewhat dour, built of large regular blocks of greyish black stone, with a frowning portico supported on substantial columns and a large, forbidding front door. The windows are divided into pairs, separated by mullions, two pairs either side of the door upstairs and down, the upper ones joined by a fifth above the porch. Higher still—sprouting from the steeply sloping roof—three gable windows gaze wistfully over the top branches of the monkey puzzle tree and into the distance. Each window is made obscure with a drift of net curtain, giving the eyes of the house a milky, sightless aspect.

Years ago the whole road was the well-to-do address of wealthy mill owners. Nowadays these properties are too rambling and draughty to appeal as homes. They are too close to town to be considered fashionable and would cost far too much to bring up to modern standards of plumbing. One or two have been converted into luxury apartments but most have been appropriated by dentists and osteopaths and accountants as business premises. But this house has no brass plaques on its stone gate posts. In fact it has neither name nor number, and the postman never calls. Without identification, hiding behind the thick planting, the house is self-effacing. Its glowering façade discourages callers. There is little indeed to suggest that the house is even inhabited.

But it is.

It is a house of women. They come and go discreetly, almost furtively, their heads down. Some have children. Some *are* little more than children; slight and vulnerable and big-eyed with fear. They arrive at a half-run, at all hours, clutching a meagre carrier bag of hastily gathered belongings or, sometimes they are coatless or even shoeless, clutching bodily injuries. They run to the house up the soft moss of the driveway, undaunted by its forbidding aspect or gloomy shadows, and they hurl themselves against the flat black door. It is always opened to them promptly. A shaft of warm yellow light is briefly cast upon the slab step and friendly arms extend to draw the women kindly in.

They don't re-emerge for some days. When they do, their bruises are faded, externally at least. They walk quickly, keeping close to the hedges, like frightened animals in a world of ever-present danger. They meet up with friends or family, to assure them that they are safe, and to receive from them clothes, or money, or essential documents. Occasionally they confront their abusers to tell them that it's over. Some of these don't return to the refuge, at least not immediately. They are persuaded back, with tearful apologies and promises of new leaves imminently to be turned over. But they never say where they're staying and they take careful measures to avoid being followed back. The address of the house, its location and its purpose, is a closely guarded secret. The only ones who know of it are the victims it has sheltered over the years, and the ones like them that they tell, and a handful of volunteer counsellors.

Megan had been told of it by a woman, another mother, waiting at the school gates. They didn't know each other; their children were in different years. She was rather older than the average, and didn't mix much. But one day she had approached Megan and looked at her squarely. Megan hadn't been able to meet her gaze, keeping her head down so that her fringe would hide a bruise on her temple. The woman had held out a folded piece of paper. As Megan reached for it the woman had caught her hand and they'd both stared down at the thin white wrist and the row of systematic cigarette burns, some fresh and dark, others partially healed, that traced a path up towards Megan's elbow.

Megan had opened her mouth but before she could speak the woman had said, 'You're going to try and tell me this is eczema or psoriasis.' She'd reached up her other hand and brushed the hair away from Megan's forehead. 'And that you did this on the cupboard door. Then you'll tell me that it was an accident, that he's never done it before, and that he's promised it won't happen again. Then you'll make excuses for him. He's depressed. Out of work. Had a rough childhood. Last of all you'll say that you deserved it anyway, for burning his dinner or nagging about money, or for not being good enough in bed. Now listen to me. It will never stop and he'll never change. It will get worse and worse until one day he'll completely lose it and kill you. It isn't your fault and you don't deserve it. No one deserves it. There *is* a better life, out there.'

Megan had looked at her for the first time. Her face was lined, free of make-up, with beetling brows and pale hazel eyes that looked back calmly into her own. Her grey hair was oddly styled around a wide, puckered parting that began above her left eyebrow and travelled diagonally across her crown. Megan had realised suddenly what it was and at the same time the woman's fingers had reached up and traced its erratic line.

'A very big cupboard,' she'd smiled. She'd proffered the paper again. 'This is a place you can go. They will look after you there, and your son, and you will never be hurt again.' She'd folded Megan's trembling fingers around the paper. 'Don't show it to anyone. Just go there. Any time. Day or night. There is always someone there.'

She'd given Megan's hand a gentle squeeze and then sauntered away to where the school doors were being propped open by one of the teachers. Then Stuart was running towards her, flapping a painting he had made. Already, aged six, his chubbiness had melted from him, leaving the fleshless, angular outlines that would characterise his pubertal appearance. Sometimes he could be moody and withdrawn, at others ungovernably over-active. She'd taken his hand and led him home.

She rarely saw the woman again; her child moved on to the high school. Occasionally they would find themselves together in the shop, or passing on the pavement. But no further word was ever spoken.

Megan kept the paper hidden. It was ten years before she found the courage to go to the address it contained.

WEDNESDAY IS ALWAYS a difficult day of deadlines, hurried re-writes, last minute changes to lay-out. A weekly paper must combine what is in progress with what is locally pertinent in the longer term, not news perhaps but newsworthy. Appearing once a week means that it can take a slightly wider view on affairs, and whereas a daily paper will be lining the litter tray in twenty-four hours, a weekly will be retained for weekend reference or even beyond, and has to offer something of interest to the casual browser which, while not hot off the press, will remain of at least passing interest. Choosing just the right stories and the right angle to pitch them becomes increasingly urgent as the clock ticks, and by Wednesday there is a fevered race to the finish. It is a pressure that Jennifer relishes, but it is wearing. In the weeks of heat wave she has noticed it more than ever; their nerves—strung out between the walls of the airless office—are shrinking in the heat. The rivalry between Shirley and Monica has become positively acerbic. Jennifer's attempts to broach the subject with each separately have resulted in tearful confessions of hormonal irregularities, sleeplessness and general weather-related ill health. Gerry, panting and pouring sweat, has taken to visiting the pub at lunchtimes. He is increasingly awkward in the afternoons, alternately somnolent and stroppy. Only Guy and Ahmed seem able to maintain their equilibrium but even they, today, are struggling. There is a choking pall of unease in the office. The reporting staff winces as though personally injured while Jennifer edits their purple paragraphs to fit around the advertising features. She is in constant conference by email and telephone with the graphics department, miles away on the Quays, who are, maddeningly, far more interested in their main publication, the *Evening Record*, than this poor relation, the *Weaver Weekly*. On more than one occasion, she finds that she has raised her voice and has to fight the urge to browbeat.

But on the whole this week's edition has come together with surprising ease. Guy has turned the lack-lustre swooning examiner story into an uplifting human-interest piece; *Blooming Students Defy Drought* paralleling Mrs Hetherington's careful nurture of the more unmanageable students with the students' own success with the tender seedlings. She is portrayed as a stalwart and longstanding champion of the academically challenged pupil, courageously combating personal ill-health to 'ensure that even the most arid and unpromising of soils brings forth fruit.' It is the best press the school has received in some time. Refreshingly, the heat-wave receives only passing mention, apropos the ingenious irrigation techniques devised by a year 10 pupil, and by Mrs Hetherington's insistence that, while it lasts, students wear hats and sun-screen. Monica's interview with the author is rather rambling—her bar bill subsequently explains why—but provides many much needed column inches in Cultural Corner. And in a pre-emptive strike on *Pirates of Penzance*, Shirley has turned in interviews with the Musical Director and Wardrobe Mistress for page 5 as well as securing two tickets for the winner of this week's Sudoku.

Also on page 5 is a heart-rending eulogy for the dead dog, and Guy's report on the missing boy. There isn't much to go on. The police's door-to-door enquiries have only managed to unearth the suggestion that the young man has been troubled by his parents' separation. His father has been uncooperative with detectives. 'A nasty piece of work,' a constable confided to Guy, 'threatened to wring the necks of the lad's pet rats. Can't blame him for doing a runner, really.' Guy has omitted this from his brief report. The rumour about the burglaries has proved completely without substance; a flier delivered door-to-door has been explained by the local neighbourhood watch co-ordinator as merely a routine call for vigilance.

Gerry has unearthed a story about a family divided over the up-coming FA Cup final; *Dad sees Red over Son's Blues*. Ahmed has excelled himself with a double page spread from the local DIY store promoting water-saving devices.

At half past five Jennifer signs off the edition and shuts down her computer.

'I'll buy you all a drink,' she says, 'I think we all need one.'

Outside the office they gather uncertainly while Gerry locks the door and lights a cigarette. They are moving onto new territory, a group of people associated professionally now making the readjustment to a social milieu. Office strains must be left there. The hierarchy must blur and then disintegrate altogether, leaving a level field, and gradually talk of the paper must transmute into more personal subjects; wives and husbands, plans for the weekend. They walk along the dusty concourse to the pub on the corner, Gerry striding ahead of them, approaching his favourite moment of the day. Monica hangs back, eyeing dresses in a shop window, and Shirley eyes Monica, noting the clothes that draw her attention and suppressing outrage at their price tags.

Inside, after the eye-searing brightness, the cool lounge bar is dark and there is a little awkward jockeying for position while they orientate themselves and decide where to sit. Eventually Shirley gropes her way to a table and flops onto a padded pew pushed up against the wall. Ahmed pulls out a chair and sits next to her. His dark skin and hair merge into the gloom leaving his eyes and teeth glowing unnaturally white. Jennifer is rummaging in her bag for her purse while reminding them, 'These are on me remember. Just give me a tick.'

'I'll get them,' Gerry says impatiently, making for the bar. 'What's yours *old boy*?' he asks Guy over his shoulder. 'A port and lemon?'

Guy ignores the jibe and says, 'A pint.' It frustrates him sometimes, not so much the inability of people to get past his accent or their tendency to treat him like a modern day Bertie Wooster, but his inability to get rid of it. It is the only remnant left of his past life, every other vestige of which he has systematically erased or overwritten, and although he jokes about being, 'A real Northerner now,' and of eagerly awaiting the imminent issue of his regulation flat cap and whippet, he knows that his accent will always prevent it.

Gerry has drunk half of his pint down before Guy's is pulled. 'What about the rest of you?' he asks, handing Guy's pint across. Shirley is driving. She asks for a Britvic Orange. Ahmed doesn't drink, he'll have the same.

'Have they any wine?' Monica asks. 'A Pinot Noir? A Syrah?'

Gerry consults the barman. 'They have red or white.'

'Of course, but what *kind?*'

'Red or white.'

Monica tuts. 'Red then, I suppose.' When it comes she takes a sip and pulls a face. 'Good God!'

Jennifer drinks vodka and tonic, 'A large one.' By the time it arrives Gerry's glass is empty, its insides coated with foam, and the barman is pulling him another. Jennifer, finding her purse at last, hands Gerry a twenty pound note. Much later on she recalls that she never received any change.

Presently they are all settled around the table and their eyes have become accustomed to the gloom. Generally, because they are so often called upon to work on Saturdays, the reporting staff takes either Thursday or Friday off, organising it between themselves to leave skeleton cover.

'Monica's right about the office, you know,' Jennifer comments. 'It really is a disgrace. I don't suppose you'd all like to come in tomorrow morning and clear it?'

'Would you be paying overtime?' Shirley asks. She had intended to take Thursday off but has nothing particular planned that could not be deferred for some extra pay.

'Sadly not. It isn't as though we need all that hard copy now, everything's stored digitally. Those filing cabinets could be done away with.' Jennifer has fairly recently taken over the editor's job from an older man who still relied on old ways. She has had to hit the floor running and hasn't managed to impose her orderly stamp on anything beyond her own corner. 'Everything on your desks, if it's over a week old, it's redundant.'

'Oh, I don't know,' Guy says, instinctively resistant to imposed organisation. 'You never know when things might come in handy.'

'Well catalogue it, then. File it, index it. At the very least stack it in neat piles.'

'There's something on your desk that smells off,' Monica comments.

'It's a bag of fruit,' Shirley says, 'it will attract flies.'

'It's a science experiment,' Guy laughs. 'Give a guy a break.' He smiles good-humouredly, then stands up. 'Another round?'

When he returns to the table the conversation has widened to the question of general attitudes to tidiness and order. Shirley, who has three teenage boys, has given up hope of it. Her house, she says, is perpetually knee-deep in filthy sports kit, take-away pizza boxes and girls in various stages of undress. Monica, who lives alone, confesses to 'a touch of OCD' about clean crockery.

'It's a good job you eat out so much then,' Shirley mutters.

Ahmed still lives at home and, 'Leaves it all to his mother.' Gerry, rather bored with the topic, but expected, like the others, to come clean, says his wife tends to deal with it all in the house, but he is keen on having his shed tidy so that he can put his hand on the thing he needs straight away.

'That's just my attitude,' Jennifer says. Her first vodka has gone and she is making inroads into her second. They are all conscious of a distinct loosening in her. In their short professional association with her they have learnt to live with what they have come to regard as her reined-in nature. 'I like things straight.'

'You don't say!' They all laugh. They realise what a relief it is.

'Well, you can laugh, but I think you spend less time keeping things in order than you do looking for things you can't find. And,' she sips and swallows, 'I'm prepared to admit that it's a bit of a throwback from when I was young. My mother was widowed and ran a business and things were always a bit of a muddle. I always swore I wouldn't be like her.'

It is the most personal revelation about herself that Jennifer has ever made to her colleagues. They all take a time to adjust to this previously uncharted territory.

Shirley, who has been trying to steer Jennifer into personal confidences for weeks, says warmly, 'It's quite true, our parents have a lot to answer for. We'll either be just like them, or completely opposite ...'

'Which tends not to go down well,' Guy says morosely, almost to himself. But his comment doesn't go unnoticed. Everyone's eyes are on him. The newest member of the team, his provenance unknown, there is a natural curiosity amongst them about him that he has so far left unsatisfied.

Monica leans forward slightly. The question, '*Doesn't it?*' is on her lips. Guy leaps to his feet. 'I didn't get any crisps!' he cries. They all protest that they don't want any but he buys several packs and in time they are all eaten.

It is cooler when they emerge from the pub. Monica and Shirley hurry off in different directions. Ahmed left half an hour before. Gerry remains inside. The concourse is in shadow and a dry breeze gusts along it blowing grimy litter in aimless eddies. Across the market square, in the churchyard, the weary leaves of the silver birch trees lift and sigh despondently. The hanging baskets suspended from the ornate lamp posts droop, leggy and brown, their mossy cradles crisp. Only a handful of people linger outside the closed shops, on their way home from work, perhaps, or waiting for friends. Guy and Jennifer walk slowly together towards the car-park. There is something cathartic about their mood; a sort of afterglow after the frenzy of the day. They bask in it as they saunter, knowing that in an hour or so the euphoria—both of the day and the drinks—will have passed, and workaday worries will re-impose themselves. They pass the shuttered library and the large windows of the new French restaurant, just open. Inside, a white-aproned waiter is polishing cutlery and placing it with precision on gleaming glass-topped tables.

'I think perhaps you ought to call your husband to come and collect you,' Guy says. He'd offer to drive Jennifer home but he's as far over the limit as she is.

'He's away tonight,' she says. 'He got promoted to Sales Manager in March, so he isn't home much.' There is no trace of sadness or regret, as he would expect a wife to feel in her situation. 'I'll take a cab.'

'Wise move.' She is quite different, he thinks. Less hectic, less tightly wound. He puts it down to the two double vodkas, to the relief of putting the paper successfully to bed, and perhaps, he speculates, just a little, to the absence of the husband.

'You?'

'I'll walk. It isn't too far. I'm renting one of those terraced houses behind the DIY store. I don't suppose you know it ...' he trails off.

Jennifer *does* know it; it's where her mother's shop was, where she grew up, but she doesn't say anything.

They find themselves lingering outside the restaurant. The waft of garlic and seafood from the open door is delicious. 'Let's go in and have dinner,' says Guy suddenly.

Jennifer shakes her head. 'Wouldn't be a good idea,' she says a little sadly. She likes Guy and would enjoy having dinner with him. But there is Kenny, and an inherent reluctance to blur the boundaries of her role.

'Probably wise,' Guy smiles, and they turn away from the restaurant and the road that would take them to the multi-storey car-park, cross the market place and enter the grounds of the church. Mock Orange shrubs are heavily laden with papery blossoms. The paving is thickly carpeted with fallen petals.

'Do you have parents?' Jennifer asks suddenly.

Guy hesitates. 'I have a father,' he says eventually.

341

'Is he ... are you close?'

Guy thinks of the distance he has put between them, his acts of rebellion, his determined rejection of his father's ethos. 'No. Not at all.'

'Ah. Well then, perhaps I can mention—perhaps you'll understand—on Saturday, at the old folks home—I'll be there, but in a private capacity. My mother is a resident.' She stops and turns to look up at him. He is a good head taller than she. Perhaps because of his comment earlier she is searching for understanding for her predicament; a parent from whom one is worlds away, the burden of it, the guilty relief. She has blossom caught in her hair. He wants to brush it out but it would be far too intimate a gesture.

'Yes. I completely understand. You don't want to get your professional and personal lives entwined. I'll steer clear.' He takes a step back, literally and metaphorically. She isn't really his type; far too confident and controlling, and at least ten years older although that, on its own, wouldn't matter to him.

'She doesn't even know what I do. I don't think she's interested, but I can't have her ... encroaching. This is just between you and me, you know.'

'Say no more.'

They walk on a little further, down some steps and towards the taxi rank. Perhaps she too feels a sudden need to restore things to safer ground. She bursts out, 'You know Guy, you're doing brilliantly well. At work, I mean. You're much too good for us, really. I sometimes wonder: what future can it hold for you? It isn't as though it will look great on your CV—an obscure little paper in a dull little town.'

'I'm a late starter on this career ladder though, aren't I? And I had to begin somewhere.' She wants to ask him how it had come about, the abrupt U turn he had taken, which, of course, she knows about from his personnel file. Perhaps she senses the begged question, and hurries on. 'Anyway, that's just why I like it.' How can he explain that this place, off the map in every political, cultural and historical sense, is perfect for his purposes; a dramatically unequivocal rejection of everything he had been expected to espouse; as low as he could sink? 'Anyway, I could say just the same for you.'

'Ah yes, but at least this is *my* little town, dull as it is.' And somebody has to stay around, she thinks bitterly, to look after Mother.

MEGAN HAS BEEN called to the Personnel Manager's office. The room, like all the others in the bowels of the dome, is stark and clinical without natural light but Mrs Rushmore and her wizened secretary, Frances, have done their utmost to subdue the utilitarian austerity of their work environment. They have pictures on the wall besides the lists of staff and rotas; a poster of Caernarfon and another of Balmoral, and a number of enthusiastic daubings created by Mrs Rushmore at Art class. Innumerable air fresheners attempt to lace the arid, manufactured air with some softness but unfortunately the flowery chill evokes something of a Chapel of Rest. Eschewing the coffee machine in the staffroom they have furnished themselves with a kettle and cheerful china and they take turns to stock the biscuit jar with homemade cookies. The barrel is in the shape of a pig, pink and jovial. Frances is inordinately fond of pigs. The hard grey chairs have hand-crocheted cushions. They have a tiny radio that they turn on at two with a delicious thrill of insubordination, for *The Archers*, to which they are both addicted.

Mrs Rushmore is on the telephone but beckons Megan towards the chair beside her desk. She motions towards a corner of the room where the tea trolley is situated, but Megan shakes her head with a smile. Then, the call over, Mrs Rushmore and Frances manoeuvre their chairs close to Megan's. They smile benevolently and Mrs Rushmore takes Megan's hand. Frances takes a small pack of tissues from her pocket and wriggles one free. Her smile, a further fissure amidst the myriad folds and wrinkles of her face, is kind.

'And so, my dear,' Mrs Rushmore says, with sweet, genuine concern, 'how are you?'

Megan begins to cry.

Later, she is working the late-shift. It is Wednesday evening. The sun slants in from the west, lighting everything lurid orange, as though fires are raging somewhere on the horizon. Since she arrived at two she has been conscious of a more than usually oppressive atmosphere at the café. Weary returners slump at tables, their ties askew, unpicking the threads of their regret. Shoppers are spent-up and fed-up, the exhilarating cup of excess drained dry; they are left foot-sore and unaccountably dissatisfied even with a boot full of carrier bags. Time spent in the car has left people tetchy and stuck with whatever prospect has failed to materialise, having to deal, during these weeks of drought, with radiators boiled dry, interminable delays. There has been a plethora of near-misses caused by drowsy, over-heated drivers.

The café is not busy. The few customers who arrive are agitated by heat, damp-lipped. Their clothes cling at first but are soon dry under the influence of the air conditioning. From feeling over-hot they turn chilly and petulant. Their food also cools instantly, fat and egg yolk congealing. They leave quickly, dissatisfied.

Megan stands at the window and watches the traffic on the road. The lowering sun glances off the cars like fingers of flame. The drivers have their visors down and their windows open. They travel more slowly than usual, subject to a speed restriction. A motorway maintenance vehicle crawls along the hard shoulder southbound. Two men in orange Day-Glo are putting cones out, forcing the three lanes of traffic into two. Although Megan doesn't drive she can appreciate that there couldn't be a worse time to begin carriageway repairs: at this moment in the day, when traffic is at its heaviest; at this time in the year, the commencement of the holiday season, and especially this weekend, when every man and his dog will be travelling south, to Wembley. She is conscious of a frisson of annoyance—although it can't possibly affect her—the ire of the motorists communicating itself like static through the laden, turgid air. There is a sense of general malaise caused by the febrile, suffocating atmosphere. And then there is the news she has just received, about the staff meeting to be held on Friday, which was to have been her day off. She has a headache anyway, from crying,

345

a ridiculous but insuperable reaction to being—for the first time in days—individually, personally addressed. This reclusive, twilight existence of hers—avoiding people's eyes, conversation, connection— only enforces the illusion that she is half invisible, so that when she is directly spoken to it is a shock, like sudden nakedness.

That is what they had wanted to talk to her about, of course. Mrs Rushmore, as well as being Personnel Manager of the Services, is the chief administrator of the private charity that funds the refuge. To her Megan owes both job and flat. Mrs Rushmore provided the furniture and appliances, passed on from an old lady who had gone into a home. Frances, a former resident at the Refuge, is now one of its most dedicated volunteers. She had helped Megan move into her bedsit, looking askance at its remote and desolate location.

'Are you *sure* this is what you want?' she had asked.

'Quite sure,' Megan had replied.

'All right then, but don't forget what the refuge is all about,' she had said. 'We help and support each other. We might be a scarred sisterhood, but we're not a closed order.' Frances certainly is more scarred than most. Her smile is curiously lop-sided as a result of a jaw injury. One eyeball is milky and sightless. Faded but still visible amongst the countless folds of her face is a tracery of dull white disfigurements.

Megan trusts them both. She knows that they want nothing but what is good for her. But the process of excision, however gently performed, is going to be painful, and will inevitably upset her poise over the quivering, delicate membrane of her deliberate evasion.

'You can't go through your life feeling afraid,' they had said, kindly.

She *is* afraid, of course, but not just of him. There are descending layers of fear; interleaved strata of hard questions and their compacted answers, a deeply embedded composite of wilful mistakes and errors of ignorance of which she, and not he, is ultimately the perpetrator. She is afraid of who she is; of what she has done; of what she allowed to happen, and most of all, of what she has left undone. Those two kindly women—ensconced there amongst the tray-cloths and flowery china—what would they think of her when they knew? But their eyes had remained on her, limpid with sympathy, seeing through her veneer. And so she had, with the courage of a patient performing surgery on herself, made an incision.

It had surprised her, the thing that rose with the most urgency from the opening. Not the festering core of it but a gush of soft sentimentality. The prospect of seeing him terrifies her, not just, as she tried to explain, because she is afraid of what he will do to her. No, it is more—and she struggled for a while to isolate it—her fear of seeing the consequences of her leaving in his bloodshot eyes. Drink and helpless rage will have debilitated him. While he had her to dominate, he could be, in his own eyes, a king. Without her he will be reduced; a little man, impotent in the world and overwhelmed by his smallness. The only way she could express this was to say that one of the things she cannot bear is to see how she has broken him.

Frances had nodded at her words. 'It is amazing,' she had said, 'but true: that even with all we have suffered, we still manage to feel that *we* are the guilty ones and that the failure is all ours.'

'What amazes me,' Mrs Rushmore had put in, 'is that after all they have done, we still care!'

'Of course I care!' Megan had cried. 'I'm not heartless!'

'It's because we invest so much in the relationship,' Frances had sighed. 'We make such sacrifices for it. We watch our friends and family give up on us because we won't leave. So in the end, he's all you have. And you're all he has.'

Megan had nodded. 'I was all he had,' she had echoed sadly.

'And you feel that you let him down, and that makes you unreliable. A bad person who doesn't deserve friends.' Mrs Rushmore had declared and Megan had acknowledged it in the wintry, wreath-scented room. Her desertions are legion, and of them, one lies profoundly implanted in the lesion of her leaving.

Frances had made tea, fussing with cups and saucers and putting biscuits on a plate with a doily. Mrs Rushmore had turned to her desk and shuffled papers around. Then, 'The problem is,' she had said gently, to no one in particular, 'it's just not true. Until you get over the idea that all your relationships are doomed to failure, that you'll be hurt, or hurt others again and again, you won't make any new ones.' Of course this is exactly what Megan feels. It is the basis of her containment—her embalmment—in social formaldehyde.

'Or pick up on old ones,' Frances had agreed, pouring tea. 'Once I'd revisited the wreckage I found there was quite a lot I could salvage. Aren't there people, *you'd* like to see again?' she had asked Megan, handing tea.

And now, as she stands with her forehead pressed against the glass, watching the world roar north and south, she breaks her own rules and thinks about the past; not of Stuart, but of the women of the Mere; her neighbours, the mothers of the children in Stuart's class. They had never taken to her really, because she was not one of them. She had arrived, out of the blue, scarcely more than a school girl, to move in with a man almost twice her age. They had frowned at her unintelligible accent and laughed at her girlish housekeeping, her avid book-reading. But mainly they had kept their distance because they knew, as she did not at first, his nature.

She sighs and hesitates, before putting her foot on the well-worn pavement of her memory. She had only known that he offered escape from her parents' dour guest house, the permanently rain-washed, grey little town and the endless bleak moorland beyond. His delivery route had brought him regularly to stay in one of their cold, over-furnished guest rooms and she had waited on him at breakfast a dozen times before he had pulled up in the rain at the bus stop and offered her a lift to school with a wink. Sometimes, after that, he took her with him for the day. She liked riding high in the cab as they trucked up and down the glens, and hiding under an old blanket while he dropped pallets of stuff off at various warehouses. He laughed at the books she took to read; *Portrait of a Lady*, *Tess of the D'Urbervilles*; and at her glassy eyes as she read them. He bought her fish and chips for lunch, and brought her back late, so she would have to lie to her mother about working in the library or trying out for the netball team. He never touched her. Sometimes he hardly spoke. Then, after her exams, in the long summer, he suggested that she come home with him. He told her to bring a few things; her birth certificate, for example, her NHS card, and any savings books she might have. She had met him half a mile up the road and gone off with him without a backward glance, as though it was all a big adventure.

She looks back now at the dimly recalled images of her parents, her school friends. More relationships reneged on. She is a bigger failure than she had let on to Mrs Rushmore and Frances; a serial runaway. None of them would want to know her now.

On the way home he had stopped and booked them into a Travel Lodge. She had thought it very high-class; the wide bed and white quilt and tiled *en-suite*—she had been as excited as a child by the little bottles of shampoo and tiny soap tablets—a far cry from her mother's candlewick bedspreads and vanity unit in chipped avocado. The sex came far too suddenly. It was unwelcome if not unexpected—dry, wordless and disappointing—but soon over. The flat too, when they got there, was a let-down. In her naivety she had imagined a penthouse with views over the city. But she had considered that having made her bed she had better lie in it. After all, she told herself, she could do her 'A' levels there as well as in Scotland. And when she was ready for University she saw no reason why he could not come with her. She hoped her parents would realise that she had lost nothing by the move and their hopes for her could all still be realised.

She had spent the summer playing house; painting the walls with emulsion he brought home for her, cleaning and tidying and even sewing curtains. She did his washing by hand—there was no machine, and he would never leave her money for the laundrette. She cooked meals, not very expertly at first, it has to be said, set the little table with flowers from the recreation field, and tried not to mind when he took his plate from the table and ate in front of the television.

But when autumn came and she began to talk about school, the violence had begun. And anyway, by then she was pregnant.

She is deeper now, bemired in the interminable questions of how and why; the twisted mechanics of emotional entrapment—sneering derision, raging fury, burning malevolence counterbalanced by periods of calm good humour and generous gestures. He kept her guessing; she never knew which man he would be. But she fell again and again into his trap and was three-times injured: by the wounds he had inflicted; by the caustic sting of her own self-castigation, and by the sidelong pity of others, who, as she haltingly explained away her wounds, thought her a patsy and a fool.

Megan realises that the sun has gone down. The sky is indigo to the east, lightening to lilac above her, pinkening at its western rim. In contrast the earth seems leached of colour; the kerbside grass as grey as the asphalt, the cars uniformly silver, the people inside ghostly shadows. Like the people from her past, they are faceless strangers.

There is only one who remains substantial in her mind, a stranger too, by the end, but not a faceless one.

GUY WAKES SUDDENLY and his senses are so dulled by the previous night's excess of alcohol that he is almost out of bed and at attention before his own cheerfully shambolic bedroom and a towering headache bring him back to the present.

In the kitchen he makes coffee. The bag of Indian food he had brought home for supper still stands on the draining board. He can see red oil congealed in its corners. He hadn't been able to face it after opening the email from his sister. She is a shrew and they have never been close but the causticity of her tone had killed his appetite and made him reach for the whisky bottle.

Dad has had a stroke. I hope you realise that it is your fault. He hasn't been the same since you left. He's hardly been to mess. Says he doesn't know where to look. I don't know where the hell you are but you must be nearer than Andrew, (who's in Afghanistan, if you're interested, where YOU should be), so you'd better come.

He opens the curtains and winces at the piercing brightness. The sitting room stinks of stale whisky and he opens the French window to let some air in. Suddenly the untidiness annoys him. In a flurry of angry activity he gathers the scattered newspapers and stacks them together ready for recycling, thumps and shakes the cushions on the sofa into shape, collects mugs and plates and drops them into a bowl of hot soapy water.

It probably isn't a stroke at all. He has known his father drive himself into an apoplexy before; shouting until he is breathless and hoarse. And he wouldn't put it past the old bastard to resort to guerrilla tactics like a feigned illness to trick his son out of hiding.

351

He damps a cloth and cleans down the bookshelves, the TV screen and the window ledges. The cloth comes away grey with grime. His coffee has gone cold and he throws it away. He climbs on a chair and flicks at a cobweb across the corner of the ceiling, then dusts the pelmets and his photographs. He gets out the vacuum; its motor is shrill and makes his head pound. He washes the dishes, wipes the surfaces in the kitchen and mops the floor.

But it is hard for Guy to think of the old man ill—seriously incapacitated—as a direct result of his actions. He has never seen his father ill. It is impossible to imagine him other than he always appeared; his uniform immaculate, shoulders set, every hair in place. The idea of him with reduced mobility or slurred speech is unthinkable. Now he considers it Guy can only picture his father in brief glimpses, coming or going for short appearances at school or, during the holidays at home—where ever home was, at the time, on whichever base they happened to be stationed—striding off to the mess for a formal dinner, or up early in the morning, dressed in fatigues, going out on manoeuvres. The most enduring image he has of his father is his eyes; steely as blades, the skin around them puckered by years of squinting into the sun and peering through binoculars but never creasing with a smile. He was impervious to humour, and whatever affection found tenuous root in his heart it never found expression in his face. Beetling brows gave him a permanent frown. A square jaw and geometrically precise moustache framed lips forever pressed together in a look of rigorous censure. No one confident in himself could remain so long under his eye. His unbending figure, meticulously uniformed and studded with brass repelled a proffered hand, much less a child's embrace.

He cleans the bathroom, heaving as he picks the hair from the plughole. He strips the bed and puts on clean sheets, loading the washing machine and closing its porthole with a slam. Outside, he sorts his recycling, and then curses as he remembers that his car is still in the multi-storey. He makes himself run into town to collect it, then drives to the municipal dump. The smell of hot, rotting rubbish is nauseating.

A plague of bluebottles swarms over everything. It makes his skin crawl.

Back at home, he hangs out the washing. The colours, in the sun, are blinding. He can barely tolerate the sight of it, blazing blocks dangling listlessly in the windless air. He stands before it, pushing his thumbs onto his eyelids and drawing his hand across his face. It is rough; he hasn't shaved. He goes back into the relative shade of the house, wondering if he has punished himself enough. He strokes the mouse-pad on his laptop. The email from his sister is still there. Her jibe about Afghanistan hurts. It had nothing to do with his decision to leave the army. He is no coward; in fact no one could know the courage it had taken to resign his commission knowing with what blistering indignation the news would be greeted by the Commanding Officer of his Brigade; his father. It was simply not what he wanted, had never been what he wanted. But his repeated attempts to say so had fallen on deaf ears, his father's the most determinedly deaf of all.

The old man would not want to see Guy, ill or not, and Guy certainly does not want to see him; there is absolutely nothing to be gained by it. He will not subject either of them to the frustration and unpleasantness that their intransigent opposing views will necessarily engender. He says as much in his reply to his sister, hits 'send', closes down the laptop, and takes himself back to bed.

IT WAS DIFFICULT to keep the flat on the Mere looking nice; everything was old and shabby and of poor quality. But she had done her best with it. That had been her mistake, of course. He would come home and note the dust-free mantelpiece, the cleaned-out ashtrays, his newspapers folded and stacked neatly behind the chair. Sometimes he would only kick off his shoes in the middle of the carpet, drop his jacket across the sofa and throw his lunchbox on the floor. But occasionally he would go into the kitchen to collect a bag of flour or rice to shake over everything with a sardonic grin.

Food had been a volatile area. She had never been a great cook but he had been inconsistent about what he would eat, taking a capricious disliking to things. Once he had developed a sudden aversion to ham and cucumber sandwiches and smeared them all over the windows.

When she annoyed him very much he would bundle her into the back of the van and lock the doors. Once he had driven up to the moors at night and abandoned her there, without a coat or money, to make her own way home.

But mainly he would content himself with a casual cuff. Or scald her with hot tea. Or trap her fingers in a drawer. Or stub out his cigarette on her arm.

He didn't use the belt on her very often. But often enough.

Now the bell-jar has been lifted the pallid, putrid contents are spilling out and the pure air of her eyrie is contaminated. She finds herself thinking of these things in the night.

MEGAN IS WORKING the night-shift. From her elevated position on the bridge she watches as the topography disappears into the thick night, the shadowy hills melding with the heavy curtain of darkness. Even the motorway—unlit—is barely discernible. The cars are merely disembodied lights in the gloom. The brilliantly lit bridge and domes glow in the dimness like hovering spacecraft suspended above the ground. Customers blink in the brightness as they ride up the escalator. In the domes, all the franchises are closed and the lights are dimmed. The piped birdsong is silent. Paul, or one of his colleagues, quarters the floor with his damp grey mop.

The night-shift can be the most difficult of all. Tiredness can cause the atmosphere in the café to become sour. Megan has known frayed tempers to erupt into domestic argument; wives and husbands literally at each other's throats, a sudden cacophony of personal accusations and intimate insults, plates and food flying. Toddlers at night are always problematic; up much too late and not to be placated by egg and soldiers, they run between the tables, their legs plaiting with tiredness, often falling and hurting themselves. From time to time a coach-load of drunken revellers, returning from a stag trip, pile into the café demanding food, dismissive of her explanation that coaches are only accepted by appointment. Their high spirits quickly turn into belligerence; they remonstrate with ungoverned language. Nobody dares look their way, fearing to give offense.

But there is the occasional drama of a more piquant type. Couples meeting illicitly, their passion scarcely contained over the Formica. There are underhand business deals; the furtive passing of documents or cash. There can be history; a pallid Cabinet Minister and his cronies

355

engaged in earnest conference over endless coffees. A soldier with sturdy boots and a bulging pack, tanned from the war and scarred from it too, on leave and hitching home to surprise his fiancée. There can be, on the night-shift, in the very darkest hour, a brief touch of humanity. For a time a young dad brought his fretful new-born daughter out in the car night after night to allow his poor exhausted wife some respite. He drove the car up and down between the junctions, passing underneath the Bridge Café a dozen times while the baby grizzled and thrashed in her car seat and would not settle. He brought her in a few times, when he felt he could not go on, looking bleary and at his wits' end. Megan would take the baby to the other end of the bridge while the man closed his gritty eyes for a few minutes. On her shoulder, it mewed piteously while Megan rocked and jiggled, alternately patting and rubbing the little back, and then would suddenly, for no reason at all, fall asleep. After a few weeks it simply stopped. Megan did not see him or the baby again.

Tonight the café is surprisingly busy with people travelling at night to avoid the insufferable heat of their cars during the day. Megan and Carlos do a brisk trade until about 2am, when things slow. He begins a deep clean of the kitchen. She takes a trolley of cleaning materials into the toilets. Their supervisor is due back from holiday the next day. Also there is to be the staff meeting. Its purpose is unclear, its prospect slightly worrying. Neither of them wants to give grounds for complaint. Everything in these difficult times is subject to review, especially staffing levels.

Later, her chores all done, she sits at one of the pristine tables and pulls a newspaper towards her. It is just after 4am. The sky to the east is growing lighter, the blackness diluted to grey and then touched with a curious yellowish green that spreads up the tent of the sky, eventually hauling a slash of purplish pink from behind the horizon to lie along its eastern length. The landscape emerges back into view, still silver grey and hazy, seeming to shift and alter, as though undecided on its final form.

The story on the front page gives Megan a jolt, two worlds colliding. The smiling, squinting faces of children from Stuart's school—his friends, children she knows from the Mere—grin out from her past like ghosts. They send out instant grappling hooks that connect up with receptors in the tender flesh of her exposed heart. Her association with them gives her back instantly a platform—solid ground—and after months of treading water and the exhumation of corpses that Mrs Rushmore has prompted, it feels good. On the Mere she was known. She had a place. The labyrinthine streets, the shops, the brooding tenements and utilitarian housing had been her environment and she had moved and lived within it. She had not always done so comfortably, often she had done it very unhappily. But they had been points of reference that defined her; Stuart's school, the houses of his friends, the shop where he bought his sweets, the field where he played. Most of all the people—nodding acquaintances—had been the cast of her landscape. His friends' mothers, Akela at the Scout hut, the teachers at the school; they had known her, and their knowing her had somehow made her real. To them, she was Stuart's mother. That's who she was, who she *is*. It is her lost identity. She has been in free-fall since she left—formless and adrift. The newspaper article reawakens the lost associations and with them a sharp stab of longing. She is homesick.

Below her, vehicles begin to materialise from the gloom. Soon breakfast will call their drivers. She rises from the table and folds the newspaper, taking it into the kitchen to put in her bag. She is conscious of a weight on her heart, a shapeless discontent. The sky is ultra-violet, weirdly charged, and the irradiated fields glow crimson, portending calamity.

357

THE TOWN HAS football fever. Even those with no particular interest in the game are caught up in the enthusiasm of others. Retail outlets cash in with generic football freebies or team-specific specials. Banners in blue and red are everywhere, emblazoning house-fronts and cars.

More than one publican has hit on the idea of re-screening each team's matches on their journey to the final in a twenty-four hour football fest. As Megan walks towards the bus station she passes pubs crowded with drinkers. They roar and gasp, exuberantly reliving each pass and corner, pontificating with the confidence that only hindsight can breed. Customers spill out onto the pavements where tables and sun umbrellas give the town a festive, continental flavour. Loose-tongued, alcohol-fuelled debate rages. Everyone is suddenly an expert, vociferous with an opinion on the best tactics and likely set-pieces. Even those on the same side find themselves at odds on the niceties of the starting line-up. A local reporter has suggested that Johnson will start off on the bench, an idea hotly disputed by some. Allegiances are declared with defiant good humour. People sport their team's colours, red or blue. The lowly Weavermen are quite forgotten in this battle of Titans. Gargantuan men and skinny-limbed boys wear replica shirts bearing their name and number, making believe they are in the team and ready to be called onto the pitch.

The town is over-crowded. Local supporters have been augmented by visiting fans who haven't got tickets to Wembley but have poured instead into the area, to be at the heart of it, to savour the atmosphere of the historic derby; a peak of bright carnival in whose shadow bloody carnage loiters. It is just midday, the day before the match. The heavy, heated air is additionally charged with the raw static of testosterone. Already beery bonhomie is teetering towards belligerence.

It will all end in tears, she thinks.

She has slept for a few hours and now, in her bag, carries a picnic and her crocheted blanket. She catches the bus to the old folks' home then takes the road across the bridge and along the lane, climbing the gate and following the pointing finger of the public footpath sign around the periphery of a mown hayfield.

Perhaps it is the heat, or the lack of sleep. She is conscious of tension in the air, a viscosity that makes movement slow and breath hard to catch. When she looks up into the arching white awning of sky her vision is prickled with small black specs that dance like thunder flies.

The path leads into a small wood, gloomy and green, the moist air breathless with waiting. Nothing moves and it is as though she has been petrified in green glass. It is a relief to emerge out into a sloping meadow, bright with flowers, and to take giant steps through its thigh-high grass. From the vantage of the stile at the far side she casts a look back at the guilty flat path of her track. The horizon is hazy, darkened by a vaporous mirage shimmering purple as smoke. Before her is another sloping pasture; this one close-cropped by cows; they huddle at the top of the slope in the shade of some trees and take no notice of her as she walks quickly across.

Finally she comes to the river. It curves in a text-book meander around a pale silty tongue of beach. The water is crystal clear, its bed a jostle of pebbles and fine sand. The far bank is an eroded cliff of brown earth studded with flints and punctured here and there with the entrances to cool, earthy burrows. On the edge nearest to her are the baked-in depressions of cows' hooves and some desiccated cowpats, but the field is empty now, apart from an old stone byre that stands in a hollow, its roof partially collapsed, housing some few badly rusted bits of farm machinery and a heap of last year's dusty straw. Megan checks it out carefully and assures herself that she is on the public right of way, before spreading her blanket on the grass and removing her shoes.

It had been so tempting to her that morning, to take the bus to the Mere, to see again the familiar places and strangely missed faces—the

Asian lady who runs the shop, Mr Mole in his ailing taxi—to re-associate herself amongst them. At least they knew her name—her *real* name, that is. The article in the local newspaper has re-sensitised her to her abject loneliness. She had also considered a trip to the school, in the hope that she might see Stuart. But he will be taking his exams now; there is no predicting his timetable. Stuart, of course, is at the guilty core of her sorrow, the fundament of her suffering. She misses him fiercely, at least some distant incarnation of him; he is soft-fleshed and affectionate in her memory. She misses his laughter—its wheezy hoarseness a symptom of its rarity, and those occasional—increasingly occasional as he had got older—moments of closeness there had been between the two of them. Latterly, in the months before her defection, she had had to acknowledge that these evidences of familiarity had all but disappeared; any vestige of tender feeling he might have retained had been deeply buried under a shell of impervious callus. Soon he would have left her, off to live with some girl perhaps, or even to college.

She wishes she could have waited just that long.

She paddles in the icy stream until her feet are numb, anaesthetised to the pain of sharp stones on its bed. Then she lies on the blanket and closes her eyes against the sun.

She is awoken by thunder, cracking the sky across from rim to rim. Sitting bolt upright, it takes a moment or two to orientate herself. It is dark, the sky above her a boiling underbelly of frowning black cloud. The short grass shivers with silvery blades in a hot wind. She thinks it must be night, but her watch tells her that it is almost three; she has been asleep for two hours and the staff meeting is less than twenty minutes away. Then the rain comes, a drenching torrent. She gathers up the blanket and stuffs it into her bag. Her hands shake and struggle with the ties of her shoes as another roar of thunder tears across the sky. She picks up the bag and makes a dash for the byre, almost blinded by rain as it pours off her plastered hair and down her face. Inside, the broken roof spouts water onto the ancient equipment but one corner is dry. She looks at her watch again, out at the rain and down at her bag, already half saturated, awkward and heavy with the damp blanket and her uneaten lunch. In an instant decision she pushes it as deeply into the gloom of the corner as she can, extracting only her purse and keys. Unfettered then, she runs out into the storm, across the field towards the stile. In a moment her cotton dress is soaked; she can feel the rain running down her back and between her breasts. In the pasture the cows are restless, lowing mournfully, and she dashes across with her heart in her mouth lest they stampede down the slope towards her. She labours up the sloping uncut meadow, the lie of the grass all against her now, the broad blades silvered with sliding beads of water like drops of mercury. In the wood the spatter of rain on leathery leaves is deafening, the path hardly discernible in the preternatural greenish gloom. Her canvas shoes are oozing.

She arrives for the meeting drenched and panting, skidding past Paul on the corridor as he lumbers along with his cleaning trolley, and takes a chair at the back of the room as the café supervisor gets up to speak. She is beautifully tanned from her holiday and has had her hair braided and beaded. There is the faintest twang of American to her voice. She has a large white screen set up and her laptop computer, and is showing photographs of food. But Megan is conscious only of the spreading pool of water around her chair, the embarrassing squelch of her clothes as she moves in the plastic seat. Her limbs and the pucker of her flesh in the chilly blast of air conditioning are clearly visible through the saturated cotton of her dress. Mrs Rushmore, helplessly marooned at the front of the room among a phalanx of suited executives, throws her a sympathetic smile. Then the door opens a crack and Paul, pink with shyness, hands her a towel with a timid smile.

Afterwards, the off-duty staff of the café gathers gloomily around a table in the food court. Curtains of rain sheet down the outside of the dome; the glass is opaque, as though varnished. The upward play of the fountain is suppressed by the volume of water coming down. The trills and squawks of the simulated wildlife are utterly drowned by the metallic ring of rain-beads on the glass roof. A premature evening gloom, sulphurous, presses down on them from a dark and angry sky.

Carlos and the other chefs are in accord for once. The café supervisor has come back from Florida wild with ideas for a new breakfast menu, American-style, a self-serve buffet including fresh fruit and jelly, muffins and bagels, rehydrated scrambled eggs and sausage patties, something called biscuits-and-gravy. There are to be pancakes made to order and served in stacks, and maple syrup to pour over everything, including bacon. The cooks mutter and fume.

'A buffet breakfast!' Carlos spits. 'Much more prep.'

'And so much waste,' someone else agrees. 'Not to mention unhygienic; everyone coughing and sneezing over it.'

'Impossible to portion-control. And *they* moan to *us* about margins!'

'What was it she said about pancakes?' someone asks.

'Stacks! One, three, five or ten. With butter and maple syrup.'

'She wants maple syrup with everything!'

'On *bacon*! Give me a break!' There is general agreement; the idea is absurd.

'I don't think they're the same as our pancakes,' Sylvie offers. 'They're thicker. More like drop-scones.'

'I don't care,' Carlos says morosely. 'Anyway, how can *one* be a stack?'

They grumble on, their sullen voices echoed by the griping thunder overhead.

Megan, of course, says nothing. She is still damp, but then so is everyone. Customers splash across the car-park in drenched droves. Unprepared for rain they use newspapers as umbrellas, and dump them—grey and saturated—in soggy heaps. The floor by the entrance is awash with filthy water; dirty footprints track everywhere across the chequered floor. Yellow A boards punctuate the ground like angular fungi, warning of the wet surface. Paul's mop works double time; he has dark rings under his arms and his round, moonish face is wet with sweat. Megan feels she ought to catch his eye to thank him for the towel, but it is something she has lost the knack of.

An unpleasant aroma of wet hair and hot damp human pervades, over-laying the scents of coffee and cooking oil.

On the dais in the centre of the dome an army recruitment team is setting up with brisk efficiency. The recruiting sergeant, supervising, is resplendent with ribbons, his uniform immaculate. He stays in the dry while the troops—smart young men in combat gear—carry display boards, an enormous television screen and a number of replica weapons in from the back of a khaki coloured truck. Their fatigues are soon dark with water; their boots squeak on the floor like trodden-on mice.

Sylvie's little boy is enthralled by the soldiers. She has had to bring him to the meeting; her childcare arrangements don't extend beyond her shifts. He stands near the dais open-mouthed, eyeing the weaponry, his dimpled hands opening and clenching in eagerness.

Sylvie sighs. 'It must be in his blood,' she says. 'His father is a soldier. He never laid a finger on me until he came back from his first tour of Afghanistan.'

Megan makes a moue; it is hard to imagine this cherubic little boy as an adult, let alone one so far brutalised as to become an abuser. But then she knows from her own experience that a child's environment and experiences indelibly imprint themselves on his psyche. She fears that nature, unless very strong, must unfortunately adapt to nurture. She watched it happen to Stuart, his innocence steadily curdled by the shouting and angst and finally extinguished by a gathering cloud of suffocating hopelessness. She watches Sylvie's child and wishes she could go back, try harder. Stuart, when she left, had been nothing like this little boy, who is transparently readable. He had been moody and secretive, monosyllabic. She had asked him to come with her, but he had been already lost; too far subsumed to see the possibilities of a world beyond the Mere.

They take the next service bus back to town. The little boy sits between them still and solemn, afraid of the storm. Megan can hardly take her eyes off him; his dimpled knees and glossy curls. He is a miracle and a mystery; what he has grown from and what he will grow into are equally impossible to assimilate. Malleable now, easy to direct and distract, in only a few years he will be fixed. He will cling with conditioned tenacity to his pathway, his helpless mother wondering where she went wrong.

The roads are already slick with greasy water. It courses down the grey-filmed windscreen of the bus and sprays from its tyres in dark arcs. All the cars have their headlights on as they crawl through the downpour, their windscreen wipers struggling to deal with the dousing torrents.

She says goodbye to Sylvie at the bus station and runs down the hill towards home. The gutters guzzle with filthy water in a turgid flow towards drains choked with litter and silt. The pavements that earlier were crowded with revellers are deserted now. Drinks abandoned on swimming tables dimple and dance with diluting rain. Water pours in sheets off parasols. Men are crushed inside; she can smell hot sweat, stale beer and tobacco gusting from the doorways. Already all but the central camber of the High Street is underwater. The uneven paving stones rock and spurt water up the backs of her sunburned legs.

It is not until she lets herself into her flat that she remembers her bag, abandoned, back in the byre.

THE RAIN HAS released a veritable feast of news for Guy; he can barely keep up with it as it breaks in waves across the town. He is up all night pursuing shrieking emergency vehicles as they attend cars crushed by lightning-struck trees, electrocutions from faultily wired outdoor lights, burglar alarms activated by thunder and some by opportunistic thieves. The storm seems to have released a pressure-valve of emotion. There are a number of domestic incidents; worried neighbours reporting shouting and violent fights. Rival football fans come to blows in the small hours. Water in the town's wiring conduits causes traffic lights to short-circuit. Chaos ensues. A motorcyclist is injured. Dawn breaks, a grim pall of bleak, cold light filtering through the thick cloud. Everything is sapped of colour, soggy and dripping. Vegetation is limp and damaged, a casualty of the storm's onslaught. The roads course with oily run-off with nowhere to go; the drains are sluggish and choked. Guy is just about to call it a night when he hears news of an incident at the motorway service station.

He is on the slip road, irretrievably committed, before he sees the twin lanes of crawling traffic heading south. He swears. He should have gone down to the next junction and approached from the other direction; the opposite carriageway is almost free of traffic. But there's nothing he can do, so he edges into the flow. Almost all the cars display an allegiance to one team or another. Scarves, trapped in the windows, hang limply down the doors.

His shoes and socks and trouser legs are damp from repeated soaking throughout the night. His wet raincoat, flung over the back seat, smells unpleasant, uncannily like a damp dog. The insides of the windows begin to fog. He fiddles with the air vent controls as a police car tears past him on the coned off inside lane. Guy swears again, his journalist's nose twitching, scenting a story.

By the time he arrives in the car-park it looks like the incident is over. Police are heavily in evidence. Burly supporters, some slightly bloodied, are being helped into the backs of police vans. Knots of fans stand around in excited exchanges of accounts; clumps of blue and red across the grey, greasy tarmac. The occasional challenging shout can be heard. 'Come on the reds!' 'Here's the blue army!' But on the whole cars are moving off to re-join the southbound carriageway.

A tearful family is being interviewed by a uniformed officer. Guy joins the small crowd of eavesdroppers, his phone on 'record' and discreetly held forward.

'We only stopped to use the toilet,' a woman sobs. 'Then we thought we'd have some breakfast. We set off at six; we've come from Carlisle. There was shouting. I don't know who started it. Chairs were pushed around. Food got spilled. My daughter was scalded with hot coffee, look!' She points out a small red weal on her daughter's arm. 'Then all hell was let loose. It was a nightmare. If it hadn't been for those army boys I don't know what would have happened.'

'I thought they came in a bit mob-handed,' commented a man on the periphery of the crowd. 'That cleaner had things under control before they even arrived.'

The mention of army personnel makes Guy swallow and look over his shoulder. He sees the military transport vehicles for the first time. At the back of one a recruiting sergeant is on the telephone. He stands stiffly and says nothing, his mobile held an inch or two from his ear. Getting a bollocking, Guy thinks.

The constable has completed his questioning and moves away. The little crowd around the family disperses. Guy approaches three men returning to their vehicle.

'Guy Crouchback, *Weaver Weekly*,' he says, holding out his phone. 'Do you think this kind of incident gives football supporters a bad name?'

'It gives *those* supporters a bad name,' one man says bullishly. 'Kicking off like that. Kiddies around, too. We haven't even had the match yet.'

'They're just getting theirs in now,' laughs another, 'before we thrash them on the pitch—and you can *quote* me on that!'

'It was handy to have the army lads on board though,' his friend smiles smugly.

Inside the dome there are ample signs of a disturbance; tables askew, one or two chairs up-ended. The floor swims with spilled drinks and in places is treacherous with squashed food. On a central dais a couple of flushed, dishevelled privates are putting a recruitment display to rights. A fat janitor, breathing heavily, is doing his best to tackle the mess. His lone, laboured efforts and his mop and broom seem woefully inadequate. Guy saunters up to him with a friendly smile.

'Looks like you've got your work cut out here mate. Did you see what happened?'

The man shakes his head. 'Not at first. I was down here. It kicked off up there,' he cocks his head in the direction of the escalator. 'It's much worse up there.'

Guy gives a confidential wink. 'I heard you were the hero of the hour.'

'Thought they'd hurt her,' the cleaner mumbles.

It *is* much worse upstairs. A line of breakfast debris is gathered like flotsam on the top lip of the escalator. Its metal teeth nibble incessantly at shreds of sausage and ribbons of bacon rind. Beyond, the floor is slick with beans and amalgamated scrambled egg, clotted with gobs of unidentifiable meat and awash with brown and orange liquid. It looks like nothing so much as an enormous pool of vomit. A wide splatter of yolk and ketchup, wearily sliding down the window, looks as though it has been disgorged with force from a distance. The smell is surprisingly nauseating. Spilled coffee bubbles and burns on the hotplate of a Cona machine. The servery is a mess of smashed crockery. Tables are on their sides, there are broken chairs.

Towards the far end of the bridge paramedics are gathered around two soldiers and a woman with tightly braided hair. The woman shows no sign of injury but both the privates have cuts and bruises. Guy marches up to them and barks, 'All right! Report!'

They both stiffen instinctively. But they have already been well briefed. 'Acting on our own initiative,' they parrot almost in unison, 'we intervened to maintain order and safeguard the public.' Guy nods, a clear picture now in his head. 'You mean you couldn't resist the temptation to throw your weight around.' The men look uncomfortable; it is pretty much what their sergeant has said to them. Guy turns away.

A slim, brown haired woman in an apron is attempting to clear up. There is something about her that arrests his attention. She is nimble amid the carnage of spilled food; sweeping, mopping, but remaining untainted as though protected by an invisible sphere. Within it, her movements are muted, efficient, designed to evade attention. Activity flows around her like water, heedless of her in its path. She doesn't speak. Her eyes remain resolutely on her task. She rests for an instant, lifting a hand to tuck a stray tress behind her ear. He sees that her hand is shaking. Just then the sun breaks out from behind a miasma of cloud and pours through the eggy glass onto the scene. The lurid colours of food debris glow brightly—fantastically irradiated—and shimmer onto the woman, lending her their hues. Suddenly she is lit up like a rainbow. Her hair—he had thought it was just brown, but now he sees it is alight with copper and gold. Guys reaches into his pocket and brings out his digital camera. At that instant she looks up and meets his eyes. Her eyes are round, and filled with fear. She takes in the camera with a start, stops what she is doing and goes abruptly into the kitchen.

Suddenly he is overcome with weariness. He takes a few shots of the scene and one of the self-effacing cleaner before driving home. By the time he gets there, showers, drinks some tea and downloads his pictures, it is gone eleven. He gets into bed. Just as he is falling asleep, he remembers that he is supposed to be covering the Open Day at the Old Folks' Home at two.

OF COURSE THEY have to close the café. The supervisor is sent home, overcome. Megan and Carlos and Brillo—when she eventually makes her appearance—spend the rest of their shift manhandling furniture, salvaging crockery and cleaning up spilled food. By two they have restored order so that when their replacements arrive they can function as normal.

As they work she and Carlos exchange no words; they are both shaken by the incident but have no basis of communication beyond bacon. To admit their distress would plunge them too suddenly and too deeply into subterranean levels of interaction.

Megan fears an imminent interrogation as the unwitting catalyst, the helpless architect of violence.

The café had been busy with exuberant, excited supporters, their big day ahead of them and everything to play for. Some good-natured banter between tables had led to less savoury exchanges. A few of the younger men had made mocking comments about the blue team's lack of recent silverware, in voices unnecessarily raised. One table, supporting the reds, had been especially boisterous; the definite hub of events. Flustered, she had made an error with one of their breakfasts; a sausage too few, an egg too many, a tiny thing but one that the customer, now attention was drawn to him, wouldn't let go. He had complained stridently, in derisive terms. She had found herself unable to move, conscious of eyes upon her and of his angry, suffused face. Her lack of response had caused his language to coarsen and his voice to rise; her startled immobility must have looked like stubborn indifference. A man at a table behind her, in blue, sitting with his wife and children, had remonstrated. The rowdy table had taken offense and turned their attention to him. The father had stood up abruptly, preparing to usher his family away, but the unruly element had misconstrued his actions and leapt to their feet.

Instinctively, Megan had reacted, folding herself into a cower, hands over her head. Everything had escalated, then; people thought she had been hit. They jumped up, jostling tables and causing spillage. The incident expanded like a rippling wave travelling down the length of the bridge. Hot food and drink flying, people on their feet, complaining because of their stained clothes, pointing blaming fingers. Customers had divided along partisan lines with astonishing speed. Shouting, flailing men, crying children, haranguing wives. The supervisor— ridiculous in her beads and braids—had tried to intervene but, wielding no authority, had been disregarded. She had dissolved into tears and it had been Carlos who had lifted the telephone from the wall to call for help.

It wasn't clear who threw the first punch; there was lots of shouting and shifting furniture, small altercations sucking others in to make larger ones, pushing and shoving. The stack of cups and saucers on the servery had been knocked over. Megan, at the centre of it all, had found herself frozen with panic and a sense of hopeless doom. Although not directly targeted she had been buffeted and jostled, utterly unable to resist or protest. The hot waft of ire had been transfixingly familiar and exerted an irresistible pull. Paul had arrived at the top of the escalator, brandishing a mop, his doughy corpulence suddenly more than a suggestion of heft and masculinity. He had shouldered his way through the melee and the crowds had fallen back, sobered. Then, behind Paul, the squaddies had surged up the stairs and hurled themselves into the fray. Things had got bloody. Those not directly involved had gathered their belongings and beat a hasty retreat, skidding on the breakfast charnel as they went, leaving only a hard-core to be separated by the police a few moments later.

She still feels shaky as she thinks of it. The raw emotion, the dull smack of fist on jaw, the suffused faces, blue-red with boiling blood and the plummeting response of her stomach. She had forgotten—how could she have done, so quickly?—the watery, debilitating fear, the dry-mouthed inability to think or speak that makes you such easy meat.

The newspaper reporter and his camera had made her feel intensely vulnerable, even here, on her bridge; the consequences of her potential exposure too awful to contemplate.

After the clean-up there is paperwork to complete; accident reports, incident reports, an order for replacement crockery. Sitting at a sequestered table she finds that her hand is trembling too much to write. She shuffles the papers together and takes them down to Personnel. But it is Saturday and Mrs Rushmore and Frances don't work on Saturdays. The cavernous corridors are dark and deserted. Only Paul is down there, tidying his utility cupboard.

'Are you all right, Megan?' he asks her haltingly, as she passes.

Directly addressed—by name—she starts slightly. He sees it; her wariness, her reluctance to engage.

'Yes thanks,' she mutters, making quickly for the stairs.

Outside the rain has reduced to a fine, persistent drizzle. Wind like a wet cloth flaps the occasional cold spray from foliage and infrastructure. She stands for a while outside the jutting entrance doors of the south-bound facility, wondering whether to wait for the service bus. But the idea of town—more over-wrought football fans, the match soon to be in progress, not to mention the mired streets and sullen, wet shoppers—is more than she can face. Anyway, she has her bag to retrieve from the byre. She sets off, past the emergency barrier, along the lane.

The welcome silence and solitude engulfs her once more as she walks between the sodden verges, the frondy grasses and heavy-headed wildflowers bowing with the weight of water down to the dark grey road. Her legs brush against them as she passes and soon her jeans are saturated and covered in tiny translucent petals. She tries to concentrate on the trees, their leaves newly glossy, and the bejewelled cobwebs stretched across the hedgerow. But the morning's incident presses on her mind and she is unable to maintain her precarious balance on the now. Her months of solitary confinement have achieved nothing, she tells herself; burrow as she might into her comfortable hibernation, she hasn't an ounce more resilience to that debilitating acquiescence that grips her when threatened. Her vulnerability is in-built; she will always be a victim.

This is the thought that assails her as she climbs over the gate into the mown field. She balances on it, for a moment, winded by the realisation. Above her a buzzard wheels on outstretched wings above the landscape, before diving, its talons out-stretched. Megan hears the tiny whimper of its helpless prey and, carried on the wind, a gaily careless commentary, the thin sound of country dance music coming from the old folks' home across the river. She climbs slowly off the gate and sets out towards the wood, her heart heavy as a rock in her chest. The cut stalks are visibly darker, revived by the rain; new shoots have emerged overnight. The rubber soles of her shoes squeak as they brush across the lush carpet. The wood, when she reaches it, is dark and dripping. The soft humus squelches underfoot and each gust of wind shakes a hail of droplets onto her denim jacket, but she is oblivious to it all, lost in thought.

The idea is sickening, but makes sense to her of the compulsion that has been growing for the past couple of days. Of her increasing sense of being lost here in the shadowlands of anonymity between the past and the future. Of her desire to step back out into the full glare of day, back to where she was—though perpetually wounded—home. The feeling that she is needed and wanted—albeit brutally—offers comfort of a sort. The knowledge that she is missed warms her lonely heart with a deceptive flame.

She shivers as she crosses the sloping meadow. As the previous day, she stands on the stile and looks back the way she has come. The sky is darkening; more rain is coming. The meadow broods in hues of dull alloys; steely grey, cold flat chrome.

Could she go back? The prospect is unspeakably bleak. Having escaped the coffin, could she voluntarily climb back in? The ruched silk and tailor-made accommodations are illusory, concealing lead-lined entombment, a pressing finality. She considers it, hopelessly.

The pasture is noticeably waterlogged; mud sucks at her shoes as she labours across it; the cows are nowhere to be seen but the cloven pits of their hooves are water-filled and oozing with liquid excreta. The slope is slick. She skids, almost slipping in the slime. She has to plant a hand in the stinking mud to save herself.

It is impossible of course; she hasn't the courage to do it. But the alternative is one she seems equally unable to embrace. She is psychologically, physiologically, unable to make good. She is like an animal, who, fatally trapped in a snare, had to gnaw off her own leg to get free. Now, though at liberty, the missing part compromises survival. Regret and guilt cripple her.

She should never have left Stuart behind.

Here is the core of it; the festering cancer of her burden. It overshadows every other regret. Of all the things she should or shouldn't have done, every alternative path not taken, each choice later bitterly lamented, this is the one that tortures her the most: She should never have left Stuart behind.

This is the territory she has not allowed herself to tread: the life she has left him to.

The rain is salty.

It is too late, now.

When she reaches the river it is unrecognisable. The small beach where yesterday she lay on her blanket and slept is submerged now under a frenzied, leaping melee of rushing brown water. It has encroached well up the field, lapping at the short turf and sucking away the sandy soil at its roots. The eroded cliff on the far bank is being further scoured, the burrows flooded. The river flows fast, an inexorable tide rushing busily to some ultimate destination, its surface effervescent with creamy froth and jostling with eager flotsam; the limbs of trees, car tyres, garden furniture. Sheets of plastic undulate like bizarre, gelatinous seaweed.

373

She stands at the very edge of the water and bends down to rinse her dirty hand. She can feel the cold chill of rain soaking through her jacket and shirt. Then a sudden surge of water covers her shoes and she is ankle deep.

The pull of the current is strong, even here at its very edge. She can feel it like eager fingers urging her to come along. The grass around her feet is soft, caressing her ankles with feathery blades. She takes a step forward and the water is around her shins, then her knees. A little backwash forms around her as she momentarily divides the flow before it closes again and hurries onwards. To her left she can see the meander straightening out. The river gushes into the next field, cascading urgently through the hedge where the water from a field drain joins the main flow with leaping exuberance. The sky, in that direction, is a little lighter; a shaft of watery sun permeates the cloud and polishes the turgid surface into burnished silver. The current entices her onwards, and she is caught up in its sense of destination. Its determined, heedless, uncomplicated journey to some objective is irresistible. She takes another step away from her stagnant slough of inaction, her pointless irresolvable dormancy.

The river is up to her hips. It is pushing her now, with rippling, liquid musculature. With the toe of her foot she can feel the lip of land that is the edge of the little beach. The drop, she recalls, is about a foot. That will immerse her up to her armpits. The pull of the torrent is tenacious. She finds that her up-stream knee is bent and she is leaning into it in order to resist its tow. She would only need to lift her feet. The river's passengers journey swiftly on their way; black branches, a punctured football, coke cans, a tennis racquet.

She is a fair swimmer, but the desire to be swept away and not to resist it is very strong. To be plunged into the swirling torrent and ride its tide to an end-point; here at last is a crossing she can complete. She lifts her foot to step into the maelstrom. Something catches her eye to the right, a tree limb, pale as matchwood and jagged where it has been torn from its trunk by the storm. It is black along its length but laced with festooning ivy, forking off into branched divisions where resolute leaves still grip. Something—a whitish shred of fabric perhaps—clings midway up the bough, tangled amongst the ivy. The branch turns slightly, agitated by the leap and lap of the restless surface. The piece of material is bigger than she had realised. It is almost translucent, curiously shaped, with separate limbs, like an all-in-one garment and Megan has to squint to make it out. Pinkish brown legs trail unresistingly just underneath the surface. Then she makes it out: a boy.

The water is cold but it isn't that which takes her breath away, it is the overwhelming force of the current that yanks her into its arms like a jealous lover. The water is brackish and bitter, and smells of pungent earth. It is thick with silt; it is like swimming in soup. She strikes out towards the branch, very afraid that it will be carried past her before she can reach it, and her arms are instantly exhausted. She just manages to grasp the leafy twigs as the branch slides by and begins to claw her way towards the boy.

The river carries them swiftly for the distance of a field or two. Then, ahead, a sturdy metal cattle bridge crosses from one side to the other. Its palings and lower supports have arrested a huge collection of debris like a beaver's dam that stretches across the width of the waterway; up-rooted trees and amputated branches, plastic sheeting and miscellaneous litter is woven in a tight and compacted mesh. The river—stopped in its tracks—has spilled out sideways over the farmland into calm, shallow lagoons. Megan, the boy and their branch slam with the force of a crashing car against the dam. Water boils furiously over them, filling her eyes, ears and mouth with the filthy, stinking effluent. She gasps as she tears the ivy that holds the boy fast, knowing she has only seconds before she is overwhelmed. Crazily, her head is filled with thoughts of Stuart; if only she had fought like this to save him.

Then he is loose, and as slippery and helpless in her arms as a new-born baby. Inch by inch, she lifts him, scrabbling for handholds in the interwoven debris, edging her way sideways, to where the water is calm and shallow.

375

SHE IS SURE he is dead. He is cold; cold and still, his skin blue-white under the film of silt. She lays him on the grass. Brown water streams off them both, off her hair and from her saturated jacket onto him, and then trickles down his fleshless little body and into the ground. She chafes his hands, strokes his hair and tells him to wake up but he doesn't move. Finally she tips his head back and presses her mouth onto his blue lips. She breathes into him. Once, twice, three times. Then he coughs and is sick.

It is raining again, and the crackle of it hitting the pool on the field is like a round of applause. The sky has gone so black she can hardly get her bearings. She knows she must get back to the byre; to shelter, to her blanket and the thermos of tea in her bag. She carries the boy. He is limp in her arms, unconscious, but he is breathing. She talks to him as she stumbles and slides over the grass. She talks about Stuart, the books he had liked, his favourite toys. She doesn't want him to be afraid. Her voice—so long unused—sounds rusty.

It is hard to get over the stiles with him in her arms. She thinks they will break; he is inert, a dead-weight. Finally she sees the outline of the byre emerge from the gloom. She lays him on the old straw and strips off her sodden jacket before pulling her blanket over them both. She draws his little body into her arms and rocks him. She can feel the whisper of his breath against her cheek.

Soon, she is sure, someone will come.

GUY LEAVES THE Old Folks' Home as soon as he sees Jennifer's car drive away. It is so banal, he thinks, so entirely predictable. He could easily have written the report without attending. There were the standard stalls, the routine raffle prizes, the usual suspects from the Council scoffing free cakes. He could even have made a pretty fair stab at the Mayor's speech, he thinks, running his eye over the précis handed to him by the press secretary. Now he considers it, perhaps that's how Shirley manages to cover so many events—she probably makes them up!

The whole shebang was such a waste of time while real news events unfold relentlessly around him.

He hurries from incident to incident, driving north through another heavy downpour to a collapsed bridge, where a police officer is feared drowned, then east to where a woman's car has been swept into a torrent. Meanwhile back in town the water levels are rising steadily. Some roads are closed. The riverside terraces are being evacuated. *That,* surely, must constitute community news. He calls Shirley's mobile, but it is switched off.

It is half past four. He hasn't eaten all day. Soon the match will be over and there'll be the inevitable aftermath to cope with. He pulls in at a café. The sight of the all-day breakfast nauseates him, after the carnage at the service station. He orders tea and a sandwich. While he waits the blues equalise.

'It'll go to extra time now,' the café owner says.

He has hardly started his sandwich when he gets a text from his contact at the police call centre. A boy in the river.

He turns into the narrow lane just past Bridge House. Things there have wound up, he sees. The car-park is empty. A gardener is struggling to untie the banner from a tree on the front lawn. Over the bridge the lane is choked with cars parked close into the hedgerows: police, a fire incident vehicle, an ambulance, other civilian vehicles. Small groups stand around on the road and in the front garden of the farmhouse. They step casually out of the way as he nudges his car past them. He can read from their pinched, pale faces that the incident is on-going, but there is no sense of haste, no busyness of organisation preparatory to a search. Instead, they show funereal resignation. Clearly, they assume the worst.

Guy parks and saunters along to where a group of grim constables sip tea from a mixed assortment of mugs and cups. A pale-haired teenage girl—stick-thin—proffers the tray and Guy lifts a mug. It has a picture of Mr Tickle on it.

'Not that one!' wails a sturdy girl of four or five who is nearby, 'that's *his* cup!'

The pale teenager gives Guy an apologetic look and puts the tray down on the grass. She gathers the child to her.

'He won't mind,' she says softly. 'It's the only one left.'

Another car edges past the house. Two more arrivals. One, a red haired youth, embraces an older man, clearly his father, very distraught.

Guy makes his way over to another group of constables, seeing one he knows. He lifts his eyebrow.

'Missing boy's step-dad,' the PC nods towards the weeping man, his voice a confidential undertone. 'His mother,' he indicates a slim, ashen woman on the front step of the house. She is being comforted by two others. Her mother and sister, Guy speculates.

'What's the latest?' Guy sips his tea. The constable makes a moue and shakes his head.

'Not good. No one knows what happened or when. The lad was playing in the garden for a while. Folks were indoors with the match on of course.'

The engorged waters sweep swiftly by; an inexorable flood.

'Will there be a search?'

'When the divers come.'

'But along the banks. He could have climbed out. It's possible isn't it?'

The PC shakes his head. 'Too dangerous. I mean,' he glances at the tumid river, 'look at it. The bank's unstable. Could go at any minute. *If* he has, we'll find him. But best wait for the experts.'

IT SEEMS IMPOSSIBLE but they have both slept. It is almost five when Megan opens her eyes to see his—grey and solemn—regarding her. She sits up. There is straw in her hair and she brushes it away with a smile.

'We did have an adventure, didn't we? Do you remember?'

The boy shakes his head. 'My mouth tastes funny,' he says.

'So does mine. It's that nasty river water. Let me see what I've got in here.' Megan draws her bag towards her, pulling out her sandwiches, a bruised apple and a crushed newspaper before finding the thermos. The tea is barely luke warm, but sweet, and the boy drinks it in hasty gulps. Just before he finishes the cup, he stops and hands it to her. 'Share,' he says, with a wan smile.

They are sitting like an old couple in bed, their backs against the dusty stone wall of the byre, the blanket over their legs. Light filters through the hole in the roof, dappling them with projected beams. She is rummaging for crisps. She won't risk the sandwiches, the ham might have turned. The boy politely pulls the newspaper towards him. He points to the picture on the front.

'This is Carmel's school,' he says. 'She knows these boys.'

'Does she?' The name rings a bell, one of the children on the Mere. 'She might know my son then. His name is Stuart.'

The boy shrugs. She finds the crisps at last and opens the packet for him.

'Barbecue!' he exclaims, smiling.

'His friends don't call him Stuart, though. They call him Skinner, because he's so skinny!'

The boy stops chewing. 'Skinner?' he says, through crisps.

'Yes.'

'Do you know where he is yet?' The boy's eyes are wide, too big for his little face. In the soft, mote-floating air of the barn he seems golden, angelic. Then she realises that his skin, like hers, is dusted with fine dry silt. She lifts a hand and brushes his arm and the powdery residue drifts away. His arm seems like little more than skin and bone; it amazes her now, that he was so heavy. He looks almost weightless.

'I expect he's at home,' she smiles. The word 'home' twangs an inner filament.

The boy turns the pages of the paper. 'No. Look.'

It is his latest school photograph. He looks uncomfortable, his eyes focussed at a point beyond the camera and off to one side, almost lashless. His thin lips are slightly parted. Even she knows that no one could describe her son as a good-looking boy. The grainy black and white of the picture disguises the worst ravages of his acne. One of his shirt collars is curled, his tie slightly askew. They hadn't sent in the money for the photograph when the proof and the order form arrived. His father would never spend money on things like that. She reads the report wonderingly. There isn't much detail.

Last seen on a Saturday evening, local boy Stuart Scanlon (17) has left his home taking few belongings and leaving no note or forwarding address. Sources suggest that he had been disturbed by his parents' separation and there is speculation that he has gone in search of his mother.

'You didn't know?'

'No.'

The byre is very quiet; the wind seems to have dropped. Even the rush of the river is hushed. She reads the report again. Restraints slip away from her, slithering into the straw beneath them like strands of silk. A hitherto trapped capsule of pressure is almost audibly released and she lets out a long, heavy sigh.

The little boy beside her finishes the crisps, assiduously consuming every crumb before crumpling the packet and handing it back to her. 'Not really allowed,' he admits sheepishly, 'I've had one packet today already!'

She puts her arm around him, pulling him close. His frail little body moulds itself to hers.

'Are you sad about your son?' he asks.

'Oh no!' she laughs. 'He's safe. We all are, now.'

Presently he says, 'I'd like to go home now.'

They leave the byre and cross the fields. The boy knows the path well.

'My house is just near here,' he says. He skips in front of her, as light as a sprite. 'We're going to sledge down here in the winter,' he tells her as they cross the sloping pasture. 'Richard says so.'

The sky has cleared. Overhead there is a washed dome of high white cloud. To the west an enormous orange sun makes everything gilt-edged and splendid. Grass and leaves groan with surfeit, rich and succulent with renewed life. A brisk breeze showers them with mischievous drips from the canopy as they pass through the wood. They climb over the gate onto the lane and the boy runs ahead of her towards the farm. He is yards ahead of her when she sees the detachment of uniformed men making their way towards her. He runs wildly through them and is lost to her sight. She hears a yell, heart-felt, and then a woman crying. She stops abruptly, suddenly wary, the consequences of what she has done crashing through her camouflaged asylum and breaking it into a thousand pieces.

Over the shoulder of the policeman a tousle-headed man she vaguely recognises aims a camera. There is a flash.

THEY DECONSTRUCT HER painstaking edifice of obscurity. Brick by brick she feels her sanctuary collapsing. Her name and address are declared and exposed on a dozen sheets of paper. She is identified and labelled in the hospital, photographed and fingerprinted at the police station. She explains it all a hundred times and her claims are queried and checked; her place and hours of work, what time she left, who saw her go.

'Do you think I stole him away?' she asks, incredulous.

'It's just for the report, Madam.'

She feels assaulted, wrenched out of the shadows into uncompromising day.

It is late when they release her. They are satisfied at last and anyway, have far bigger issues to concern them. The police station is chaotic, packed with drunken, obstreperous football fans and damp police constables; the smell of alcohol and wet gabardine is overwhelming. She can hear chanting from the cells. She slips away into the coolness of the night air. The town reverberates with the sound of sirens and burglar alarms. She walks away from it all, towards the refuge.

SUNDAY AFTERNOON IS a quiet period in the café and a coveted shift she had not wanted to give up despite being told that, in the circumstances, it would be all right. The opportunity to be paid double time while the world passes beneath your feet, replete with Sunday lunches enjoyed in cosy country pubs, or *en-route* to sumptuous afternoon teas at riverside restaurants, is not one to be passed up. Besides, now she knows that Stuart is out there somewhere, perhaps quite close, and she doesn't want to hide from him.

Quite apart from the usual respite of the shift there is a sense of something expended—a languorous torpidity—that lays itself across the whole town after the excesses of Saturday night, and reaches out even as far as the twin domes. Everyone is dazed, released as if from a satanic possession, and aghast at the damage their crazed selves have wrought in the grip of it. Desultory efforts are being made to clear up as she picks her way through the detritus of rubble and glass, splintered wood and smashed pub furniture. Men are laboriously boarding up shop-fronts, sweeping the pavements, assessing their losses. The bus station is a mess; several disabled buses, broken glass, vandalised seating. It is a relief to see the mini-bus creep cautiously into its bay; a tiny triumph, a sign of survival.

She feels something of it herself; a sense of emancipation, something let go.

The café is entirely empty when they arrive, riding up the escalator, neatly dressed and solemn. The woman wears her long hair loose over her shoulders. The man sports a nicely pressed shirt and conservative tie. The little boy is hidden behind an extravagant bouquet. She is their intended quarry and there is nowhere she can decently run to avoid it. She isn't able to help looking over her shoulder, to see who is watching her exposure. But Carlos is in the kitchen cleaning the ducting, a job he always saves for Sunday afternoons. If he is aware of the little delegation on the bridge he makes no sign. They too, as they cross the polished linoleum towards her, show evidence of strain, the ravaged emotions of the previous day have taken their toll.

She knows the woman, of course. She is the oldest of three girls. They had lived in one of the maisonettes behind the shops on the Mere. The recognition is mutual and Megan faces it with a brave, resigned smile. The boy comes over all coy, their reciprocal confidence of only the day before swamped by the enormity of the bouquet, his best clothes and the words he has been schooled to say, which he does, in a breathy whisper, with a furious blush.

'We want to say thank you,' the man says. He is rather older, with red hair and a pleasant, freckled face. And when she tries to demur, saying that it was what anyone would have done, he becomes earnest and says, 'No really. You don't know what it means. To have lost him, and then for him to have been saved.'

'Oh I do,' she says. 'Yes. I do.'

They refuse tea, orange juice. She walks them to the top of the escalator. Then the woman murmurs, 'No one will hear from us, you know, where you are. We understand your position. I've explained it very carefully to him,' she indicates her son, 'and I left my daughter with her Grandma today. *She* couldn't be trusted, but *he* can.'

'I'm afraid there's no hope now. Don't worry,' Megan says sadly, as they glide away from her, down into the dome.

It is then that she feels it; the last tenuous shred of the veil, slipping from her almost as though they are pulling it away as they descend, leaving her uncovered, the bouquet trembling in her hands.

THE ATMOSPHERE IN the office is strangely tense; edgy, with snide undertones. For both Guy and Gerry the weekend has been a hugely productive source of news. They arrive together like conquering heroes, bristling with booty. Some of it is written up in draft form and stored on memory sticks but much of it in a raw state, on mobile phones and digital cameras. But Jennifer, behind her immaculate desk, immediately dampens their mood.

'I thought you were going to clear this place up,' she snaps. 'It's a disgrace.'

In his corner, Ahmed slips an inch or two deeper into his chair. Shirley, alerted earlier to the lie of the land, is self-righteously wielding a bin-bag already and smiles smugly as the two men exchange looks. Monica, of course, is absent.

'I didn't get back from London until yesterday,' Gerry mutters defensively. Guy, who, until last night, hadn't slept since Thursday, says nothing, but notes the dark circles under Jennifer's eyes.

'You've got an hour,' Jennifer says. 'In the meantime, give me what you've got so far.'

It takes more than an hour, of course. Guy has to go out for more bin-bags. He comes back with cappuccinos and Danish pastries all round but it doesn't mollify Jennifer, who resolutely works her way through the draft outlines they have given her.

'We ought to be recycling all this paper,' Shirley simpers at one point.

'*You* recycle it then, if you want,' Gerry snaps.

As much as he abhors the activity Guy has to admit that Jennifer is right, really. Some of the post-its on his screen are so out of date that they have grown a layer of soft grey down, like juvenile facial hair. The fruit in the bag, definitely, is beyond anything; he can hardly recognise what it was. He sorts briskly through files and folders and stacks them perilously on top of the bursting filing cabinets.

'All those,' Shirley nods towards them, 'are being archived. Jennifer's arranged it. She knows a man with a van.' She is inflated with her inside knowledge, only gleaned by eavesdropping on an earlier telephone conversation, but imparted like a prophecy divinely received. The men glower at each other. Jennifer throws Shirley an icy glare.

They are repeatedly interrupted by the ping of the bell down in the vestibule. People want to report cats missing since the storm. A handyman hopes to capitalise on the disaster by advertising his services to make good flood damage. A tree surgeon proffers a poorly punctuated small ad.

'Why can't people make appropriate use of the apostrophe?' Shirley crows. 'Look at this: "Storm damaged tree's made safe. Log's supplied."' She indicates the superfluous apostrophes with a crooked finger.

Eventually Jennifer indicates that she is ready to begin the meeting. The staff perches uncomfortably like chastened school children.

'A pity about the Beaver Olympics Shirley,' she begins.

'Yes, poor dears. A complete wash-out.'

'You could have done the Bridge House Open Day after all,' Jennifer goes on. 'You'd have made a better job of it I'm sure.' She turns to Guy. 'How long exactly did you stay?'

'Long enough, I thought,' Guy says, frowning quizzically.

'You missed the main event. An elderly resident fell and broke her hip. The *Evening Record* got it.' Jennifer's look is venomous as she flings a copy of Saturday's evening paper at him. It is almost as though she holds Guy somehow to blame. Clearly the incident has more than ordinary significance to her.

Guy is quick to put two and two together. 'I'm so sorry,' he says. 'How is she?'

Jennifer ignores him. 'All this other stuff you've got,' she shakes her head. 'I'm sure it was very exciting, *ambulance chasing*,' she sneers, 'but this will all be old news by Thursday; you know that, Guy. And the street fighting on Saturday is old news *now*. It was all over the television, yesterday. I'm amazed you spent so much time on it.'

Guy is crushed. He'd been out until dawn on Sunday, keeping close behind the riot police lines, observing pitched battles and photographing the wounded. He'd planned an extended piece on it, using the fracas at the service station as a preamble, references to tactics and counter attacks and an analysis of the psychology of football rivalry.

'Anyway,' Jennifer goes on, her tone reproachful, 'it isn't exactly the kind of thing the town can be proud of, is it? Not our finest hour. I don't think we want to dwell on it.'

'Such a shame,' Gerry says smugly. 'The behaviour at the match was impeccable. I can't think what set them off.'

'It's the weather,' Shirley puts in archly. 'Those weeks of drought, the high pressure, water shortages, and then the storm. It just threw everyone over the edge.'

'*That* would make a good feature,' Ahmed comments quietly.

'If we worked for *The Guardian*,' Gerry scoffs.

'*This*, story, however,' Jennifer says, waving a print-out, '*woman rescues child from river in spate*', this is something I think we *can* run with. It's *good* news, for a start, with a positive outcome, local hero—a *woman*, to boot—the pathos of the child; it's got the works. Secondly,' she selects another sheet, 'obviously we're going to have to cover the collapse of the bridge and the death of the police officer, although they happened so far out they're barely in our catchment, but if we counterbalance *that* with *this* ...' she trails off, looking round the room expectantly. 'Are you with me?'

'You mean,' Guy speaks up hesitantly, 'all the rest of the stuff; the car in the river, the evacuation of river-side properties, the incident at the service station, the riots, the looting ...'

'Shirley can pick up the riverside evacuations,' Jennifer concedes. 'I want human interest, Shirley; true grit; heart-warming stories of neighbours pulling together—that kind of angle. Some church is putting on a soup kitchen. Look into that, ok?' Shirley is visibly thrilled as she takes the brief. 'Guy I want you to mothball all this other stuff and concentrate on this woman-rescues-child story. Who's the boy? How did he come to fall in? The woman: who is she? What does she do? Why was she by the river? Then a blow-by-blow account of the rescue. I want drama. Let's see if we can get Stephen Spielberg interested. It's just what we want for the front page.'

'The front page!' Gerry ejaculates. 'You promised that to me! I've got reams of material; in-depth interviews with both managers! I've got stuff Gary Lineker would kill for!'

'I know Gerry and I've read it. It's informed and analytical; its ... well frankly it's just too anal, Gerry. And the match itself was disappointingly lack-lustre wasn't it? Really? One-all and then a penalty shoot-out. Nobody exactly covered themselves with glory, did they? We'll put the picture of the winners lifting the cup and a précis on the front page. The rest is much better placed on the back—don't you think? Let's face it,' she gives Gerry a thin-lipped, ingratiating smile, 'that's where the real pundits go anyway to find out what they think about the game.'

'You patronising bitch,' Gerry splutters.

Jennifer starts, and visibly pales, and then says, 'This meeting is over. I think we all know what we're doing.'

Later that day Guy says quietly to Jennifer, 'Come and have some breakfast with me.'

'What?' she looks up.

'You need a break, and I need to go to the services café anyway to follow up this story. And you can tell me about your mum,' Guy smiles winningly.

'No,' Jennifer slams the shutters down on him. 'I'm busy.'

Megan is not there anyway. Guy wanders around the south- and north-bound facilities and across the bridge, looking for her. The domes are an oasis of brightly lit greenery, buzzing with travellers and alive with the chirrup of cash registers. The air is heavy and humid with the scent of coffee and sweet hot fat. A coach party of Japanese tourists swarms around the displays of the souvenir shop, making indiscriminate purchases of short-bread and stilton, clotted cream and Norfolk honey; nothing indigenous to the region.

The bridge is gleaming, bathed in sunshine. Another girl is serving breakfasts. Guy orders bacon and two poached eggs, toast and tea. Below him traffic pours north in an endless stream, almost as though dispensed from some hidden slot in the platform beneath his feet; it shoots out from nowhere in three parallel trajectories. He is mesmerised by the incessancy of it as roofs of cars and lorries materialise out of nothing, and hurtle off down the broad grey runway.

He has heard again from his sister. She has adopted a more placatory tone.

Dad's gone into Postlewood. You know what that means and you can imagine how he feels about it. But he's had to accept it. If he can swallow his pride, can't you?

Come, Guy. I know he wants you to.

Postlewood is a nursing home exclusively for retired army officers, affectionately known as the Last Post but privately dreaded as the end of independence; days of inaction made indistinct by unreliable memory, food little more than slops—amorphous and unappealing—a dress code of dressing gowns and tartan bedroom slippers. How galling it must have been for his father to agree to give up his well-ordered, pompously furnished apartment overlooking the parade ground, and Pettigrew, loyal batman of twenty years' standing. He would resent being fed and fussed over by strange female hands. Guy sees his father suddenly with a renewed vision; the iron-grey, upright pillar softened and reduced to a toothless old man in a basket chair. He finds his instinctive resistance lessening. What is there now, to be afraid of? The worst thing will be approaching Jennifer for leave at short notice. She has turned alarmingly pugnacious.

'Isn't Megan working today?' he asks the girl when she brings his food. Her smile fades immediately, replaced by narrow suspicion.

'Megan who?' she says.

Guy assumes a bashful demeanour. 'I met her here on Saturday morning, and then again on Saturday evening. She,' he smiles coyly, 'she made quite an impression!' He waits a moment to see whether the girl will succumb to his implication, as many women—suckers for romance—will. But she places an indignant hand on her hip. He laughs then, and pulls a business card from his shirt pocket. 'I'm Guy Crouchback from the *Weaver Weekly*,' he says. 'Would you give her this and ask her to give me a call?'

The girl humphs and stalks away, but she takes the card and slips it into her apron pocket.

As he is leaving he notices a huge bouquet of flowers on the end of the servery. There is no card.

'Somebody's very grateful,' he remarks.

'We make very good breakfasts,' the girl says tartly.

Down in the gloom of the gents he encounters the hefty caretaker and attempts to engage him in conversation.

'I met your Megan,' Guy winks conspiratorially. 'No wonder you were so quick to jump to her defence. Quite a looker!'

'She's not my Megan,' the man blushes, clumsily rearranging antibacterial sprays in his cleaning cart.

'Shame, eh? How long has she worked here? Known her long?'

The man considers for a moment before saying, 'She wouldn't want me to say. She's very private.' He seizes an enormous rubber plunger and disappears into one of the cubicles.

It's the same story all over. Everyone Guy asks about Megan denies knowing her, or anything about her, or even ever having seen her. The woman's an enigma, Guy thinks, intrigued, as he climbs back into his car.

Back at the office everything is different. The vertical blinds are pulled right back and the room is dazzlingly illuminated. Ahmed, the only person there, blinks and cringes in its glare. The place where the filing cabinets were is vacant, the deep indentations in the carpet the only sign that they ever existed. The long shelves are empty and the window ledge is clear; every bluebottle has disappeared. Lozenges of radiance dance across the ceiling, refracted off gleaming surfaces and the mirror-like chromium of polished desk legs. Guy, on the threshold, wrinkles his nostrils. The room smells odd; unpleasantly astringent and perfumed by a number of conflicting scents.

'Lemon polish,' Ahmed mutters darkly. 'Windowlene. Febreze. Shake 'n' Vac. Playing havoc with my asthma.'

'Oh my God!' Guy takes a few steps into the room. The boundary that used to demarcate so clearly the pristine precincts of Jennifer's domain has disappeared. It's *all* immaculate, now.

'Never seen anything like it,' Ahmed says gloomily. 'Those two women, like whirling dervishes. Boxes and packing tape, then rubber gloves and ...' he shudders and enunciates soundlessly, as though blasphemies '... hot soapy water.'

Shirley enters and bustles across the room to her glowing, neat desk. 'What do you think?' she smiles, ebullient with her achievements. 'Better, isn't it? Now it's tidy we're going to get the decorators in.'

Guy raises an eyebrow in the direction of Jennifer's desk. Shirley wriggles self-importantly on her chair. She is bursting with privileged information.

'Gone to the hospital,' she announces with a sanctimonious smile, 'to visit her mother.'

'Oh yes,' Guy remarks, off-handedly. 'She did mention it.'

Shirley's smirk evaporates.

MEGAN'S SHIFT BEGINS at 10pm. As they pass each other Sylvie hands her a small cream-coloured card. **Guy Crouchback,** *Weaver Weekly* it reads. 'He came here today,' Sylvie says, 'asking questions.'

'I knew he would,' Megan says.

She recognises the name: it is the name of a character in a book.

That interests her.

GUY MAKES ANOTHER abortive visit to the services on Tuesday. This time he shows Megan's picture to the girls in the book-shop, the coffee shop and sundry watering holes around the dome. They all shake their heads.

The beaded supervisor is back in the café.

'I'm not at liberty to discuss any members of my staff,' she says archly.

Clearly, it is a conspiracy of silence.

He goes instead to the farm. It is a bright, sun-washed day with a stiff breeze that sets flower-heads nodding. The front lawn is recovering from its onslaught on Saturday afternoon. As he waits on the doorstep for an answer to his knock a car pulls into the drive and the boy's mother climbs out. The children spill out of the back seats. The boy seems miraculously recovered, as though his ordeal had never happened. He pushes past Guy and into the house, dropping his school bag and lunch box in the hallway. The girl trails after him. She looks hot and irritated. The woman invites Guy to follow her into the kitchen, where she makes tea.

'I've been expecting you,' she says.

He looks around her kitchen. It is the kind of family environment he had dreamed of as a child. The worktops are cluttered with unwashed breakfast dishes and shopping in the process of being put away. There is a half-made Lego vehicle on the end of the table. A party hat and a pair of swimming goggles dangle from a cupboard handle. There are crayon drawings stuck to the fridge with magnets. Aromatic line-dried laundry nestles in a plastic basket. More washing–a swirl of pink, girlie things—presses onto the window of the machine, ready to be hung out. The window ledge is in need of dusting but it would be too difficult because of the collection of cotton-wool filled polystyrene cups that are sprouting with pale, leggy, nutrient-starved cress.

He thinks it is glorious.

The woman smears brown bread with peanut butter. Guy makes a mental note to get some. Peanut butter—another thing that was denied him in childhood, sneered at as 'plebeian' and 'American'. Presently the children descend and fall on the sandwiches. The boy is dressed for Cubs. After tea the mother suggests that the boy shows Guy the garden, with a significant look.

He shows Guy the site of his den, describing in detail its construction and appointments. He even shows him the place at the bottom of the garden where the branches and hedge trimmings came from. They discuss the finer points of the ideal bivouac as though they are two experienced commando colleagues just returned from behind-the-lines deployment.

'It was quite a project. You did well,' Guy concludes. 'All on your own?'

'I helped,' the girl says. She has scampered after them despite her mother's efforts to detain her, and is bouncing on the trampoline with exaggerated movements, trying to attract his attention.

'You didn't!' her brother shouts.

She bounces on. 'I'm practicing for the 'lympics,' she says.

'No you're not,' the boy says scornfully.

After a while she runs self-importantly to her own den—a tepee—and makes a great show of going inside and coming out again.

Guy asks the boy how he fell in the river and hears about the attempts to save the precious contents of the den. The bedraggled blanket, draped over a garden chair, is shown in evidence. The binoculars are proudly displayed.

'I couldn't get the torch though,' the boy says heavily.

The river has retreated to normal levels and is clearing, regaining something of its silver lustre. He stares across it, lost in thought for a moment. 'That's what I was trying to do. I thought Richard would be cross. It was his torch.'

'Tell me about Megan. You remember her, right?'

The boy's eyes suddenly become shifty. 'Not really.'

'Tell me how it happened. Did you shout out to her? How far did she have to swim?'

'I can't remember.' He concentrates on the toe of his trainer, scuffing a depression out of the sandy soil.

Guy squats down to try and get eye-contact. 'What did she say to you? What did you talk about? It must have been quite a walk back here. I expect the river had taken you quite a long way.'

The lad's eyes slide away. 'We talked about S ... about sledging. I have to go now; it's nearly time for Cubs.' He begins to trot back to the house.

'Wouldn't you like to see her again?' Guy calls after him, trying not to sound desperate. But the boy disappears indoors.

'He *has* seen her again,' the little girl, close behind him, says sullenly. 'On Sunday. And they wouldn't take me with them.'

'Really?' Guy pivots on his heel. 'I wonder why?'

'I don't know. Come and look at *my* den,' she says, and runs through the yellow flap of the tepee.

Guy calls in at the office on his way home. Even though it is after six, Jennifer is still there. She looks drawn. Her hair, usually sleek and immaculate, is dull and mussed up where she has been raking it out of her eyes.

'You need a drink,' he says to her kindly.

She shakes her head. 'I have to go back to the hospital at seven,' she says.

Guy perches on the chair in front of her desk. 'How is she?'

She sighs. 'Not good. She has a chest infection. They won't do anything about her hip until they've got on top of that. They've got her sedated but they keep on moving her from pillar to post. The hospital is packed. She spent most of yesterday on a trolley in a corridor.'

'How awful,' Guy says, thinking about his father. 'But she probably isn't aware of it.'

'She isn't aware of *me*,' Jennifer says bitterly, 'and there're things I need to tell her before he gets here.'

'He?'

Jennifer throws him a look like a twisted rope of complex emotions; hopelessness, anger, guilt, resentment. 'My brother. I've sent for him. They've been estranged for years but ... well, I know she wants to see him again.'

The rope ties itself, like a noose, around Guy's neck. 'My father's ill too,' he finds himself saying, 'I was thinking that I would go and see him.'

'Go tomorrow,' Jennifer says. 'Don't put it off. Is your story ready?'

'It will be, in a couple of hours, such as it is.'

'Email it to me when it's done. Go tomorrow,' she says.

He writes the story there and then, at his spotless desk, utilising his lack of solid information about Megan to add a dimension of mystery. He describes her as romantically elusive, a self-effacing heroine who emerged like a wraith out of the storm, battled the tumultuous river and then melted away into the night. He calls her an enigma, a shadow, with an uncanny ability to merge into the background, and tells of the veil of secrecy that has confounded his efforts to get her account of the incident. It adds a poignant—not to say gothic—note to the story that will have to suffice in the absence of hard facts. He uses the picture he took of her that evening, as she walked out of the setting sun towards them. It is a close-up shot. Her face, though partly in shadow, is clearly visible and yet somehow inscrutable. Her eyes are veiled. Her whole demeanour is closed or shrouded, overlaid by some indistinct layer, making her seem, though present, incredibly far away. Her hair is dishevelled, as you would expect after her ordeal, but lit up by a golden aureole, like an angel.

He attaches the report to an email and presses 'send'. His second message, to his sister, is brief: *Will go tomorrow. Guy.*

It isn't until he leaves the office that he notices the icon on his phone that denotes a missed call. A voice message from Mrs Rushmore, Personnel Manager at the services, invites him to contact her.

MEGAN HAS EMERGED as though from a chrysalis and for a time she rests in the sun while her wings unfurl, and the beautiful subtleties of their colours materialise. Behind her, the old carapace is shrivelled and redundant. She can see it now for what it is: fragile and never designed for long-term habitation. It had been a place for change and readjustment; a bridge from one condition of life to another. But she had lingered there too long, becoming too comfortable within its confines. Rather than energising her, equipping her with a new vision, it had begun to limit and debilitate her, sapping away at her self-esteem so that the longer she spent cocooned in its papery, desiccated layers, the less able she felt to survive outside it.

As a girl—and later, too, as an adult, but clandestinely—she had read books about children who ran away from home and survived quite happily in tracts of ancient woodland for weeks on end, gorging themselves on wild strawberries—perpetually in season—and finding cosy shelter in the dry hollow of a tree, befriended by foxes. Of the inconveniences of such existence no mention had been made; the many-legged creatures that scuttle on the forest floor, the difficulties of sanitary arrangements. It had never occurred to her before that the climax of the story was always the point of discovery; a bright torch shining through the gloom, being gathered up into strong arms and carried to where there is light and welcome, warm milk, clean sheets. But the last thought in the wanderers' heads as they sink into their familiar feather mattresses is how silly they have been to deny themselves the comforts of life for so long.

Megan spends most of Tuesday similarly employed, sitting in her tiny cell and wondering at herself. Why had she chosen this backwater of a place, surely the loneliest most desolate part of town, away from any residential district, with no neighbours? With no chance of an eye to catch, a smile to return or a word to exchange? Why hadn't she, like the other women, opted to share a house of ceaseless comings and goings, where the kettle is permanently on, a constant curtain of hosiery dripping from the shower rail and a regular three day period of mutual acrimony when everyone's monthly cycle coincides? Why had she eschewed the comfort and therapy of whispered confidences over chocolate digestives in the dark, and the safety of numbers in the light? She sees it now as only this: a fruitless attempt to wither and shrink beyond substance, a social starvation, self-castigation on an insidious scale. She had worn it like invisible sack-cloth, and the doleful note of an unclean bell had rung, like tinnitus, in her head. As long as she had refused to expurgate the tumour of self-loathing and failure it had continued to fester, wounding her as surely on the inside as he had wounded her on the outside. She had been, for the past six months, the architect of her own abuse.

Well she is done with it now. It is time she forgave herself.

She goes out in the afternoon and buys herself flowers, and meat for her supper. She takes the little cream card with her and makes a telephone call.

When the bus comes out of the mizzling rain of the early grey Wednesday morning she finds she is quite able to take a seat next to the girl from the book-shop, and they make sporadic conversation while the bus makes its way to the site. She walks down to the staff room with Paul and they hang their coats in their lockers. They hardly speak; Paul is tongue-tied and awkward. She is too, a little, out of practice at friendship. But the companionable proximity is something.

Carlos is his usual early-morning self, spitting out Spanish expletives like pips from a ripe watermelon. The kitchen has been left in a state *again* with no prep done for the session. The bins are over-flowing. There is no sign of a delivery that should have been brought upstairs and decanted into the cold store overnight. Megan makes coffee and places a cup on the workbench inside the door.

401

'Shall I take a couple of those down for you?' she asks, nodding towards the bin-bags. 'I could look for the delivery if you like. What is it? Mushrooms and tomatoes? Things are quiet just now.' Carlos' stream of invective is halted mid-syllable. He looks as Megan as though he has never seen her before.

The world comes and goes as it always does, people going somewhere else briefly pausing on their way. There is a family, sombre in funeral clothes. Two salesmen in shirtsleeves argue about their pitch and which of them will close the deal. A couple who are house-hunting have particulars spread out amongst their crockery. She likes the cul-de-sac property backing onto the golf-course. He says it's out of their price range.

The supervisor arrives at ten. Her hair is beginning to escape from her braids. The tan is peeling from her legs in ugly white flakes.

The rain gets heavier, rattling on the roof like falling pellets and beading down the windows of the bridge. Down on the southbound carriageway there's a shunt. Heavy spray causes poor visibility and the road surface is slick and greasy. An ancient Citroen goes into the back of a sleek black saloon. They both limp across the coned off lane and onto the hard shoulder. The drivers exchange details and make phone calls. The AA arrives and tows away the saloon. A long time later a tow truck from a local garage takes the Citroen away.

Towards lunch time several men in suits ride up the escalator. The supervisor bustles up to meet them. They take up two tables, pushing aside the condiments to spread out their plans, pointing out lighting circuits and ventilation ducting. Then the supervisor walks them along the bridge, making gestures with her arms indicating a change in the seating arrangements that will clear a central aisle for the hot and cold buffet tables. The men glance into the tiny kitchen. Carlos scowls at them as he scrambles eggs. The suited men frown at the limited food storage and preparation facilities. One of the men opens his laptop. Another unfurls a tape measure and begins to pace out the space. He looks doubtful; they all do, except the supervisor, who rabbits on about customer volume and table turn-over. Meanwhile another of their number saunters over to Megan where she is cleaning a table.

'What do you think about this scheme?' he asks her.

She hesitates a moment before replying, 'I think you should ask the customers.'

'Good idea,' he agrees, and makes his way over to one of the tables. The customers look up from their breakfasts—a sea of egg yolk and bean juice, islands of sausage and toast—and frown. 'Pancakes? Jelly? Is this a joke?'

'MEGAN GAVE ME your number from the card you left for her,' Mrs Rushmore explains, pouring tea. 'She wants me to explain why she doesn't want to be interviewed. In fact she wants me to persuade you not to run this story at all.'

'As a member of the press I'm afraid I must defend the right to print any story, Mrs Rushmore,' Guy says firmly.

'I understand that,' she replies, adding sugar. 'I'm rather hoping, though, to appeal to your better nature as a member of the human race.' She is very frank with him, 'off the record'. Her flowery-scented bower seems an anomalous place to be discussing such horrors.

'Why doesn't she get a restraining order, if he's so dangerous? Or file a complaint and get him arrested?' he enquires when the grisly facts are before them.

'You're right, of course, she could do either of those things,' Mrs Rushmore agrees, stirring her second cup of tea with a tiny silver spoon, her little finger impeccably curled, 'but she doesn't choose to and, at the refuge, we respect the choices the women make. And anyway, you know, it isn't as simple as that.'

'What do you mean?'

'Well ... do have another biscuit—good aren't they? Homemade, you know ...' Mrs Rushmore proffers a caddy in the shape of a pig. In another part of the room a withered, disfigured old woman hammers relentlessly on her computer keyboard. Mrs Rushmore throws her a glance before continuing, 'Imagine living with someone for years and years. Almost every adult memory you have includes them. Every significant point of reference you have involves them; the big milestones of life—your marriage or the birth of your children, the death of your parents, national events like Princess Diana's funeral. Fundamental things about you have been influenced by them; who you vote for, issues of faith, your sense of self. Even the small things are built around them. The food you cook is based on their preferences. The clothes you wear are what they like to see you in. The programmes you watch on TV are their choice. It's an exclusive relationship. You have no life at all apart from them, no friends, no activities that don't include them. For a loving couple it's a perfect scenario isn't it? But imagine that person physically abuses you. Or maybe he just criticises you and dominates you, controls the choices you make, doesn't listen to you, belittles you, or quite simply just dismisses and ignores you ...'

'I'd want to get out.'

'Of course you would,' Mrs Rushmore shifts in her chair, adjusting a crocheted cushion more comfortably into the small of her back, 'and for most women, that's quite enough. They don't need to inflict punishment; they're just glad to be free.'

'But if they have to go into hiding for fear of discovery ..?'

'It's *their choice*. See? And often it's quite enough to deal with for them ... beginning a whole new life without that central pillar, which has directed and controlled their every impulse for almost as long as they can remember.'

'Well, yes, I do understand that,' Guy agrees, with a note of inner irony.

'Of course you do.' Mrs Rushmore picks a crumb from her lap and eats it. 'The idea of police interviews, court appearances, cross examinations ... It's more than they can cope with although of course,' she raises a hand slightly, 'if they choose to, we support them.' She leans forward now, and goes on in a more confidential tone, 'The thing is, you know, that most abusers are very weak, very frightened, very insecure people. It's the secret that their victims know and, even after everything, it makes them have ... compassion.'

'I understand that,' Guy says softly.

It is, after all, why he is on his way to see his father.

JENNIFER CONDUCTS THE meeting with brusque efficiency. Guy's story has the front cover. Gerry glowers. The Press Association photograph of the cup winners and his pithy résumé of the match have been relegated, in the end, to page 3 to make way for a banner advert for hardwood conservatories, windows and doors that occupies the bottom third of the front page. Page 2 has the story of the collapsed bridge and the fallen policeman, carried courtesy of their sister paper from a town more local to the incident. Shirley's community interest report on the evacuations shares page 3. She's managed plenty of photographs of welly-wearing neighbours drinking tea and smiling broadly in kitchens knee-deep in sewage, and home-owners turfing out sodden, irreplaceable family mementoes with cheerful unconcern.

'Well done Shirley,' Jennifer says. 'Just the thing I had in mind.'

'You didn't use the material from the soup kitchen?' Shirley is disappointed. 'Such a friendly bunch.'

'No,' says Jennifer. 'I thought enough was enough.'

Jennifer has put together a collage of Guy's other reports, comprising the submerged car, the fracas at the service station, a couple of domestic incidents and a near-fatal electrocution, together with the briefest reference to the pitched battle between fans, and the looting. This takes up two further pages. Cultural Corner has Monica's assessment of a new exhibition of modern sculpture in the garden of a stately home—'the viscount escorted me in person,' she crows—and her experience at an 'all you can eat' Asian buffet restaurant; 'dreadful'.

Shirley's review of *Pirates of Penzance* is included alongside.

'Not very *incisive,* darling,' Monica sniffs.

'You mean not rude and heartless,' Shirley mutters.

The Coroner's verdict on last week's suicide is crammed onto a page in unhappy juxtaposition with the Bridge House Open Day, the Talented Pets at the Animal Shelter and a plethora of washed-out fetes and bazaars, after *Reader's Letters* and *Births, Deaths and Marriages*. Gerry's interviews, reports and analyses occupy the back three pages.

'I've been up literally all night.' Jennifer says finally, 'trying to rush this through. There are reasons why I may have to leave at any moment. Unless there are any *really burning* objections I'm proposing to sign this off right now.'

Gerry juts his bottom lip out even further than usual but says nothing. Monica shrugs and Shirley says, 'I think you've done a marvellous job, under the circumstances.'

Jennifer's telephone rings half an hour later. She pales as she takes the call. 'That's it,' she says, grabbing her bag. 'I have to go. I won't be back today.'

'Don't worry darling,' Monica croons, totting up her expenses. 'You've done everything that you need to do. It's in the bag.'

'Leave everything to us,' Shirley says.

'The thing's a complete dog's dinner!' Gerry explodes as soon as Jennifer is out of the building. He wrenches his jacket from the back of his chair. 'I don't know how much more I can take of this. I'm off to the pub.'

'It's barely half past eleven,' Shirley remonstrates, but Gerry is already halfway down the stairs. Ten minutes later Monica leaves. 'Off to interview the director of a new play at the Lyceum,' she says.

Shirley and Ahmed look at each other across the room.

'I don't suppose there's any point in us staying,' Shirley says.

They leave, and pull the door closed behind them.

GUY HURRIES OUT of the dome, weaving through the tightly packed cars to get to his own, a beautifully restored, bottle-green MG. Once in the driver's seat he takes a deep breath and rings Jennifer. He has to get her to kill the story.

Her phone goes to voice-mail and Guy can only leave a message asking her to contact him urgently. He tries the office but the phone rings on and on. He calls Jennifer again, and leaves another message, more specific. Then he starts the engine and takes the road south.

His meeting with Mrs Rushmore has made him later than he expected and the motorway is busy enough without the additional delays caused by the coned off lane and a 50mph speed restriction. The rain gets heavier and bounces off the windscreen. The wipers thump relentlessly from side to side and Guy hunches forward, squinting through the grey curtain to keep the rear lights of the car in front in sight. He realises, after a few miles, that his heart has speeded up to the rhythm of the wipers and his shoulders are rigid, his hands white on the wheel. He eases himself more comfortably into the seat and takes some deep breaths.

This is nothing new. The idea of an interview with his father has always been enough to turn his stomach to knots at the very least, and at worse, his bowels to water. From Guy's childhood his father has been remote, a figure to be feared and avoided, whose sole purpose was to dispense disapproval and discipline. In later years, and especially after the death of their mother, from cancer, time spent with their father had been a duty to be endured through gritted teeth. The old man would address them as though they were raw recruits, handing down orders concerning their lives in which they had no say at all. Argument was futile. They had all applied to the colleges and read the subjects dictated by him and after graduating both brothers had gone to Sandhurst while their sister had done the next best thing and married a fellow cadet in Andrew's division.

Guy had passed out and served in an active regiment including three tours of Afghanistan with a Commando unit; no one could say he had had it soft. No one could accuse him of not giving it a chance. He had given it eight years. Eight years of feeling like a round peg in a square hole, driven into it by the relentless, irresistible hammer of his father's adamantine will.

Guy's tyres eat up the miles. The rain clears and a dilute sun begins to burn off the surface water. The grey road lightens in a seamless succession from charcoal to iron then pewter to platinum until it is soft and pale as a dove.

He rehearses in his head, with arguments smooth and reasonable, the causes of his defection. He imagines fixing his father with an earnest and honest eye and appealing to his softer nature but doubts, in his heart, whether such a thing exists. He recounts, from harrowed memory, the many opportunities over the years just to listen that were thrown away by his father in favour of ballistic explosions of rage, threats and imprecations. In the end, Guy decides with a grim resolve to offer no explanation at all. The thing is done and can't be undone. He has, at last, had his way. He will allow his father to take the lead and let him, if he wishes, do his worst.

He pulls off the motorway at last and fills up with petrol. He is back on home territory now but it is eerily foreign to him; in some way skewed as though viewed at a strange angle or through a distorting lens. It is almost impossible to see himself walking these pavements or frequenting these shops, as though he did it in a different life a thousand years ago. If he walked through the doors of his barber, he feels that the man would see a stranger. Yet also there is a sense of wariness, as though he is a fugitive and liable, at any moment, to capture. He both desires and dreads recognition.

The petrol attendant swipes his card and puts his purchases in a bag. Guy drives into one of the parking bays and tries Jennifer's mobile and the office again. He tries ringing the other reporters but nobody has their phone switched on. He leaves messages, conscious of a pleading note in his voice. He wonders what on earth can be happening and kicks himself for driving south at all. He should have gone back to the office and killed the story himself. Ramming the car into gear he drives on into the well-known countryside.

Given their history it is hard to understand why he has succumbed to his sister's heavy-handed attempts at persuasion. He has shaken off her implication that he is the cause of the stroke; if that were the case it would have happened six months ago. And he does not at all expect that it will have softened by a single fibre the unyielding hawser of his father's character. But perhaps the old man's agreeing to retire to Postlewood suggests that the opportunities for future reconciliations may be few. Nothing, Guy is sure, short of serious bodily deterioration, could have prompted it. And for once, perhaps Guy is able to empathise with his father, at least in the feelings of dislocation that such a move will inevitably have engendered for a man so entirely regimented in his daily habits and contacts. It is this unwonted experience—of being able to place a tentative toe into the flawlessly polished leather of his father's engulfing shoe—which has made the difference. He has what Mrs Rushmore identified with such unnerving acuteness as a cause to overlook evil: compassion.

He drives through the old stone gates of Postlewood and parks his car on the gravelled sweep. An attendant in the hall gestures to a pair of ancient carved doors and Guy, with a deep breath, steps through.

The brigadier is not, as Guy expects, wearing a dressing gown, but is smartly clothed, albeit in civvies. The room where he is waiting is the library, where deep leather chairs and towering shelves of beautifully bound books suggest a gentleman's club more strongly than a nursing home. There's a huge fire place with a high fender perfectly placed for the perching of distinguished military posteriors, and tall glazed doors give access via a discreet ramp to a manicured square of well-disciplined lawn. Guy is clearly expected—his sister must have forewarned their father. The library is diplomatically deserted and a tea trolley is laid for two. He resists the urge to come to attention and tries a smile. The brigadier's face twitches minutely and there is a moistness in one notably drooped eye. He levers himself out of the chair and crosses the red and gold carpet with a slow stride that almost, but not quite, disguises the stiffness of one leg. They eye each other across the space between them, the brigadier gives a curt nod and then turns and indicates the tea trolley and a conveniently placed chair.

'They'll bring tea directly,' he says.

Immediately a uniformed orderly arrives with the hot water and pours.

'I'd expected female nurses,' Guy exclaims.

'Humph!' his father blusters.

The room is crowded with elephants. Guy chooses the least intimidating one. 'How are you settling in, sir?' he asks.

The brigadier has not yet regained discursive speech and communicates in short, grumbled phrases, like bullet points. 'Pretty comfortable billet; decent cellar, general morale rather low,' he says, his eyes fixed on a spot on the wall across the room. His words, though comprehendible, are slightly slurred.

'*Your* morale, sir?'

The brigadier jumps as though physically assaulted; he is not used to being asked personal questions. Guy might as well have asked him how his bowels are. '*General* morale. A lot of chaps not quite with it. Old Piffy thinks he's in the Falklands.'

'Good lord! That's thirty years ago.'

'I suppose it is.'

'Two years after I was born.'

'Yes.' The brigadier turns his head then, and looks at Guy. 'I missed your birthday.'

There is a beat. Guy swallows; his mouth is suddenly dry. 'Shall I pour the tea, sir?' he asks thinly. Presently Guy observes, 'I think you'll do splendidly here, sir.'

'Not *staying!* the Brigadier splutters. 'Only here for a spot of R & R, you know. Good God! Not ready for the Last Post yet!'

'Really?' Guy purses his lips. He has been tricked. But somehow, he doesn't mind.

They discuss—haltingly—non-controversial topics; the weather and the wars—on which, of course, there can be but one opinion. Guy bowls a steady stream of soft-edged questions for his father to return while the older man wrestles painfully with his tea, sandwiches and a scone. The accoutrements of the meal seem inordinately cumbersome in his stiff, disobliging fingers. Guy takes a surreptitious glance at his watch. He needs to call Jennifer again. He excuses himself and makes his way to the lavatory—oversized cubicles girded with hand-rails; buttons and pull-strings in case of emergency. Still there is no reply. He leaves a last, plaintive message. Surely by now someone will have pulled the story, but he wants to know for sure.

Afterwards they walk around the gardens. Gravelled paths meander through prick-neat beds of summer planting. Guy's father gives a staccato potted history of the house that dates back to the Tudors and has been, in its time, a country mansion, a convent, a military hospital, an hotel and an asylum. The elephants shamble after them in the cooling air of the late afternoon. Unexpectedly the brigadier tackles the largest. 'So,' he says, 'a journalist.' He is trying, Guy can tell, not to pronounce the word as though it were a debilitating disease.

'Yes, sir. Just in a small way, while I find my feet.'

'Humph!'

'But it suits me, sir,' Guy adds significantly.

There is a long pause. The shadows on the lawn lengthen. The brigadier seems to be engaged with an inner struggle. Then he says, 'Old friend of mine in the War Office,'—he stubbornly refuses to give it its modern title—'has a son in the same game.'

'Really? How interesting,' Guy says, suppressing the instinct to offer condolences. He wonders if they have exchanged commiserations over their mutual tragedy.

'Looking for a chap to cover things in Iraq. Needs someone who knows the Military ropes; won't get in the way.'

'A war correspondent? Who did you say he works for?'

'Not the BBC. One of the others.'

'Good Lord. And he'd consider me?'

'Said so. Got his card, anyway. Time I went in now. Nearly time to dress. You'll stay?'

'I can't, I'm sorry.' To his surprise, Guy genuinely is sorry. His father is different, by no means a broken man. He is still formidable, mentally as sharp as ever if physically somewhat constrained, but in some profound way he has been smoothed and soothed by the stroke; his cantankerous creases have been softened, his rage has cooled.

They arrive back in the library. The tea things have been cleared and a trolley of decanters and heavy lead crystal tumblers has taken its place. It is dark in the room, after the brightness outdoors. They stand on the rug before the fireplace. Slowly, the brigadier reaches into his jacket pocket and brings out a business card. He tenders it reluctantly. 'Can't do anything for you in this field,' he mumbles, frowning, and then, more quietly, almost to himself, 'Just wanted to keep them all where I could see them.'

Guy reaches into his own jacket pocket and draws out a red and white tin of strong mints, his father's favourites. He removes the card from his father's hand and places the tin in its stead. His father makes a small choking noise in his throat that he turns into a cough before slipping the tin into his pocket.

Out in the hall there is a swish of wheels as residents are wheeled away to dress for dinner. A gong sounds softly. 'Time you went to dress, Father,' Guy says. The old man takes Guy's right hand in his and with

413

the other makes an awkward, hesitant reach inside the flap of Guy's jacket and presses it momentarily on Guy's flank. Guy can feel the warmth of its tremulous pressure through his shirt.

'Humph,' the brigadier says, releasing himself abruptly and turning to the door, 'not quite combat-ready!' While it's true that Guy is no longer at an operational peak of physical fitness, he has kept himself well in shape at a gym. But he has neither the heart nor the words to defend himself. His father's gesture—brief, uneasy, and regardless of the disparaging comment that had accompanied it—is the closest he has ever come to an embrace.

It is enough. More, far more than enough.

HIS PHONE RINGS before he gets to the motorway junction. He swerves the MG towards the kerb and mounts it up the pavement before answering the call. It is Jennifer.

'What's all this, Guy?' She sounds harassed.

He explains. 'I want you to pull the story,' he says. 'You'll *have* to.'

'I don't *have* to do anything,' she snaps. Then he hears her sigh. 'I can't, anyway Guy. It's too late.'

He looks at his watch. It is only just after seven. 'We've been far later than this before signing off the paper,' he says. 'You must be able to do something. I've got an alternative story for you. The street fights. I wrote it all up, anyway.'

'It isn't that,' she says. 'I signed off this morning. I've been at the hospital all day.'

'I see.' He bites his lip. 'Is she ..?'

'Still clinging on,' He can hear the sardonic note in Jennifer's voice. 'She'll wait until he comes. He's due later tonight.'

Guy stares through his windscreen. A group of pedestrians has to break ranks to edge past his vehicle; the blokes admire its sleek lines. 'They don't make them like that anymore,' they agree. Guy lowers his voice. 'Jennifer, this woman's in danger if we run the story. Her husband's an animal. He may well kill her. There must be *something* you can do.'

'The story's very non-specific about her,' Jennifer reasons. 'It doesn't name her at all. It doesn't give her address ...'

415

'Her picture's there and it suggests that she was on her way home from work. It wouldn't take a genius to work out where that is!'

'I've told you Guy, I can't pull it.'

'You mean you won't.'

There is silence for a moment. 'It's a good story,' she says, with that hard edge to her voice that he is coming to know. 'I'll take full responsibility ...'

'Your name isn't on the by-line.'

'Neither is yours,' she says, and hangs up.

STUART FINDS HER first. He arrives at the site at the end of Thursday afternoon, riding up the escalator in an unspeakably filthy parka and disintegrating trainers, a substantial haversack in tow. He stands on the threshold waiting for her to notice him, blinking in the brightness like an underground creature just emerged into the light, gnawing the skin on the side of his thumb. She walks towards him quickly, wiping her sudsy hands on a towel, putting her arms around him. He doesn't resist, neither does he respond. Inside his layers, he is skin and bone. He smells like an animal; rank and sour.

'Saw your picture,' he mutters, his eyes sliding off her face. 'Thought I'd better come.' His voice, ever high and reedy, is almost a whisper, as though long unused.

'I'm so glad you have, Stuart,' she says.

He allows himself a long, appraising look around, his eyes wide and almost uncomprehending, as though he has found himself on a starship in another universe. 'This where you work, then? Is this where you came?'

'Not at first,' she says. 'But we can talk about all that later.'

His skin is dull and grime-impregnated and as severely pustular as ever. His hair is matted and coarse, like fur. His eyes, when she can get a clear look at them, have a clouded appearance, denoting illness or trauma. They are like shuttered windows, telling her nothing of the person within.

People in the café are looking at him askance. He looks like what he is—a vagrant—and they are both repelled and unnerved by him. Their attention disturbs him and he ducks away with a shrinking, withdrawing movement of his shoulder to re-concentrate his attention on his thumb. The supervisor, engaged with customers at the other end of the bridge, keeps giving the two of them apprehensive, inquisitive glances.

'Just a minute Stuart,' Megan says. She moves him gently to one side of the bridge, right to the back where they have stacked the furniture broken in Saturday's disturbance, and drags his rucksack across to join him. It leaves a damp dark smear across the linoleum. His shoes, she notices, are oozing brown water. She goes into the kitchen and comes out a few moments later with a tin-foil wrapped parcel. She fills one of the polystyrene take-out cups with milk and presses on the lid. Stuart has remained exactly where she left him. He is staring out of the window at the traffic passing below. As she carries the food towards him Megan is aware of the supervisor making her way along the bridge. Megan's suggestion that customers be polled on the proposed new breakfast offer has caused a hiatus in the plans for redevelopment and resulted in some spiteful treatment from her superior. She only needs to put a foot out of line to find herself without a job.

She turns to Stuart and hands him the food and her precious door key. 'Can you get back to town? This is where I live.' She describes carefully the location of her flat. 'Go there and wait for me,' she says. 'Have a shower—a good long one. Eat what you want. Have a sleep in my bed. I'll be back about eleven.'

'No,' he says, shaking his head, and looking at her straight for the first time. 'I need to stay here. He'll come, you know.'

'Maybe. But not today. He won't even have seen the picture, yet, and he won't be as quick to work things out as you.'

'Megan!' the supervisor is right behind her. 'What are you doing? We don't give food away to ...' she looks Stuart up and down, 'people of that sort. You know the policy.'

'This is my son,' Megan snaps, rounding on her. And then, in a more conciliatory tone, 'I'll pay for the food. He's not staying, anyway.'

'Why did she call you Megan?' Stuart asks.

'Come on,' Megan turns him gently back towards the stairs. 'I'll explain on the way down.'

They pass through the dome. In the news-stand outside the book-shop the *Weaver Weekly* is prominently on display. At the entrance, the six o'clock shuttle bus has just pulled up. Megan speaks to the driver and he agrees to take Stuart back to town. He steps on board, the tin-foil parcel and cup of milk still clutched in his grimy hands like souvenirs from an inter-galactic tourist attraction. He looks bewildered and lost, as he had as a small child when left out by the other children because he was too puny to play their games. His erratic behaviour—sometimes manic, sometimes moody—was too unpredictable to include him in party invitations. He was the ugly boy whom nobody wanted as a friend. She feels again as she had then; fiercely protective, believing that her love for him would conquer all his foes.

'I wanted to look after you,' he says, and she realises that he is close to tears, and that he feels that she is sending him away.

She steps up and hugs him again. 'You will,' she says warmly. 'But you need to eat and sleep first. Try your sandwich,' she smiles then, and nudges him gently further into the bus. 'I put brown sauce on it. Your favourite.'

He sinks down on to the seat with the weariness of a man sixty years his senior, and as the bus pulls away Megan mouths 'see you later' and gives him her bravest smile.

Guy comes next, much later in the evening. In spite of his tallness and broad shoulders he looks weighted, burdened with responsibility and apology. He orders breakfast because that is all there is at the bridge café, and takes a seat at a remote table.

'Just give me chance to try and explain,' he says as Megan pours his coffee.

The café is quiet. The supervisor has gone home. Megan slips into the chair opposite him. Before he can speak she holds up her hand.

'Your name isn't Guy Crouchback,' she says. One eye is mischievously narrowed and the corresponding corner of her lip is curled. He had expected an emotional outburst. Her gambit takes the wind out of his sails. He smiles ruefully. 'You've read the books?'

She nods. 'A long time ago. It took me a while to place it.'

'I really am Guy,' he begins, 'but, no. Not Guy Crouchback. There were reasons why it seemed expedient and ... ironic.'

'You don't need to explain,' Megan says. 'My name isn't really Megan, either.' They look at each other then, across the white Formica.

Dusk is falling beyond the slanting windows of the bridge. It is that breathless moment when day has ceased to hold sway but before the mantle of night descends. To the east the sky is indigo and pricked by the first stars, to the west it is the blue of a cameo. It neither emits nor absorbs light and briefly the landscape beneath is illuminated by its own inherent radiance, a silken purple gloaming; lavender grass and lilac trees smoulder with an inner luminosity; the road is a river of mauve strewn with amethysts.

Behind them, around them, the bridge vanishes into the air and they are suspended, the two of them, on an ultraviolet cloud over a gorge of dusky shadow. Then the automatic sensors cause the fluorescent strip lights to flicker and surge into life, and Carlos rings the bell. Guy's breakfast is ready.

Other customers come and Megan takes their orders and serves them before returning to Guy's table. He watches her, tripping up and down the bridge with beverages and breakfasts, stacking dishes. Her movements are as contained as ever, she does not draw attention to herself, but her protective sphere is missing. She looks small and incredibly vulnerable.

'I tried to pull the story,' Guy says, toying with his toast. 'But the editor's mother is dying and ...'

'I'm glad you didn't,' Megan interrupts. 'Or Stuart wouldn't have found me.'

Guy stares at her. 'Stuart's your ...' He struggles for a polite title for the kind of man who would abuse the woman in front of him.

'Oh no. Stuart's my son. And I wouldn't have known that he'd left home without your report last week. And that made—well—quite a difference. So, you see ...'

'It was your son who went missing from the Mere?'

She nods. Guy laughs, and shakes his head slightly.

'What is it?' Megan asks.

'Just the way separate things end up being connected,' he says.

He finishes his food and pushes his plate away, but regrets the unconscious gesture when she takes it as a signal that their conversation is over. She stands up and pulls it towards her. Guy gets to his feet. He is much taller than her. He looks down at her, his face serious. 'What do you think will happen?' he asks.

She shrugs. 'I don't know.'

'Will you ... will you ... go away?'

'Oh no,' she shakes her head. 'I won't do that. I'm sick of hiding.'

'I'm glad,' he says.

He follows her to the servery where she deposits his crockery. She walks down the bridge and tops up the other customers' coffee cups. On her way back she stops and fusses with the tables, putting chairs straight, tidying cruets. Guy watches her for a while. He is reluctant to leave her here, alone. Responsibility weighs heavily on his shoulders, as heavy as any Bergen he ever carried across the desert.

'Do you think he'll come?' he asks her directly when she gets back to the counter.

She has been thinking of nothing else. She knows him. He won't have seen the newspaper until the afternoon and by then it would have been too late to do anything about it. He'll brood over it all night. He'll come up with a plan but it will be whisky-fuelled and ridiculously gung-ho, and he'll be beyond putting it into action. Then, in the morning he'll reconsider. He'll think more rationally. He'll calculate and scheme. 'If he's going to do anything, it will be tomorrow,' she says.

'And are you working tomorrow?'

She nods. 'The night-shift.'

THE MECHANICS OF conversation have exhausted her; she has felt like someone picking up an instrument after years of neglect. It is a relief to sit on the bus by herself and ride through the night back to town.

Things are righting themselves after Saturday's furore. The shop-fronts have been re-glazed and a burned-out car towed away. The broken glass and discarded beer cans have been swept from the streets. The river is back between its banks; a tangle of branches and plastic strapping and some sinuous strings of green slime are marooned on the high-water mark. These are all that remains of the flood except for a posse of white vans that has arrived; builders from out of town contracted by insurance companies to make good the damaged houses.

Stuart's coat and backpack are just inside the door. The orange nylon lining of his parka glows luminous in the light of the small lamp he has left on by the bed. Wet trainers sag in a pool of brown liquid on the linoleum in front of the sink. The draining board is cluttered; he has gorged himself on cereal and toast. He does not wake as she steps inside and closes the door behind her. She holds her breath, as she used to do when he was a baby, when she would check on him before she went to bed.

He is in her bed, the sallowness of his skin made starker by the white of her linen. He lies on his back, the sheet pushed down to his hips, one arm flung back above his head, the other by his side. The lamp throws his contours into exaggerated relief; his bones and their angular shadows are indistinguishable. His ribcage is sharply defined, like ripples etched into sand at the retreat of the tide. It rises abruptly over the cavernous hollow of his belly. The one hipbone she can see protrudes in a gaunt promontory, falling away into the undercut of his

423

flank on one side and the dark pubic shadow on the other. His shoulders have broadened, even in the six months since she saw him. His arms are longer and his hands are bigger; they pulse, slightly, in the clench-and-unclench motion she has observed since babyhood. She reaches out and takes the hand that lies closest to her, gently uncurling the bony fingers and smoothing out the palm with calming, reassuring strokes. He is dreaming; his eyes flicker beneath translucent lids and an occasional furrow creases the roseate surface of his forehead. Spots in various stages of inflammation plaster his cheeks and his nose is a rash of blocked pores.

'Poor thing,' she says tenderly, drawing her thumb across the taut, erupting skin of his face.

He is cleaner, the worst of the dirt of vagrancy scrubbed away—she sees, from the corner of her eye, her towels, abandoned in a heap on the floor—and smells pleasantly of soap and shampoo. She wonders what other marks his fortnight of drifting will have left him with. Insatiable hunger, perhaps, an aversion to cold—her own response to a winter night incarcerated in a garage—or a cavalier attitude towards other people's property. She wonders how he has survived; what he has thought and felt; where he has been. He is fathomless. He is her son, her baby, flesh of her flesh. But she has allowed him to become a stranger.

She perches on the edge of the bed as he sleeps, deeply, lost in his dreams. Her foot catches something on the floor. She reaches into the gloom to get it. A collection of leaflets; he must have been reading them before he went to sleep. She picks them up and holds them towards the light. They are Army recruitment pamphlets.

Then he stirs, and drags his arm across his eyes. She thinks he will wake, but instead he rolls towards the wall and she loosens her hold on his hand. Then she sees his back. At first she thinks it is a trick of the lamplight, or crease-marks from the sheet. She leans in closer and puts out a tentative hand. Then she claps it, horrified, to her mouth. It is a topography of violence; the harrowing story of her absence and the profoundest proof of how she has failed him. She rises slowly from the bed and surveys the ravaged map of his skin. It is sickening but there is a part of her that is fascinated; she has, after all, never been fully able to survey her own.

JENNIFER IS PALE and harassed, dismissing Shirley's attempts at friendly condolence with an irritated wave of the hand. As a result Guy offers no words of sympathy. He is, anyway, still disturbed by her refusal to replace Megan's story. He wonders what kind of woman would put another in such danger. It has cast his impression of her in a new light. Whereas previously he had rather admired her business-like, unsentimental approach to office management it occurs to him now that it is more than just a front; she is intrinsically hard. The understanding he thought they had attained, just a week ago, has evaporated. He feels fundamentally at odds with her editorial policy; his report on the street-fighting should never have been suppressed. It had gone beyond the sequence of events to examine the culture of mob action and to ask questions about why a group identity could suppress personal accountability. It is good; he knows it is. He fingers the business card in his pocket. Too good, maybe, for the *Weaver Weekly*, after all.

Guy has drawn the office blinds. They rattle softly in the breeze from the open window. In the comparative gloom of the office the various expressions on the faces of the staff are obscured. Gerry is absent altogether, a fact that is apparent to everyone but which, given Jennifer's prickly, possibly unbalanced state, no one openly remarks. Her studied refusal to mention it, however, suggests powerfully that something is wrong; there has been a rift. Shirley bristles with curiosity but having already been rebuffed by Jennifer dares make no enquiry. Monica remains impassive. She is due a large expenses cheque and doesn't want to say or do anything that might delay its delivery. Guy can't be bothered to ask; the small-town mentality of the *Weaver Weekly* is beginning to irritate him.

Perhaps Jennifer regrets the decisions she made in the fraught few days between her mother's accident and her death. She does not, as she habitually has, review with the team the edition that finally made the streets but moves straight on to the one currently in compilation. It is sketchy, at this early stage, and she hands out assignments for the weekend; school fetes, a farmers' market, a Head Teacher's retirement and the re-scheduled Beaver Olympics for Shirley, who purses her lips as she takes the pink sheets. She had hoped, after last week's success, not to have been relegated to tea and tombola. Monica is to attend a literature festival at a local theatre and a party-in-the-park. Jennifer hands over the tickets.

'From the sublime to the ridiculous,' Monica sighs, as she tucks them into her handbag.

Jennifer turns to Guy. 'There's a gay-rights demonstration on Saturday I'd like you to cover, please. Keep a weather-eye out for celebrities. I think that's all for you, for now. I know you worked all last weekend. But keep your ear to the ground. You never know what might turn up.'

Guy suppresses the sardonic suggestion that there might be a murder.

There is a pause. They all look at the sheets that remain on Jennifer's desk; sports fixtures, they assume. Jennifer picks them up and shuffles them before laying them, significantly, back down in front of her. But nobody is in any mood to help her out. Eventually she picks them up herself and puts them in her 'in' tray.

'The office will be closed all weekend,' she announces snappishly. 'We're being decorated.' If she expects the news to be greeted with pleasure she is disappointed. Just then the vibrato notes of an accordion rise up from the street and filter through the window in a mournful lament.

'Oh God,' Jennifer groans.

THEY HAVE THE nicest day, Megan and Stuart.

She goes out early to the laundrette and washes his clothes, coming back as he stirs at last from his slumber. He showers again, at her insistence—rolling his eyes with typical teenage hubris when he says that it's something young men should do at least once every day—and she makes breakfast. They eat it at the little table; he sits on the chair, she perches on the bed.

He doesn't say much and she refrains from asking questions. In any case she is reluctant to hear the answers, and she knows that Stuart is taciturn by nature. She has brought him up that way; to watch and listen but to say nothing controversial that might rile an irascible temper. It has made him devious, she knows, and emotionally stunted. Also self-reliant and resourceful and a good keeper of secrets. She keeps up a steady flow of inconsequential chatter, as though he is a baby who needs the reassurance of her voice.

They take the bus to an out-of-town shopping complex where she buys him new jeans and t shirts and trainers and underwear. It is hard to get him to choose. He agrees to whatever she suggests with a shrug. Only once do his eyes light up with anything like enthusiasm, when she holds out a denim jacket from a rail.

'Maxwell's got one of those,' he says, reaching out to touch its sleeve.

She knows about Maxwell; all the kids on the estate idolise him. 'Now you'll have one, too,' she says, taking it to the till.

'Bet he didn't pay for his,' Stuart grins as they stand in the queue.

'Probably not,' she smiles.

She buys stuff for his acne. 'You haven't been taking your tablets,' she observes, as she selects facial scrub and medicated lotion from the shelves. He makes no response. They both know that it's because there has been no one to organise the prescriptions.

Over lunch she mentions school. Stuart frowns and looks away.

'Have you been going?' she queries lightly, as if it were just a matter of interest. He nods.

'But you didn't take your exams?'

'No point,' he says, taking a bite of his burger. 'Hadn't done the coursework.'

'It doesn't matter,' she says. Nothing seems to matter today. She pushes her untouched lunch towards him. 'Help me out,' she says. He wolfs the lot.

After that they don't speak of the past, or of the future, but only of what they can see at that moment, as if it is all they have.

In the afternoon she dozes a little on the bed. Through half-closed eyes she watches him read laboriously through the army leaflets, his finger tracing the lines of print, his lips forming the promises. Afterwards he sits and does nothing, entirely at rest, basking in the stillness. It is a condition she recalls from her early days at the refuge; the bliss of being where no angry word is spoken, where the tranquillity is not subject to sudden seismic shifts but remains rock-solid, hour after hour. At first you can only marvel at it as it caresses your skin with a velvet hand, but gradually you absorb it into yourself. You feel it oozing like sweet, warm honey through the hurt apertures, and it fills you up like alcoholic nectar, occupying every raw and lonely void until you are satiated and drunk with its wonder.

When she opens her eyes he is watching her, patiently waiting for her to wake up. 'You haven't got a telly!' he declares.

'No,' she says, getting up and stretching. 'I don't need one. I like reading instead.' She points to her pile of library books.

'Oh,' he raises his eyebrows. He hadn't known that about her. It hadn't been allowed, of course, at home. They exchange a glance of understanding. 'What else do you like?' he asks.

They know everything, and nothing, about each other. It is hard for both of them to make the transition. They are like novice dancers who don't know the steps; reluctant and stumbling. Their entire relationship is based on the unsaid, things not openly acknowledged but mutually understood; that *he* must be placated, his ire diffused; that certain situations were to be avoided and some information was better suppressed. Home for Stuart has been a territory of no-go areas; his father's chair, the remote control, his parents' bedroom. There are some things about his mother it has been better not to know. Not just why she locked his bedroom door at night and the source of her bumps and bruises—those questions he had answered for himself, in time—but what her treasures were; what made her happy. If he had known them he might have been compelled to tell, and then they would inevitably have been spoiled, so it had been better not to know.

She tells him about the café, the people who arrive and disappear again, the traffic and how she likes to imagine where it has come from and where it is all going. She describes Carlos and Sylvie, the wire-wool woman and the beaded supervisor. She makes them all sound like improbably silly characters from a sit-com.

Finally she explains about the refuge and the women who go there.

It is a new landscape for them, vast and fragile, but at last they have breached its borders.

'I should have taken you with me,' she reaches out and touches his back significantly, through the layers of his new t shirt and jacket. 'I wish I had.' He looks uncomfortable and she drops her hand, turning to the sink where she is drying dishes. There is silence for a while. When she turns back into the room he is standing by the window staring out into the deserted yard. He has picked up the little photograph of the two of them and is turning it absent-mindedly in his hands. He is thinking of the night with the bonfire, of Spencer and

Maxwell, of Carmel, and how he had suddenly known then what he could not have seen six months before: how empty it all was.

'I wasn't ready then,' he says.

She realises with a jolt that of course he is right; there are some choices that everyone has to make for themselves. She calls to mind the time she had first heard about the refuge—the kindly woman with the jagged scar—and the ten years it had taken her to be ready.

'I'm glad it didn't take too long,' she says.

Later, when it is time for her to go to work, she tries to persuade him to stay behind. But he will have none of it. She closes and locks the door carefully and they walk together through the dusk to the bus station.

Paul is waiting at the stop. Megan introduces Stuart.

'You don't normally work this night-shift do you, Paul?' she asks.

'I swapped,' he mumbles.

IT IS EVENING when Guy gets in from the gay-rights rally. He sits down at his laptop to write his report, but his mind is too distracted and he gives it up after half an hour. He makes himself a sandwich— peanut butter, to which he is becoming addicted—and takes it outside. His little patio is joyous with colour. The nasturtiums are clambering over everything; tendrils have woven themselves around the ironwork of his chair and table. He gently detaches them and encourages them instead to climb up the drainpipe. He nips off seedpods and dead heads to prompt more flowers and gives the tubs a good dousing with the watering can.

A few doors down someone is barbecuing; the smell of charcoal and charred meat wafts over the fences on the lively breeze and he can hear the buzz of garrulous company. It isn't the nicest evening for eating outdoors. Since the storms the weather has reverted to English type; brisk winds bringing a succession of squally showers, the sun as often hidden behind banks of racing white clouds as visible in the blue. He stares up at the sky now, but sees in his mind's eye only the little white card that his father gave him, propped on the mantelpiece in the room behind him.

He is bored and lonely in this little town. The opportunity to get back to the world he knows without having to sacrifice his autonomy is seriously attractive; to be of it but not in it; to be able to tell the uncompromising truth—both good and bad—without the need for fact-obfuscating euphemisms. It hadn't been the work of the army that had frustrated him, or the people, just the bullshit, and the way it had crushed his soul.

But he doesn't want to do it on the back of his father's recommendation. He will earn it on his own merit, or let it pass by.

He gets to his feet and goes indoors. Booting up his laptop once more he sends an email to the address on the card, and attaches his report on Saturday's street riots. He signs it Guy Crouchback and presses 'send'.

When he has finished it is almost 9pm. He goes upstairs to change. He has a date.

A DARK, MOONLESS night. Black clouds billow low over the land, blown by a warm southerly wind. On the peripheries of the car-park saplings lash at each other with thin, supple branches; their leaves clashing like distant hands. Between them, sprouting flagpoles wave and moan in the gusts. Their flags are sails, flapping and bulging, their wire fixings bash dementedly against the poles. The sodium phosphorescence of the lights is weakly against the pressing dark of the night and the sky. Far across the car-park the petrol station is a bright beacon but in between there is a gulf of unrelieved blackness. Earlier, travellers parked up close to the dome and hurried inside, their inadequate jackets wrapped closely around them against the snatching fingers of the wind, their voices torn from their throats as they ran, laughing, towards the automatic doors. But now the car-park is virtually empty. A very few vehicles stand fast against the currents of dust and litter that swirl in manic eddies around the empty space. A clapped-out Escort, a silver sedan, a crouching green MG.

The domes are in semi-darkness; napping meteorites emitting a dull greenish glow. Inside, pinpricks of red show where coffee machines slumber and pizza ovens rest. The forest canopy is an umbrella of shadow. Tables and chairs drowse in the dim. Through the impenetrable gloom it is impossible to see who might be lurking amongst the arbours. Only over the escalators, up and down, is there a cascade of welcoming yellow brightness, and the bridge arches out over the small-hours gloom like a splendid ocean-liner over a vast, endless sea. High up here the wind is ferocious, buffeting the plate glass windows with frequent shudders, shrieking around the lacework of girders like a host of harridans before screeching off into the night.

The café is empty. Carlos sits at one of the tables scanning a newspaper. In a far corner, Stuart has given in to fatigue and sleeps with his head on his arms. At the western end of the bridge yellow A boards indicate that the toilets are being cleaned. Megan is inside replenishing toilet rolls and the machines that dispense sanitary towels and chewable toothbrushes, coating the porcelain with anti-bacterial spray. The wind is whistling through the ventilator grilles, making their fans whirl backwards and rattle in their plastic housings. She is smiling. She has a feeling. It is like a fountain deep down in her abdomen that keeps squirting excitement in intoxicating jets up towards her heart. She wants to clap her hands. She wants to giggle and run about like a girl. Guy has been here *again,* eating breakfast and drinking cup after cup of coffee, and making her laugh, and asking her about the books she is reading. And he had stepped up close to her and murmured 'any sign?' and she had been able to feel the warmth exuding from his black long-sleeved shirt and smell his skin. She had laughed and nodded towards Stuart and said she had her own personal bodyguard and he wasn't to worry.

She knows it is ridiculous and she mustn't even think about it.

But she can't help it.

She is out of liquid soap. She drifts along the café and rides down the escalators to the wide tiled corridor that goes past the main lavatory facilities and on to the utility and office areas under the dome. Paul's trolley is parked outside the Gents. She can hear a toilet handle repeatedly pumped and the suck and squelch of a plunger.

'Nasty job,' she thinks.

The corridor is draughty. The wind is a whining puppy scrabbling to get through the gaps of the double doors that divide the public area from that reserved for staff. As she passes the Ladies a woman and a small child emerge. The child is as white as a sheet, with dark circles around her eyes and pale, bloodless lips. 'I'm so sorry,' the woman says to Megan. 'My daughter's been sick. We didn't quite make it to the cubicle.'

'Oh dear,' Megan gives the child a sympathetic smile. 'Are you feeling a bit better now?'

The child nods wanly.

'It's my own fault,' the woman says. 'It's far too late for her to be up.'

'It's almost two in the morning!' Megan agrees, addressing the child, 'time little girls were in bed.'

The woman bridles a little, inferring criticism. 'I'm sorry about the mess,' she says stiffly. She takes the child's hand and leads her toward the escalator.

'Don't worry,' Megan calls after her.

She looks over her shoulder briefly at Paul's trolley but then continues on her way; she needs to get the soap anyway and Paul already has a nasty job on his hands. She'll deal with the mess in the Ladies. She pushes through the doors to the staff area. A gust of trapped air howls past her like a released hound. It is gloomy. The offices are all empty and unlit. A weakly green emergency exit light is the only illumination, pointing the way to the extreme end of the corridor. She can hear the bolts of the fire door rattle in their housings. The cleaning storeroom is about halfway down the corridor, on the right. She uses her staff key. The light comes on automatically as she opens the door. The room is about five feet wide and around eight feet deep and lined with well-stocked shelves. She knows where the sand and shovel are kept, towards the back. She makes her way down the narrow space.

It happens quickly, taking less time than the telling. She is shoved violently from behind, crashing headlong into a row of metal buckets that lines the wall at the back of the store. Their metallic clatter is like a symphony of dropped cymbals. She falls heavily with her hands underneath her. They slap and smart as they meet the tiles. She twists her head as she falls, smacking her cheekbone on the sharp rim of a bucket just where the handle is joined; she feels it hook into her flesh and tear. There is a second while her brain catches up. She opens her eyes to see blood on the tiles and, behind her, his feet. She would know them anywhere. The old black lace-up shoes, the left one bulged by his bunion. At least, she thinks, it isn't his steel toe-caps. Then he closes the door. The light automatically goes out and they are plunged into darkness. He hadn't expected this. She can hear him running his hands up and down the walls adjacent to the door. She finds herself smiling; there *is* no light switch. Ridiculously, she thinks that the darkness will protect her, that she has only to lie very still. The tiles are cold and she can feel the chill of the wind as it winnows under the door. Her blood is sticky underneath her cheek, quickly coagulating. Then she feels him, his feet shuffling and probing for her across the space, finding her legs. His hands, working their way up, are hard and bony on her back, groping for a purchase. Her first instinct—born of long conditioning—is not to scream lest she wake Stuart, but she shakes it off and takes a breath. It is jerked out of her throat, left hanging in the air as he grasps her collar and yanks her up. She dangles for a second, limp as a doll with useless limbs, the collar of her uniform tight against her windpipe; she can hardly breathe. Then he pulls again, sharply upwards, and the back of her head hits the underside of a shelf with a smart crack. She can hear the cans of oven cleaner and air freshener on the shelf jostle and jump; there are fireworks in her head.

He throws her sideways with a grunt and she lands in a stack of brooms and mops. They go everywhere, slewing across the floor at all angles with a terrific rattle. He lunges after her, half-bent, his arms flailing in the dark. He trips over the brooms and lands heavily on top of her. His face is close to her; she can smell him; the stale alcohol and the meaty reek of his breath. He is wearing that old frayed pullover. She can feel the feathery edges of its neck on her cheek. She turns her head away; the smell and the feel of him is worse than the blows. From her position on the floor she can see a filament of light shining underneath the door; a strand of hope. He struggles off her. She has somehow managed to get her arm wedged under the broom handles. He must be standing on the brooms because when he grabs her collar and wrenches her up again she is stuck fast, her elbow and shoulder jar as he pulls again and again. Tendons twist and twang sending showers of pain like needle-sparks into her fingers. Finally he shifts his position and hauls her again. This time she lifts up as though propelled and they almost over-balance. He man-handles her as though she were an empty sack, grasping her clothing and hair. His sinewy arms and claw-like hands have incredible, prehensile strength. Then he lands her with a vicious punch across her jaw; she hears it separate with a gristly snap. She lands against another shelf, where industrial-sized tins of floor polish and de-greaser are ranked in orderly rows. She begins to pull them off the shelf and fling them into the darkness. A few catch him with swingeing blows, the rest ricochet off the walls and floor.

He lunges towards her, kicking and hitting out wildly, blindly, slipping and tripping on the jumbled collection of tins and handles that litters the floor. She dives towards the door but he catches her a penetrating blow in the kidneys and she goes down. She falls in an awkward twist, across the brooms and aerosols, and the back of her head hits the tiles. Lights explode behind her eyes. Then he is on top of her, his hands around her throat. Chest pumping, sucking nothing. Hands grappling wildly with his at her throat, then up at his face, reaching for his eyes, but he is unstoppable. She thinks her head will burst, it is inflating, eyes and ears bulging, tongue swelling. Then she feels it draining away, she is falling, shrinking. The past, the present and the future become more distant and indistinct. The dark of the storeroom is overlaid by a thick, suffocating blanket of black.

There is thunderous roaring and simultaneous lightning; it sears her eyes and makes her blind. Its forks are electric wires in her head and jaw, her arm, her back. Then it passes and darkness envelops her again. Another storm has come and it is such a relief. The pressure—the weighty, tiresome burden of it—is lifted off her chest as palpably as a stony sarcophagus winched away. Only now that it is gone can she feel what a crushing load it has been, entombing her in its leaden grasp. Now she can rise and float, as light as a wisp on the back of the boisterous wind.

She can hear it coming for her down the corridor, panting and gusting, a thoroughbred, anxious to be off. A pure white horse with a long silk mane and hooves of silver to ride the storm. It will bear her up, through the cleansing rain into the peeling shadows of the storm clouds, and away to journey's end. Down a dim passageway of confusion the roars of thunder become the shout of a river in spate. She can hear the smack and ricochet of angry flotsam in its tumid stream. Hurried footsteps: people running to see the flood, to fling in the bad things and watch them borne away on its tide. Then the wind finds her; she feels the first touch of it on her hair, gentle as angels' breath; its arms enfold her and she spreads wide her eager wings to let it sweep her up, up and away into the maelstrom of the night.

THE HOSPITAL WARD is just the same as the café on the bridge; a place where nobody desires to be, just a necessary staging post between illness and health, or death. She is conscious of people coming and going. Not that she sees them—one eye is closed, swollen shut by inflammation from the stitches in her cheek, the vision through the other dazed by strong pain killers—she can make out only blurred outlines. And not that she can really hear them, either. Her head feels strangely buried inside some mushy, grotesque vegetable. Everything comes to her through the muffling filter of dense, fibrous pulp. She feels people pass; the slight draught as they pass her bed, the evocative aroma of the outdoors exuding from their clothes.

Her jaw has been wired back together; it is agony to speak, eat and swallow. The tender skin of her mouth feels flayed and tastes ferrous, barbed with cat-gut; the teeth oddly displaced and angular as old tombstones. She feels that if she tries to speak the voice of another person altogether will rasp from her throat. The pain of her head puts it all out of proportion to the rest of her body. It is a gross gargoyle on the pillow. The rest of her is flimsy and insubstantial in the bed.

The details of the attack are hazy; she indicates as much to the police officer who comes to interview her. She responds to his questions with the slightest, wincing nod or shake of her head, her inability to articulate further a blessed relief. She had been attacked in a pitch dark storeroom and left for dead. A friend had found her and called the ambulance. That's all she allows him to gather.

She drinks sips of cool water through a straw eased between her parched lips; she can't even manage to lick them properly.

After a day or so she is moved to another, busier ward, and put into a bed at the end of the row. Here, it is hoped, her swollen black and purple face, the livid puckering of stitches, the flinches and grunts she makes through clenched teeth as she is moved for washing and the toilet, will least disturb the other patients.

She thinks of herself as the elephant woman—grotesque and repulsive—and it is impossible to ignore the startled glances of other patients' visitors. After months of anonymity the exposure of ugliness is unnerving and she is of course sad to contemplate her permanent disfigurement, but even so it feels more honest than what has gone before, and she is not afraid.

She tells the boy's mother so, when she appears one day at her bedside, to express her sorrow at Megan's state, its cause implicitly understood between them.

'It's all right. It's over, now, at last,' Megan manages to get out, wanting genuinely to reassure, but her tongue is huge and cumbersome within the unfamiliar cage of her teeth and she is afraid that her assurances might sound hollow.

Jasmine regards her for a few moments before saying, 'My sister's in a bed up there at the far end of the ward. Coincidence, or what?'

'How's your son?' Megan asks.

'Oh! Fine! Any news of yours?'

Megan nods. 'Fine too.' She tries to smile but the skin of her cheeks is too taut to allow her mouth the proper elasticity for such an expression and she fears that she has only managed a grimace.

Sons lost and found. Unseen parallels and tessellations. Reflections of experience between one stranger and another, making for tenacious correlations. The way a random occurrence will throw repercussions far and wide and tie disparate things irrevocably to itself. Like Guy had said: separate things ending up being connected. Megan muses on it; the years she spent cheek by jowl with this family, all unsuspecting of the ties that lay deeply buried in their future relations. If only she had

441

known. But then, perhaps the knowing would have changed the relation, skewed the outcome in some way to precipitate a different, perhaps tragic, result.

Jasmine visits again on subsequent days and introduces her family. She is connecting up the pieces, assembling a whole of what could have been from the incongruent fragments of what fell out; garnering Megan into the fabric of their lives. As a result Jasmine's wisp-like sister takes to shuffling down the ward and perching for a while on the end of Megan's bed. She doesn't speak much. A burden of sorrow stops up her words and Megan of course has limited dexterity of articulation, but they build up an understanding of companionship in swapping magazines and truncated gossip about the nurses. The fragile association that they have from beyond the ward reinforces the hot-house hospital friendships that spring to life in the cloistered, unreal environment.

Stuart comes also, day after day, to sit at her side. Her ravaged features are difficult for him to contemplate, though. She suspects that he is having difficulty suppressing tears.

'Are you staying at my place?' she asks him. 'Are you eating properly? Do you need any money?' He looks clean enough, and well fed.

'Stayed there for a bit,' he tells her. 'The woman with the earrings wanted me to go to that place you told me about.' He grimaces and shakes his head. 'Didn't fancy that though.' He brightens. 'Anyway, then Guy said I could doss at his for a bit, till you're better.'

'Did he?'

'Yeah! It's ok. Lots to eat.'

'That's good then,' she says, twisting her lips into what she hopes will be a smile. She nods towards the girl in the far bed. 'Do you know her, from …' she hesitates to say the word—such a travesty it had been, but she can think of no other, '… from home?'

Stuart blushes. 'Yes. No. Not really.'

'Is Guy your boyfriend?' he blurts out one day.

'No,' she tries to sound as though the idea is ridiculous, which, of course, it *is,* now. 'I hardly know him, really.' To herself, she adds, 'Poor bloke. I expect he just feels responsible,' but she will not make Stuart feel like a burden so she adds, 'I expect he's enjoying having you for company.'

He likes that idea. 'Yeah!' he grins.

Guy comes too, from time to time, a diffident attendant rather than an actual visitor. He hangs aloofly just beyond the curtain, poised to fetch things from the shop, or sometimes darting forward to lift the water beaker to her mouth, or to adjust a pillow.

'It's good of you to look after Stuart,' she croaks one day.

'No trouble. Least I could do,' he shrugs her thanks away.

Yes. He feels responsible, she tells herself. She dare not allow herself to contemplate any alternative.

One day the girl is discharged. She walks down the ward to say goodbye, looking strange and somehow remote in her outdoor clothes, disqualified from the enforced intimacy of pyjamas.

'I'll see you again,' she says.

'I hope so,' Megan replies. She has no idea how far these newly anchored strands of friendship and involvement will stretch.

A few days later Megan herself is discharged. She goes back, despite strong opposition, to her little bedsit.

'You should come to us,' Mrs Rushmore had urged, meaning back to the refuge.

'Or to me,' Guy had offered.

But one would be an unacceptable backwards step, the other an advance for which she does not feel ready.

Her flat though, when she returns to it, is bleak and unsatisfactory, and she knows she will not stay in it long. It had served its purpose, she thinks.

443

When she looks at herself in the mirror however, the view is not as unnerving as she had expected. The swelling has subsided. The mottled discolouration of bruises and suturing is fading to a stale, yellowish heliotrope. The scar on her cheek is right-angled, the skin puckered into a seam, but it will fade in time she supposes, like the others.

STUARTS WAITS UNTIL she is out of hospital to show her the forms he has to fill in, pointing out the parts he needs help with.

'Don't look at me,' Guy says, carrying mugs of tea from the kitchenette to where they are sitting on Megan's bed. 'I've done my best to put him off. I've told him it will be endless square-bashing and shouting sergeants.'

'I'm used to being shouted at,' Stuart says, with a dry humour that is new in him.

It is pure Guy. In the week of her hospitalisation Guy and Stuart have spent many hours in each other's company. She knows she is the link between them but she is also aware of another bond, something between the two of them that she is in some way outside of. She doesn't mind. Stuart is a different boy, as though released from a grim shadow; a layer of dead skin has been sloughed off. That shifty, shrinking demeanour has entirely gone and in its place are the nascent beginnings of Guy's reliably good mood energised by occasional bursts of spontaneous exuberance. She smiles and then winces; her jaw is still agony.

Guy hands her tea. 'Try not to dribble dear.' He winks at Stuart, who disintegrates into reedy, warbling laughter.

Later, when it is just the two of them and they are sitting quietly side by side, Stuart turns to her out of the blue. 'It says ... in the leaflet, it says you get to be like ... like brothers, in your troop.'

That's when she sees it; a light inside him she has never seen before, and the way it illuminates for him a path that is solid beneath his feet

445

and that he feels he can tread with confidence. It will not crumble. It will not throw him off balance. Although she has only got just got him back she knows it is time to let him go.

There are aptitude tests and medicals, but none of it takes long. The preliminaries are unaccountably expedited by an invisible hand. Before she knows it she is at the station to say goodbye. As he glides away from her she thinks: this is right. This is the way it should be; a son leaving his mother; not the other way round.

GUY IS GOING AWAY too. Between him and Megan there is something that might be—but that is not yet—marvellous. The wonder of its possibilities keeps Megan awake at night; the splendid blessing of the second chance. They are both approaching it warily, treading like explorers on virgin territory. They are mapping it out, sampling its riches in delicious, experimental morsels. But there is also a sense of testing—for hidden pitfalls into which they might, in their inexperience of the ground, inadvertently stumble. He in particular moves slowly, loath to startle her into flight. He never makes any sudden moves and never raises his voice. He handles her with extreme gentleness as though she is a rare, exotic but wounded bird and he that breed of twitcher to whom a glimpse of a wingtip would count as a rare boon. He is someone to whom possession or entrapment constitute no part of the science.

In a strange way his new job, overseas, is part of their exploration of this new terrain. He will find the outer boundaries of it while she, at home, will be free to establish base camp. Her own, independent life.

For the second time she is at the station. The windows have been re-glazed after the riots but the exterior of the building is still blackened from the fire. Guy is packed and standing by her side. The tannoy squeals into life and his train is announced. He turns towards her slowly and slides a gentle arm around her.

'I've never had a girl to see me off before,' he whispers.

'A *girl!*' she demurs.

447

He has had his hair cut; not a brutal shave like Stuart but a considerable crop. She had collected a lock of it, secretly, from the barber's floor, and felt a fool.

He kisses her then, very softly, and it is a sort of promise, a deposit on account. She wants to weep at the wonder of it but finds the resilience from somewhere to offer, as a receipt, 'I shall see you every night, on the television.'

'And it will only be for a month,' he smiles, 'this time.'

'It *is* dangerous,' she frowns.

'So is going to collect soap,' he says wryly.

The train arrives and there is the usual jostle around the doors. Gritty pink children—weary from summer day-trips—and tetchy commuters are barely able to get off before others push to get on and claim a vacant seat. Guy smiles down at her and then he is lost in the fray.

She watches the train pull away but then she hurries away from the station to go home. Not to the lonely little flat, but to his home, where she is going to stay while he is away, to water his plants and keep her eye on things, and where there will be room for Stuart when he comes home on leave from basic training. She walks quickly, with her head up. She has Jasmine and Richard and the children coming for tea.

Man's body discovered by motorway maintenance team

Police are investigating the discovery of an unidentified man's body on Monday this week. Motorway maintenance men, working to clear cones that have closed off a nine mile stretch of the southbound carriageway between junctions 20 and 21 since June, discovered the decomposed remains in the long grass of a steep embankment immediately beneath the eastern dome of the services. Forensics will be needed to identify the man, thought to be in his early to late fifties, as well as the cause of death, which could have occurred as long as three months ago.

A spokesperson for the Highways Agency said: 'I have no idea why those cones were there. No work has been carried out or is scheduled for that stretch of motorway at all. I discovered they had been put out in error and I had a team remove them as soon as possible. I apologise for the unnecessary delays caused to road-users all summer.'

A spokesperson for the police confirmed that no men fitting the deceased's description have been reported missing and that they are not seeking anyone in connection with the death. The man's injuries, as far as they can be determined at this late stage, are consistent with a fall from the structure above. The design of the building, with its many exposed girders, and its elevated position close to the carriageway, is now under question.

Paul folds the newspaper up and pushes it down into his rubbish bag. Then he picks up his mop, and begins to quarter the floor with long, easy strokes.

BOOK 4

STEP OF FAITH

JADE IS LATE getting to the pizzeria. The afternoon of titivation she had promised herself in the cramped, crack-tiled bathroom—strictly reserved under threat of physical disfigurement for her own personal and exclusive use—had been abruptly curtailed by her nephew's adventure in the river. Her mother had summoned Mr Mole's seedy taxi and they had hurried over to Jasmine's house—Jade literally mid-wax—as soon as they had received Jasmine's stricken call.

The crisis had united them, albeit briefly. They are a family whose normal relations are scratchy and acrimonious. Over the years their antipathies have taken on the characteristics of an endurance sport; the endless, wearisome parry and thrust of bitchy remark and snide non-sequitur; the compulsive purloining of one another's personal belongings. It is a circadian round of querulous irritation and reciprocal annoyance. They are all exhausted by it but, like marathon competitors, none will admit defeat. Their rancour inhabits the house like an additional resident with a personality of its own and no one will admit to spawning it, either severally or individually. Occasionally the brooding atmosphere is relieved by ferocious, physical hostilities; tempers unleashed in vicious tirades, objects hurled, hair pulled out in handfuls, bites that puncture the skin.

But regardless of internal wrangling a family catastrophe is certain to reunite them in fervent, clannish accord. A disaster spells importance—personal aggrandisement; a sudden bringing to the fore from the nether region of obscurity where they resentfully reside—and for that reason alone they relish it. It puts them centre-stage and any sense of ignominy they might experience at having their dirty laundry aired, as it were, to the public gaze, is wholly eclipsed by the brief but glorious focus of the world's attention. It is the Jeremy Kyle effect.

But in truth this afternoon's calamity had had the makings of real tragedy. There had been nothing tawdry, nothing shameful about it. It would have been nothing less than a blameless, heart-breaking accident; the loss of a child.

Jade is not certain—even as she throws on clothes and smears foundation over her skin—that she wants to join the others in town after all. After all, it is only the birthday of a girl she hardly knows. She is tempted to abandon the whole thing. But she promised she'd go and she's paid a £10 deposit. So she finishes dressing with all speed and runs down the road to catch the bus.

Once on her way along the all-too familiar street—the bus lurching past parked cars and narrowly missing a child who runs out after a football—she allows herself to think, now that the danger is past, what life without Mikey might have been like. He is their family anachronism. His unique maleness sets him apart from their feminine commonality, far above their shrill, interminable bickering. Even his little sister Lilly is tuning into it. The youngest of the coven, she can sulk and whine and pester with the best of them. But Mikey has always floated, removed from their turbulence, sailing serenely on a quieter sea. He regarded them, even when a baby, with the detachment of a visiting extra-terrestrial. He had been ever tolerant, mildly curious, but never sucked in. Since his arrival, to stay—another startling phenomenon; no other male in their lives has ever achieved it—he has reminded them that something else is possible, even from them. Nothing is inevitable. Without Mikey, Jade supposes, they would have descended quite literally to bitch-eat-bitch.

That afternoon, before he had been found, they had congregated on Jasmine's porch. The grim uniforms had gathered at an obsequious

451

distance, muttering darkly and drinking the weak, lukewarm tea that Carmel had eventually roused herself to make.

That girl, Jade thinks now, shaking her head as the bus makes its tortuous way to town, can never make a decent cup of tea.

The four of them—Jasmine, their mother Sadie, Carmel and herself—had trembled uncontrollably and smoked cigarette after cigarette, (even Jasmine, who had given up), and tried to comprehend it—that this was real and really happening to them. They had not been able to meet each other's eyes, unused to this unwonted concurrence, but their hands had fluttered and rested briefly on each other as the agonised minutes ticked by. She, with the remains of a face-pack making a tide-mark around her jaw and hair-line, and a wax strip still adhering to one shin, had had difficulty adjusting to her unexpected role in this sudden drama.

It's like waking up on the set of *The Bill,* she had said, and being expected to know the lines.

The bus crawls as slowly as possible into town. A bridge has collapsed and there is a long diversion. The recent floods have shut some streets. The minutes tick by, making her more and more late. She wonders, briefly, is she should abandon the whole plan and go to the hospital instead, where Mikey was taken to be checked over. But she is hungry.

THE HOSPITAL ACCIDENT and emergency department is busy. Jasmine and Sadie and Mikey have already been there two and a half hours. The two women had ridden in the back of the ambulance buoyed up on the adrenalin that had flooded in while the child was missing; a cocktail of fear and anxiety. They had been relentlessly bombarded by unthinkable thoughts and unimaginable possibilities; that he was lost, taken, afraid, injured, dead. Each one was a red-hot platform—agony to stand on, impossible to tolerate—and yet no cooler, more comfortable likelihood offered itself as an alternative. They had leapt from one excruciating scenario to another, their blood thinning to water in their veins.

The crowd that somehow assembled itself—men in uniforms, experienced in crisis—strangely offered no reassurance but only exacerbated the sense that the un-faceable would have to be confronted. Sadie, as always, had resorted to the blame-game: who had been watching him? Who had allowed him outdoors unsupervised? She had absolved herself with the cheerless benediction of hindsight: *she* would never have allowed it. It could not have happened if *she* had been there.

Jasmine—and Richard—had let the implied criticism wash over them. It was only Sadie's way, they knew, to appear always to know best, to have the monopoly on right. It is purely a defensive mechanism, a smoke screen for her myriad mistakes. Richard had led Jasmine behind the jut of the little porch, away from those waiting to see her register the loss. She had buried her face in his shoulder, that comfortable hollow above his collarbone where she was learning to find such solace, while her mother had droned on and on to anyone who would listen.

453

'I don't like this dream,' she had whispered. 'I want to wake up, now.'

And then there he had been, running down the lane and into her arms, slippery with silt and smelling of river and barbecue crisps, and she had thought that if she could she would crush him back into her body, back into her womb, where he would always be safe. Fight had metamorphosed into flight. She wanted nothing so much as to get him away, away from the river, away from the dour officialdom, away, even from the woman who had brought him back. They had been carried into the ambulance in a rush of action like a film on fast-forward, and the ambulance itself had torn off, hurtling through the streets.

But now reality has kicked in. Their paramedic has deserted them, off to other jobs. The woman—Jasmine knows her of course, it is Skinner's mother—has been escorted into a side room by a female police constable. Now they are only three amongst fifty waiting on hard plastic chairs to be seen by the over-stretched hospital staff.

It is the most bizarre of 'come as you are' parties; people hurt in the course of different activities. There is a man in wellington boots, another in an apron that says *Danger—Man Cooking*. He sits between a climber in a harness and a cyclist in Lycra with the number 465 safety-pinned to his back. There is a girl in a bathrobe. They all grin at each other sheepishly and survey one another's injuries. There are various gardening wounds—cuts and burns, a toe crushed by a loaded wheelbarrow. The results of motor car shunts—whip-lash and facial abrasions. Children with feet perforated by rusty nails, gaping cuts to their skulls from falls and mashed, bloody fingers eye each other across the aisles. A woman with a black eye and a broken arm sits and cries quietly into a sodden tissue. A scalded toddler whimpers on its mother's knee, the affected part obscured with damp teabags and wrapped in cling-film.

They have exchanged stories, as people do, Sadie pointing again and again to her grandson. 'He fell in the river,' she says. 'Got carried for miles.'

The other women smile thinly. In comparison to their gouged and lacerated children Mikey looks the picture of health. He sits in an area reserved for children, engrossed in a dog-eared book about aeroplanes.

They have all arrived at a place where their personal crisis has been put into perspective. They have had accidents but they are scarcely emergencies. The twisted, prone, empurpled bodies bristling with plastic tubing that arrive from time to time in ambulances—*they* are emergencies. They look at their own wounds. They probably don't need stitches, they are up to date with their tetanus shots. It is really nothing that a thorough cleaning with some antiseptic, a sterile bandage and a couple of paracetamols couldn't put right. More than likely that's the most that any of them will get, after hours of waiting. And yet the right—however briefly—to be a victim, to be the injured party, the right to all that attendant kudos, is a nagging imperative. They sit tight and time ticks by.

Every so often there is a flurry of activity outside the automatic sliding doors. Their eyes are irresistibly drawn. Anything, beyond each other's drawn, bored faces, beyond these flat magnolia walls and the posters about AIDS and Chlamydia that they have read a hundred times, has to be a distraction. An ambulance arrives or a car skids to a halt. Another patient is brought in. The people crane, ghoulishly, to catch a glimpse of blood, a protruding bone, a slither of escaping entrail. The patients on ambulance stretchers are wheeled immediately through the double doors to the mysterious regions beyond, where white-coated doctors and nurses in cotton two-pieces like pyjamas flit from cubicle to cubicle. The others are helped into seats while their relatives book them in at reception. They hold blood-soaked bandages to themselves, or wince and gasp as every movement jars an unseen hurt. They are sure they are mortally wounded, but they must take their place in the long line of patients and before long they too begin to wonder if they really need have come.

JADE HAS ABSOLUTELY no hope of enjoying herself. Hope is a word—and a concept—that is absent from her lexicon. As the bus makes its tortuous way into town she broods and fumes, the flavour of gall familiar in her mouth, and wonders again why the hell she is even bothering.

It is almost eight o'clock. The others were going to meet at seven for cocktails and go to the restaurant together. She will be late. Left behind, left out, as always. She lives with shrunken horizons, confined and groping in dark tunnels of hopelessness.

Poor Jade. Life has buffeted her. Not with tragedy—she has not been orphaned or bereaved, she carries no physical or mental impairment—but it has dispensed its blessings with a parsimonious hand. Her disadvantageous upbringing on the Mere, a mother too overly preoccupied with her own disappointments, the tooth-jarring discord of sisterly rivalry and, most of all, the lack of personal spark that might have mitigated all the rest. If she'd had extra-ordinary intelligence, unusual talent, remarkable beauty, particular kindness … Any of these might have lifted her onto advantageous ground. But they have stubbornly passed her by. Her umbrage has grown into a gremlin grafted onto her shoulder. It is her familiar; she is always conscious of its sullen, dissatisfied weight. While the town is in chaos—the floods throwing out aftershocks of dismay to householders and spelling ruin for business owners whose stock is reduced to mush—Jade's predilection is to take the nuisance of it all as a personal affront. It seems to her that wherever she goes, whatever she does, things always go awry on the whim of a malevolent power holding malicious sway over her fate. She is engaged in constant battle with it; the unfairness of things. It dogs her like a demon. When she is not railing at its unjust interference she is sulking at what she perceives to be the results of its influence; the smallness of her inconsequential life, her bleak future.

She lifts smudged, too-hastily painted fingernails to stroke her freshly plucked eyebrows. She is sure they are uneven but there was no one at home to ask—not that she could have trusted either of *them* for an honest answer.

The throat-clutching anxiety of those few hours this afternoon have left her feeling spent, disinclined for celebrations of any kind—certainly not for a virtual stranger from the shop where she has only worked for a fortnight. She would have preferred to stay at Jasmine's, to have celebrated the child's safe return, to have taken advantage of that mellow, forgiving catharsis that had engulfed them after the relieved tears and before the squabble over who should accompany Jasmine and the child in the ambulance. Their mother, of course, had prevailed. Carmel had remained with Lilly. Richard had gone off with his real son and she, Jade, had been left behind, wanted, chosen, needed by nobody at all.

Alone in their dismal maisonette she had returned to her preparations without enthusiasm. Even having the house to herself—a rare enough occurrence—could not give her solace. She found that, after all, there was no fun in locking the bathroom door when there was no Carmel to howl and hop and demand admittance. There was no satisfaction in drinking the last of the milk or leaving the sink in a mess, when there was no Sadie to complain. The opportunity to rummage unchallenged through Carmel's things, and to borrow her amber earrings and matching necklace, had seemed like scant recompense.

Perhaps Jasmine, had she been there, would have told the truth about the eyebrows. Jasmine is *good,* in a distant, beatific, saintly way that irritates Jade. Her departure with the two children from the cramped little house has relieved things slightly. Jade and Carmel have separate rooms now, and it is possible to get some hot water for a bath or her clothes in the washing machine, which is rarely was when Jasmine and the two children shared the house.

Even so, in a way she cannot explain, Jade misses her.

Jasmine is thirteen years older than Jade—a larger gap than most sisters have to bridge. For a time, when Jade was tiny, Jasmine enjoyed playing mother (enjoyed it, in fact, a good deal more than Sadie did), dressing her up in different outfits, arranging her coarse, uncooperative hair in tufts that sprouted, like fibrous palm trees, from her scalp. Jade took her place in the prick-neat parade of dollies and soft toys with which Jasmine's room was populated. As long as she sat quietly and did not disturb the whispered, fantastical dialogue between Jasmine and her entourage she was tolerated and even—alongside the real-tear-crying baby dolls and soft-furred, doe-eyed Disney animal collection—petted and loved.

But Jade had grown impatient of this passive role amongst the silent, plastic multitudes. Aged about eighteen months she had one day gained access to Jasmine's room and played with the toys on her own, releasing them from their clinical imprisonment, carrying a few of them down for some fun in the garden and, later, for a splash in the bath. The furore after their discovery—naked and buried head-first in the flowerbed, or bedraggled and damp, their once-silken tresses now as unkempt as Jade's own—had been electrifying. Jasmine had been beside herself, inarticulate with fury and almost sick with grief. Their mother had been unable to console her, or to convincingly chastise Jade. The fact was that Sadie didn't really care about the dolls and at least the toddler had been kept beautifully quiet all afternoon. In the end Jasmine had been sent to Granny Annie's house for the weekend for some calm, soothing cake-baking and to help look after some puppies: her neighbour's dog had just had a litter. But the lesson, for Jade, had been well-learnt. Her sister's sensitive buttons had been all too clearly revealed and Jade knew how to push them.

As Jasmine's preoccupation had moved on to Leonardo Di Caprio and The Backstreet Boys, and as the dolls had gradually been replaced by make-up and trinkets, Jade had continued to invade and interfere from time to time, but it had become harder and harder to provoke a satisfying response. The older girl became increasingly distant, occupying a space that seemed secret and remote, a private world of sighs and dreams. It was is if she knew, even then, that she need only wait, sure in the knowledge that one day her prince would come. It lifted Jasmine above their seedy house on the run-down estate to a place where Jade could not reach her; there hovered, between the two of them, an arctic, distrustful chill. Their mother too had been in pursuit of something beyond Jade's comprehension. A succession of 'uncles' came and went. The bedroom door was often locked, at first for what was explained as 'moving the furniture' and then for paroxysms of disappointed tears, presumably—she had thought, at the time—as a result of the furniture stubbornly remaining in its accustomed position. In between the uncles were periods of ill-health. There was always something with Sadie—a bad back, a mysterious lump or suspicious mole, dizzy spells, low moods—that gave her something to complain about, which she did, in an endless monotone, to anyone who would listen.

The frustration had been almost unendurable. Jade had felt invisible, as though locked in a cupboard and forgotten about, or otherwise bound and restricted; completely unable to exert any influence or get herself noticed. She started school expecting to shine, but found herself cloned in an ugly uniform, unremarkable, a pouting face in a crowd. In early school photographs she is always scowling, or poking the person next to her. In later ones she is invariably stationed immediately adjacent to the teacher.

Then Carmel arrived and all, for a time, had been well. There had been a smaller person to hold in thrall, to prod and annoy, to make her feel like somebody.

ANOTHER HOUR GOES by and still there is no sign that Mikey will be seen by a doctor. Other patients—the bleeding and broken—have been gradually garnered into the region beyond the double doors.

Sadie is ready to rattle some cages. 'This is ridiculous,' she says, quite loudly enough for the receptionist to hear. 'We've been here *hours*. We were told the child might have concussion. I mean, that's the kind of thing you can only tell with a brain scan, isn't it? He could be *seriously damaged* and we wouldn't know.'

Jasmine sighs. 'I think they're more concerned he might have picked up a bug in the water. They'll fit us in when they can, I suppose. Do you want another cup of tea?' The tea, from a vending machine, is execrable.

'I'd rather have a wine,' Sadie says. It is her one comfort, she always says, her only treat; a glass of wine of an evening. More often than not one glass becomes two or three—and they are large ones. Mikey has finished his book and exhausted the sorry collection of chipped and battered toys in the children's area. He climbs onto his mother's knee. 'I'm tired,' he says.

'Don't let him go to sleep!' Sadie cries. 'He might go into a coma!' Something about her tone suggests she almost wishes he would; at least then they would get some attention.

The automatic doors slide open and a blonde woman hurries in. Clearly not injured, she is taut as a spring; the knuckles of the hand that grips her bag are bleached white. She marches up to the reception window.

'Well I'll be ...' Sadie gasps, 'it's Jennifer Fairlie.'

Jennifer is a figure so consigned to Sadie's past that she has closed the door on it; a heap of dusty mementoes in a dark attic, neglected but not disposed of, so that a shaft of light, or, in this case, the swish of the automatic door, can kindle it instantly back into pulsating life.

Jennifer has adopted that imperious hauteur she finds effective when dealing with what she thinks of as pointless, obstructive bureaucracy. 'Iris Fairlie—F A I R L I E,' she spells it out with patient enunciation. But the stolid, unflappable woman behind the screen seems undaunted. Jennifer sighs affectedly, and begins to sketch in more detail. 'I had a call,' she checks her watch, 'about an hour ago. She was brought in around five, I believe. I had to find *that* out from Bridge House. I can't think why it took so long for me to be contacted. It's a suspected hip fracture.' Jennifer recites these facts as though they are counts on a charge-sheet and the receptionist is the accused, but the woman remains impervious, scrolling doggedly through her list of patients.

Jasmine and her mother are leaning conspiratorially together. 'Wasn't Iris Fairlie the woman who used to live next door to Granny?' Jasmine asks in a murmur.

'She might still live there, for all I know. That's the daughter. Never showed her face. That's why the old girl used to come to us for Christmas.'

Jasmine has memories of Christmases at Granny's. The house was always heaving with people—Sadie's brothers and sisters, their spouses and children. The table was laden with food and drink. There had never been enough chairs—the children had to sit on the floor. But always in the big chair by the fire, in pride of place, was the lady from next door. She would be dressed in her festive best, and hold court while Granny bustled between the sink and the stove with tureens of vegetables and vats of gravy. In later years the crowds were thinner— aunts and uncles chose to stay at home or celebrate with friends. In the end only Sadie and her daughters and Mikey and Lilly had kept up the tradition; the alternative of Christmas at home together with their squatting seventh—their mutual spite—being untenable. But still there was a place laid for the redoubtable Mrs Fairlie.

'I never knew she had children,' Jasmine says in a low voice.

'Oh yes, she did,' Sadie's face is suddenly illuminated, alive with memory. Her eyes sparkle—a long dormant inner light curiously reignited. 'She had two. That one,' Sadie nods her head towards the blonde haired woman, 'she's my age, more or less. And there was an older brother, Michael.'

At the window Jennifer is becoming obstreperous, 'Still awaiting assessment? She's been here *hours*.'

The receptionist recites her mantra. 'We've been extremely busy; there have been a number of major incidents ...'

'And I suppose one elderly lady doesn't qualify.'

'It's a matter of prioritising.'

Jennifer decides to take another tack; perhaps pathos will be more effective. 'She'll be so afraid, all alone for so long.'

'She isn't on her own. There's a nurse from the home with her ...' The receptionist checks her screen, 'Rosie Fairbanks booked her in.'

'Oh,' Jennifer is somewhat mollified. 'Well I can take over now. I'm her daughter, after all.'

'I'll call someone to come and show you through.'

Sadie and Jasmine have been eavesdropping. As Sadie makes to rise to her feet and intercept Jennifer, Jasmine shrinks into her chair and puts out a restraining hand. 'Did you hear that?'

'What?'

'Rosie Fairbanks. That's Richard's wife.'

As the bus pulls at last into the station Jade remembers the card, pulling it out of her bag and signing it with a kohl pencil—all she has to hand. She encloses a ragged £5 note—somewhat reluctantly—and seals it up.

It is ten past eight.

Why am I always late, she laments. She casts a glance over her shoulder as though expecting to see some crouching, wart-covered goblin at her back. She has a fleeting idea of it stretching elastic lips back over toothless gums and rubbing its bony hands in glee at the annoyance he has managed to cause her. Why am I always last?

The town is busy, even for a Saturday night. Groups of girls are still dressed for heat-wave—exposing flesh—although the weather has broken now and low cloud threatens further downpours. The streets are slick with brown, tread-marked sludge, and oily pools stand over blocked grids. A youth on a bike cycles through a puddle and Jade's white skirt and legs are tattooed with dark brown splashes. Her rage explodes and she shouts after him, a string of obscenities. He raises two fingers in salute. She is almost disappointed that he does not come back to debate the issue. She could cheerfully have hit him.

The town is on the edge of craziness; a potent cocktail of mania, shock and euphoria. The pure-proof kick of the storms and flooding has been further energised by the effervescence released by the end of the heat wave. It quivers at the brim of the chalice of the football cup which has, that very afternoon, come to its unsatisfactory conclusion. Everything is upside down, up for grabs. Amid the ruins of humdrum, it seems like anything is possible. The populace are like escapees from

463

an institution, unexpectedly at large but at a loss to know how best to employ their liberty. She can sense it, as she hurries along the busy concourse and across the market square; a firework whose touch-paper has been lit.

There are fourteen of them in the pizzeria celebrating Charlene's birthday. They are the lads and girls from the discount supermarket plus three others—the birthday girl's brother and two cousins. The party has divided, as it always does when an attempt is made to mix disparate strands of social association. All but one of the supermarket colleagues—alien out of their dreadful uniforms, the boys gelled and pungent with after-shave, the girls made up to the nines and giggling with excitement—are loud and boisterous down at one end of the table, already swigging house Chianti. Charlene, her brother and cousins are seated together, reminiscing hilarious old-times to the exclusion of the rest of the party. At the far end of the table, marooned from her workmates, is Maureen. Maureen is the supermarket deputy manager, leathery from too much time on the sun-bed, her skin is as tough as a dry chamois. She is by far the oldest of the party. She was only invited as a matter of politeness and her acceptance has cast a pall of apprehension over the occasion.

'I never actually thought she'd come,' the birthday-girl had confided gloomily, 'I might as well have asked my effing mother.'

A concerted effort on arrival at the restaurant has got Maureen relegated to the far end of the table from where she has attempted to preside over proceedings until it is evident that her recommendation that wine ought not to be ordered in quantities greater than a single carafe is going to be ignored. Now she has withdrawn into moody silence, her mouth a hard, pursed line of disapproval, perusing the menu with an eagle eye to the prices.

Jade, arriving late, is forced to take the only unoccupied chair, opposite Maureen, with annoyed resignation. Typical, she thinks, draping her shoulder bag over the back of the chair and squeezing into the seat. Her heels are already rubbed raw by her new sandals. She drops a discreet hand down to loosen them before glaring down the table. The other girls are dressed in loose, elegant summer dresses. I bet they all planned it, she thinks, feeling bitter and left out. Her clingy skirt and tight, strappy top are way off-message. She now realises that they were the wrong choice of attire for a meal, and one she would not have made if one of her useless sisters had been at home to advise her.

Nobody pays much attention to her. She wonders if she, too, was only asked as a matter of form, because she is the new girl. Her thoughts teeter on the edge of self-pity before landing in their habitual receptacle of resentment. She is sick of being friendless; the odd one out. At school she'd invariably been the one without a partner, a hanger-on on the periphery of the crowd. None of her associations had lasted beyond the final term. She has never found friendship easy, finding the small-minded bitchiness or sheer dim-witted idiocy of girls just too infuriating. On the whole she has always found boys easier to relate to but not, in the end, any more trustworthy. She *wants* friendship, nonetheless. Her seeming inability to make an essential connection frustrates her. This, she thinks now, looking disconsolately down the table, this is probably her last opportunity. In another couple of years these girls will be engaged or married and preoccupied with domestic responsibilities. They won't have time for her then. No, she sighs. As meagre as it is, this had been an opportunity, but now it is wasted.

'Happy birthday Charlene,' Jade says, with the brightest smile she can muster, handing over the crumpled envelope from her bag. Immediately after the transaction—too late—she sees the row of gift-bags and extravagantly be-ribboned presents on the low window ledge adjacent to her seat.

'Thanks!' Charlene replies, almost throwing the card—unopened— amongst the other offerings. She indicates Jade's neighbour, 'this is my brother Ryan.'

'Hi,' Jade says, smiling.

He nods and hands her a menu. 'Bus late?' he asks, pouring wine into her glass.

'It's been a nightmare of a day,' she says.

'Yes,' he says. 'It has.'

She wonders how he knows, but then realises he is referring to the flooding and its attendant tragedies of which theirs has been only one and an insignificant one at that.

The crowd has already ordered. Jade hasn't time to look over the menu properly. She points to something on the card and the obsequious waiter writes it down on his diminutive pad. When it arrives it is a roiling tangle of pasta threads smothered in red sauce. It is delicious, but a demon to eat, slithering off her fork as if alive. Afterwards, she sees that her white top is sprinked with sauce, as though it has developed measles. It is her mother's—there will be hell to pay. Whilst tussling with her food Jade is subjected to a diatribe from Maureen, comprising the weighty responsibilities of the deputy manager, back-office politics, unreliable delivery drivers and the increasing pressure to dispose of packaging in an environmentally-friendly way. To Jade, who has only just been allowed to operate the till unsupervised, it is all meaningless. She can only nod and say, 'I see. Oh. I see'. To his credit, Ryan keeps her glass topped up with wine and she catches him, once or twice, giving her a sidelong glance. Her gripes finally exhausted, Maureen subsides into moody silence and takes tiny, shrivel-lipped sips at her lime-and-soda as though it is something she is required to force down against her will.

Down the table there is laughter and fun. The girls are giggling at the boys' jokes. But Jade can't hear what's being said and to giggle anyway just to seem like part of it would make her look stupid. Without an eye to meet or any part to take in the conversation, she stares through the window. It is festooned with artefacts designed to conjure the Mediterranean—fishing nets and oars and skeletal fish jaws, and along the sill is a row of wine bottles encased in woven raffia. The bottles are dusty and enmeshed in grey cobweb. Outside, on the market square, there is lots of activity. The ornate lights have flickered into life as the dusk descends. Groups of girls are off to clubs, lads in football regalia cruise the pubs, there are couples heading to restaurants. She watches them all, envious of their companionship, their inclusion. Wherever she looks, people are together; nobody is on their own.

'Penny for them,' Ryan says, nudging her from her reverie.

'Oh,' she shrugs, 'nothing, really.'

The waiter brings a cake with a crackling sparkler and the table sings a raggedly self-conscious chorus of 'happy birthday to you'. Charlene beams and begins to open her presents. Jade is relieved to see her dog-eared envelope disappear beneath the discarded wrapping paper as expensive toiletries, a pashmina, DVDs and—to much sniggering amongst the supermarket boys—a rabbit vibrator are unwrapped. It is the last straw for Maureen, who pushes her chair back with a violent scrawp on the tiled floor, arresting everyone's startled attention, before disappearing between the crowded tables. She must have paid her share of the bill because the next time they see her she is at the door and saying goodnight. As the door opens it admits the briefest snatch of noise; an anxious, tight-strung note that pulsates through the evening air. Sirens.

JENNIFER HAS TAKEN up a position just outside the double doors that lead to the treatment area. It looks like she is lying in wait for the first unsuspecting member of the medical staff who might emerge. A spider poised in a web, she will snatch them and coil them in silk and bundle them back through the doors, a hostage to exchange for her mother. She carefully avoids eye contact with the other lost, languishing souls in the waiting room. Her case, she tells herself, her mother's case, is quite different, more serious. It *must* be, otherwise Mum would be out here and they would be inside. Casualties, she has been told, are strictly prioritised. Clearly, she has precedence.

She and Kenny have had a row. He has been on edge all day; pumped up about the football, as though it really mattered. He had accompanied her with bad grace to the Open Day, and moaned about it all the way home, even though she had only stayed there the briefest time. She had had to cajole him into putting his hand in his pocket at the stalls. 'That's the point,' she had hissed, 'of course this is just to raise money.'

'They're bleeding us dry as it is,' he had said, which wasn't true anyway. Her mother's affairs are now in order and she is paying her own way.

'It isn't for Bridge House,' she had clarified, 'it's for the voluntary groups who come in and do things; the church and the WI.'

She had hated to leave, really. Walking away from her poor mother, abandoning her in the over-crowded lounge had felt dreadful. And of course the old woman had chosen just that moment to mention Michael, when it was *the* most impossible moment to explain.

Who could blame her, then, for being a little withdrawn afterwards? Kenny had accused her of being moody and sour. They had got home just in time for kick-off and when she'd suggested that perhaps she might leave him to it and pop to the garden centre he had blown his top.

'You're always complaining that we don't spend any time together,' he'd roared. He had pushed—no, not really pushed—pressed her into a corner of the sofa and positioned himself in such a way that his shoulder and hip kept her pinioned there. She couldn't even see the television! Her only view had been the back of his neck, the way his short hair bristled from the roll of flesh that was developing, the result of too many business lunches. From that angle he looked like a Rottweiler. He had yanked open a can of lager so that some of it spilled on the white leather sofa. She had eyed it uncomfortably, wanting to get a cloth, but his demeanour had dared her to try it and she had had to watch it dry into a sticky, scummy stain. He hadn't spoken another word to her for nearly two hours.

He can't have been comfortable, sitting against her like that, and eventually he had moved so she could at least see the action, what there was of it. She had made the obligatory gasps and gripes whenever it seemed that something conclusive would occur. At half-time she had fixed snacks. But all the time her mind had been on her mother; the look in her jewelled, frightened eyes when she had asked, 'Is he dead?' The courage it must have taken to face it. How alone—how very, very alone she is.

Kenny's team had won and she had expected that to improve his mood. But it hadn't. The victory was in some way unsatisfactory, unconvincing. Expectation remained in the air like an unanswered question; an itch unscratched. Kenny had roamed around the house, changing his clothes, pouring a whisky. She had made a series of suggestions in a voice unnaturally bright and tight; dinner out somewhere; take-away; barbecue. Even—in desperation—an early night. He had only shrugged and scowled and flicked disconsolately between sports channels as though some other network might report a different game with an alternative result; a resounding, unequivocal victory. He complained—about the players, the manager, the tactics, the pitch, and especially about a controversial decision by the referee. He had complained about her, sitting there all afternoon with a pained expression, wishing she was somewhere else. Then the telephone had rung. The hospital.

He had really expected her to ignore the summons, to abandon her mother …

When she gets back, he said, he wouldn't be there.

She doesn't care. She is beginning to prefer it.

She doesn't at first recognise the stumpy, round-faced woman who approaches her, but when Sadie speaks identification is swift. It is Annie who speaks from Sadie's mouth; the same carked, unmusical voice. She hears an echo of it, a tuneless croon while she rolled pastry or kneaded dough. And, now she has placed it, the same hard-luck-story chin and badly-done-by eyes. And because she has spent all afternoon thinking about her mother—her isolation, there, amongst strangers—it is like a wish-fulfilment and she is conscious of a leaping surge of optimism, of gratitude. This familiar figure from her mother's past means she is not alone, after all. Although with her logical mind Jennifer knows that Annie is dead and gone, the surge overtakes logic, deluging it like a downpour over parched land, so that she greets Sadie more warmly than she otherwise might have done, with a swift, fierce hug.

'Sadie!'

'Yes. I knew you the minute you walked in. You haven't changed.'

The inundation is momentary, leaving Jennifer high and dry and needing to retreat from the level of enthusiasm she has brokered. For a start she is unable to return the compliment. The Sadie she remembers was plump and pleasantly dimpled, with an engaging smile and curly hair Jennifer had always envied. This Sadie has run to seed; her complexion is woeful, riddled with lines, especially around the mouth where smoking has stitched a row of vertical seams. The lipstick she applied earlier has retreated to the creased perimeter of her lips and lodged itself in two greasy reservoirs at their corners. Her hair is bottle-black, harsh and unnatural. Her clothes—even given where they are and the allowances for haste and heedlessness one might make—are awful. Pilled black leggings sagging at the knees, a sleeveless black t shirt and a vivid raspberry pink shirt that looks like a man's. On her feet is a pair of discoloured flip flops. Her feet are dirty.

'How have you been? What are you doing here?' Jennifer asks, with forced brightness.

Sadie begins her well-rehearsed story. At its conclusion she points to Mikey, curled in his mother's lap. 'That's my daughter Jasmine,' she says. 'My oldest.'

Just then the double doors swing open and Rosie steps through them. Her ears catch Jasmine's name and her eyes follow the pointing finger. The two women look at each other across the room. What passes is a complex, many-layered exchange of mutual reproach, envy, sadness and shame. There is nothing caustic about it; their natures allow of no explosion, no haranguing or blame. What one allowed to slip away, piece by infinitesimal piece, the other collected with surprised, grateful hands. Rather than dividing, it binds them in a shared, astonishingly intimate union; a common appreciation of the lost and found. It is an uncomfortable, startling, indelible alliance.

THE PIZZERIA IS filling up and presently the window is clouded by condensation; a misted curtain. Jade cannot keep on gazing through it. She is desperate for a cigarette and considers—in the guise of going outside for one—slipping away.

The girls and boys at the bottom of the table are becoming unruly. Charlene has abandoned her seat and is perched on the knee of the forklift truck driver. He plays the vibrator over her breasts. Ryan blushes and looks away, down at his watch, then at Jade.

'Sisters,' he says hoarsely.

'Stupid bitches, aren't they? I've got two of them,' Jade agrees too vehemently.

Ryan looks a bit startled. He is older than Charlene, she guesses, but not more than twenty two or three. He has thin wrists and large hands, shy eyes beautifully fringed with pale lashes, good teeth, curly hair. He cocks his head in the direction of the other guests, 'Do you know all these people?'

'Not really. I've only worked at the shop a couple of weeks. They've been quite friendly, though, especially Charlene.' This isn't quite true but she feels she must retreat from her implied criticism of his sister.

'I've got a new job, as well,' he offers. 'It takes a while to find your feet.' He smiles at her then and there is a leap of frisson between them, a sympathetic tie, gossamer fine and so quickly gone in the charged atmosphere of the restaurant that it is lost almost as soon as it is felt. Ryan must have felt it too; he blushes and nods suddenly towards the window. 'Something's happening out there.' He stands up and leans across her, wiping the condensation from the pane. In the orange-electric glow of the street lights they see a solid body of people walking swiftly by. He smells of citrus. His shirt, as it brushes Jade's bare arm, is soft, and she can feel the warmth of his body through it.

The waiter brings the cake, cut into squares. The icing is sickeningly sweet, the sponge the colour and consistency of foam rubber. It makes Jade think of Granny Annie. She could bake a proper cake.

Her granny's house had been a haven. The place where they were sent if ill—to be wrapped in a crocheted blanket, fed with chicken soup and have their rashes dabbed with calamine—or when sibling contention escalated beyond Sadie's ability to cope. Or when Sadie—and latterly Jasmine—was going out and there was nobody to look after the younger girls. Or sometimes for no reason at all, just because Sadie had had enough of them. They would be ferried by bus to the tiny two-up, two-down house on the harsh, narrow little street where no tree or verge softened the kerbs. Sadie would bundle them into the house with a carrier bag of hastily gathered belongings that did not always include necessaries like knickers and toothbrushes, and close the door without a word, leaving Granny to cope. She would stop what she was doing, dry their tears, soothe their sulks and feed them. Somehow, in her house, all enmity seemed pointless. It was as though the walls had seen more angst already than three sullen girls would ever be able to generate, as though Granny herself had witnessed and lived through every vicissitude, and not even their most determined assaults of spite could move her. The house had a front room where no one ever went, with its stiff, scratchy sofa and glazed animal ornaments. A narrow, steep, dark stair led to two bedrooms and a tiny, incommodious little bathroom, but in the back was the kitchen, with a real fire and always a tray of scones or gingerbread just out of the oven. There was a radio—Granny called it a wireless—and some interminable piece of knitting tucked down the side of the armchair. Jasmine and Granny would roll up their sleeves and make pastry—short-crust, rough-puff, choux, flaky—as absorbed as alchemists in their laboratory. In a cupboard built into the side of the fireplace there was Granny's button box, an old Quality Street tin. It was a treasure trove of beautiful buttons; tiny pearlised penny-sized counters, bold embossed brass doubloons, diamante-encrusted lozenges, shiny jet beads. There were buttons made in the shapes of flowers and shells, of every size and colour. Carmel would take the box under the tent of the table cloth and spend hours sorting them out into piles according to type or size or hue, small heaps of booty wrested from an imaginary dragon's lair. Jade would bide her time until the last button had been painstakingly weighed, considered and allocated before pushing her way into the space and grasping the piles, letting the buttons cascade through her fingers, spreading them far and wide in a glorious disorder, obliterating Carmel's taxonomy and making her cry.

Behind the houses was a passageway that ran the length of the block, but behind that was a secret garden, with mysterious locked outhouses where once cream had been made into butter and cheese and sacks of vegetables stored. The garden belonged to the house next door to Granny but the girls were allowed in to it because the lady was Granny's friend. She always had dogs with laughing mouths and lop-sided ears. They had raced the grass away in a circular track but around the perimeter of the garden was an overgrown forest of flowering shrubs and fruit bushes. Jade, exiled from the kitchen, would cram raspberries and blackcurrants into her mouth as quickly as possible before Carmel came out and she would have to share.

When Jade returns from her day-dream, Sarah from the deli counter is snogging Wayne from fruit and veg. Two check-out girls have swapped seats and are moving in on Ryan and the boy cousin. They bring what's left of a carafe of wine and empty it into their glasses. Jade is excluded. Whatever embryonic connection she had discerned between herself and her neighbour has gone. Her famous temper is welling up and she knows that she has begun to glower. She starts up from the table, scrawping her chair as Maureen had done, appealing to somebody to notice her, invite her to join them, include her, but nobody gives her a second glance. Her initiative having failed, now she is standing she must do something, so she makes her way to the Ladies between the crowded, sociable tables. Her shoes are agony. They'll be going in the bin the moment she gets home.

JENNIFER'S MOTHER IS on a bed in a curtained cubicle, covered with a white sheet and a thin, much-washed blue cellular blanket. She looks uncomfortable; one leg juts at an awkward angle. She has a cannula in the back of her hand and a thin clear plastic tube snakes away from it to a pouch suspended on a metal stand. Another tube, under her nose, delivers oxygen. She looks quite different, lying down. The flesh of her face has fallen away taking with it the familiar features and expressions, leaving only the smooth promontories of cheek bone and eye socket and jaw. The result is strangely lifeless, like a marble effigy. They have taken away her teeth and her lips disappear into a hollow cave. It is as though she has withdrawn inwards, pulling the essence of herself to some central nucleus where she can husband it. She mumbles occasionally and her eyelids struggle to open, but her eyes are filmed over. It is impossible to read any sense in them.

'She's heavily sedated,' Rosie says.

'What happened?' Jennifer asks. They both use lowered voices as though they might wake the patient but she is clearly oblivious to her surroundings and the noise of bustle in the department is deafening anyway. Nurses come and go constantly, their shoes squeaking on the linoleum, flapping files of notes. Porters manoeuvre trolleys to and fro, 'Off to X-ray is it my darling?' they say with a wink, as if off to the seaside. A telephone rings on and on. Patients cry out and sigh and groan and describe their symptoms with excruciating frankness—between the dividing curtains there isn't an iota of privacy. The blip and bleep of monitoring equipment makes a syncopated percussion beneath and around the injured.

Rosie shrugs. 'Nobody saw. She was half way across the lawn going down towards the river. I've caught her out there before at night. She likes to look at the water and the fields, I know that.'

'Does she?'

'They remind her of when she was a girl, I think.'

'Oh.'

The woman under the sheet is a stranger. Jennifer knows nothing of her likes and dislikes, her girlhood, the significance of water and fields. Suddenly she is conscious that the capable, substantial figure of her mother has ebbed away. In the past—what would it be? Three months?—since going into Bridge House she has diminished, reduced to this collection of apparently fragile bone and strangely foreign tissue. An unpleasant, guilty claw clutches at Jennifer's innards.

The patient in the neighbouring cubicle is pressing his call button insistently. His companion calls, 'Nurse! Nurse!' Then there is the unmistakable sound of regurgitated semi-solids hitting the floor. Somewhere else a child is crying. A male voice, perhaps his father or a nurse, tries to soothe and reassure. 'It won't hurt, I promise. Try to be brave.' This mixed message puts the child on his guard. His scream is falsetto, setting the teeth on edge, denoting panic and betrayal. '*It does* hurt! No! No! Daddy! Don't let him!' The curtains billow as they struggle. Then, in another area of the room, an argument erupts between a gruff-voiced man and a doctor. The patient is clearly inebriated, his language is obscene. It serves to silence the child into shocked submission. 'There now,' the male voice says. 'All over. Good boy.'

'You can go now, if you like,' Jennifer says, although she is reluctant to be left here in this bear-pit of distress. Reluctant, also, to be left alone with her mother who is an uncomfortable mystery she feels ill-equipped to fathom.

Rosie picks up Mrs Fairlie's mottled, misshapen hand and strokes it tenderly. 'I don't like to, poor thing.'

477

The implication—that Rosie too recognises Jennifer's inadequacy to the task of taking care of her mother—and the evidence of comfortable kinship demonstrated in Rosie's gesture, take Jennifer aback. She cannot remember holding her mother's hand for many years. But she is not one to shrink from unpleasantness.

'If there's any news, I'll call Matron,' she says, by way of dismissal.

'All right then,' Rosie smiles, and bends and kisses the old woman on her leathery cheek. 'Good bye Iris,' she says.

There is one plastic chair in the cubicle and Jennifer sits on it gingerly. She eyes her mother's hand, where Rosie has left it, lying by her side. The thumb is awry. Dimly she recalls some tale about it having been kicked—or trodden on—by a cow. All the joints are swollen and purple as blighted plums. For the first time Jennifer considers whether they had been painful. Her mother had never complained but it seems impossible to think that such inflammation could have been painless. The fingernails are yellow but neatly trimmed. There are still calluses on the sides of some of the fingers, but they are clean now, whereas in her youth she remembers her mother's hands were always dirty with the soil from potatoes, or smelt of sour milk.

Her childhood is something she rarely thinks about. If she is honest she is ashamed of her lowly origins. But seeing Sadie out there in the waiting room has brought back a flood of recollections. The two of them aged, perhaps, three or four, running naked in the garden while Michael, or one of Sadie's older brothers, squirted water at them from a hose-pipe. They had shrieked, almost hysterical with shock and joy. One Christmas they had both been quarantined with chicken pox. Annie had nursed them both because Jennifer's mother had the shop to look after, and they had sweated and itched together in the tiny back bedroom while the other children enjoyed Christmas parties and went carol singing door-to-door. They were banned from the church nativity, a prohibition Jennifer had railed against for days—it had been her turn to be Mary. She had eventually taken her anger out on Sadie, making her stand in the draughty corner and recite her times tables and spell difficult words while she shivered with fever. Jennifer was always the quicker-witted of the two. She did much better at school, and if they got into trouble it was because Sadie was too slow to think of a ready excuse, or a plausible one. It was always Jennifer who took the lead. Sadie had been a plodding acolyte, a convenient companion and at times a useful scapegoat. Aged eleven they had begun to drift apart. Jennifer passed to go to the Grammar school and Sadie didn't. It reinforced the unvoiced but acknowledged gulf between them—so much more than the thin skin of brick that divided their houses. Jennifer's mother was the employer, Sadie's the employee. Jennifer's father was respectably deceased, Sadie's disgracefully alive, a drunk and a bully. Experience, expectation and ambition drove them inexorably apart for the next few years. Jennifer associated with nice girls whose fathers were accountants and solicitors. Her home-life was something that she kept firmly in the shadows. At school she was one of a few students identified as possible Oxbridge material, and given extra lessons. By that time her brother was already heading off the rails and the shop was on its last legs. All in all home was something she felt she could not get away from quick enough.

But one summer, a June day in 1977, there had been a brief, surprising reconciliation between the two girls. She would have been seventeen, Sadie a few months younger. There had been a street party for some royal occasion, everyone out of their houses dressed in red, white and blue, food and drink flowing. She had intended to have nothing to do with it—it was too plebeian for words—but Sadie had come to find her. Against Jennifer's own stick-thin, flat chested figure Sadie was voluptuous, like a ripe fruit, with big brown eyes and dark lashes, her hair worn long and loose and glowing with auburn highlights. For the first time in their relationship Jennifer had felt at a disadvantage, as though Sadie had gained ground and left her behind, gawky and awkward. Sadie had led her into the garden where one of her brothers had a stash of cider. They had raided it repeatedly as the warm afternoon wore on to balmy evening, and the event, as it turned out, had been quite good fun. Later, Michael had come and played for them, and they had all danced—her and Sadie very unsteadily—on the cobbles, until her mother had come and led her indoors. Her mouth had been downturned and disapproving, but now, she wonders if there hadn't been a suggestion of humour in her eye. Later, she hadn't been able to find Sadie, or Michael either, come to that.

'Are you here with Mrs Fairlie?' the doctor asks. His white coat is buttoned up wrong and his eyes are hollow with fatigue. He opens his sheaf of notes and clicks the top of his ball point. 'Just some details then, if you would.'

She takes him through what she knows; age, address, GP's details, known medical history, allergies, medication.

'I'm just going to examine you Mrs Fairlie,' he says loudly to the body on the bed, exactly as you would speak to someone in a remote area of the building. His voice is raised but retains a genial, conversational tone; shouting *to* rather than *at*. It is as if he knows that she has retreated to some inner sanctuary. He lifts the blanket and manipulates the leg. She jumps and cries out, a string of gabble made incoherent by her toothless, doped-up state. Something about her voice arrests his attention though; he cocks an eyebrow and inserts his stethoscope into his ears, listens intently to her chest. Jennifer can see her mother's breastbone through the mottled parchment tissue of her skin. It rises and falls like a bellows in a smithy; a laboured, industrious action.

'Hum,' the doctor says. He inserts a device into Mrs Fairlie's ear. After a moment he removes it and regards it, closely.

'Hum,' he says again.

MEN POUR FROM the pub and out into the street in a zealous surge. The FA Cup Special carrying 'our lads' is due in any moment and there is word that the streets down by the station are mobbed by opposition supporters, ready to kick heads in. It is primeval, the most ancient of instincts to defend the clan; a visceral call to arms. They down their pints as one and shoulder their way through the doors, emboldened by numbers, a common cause and the caramel glow of best bitter.

Most of them have been in the pub since early afternoon and are acclimatised to its sweaty yeast-and-hops ambience. After its fetid heat, the outside air is chill and damp; it hits them with the kick of a whisky chaser. The dark surprises them, as though time has accelerated while their backs were turned. They jostle around in the narrow cobbled street, paddling heedlessly in the turgid puddles and smoking cigarettes, stoking each other's bile. There is some swift texting and a few terse phone calls to gather intelligence, enlist additional support and cobble together a strategy before an intuitively felt signal draws them as a body down the hill. They walk quickly, shoulder to shoulder, united by their identical club-shirts and their grim purpose, with neither the time nor the perspective to analyse it. At the corner they encounter another phalanx, trooping down from a different part of town. They are strangers to each other but their colours identify them as comrades and the two groups merge seamlessly into a broad, bold brotherhood.

It is almost 9.30pm and darkness has done nothing to ameliorate the gloom of the damp, bedraggled town. It wallows in a dank malodorous murk. The lowest-lying streets are coned off, still a-swill with brown river water. Saturated circuitry causes manically flickering traffic lights to reflect demented disco rainbows in the pools. A pungent smell of sewage is carried on the air.

Unleashed but not exhausted by last night's storm, there is a residue of angst from the weeks of drought that the football match should have— but has not—purged. The weeks of build-up—endless speculation and increasing club-apartheid—coinciding with the brutal oppression of the weather, has bred an aggressive plume of confrontational spores that the lack-lustre final did nothing to expurgate. They all agree that the much-vaunted clash of the titans turned out to be little more than a fairy-footed ballet dance on Wembley's grassy sward. Tribal pride has not been satisfied; the question of supremacy is still decidedly moot. They have brooded since the final whistle, licking their wounds in the pubs and bars, feeding a nagging, persistent pocket of frustration that only spectacular victory or crushing defeat can finally resolve.

The numbers swell as the men march through the streets of the town. They are loud with beery confidence. Distantly, but ever closer, they can hear an amorphous hubbub filtering between the buildings. They meet, by arrangement, with a detachment of allies in a car-park about five minutes' walk from the station. A runner reports large numbers on both sides already assembled at the station and being kept apart with difficulty by lines of riot police. More police are lining the route with the intention of funnelling fans away from the station. A hurried conference results in a decision to skirt back through the streets, across the market place and come down by the second-hand motor dealership onto the rear of the opposing forces. They set off through alleyways and back-streets, their ebullient mood of only moments before suddenly subdued, darkly hostile. They tread quietly, tuning in to the clamour that roars now in disembodied gusts towards them; the bellow of boiling blood. If any of them are having second thoughts, now is not the time to say so.

They go quickly through the gloom behind the discount supermarket and past the gym; the acrid chlorine stench wafts out in warm billows from the ventilation ducts. Occasionally, in the dimness, they see skulking individuals hurrying in the opposite direction and gaggles of scantily-clad females, oblivious to the thunderous mood of the town.

They turn right and begin their descent.

By the time they reach the second-hand motor dealership there are perhaps a hundred of them. The battlefield is before them. By the bright illumination of the station's arc lights they can see, in the wide hollow at the bottom of the hill, a writhing mass of men, boiling and erupting in waves towards the sturdy breakwater of police. A volley of stones and bottles flies in an arc over the police lines and into the crowd beyond, which is equally numerous, equally agitated. A reciprocal cascade soars back. They glint and shimmer in the lights like shooting stars. The cacophony has clarified now. The amalgam of sound has separated out into its individual components; enraged voices, the smash of glass, the clash of missiles on riot-shields and the high-pitched shriek of sirens.

There is a momentary hesitation. Even in their considerable numbers, and with their advantages of high ground and surprise, they are overwhelmingly outnumbered. Then, very suddenly, before there is time to reconsider, they are in the fray. A shower of stones hits them from amongst the tidily parked cars on the forecourt. Now they look properly all the windscreens are smashed into frosted mosaics. A cohort of opposition fans hurls themselves from their crouched positions amongst the vehicles and a section from the back of the crowd below detaches itself and begins to move like an inexorable tide, up the hill.

Then, overlaying the savage bawls of the rival fans, the barked orders of the police and the piercing shrill of whistles, a deep rumble makes the ground tremble and the Cup Final Special pulls into the station. Its doors slide open and the carriages disgorge hundreds more frustrated fans. They pour across the platform and swarm down the steps. The police lines buckle and break, and the officers are overwhelmed as blue meets red in bloody retribution.

THE LADIES LOO is wholly and unrelievedly pink, conjuring idealised babies and iced buns and piglets and Barbie dolls. The walls and ceiling are candyfloss pink. There are shell pink tiles and the porcelain is baby lotion pink. The toilet paper is pastel pink, the soap strawberry pink, the towel powder pink on a shocking pink hook. In a pearly pink vase are artificial flowers in every hue of pink: coral, salmon, peach, blush, rose, flesh and cherry. In the mirror Jade regards herself—pink also, with alcohol and anger. She has a ridge, a frowned-in crease between her eyebrows—evidence of a sulky nature—dark eyes and a mouth that is tending to droop at its corners. She is, she considers gloomily, a clone of her mother, with 100% maternal genes unrelieved by any ameliorating contrast of paternal input. Her sisters on the other hand have entirely escaped Sadie's petite, dark-complexioned DNA, but have a correspondingly insubstantial quality. There is something miasmic about them both, a wispy remoteness in keeping with their fathers who disappeared into the ether before any of them made it, gasping and mewling, into the light of day. She considers that she is plain; pleasant enough, but unremarkable. Next to her sisters—angelic, honey-gold Jasmine, who exudes goodness like sweet, sticky, irresistible resin, and Carmel, who has a pure, icy elegance that is almost appalling—her dark colouring and diminutive, plump stature makes her look like a swarthy dwarf.

The skirt, she sees now with despair, looks awful, riding up into nasty creases across her groin. It is something only someone as skinny as Carmel can wear. And although she is nicely tanned—who is not, after the weeks of baking sun they have endured?—there is far too much flesh on show. In fact her figure is better than she knows—curvaceous and velvet-smooth, and her brunette curls and dark brown eyes suggest something of the Romany; a deep, mysterious fire. But in truth she does not always choose her clothes well, mistakenly believing that less is more, and she suddenly feels even here, in this womb-like environment, uncomfortably exposed; more naked than dressed, vulnerable and very, very lonely.

Bleakly, she considers her options. She can go home and binge on crisps and chocolate, pick a fight with Carmel and row with her mother. Or she can stay and get drunk.

When she gets back to the table she finds the boy cousin has ordered a round of shots and it feels as though the decision has been made for her. They arrive on a tray, tiny glasses of clear liquid, but before he distributes them he applies his lighter to one of them. A curl of blue flame flickers briefly before he pours the drink into his mouth. There is a gasp, and then everyone is reaching for the drinks. The girls squeal and hesitate while the flames heat the glass and burn off the alcohol but the boys throw the drinks back swiftly and order more. Jade, unnoticed at the end of the table, drinks hers with a rapid swallow, and when another comes, she drinks that too.

Things progress rapidly between Charlene and the forklift truck driver. They are soon engaged in a fierce embrace, hands roaming, quite oblivious to the startled glances of diners at other tables. A check-out girl and the female cousin are also embracing, having discovered, in their inebriation, a deep affinity of ancient sisterhood. They discuss past lives as medieval maidens and Egyptian Empresses with slurred enthusiasm. Another girl, with smudged makeup, has draped herself across one of her colleagues. She has become maudlin and is close to tears. He looks uncomfortable, and pats her shoulder awkwardly, looking to his co-workers for aid, but none is forthcoming. The rest of the boys are becoming aggressive, discussing with raised voices the afternoon's football match. The boy cousin has found himself in a minority over a controversial referee's decision and argues his case with a voice too loud and in a tone too truculent. Ryan fends off Sarah's determined advances—she has abandoned Wayne without compunction and moved on to new prey. Jade watches them all as though from some high eyrie, with a scathing, resentful eye. Through the window she is conscious of urgent activity; many feet passing, motor vehicles—usually debarred from the pedestrianised market place—shouts and breaking glass.

As though infected by whatever furore is brewing without, diners in the restaurant show signs of increasing uneasiness. At the centre of their disquiet is Jade's table; the pawing and mauling, the raised voices and inappropriate language, the naked flames in close proximity to discarded wrapping paper and their obvious intoxication. It all adds up and eventually someone goes to make a complaint.

Almost immediately the waiter comes and suggests that it is time for them to leave. He needs the table, he says. He places the bill in front of Ryan, who pulls it towards him and gets out his mobile phone to use as a calculator.

Then, there is an ear-splitting crash. The window next to Jade fractures into a million frosted facets. Through its centre, as though erupting through ice, comes a solid, square missile. It lands on their table, knocking over glasses and bottles, narrowly missing Ryan's head. He snaps back in his seat, as though shot. Brittle red brick fragments and splinters of glass strew the table and the diners, the plates of left over cake, Charlene's gifts. Women scream and everyone is on their feet. Jade is conscious of something warm trickling down her scalp and onto her forehead. She passes her hand over it and it comes away bloody.

MEGAN IS BROUGHT out of the side room and left alone while the police constable steps through the sliding doors to speak into her radio. She looks ash-pale and trembly, perched on the edge of a chair with her hands clasped tightly in her lap.

'Have *you* been seen?' Sadie asks sharply.

She nods, a little apologetically. It had been cursory; a quick assessment of her scrapes and bruises, her temperature taken—more of an insurance policy for the police than a genuine examination.

'Well I like *that!*' Sadie cries. She seems to be in some confusion between the means by which Mikey had been restored and the cause of his disappearance. The behaviour of the police has facilitated it, and she thinks of Skinner's mother now as in some way culpable in the afternoon's adventure.

'Mum!' Jasmine admonishes under her breath, but to no avail.

'Well I don't see why *she* should get to be seen before us!'

'She saved his life. She probably risked hers,' Jasmine hisses.

'Is *he* all right?' Megan nods at Mikey, asleep on his mother's lap.

'Nobody's looked at him! He could be unconscious for all we know,' Sadie cries, looking daggers over her shoulder at the imperturbable receptionist. Of the original group gathered in Accident and Emergency only Mikey and a woman who cannot turn her head more than twenty degrees to right or left remain. The others—the mashed-toed, black-eyed and broken-boned, the scalded and sprained, cut and concussed—have gradually been absorbed through the double doors.

487

Others have taken their places of course; the barbecue-burnt and skateboard scraped, the blistered and sliced, the crashed and whiplashed. There is a child suspected of having consumed a raw sausage and another with a pea up his nose; they all wait in agonised, hopeless line.

Megan's police officer returns. 'You'll have to come to the station, I'm afraid,' she says with a weary sigh. 'There's paperwork to complete.'

When she has gone, Sadie turns to Jasmine with a complacent expression denoting the satisfaction of having been right all along. 'There you are: she's got to be questioned. There must be something suspicious ...'

'She's nice, Grandma. She didn't do anything wrong,' says Mikey sleepily.

Time passes. Outside, night has fallen, bringing a mizzling rain so fine it is almost vapour.

'I'm hungry,' Mikey says.

In the receptionist's booth, a telephone rings. Presently an agitated hospital administrator backed up by a brawny-armed security guard reads an announcement from a type-written sheet. 'Ladies and gentlemen, we're getting news of a major incident in town, which has been classified as a code 2. This means that this department is closed to anyone not involved in that incident unless their condition is of a life-threatening or extremely serious nature. I'll be posting the list of conditions that are considered to fall within that category on the notice board. If your complaint is *not* on the list I would urge you to go home, or to an alternative hospital. I am very sorry for those of you who have already been waiting for some time. If you wish to lodge a complaint, the address can be found on the list I am going to put up.'

There is a concerted groan, a weary groping for bags and belongings. A few people hobble over to where the list has been pinned to a board.

'Brilliant!' crows Sadie, throwing up her hands.

Jasmine gets out her mobile and calls Richard, luxuriating in the delicious assurance that he will come for them and take them home.

THE BATTLE RAGES on, supporters from both sides storming the inadequate ranks of riot police, hurling anything they can find into the lines of the opposing fans. From a distance they look like a surging sea of flotsam ebbing and flowing in reciprocal rushes against a wavering levee. Occasionally the currents meet in a turbulent rip-tide of hand-to-hand fighting; brutal and bloody. The noise is deafening; the tumultuous cries of the antagonists as they goad and incite, an antiphonic exchange of insults sharp as spears, called in contrapuntal chorus across the divide. The shrill insistence of sirens is like a legion of unleashed demons. Emergency vehicles screech along the back roads, tyres shriek and skid on the greasy macadam. And underscoring it all is a rumbling, malefic resonance, more of a sensation than a noise, a growling vibration denoting malevolence untamed by reason. Aggression unleashed and beyond all control. The tremors of it pass along the pavements, echo between the buildings and pulse in the air like a distant, primeval drum.

In the second-hand car lot an enterprising detachment siphons fuel into crates of empty beer bottles looted from behind a pub to make petrol bombs. They soar in arcs across the swarming road, their flames painting the fine rain into momentary rainbows. Presently they have the idea of setting fire to the cars themselves and let one roll down the hill towards the station. Men on both sides, and the police, scatter in chaos as it hurtles down the incline in a ball of white heat. The carnage that ensues is cataclysmic; people injured in the crush, skin scorched, the police lines decimated, ancillary fires, a hail of flying debris as the car explodes. The glass façade of the station is smashed into smithereens and a group of terrified, innocent passengers who had been taking shelter inside narrowly escape being crushed or burnt alive only by swarming out onto the platform and leaping recklessly across the tracks.

From the fiery heart of the battle, burning embers of anger and a sort of lunacy are spreading out across the town in bright billows of red and blue. They drift along the dark, narrow streets in search of easy-pickings, lone adversaries they can corner and kick. They are armed with rudimentary weapons; splintered wooden staves torn from a pallet, lengths of scaffolding lifted from a building site, bottles and stones. A few have batons taken from the police. They all have fists and stoutly booted feet. Hardly any have escaped injury. They are ghastly with cuts, their faces disfigured by swollen, pulpy eye sockets, broken noses and split lips. They wear their wounds with grisly pride. They have been blooded in the savage exchanges of blows and missiles. There is a kind of defence in them too. Their maimed faces have become masks to hide behind; individual accountability has been subsumed by their gory disguise. They are a mob, nameless and almost literally faceless. In the frenzy of the hour they lose sight of their object. Anything, anyone, is a target. Their sudden potency is intoxicating. Windows are smashed and shops looted. The doors of the evacuated houses by the river are broken in and the mob swarms up the sodden staircases to rummage amongst the small stacks of salvaged belongings. Lone pedestrians are beaten up, a woman is raped.

'I'M TERRIBLY SORRY,' the nurse says, 'but I'm going to have to move your mum out of this cubicle.'

Jennifer jolts to consciousness. She must have been dozing. 'Why?'

'There's a major incident. We need to clear the department.' The nurse hangs Mrs Fairlie's notes by a clip to the frame of the bed and checks the identity bands on both wrists.

'Is she going into a ward?' Jennifer stands up.

'Eventually. She will be admitted. But I'm sorry I can't tell you when that will be.'

'She'll need surgery, surely? She's broken her hip.'

'I'm sorry. You'll have to talk to the doctor about that. I'm not qualified to make diagnoses. Could you wheel this, please?' The nurse, diminutive as she is, is man-handling the bed on its awkward castors through the department and into a long, green corridor. Jennifer finds herself trotting after her, sliding the metal stand with her mother's drip besides her. A number of other beds are already stationed along one side like lorries along a hard shoulder when high winds on an imminent hilltop threaten to overturn them. Concerned relatives mill around, getting in the way of hurrying hospital personnel. Florescent strip lights give them all a ghastly, jaundiced hue. There are no chairs and no space to put any. A damp draught gusts periodically from the far end of the corridor where presumably there is a door. At a distance, but getting closer, Jennifer can hear a cacophony of sirens.

'You can't leave her here!' she remonstrates, placing her hand on the nurse's arm.

491

'She'll be regularly monitored and moved when we can find a bed. I'm sorry; it's the best I can offer. Look. She'll sleep for hours. What you ought to do is go home and get some rest. Get her a nightie and some toiletries and come back in the morning.'

'I couldn't possibly leave her!'

'There's absolutely nothing you can do here.'

HINDSIGHT IS A dragon that follows behind us breathing the hot, foul breath of recrimination. It shrieks out should-haves. As Jade hurries down the pedestrianised concourse towards the bus station she can feel it panting on the back of her neck. Now she is out in the streets, now the pizzeria is too far behind her to go back, now it is too late to agree to the suggestion that one of the blokes accompany her, *now* she can see the extent of the danger. Her gung-ho assertions that she is a Mere girl and not afraid of a few football fans have been proved to be—by the watery tremor in her knees and the clutching spasms of anxiety in her throat—so much hot air. *Now,* she realises at last, she should have stayed with the others.

The streets of the quiet, dull little town have been metamorphosed into scenes reminiscent of some war-torn Middle Eastern city. The people too, have been temporarily changed, enraged, infected with the wild-eyed lunacy of opportunity. Boundaries of law are momentarily removed. The police are too few and stretched too thinly to keep order. Their entire resources are engaged down by the railway station where the opposing supporters remain in huge, volatile numbers. The ineffectual attempts of restaurant managers, pub landlords and law-abiding bystanders are wholly inadequate as hordes course through the town wreaking havoc. Here and there the dazed and wounded clutch blood-soaked handkerchiefs to their faces, nurse kicked shins and purple eye sockets. Shop windows are smashed, their alarms ringing out unheeded as, within, scavengers carry off electrical goods, armfuls of designer clothing, jewellery and tobacco. The pharmacy door is off its hinges and a group of men inside is working at the metal grille that protects the prescription drugs. An off-licence has its plate window completely shattered, the shards glint and wink like yellow diamonds in the unnatural orange glow from the street lights. Rioters carouse in the streets guzzling strong spirits, or carry off liquor by the crateful. Car windows are smashed, stereos and satellite navigation systems ripped from within, their monotonous, bleating horns filling the air with a doleful din. Jade keeps her head down, dodging the looters, ignoring the drunken cat-calls, shying away from the injured and distressed. Her feet—bare, the torturous sandals abandoned—are filthy and cut as she covers the rubble- and glass-strewn cobbles towards the bus station. She thinks of it as a refuge, a means of certain escape. But when she gets there it is a shambles. One bus is alight, others have been variously disabled, their windows broken and tyres shredded. Around the ticket office and waiting room every window is an open, saw-toothed mouth. There isn't a driver, an inspector, not a single uniform or figure of authority in sight. Jade stands and gapes at it, and is suddenly aware of fear—a cold, clammy hand on her scalp—and panic—an icy knife rummaging amongst her guts.

She wishes Jasmine were here, Carmel. Even her mother.

She runs down a narrow alley, between a discount book store and a carpet shop, in the direction of the taxi rank. Four men pass her on their way up, carrying an up-rooted bench between them, intent on battering down some barricaded door that has frustrated their efforts so far. At the bottom of the hill the street widens out. Where the taxis should be waiting is just an empty lay-by. Her heart slips further into her bowels.

She is frightened now, really frightened. She has no way home from these mutinous streets. It is a new sensation. Angry she has been often. Bitter, resentful, even furious with an occupying, hysterical rage—her malicious familiar has provoked all of these. But never this empty-bowelled fear.

To her left, towards the railway station, she can hear the sounds of fighting. Voices bay like animals. There is the ricochet of missiles, the burst and spurt of small explosions. She turns instead to her right, hurrying along a road she does not recall having been on before, not knowing where it leads. She is panicking; she knows it, not thinking straight, acting on impulses that are driven by fear and not by reason. She turns left and then right, past an old mill building and a row of sorry-looking, run-down shops, and hesitates at the head of a flight of steps that offers itself unexpectedly between a shoe repair place and an old fashioned haberdashery. Damp, cool air rises up the dark aperture. Her bare arms, legs and shoulders pucker into goose-bumps. She begins to descend. The steps are steep, slimy and uneven. The high walls cast the way into impenetrable shadow. When she reaches out to steady her descent her hands meet damp, crumbling brick sprouting tendrils of wet, leggy, sun-starved growth. Looking down is like staring into a black throat of uncertainty. From the street below she can hear the crash of doors being broken down and of windows shattering, the whoops and hollers of looters as they rampage through the closed-up houses down by the river.

She stops, paralysed by indecision, by fear and an overwhelming feeling of being hopelessly, utterly, irredeemably lost.

From behind her, back up the steps, her ears catch a steady marching stomp of military feet. She turns, and in the feeble glow of the single street light at the stair-head, she sees the shadowy forms of riot police as they progress in grim phalanxes towards the station. They are black-suited, their faces rendered featureless by the visors affixed to their protective helmets. They clutch body-length shields and long batons. Rank after rank passes the stair-head to break up the disturbance at the station and restore order. In her disorientation they are as intimidating as the rabid plunderers in the town and the hooligans at the station. Jade crouches on the cold, wet steps. She is soaked, with cold sweat and with the fine, saturating drizzle. At her back the wall exudes an ancient chill. She is trembling, engulfed for a moment in self-pity and an unaccustomed tight, tense, helplessness. But presently, from some deep resource, she summons a reserve of courage and retraces her steps back up to street level.

She pictures the town in her mind's eye. It is built onto the side of a hill, a series of terraces descending down to the river. She doesn't drive and the only way out that she knows of is the route the bus takes, from the bus station. It goes down a hill and across a big junction. From there a road bridge carries traffic in and out of town, over the yawning gulf of the river and the railway and the cluster of dark, semi-derelict mills. She has no idea if it would be the best way to take but it is the only one she knows. She regrets now the countless times she has ridden it blithely unseeing, oblivious to landmarks.

Down towards the station the buildings are weirdly illuminated by the dim orange glow of flames, and on the wind she can smell burning, but because of the heavy, rain-soaked atmosphere it is the charred, ashy smell of old fires. Beneath her bare feet the ground is reverberating, the very air, trapped between the tall, dour buildings, is alive with a clamorous thrum like prisoners' hands hammering for release. It is suffocating; the vapour-laden air, the acrid fumes, the sense of entrapment all weigh down on her and all at once she is overcome with weariness and sinks against the rough brick wall feeling that nothing could possibly increase her desolation and misery. Then the hue and cry from the station increases. From out of the false sunset of fire the silhouettes of a multitude are jostling and charging towards her. They are an impermeable wall, occupying the whole street, ricocheting off the seedy shop-fronts and the blank brick façades. Brandishing make-shift weaponry, a routed mob—blue and red—stampedes before the augmented ranks of riot police. They cover the ground like a moving swarm, a plague of rats, heading straight for her. Instinct makes her shrink back down the stairs but from the bottom of them, out of the shadow, she can hear the swift pounding of feet ascending. Perhaps they too are being pursued, or perhaps they have been recruited as reinforcements against the police, the new common enemy. It is clear that she will be thrown down the cruel flight or crushed underfoot in an instant. She starts off in the only direction left to her, left, further along the unknown street. The way ahead is dark, narrowing, seeming to be leading to a dead-end. In the gloom perhaps a hundred yards ahead she makes out a shadowy underpass beneath what she recognises with relief as a road bridge. Perhaps, beyond the underpass there will be steps up to the road. But something about the shadow unnerves her; it is too solid, suspicious. Even as she approaches it she baulks at entering its inky recess. Behind her she can feel the pavements pounding with panicked footsteps, the roar of many voices. They are almost upon her. She is running. Her bare feet slap the wet slabs. Her heart erupts from her throat. Then she sees them lurking in the darkness; her way, and the way of the mob behind her, is blocked by a solid barricade of riot shields bristling with batons. The shadow hides the jaws of a malevolent trap ready to snap shut on the vandals, the looters, the hooligans and thugs, and on her, a hapless casualty of the night's mayhem.

As she covers the yards between them the officers step out into the light. The crowd behind her sees the glinting shields, and its voice bellows with indignant fury. Above her head and past her ears a hail of sticks and bottles sails into the police lines, landing with an ear-splitting clatter and the far-flung spray of glass shards. The rabble is gaining on her with every step, it is a maddened beast. She can feel its scorching breath, the heat of it almost blistering her back, the stamping crush of its boots is at her heels. Then someone tackles her with a violent shove and she is knocked abruptly off the pavement and into an open porch. The speed of their impetus is arrested by an inner door and they half collapse against it. She struggles in the dimness with her assailant. She is splintered on her thigh from some low, rough, wooden bench that straddles one side of the porch. Her feet, already cut and sore, are trodden on as they wrestle. She is pushed into the darkest corner and held there, her face buried in his chest, her cries deadened. He makes himself a shield between her and the raving pack. His shirt is soft, and smells pleasantly of citrus. Past their insubstantial sanctuary, the throng thunders past them in an endless stream to hurl itself upon the waiting ranks of police.

IT TAKES JENNIFER a long time to get home. It seems like every road is blocked by flood barriers or barrel-chested policemen in fluorescent gear sending her on meandering diversions—any route at all that keeps her away from town. In contrast, chequered police vans, ambulances, fire engines and a plethora of other emergency response vehicles are hurtling towards the town centre like bees to a hive under threat.

When she gets home the house is in darkness and Kenny's car is gone. He has not—as she half expected—trashed the place, other than to hurl his heavy, crystal whisky glass at the beautiful polished marble fire-surround. He has chipped it, she sees, and she strokes the blemish with a regretful hand, as though soothing a wound. The pale carpet winks with a million malicious splinters. Her bare feet are at perilous risk—he will have known that; she *always* removes her shoes at the door. She collects the biggest fragments, wraps them in newspaper and puts them in the bin before fetching the Henry vacuum from the garage to deal with the rest. Then she gets a damp cloth from the kitchen and wipes the sticky lager stain from the leather settee, kneeling on the floor as she rubs and polishes the leather back to pristine white.

She looks up suddenly and stares at the place on the settee where he had sat all afternoon, seeing his scratchy unshaved chin, his stomach spilling over the waistband of his trousers, the resentful glaze in his hooded eyes. She sees beyond those things too; his moodiness, his self-absorption, his increasing outbursts of temper that are becoming uncomfortably physical. She blinks him away and the place is empty, just a vacant space, an exact echo of her heart. She imagines what it would be like, how she would feel, if he were to be gone for ever. She is not even mildly surprised to find that the idea holds no clutch of panic, no ache of loneliness, no sting of regret at all. The only sensation she can identify at the thought is a warm seep of relief.

'I don't love you,' she says aloud, a little experimentally, to the empty seat. She waits, in the silent house, for the fallout; for a rush of returning sentiment, a deluge of guilt, a tearful retraction. But there is none. There is no sudden impact of dire consequence. The sky does not fall. Her heart, her head, like a Geiger counter, maintains a steady, untroubled zero. It is a simple statement of fact.

'I don't love you Kenny,' she says again.

.

FOR THE FIRST few moments they can think of nothing but their relative sanctuary here on the far side of the heavy wooden door. Its rusty round handle had unexpectedly yielded to Ryan's hand and they had slipped thankfully into the interior with a view only of putting a solid barrier between themselves and the commotion. Jade has asked no question of Ryan and he has offered no explanation. Words are beyond them. It is a mystery that remains to be plumbed. A stroke of luck which, to Jade, with her habitual expectation of the rawest deal on offer, is as welcome as it is surprising.

They lean against the door and allow their breathing to level out. The building, whatever it is, offers a benign reassurance to their frayed spirits as real as a cool hand soothing a fevered brow. They inhale it, with the slightly musty air. It is amazing how completely the closed door has excluded the sound of the insurgence outside.

'What kind of place *is* this?' Jade asks. Her mouth is dry, her voice unsteady.

Sensing distress simmering like milk under a thin skin, seeking to give her space in which to subdue it, Ryan offers suggestions in a low, musing voice. 'A concert hall, maybe? A lecture theatre?' He indicates, at the far end of the large, dilapidated space, a sort of stage. It is bare apart from a lop-sided lectern and a crop of skeletal music stands. 'Maybe they were in the middle of something when the trouble started and just left,' he speculates.

'And forgot to lock the door,' Jade murmurs.

The interior of the large hall is dimly lit by an impossibly grandiose and ornate chandelier that hangs high above them, suspended by a weighty chain from some even loftier anchor in the invisible ceiling. Of the thirty or forty dusty bulbs only about five are illuminated, low wattage, emitting the feeblest of glows. In the faint pool of light, through a miasma of dancing dust-motes, and as their eyes adjust, is a jumbled collection of chairs—folding wooden, plastic garden, old fashioned wheel- and ladder-backed, semi-upholstered—arranged in ragged rows and facing the platform. Peripherally, stacked anyhow, is an equally disparate collection of tables. Other bits of furniture are casually distributed about. An old trestle table is stacked with cups and saucers, an urn—steaming eerily—a soup kettle and a basket of greetings cards. Underneath is a box of bedding and another of tinned food. Against a wall a book case has been hastily covered with a balding velvet curtain. An upright piano is precariously held level by a stack of books under one corner. Its stool has a threadbare and faded tapestry-work seat. Towards the back of the room, in a shallow recess partially obscured by a musty curtain, is a crate of old toys containing a grubby dolly, a shape-sorter tacky to the touch, a one-eared giraffe and a few battered books. The walls are flaking, showing patches of bare plaster. The carpet is worn almost to its hessian backing, fraying into holes by the door and down the centre—the suggestion of an aisle—that divides the room.

'Looks like there's going to be a jumble sale,' Ryan whispers.

Jade doesn't wonder at his need to whisper. The dereliction of the place—the air thick with dust and the strong impression of grey, laden cobwebs looping across the space—makes her feel that any sudden noise will dislodge an avalanche of dead skin cells and desiccated insects. Above their heads, far beyond the reaches of the meagre light bulbs, there is a sense of unfathomable height into which sound will be sucked and amplified. The least murmur, even an unvoiced secret, would be made audible to a celestial ear. But there is something else. Perhaps it is just the intense quiet contrasting with the cacophony outside, perhaps only a sense of relief at her escape from the threatening gangs, or the relative warmth after the damp, chill night. But there is something enveloping, a weighty, almost palpable aura, a pressing, penetrating, numinous calm that Jade can feel. It is a soft, reassuring shawl around her shoulders. It is overwhelmingly comforting, also exquisitely special; an ornamented ceremonial robe, the gossamer of an angel wing. She stands in the cavernous, curious space and realises that she is barely breathing, that every sense, so recently assaulted by fear and agony, is intensely tuned to this new frequency. It is surreal, a revelation, almost like an enchantment.

'You're shaking,' Ryan says quietly, pressing her gently into a chair. He drags the dust sheet off the book shelf and drapes it over her shoulders, tucking it carefully around her bare, trembling legs. She realises that she is crying; silent tears. She tries to conjure up some of the obdurate resilience she is famous for, to look defiant, to dare him to mock, but finds that she can't be bothered.

'You're in shock,' he says, 'but, if it's any consolation, you look like a fairy-tale princess, trussed up like that.'

She looks down at the faded red velvet material, and then at his face, with a narrowed eye. She suspects sarcasm, but finds none. In any case she hasn't the will or the ability to come up with any cutting retort.

The furore without seems like a million miles, a lifetime away. Here in this strange, forsaken chamber, amongst the motley furniture, with Ryan—her surprising rescuer—she has an unaccustomed feeling of profoundest peace. It is as though some tightly wound binding of chafing cord has been unravelled and she realises, suddenly, how constricting it has been, how sore and irritable it has been making her. But now it feels as though the teeth of injustice have ceased to gnaw at her bones.

Presently, through the benign stillness—it is thick, and, in the weak, diffused light, golden, like syrup—they discern a low, distant hum, a drone of quiet speech from a narrow, previously unremarked corridor leading from one side of the platform. Ryan and Jade—trailing her borrowed finery—creep down the aisle and hesitate on the threshold of the passageway. From a partially open door at its end an envelope of bright light is projected onto the dull tiled floor and the murmur of speech drifts in jumbled phrases from the room to their curious ears. It seems at first as though they are eavesdropping on some fervent negotiations. First one voice then another is raised concerning the situation in the town. They gather as much from the tone—of imminent emergency, of heart-felt distress—as from the actual words, which are muffled and come to them in disjointed snatches. Whoever the authority addressed, he remains silent. It dawns on Jade that they must be speaking on the telephone, taking turns with the handset, but then a clamour of voices speaking all at once makes the idea impossible. It must be, she thinks, a meeting with the police chief or a government official hastily convened to orchestrate the crisis. But even this scenario does not quite fit the facts. Words like peace, calm, reconciliation and healing are bandied with ardent advocacy, as though their interlocutor has power far beyond the strategic distribution of personnel or the future allotment of finance. It is weirder than weird: *they* must be weird, to think that any appeal, however passionately made, to any authority, could achieve what they ask.

'Who are they talking to?' she mouths at Ryan, her forehead furrowed.

He raises his eyes towards the ceiling. 'God,' he says.

It is the last straw, or almost. She feels it welling up from her solar plexus, trembling, uncontrollable and irrepressible. Physically and emotionally, she is spent, and this is all that is left to her. Tears pour from her eyes like fountains. Hysteria shakes her limbs. For a dreadful moment she thinks she will fall, wet herself, convulse. Something, certainly, is going to give. It is too bizarre, too incredible for words. What has happened to her today—her emotions have yo-yoed beyond her capacity to cope. The agonised hour by the river. Little Mikey—unthinkably lost, the doldrums of despair, the chasm of his absence already yawning. And then, amazingly, found; the euphoria of his restoration. The hellish meal, the uproar at the restaurant and her terrible journey through the town. Imminent danger, unexpected rescue. All these things have brought her to this; crouching in a dilapidated old building wearing a tattered curtain, cut and bleeding and eavesdropping on the earnest conference of God-squadders with their imaginary leader. Outside, hordes of ravening lunatics tear each other limb from limb. It all passes through her mind like a post-modern film of ridiculously juxtaposing scenes—Alice down a rabbit hole—ever more fantastical layers of absurdity descending into crack-brained lunacy. She knows that in a moment she will lose her battle to suppress it. She will laugh; a great burst of mirth, a shout, a wild release. It will burble and shrill and rise to the unseen roof like a mocking banshee. Ryan sees it too. He pulls her into his arms and once again presses her face against his shoulder.

Then, one last thing, as sobering as a corpse and as shocking; as wondrous, as uplifting as light in a dark cell. A new voice issues from the room at the end of the corridor, one they have not heard before. It is a woman's voice, deeply sonorous, smooth and dark as rich chocolate, mature in timbre but in tone as awestruck and amazed as a child. It carries clearly to Jade and Ryan as they lean together helplessly on the cold step.

'We know,' it says, 'that these things are not small things to ask. But we're asking anyway because we have confidence in you and our confidence comes from the fact that when we ask, you answer. We want to say 'thank you' for saving that little boy today—the one who fell in the river. It seemed ... impossible ... that he *could* be saved. I admit that when we asked I doubted. But he *was* saved. *You* saved him. Thank you.'

'Thank you,' the other voices echo.

A kite being yanked from the sky. A genie sucked back into its bottle. A rocket falling back to earth. Her rising fit plummets and she is staring, wide-eyed, down the passageway towards the light.

THE RIVER SLIDES between the old folks' home and the farmhouse like a brown snake sullenly contained within its banks, a malevolent presence not to be trusted. The plash and ripple of its turgid waters infiltrate the dreams of the over-wrought residents, the last of whom have been variously placated and sedated with Horlicks and diazepam. The unusual stimulation of visitors and emergency has made them tetchy and querulous. The staff is thinner on the ground than usual because of Rosie's absence at the hospital. Burdened with the extracurricular responsibilities of the Open Day, they have found their tempers abnormally frayed. Mrs Terry, in her office with its notoriously open door, considers the disasters of the day through the lens of a large Scotch, her bright hopes and the gay awnings on the lawn in equal tatters. On her desk is Mrs Fairlie's file, all in order, all-but closed. Matron's long years of experience tell her that it will only be a matter of days before she can stamp it with the word 'deceased'. However, on the bright side, she has four new names on the waiting list, the reservations of their reluctant owners over-ruled by the kindly insistence of sons and daughters. The Open Day, perhaps, for all its tribulations, has not been an unmitigated failure.

Across the river Mikey sleeps profoundly. He has gorged on peanut butter and toast, bathed, and, in spite of the lateness of the hour, been regaled with the penultimate chapter of *Stig of the Dump,* which Richard has been reading to him. The mesh of the childish mind is accommodatingly widely woven. Even the most traumatic of experiences filter with extraordinary ease through its lattice. They will be stored in some remote repository, perhaps to exert malign influence on later life. Or perhaps they will only be revisited in old age and even then, often be confused with dreams. Whatever the difficulties to come from the day's ordeal, at present Mikey's dreams are peopled only by cavemen and standing stones. They are untroubled for now by the chill grip of an insistent current or the pervading taste of brackish water.

Downstairs, in the low-beamed lounge, Jasmine and Richard are entwined on the sofa. Richard has lit the fire; it isn't cold, but the wildly fluctuating emotions of the day—sons lost and restored—have had the effect of draining them both. Now its cheerful glow and the snap and crackle of the iridescent logs bathe them in languorous torpidity. She is wearing his pyjamas in pursuance of her compunction to be ever close to him. From time to time they exchange comments, reflections on the past few hours. Richard relates, in halting phrases, his reconciliation with Matt. His son's acknowledgement has been hard come-by and harder still to articulate. But he has at last seen that beneath the layers of anger, confusion, resentment and hurt—still raw and very real—there remains a fundamental, impermeable connection between them. It cannot be denied, however hard the young man might, in his instinctive umbrage, try. With an enormous leap of maturity he has discovered that his father might be human, fallible, yet still just as lovable. At the bottom of it all is a selfless desire that Richard should, in spite of the consequences to others, grasp happiness if it is within his reach.

'It is humbling,' Richard says, his voice—his heart—broken with the hugeness of it. 'I don't deserve it really.'

'That's for him to say,' Jasmine smiles.

The clock on the mantel marks off the peaceful minutes. A log falls in the grate showering sparks onto the flue; they attach themselves and glow like fireflies in a tropical sky.

Later, when the fire is a mound of glowing ashes, Jasmine tells him about seeing Rosie at the hospital.

'I did not expect her to be so beautiful, or so kind,' she says ruefully.

'She is,' Richard replies, 'both those things.' He thinks of the little girl that was lost, Matt's sister, the tiny child who hardly drew breath long enough to be christened, in haste, by the hospital chaplain. He thinks of the prickly, poisonous plants of loss and isolation that sprouted from her grave. They had created an impenetrable barrier between Rosie and him ever afterwards; thoughts unspoken, feelings not shared, tears un-witnessed. They had borne the loss separately, mourning year after year in different rooms. It had been an icy wedge between them, widening and ever widening as the years passed and the child's little frame ebbed back into dust; the saddest memorial, but as stark and undeniable as any granite effigy, any cold marble stone. He thinks, with a rush of love—and how it would surprise and relieve Matt to know it—of the little girl upstairs; stroppy and wheedling, his iron-willed little Lilly, and smiles. He pulls Jasmine closer to his side. She is warm, so soft and yielding, his embraces ever-welcome, she drinks him in like a flower turning its head to the sun. The loneliness of years loses itself amongst her petals.

Jasmine sees his smile, and traces it with her finger. Still, after all these months, when usually the burning obsession, the unquenchable thirst is past its zenith, her feelings for this man undo her. He is her world of security and stability after a lifetime of flux and difficulty. The collision of progesterone in a house of women, the frequent incendiary of Jade's temper, her mother's sequence of flaky relationships and non-specific illnesses have all taken their toll. Add straitened finances, the negative social consequences of living on the Mere and a constant struggle—not always won—to eschew the spurious escape offered by alcohol, drugs, ill-advised sexual couplings and criminality. She clings to his goodness. The fathers of her children—one a feckless waster and the other a villain—had almost exhausted her faith that it might ever be found. She feels he has reached inside her soul and discovered there the things that have been trodden on and discarded, or ignored, or reviled, by everyone else. He has drawn them, with reverence and gentleness, to a place of prominent display. How she loves him! She is helpless with it sometimes, at other times buoyed up, almost intoxicated. He is a magnet she cannot resist, her pole star.

In the small hours they climb the narrow creaking staircase to bed. She drops, under his hand, string after string of warm, honeyed pearls, each one bigger and more delicious than the one before. They gasp—they both do—at their sweetness and number; her very essence exuding. Then the last, the purest gem of polished marrow; her body filled with imperative to loose it and then, the moment it is gone, with aching regret at its loss.

ALL THE FURNITURE in the mansion of Jade's expectation is being over-turned. She is dizzy with the wildly contrasting circumstances that seem, minute by minute, to veer her from one extreme to the other. She feels that she has been picked up and shaken, deluged with hot and cold water in quick succession, repeatedly blinded with light and then plunged into the dark. She has come to a point where none of it— neither the hot nor the cold, the light nor the dark—seems entirely real, quite reliable. The inhuman savagery in the streets—was that a terrible fantasy? Was the almost audible, almost palpable, almost personal sense of calm and peace she had felt here in the gloom only a glorious delusion? How could the metaphysical interaction in the sequestered room give way to this homely banter? Jade and Ryan sit in the midst of the small, unpretentious, comfortable crowd, blinking and amazed. It is curious and unreal, verging on the absurd. She wonders whether, tomorrow, the building will be bolted and boarded, long-deserted, an echoing ruin. Will the motley collection of chairs, the pendulous chandelier, the bright-eyed intercessors all prove a figment of passing enchantment?

Somewhere beyond the peripheries of it—out where the charged air of wonderment and confusion is less potent—something is waiting, as it were, in the wings. Waiting until the bewildering succession of scenes has run its course, and the actors have left the stage. It is a question awaiting answer, a bigger picture that has somehow escaped her notice. It hovers patiently, beyond her ability to encompass it just now.

The church members have exited their prayer room in easy, ebullient conversation; tea cups and tray-bakes, umbrellas, pay-and-display; the ordinaries of life. They are a world away from Jade's imagining. They are not wearing cassocks or wimples, or weighty wooden crosses, or sandals or bad beards. They are not of the pinched, dry, vinegary type she has glimpsed briefly on *Songs of Praise*. They are industrious and cheerful, gregarious, carefree. The concerns they expressed only moments before seem lifted from their shoulders. Over by the trestle table a jolly woman with garish earrings is pouring tea from an enormous tea pot. A tall, wiry, tousle-haired man with a broad grin offers homemade cake from a Tupperware container. A pale, unshaven man in his late twenties lounges on a wobbly plastic chair and chats amiably to a plumpish girl and her mother. Others sort efficiently through the box of tinned goods. They have greeted Jade and Ryan with kindness and pleasure, like guests long awaited and much anticipated. Their spattered, tattered garb and Jade's fantastical cloak has been ignored, their presence taken as a matter of course. Pleasant-faced women and genial men have simply assessed their visitors' needs, provided with open-handedness, and absorbed them into their fold. Jade has been given a washing-up bowl of warm water for her feet. While they soak, her cut head is bathed with clean gauze from a first aid box by a minute, much-wrinkled woman uttering a series of sympathetic tutting and wincing noises as she probes, carefully, for glass. 'Poor thing, poor thing,' she mutters, 'just another minute, my lovely.'

'What *is* this place?' Jade asks again. The hall, even with more lights on, and the cheery rattle of tea cups and jovial conversation, is nothing like a church; nothing, at least, like her stereotypical conception of one. There are no carved pews or stone columns, no stained glass or candles. The mouldering walls are bare of inscribed tablets to the deceased, the shadows empty of recumbent statues atop chilly tombs. No bells, no smells, no old brass or faded frescoes. No historic draperies or antique hassocks. No ancient worshippers in aged hats. No holy silence. '*Is* it a church?'

'Oh no.' The woman smiles, her lined visage creasing into further wrinkles. It is a lop-sided smile. One eye is grey and limpid, the other sightless. In an alternative dream she would be a wicked witch, perhaps, but in this one she is a fairy god-mother. '*This* is just a building. *We're* the church. There now. I think that's clean, and it's above the hair line so the scar won't show, if there is one. What lovely thick hair you have. I'm Frances,' she says.

She kneels down then, and begins to wash Jade's feet. The selfless intimacy of the act would be shocking, if not entirely in keeping with the bizarre sequence that has become a characteristic of the evening.

'Just—I mean—how many ...' Jade can think of no term that, in her mouth, would not sound as though she were being scathing; congregants, worshippers, believers—in her mind's eye they are all stuffily self-righteous and hopelessly deluded. Dyspeptic spinsters and florid bachelors, the widowed and lonely, the lost and semi-lucid, the stuck-up and messed-up, oddballs and throwbacks. But looking around her now she sees only ordinary people. An onlooker, asked to identify the oddball, would point unerringly to Jade herself, eccentrically garbed in her moth-eaten gown.

'How many are we? Oh! More than this of course. A few of us just got together in a hurry tonight because of what's going on outside. But normally, on a Sunday, there are sixty or seventy of us, including children. We have a ball!'

'So you're not—like—a regular church?' Ryan asks, to fill the moment.

'No. Definitely irregular!' Frances laughs, deftly checking Jade's feet for foreign bodies.

The jolly woman brings tea. 'I haven't any money,' Jade says. Now she thinks of it, she hasn't an idea where her handbag is. Perhaps she left it in the restaurant. Ryan delves his hand into his pocket.

'Heavens poppet, you don't need any,' the woman gushes, handing cups. Hers is the deep, resonant voice that had arrested Jade's attention earlier. Jade looks at her narrowly, taking in her elegant chignon and gaudy earrings, feeling a connection as fine and as strong as silk between them. This woman had *cared* about Mikey and in Jade's mind his extra-ordinary salvation that day from the tumid river is now indelibly associated with *her* concern and the intervention of *her* God. It

511

is wildly unexpected; a dominant brush-stroke in the larger canvas of which Jade is becoming conscious.

The longer she sits here, amongst these kindly, easy people, the more surprising she finds them, and yet her astonishment is by no means alienating. The old Jade might have rejected the whole episode as surreal, a fantastical adventure. She would certainly have dismissed these people with a cynical sneer as well-intentioned do-gooders, sure to be taken advantage of, rather to be pitied. But for reasons that she can't begin to fathom the view around each unexpected corner of this dream-like labyrinth of experience is drawing her onwards, opening up new horizons. And central to that unforeseen landscape is Mikey, placed there, with loving hands, by this woman. *His* extra-ordinary presence there begs a number of questions—not least, about *hers*.

Their kindness is a foreign and bewildering outlook. It is entirely new to her, this altruistic web that binds strangers. Skinner's mother had felt the tug of it, enough to wade into the raging waters and pluck Mikey from their murderous grasp. Ryan, by her side, quietly attentive, must have answered its pull when he followed her from the relative safety of the restaurant through the tumultuous streets. What other impetus could he have had? He had saved her in the nick of time; a risky, noble action. It is a seismic shift in Jade's world-view; that anyone should give a moment's thought to anything not immediately connected to them. Why would they? Don't their own narrow lives sufficiently occupy their attention? Are they not, like her, too intimately enmeshed in the demon-filled paper bag of their own embattled existence to spare a glance at a longer perspective?

The answer is clearly that they are not. It assaults Jade as she lifts the teacup to her lips and she winces at its rebuke.

'I'm so sorry,' Frances says. 'There's quite a lot of grit in these cuts. It'll have to come out. Can you be brave?'

Jade nods wanly. Ryan puts his arm around her and gives her an encouraging squeeze, but when she looks in his eyes there is nothing predatory there at all. He too, is only being kind.

ON SUNDAY JENNIFER eventually finds her mother in a side-ward, still sedated. She is glad—of both these things. The hospital is over-crowded, the wounded stacked in A & E nursing concussions and cuts, broken noses, split lips, sprains, splinters and dreadful hang-overs. They spill into the corridors and gather in bruised and bloodied groups on the ambulance approach, scrounging cigarettes. Weary policemen take statements, bewildered relatives wander dazed through labyrinthine by-ways between departments pushing their injured loved ones in uncooperative wheelchairs from X-ray to the fracture clinic. There's a lacerated queue awaiting triage. Clinicians are suturing with the intensity of sweat-shop workers sewing replica designer-wear.

She pulls a chair closer to her mother's recumbent form. She seems, in the night, to have shrunken further, her flesh and bones dissolving away. In contrast her spirit—some reserve of inner strength—is stirring. She is moaning and restless, an incomprehensible string of verbiage issuing from her parched, sunken lips. Jennifer bends close to her but can make nothing of the diatribe. She is as unfathomable now as she always has been. Jennifer finds that she is examining her mother's face. The deep-scored wrinkles on the puckering, troubled forehead. The frowning, beetling brows. The tracery of red veins on her downy cheek. She knows she ought to speak words of reassurance, to try and soothe her, but can find no basis of relationship that could support it. Her mother is such a mystery to her that even if she felt she had the right, she would not know what troubles, what regrets, what remorse might be the cause of her evident distress. She scans through a catalogue of images: her mother moving sacks of vegetables, whelping innumerable dogs, treating and excusing Annie's frequent injuries,

513

wearing a ridiculous hat at Jennifer's A level presentation ceremony. In all the images her mouth is a pursed line, her eyes stoic. Did she have dreams? Did her heart yearn? Was she happy? Jennifer has no clue; their estrangement is immense, and never more so than now, when they each have such need of comfort.

She has heard nothing from Kenny. She supposes he is on one of his benders and will not return for some days, red-eyed, stinking of stale alcohol, perhaps sporting an injury for which he is unwilling or unable to offer any explanation. She will have covered for him at work, inventing some virus or other. Later, the bank statement will reveal something of his exploits; huge hotel bills, extensive bar tabs, profligate spending on race tracks and at casinos. Once there had been a first class aeroplane ticket, another time evidence of payments at what turned out to be a massage parlour. All these things she has not been able to tell her mother because she never liked Kenny and never trusted him and Jennifer would not give her the satisfaction—nor herself the shame—of admitting that her mother's instinct had been right all along.

Her mother's muttered soliloquy continues, her hands fluttering and plucking fretfully at the sheet. She is shaken by the occasional shiver that convulses her whole body. Her forehead is beaded with sweat. Her distress, if anything, is mounting.

Jennifer puts her hand tentatively onto her mother's inflamed fingers. They are hot, the skin taut. 'It's all right,' she says vaguely, 'don't worry. It's all right.' But the hand is snatched away from her and her mother's querulous rhetoric intensifies. In desperation Jennifer pulls the *Evening Record* from her handbag and scans its pages, looking for something she can read aloud. Perhaps the sound of a voice is all that her mother needs, perhaps the words, after all, don't matter. The front pages are full of the disturbances in the town. Poor quality, blurred photographs of burning vehicles and ranks of riot police, faceless hordes of football supporters, a town plan showing the progress of the fracas. 'Rival Gangs Blitz Town,' she declares self-consciously. In the cubicle her voice sounds unnatural; loud and taut as stretched elastic. But she goes on doggedly, 'Costs Estimated in the Millions.' She turns the page.

'River Inundates Homes,' she reads. 'Woman Feared Drowned as Car Swept Away. Bridge Collapses Isolating Community. Policeman Feared Dead. Fifty Percent Off Selected Potting Products.' Her eyes are skipping across the bold headlines, scanning the print, leaping inconsequentially from story to story. Her mother's inarticulate whimperings do not abate. Jennifer raises her voice a little. 'Weavermen in Bidding War for Peruvian Goal-Keeping Talent. Ikea dining table and four chairs, light oak, good condition, £50 or near offer. Beaver Olympics Cancelled. Straight female (late forties) seeks non-smoking male for meals out, companionship and more.' Suddenly her eye and her fevered reportage are arrested by a picture in the bottom right hand corner. It is a report covering the Bridge House Open Day and her mother's fall. A segment of a group-shot of residents in the day room has been enlarged to show the accident victim's anxious, eager face in grainy detail. It is a terrible picture, poorly focussed, but what strikes Jennifer most is that whereas the other residents are facing the camera, their smiles fixed, her mother is looking in another direction, over the heads of her fellows. Her whole body speaks expectancy, her eyes, trained on the doorway, and her craned neck shout hope at a hundred decibels. It is almost possible to see her bated breath, to read, in its eagerness, a volume of wishing. She is looking for someone, waiting for them, expecting them to come. Jennifer goes back in her mind, to her own arrival in that day room, her own approach through the crowds to her mother's chair, and the immediate question: where is your brother?

Outside the side-ward, nurses are hurrying to and fro, tending patients, ushering visitors, carrying bedpans and files and pushing trolleys of medication and tea cups. Presently a junior doctor arrives, with eyes so shadowed they look bruised. She tells Jennifer that her mother has been diagnosed with a severe chest infection and is being treated with antibiotics. A general anaesthetic to replace the hip would be too dangerous until they take hold. She prepares her, kindly, for the possibility that her mother may not recover at all, may not even regain proper consciousness. At her age, the shock of the fracture might be enough to carry her off, even without the infection, but the two in tandem ...

'If there are any other relatives ...' she suggests cautiously.

Mrs Fairlie's moans redouble. The doctor leans over her patient.

'Shush now. Shhhhhhh,' she says.

IT IS LATE afternoon when Jade wakes up. She has slept like the dead, or the un-dead, her dreams vividly troubled by a plethora of threats kept at bay by the kindness of strangers. The bandages on her feet are a Cinderella slipper; proof that the previous day's events were more substantial than her dreams. She gazes at them for a long time. When she goes into the bathroom she gives similar scrutiny to her face in the fly-blown mirror. It is streaked by yesterday's make-up. A place up past her hairline is tender to the touch and the hair close to her scalp is crusty with dried blood. But these evidences are not what she looks at with amazed intensity before climbing into the shower. She looks at herself, the inner part of her, and at the ashes of the glowering fire of indignation that she recognises, spent and benign, at her core.

The pale man, Patrick, had driven them home in the small hours, through streets ravaged by riot and heavily policed but eerily silent and ghostly. A post-Armageddon landscape of burnt-out cars and broken windows, shop shutters hanging loose as though blown open by an explosion or a tornado. Ryan had sat next to her in the back seat. He hadn't touched her. They had barely spoken. This had been a new phenomenon for Jade, for whom the back seats of cars have been a traditional arena for contact, either combative or coital; she is used to both leading men on and fighting them off in that locale. But she knows that Ryan is not like those men. He is—and she had named it to herself a little reverently—a gentleman, like Richard.

The day Jasmine had introduced Richard, Jade had seen at once that he was the prince that her poor princess sister had been waiting for all her life. It explained—and justified—her aura of long-suffering detachment from the Mere and its assaults of hyper-real brutality. She had been *in* it but not *of* it, exactly as though placed there by a wicked step-mother, pending a rescue that she had every faith would come. With Richard Jasmine had blossomed, her wispy, dream-like quality taking on flesh. Mikey and Lilly adored him. Sadie had flirted like an old courtesan. Jade had stubbornly persisted in searching for vestiges of frog-like characteristics, but found none. What she *had* found was a little reluctant gladness for her sister and a large wallow of bile for herself. She, no doubt, would be doomed to make do with some riddling Rumpelstiltskin, whose conundrums she would never be able to fathom.

But Ryan was no Rumpelstiltskin.

Patrick had made small-talk to cover their silence. He has a wife and two small children and lives not far from Jade, near the ice-cream factory where his wife works as a supervisor. Surprisingly he is the church leader. Not a vicar, he had clarified, with self-deprecating laughter, banishing the image that had risen spontaneously in the vehicle like a hitch-hiking apparition—balding, buck-toothed, unctuous. He told them that the church has only just taken over the building in Bridge Street, which explains its disorganisation, the make-shift furniture, its dilapidation. It has been disused for years but they had signed the lease just in time to be able to throw together some kind of facility to help the poor folks flooded out of their homes. A refuge, a soup kitchen … he didn't know yet, quite what it would be, but he knew it would be something useful because he didn't believe these things happened by accident. They were always short of volunteers, he concluded, if either of them found themselves with any spare time.

He had left her and Ryan at her gate just as the birds were beginning to stir in the bluish dawn twilight. The drizzle had evaporated leaving chill air in a sky that was a towering vacuum above them.

'How will you get in?' he had asked. 'Weren't your keys in your bag?'

'Yes, but there's a spare one under a plant pot.' She had looked up the narrow pathway to where a cracked planter with the skeleton of some long-dead bush moped forlornly by the front step. She had wanted to say thank you, to make, if she could, some acknowledgement of his actions. She wanted to let him know that it was not a small thing, what he had done for her. In fact that it had been, in her experience of life and human nature, entirely unprecedented. But the words wouldn't come. His kindness and chivalry had left her in new territory. The language of gratitude was too foreign for a tongue familiar only with complaint. The moments had ticked by and their silence on the empty, shadowy pavement had become more uncomfortable. But she had hesitated still, not wanting to say goodbye without offering—making available to him—some opening for future association. She had already realised that her usual ploys on such occasions would not serve with him. He was of a rarer ilk and would recoil if she were to lay herself on a plate or to imply, with a twinkle and a deliberate twitch of her dimple, that she would do so at some future date. Now it was all over, their concert—forcibly orchestrated by the crisis—had unravelled. He had stood awkwardly in the shade of a leggy mallow in next door's garden, his hands in his pockets.

'I don't know anything about you,' she had said with an embarrassed little smile, meaning really, that she did not know what to say to him.

When Jade gets downstairs Carmel is in the kitchen eating Rice Krispies out of the packet. The sink is full of dirty dishes. Jade's laundry has been taken out of the machine and left in a damp heap on the kitchen table. It is her uniform and she needs it to be dry by tomorrow. The script—accusation, denial, counter-charge, blame apportionment, indignant repost—hangs in the kitchen alongside a tendril of tinsel that has been there since Christmas and an enormous cobweb that has had tenancy for even longer. The roles are familiar to them both, interchangeable depending on the circumstances, a hackneyed diatribe they can parrot automatically.

'You might have hung my washing out,' it might begin.

'It's *your* washing,' would be the immediate repost.

She would counter with, 'It's *your* turn to wash up, though,' with a glare towards the loaded sink.

Carmel might shrug and whine, 'It isn't my fault there aren't enough cups,' to which she would fling back, 'You're right. We should just keep on buying more, then nobody would have to wash up.'

It is only a matter of finding the cue, the opening line. The rest will follow, as well rehearsed as a long-running play.

Jade fills the kettle.

'No milk,' Carmel says through cereal, making her gambit.

Jade looks at her, the kettle still suspended over the sink. The reply, 'I brought two pints home from work on Friday,' is on her lips. But suddenly she hears an alternative line whispered from the wings, as though from a prompt with the wrong—a different—book. It is ridiculously easy, absurdly obvious, and she can't think why they have always insisted on battling with the guttural idiom of contention when more fluent, co-operative discourse is so blindingly available to them.

'That's ok,' she says experimentally, as though getting her tongue around a new dialect, 'I'll go and get us some.'

Carmel is so startled she almost chokes on her Krispies.

When Jade comes back Carmel is on her way out.

'Where's Mum?' Jade asks.

Carmel shrugs. She *does* know, of course, but to volunteer the information would just be too helpful, and is therefore against the rules.

'I suppose she's at Jasmine's,' Jade speculates.

Carmel looks at Jade's feet, giving them an enquiring nod. 'What happened?'

'It's a long story ...'

'Suit yourself.' Carmel tosses her hair and fusses with it in the mirror, demonstrating her utter lack of interest.

'No. I meant, if you're going out, there won't be time to tell you.'

Carmel is pale, paler even than usual, as white as the milk in Jade's hand. The peachy tan she has accumulated during the weeks of sun seems to have gone overnight as though sloughed away in the shower. While she is checking her hair in the mirror, Jade eyes her. Her whiteness is somehow more than just a skin tone. It is deeper than that; as though her flesh is fish-white. She looks ill, her eyes like enormous pools rimmed with tiredness. Her lips are bloodless.

'Are you all right, Carmel?'

'Yes! Of course,' she snaps, stepping through the door, but not before Jade sees the pools gathering in her eyes.

That boy is no good for her, Jade thinks, as she shuts the door.

She makes tea, clears the sink, hangs out her laundry. She surveys the rest of the house. It is strewn with discarded clothing, dog-eared magazines, odd shoes and dirty dishes. There are piles of things stacked on the stairs, supposed to be claimed by their owner and taken up; some of them have been there weeks. Carmel's school things are abandoned in a heap in the hallway. There is a line of grime around the appliances on the kitchen worktops where a hasty dish-cloth has been smeared past them. The lounge, which is rarely used because it is too tempting a forum for argument—they tend to keep to their own rooms, where they each have televisions, their own jealously guarded territories—is dusty and unappealing, a dumping ground for stuff. Boxes of mysterious documents and awful ornaments brought home from Granny's are still stacked there even though it is months since she died. Her mother, who cleans other people's houses for a living, never has the energy to pay any attention to her own and anyway says that with two girls living at home she shouldn't have to. Experimenting with kindness, Jade tidies up, and not only her own belongings. Nevertheless she is conscious that her attempts will be misconstrued as 'messing with things.' She considers making a meal but the cupboards are bare and, without her bag, she is penniless.

In her own room she surveys the damage to her mother's top—really it is beyond redemption—and realises with a sinking sense of gloom that

Carmel's amber necklace is missing, lost, she supposes, at some stage of the previous evening. The chink of possibility she had discerned seems suddenly very small, the merest glimmer through the impregnable walls of their self-absorption. She sighs and lies down on her bed. Her feet, inside their bandages and the unlaced trainers that are all she can get on over them, feel raw and tender.

She spends a long time looking out of her window, wondering if Ryan will come, and whether Patrick could be right, about these things not happening by accident.

RICHARD AND JASMINE take Mikey off to thank Skinner's mother and Sadie is left with Lilly, who screams herself purple at being left behind. Sadie leaves her to it and goes into the garden to smoke. Across the river, at the old folks' home, a few withered souls are being subjected to their dose of fresh air. They cower under rugs, the brisk breeze carrying away the sun's warmth before it can heat their turgid blood. The river, still high and running swiftly between its eroded banks, is almost orange, like tea left to stew too long.

When they come back Jasmine begins to prepare food. 'Matt is coming over,' she says, adding significantly, 'to meet Mikey and Lilly. And me.'

'I'm looking forward to it,' Sadie says, folding her arms and eyeing the food. 'It's Old Mother Hubbard's at my house.'

'Richard could take you to the supermarket on the way home,' Jasmine offers.

'No point,' Sadie replies flatly. 'No money till I do Mr Pickering tomorrow.'

'You've started back there, then?'

'Yes, he rang me last week. What a state the place was in! Told him I'd have to do double hours for the next few weeks to get things back straight.'

'And will you?'

'No, but he won't know. He'll be back at work. Anyway, he owes me; laying me off like that. I'll teach him. Did you think she looked younger than me?'

'Who?' Jasmine stirs onions in a pan. She has been asked to make curry. It is Matt's favourite.

'Jennifer Fairlie.'

'I didn't really notice.' Jasmine is diplomatic. 'Her hair was dyed.'

'So is mine.'

'She had expensive clothes on. I'd say she's done OK for herself.'

'Nothing like money to hold back time.' Sadie sniffs. 'Not that I'd know. Have you got any wine?'

'It's a bit early.' It is four o'clock.

'I'll be the judge of that. It's my one comfort, you know that, and I think I've earned it this weekend, don't you?'

'In the fridge, I think there's half a bottle of Chardonnay.'

'That won't last us long.'

Jasmine selects spices from a rack. 'I don't want any.'

Sadie pours the wine. 'I think I'll visit.'

'Who? Jennifer?'

'No, the old lady. She was practically family to us. Whose sauce are you going to use? Patak's sets off my hiatus hernia—it's too spicy.'

'I'm not using a jar. I'm going to make my own.'

'Oh! Excuse me!' Sadie folds her arms. The air in the kitchen begins to smell of pungent spices and garlic.

'I think that's a good idea.'

'What?'

'To go and visit Mrs Fairlie.' Jasmine drops chopped chicken fillets into the pan.

'Oh yes, I will. Then I can find out all about what they're up to, Jennifer and Michael.'

'He's the brother?'

'Yes,' Sadie says, lighting another cigarette.

Richard comes in from the garden where he has been playing with Lilly. He gives Jasmine a hug and sniffs appreciatively at the curry. 'Smells fantastic darling. I'm going to pick Matt up now. Lilly's on the swing.'

'All right,' she smiles.

'Can I run you home Sadie?' Richard lifts his keys off a hook behind the door.

'No thanks. I'm staying. Want to meet this lad of yours.'

'Ah.' Richard and Jasmine exchange looks. She gives an almost imperceptible shrug. 'All right. See you later, then.'

He has hardly been gone a minute before Mikey comes in from the lounge. 'Where's Richard?'

'He's gone to collect Matt. He won't be long.'

Mikey looks a bit crestfallen. 'He said he'd test me on my spellings.'

'He will do then. Or I can. Don't worry poppet. Play outside for a while.'

'All right.'

'Stay away from the river,' Sadie calls after him, as though it is enormously funny.

Later, when the curry is in the oven, the two women move to the garden. Mikey and Lilly are on the trampoline.

'It's like yesterday was just a bad dream,' Jasmine says wonderingly, watching them. Its horrific anxieties are blurred in her memory conjuring images of a storm at sea, endless tracts of formless menace, the dark, disorienting peril of amorphous sea and sky without a beacon of light—neither star nor shore—to offer comfort or direction. But then afterwards the very uniformity of its terror makes it impossible to describe or remember. It has become the stuff of fevered delirium. In comparison, everything today is intensely real and strangely beautiful.

Even the ordinary things like the laundry on the line and the warm mug of tea in her hand. The solid house behind her, and even her mother—despite her obtuseness—represent emblems of security; unsuspected blessings. Her children, rising and falling on the trampoline—sturdy, vital and reassuringly alive—are miraculous, and she is conscious of a swell of gratitude towards who or whatever has brought her to this peaceful haven.

'Do you believe in fate?' Sadie asks, with such unaccustomed intuitiveness that Jasmine finds herself staring.

'What do you mean?'

'Well, I mean, do you think that you would have ended up with Richard no matter what? Even if you hadn't gone to work at Pickering's—that somehow or other fate would have brought you together?'

'Oh! I see. That it was 'meant to be'? Oh yes. I do believe that.'

Sadie grunts and drains her wine glass. 'I wonder why it has to take so long,' she says, almost to herself.

'We might not recognise it first time around,' Jasmine suggests, although she doubts it. 'Or appreciate it, anyway. I mean, look at Skinner's mother. I've known her for years—known her to look at, anyway—I must have passed her in the street a hundred times, seen her in the shop. But I never took any notice of her. I didn't appreciate who she was because I didn't know what she would do for me one day. Only time has made that clear. The interesting question is: if I *had*, you know, if I had made friends with her, would she have left Skinner's dad, would she have been in the right place at the right time to save Mikey?'

The conundrum bewilders Sadie, who pounces for refuge on the subject of Skinner's mother. 'So. Did she tell you all about it? Where she's been, I mean. Has she got some-one else?'

'I didn't ask, and you mustn't breathe a word about where she is.'

'I don't *know* where she is—you didn't deign to tell me where you were going,' Sadie says archly.

'But I mean, it, Mum. You mustn't tell anyone you've even seen her.'

Sadie sniffs. 'I can keep a secret,' she says at last, twirling her empty glass with a pointed sigh.

Jasmine goes inside to check the curry, and to find more wine.

THERE IS NO sign of Kenny on Sunday, and no message, and Jennifer spends the evening and half of the night wandering restlessly through her house feeling angry and impotent. Everywhere she goes are evidences of his brief enthusiasms. The exercise machine in the spare bedroom, his wet-suit in the closet, boxes of filters and lenses for the expensive digital camera he had insisted he was going to master. She feels like packing it all up and getting rid of it. None of it has seen any use in years. Now she has cleared her mother's place she knows how easy it is to dispose of the useless, the unsightly, the unwanted.

The more hours that pass without his key in the door or his voice on the telephone, without even so much as a text message, the more incensed she becomes. She is quite ready to throw vitriol at him the moment he appears. If he thinks his actions will chasten her he is in for a surprise. She is rabidly angry at him for deserting her in the way—and at the time—he has. In the small hours she does in fact fetch a suitcase down from the loft and begin to throw his clothes into it, telling herself she will drop it at Pickering's on her way to work and call a locksmith to come and change the locks of the house.

For the rest of the night the case sits in the bedroom drawing her eye; the embodiment and the object of her ire. Silhouetted in a patch of moonlight, a dark obelisk against the moon-washed wall, it reminds her of a gravestone and she cannot help thinking what a pathetically small thing her marriage has been reduced to, its personal effects buried carelessly and in anger. The case is a sorry testament and she is, in a hollow place beneath her rage, sick with sorrow. The two emotions yo-yo all night. It is partly the sadness of it—its death incontrovertible and impossible to ignore now she has exposed it to the light—and partly the thought of his wrath at being so publically exposed, which makes her, in the morning, unpack the case and put it away. It is a period of mourning between death and interment where anger and sadness vie.

But I'll be damned, she thinks, with annoyance for a while in the ascendant, if I'll ring the office and tell them he's ill. He can make up his own excuses.

When she rings the hospital to check on her mother the ward sister is vague. 'As well as can be expected,' she says. When Jennifer presses her it transpires that Mrs Fairlie has been moved somewhere else and, in the furore, the sister isn't too sure where.

'This is appalling!' Jennifer shouts. 'She could be anywhere. She could be in the mortuary!'

When she gets to work the dirt and disorganisation is more than she can bear, spilling off desks and out of filing cabinets. The slovenly complacency of her staff is infuriating. She pours out her frustrations on them, brazening out their astonishment and offence as she forces them to tidy up and pours scorn on their weekend labours.

She enlists the aid of a female member of staff and together they scour the office, chucking out old files, ravelling cobwebs, scrubbing paintwork and vacuuming the hair and fluff and mouldy crumbs of years from every nook and cranny. It is cleansing and satisfying to exert herself, both physically and mentally, onto the situation, to impose order on a small corner of the chaos that her life is threatening to become.

At the hospital she finally locates her mother in a reasonably sequestered corridor not far from the geriatric ward. Four or five other recumbent old people are distributed on trolleys nearby. They might as well be corpses; only the occasional flutter of the hand signifies there is life. One old gentleman has shifted in his bed, disturbing his bedclothes and his gown, exposing mottled, shrivelled buttocks to public view.

'This can't be right,' Jennifer appeals to the administrator she has recruited to help her find her mother, 'it's so disrespectful. What about their dignity?'

The administrator shrugs. 'This is within the parameters of flexibility dictated by the guidelines for a code 2,' she says. 'Each patient is regularly monitored. These patients are all under sedation anyway.' She does, however, a little shamefacedly, twitch the gentleman's bedclothes back over his bottom before leaving.

'I'd like to see the doctor,' Jennifer calls after her.

'Wouldn't we all dear?' an old woman further down the corridor croaks.

Mrs Fairlie's breathing is very laboured. It whistles and wheezes as though coming from subterranean caverns. When Jennifer speaks to her, her eyelids flutter but do not open. Her skin is distinctly yellowish and the texture of warm wax. But her fretful whimpers have been stilled and she appears to be at relative–though remote—peace.

When Jennifer looks up it is to see Sadie bearing down the corridor towards her. She is wearing jeans–far too tight—a saggy red t shirt and the same disreputable flip-flops. Jennifer's heart, already heavy, sinks six inches in her chest. 'Oh God,' she sighs.

'Isn't this terrible? You should complain! I wouldn't have let them treat *my* mother like this,' Sadie says, bustling up. She is hot, her hair damp with perspiration. She radiates heat and a complex bouquet of aromas; stale alcohol, tobacco, cheap perfume, body odour. Her voice has a harsh, unmusical edge to it, like a dull blade being sharpened, just like Annie's. 'I've been here half an hour trying to find her, and I'll have to leave at quarter past to get the bus home. Unless you can run me.' She puts her hessian shopping bag down on Mrs Fairlie's bed as though it is no more than a convenient shelf. 'Now then,' she says more softly, turning to the patient, 'how are we today, then?'

'She's asleep. That is, she's sedated,' Jennifer says, moving in proprietarily.

'Is she? Poor thing.' Sadie lifts Mrs Fairlie's notes off the foot of the bed and begins to scan them.

'I think they're confidential,' Jennifer says with a frown.

'That's what I mean,' Sadie agrees, continuing to read. 'They shouldn't park them out here like this. Anyone could see them. *I* wouldn't stand for it.'

'I'm not going to either. But I've only just got here.' Jennifer's indignance is weary though, as thin as old skin and, she fears, as likely to flake.

Sadie puts the notes down and looks at her. 'You look worn out. Let's go to the WRVS place and get a cuppa, shall we? We can't do her any good here.' Jennifer nods wanly.

Jennifer buys the tea—and a sandwich and a cake for Sadie, who declares that she has skipped lunch to get to the hospital in time for visiting. Sadie does most of the talking, giving Jennifer a potted history of her life since their teenage days. It is a roller-coaster ride through a landscape of tricky births, romantic disappointments, dysfunctional daughters, suspicious lumps and investigative surgeries, all related *fortissimo* in the little enclave of tables and chairs outside the WRVS hatch. Even as she listens Jennifer recognises each anecdote as a deposit in the bank of their renewed relations, which Sadie will presently draw on in reciprocal confidences. She has no idea how she will make the payments. Her new prospect is too bewilderingly raw, much too tender to tread on and yet to talk about her life as it has been will be like walking amongst corpses. It is over, she is sure of that, although how its demise will play itself out, and what its replacement will look like, she has no idea. She feels as though, having been cooped up in some constricted space, a diving bell or a tiny space craft, she is on the point of exit with the fearsome prospect of endless free-falling before her.

But then, as Sadie's biography comes to an end, she thinks, well, what does it matter? She knows the worst there is to know about me anyway.

Sadie, however, draws a surprising cheque upon their new-found association. 'So, tell me about you. Tell me about *Michael*,' she says, wiping cake crumbs from her mouth with the back of her hand even though, Jennifer notes, there is a napkin dispenser on the table.

531

'Michael?' What is there to say about him? How can she possibly describe the journey he has been on since this woman, as a girl, idolised him? 'Well, you know. The world was never quite big enough for Michael, was it?' It is true. His appetite—his zest—had been voracious; to go, to be, to see and experience. Nothing too big or too small, too weird, too profound but he must delve into it and drain it to the bottom. But satisfaction had evaded him; he had always needed more.

'He's travelled then? He always said he would.'

'Oh yes, he's travelled.' To the world's end and beyond, into realms of consciousness uncharted, and still his hunger is unappeased.

'Where to?'

'Where has he *not* been,' Jennifer laughs uneasily. Images roll across her mind's eye: mountain-top monasteries, the seediest dens of drugs and prostitution, palaces, slums. She sees him on psychedelic trips and wretched withdrawal treks, borne between the sublime and the sick. He has been ensnared by sects and absorbed by communes, and exiled himself for weeks and months of physical deprivation in search of elusive spiritual enlightenment. But always, *always*, he has returned to the same hollow discontent, a burning thirst that nothing can quench; the corporeal limitations of being Michael.

'And is he happy?' Sadie's question surprises her. She supposes she wants to know if he is settled, married, the father of children, a contented man.

'What you need to know about Michael is that he's ...' she gropes for the adjective. Mentally ill? An addict? An itinerant? Broken? Dangerous? 'Gone. The Michael we remember has gone,' she says at last, resorting to the explanation she had given her mother only two days before.

'Do you mean he's dead?' Sadie's complexion is ashy.

'He once told me to consider him that way. But no, he isn't dead.'

'Well,' Sadie sniffs, and drains her tea cup. 'We're none of us quite what we used to be. Doesn't mean there isn't hope. I was only saying to

Jasmine yesterday. Things sometimes take a long time to come right, because we're not always ready for them, or because things aren't quite set in position. But you've got to believe they *will* come right in the end, otherwise, what's the point?' She sits back, giving Jennifer time to absorb this pearl of wisdom. Then, 'I think,' she leans emphatically towards Jennifer and cocks her head in the direction of the wards, 'I think you ought to send for him, Jennifer. Your mum, you know. She hasn't long.'

Jennifer looks at her, knowing it's true. 'I know,' she says at last. 'I will.'

THE DISCOUNT SUPERMARKET has escaped relatively unscathed from Saturday's excesses. Its shutters resisted attempts to prise them from their runners and although the car-park is littered with detritus the interior is undamaged. In truth the store rather benefits than otherwise from the townspeople's temporary madness. Where rival shops are closed pending clear-up, this one is open for business on Monday and only the bruised and haunted aspect of some of its staff remind shoppers of what has been.

By Tuesday a concerted effort in the town has restored things to something like normality. A kind of community cohesion has been forged in the furnace of wanton irresponsibility, and those who, on Saturday, looted and rampaged, now present themselves for volunteer work-parties with stiff-bristled brooms and short-handled shovels. Their grim willingness recalls the old Blitz spirit. They tend to talk about the incursion in the same terms as the floods, placing them in the 'natural disaster/act of God' category of experience; truly awful, tragic, very sad—but nobody's fault. Thursday's *Weaver Weekly* will confirm their approach, making scant mention of the episode which, everyone agrees, is better forgotten, consigned to history as a lamentable aberration in the annals of a town remarkable for its dullness.

For Jade too, it seems that out of the darkest day in her dark, frowning, narrow life, something good has come. The parameters of her world have simply opened up, her horizons enlarging and stretching, becoming as transparent and iridescent as a soap bubble. Through its shimmering rainbow lens things have been brought dazzlingly into focus. Within its gentle membrane she finds that she can breathe. The crushing weights of scowling self-regard and terminal envy have been lifted away. After what feels like a life-time of being passed by she has been, not once, not twice but three times blessed; she has had her three wishes, and they are all good. It is a revelation to her—how big a little kindness can be. She thinks of Skinner's mother's, Ryan, the people at the church, and she finds it as delightful and infectious as a fit of giggles. Looking out over her newly broadened life-view it seems to her that rather than the cruel malevolent spirit she has always imagined crouching over her determined to deprive, there might be a gentler, wiser authority with a mind to give.

At lunch time she goes down to the Bridge Street building. Inside is a whirlpool of activity. Volunteers serve soup and sandwiches. They sort through donations of food and clothing, handing them out to the flood-victims with broad smiles. On the stage a number of makeshift booths make private interview spaces, where people can get help with the endless form-filling for insurance claims, or finding alternative accommodation. A huge notice board carries cards from each church member offering what help they can, from carpet fitting to cat fostering, or just messages of concern; their gist: 'you are not alone.' In a discreet corner there is prayer. Gentle hands are laid on weary shoulders. There is earnest entreaty, the balm of assurance. It is a moment's respite from the on-going nightmare of saturated plaster and blown electrics, decimated treasures, the stink of silt and sewage. And whether it is the patient attention of those who pray—the comfort of their murmured compassion—or the movement of the Spirit isn't clear, but each crumpled and careworn person who emerges from the dim enclave seems to do so with a little more strength to endure.

Patrick greets her warmly and is all for finding her a job to do until she tells him that she has only popped down in her lunch hour to say thank you.

She looks wonderingly around her at all the happy, busy giving. 'This isn't what I imagined church to be.'

'No,' Patrick says with a knowing smile. 'Lots of people tell me that. It's a shame. It's just what it ought to be, too. It's *exactly* what it was, in the beginning.'

Jade smiles awkwardly, sensing the imminent proffering of evangelistic literature or even that Patrick will produce a bible from his back pocket and refer her to the chapter and verse. What he actually offers is a chocolate bar. 'The cash and carry just donated these,' he smiles. 'Now, if you'll excuse me, I must get on.'

'Well, thank you again,' Jade says.

'I've told you, we were thrilled. And so was He.'

'Ryan?' Jade feels herself blushing.

'No Jade. Your father.'

ON TUESDAY JENNIFER works late at the office, trying to knock the week's edition into shape. She is a day early with it really, and a lot can happen in twenty four hours, but she has a premonition that Wednesday will be hi-jacked and knows that she must, regardless of her personal burdens, safeguard the paper and her job as its editor.

She has remained in the office even though she could as easily work at home. There is coolness and composure in her dining room. A breeze wafts garden scents in through the patio doors. But her pristine house has lost its appeal to her. She is restless there, roaming endlessly through the rooms, like someone expecting guests but ready far ahead of time. Every single thing is minutely in place. There is nothing more to be done at all but just to count each infuriating second that must pass before the time comes to open the door. She is entirely resolved, and it is a fundamental aspect of her character that once decided she must act immediately. Kenny's continued absence is enforcing a delay that is anathema to her determination; she simply cannot bear loose ends.

She looks up now from her computer screen. The front page story is woefully flimsy, short on facts, the gaps filled with hypothesis. 'It is thought that,' 'sources suggest', 'commentators speculate', but the reporter has harnessed his lack of detail to create an enigmatic and appealing heroine, giving the story exactly the inspiring angle Jennifer wants. The picture is very good too, and Jennifer pulls the corner of it on her screen to make it bigger; the most dominant image on the page. Clearly, the woman has her reasons for remaining reticent, hiding herself away and getting her colleagues to cover for her, but Jennifer's loyalties lie with her readers who deserve—and, just now, really need—some good news.

In any case, she has no patience with ostriches. What else is Kenny doing now, than lying low and hoping it will all go away? The first flush of his angry departure will have evaporated long ago. Wherever he went, whatever he did, it will be clear to him now from his heavy head and empty wallet that he has punished himself as much as her. His main preoccupation will be to ensure that he can portray his ignominious crawl home as a victorious homecoming. In the meantime she is in limbo, unable to move on, her marriage denied its swift despatch from the axe she has poised over it.

At least she has got the office in order. Its newly imposed tidiness pleases her. It is something completed; a box she can tick. It is her vehicle. She knows every inch of it now, having inspected each document and file and discarded with a sense of glorious finality the obsolete and out-moded, the broken, the useless, the shabby and the spent. Nothing can happen here that she does not feel equal to handling. She is wholly in charge. It is how she likes it.

This is more than can be said for her home, which is proving pregnable to her problems. Kenny's boss, Mr Pickering, just returned from a prolonged period of convalescence, has left a telephone message, enquiring, not unreasonably, where his Sales Manager is. She supposes she will have to respond to the call. She will not lie for Kenny but neither will she run telling tales. Mr Pickering's reputation is formidable and if Kenny is to feel the full force of it, it will be entirely on his own head; he will not be able to lay it at her door. She is fully aware that he will have a complete arsenal to throw at her once she has made her position clear, without her adding to it.

Sadie has made early use of the telephone number Jennifer had been pressed to exchange. Has she contacted Michael? When does she expect him?

She has sent for her brother with a sense of ludicrously adding to her already unwieldy pile of problems. But having decided to do it she had done so immediately, sending the newspaper clipping of their mother's fall and some money in an envelope to an address that Michael had given her; a refuge for the homeless in the City of London. She has no idea if he will get it, or when, or what he will be like if he comes. He is an unknown quantity. The only thing she can be sure of is that if he comes, he will not stay long.

Sadie has again been to the hospital, insinuating herself rather too eagerly into the Fairlie emergency. She inveigled her way into the high dependency ward where the patient is now lodged by describing herself as Mrs Fairlie's daughter-in-law, brushing aside Jennifer's reservations with, 'Well, we're *practically* family aren't we? And I'm not going to stand by and watch you cope all on your own.' Rosie has also been there and Mrs Fairlie had been washed and dressed in her own nightgown when Jennifer visited the previous evening. The sight of the homely rosebud print and the ruched elastic round the bony yellow wrists had given Jennifer a multiplicity of stab wounds. Guilt, that she had not thought of it, jealous resentment—this is *her* mother, after all—and also a kind of relief, that there are others prepared to share the burden with her. She cannot be sure of Sadie's motivation—although she can guess it—but Rosie is clearly moved by genuine attachment. *That* gives Jennifer pause for thought as well, and, looking down at the waxy, wasting woman, she wonders where on earth she went wrong.

The doctor, the third or fourth that Jennifer has seen—this one a Sikh with a bright red turban and a bright white smile—was kindly bleak. The antibiotics weren't being as effective as they had hoped. There was evidence of encroaching organ failure. A rally, he said, is very unlikely. He predicted that twenty four hours would see a conclusion. In the meanwhile they would keep her comfortable; it was all they could do. They had stood either side of the neat bed, the dolorous, muffled bing of a heart monitor the only sound, the last discernible residue of the woman between them.

IF PATRICK HAD sought to gratify Jade by his reference to her father, he has wildly mis-fired. It is a word that is loaded with negatives for her. In its abstract, when she tries to conjure a father, a daddy, in her mind, her only aids are television commercials. They are gravy-eating, Tesco-shopping, Gillette-shaved dads—a brittle, fickle concept of the best a man can get. Nothing in her experience can put flesh on the idea. Her real uncles live too distantly and, now that Granny has gone, never visit. Her spurious ones—the ones her mother brought home from time to time—kept their distance from the round-eyed toddler or gawky, dishevelled school girl who regarded them through the banisters when she was supposed to be in bed, or, awkwardly, over Weetabix at breakfast. She can't remember anything about them now, expect for the one thing that they all had in common; they did not stay.

She supposes that, if she really wanted to, she could find out about her father. She has enough confidence in her ability to badger and harass Sadie into revealing a name, assuming she knows it. It could prove important one day, to know what elements—genetic aberrations—of paternal residue she might be harbouring, good or bad. From time to time curiosity has gnawed at her, and she has not been immune to flights of fancy that he is living prosperously somewhere, with room in his life for a long-lost daughter. But her expectations, jaundiced by disappointment, supply only the likelihood that, if found, prosperous or not, he would have no interest in her. Why would he? Those of her friends who have fathers, whom they tap for loans or call on for lifts at unsociable hours, describe them as 'embarrassing', 'old fashioned, and 'grumpy.' On the whole Jade has convinced herself that a father, like everything that life has denied her, is simply a dispensable asset.

So it is a challenge. The label of 'father' produces for Jade no image of paternal comfort, but only the vivid potential for being let down. Her burgeoning spiritual consciousness teeters. But the benign overseeing force, which—or who—is increasingly coming into focus in Jade's awakening perception in large ways and in small, does not fall. The possibility of it as the power behind Mikey's rescue is its grandest and most dramatic manifestation, but she is seeing it more and more in less spectacular but no less notable ways. In the benevolence that one person can show another, in the sudden dawning possibility that all need not be dour and dry and disappointing. Good things will not necessarily gnarl and wither in her hands. Her path need not be perpetually blighted. There is hope, even for her.

She does not give up hope, for example, on Ryan, even though day follows day and he does not come. This in itself is evidence of how far she has come. Four days before she would have been telling herself that he was not her type anyway, and had probably only knocked her into that porch-way by accident, trying to save himself.

She makes discreet enquiries with Charlene, who declares with a shrug that she hardly sees her brother these days, since his move into Sales. He is often away on the road in the car that has come, as an unexpected bonus, with his new job.

'I never even got to ask him what he did,' Jade says. And then, fishing, 'Did he tell you what happened to us?'

'No, but he never tells me anything anyway and definitely not about his work. They make little things out of metal—that's all I know.'

From what Jade can gather they are a nice, middle class family. The father is a commercial estate agent, the mother teaches piano. There is an older sister, doing accountancy. Ryan went to college and did two years of technical and engineering drawing before starting work. Charlene says she is a disappointment to them, flunking her exams and drifting from job to job. Jade thinks that in that case they are unlikely to welcome *her* into the bosom of their family. She is a girl from a broken family in a rough neighbourhood. She has no qualifications and more than one or two tours around the block to her credit. It is more than possible that it will serve as a deterrent to Ryan, yet in her heart there stubbornly bubbles a geyser of optimism that will not be quelled. It isn't even that she has to fuel it with positive thinking. It seems to spout under its own volition. She wakes up with it each morning, a giddy thrill of expectation. She doesn't know if it has always been there, buried in the rock of her scowling obduracy, waiting for something as cataclysmic as the quake of Saturday's several ordeals to release it. A spookier explanation still is that it has been planted there, that there has been some mystical in-pouring from the charged, uncanny air of the church. Either way, she doesn't care. She likes it; she likes herself more, with it.

Sadie is often away from home, hospital visiting. It is left to Jade to keep an eye on Carmel, which she does, at a carefully obtuse angle so as not to antagonise. There is definitely something wrong. Her eyes— usually cold and almost vacant—have a startled, hunted expression Jade hasn't seen in them before. The girl, already stick-thin, hardly eats. This, and evidence in the toilet, make her suspect an eating disorder. Every evening Carmel sees her boyfriend Spencer. Jade, who at one time, briefly, but with very unpleasant consequences, had been involved with Spencer's older brother Maxwell, knows that it is a recipe for disaster. Her concern is overwhelming—a deep pool of compassion—but their past relationship is such that broaching the subject is almost impossible. She decides she will talk to Jasmine.

MR PICKERING IS not as Kenny has described him. He is reduced, less florid and certainly less arrogant than she had expected. He stands on her doorstep early on Wednesday, apologising for the hour, enquiring kindly for Kenny.

'Is he ill, Mrs Roach? Only we haven't seen him in the office and I know there are some appointments he has missed.'

'You'd better come in.' Jennifer stands to one side and he steps into the hallway. 'I did get your message but by the time I got home it was far too late to call.'

'It's never too late to call me, Mrs Roach. I'll always make myself available for my staff, especially if they find themselves in difficulty.' He says it with fervent, almost evangelistic zeal. At the same time she can see him casting glances around the hall and through the open lounge door, looking, she supposes, for evidences of a malingering Kenny. There are none, of course. In fact there is no evidence at all of Kenny. By now she has cleared every remnant of him into the spare room; the shoes he kicks off and abandons in inconvenient corners; his coat, draped, habitually over a chair even though they have ample hooks in the cloakroom; half-read newspapers he hasn't quite finished with; letters opened to be dealt with 'later'. She has removed it all and stored it away out of sight. It is a half-measure that is unsatisfactory. She wants it all—she wants *him*—completely gone.

There is one mug and cereal bowl on the kitchen counter—clearly breakfast for one—so that when Jennifer says, 'I'm sorry, Mr Pickering. Kenny isn't here,' she can see that he believes her immediately. 'And the truth is,' she goes on, 'I have no idea where he is.'

'I see,' he says.

She expects an explosion but none comes. He takes a deep breath, and then another. If she didn't know better she'd say he was counting and she suddenly hears her mother saying, 'Now, Jennifer, count to ten. Count to ten while you calm down.' She doesn't know where the memory has sprung from. Some echo from the past, when she would lose her temper and go off like an incendiary. Her mother would look at her as though she was an alien; an utter, incomprehensible mystery. She would shake her head and say, 'I don't know where you get that temper from, girl. I've never seen anything like it.'

'I'm in something of a dilemma Mrs Roach,' Mr Pickering is saying. 'On the one hand your husband's appointment as Sales Manager was temporary, to be reviewed on my return. I must say that on examining the order book things aren't quite as they should be. Then, you know, to go absent without notice is, well, it isn't what I expect and it's left poor Ryan high and dry. The lad's been trying to cover both their appointments these last few days but he's in way over his head.'

'You're going to sack Kenny,' Jennifer interrupts, cutting to the chase. She doesn't blame him. It is what she would do, without compunction, in his shoes. Kenny's behaviour, especially in his probationary period, is untenable and has been since the start. His promotion has gone entirely to his head, and in the absence of Mr Pickering, under the less authoritative eye of Jack Perry, he has been carried away with the opportunities for golf, long lunches and so-called sales conferences.

'Well, no. I don't want to do that, especially if, you know, if Kenny is having difficulties that are temporary, or that I might be able to help him with,' he looks at her significantly. 'I wouldn't want to act too hastily. People do have troubles, I know that, and sometimes they just need a little time to organise things ...' He places this suggestion in the air between them. She could grasp it, if she wanted, but she leaves it floating.

'But on the other hand, you see, I have to consider the company and do what's best for the other employees. If there are no orders there can be no manufacture. That's the bottom line.'

'I quite understand. I wish I could be more helpful.'

'You have no idea at all where he might be, or when he'll be back?'

'None at all.'

'You don't suspect, do you, some,' he hesitates to say the word, 'some mishap?'

'Oh no.' She even laughs a little. 'Kenny is indestructible. He'll turn up sooner or later like a ...' The words 'bad penny' drop with an unpleasant, off-key clatter onto the laminate flooring.

'I take it things aren't so good at the moment Mrs Roach.'

'My mother is dying,' Jennifer says.

'I'm very sorry to hear that,' Mr Pickering says sincerely. 'If there's anything I can do ...'

The production meeting at the newspaper office is very tense, with no Guy there at all and Gerry, the sports reporter, clearly furious that he has been denied the front page. She takes no prisoners however, pushing through the edition she has cobbled together, conscious nonetheless that her work—the one thing that will have continuance after everything else is finally wrapped up—is taking the brunt of her frustration at the things wending, with such lingering sluggishness, to their end. The unresolved relationships in her life are appalling. To her minutely organised, compartmentalised life they are as untenable as a multiple car pile-up on the motorway, the carnage left by fire or flood. Nothing whatsoever can be saved from them and their consequences ricochet across the otherwise ordered landscape of her life, tainting it and knocking things out of kilter. She cannot bear the waiting, the need for polite patience. It is cruel and only prolongs the pain. As a child she always ripped plasters off, yanked out wobbly milk-teeth, preferring the swift discomfort to the torture of prolonged easing and experimental pulling. Once she had smacked the head of an ailing hamster against a wall, saving it the drawn-out misery of a long death. That's how she feels now; that her mother's slow decline, Kenny's continued absence, even Michael's uncertain arrival, are just vehicles to make an inevitably bad situation a dozen times worse.

Facing things is always better than hiding from them. This is why she would not cut the front page story even though the reporter is adamant that its publication could put a woman in danger. People should confront their demons.

All afternoon she sits on the hard, uncomfortable chair provided by the hospital at the side of her mother's death bed. She has been told that a few hours will see the end of it and she is anxious for it, for all their sakes. What remains of her mother is barely more than an effigy of plasticised skin and chalky bone. Only her dry, rasping breaths and the bing of the heart monitor prove the continued operation of her inner mechanics. And yet—Jennifer smiles at the irony of it—this tenacious grasp is the purest manifestation of her mother; she is defined by stubbornness. It is as though life has boiled her down, refined her to her purest element, the central nerve of her existence, and it is Michael. She will wait for him before letting loose the last frayed thread of her life to set them all free.

AFTER WORK JADE catches the bus to Jasmine's house but when she gets there her mother is already *in situ*, perched on a chair only just outside the back door, smoking and drinking tea.

'What are you doing here?' Sadie asks narrowly. She likes to appropriate the happily-circumstanced Jasmine to herself, leaching a vicarious satisfaction from the success of her new relationship and pleasant situation here in the farmhouse.

'Nothing,' Jade puts her bag down on the kitchen table. 'Just thought I'd come and see how Mikey is.'

'Tea in the pot,' Jasmine says, 'if you want.' She is up to her elbows in some meaty mixture, rolling it into balls before dipping in flour. She makes a mental assessment of the quantity; can she stretch it to feed one more?

'Turned into a proper Nigella, hasn't she?' Sadie comments, nodding at Jasmine's culinary industry. 'She made curry from scratch on Sunday.'

'Useful stuff, scratch,' Jasmine mutters with a smile. It is something Richard says.

The children are watching television. Mikey is crouched on the floor, all angular limbs and sharp knees, a smear of something down his aertex school shirt. Lilly is primly perched on the sofa, her uniform prick-neat even after a day at school. They greet Jade absently as she enters, absorbed in google-eyed American puppetry, and she nudges Lilly over to make room.

'Not been swimming again today?' Jade asks, in a lull of frantic fake-fur frolics. Mikey rolls his eyes. Lilly takes her thumb out of her mouth and says, 'A man from the newspaper came. He looked in my tent.'

'Did he? Lucky him.' She wriggles an arm around Lilly and draws her into a cuddle. The child smells slightly rubbery and sour, like sweaty plimsolls. 'Today?'

Lilly shakes her head. 'Yesterday,' she says, around her thumb.

Jade observes Mikey obliquely. He is such a scrawny little scrap, all eyes and elbows, jangle-jointed as though his connections need tightening. But now he is connected also, in her mind's eye—via unsuspected links and surprising junctions—into a mysterious, all-encompassing network. He is cared about by strangers. His fate is safeguarded by an intervening hand.

He seems entirely unaltered by his experience. She had expected that she might be able to glimpse, in his eyes, a new, otherworldly level of wisdom, something profound or ethereal, evidence of an angelic touch.

'What did he want to know Mikey?'

Mikey does not take his eyes from the television screen. 'Just about what it was like in the river,' he says.

'And what *was* it like?'

He shrugs. 'Cold. Wet.'

'You didn't hear anything, like a voice in your head or anything? Or see anything?'

'What do you mean?'

Jade doesn't really know. She is recalling bits and pieces from programs like *Amazing but True* and *Out of this World*. 'A light? A garden?'

'I saw an old lady.'

'*Did* you? Did she have her hair in a bun and big earrings?'

'No, she had a walking frame. She lives at the old people's home. Why?'

'It doesn't matter.'

'When is Richard coming home? He could run us home after tea,' Sadie says. She is milking the usefulness of a man while he is still in attendance. Bitter experience tells her, despite evidence to the contrary, that it will not last forever.

'Aren't you going to the hospital today?'

'Not today. Tomorrow perhaps.'

Something about her mother's tone catches Jasmine's attention. Something is brewing. Now she looks closely she sees that Sadie has been to the hairdresser's, plucked her eyebrows and waxed her legs. She is basking in an envelope of evening sunshine like a cat.

'What's going on?' Jasmine asks, narrowing one eye.

'Oh, nothing,' her mother replies.

'Mmm,' Jasmine says sceptically. She drops the meatballs into a casserole of rich, bubbling gravy before sliding it back into the oven.

'As a matter of fact Richard won't be home until later. He's taking Matt to play squash after work.

'*Is* he now?' Sadie draws heavily on her cigarette. She says gloomily, 'He'll always be seeing Matt now, I suppose,' in a tone that implies the battening of a coffin lid.

Jasmine discerns it. 'They used to spend all their time together, before. It's only to be expected,' she says defensively.

'You should put your foot down.'

'I certainly won't. How could I, when he's been so good about Mikey and Lilly?'

Jade ambles in and puts her empty tea cup on the table. Then, with a second thought, she picks it up again and rinses it at the sink.

'What won't you do?' she asks.

'Put my foot down about Richard seeing Matt. I'm just so pleased he's come round.'

'Of course he should see him. He's been hanging out with Spencer and Skinner. Carmel told me. Can't be a good thing.' Mentioning Carmel reminds Jade of the purpose of her visit, but Sadie's presence makes it difficult to pursue. Jasmine is at the sink, scraping new potatoes. Jade picks up a tea towel and begins to dry the dishes stacked on the drainer. They both have their backs to their mother, who, reluctant to be excluded, and catching mention of Skinner, calls from her seat by the doorway, 'Any news of Skinner, by the way?' She lights another cigarette.

Jade shakes her head. 'Not that I've heard. Can't blame him though. That Scanlon's a bastard.'

'You know,' Jasmine muses, thinking of Skinner's mother, 'now I think about it, her life must have been a nightmare. I feel bad now, that I never got to know her.'

Sadie opines sagely. 'You don't want to get involved with people like that. We've got enough problems of our own.'

'Good job *she* didn't take that attitude on Saturday afternoon,' Jade mutters, with a sidelong smile.

'Yes. Look what kind of person she is,' Jasmine says. 'And all that time we never knew. And now he might find her again. It'd be awful if anything happened.'

'Skinner might find her too, though.'

'There is that.'

'He'll be long-gone,' Sadie says with glum certainty.

Jade doesn't stay for tea at Jasmine's but walks over the old stone bridge and past the old people's home to wait for the 457 back into town. Whenever she is away from home she wonders if she has missed Ryan. She supposes that he knows that she works at the discount supermarket with Charlene but feels it is unlikely that he will come to find her there. Her house is the only place he can be sure to contact her and she is as certain as she can be that if he comes—*when* he comes—it will be there. She can't explain why she feels so sure of him but it springs from the events of Saturday. Chance, coincidence or destiny had led him to her as surely as it had led Skinner's mother to Mikey, their courses as pre-ordained as a railway timetable and their destinations as inevitable. At one time Jade would have been pro-active in tracking Ryan down via Social Media, but now, although wondering at the strangeness of it, she is content to leave it in providential hands. It is such a relief, after years of wrestling with circumstances, simply to give up the fight and let things work themselves out, and there is balm in the belief that somewhere, somehow, a kindly hand is at the helm.

It is obvious immediately, when she steps into the cluttered hallway, that something is wrong. Carmel's school things are, as always, abandoned there, but they are accompanied by other paraphernalia; a scuffed, much-scribbled-on Adidas sports bag and a pair of large, filthy trainers. The air in the house is stale and thick, as you would expect of a place with smokers and where the windows are never opened. It is a curious cocktail of old tobacco, the competing scents of different deodorants, burnt bacon fat and toast. But today there is an additional, feral tang; an anxious, animal air. She hears voices from upstairs, and they too are weighted and discordant. She picks out Carmel's voice, shrill as broken glass, and another, strident but strained almost to cracking; the voice of a boy who is almost a man. Jade closes the door quietly and mounts the stairs.

Carmel has the front bedroom, the second largest, the one that Jasmine and Jade had shared. It had been like a cold war then; their belongings kept strictly separate. Jade's side of the room had been a shambles while Jasmine's was prick-neat and organised, fussy with knick-knacks, her bed always tidily made and guarded by ranks of solemn-eyed stuffed toys. Later, when Jasmine had reached eighteen and declared herself too old to share, she had moved into the small room while Jade and Carmel had joined open battle in this one, wilfully damaging each other's possessions, hiding or stealing them, their conversation a constant cacophony of bickering sawing on into the night. Only

551

Jasmine's departure to live with Richard had released them from their enforced proximity, and a tossed coin falling—inevitably—to Jade's disadvantage had secured the larger room to the younger girl. It is always in total disarray. The bed is never made, the dressing table is crowded with make-up and hair accessories and belts and Cds and dirty cups, all covered with a bloom of face powder and eye shadow as thick as pollen. The floor is always strewn ankle-deep with clothes, rendering the carpet completely invisible. School books are tossed anyhow in amongst it all. The floor is a hotchpotch of history coursework and dirty knickers and mouldy apple cores. There is the vaguest suggestion of a track ploughed through it all between the door and the dishevelled bed, like a pathway trodden through multi-coloured snow. As Jade enters the room it strikes her almost as a psychedelic landscape, the colours and textures of it all, the tumbled bedding and dust, the bright evening sun filtering through the half drawn curtains picking out two immobile figures in the room. Spencer perches awkwardly on the mattress, filling the room with his masculinity. Carmel is poised precariously amongst the heaps of clothing and damp towels as though picking her way between slippery rocks at the seashore.

At Jade's arrival their conversation is abruptly halted and they both turn to her. Their faces and bodies speak volumes, though. Spencer is flushed, a sheen of perspiration on his forehead and upper lip, his eyes bright and sharply malevolent. His body is in some way inflated, like a dog with raised hackles, trying to make himself seem bigger and more intimidating than he is. He exudes denial, defensiveness, his muscles primed ready for fight or flight. He is a snarling, belligerent display of a boy under threat. In contrast Carmel is almost see-through, her colour drained entirely away. She is so nebulous that Jade imagines at first that she can see the bright hues of discarded garments through her porcelain-pale transparency until she realises that she is only seeing their reflection on Carmel's skin, which is glazed by tears. The thing in her hand speaks for her; it is a pregnancy testing appliance, showing positive. It, and every distraught, bereft line of Carmel's waif-like body tells the awful truth; that she is being left, quite literally, holding the baby.

Spencer rushes past Jade. They hear him taking the stairs three at a time and the slam of the door behind him. The sisters are left looking at each other across the wasteland of Carmel's bedroom. In the wilderness of their traditionally unsympathetic relations it seems impossible that shelter or aid can be found. Carmel sways, the last vestige of her resilience turning gelatinous. She looks as though she will collapse, a slow, viscous descent into the laundry around her. Her skin and bone, the white blonde feathers of her hair, her pale eyes and her baby will join the tangle of sheets and tights and tops that strew the floor, an extra strata of tissue to add to the multi-layered hoard. What Carmel expects from Jade is a tirade, a smug intolerable stream of gloating told-you-sos, and it is more than she can bear. What she gets is a swift and enveloping embrace as Jade wades across the floor and leads her, trembling, to the bed. It calls up a geyser of emotion and tears more copious than you would think Carmel's emaciated body could contain; louder, stronger and more profound. The more Jade holds her, stroking the sharp protrusions of her shoulder blades, smoothing the silky threads of her hair, clutching to her the bird-like bones of her sister, the more anguished the distress that is called forth. Her spasms are almost like retches. It is a process of evisceration that will not stop until her very heart and lungs and bowels and the tiny bunch of cells in her womb have been sobbed away.

Their tears begin to scour away the years of bitter rivalry in the same way that the flood has washed away the scum and slime of stagnant waters, the dead wood on river banks and the pent up angst of drought. And it is just at this moment that they both hear, down below, the brisk rattle of their door knocker. Carmel grasps Jade tightly.

'Don't go,' she whimpers. Her eyes are round and wild, fearful—not of whoever is at the door—but of the crushing burden of being left on her own. Jade squirms onto her knees and peers over the window sill. A smart, sporty little hatchback she does not recognise is parked on the road. Below, on the untidy path, between the leggy, over-grown shrubs, a curly haired young man in jeans and a light, short-sleeved shirt is hovering. His shoulders are set boldly, almost bravely. They belie the

553

message of his hands, which are thrust deeply into his pockets, and the nervous shuffle of his feet against the threadbare mat.

It is Ryan.

There is a beat, an inner struggle, a silent sigh. Jade turns away and settles herself back on the bed next to Carmel.

'It's ok,' she says quietly. 'It's nobody.' And presently she hears the solid clunk of the car door, and the purr of the engine as he drives away.

IT TAKES UNTIL well after midnight to sort out the paperwork. Their mother lies for hours just waiting for a doctor to find time to confirm that she is dead. Michael is impossibly restless, pacing up and down the corridor, in and out of the thick, swinging plastic doors at the end of the corridor. He wanders to and fro under the night sky, smoking thin little cigarettes that he rolls himself with deft, practiced hands. His dog watches him with attentive eyes from where he is tied to a railing with a piece of string. Every time Michael disappears back through the doors the muscles under Snowy's black, wiry coat contract, making the fur bristle. His ears lie back along the sides of his narrow skull and his eyes, already rather protuberant, start a little more anxiously from his head. It makes him look like a gargoyle and the few pedestrians that there are—porters, laundry workers and kitchen staff—give the dog a wide berth.

In the ward, waiting behind the drawn curtains, Michael and Jennifer exchange few words, but those they do say are uttered in a whisper, partially in deference to the other elderly patients, who they can dimly hear whimpering and muttering in their sleep, but also because they have still not separated sleep from death in their minds.

Indeed in Michael's mind many boundaries are blurred. When he speaks he does so almost to himself, or addressing his dog, whether present or not, as though he has given up expecting anyone to answer him and is reduced to speaking to the only interlocutor who can be relied upon to listen. He has been relegated to that invisible class of society: the drunk, the down-and-out, the mentally ill, the displaced. When someone speaks to him he cocks his head, much like Snowy, his eyes refusing to meet those of the enquirer, as though he only half believes they exist anywhere but inside his head.

Whatever had passed between himself and his mother in those few brief moments between his cacophonous arrival and her easy, contented departure, it had been silent, a meeting of eyes, a reconnection of relational ties long severed. When it is over Jennifer expects him to cry, to show anguished remorse or guilty grief, but what she gleans from his muttered comments and inappropriate expletives, is that he is angry.

'*Why* was she in the fucking home?' he asks again and again. 'I mean *why?* I mean of course you're going to get ill if you go into one of those places. Death's what they're about. Stands to reason. Just wait till I get my hands on them Snowy. *Note to self:* just wait.'

'She was crippled with arthritis Michael. She couldn't get upstairs to the toilet. And she was getting forgetful. She nearly burnt the house down.' Jennifer tries to explain but Michael shakes off her comments with a flick of his greasy hair as he might an annoying wasp near his ear.

'And nobody *told* me,' he says emphatically. 'I didn't know, or I'd have been here, wouldn't I? Ha! I'd like to have seen them try then, that's all!'

Jennifer summons patience with a heavy sigh. 'You'd have seen what she was like, if you *had* been here. But you never are Michael, are you? That's the point,' she says bitterly. He gives no sign of hearing her. She might just as well not have spoken.

She gives up trying to reason with him, or to get through to him at all, but gives her attention to thanking the nurses and politely but firmly sending the hospital chaplain away. She nominates a funeral director and signs innumerable forms and then they are done. But for all that she has longed for the closure of it—the neat tying of the loose end—it is very hard to walk away from the still, recumbent figure in the bed. It is as though a fine filament, like a pulled thread on a cardigan, has been hooked there, and as she leads Michael down the corridor and out through the doors, she feels as though she is unravelling inch by inch. By the time she gets to the car-park she feels naked and begins to shiver although the night is warm. She suddenly wonders if she'll be able to drive, and is conscious of a brief storm of anger at Kenny, for abandoning her to this, alone. Snowy is reluctant to get into the car, and Michael spends a lot of time soothing him and coaxing him in, and stowing his accordion and duffle bag away. By the time they are ready to go she has conquered herself somewhat and she manages to get the key into the ignition and do the necessary with the car-park ticket with a semblance of regained composure.

It is not until they are out of the hospital grounds and on the by-pass that she realises that she has no plan at all for Michael's accommodation other than the fact that having him at her house is out of the question. They drive for some time in silence, apart from Michael's occasional murmurs of reassurance to the dog, who sits in the foot well between his knees, his eyes staring fixedly at Michael's, trembling. Eventually she pulls into a *Little Chef* situated close to the motorway junction. Its lights are on, but every booth and table is empty. Only a lone employee in uniform leaning over the counter indicates that the place is open. Behind the restaurant is a motel, an old fashioned place built in the American style, with the doors of its rooms opening directly from the car-park. It is a shabby, little-used place. She isn't even sure if it still operating, but a dimly lit office at the end of the block has the word *Reception* in illuminated red, fluorescent tubing in the window. Apart from that the place is in darkness.

'Are you hungry?' she asks. 'I am. Let's go in here.'

'Is there a bar?' Michael asks, brightening.

'No.'

She orders them tea and two dishes from the brightly coloured pictorial menu, but when the food comes neither of them eats with much relish. They do, however, drink cup after cup of tea, Michael sitting hunched into the fixed plastic seating with his cup cradled between his hands, alternately blowing at his tea and gulping down scalding mouthfuls. He glances about him with a tense, wary demeanour, uncomfortable with the bright lights and the garish furnishings. He refuses to take his malodorous coat off and has insisted on bringing his luggage into the restaurant with him. Snowy he has reluctantly left tied to the door handle of Jennifer's car where he sits now, staring intently in through the plate glass window, a pool of dark shadow on the flood-lit tarmac.

'I need a drink. Have you got a drink?' he asks repeatedly, of Jennifer, and even of the sallow-skinned waiter when he delivers their order.

'It's too late to get a drink anywhere now Michael. What we need is some food and then sleep. I think I'm going to book you into to this hotel here.' Jennifer's brisk assertion barely conceals her misgivings. Michael's appearance is shocking. She doubts that the hotel will accept him. He is unspeakably grimy and exudes a fetid smell. His hair is dirty, his chin unshaved, his fingernails filthy. More than this, his every gesture confirms that his dereliction is more than skin deep. There is a wild unpredictability about him, sudden expansive movements and loud, barking comments give way to periods of sullen, suspicious reserve. He seems unaware of his surroundings or of other people, or, if he is aware of them, completely indifferent. The next moment he seems cowed, overwhelmed. At times it is as though he is the only concrete thing in a hazy, insubstantial landscape. At others, that the environment is rising up in solid, crushing cliffs, towering over the tiny spec of himself.

He looks out of the window of their booth and mouths to Snowy, 'We're going home, lad, *home* to my mum's house. She'll look after us.' His breath mists the window. Jennifer looks at him in despair.

'Michael!' she says sharply, reaching across the Formica table and taking his hand firmly in hers. 'Michael look at me!' He drags his eyes from the dog and looks at her, not into her eyes, but at her lips as they speak. 'Mum just *died*, Michael, in the hospital. You were there. Don't you remember? She isn't at home. There's nothing there, now.' He frowns as though she is speaking a foreign language.

'I need a drink,' he says.

She leaves him standing by the car smoking while she goes into the motel reception. At the ping of its dusty bell a large-bellied, grizzle-faced man in a disreputable grey pullover shambles through from a back room. She books a room for the night in her own name and pays with her credit card. He gives her a key and indicates a room a good way down the row. The room is poorly furnished and in need of decoration. The tiles in the bathroom are dull with soap scum and the grout is mouldy, but there is a small supply of toiletries, the bedding is reasonable and there is a television, which Michael immediately switches on. He perches on the end of the bed and is lost in the fuzzy screen. Snowy settles himself on a mat by the door. Jennifer has no idea whether dogs are permitted. She has simply neglected to mention Snowy to the man. She leans close to Michael and says, 'Have a shower Michael, and get some sleep. I'll come and collect you in the morning, all right? I'll bring you some things then.' He makes the barest indication that he has registered her words, craning round her to regain his view of the programme. She sighs and closes the door behind her. As she drives away she half hopes and half expects that, in the morning, he will be gone.

BY THE TIME Sadie gets home Jade has put Carmel to bed. They have agreed, for the time being, to keep the news to themselves. Carmel assures Jade that the pregnancy is in an early stage. She has only missed one period.

'We only did it a few times,' the girl says miserably.

'And you didn't use anything?'

Carmel shakes her head. The old Jade would have said, 'You idiot, what do you expect?' But the new one asks, 'Do you want to tell me about it?'

Carmel takes a deep breath. 'I didn't really want to do it but Spencer was all riled up over something to do with Skinner and Maxwell. He took me up that path that goes past the golf course ... You know what boys are like when they want something.'

'Did he force you Carmel?'

She begins to cry again, hard, dry sobs. 'I didn't like it,' she weeps, 'but I thought that if I let him he would really be mine.' It is the age-old story; the female need—as powerful and imperative as stampeding horses, and as dangerous—to secure for all time and only for herself at no matter what cost the protection and shelter of her chosen mate. The countermanding male need—ruthlessly indulged—to spread himself amongst many. The inevitability of it—and its hopelessness—are stamped with indelible strokes on the history of their family. Jade shudders at the ease with which Carmel has placed her foot on the path so well-trodden by her mother and sister. But if she quails inwardly at what will come—the repetitive pattern of their lives—she says nothing. She lies alongside her sister on the narrow, tumbled bed, soothing and stroking and murmuring words of comfort. The confidential press of Carmel's thin frame against her own, the nearness of their faces on the pillow—so close that she can smell the fragrance of her shampoo and feel the whisper of her shallow breaths on her neck—inflates Jade's heart within her until she feels that she might burst. She looks back with dismay on a life spent struggling for dominance through spite and bile. So much wasted effort, yielding only blighted crops of antagonism, while all the while this alternative facility lay within her grasp. A delicious, satisfying harvest of closeness; all—she realises now—she has ever really wanted.

Later, when Carmel is sleeping soundly, Jade gets up and creeps from the room. On the way across the landing she pauses outside her mother's bedroom door. There is a sliver of light showing from underneath it and the muffled blare of the television. She pictures Sadie within, sprawled on the bed in her too-brief nightie, the slack flap of her stomach, her thread-veined legs, a glass of wine in her hand. She has no desire at all to go in, to share her burden. It is too precious to her, too vulnerable and new, to expose to Sadie's crowing dismay and harsh, hard-mouthed indictment. Sadie will behave as though Carmel has acted deliberately to spite her, taking to herself the lion's share of angst and alarm. It will be the excuse, no doubt, for an attack of nerves or similar emotional prostration that will place her squarely in the centre of Carmel's crisis.

Jade tiptoes past the room and creeps down the stairs. Downstairs the rooms are eerie, moonlit, colour-drained, and self-consciously still as though she has disturbed some fantastical midnight party. The furniture and curtains seem just to be waiting for her to go before resuming their revels. Carmel's strewn belongings look strange and almost animate on the hall floor, like small creatures that might suddenly dart away. The battered old hall table is gilded with silver light that pours like skimmed milk through the panes of the front door. As always it is a jumble of bits and pieces; keys, a bus pass, hair grips, bills to be paid. Amongst them is an unopened envelope, her name written in a bold hand across its front. She tears it open and into her hand slithers a fine metal chain and Carmel's amber pendant. On the back of the envelope he has written, 'Found in my shirt pocket,' and that is all. Her heart contracts a little. No number. No suggestion that he will call another time, and now that he has returned the pendant there is no reason at all to hope she will see him again.

But, regardless of reason, and in spite of the shadow in Carmel's room, she does hope. As she wanders through the quiet rooms of the house, and out through the back door into their tangled, neglected garden, as she smokes a cigarette and gazes up at the dark ochre sky and the bright slice of moon, her hope is like a lamp and its light is gladness.

IN THE DARK hallway of Jennifer's quiet house the light on the answering machine blinks like a tiny red eye. There are several messages from Sadie, one from Mr Pickering and one from the wife of her sports reporter. This last message is spoken in a rush, almost as though from a memorised script, anxious in case she should falter. Gerry is unwell. The doctor has signed him off for a fortnight due to stress. He needs complete rest, she says.

'Stress my foot,' says Jennifer aloud in the silent house. 'More like his nose is out of joint.'

The last messages are empty, just the crackle of static on the line and the faintest possible susurration of someone breathing. She knows it is Kenny, building himself a body of defensive evidence. She can almost hear his voice insisting that he had 'called numerous times' and that she had 'always been out.'

It is gone three o'clock in the morning by the time she climbs into bed. She is beyond tired and watches the moon-bright darkness give way to dull blue dawn. She hears the birds stirring in the hedges, the whir and jangle of the milkman in the close. Her mother has gone and her brother has arrived and all in all it seems to her that she has exchanged one unwieldy burden for another. But she comforts herself with the knowledge that in a few days they will both be out of her life for good. She will organise the funeral as swiftly as possible. It will be small and executed without fuss. Nobody will go. She does not even expect Michael to stay for it. Any formal, ceremonial occasion is bound to be more than he can cope with and it goes without saying that she will be left to endure it on her own.

563

She does not mind. On her own is what she desperately wants to be, unfettered by the demands of others, unburdened, free to tread her own, straight and unwavering path. But when she does fall asleep she is troubled by dreams; her mother's funeral, the quiet of the crematorium disturbed by a series of sharp, insistent raps from the inside of the coffin and the maudlin yawl of Michael's accordion. She is wearing a white suit and it is covered with black dog hair. No matter how she brushes it the short, wiry hair clings to her. Across the aisle, Kenny, in sombre black, looks at her with such cold disgust that she wants to slap him. The mechanism that will roll the coffin away chunters into life and the coffin gives a number of sudden ungainly jerks before being borne slowly backwards. The knocking from within becomes more frantic as the clankings and rumblings of the apparatus get into gear. Michael is playing two notes over and over again, mournful, like emphysemic lungs expanding and contracting. Suddenly it is full daylight, someone is ringing her doorbell and hammering on her door knocker, and the engine of a taxi is idling outside.

It takes both Jennifer and the taxi driver to get Kenny inside the house and up the stairs. She pays the fare and tips generously, asking no questions. Kenny is sprawled on his back on the bed in the spare room, utterly insensible with drink. He has a three day growth of stubble on his florid cheeks and jowls. His eyes are bloodshot and glazed, horribly puffy and crusted. His lips are woollen; it is quite impossible to make out anything that he says. His shirt is stained with food and vomit and the smell of him is so rank that she suspects he has soiled his underwear. She brings him a glass of water and an old washing-up bowl and places both beside the bed, removing his shoes and rolling him with difficulty onto his side. He is a dead weight, as though stuffed with boulders, and he is already snoring as she walks towards the door. She stares across at him for a moment, his comatose state allowing her a long, dispassionate assessment both of him and of her own feelings. She trawls her heart for a flicker of emotion but finds none beyond a crawling distaste and a kind of grim satisfaction to see him here, neatly reunited with his belongings. His clothes, his Cds, his golf clubs and squash racquet, the various trophies for his snooker triumphs, his birth certificate and savings bonds, his driving licence, his motor magazines, the *Stag at Bay* picture she had always hated, they are all packed up around him, carefully wrapped and neatly labelled, and ready to go.

It is still very early, not even eight o'clock, when she drives to the out-of-town hypermarket. The traffic is still relatively light; the most tortuous of the diversions have been taken away. The mizzling rain of recent days has entirely cleared leaving pale washed blue skies and thin high cloud. In her head she enumerates the list of things she must do; call the undertaker, make an appointment with the registrar, contact Mrs Terry at Bridge House, ring Sadie, as well as the work itinerary for the day. She is undecided at how to present Gerry's absence to the team. She feels slightly light-headed from lack of sleep. She buys coffee at the tiny *Starbucks* counter in the corner of the store, and sips it as she tours the shelves, selecting toothpaste and a brush, shaving tackle, underwear, shirts and jeans, and a collar and lead for the dog. But when she gets to the motel Michael's room is empty. There is no sign that the bathroom has been used; the towels are dry and still folded on the rail. The bed is barely dented. The television is on, cheery newscasters reading the news to the empty room.

The next time she sees him he is in the market place, sitting cross-legged on his out-spread Afghan. It is a breezy day, but dry. The wind is lifting Michael's greasy hair and putting some colour into his face, but instead of making him look healthy it gives a hectic flush to his pallid cheeks. She cannot see his eyes, they are tightly closed. He is in a world of his own. His arms open and close the bellows of the accordion with smooth, practiced strokes. His fingers wander over the keys as though exploring. The music is a dirge, full of mournful cadences and tortured harmonies, as though played on broken heart strings, and indeed its notes have a way of worming themselves into the most tightly locked casket of emotions. They reverberate around the square and rise up to the swiftly moving clouds like a heart-torn requiem. Snowy, at his side and echoing his mood, wears a forlorn expression and occasionally gives a sympathetic whine. Shoppers are giving them both a wide berth. Not surprisingly, a shapeless hat laid on the stone flags of the market place is almost empty.

565

'You don't need to do this,' Jennifer hisses. 'I can give you money.'

'I'm not doing it for the money,' Michael snaps. When he looks up at her, she sees his face is wet. 'This is what I do.'

She understands him. His grief has permeated down through the addled by-ways of his mind and finally found a resting place in his consciousness. This is how he will cope with it. His pain will be exorcised on the wings of his song. The words he cannot speak, the feelings he cannot give voice to will ooze from his accordion, his mouthpiece.

She goes into a coffee shop and comes back with food and two polystyrene cups of tea. She drinks hers perched on one of the decorative wrought iron benches of the square. Presently Michael lays his instrument aside and drinks his too. Most of the sandwich, though, he gives to Snowy. Then he comes and lowers himself onto the bench beside her.

'The funeral will be on Monday,' she says.

They both look across at the old stone church. It is where their father is buried. 'Not there,' Michael says, frowning.

'No. I read her Will. It doesn't say anything specific about that. In fact it was written years ago, before dad died. Most of it's irrelevant, now. Anyway, I did ask the undertaker but a burial costs a lot more and would take longer to organise. And after all,' she shrugs, 'what does it matter?'

Michael shudders. 'We mustn't put her in the ground,' he says brokenly.

'No,' gingerly, she takes his hand. In the fresh air she finds proximity easier to handle. The fingers are long and slender, but dirty with the grime of a dozen countries. 'No, I remembered how that had upset you. I wouldn't put either of us through it.'

'Burning is quick and clean, and it releases the spirit into the air,' Michael says with a flash of lucidity.

'Yes,' she says. 'Well that's how we'll do it, then.'

They sit in silence for a while, watching people going about their lives. Glaziers are refitting the windows of the pizzeria. Further down the concourse the pharmacy is having a new security shutter and a delivery van is restocking the wine shop. People hurry by, shopping, on their way to meetings, or dawdling, idling away the minutes until their bus is due.

'I think,' says Jennifer, 'that we were both a bit of a mystery to her, you know. But she did love us, in her way. She loved you. She asked me about you, only on Saturday.'

'There were never ...' Michael tries, but stumbles.

'No, there weren't.' She knows just what he wants to say, and the very fact that he can't is all the illustration he needs. There were never the words. The Fairlies suffered from a congenital lack of them, or an inability, at least, to grasp them. They would flit around the ceilings like tiny darting birds, eluding capture. The air would be thick with thoughts and feelings rendered mute through inadequate vocabulary, their inflections beyond the family palate. Sometimes it had been like screaming in a dream. Screaming, screaming, screaming, but no sound would come. But sometimes words would tumble out of Jennifer's mouth, propelled by an imperative inner mechanism. Gouts of anger would pour forth, sour as vomit and as irrepressible, and her mother had simply stared impassively on, as though she was speaking in a foreign language, or uttering mysteries in tongues.

Jennifer reminds Michael where the crematorium is, and tells him the time of the service. 'Shall I collect you? Or meet you there?' she asks. But he is gone from her, sunken in a reverie, his eyes fixed on some point across the square. She squeezes his hand, which still lies, unresisting, in hers. 'Will you go back to the hotel? I'll pay, of course.'

He rouses himself enough to shake his head a little. 'There's no sky,' he mumbles. 'Snowy and me like to see the sky.'

She thinks of them in her neat, flawless house. Michael's rangy, uncoordinated movements and sudden bursts of spleen threatening her

Lladró figurines, Snowy' s black fur matting her white carpets, the smear of his nose across her immaculate patio windows. 'So there's nothing at all you want from me?'

He shakes his head again.

'All right.' She sighs, and stands up, moving the carrier bag across the bench to him. 'I got you some things, and I hear there's a refuge on Bridge Street. It's for the flood victims really but they'll give you a meal, I should think.' She stands in front of him. Besides his battered duffle bag and stained coat, the pristine carrier bag is an anachronism and she half expects him to dump it in the nearest bin or even to walk away and leave it on the bench. She wonders about giving him money but is reluctant; he is all too likely to spend it unwisely. 'I suppose I'll see you around, and on Monday,' she says.

Walking away from him is harder than she had expected. The loose ends she has been so keen to tie off have barbs.

'I DON'T KNOW what to do,' Carmel wails. 'I don't want to have to decide.'

Jade has been to a clinic in her lunch hour and collected leaflets. The two girls have read through them together, sitting side by side on Carmel's bed amid the carnage of her bedroom.

If their mother wonders about their new-found relation she does not mention it. In any case she is preoccupied with the death of an old lady and the funeral on Monday, rearranging her cleaning jobs to make sure she can attend, going through her wardrobe. She had cooked them supper; dry fish fingers as stiff as pegs and oven-chips like cardboard. While her daughters stared at their plates Sadie had announced that she wished the whole family to attend. 'Mrs Fairlie was family,' she'd said. 'You all remember her. She was the best friend your granny ever had.' She had suddenly erupted in floods of tears, exiting the kitchen with her hand clasped to her mouth and running heavily up the stairs. It is her way—to leach other people's tragedies—but there is something tightly strung about her. She is on edge, an elastic band ready to snap. Jade and Carmel had regarded each other wanly as their mother's sobs echoed through the house. They knew she wanted them to follow her, to offer comfort, but the weight of their own burden is as much as they can bear for the time being. Carmel looks faintly green at the sight of the cold, unappealing food on her plate. Jade scrapes it all into the bin and they retreat with toast and tea to Carmel's room. Sadie's tears soon dry and presently, at a distance, they hear the familiar squeak-pop of a cork being drawn.

'I don't want to be a mum,' Carmel whispers, as though it is sacrilege she ought not to voice. Looking at her, the idea is ridiculous. In her school uniform, her face free of make-up, she is a child herself; thin-limbed, with only the slightest discernible swell of breast. Burrowed as she is into a nest she has made of her duvet, she looks vulnerable and afraid, in no position to make life-changing decisions. 'But then again,' her face begins to crumple, her pale eyes swim with tears, 'but then again, when I think about ... getting rid of it ... I can't help thinking about Mikey and Lilly, and it would be like throwing one of them away. Like *pushing* Mikey into that river ...'

Jade selects one of the leaflets from the pile on the bed and peruses it again. 'There's adoption. You know, some people ...'

'No, no, no,' Carmel cries. 'I couldn't do that. I couldn't carry it around for nine months and then give it away.' Her expression is one of perfect hopelessness, over written with the agony of an impossible decision. It is eroding her. Her skin is transparent, the juts and branches of her bird-like bones protruding through it. Soon, Jade thinks, she will get really ill.

'Eat your toast,' Jade says, edging the plate towards her.

'I can't. I can't swallow it. I can't swallow anything,' Carmel's voice is husky, exactly as though her throat is constricted. Suddenly she sweeps the plate and all the leaflets onto the floor. 'I can't decide,' she says again. She fixes Jade with an anguished stare. Her eyes are pale hollows and there is a light in them Jade doesn't like, a burgeoning hysteria. She reaches out and grips Jade's arm. Her fingers are like a bony vice. 'I just want someone else to decide. Isn't there anyone who can do it?' she asks.

In Jade's pocket the amber necklace presses against her thigh. She hasn't given it back, yet. In her torment, Carmel has not even noticed that it has gone.

Jade likes to have it near her. It is a sort of talisman, reminding her. Its warm golden light and ancientness is a sort of symbol.

'Well,' she says, 'perhaps there is.'

KENNY SLEEPS FOR a full forty eight hours, staggering blearily to the toilet from time to time and drinking copious amounts of water. At some stage he strips off and has a shower. She finds his clothes—meeting all her expectations of dreadfulness—in a heap on the bathroom floor. She puts them all into a bin bag and ties the neck of it tight. He remains in the spare room and they manage to avoid meeting. In the meantime she is busy with arrangements, with work, and with the extra duties occasioned by Gerry's absence. She attends a county athletics meeting, a charity golf tournament and a surprisingly exciting crown green bowls match. She is writing this up when he treads down the stairs.

He has made every effort to look normal. He is showered and shaved, and wears his usual weekend attire although he must have had to search through the suitcases for it because she has emptied all his drawers. But no ablutive effort can erase the effects of a five day binge on his system. He is coursing with toxins, as though poisoned. His skin is dull and deadly grey except around his jaw, which he has scraped raw shaving. The whites of his eyes are the colour of parchment, the rims red, their membranes inflamed. They dart around the room, glancing off Jennifer, reluctant to meet her cool gaze. An expectant pall hovers between them, taut and laden with what will come. In sympathy the sky outside is low with fast scudding cloud, presaging rain. A brisk wind thrashes the decimated spikes of spent wallflowers and the weedy, confused perennials that have been alternately dehydrated and drowned in recent weeks.

Jennifer feels a clutch of anxiety in her gut, the quiver of nerves. Her throat is dry. Normally in these encounters Kenny will take the upper

571

hand quickly by launching a pre-emptive strike on something; complaining about the state of the house, the lack of some commodity he wants, a poorly ironed shirt, putting her immediately on the defensive and diverting attention from the burning issue. She steels her nerves and takes a long, hard look at him. He stands in the doorway, shuffling his feet. He smiles but it is an uneasy expression that does not reach his eyes and seems to distort his skin with the effort of it; it is more, in fact, of a grimace. He exudes fretfulness and stale alcohol. The silence is like a bomb.

'You look terrible,' she says at last.

'Tea?' he asks.

He makes them tea and brings it to the dining room table. While he is in the kitchen her fingers continue to dance across the keys of her laptop but she is typing gibberish. When he brings the tea she stops typing and sits, waiting for him to speak. She will not put a stake in the ground by asking him where he has been. Nor will she allow any procrastination by making small talk. It is his move.

Eventually he says, 'Why are all my things packed up?'

'Why do you think?'

'Jenny,' he says, with a reproachful moue, 'that isn't what you want, is it?' There is an unpleasant, wheedling edge to his voice that makes her shudder. He tries a boyish, mischievous grin. 'I messed up *again*,' he says, 'I'm sorry.' If he is trying to engage her his effort is off-target. She continues to stare at him with stony directness. 'Don't you think,' he says, mustering a flicker of belligerence, 'that we might be over-reacting?' She gets up from the table then and disappears into the hall, returning with the telephone directory and the telephone. 'What's this?' he regards them, nonplussed.

'You'll need somewhere to stay so you'll have to make some calls. I think you should also call your boss. I rather think he's going to sack you.'

'Old Perry? *He* won't sack me!' Kenny almost manages a laugh but his bravado is hollow.

'Not Perry. Pickering. You picked the week he came back to work to go AWOL.' Kenny blanches then, and opens his mouth, but Jennifer interrupts him. 'And, no, I didn't tell him you were ill. I told him the truth: that I had no idea where you were, and that my mother was dying.' He flinches at that, quite markedly, as though she has dealt a physical blow.

'Dying?' he manages to say hoarsely.

'She's dead now, Kenny. She died on Wednesday. The funeral's on Monday. You can come if you like, but I want you out of the house by then.'

He stands up. 'Jenny, darling. That's so awful,' he says. 'No wonder you're angry. It's been horrible for you.' He extends his arms and she knows that he is going to try to hold her. He covers the few feet of carpet between them but it might as well be a million miles. She steps briskly away from him and takes up her tea, a shield between them; it is impossible to embrace a person holding a cup of hot tea.

'Yes,' she says, but without a trace of self-pity, 'it has.' She turns from him and looks out through the patio window at her ravaged garden. She has been trying to find time for weeks to get into it; its raggedness infuriates her. Perhaps she should engage a gardener. The juvenile trees of the estate gardens are whipping wildly to and fro in the wind. As she watches, one of her plastic patio chairs shifts across the decking. She ought to go out and stack them up, she thinks. So much to do, when this is all over. She can almost see the end of it now. It is only a matter of being firm. She turns back to face him.

He must be able to read, in her face, and through her voice, the level of her quiet, cold determination. Normally he would inflate his own resolve to equal hers and embark on an extended campaign that might result in days of acrimony. Blazing argument would alternate with cold shoulders, hours of stony silence be interspersed with vitriolic outbursts. But the result would always be Kenny getting his own way. Now he seems unable to summon up the strength for it. His other tactic—charm—he must know is hopeless. The detrimental personal impact of his spree coupled with her extreme—and justified—predisposition against him makes it a forlorn hope. He deflates in front of her eyes. His shoulders sink, his knees buckle and he sits down heavily on a nearby chair. The very skin of his face seems to sag. He rests his elbows on the table and puts his head in his hands. She regards him doubtfully for a few moments, gauging his tactics. When he lifts his head from his hands his eyes are wet and his face is a mask of misery.

'I'm sorry Jenny,' he says brokenly, 'so very sorry.'

She hadn't expected this and it gives birth to a worm of sickening guilt and self-loathing. It is terrible to be the author of another's pain, and even though he has coldly caused her tears on numerous occasions there is no satisfaction in returning the blow. She feels her resolve weakening. While she wrestles with it she saves her work and shuts down her laptop, tidying away her notes and clearing the dining room table. When she comes back she is wearing a waterproof and holding her keys. He is still sobbing, like a child and like a man.

'I have to catch the dry cleaners before they close,' she says. 'They've got my suit for Monday.' He makes no sign of having heard her. 'Look, Kenny, I'm sorry too. I know this is awful, believe me I've been through it all, while you've been away. But when the shock subsides you'll see that there's no other option.' Her icy pragmatism belies her inner turmoil. She is surprised at how profoundly his grief is moving her, on a personal and on a human level. She wants to comfort him, to relieve him of his anguish, but the harsh, undeniable facts remain unchanged and she knows that it would be cruel, giving false hope. Their sand-founded marriage will only collapse again. And again and again and again, subject to awkward props and makeshift patching until they are living amongst the rubble of it, too entrenched in the cycle to see it for what it is. Plus, knowing Kenny as she does, any chink she might show in her armour will be widened in his perception to admit the possibility of return and he will add tears to his arsenal for future deployment.

So she leaves him, and goes out into the gathering storm.

IT IS LATE when Jade eventually manages to slip away from the house. It has taken her all evening to settle the children, who are sleeping over while Richard and Jasmine take Matt out somewhere grown-up and special for the evening in early celebration of his starting work at Pickering's. Lilly has been as stroppy as a bag of cats. She was overbearingly dictatorial about the evening's television viewing and complained about the paucity of snacks. Then, when it seemed like they might at last be on the home strait, she had insisted on dramatic renderings of the usual bedtime stories. This is a recent precedent set by Richard, who moves heaven and earth to get home in time to supervise the bedtime routine. Sometimes, Jasmine has told them, he makes Lilly almost sick with laughter as he leaps round the bedroom brandishing a comical selection of props, draped in makeshift costumes and declaiming the various characters' voices. Even between them, Carmel and Jade had managed to produce only the palest shadow of his performance. Lilly, in high dudgeon, went on to be awkward about the sleeping arrangements, eventually consenting to a nest of duvets and pillows on an area of Carmel's floor, which had been hastily raked clear of detritus. In contrast Mikey went to bed without a fuss, as though already resigned to the fact that, against a family full of women, his only chance is to follow the path of least resistance. Carmel, translucent with exhaustion, had crept into bed as soon as the children were asleep, regarding Lilly—metamorphosed in repose from harridan to cherub—with troubled ambivalence from her pillow.

The Mere is strangely energised on Saturday nights. Whilst its weekday current is dilatory—a muted, lackadaisical flow—on Saturday the stockpile of its workaday economies is released in a pent-up surge. The boom and throb of a dozen sub-woofers echo around the cul-de-sacs and tenements. A cacophony of shrill voices pierces the night. People are pressed into rooms, wedged into stairwells, talking, laughing, drinking, smoking manically as though to make up for the dearth of the week. Cars come and go with a roar and a squeal, delivering party-goers, Pilsner, pizza. People on foot clatter and chatter along the pavements, revitalised, as though awoken from an enchanted sleep. The social club is lit up like a beacon, its car-park jammed with vehicles, its various bars and function rooms packed with fast-drinking revellers. Sadie is there, of course, on her habitual bar stool, a large glass of wine in her hand.

The convenience store is doing brisk trade, and there's a queue outside the takeaway, but Jade walks away from the lights and the people, down the slope past the lock-up garages, and onto the recreation field. She lets the night envelop her, sensing, rather than seeing the grey macadam ribbon of path through the night-blackened grass as it takes her to the bridge. She pulls the darkness around her like a cloak, a veil behind which she will perform her task, shielded by its dimness. In the middle of the field, where the broken lamp post is, the wind is at its most crazy, careering around the periphery of the field in ever decreasing circles, arriving here in a twisting vortex. It lifts Jade's hair off her shoulders and fills the loose folds of her shirt in billows. The sky is the colour of churned mud photographed in sepia. A million frantic secrets are whispered between the agitated trees. Beneath her feet, the grate and grind of broken glass makes her wince, even though her feet are practically healed and the soles of her trainers are thick. Across the weir, the fallen tree makes a bulky, grotesque shadow; the lighter barbs of its exposed roots feebly pale as the occasional glimmer of moonlight pierces the racing clouds. Here and there stray moonbeams glance off the water of the weir, but the river upstream slides dark and sullen.

She crosses the bridge and turns right, taking the track that leads up past the golf course, towards the viaduct. Presently she arrives at a place where, between the path and the course, there is a rough area of long grass and native trees, a place where two people, lying low, would be hidden from view and well out of earshot. The thick darkness and wildly thrashing wind makes the spot eerie and although the wind is warm Jade finds that her skin is puckered into goose bumps. The grass, insubstantial as feathers, bends to the will of the wind but the trees creak and groan in complaint, and their leaves tremble in anxious multitudes. Jade trembles too, and her innards flutter as though filled with trapped insects. It is impossible that she could be observed or heard here in this enclave of wilderness yet she feels as self-conscious as though she were on a stage, illuminated by a hundred spotlights and amplified by as many microphones.

For a few moments she peers around her, squinting into the gloom. Her face, lit up momentarily by a stray glimmer from the shrouded moon, is white, and her dark hair, roiled and restless in the wind, whips around her head and shoulders like snakes. She hesitates, on the threshold of a new unmapped territory, led to it by unexpected by-ways and surprising landmarks—coincidences, signs—but now needing to make the last leap based on nothing more than her choosing to believe.

She wades a little way into the area, imagining Spencer's long imperious stride and Carmel's reluctant steps behind him, and sinks down into the grass. It has long recovered, of course, in a way that Carmel will not do. The night was still, then, which now is energetic and portentous. The ground had been parched, baked hard, the grass as dry as straw perhaps, sharp-bladed and uncomfortable, whereas now it is soft and yielding, squeaky with moisture. Nothing, in fact, is the same except— she must believe—the presence of an all-seeing, benevolent eye. She re-treads, in thought, her fantastical journey, recreating in her mind's eye the earnest petition in the sequestered room, the happy, unperturbed faces that had emerged from it. She repeats in her head the words of the velvet-voiced woman, sees Mikey's silhouette on the golden lane and his skid, all arms and legs and silt-dulled hair, into Jasmine's arms. She hears the pounding feet on the road behind her, and smells the lemon-scented softness of Ryan's shirt. All these were real. It—He—was real.

Her voice, when she tries it, is snatched away by the wind, unnaturally strangled, hesitant and self-conscious. 'It wasn't *fair*,' she hisses, but immediately recognises the voice of her old familiar in its habitual complaint. She swallows hard and licks her lips to try again. 'Please,' she says at last, in a small voice, 'make it come right. I believe you can do it.'

It feels like all there is to say. The simplicity of it calms her. Presently she lies down in the grass as she imagines Carmel will have done, and as the dull brown clouds skim over her and the scandalised grass susurrates on every side she puts herself in her sister's place, and accepts, along with her, whatever consequence may come.

Later, she finds her face is wet with weeping, and she is spent as though from a fit, but an irrepressible flame of hope warms her heart as she walks home.

LILLY'S SCREAMS WAKE the whole house. She runs into Jade's room shrieking like a banshee, her mouth a red gash, her eyes wide and stricken. 'Carmel ...' she manages to gasp out.

Carmel's bed is soaked with blood, purple and viscous, pooling beneath her hips. Its dark, iron tide creeps down the sheet and lards itself around the outside of her body as though in a confused attempt to get back in. Her puny thighs are stained red. The rest of her is smeared red where her hands have unconsciously spread the sticky gore in the night. Her short, flimsy night dress is rusty, in places crusty, with blood. Against its livid brightness Carmel herself is bleached, leached of pigmentation. Her belly is concave and white as marble between the promontories of her hips, their porcelain paleness all but visible under the tissue-like membrane of her skin. Her eyes are opaque and dull, like sea-glass. Her lips, her nail-beds, the rims of her eyes beneath their fringe of pale lashes, are white.

Sadie staggers into the room. In contrast to her daughter she is a bright, chaotic palette of colour. Last night's eye makeup is still bright but sliding onto the lower regions of her face. Her newly dyed hair is too dark and stark against the mottled milkiness of her shoulders and chest. The ruffled nylon and lace of her scarlet robe is an artificial echo of her daughter's organically painted attire.

'Call an ambulance,' Jade shouts at her mother. 'For God's sake, call an ambulance!'

SUNDAY IS A damp, sombre day, grey with moody cloud. The air is laden with rain that will not come. Jennifer spends the day in her garden, tackling at last the rampant spread of weeds in the borders, pulling out the spent wallflowers and staking up the wind-damaged delphiniums. She hoses down the decking and sprays it with a proprietary brand of cleaner, watching the slick, green slime lift away under its caustic influence. She cleans the furniture with hot water and a cream cleaner and rinses it off, satisfied by the newly gleaming whiteness of the PVC. She goes to the garden centre and buys trays of annuals. It is late in the season really, and the plants that remain on the wooden stages are past their best, but she chooses the best of the bunch and spends the rest of the day filling the blank, grey soil with life.

She and Kenny had spent the rest of the previous day and a good deal of the night going over the same acre of ground; he pointing out signs of life and potential in their marriage plot, she patiently indicating the thin, infertile quality of the soil, the arid conditions, the bleak, barren situation. As she had expected he had used every argument at his disposal, being by turns blisteringly argumentative, charming, imploring, martyred and broken. To each of these alternating sallies she had been equally implacable; calm, kind but firm. It had not been easy. She had been wholly convinced by his sincerity, and surprised by it also; the genuineness of his grief and dismay could not be doubted, and it made her wretchedly sad because it was just too late.

Now, as she works in the garden, she is aware of him in the house, supposedly gathering his things, making arrangements. Periodically she finds him staring at her mournfully from an upstairs window or creeping towards her across the foaming decking with an expression like a whipped dog, bringing a mug of tea.

'You're not listening to me,' she says to him at one point, as patiently as one might speak to a confused child.

'What do you mean?'

'You're only thinking about what *you* want, and you're trying to make me want the same. You're not listening to what *I* want. What I have *already decided* that I want. Don't you get it? The more you try to make me change my mind the clearer it is to me that I am doing the right thing.'

He shakes his head. 'What about what *I* want?'

She turns from him then, and picks up her trowel. 'We've had twenty years of what *you* want, Kenny, haven't we?'

Towards the middle of the afternoon he goes, at her recommendation, to see Mr Pickering.

'Much better now,' she says, 'than tomorrow in the office. Don't you think?'

'You just want me to lose everything I have,' he says bitterly.

'Don't be silly,' she says.

He is standing behind her as she kneels on the grass. 'Please Jenny,' he says. '*Please ...*' He drops down behind her and gathers the loose pleats of her gardening sweater into his desperate hands.

'No,' she says, scrambling to her feet, appalled at what she has reduced him to, appalled at herself for so reducing him, astonished by her own cruelty. She teeters between two dreadful futures; one with him in her life, one with him on her conscience.

'You'd better go,' she says to the top of his drooping head. She is glad that he cannot see her face.

He is gone a long time. The smell of next door's roast has wafted well away by the time she has finished the garden. She can hear the theme tune of *Countryfile* from the neighbour's open window. She puts away the tools, hoses off her wellingtons and rinses her gloves, pegging them on the line to dry. Inside, she peels off her gardening gear and puts it straight into the washing machine. She pads upstairs in her underwear and runs herself a deep, hot bath. It is almost dark when she gets out of the bath, cleaning and drying it carefully with an old towel she keeps for the purpose in the Vanity unit. The house is silent and dark as she wanders into her bedroom to pull on pyjamas and a dressing gown. As she closes the curtains she sees that Kenny's car is still missing. Crossing the landing she glances into the spare bedroom; it is empty. His cases, boxes, holdalls, suits, shoes are all gone. He is gone.

On the mat in the hallway a faint gleam from the streetlight picks out the forlorn sheen of his latchkey.

She sinks down on the top stair and cries then, for a long time.

In the morning, when she lifts the dry cleaner's cellophane off her suit, she finds that it has been slashed to ribbons.

CARMEL, CLUTCHING FEVERISHLY at Jade, begs her sister to come in the ambulance as the paramedics settle her on the gurney and prepare to wheel her out to the ambulance. But she is over-ruled by Sadie, of course, who thrusts herself into the nucleus of the crisis, almost, indeed, onto the stretcher itself, so proprietarily does she insist on walking by it, even though doing so makes their progress down the narrow, overgrown path scarcely achievable.

The paramedics shut the patient inside, firmly excluding Sadie, deaf to her protests that Carmel is a minor whose human rights are being violated, while they ask some searching questions and set up a drip. Sadie paces furiously around in the road, smoking voraciously and regaling the neighbours—who have all emerged at the sound of the sirens, to partake of whatever left-overs of emergency there might be— with the gory details of the morning's calamity. Dishevelled, wearing a disreputable old tracksuit and last night's makeup, she is the picture of anguished tragedy.

'Why doesn't she shut up?' Jade asks herself angrily. 'Doesn't she realise what has happened? Everyone else will put two and two together, even if *she* doesn't.' For this is a catastrophe that Jade feels should be kept small and insignificant, in the nether region of obscurity, where its chief protagonists will best recover without the aid of the public gaze.

While her mother has wrung her hands and wept and wailed, Jade has hastily dressed herself and the children, telephoned her sister and summoned Mr Mole's taxi to take them to the hospital. Her body functions automatically while her innards quail at the enormity of what

583

has occurred and the possibility—ungraspable, terrifying, but how else explained—that it is connected to her previous night's foray into the wind-tossed night. The sense of having unlocked an unpredictable power—one which, once acknowledged, might demand more, might go further than she had envisaged—is very real. Her foot, placed so tentatively on the experimental bridge of faith, trembles.

Later, they sit in a sequestered relatives' room while Carmel is in theatre. Sadie, exhausted by a vociferous display of maternal grief, as well as a late and alcohol-fuelled night, dozes awkwardly in the most comfortable chair. Jasmine and Jade exchange white-gilled glances of anxiety, their thoughts running along the same lines: the consequences—physical, emotional and legal—that could accrue from Carmel's condition. The condition itself they do not name, using euphemisms supplied by the medical staff; haemorrhage, menorrhagia, endometrial hyperplasia, endometriosis.

Matt, sitting a little apart, his elbows on his knees, squirms at the gynaecological terminology but doggedly remains even when Richard takes Lilly and Mikey home. He feels, with a sinking heart, that he is in some way responsible. He runs over in his mind again and again that hot, hectic night by the bridge, Spencer's volatile mood, his imperative stride into the twilight and Carmel's reluctance to follow. He recalls the wince with which she had lowered herself onto the grass afterwards. He remembers too, the night of the fire; Skinner in the mist crouching over Carmel's body, the sudden, guilty surge of his own desire. The memory makes him start to his feet, mutter an excuse and leave the room, and he paces around for a while, breathing in the hot antiseptic smell of the wards. There is a constant coming and going along the marbled, pistachio-green corridors. Patients shuffle past him trundling their drip-stands, or stand at windows staring dazedly out into the gloomy day. Doctors walk briskly from one place to another, their white coats flapping. Nurses and porters scurry along on important errands. Visitors are beginning to assemble outside the wards.

Eventually Matt finds a place to lean where he is not in the way, close to a double doorway that leads into a quadrangle, and stares out at the raised beds. Only one short week has passed since he was reunited with his father. It has been a week of squash tournaments and crazy golf and bicycle rides and hanging out at the farmhouse, almost a holiday, before the excitement of starting work at Pickering's. It has blotted from his memory those unhappy weeks with Spencer, the ambivalence of his feelings for Carmel, the veiled threat from Skinner's dad and from Maxwell, the disappearance of Skinner himself. Now those two seemingly irreconcilable worlds have collided, the past hitting the future like carriages on a derailed train.

As though conjured by the thought, Skinner walks down the corridor towards him. A cleaner Skinner, though—if possible—leaner, dressed in new clothes and holding in front of him with awkward ceremony an enormous bouquet of flowers. Even as he covers the few yards between them Matt can see that Skinner has changed in more than appearance. He has lost that sneaking, cringing demeanour. He walks tall, with his shoulders back, as though some unsupportable weight has been lifted away from him. Assuming he has come to visit Carmel, and putting aside the question of his disappearance, Matt steps forward and puts his hand on Skinner's arm.

'She's still in theatre,' he says.

For an instant, shades of the old Skinner flicker across his face and in his eyes. There is a slight recoil, the sense of a veil being hastily drawn down. One hand relinquishes the flower stems and a finger nail strays towards the sharp, yellow teeth to be gnawed. But then it is gone, and Skinner's pale eyes meet Matt's in frank encounter.

'Who is?'

'Who's this, Stuart?' A tall, tousle-haired man at Skinner's side enquires with a genial smile.

'I'm a friend from ...' Matt hesitates, 'school,' he says eventually. 'Another friend of ours is having an operation. I thought that's who you'd come to see.'

'Who's having an operation?' Skinner asks.

'Carmel,' Matt says, and then, forestalling further enquiry, 'girl-stuff.'

585

Skinner's head swivels on his thin neck and his face takes on a slightly bullish expression. 'Is Spencer here?'

Matt snorts derisively. 'What do *you* think?'

The boys look at each other then, with the understanding of men. In a few short weeks, they have come that far.

'I've come to visit my mum,' Skinner offers.

'You found her then? That's where the papers said you'd gone.'

Skinner throws a smile over his shoulder at the man behind him who has taken up a position a pace or two away to check his phone. 'Yeah!'

More visitors are arriving, bringing flowers and fruit, newspapers, toiletries. They make a ragged queue outside one of the wards.

'Where did you go to, Skinner?' Matt asks. 'I know you went over the weir.'

'Yeah!' Skinner says again. He shifts the bouquet to the other hand. 'I holed up in one of them garages for a bit,' he says, 'and then made a bivvie out past the viaduct. Went into town now and again to scrounge some food. It was all right; warm, dry—like camping. Then that rain came. Wasn't so good after that.' He smiles ruefully.

Matt takes a step closer to him, 'And what about your dad?' he asks in a low voice.

'Oh,' Skinner's eyes slide off Matt's for the first time. 'Don't need to worry about him,' he mutters. A shrill bell indicates the commencement of visiting time, and Skinner and his friend walk into the ward.

When Matt gets back into the relatives' room the women have been joined by a man in blue scrubs and white wellingtons.

'Considerable loss of blood,' he is saying, 'requiring a sizeable transfusion. But no permanent damage, I'm pleased to say. With rest and a good, wholesome diet we should see a complete recovery.'

Jade slides off the edge of her chair to her knees.

'Oh thank you,' she says brokenly, tears pouring down her face. 'Oh thank you, thank you, thank you.'

THE WEATHER, HAVING grieved all weekend with morose, low-browed cloud and a restless, distressed wind, is inappropriately cheerful on Monday, the day of Mrs Fairlie's funeral. A bright sun shines from a jovial blue sky. Within the precincts of the crematorium birds twitter and chirrup in the trees with holiday ebullience and even the gravestones seem to recline in carefree abandon amongst the luxuriant grass.

Jennifer arrives early. A huge group is assembled outside the chapel doors and at first she thinks—wildly—that they are there to pay their respects to her mother. That they are old friends, neighbours and associates come out of the woodwork. That word must have spread in that mysterious way that it does, drawing long-forgotten acquaintances out of obscurity to accompany the departed to her last resting place. And that afterwards, with guffaws of unseemly laughter, they will regale each other with life-histories over a free buffet and sweet sherry.

'They will be disappointed then,' Jennifer thinks to herself dryly, having planned neither buffet nor sherry. She scrutinises the faces however, and soon realises that this crowd belongs to the previous bereavement. A red-eyed family, smart but over-heated in dark coats, and clutching sodden handkerchiefs, comfort each other supported by ranks of condoling sympathisers. Their empty hearse has disappeared down the one-way cortege system that meanders between the graves and terminates in an awkward junction onto a busy road. Their loved-one too, has been whisked from them onto the conveyor belt of no return. Three long, sleek limousines stand ready to transport the bereaved to their funereal meats.

With surprising swiftness the crowd disperses, and she is alone before the yawning doors of the chapel. Like the weather, the chapel seems determined to contribute no note of gloom. The doors are neither sombre nor forbidding. They are solid and wooden—cedar, perhaps, or light oak—and lead into an inoffensive vestibule. A further glass door set into a delicately etched glass partition gives access into the chapel but makes visible only her own solitary reflection standing in the sunshine. The building itself is without ornament but elegantly proportioned, windowless, built in unobjectionable pale brick, thickly planted around with innocuous evergreen shrubs. Here and there are urns of gay geraniums. In front of the door a broad, pleasant, paved area is partially sheltered by a covered walkway that projects to the grey macadam of the drive, a considerate design feature to protect mourners from the weather. A narrow, utilitarian chimney rising into the blue from the nether regions of the chapel is the only sign of the building's grim purpose but it is completely invisible from this public vantage point.

The funeral director had tried to get her to name her mother's favourite hymn, or some other suitable musical accompaniment. The minister, during a telephone interview, had suggested various bible readings and poems. To them both Jennifer had simply said, 'I just don't know. Whatever you think.' She had sketched in, as far as she knew it, her mother's biography, a few threadbare sentences. She is sorry, now that the moment has come, not to have chosen some significant words to comfort her mother on the journey, and sorrier still that her failings as a daughter have rendered her so inadequate to the task.

She is joined by Sadie and two of her daughters. One—the younger of the two—is the image of Sadie herself thirty odd years before; rather small and edibly plump, with soft smooth skin and dimpled cheeks and abundant coils of glossy dark hair. The other is nothing like Sadie; a tallish, elegant figure, that, in a man would tend to ranginess. She is fine boned, earnest-eyed, with light golden hair. Sadie introduces them briefly, Jade and Jasmine, before launching herself onto centre stage.

'Carmel's in hospital,' she announces loudly, although there is only the four of them present. 'We nearly lost her yesterday.' She clutches Jennifer's arm and displays a stricken face. 'Thank God, thank *God,* the doctor says she'll live.'

The older girl murmurs, 'Mum,' with an alarmed, awkward emphasis; this is hardly the time or the place to glory in being spared death.

Sadie steps back and recovers herself with remarkable speed. 'Where's everyone else?' she asks, brightly.

'I don't think there'll *be* anyone else,' Jennifer says.

'But surely, Michael ..?'

Jennifer shrugs. 'Who knows?'

'Here's someone now,' Sadie says, but it is only Guy and Shirley from the newspaper office. Jennifer is surprised to see Guy. Since the heroine of the river-rescue has become the victim of a vicious assault—as he had warned that she would—she had hardly expected any quarter from him. But then she realises of course that they would have 'drawn straws' in the office (and had a collection for flowers too, no doubt) and that there is nothing significant to be read into the arrival of these specific colleagues. To do Shirley credit though, she is throwing herself whole-heartedly into the role, magnificently dressed in black organza and already dabbing her black-edged handkerchief to her eye. She is the picture of abject grief, as creditable and enthusiastic a mourner as any hired mute.

'So very sorry,' she sobs, leaning towards Jennifer to offer a kiss.

Jennifer recoils. 'Thank you for coming,' she says stiffly.

Guy says nothing, but squeezes her hand, and she thinks she sees real compassion in his eye. She recalls, suddenly, that she never asked him how his visit to his father had gone. 'Perhaps he's dying,' she thinks.

A vehicle is approaching and they stiffen themselves for the arrival of the hearse, but it is only the Bridge House minibus. Mrs Terry, in an immaculate grey wool suit and lipstick a shocking shade of puce, steps out, followed by Rosie and an impossibly stooped rather corpulent elderly lady in a sombre blue dress, a sprigged Alice-band and a pair of bedroom slippers. As she is helped from the bus she maintains a constant stream of urgent verbiage that occupies Rosie's whole attention and makes it unnecessary for her to acknowledge—or be acknowledged by—any of the other mourners.

'Mrs Baker,' Mrs Terry says discreetly to Jennifer. 'Your mother's particular friend.'

Jennifer introduces Sadie and her girls and walks over to shake hands with Mrs Baker. The old woman is so bent over that she has to screw her head round to look up at Jennifer. As a result her eye, swivelled in its socket and revealing much greyish, veined white, is unnerving.

'I'm so glad you're ...' Jennifer begins, but Mrs Baker interrupts her.

'She *never* put smalls on the line; that wouldn't have done at all, no, and I never did afterwards. No, it would never do, it would never do,' Mrs Baker says in an imperative tone and with earnest, tortured eyes, as though trying to convey some vital sub-text.

'Of course not,' Jennifer says, looking with bewilderment at Rosie.

Rosie smiles and takes Mrs Baker's hand, 'There now, there now, Pearl,' she soothes.

The vicar makes his approach, his black surplice flapping around his legs in the lively breeze, revealing brown shoes imperfectly polished. He holds out his hand to Jennifer, who takes it reluctantly; it is ice cold and almost fleshless. His head is bald, just a few tenacious strands of iron grey hair cling to it. Lifted by the wind, they dance on end like charmed, emaciated, monochrome snakes.

'It's almost time,' he says to her in an undertone. 'The cortege is making its approach. The mourners should take their seats. If the chief mourners,' he gives a tiny cough, 'hold back, they can follow the departed into the chapel.'

Mrs Terry, Rosie and Mrs Baker, Sadie and her girls, Guy and Shirley step out of the sunshine and are swallowed by the cool shadow of the porch. As they push open the glazed door, Jennifer hears strains of cello music floating from within. Her throat constricts and she feels the pin-prick of tears behind her eyeballs. She is swamped by utter loneliness as she waits alone on the empty paving stones for her mother to come. The crunch of obsequious tyres on the tarmac heralds the hearse's approach and just at that moment she hears hurried footsteps approaching from the other direction, beyond a grassy mound. Mr Pickering and Kenny march into view. Mr Pickering has Kenny firmly by the elbow. Kenny looks wretched; bloodshot eyes and a deathly pallor are not compensated for by his smart dark suit and immaculately knotted black tie. Mr Pickering parks Kenny at Jennifer's side exactly as a kindergarten teacher might position a pre-schooler for a role in a play, gives him a speaking, deliberate look and then disappears into the chapel just as the bearers emerge from their vehicle and open the tailgate.

Kenny opens his mouth and inhales but before he can speak Jennifer says, 'Do not even *start* to make this about *you.*'

The coffin is surprisingly small. Her mother had always appeared to her, in life, such an imposing figure; her strength and will-power giving her formidable stature. The men raise it to their shoulders so easily that Jennifer wonders if it can really contain a body at all. It makes her sick to think of her mother's limp unresisting body jerking and shifting around inside, her teeth dislodged, her hat knocked askew, and she wonders with a sudden macabre flight of imagination if it is in some way restrained, in the way that delicate goods are for transit, by rigid plastic strapping to the wrists and ankles, or packed in polystyrene chippings. She pushes the thought away as the men steady their burden and carry it past them into the chapel. She concentrates instead on the coffin; the fine grain of the wood, the ornate handles, the arrangement of white lilies and purple iris on its lid. As it passes them she hears Kenny breathe out, a huge, pent up billow, and she realises that he has been holding his breath. It makes her relent a little and she takes his arm, but the sleek veneer and polished brass of the coffin makes as substantial a barrier between Mrs Fairlie and her daughter as the one that divides Jennifer and Kenny as they follow it into the chapel.

The interior is unadorned and bland. Carefully positioned lights scan the ceiling, as English people do when confronted with displays of emotion. The mourners have considerately spread themselves around as if in doing so they might appear more numerous. The cello music fades as the vicar intones prayers and the coffin in placed on a raised slab of beautifully patinated timber. Jennifer and Kenny take their seats on the front pew and the attendants retire. The voice of the vicar rises and falls. His words are as meaningless as wind in a chimney; hollow, chasing themselves in circles, trapped and at the same time maddeningly random, without meaning or beauty or comfort. She takes no notice at all of what he is saying, or of the building, or the other people, or even of the casket that contains her mother, but sits with her eyes fixed on her knees, which tremble involuntarily against the silk lining of her second-best suit. Mingled with the vicar's litany is Mrs Baker's muted diatribe, an antiphonic narrative whispered into the hush, punctuating the psalms and making a plangent undertow to the vicar's brief, glutinous sermon. At one point they stand, and Kenny's hand under her elbow raises Jennifer to her feet. They sing *Abide with Me*, their voices thin and reedy in the empty air. Only Mr Pickering and Guy make any serious attempt at it, and Shirley, in a surprisingly velvet contralto. There are more prayers and then the tribute: a ridiculously vague, woolly-edged and rambling homage to a woman whom none of them had known. They stand again for the committal, and it is at this juncture that Jennifer becomes conscious of a disturbance at the back of the chapel. She hears the squeak of a door, low, imperative voices, a dog whining, and then Michael's voice, inappropriately loud and dangerously taut with emotion shouting, 'She's my *fucking* MOTHER!'

Jennifer closes her eyes and sags forward until her forehead is almost resting on the rail that holds the service books and hymnals. There is a breathy wheeze, an anguished squeal as tooth-jarring as an acutely injured animal, and then the music of the accordion begins to swoop and soar above their heads like a flock of nightingales. It is a eulogy of sound that fills the lofty heights of the chapel and tugs at their hearts' strings, an angel throng of beautiful, mournful, iridescent notes. The vicar, arrested mid-spiel, is waiting for a signal from Jennifer. She nods her head slightly, he presses a hidden switch and the curtains begin to close.

Walking out of the chapel feels like a betrayal; she knows that her mother is still there, behind the curtain. She will always be there, her mouth a hard line of disapproval. But somewhere deeper—buried—a soft core of caring that she never has and never will, now, reach. It is a shame—it is Jennifer's shame—but she dare not dwell on it. It is done, now.

The hearse, of course, has gone. The funeral director's men are arranging the meagre floral tributes on an area reserved for them across the drive. Jennifer moves to stand next to Michael who is hunkered down next to Snowy, stroking the dog's narrow head, whispering soothing reassurances. He is oblivious to the short line of people who file past and shake Jennifer's hand. At least, she thinks, he is wearing the new clothes she has bought him, and he looks clean. She makes no effort to introduce him or Kenny, who hovers behind her, conscious of his ambivalent status. Stationed between the two of them, she feels lonelier than ever. Presently she walks across to inspect the flowers, reading the cards with an appearance of intense interest, half hoping that when she turns back they will all have gone, whisked away by the warm wind. But when she turns they are all still there, the summer breezes winnowing their hair and tugging away their sombre smiles. In a different setting their studiedly cordial greetings might lend themselves to an august garden party on the lichen-soft terrace of a stately home.

Mr Pickering has taken renewed custody of Kenny with grim authority, and Jennifer wonders what her husband's fate will be. Clearly he has been taken in hand but it seems improbable, after such a display of truancy and malingering, that Mr Pickering will allow him to retain his position.

Guy stands a little apart, his hands behind his back and his eyes fixed on an invisible point in the distance, physically present but psychologically at a respectful distance. Shirley, in contrast, circulates freely, glad-handing and making rather pointed enquiries as to people's relationship to the deceased. Of all of them Rosie seems the most moved, and has to hand Mrs Baker to Mrs Terry's reluctant care while she attempts to regain her composure. She is rummaging in her handbag for a fresh tissue. Mr Pickering offers his handkerchief and she takes it with a sad smile. When she is collected, they begin to talk, quietly, away from the others.

Sadie has quickly appropriated Michael and they sit on the grassy mound and smoke cigarettes, attracting disapproving glances from the funeral director and the vicar, who is preparing to take his leave. Michael seems bewildered but not distressed. The foregoing episode in the chapel has been reduced or eclipsed in his mind to an aberration of memory or a bad dream. He surveys the assembled people on the paving stones with a certain quizzical distance, as though they are projections on a screen. Only the hard, warm head of Snowy under his hand is reliably real to him.

'Where are you staying?' Sadie asks him. 'We must get together. It's been too long.'

He turns his eyes towards her, waiting a long time before answering, 'There's a refuge at a church on Bridge Street.' He waits to see whether his words will drop like stones into an empty pool.

'I know Bridge Street,' Sadie nods.

'But Snowy and me like to be able to see the sky,' Michael concludes. He looks up at it, now, garnering reassurance from its wide, open, blue vastness.

'Oh so do I,' Sadie gushes. Her daughters look at her askance; they would never have described their mother as the outdoor type.

'I know that place, on Bridge Street,' Jade puts in. 'Do you know Patrick?' Michael looks at her narrowly. The sight of her seems to add to his uncertainty, as though time has played a trick on him and whisked him backwards thirty years.

'Sadie? *Sadie?*' He reaches out a tentative hand to see if she is real.

'No Michael, *I'm* Sadie,' Sadie laughs, a little shrilly. She puts her hand on his arm and jerks it back. 'You remember me, don't you? I lived next door for *years*, with Annie. You remember Annie?'

Michael nods, but keeps his eyes fixed on Jade.

'That's Jade, my middle girl. And *that* one's my oldest, *Jasmine*.' She speaks the name with such significance, laden with latent meaning, it is impossible—even for Michael—to ignore. He looks at Jasmine where she stands on the path at the bottom of the knoll, and she looks at him.

Having them both in view makes it suddenly so obvious to Jennifer, even from across the path. They have the same colouring and bone structure and spare, lithe figure. They share the same other-worldy expression of eye suggesting an inner life of more than ordinary potency. Jennifer sees at once what Sadie hopes will come of it, and as quickly how hopeless it is. She strides across the paving slabs. 'Time for us to move on, I'm afraid. The next group will be here soon.' She resists—just—the temptation to clap her hands like a teacher marshalling her pupils, or a farmer's wife her hens.

'Is there a wake?' Sadie asks with an eager smile, scrambling to her feet and brushing grass-cuttings from her skirt. 'Funerals always make me thirsty.'

'No, I'm afraid not. I didn't expect anybody to come,' Jennifer says firmly.

'You're kidding!' Sadie remonstrates, looking to Michael for support. 'We've got to send your mum off properly, haven't we, Michael?'

'Mum had jasmine in her garden,' Michael says with a frown, as though trying to connect up the ragged edges of memory. 'A shrub with a little white flower. She made tea out of it. It smelt lovely in the evenings.'

'Yes, it *did*,' Sadie says emphatically. She can see her opportunity slipping away from her. 'That's why I picked it, Michael.' Her words are weighted down; her eyes bore into Michael's confusion.

'You picked the jasmine?'

'I picked the *name*, because it reminded me of the flowers, in the evening, especially *one* evening.'

'Come on Sadie,' Jennifer takes her arm and begins to draw her away. 'I'll give you a lift home.'

'I came with Jasmine,' Sadie remonstrates, resisting. Jennifer almost drags Sadie through the little crowd. 'What do you think you're playing at?' she hisses. 'What good will it do? You can see what he's like! Would you really saddle her with *him*?'

'I wasn't thinking of *her*,' Sadie rejoins sulkily.

'Well perhaps you ought to.'

Mrs Terry is extending a general invitation to Bridge House for a funeral tea. 'We'd be most glad to welcome you all,' she cries, 'and also of course,' she lowers her voice and steps in front of Jennifer and Sadie as they cross the slabs, 'there's the matter of your mother's personal effects. Her room ...'

'I'm afraid I can't come today,' Jennifer barks, side-stepping the obstruction. The prospect of going there, of collecting those few pathetic belongings, of confronting the cruelty of it, is too much. 'I'll come over soon,' she offers, over her shoulder.

Mr Pickering and Kenny walk away together. The Bridge House minibus rolls up to collect the inmates. As Mrs Baker is loaded she gets stuck on a snag in her story, 'A bit awkward with his trombone, his trombone, a bit awkward,' she repeats as Rosie and the driver haul her into the vehicle. Guy and Shirley stroll away towards the car-park. Jade, Jasmine and Michael are left together in the sunshine, their awkward relation tying them in place. Jasmine and Michael are mirror-images of pale disorientation, a bridge reflected in water; perfectly detailed, showing nuances of shade and light, arching spans leaping elegantly across the shimmering void, but insubstantial, connecting nothing with nothing, it will break up in the first breath of breeze. Jade shifts slightly. It is enough to shatter the image and they are released.

'Very nice to have met you,' Jasmine says softly. 'Goodbye.'

Then the area in front of the chapel is empty, and only Michael remains with Snowy on the grassy mound. In just a few moments the next party of mourners will arrive.

'Ah well, Snowy, lad,' says Michael. 'Ah well.'

JASMINE AND JADE are slightly late for visiting time. Most of the other patients in Carmel's ward have attracted visitors. They perch on plastic chairs and listen while their visitee regales them *sotto voce* with the technicolour intricacies of their fellow patients' illnesses. It is the only news they have to offer. The outside world seems so very remote and it does not touch them. It is astonishing how intimate these languishing strangers have become in the sequestered ward, confidences exchanged between beds, the oblique angles and intervening curtains making it easy to share the most personal of details.

Carmel lies pale and still in her bed, her eviscerated body making hardly a wrinkle under the covers. She is as white as the sheets except for two hectic blotches on her cheek bones. Her hair is lifeless and transparent on the pillow. Her eyes and teeth are too big for her. When she closes her eyes the lids can barely make the stretch. Occasionally she passes her tongue over dry, cracked lips. Jade puts a spare nightdress, toiletries and a magazine in Carmel's locker. Jasmine produces enthusiastically coloured-in 'get well soon' cards from Lilly and Mikey and puts them over the rails of the bed-head. They pass on messages from Sadie and Richard.

'And Matt says to say hello, too,' Jasmine says. 'He was here yesterday, you know, but he wouldn't come onto the ward. I suppose it's awkward, for a boy ...'

'Spencer ought to come,' Jade says darkly.

Carmel's reply is quiet. 'I don't want him to,' she says.

599

A pouch of clear liquid is being dispensed drip by drip into the cannula in Carmel's hand; Jade wants to squeeze it, to accelerate the rehydration process. Beneath the bed, another, larger pouch, dangling like an udder, collects waste product the colour of topaz.

'Lucky thing,' Jade jokes, to disperse the tension, 'getting intravenous Lucozade!' Carmel smiles wanly, and reaches for her sisters' hands. Two tears well from the opals of her eyes and roll down her cheeks.

'Don't cry Carmel,' Jasmine soothes. 'It's all over now. It wasn't your fault.'

'I feel so *sad.*' Carmel cries without sobbing. Her body seems to lack the energy for it. The tears just ooze from her eyes, clear and slightly viscid, almost as though channelled directly from the drip-pouch. 'But glad, too, and then ...' she swallows, 'you know ... *bad* about feeling glad.'

'Of course you do,' Jade says, wiping Carmel's tears away with a tissue. 'But it wasn't your choice, none of it was. Not the beginning or the end. You must remember that.'

'Yes,' Carmel nods, 'I'll try.'

The three sisters remain in silence for a few moments in the hot, humming ward, their hands joined. Their communion in those quiet minutes is more frankly comprehensive—their sympathy more alive—than it has ever been.

Carmel appears to draw some vital element from her two sisters. Presently she stirs a little in the bed. Her colour seems improved. There is a glimmer of animation in her eye.

'That lady down there,' she says confidentially, 'the one with the terrible swollen face and bruises,' Jasmine and Jade follow Carmel's glance, 'it's Skinner's mother.'

Jasmine starts to her feet. 'Oh God, no!' she says.

'She was brought in from another ward this morning. She's had her jaw all wired up. I heard them say her name, otherwise I wouldn't have recognised her.'

'Oh God,' Jasmine says again.

'He must have found her,' Jade observes. 'Bastard.'

'I think ...' Jasmine begins, 'I think I probably ought to go and speak to her.'

Later, in the car, Jasmine says, 'Shall I run you home?'

It is half past five. The traffic is backed up at every junction and roundabout. From the hospital the Mere lies in the opposite direction to the farmhouse.

'Can I come home with you?' Jade asks, not particularly because she wants to save Jasmine the trouble of the extra journey, although she is glad to do that too, but mainly because she doesn't want to separate from her sister.

'Of course you can,' smiles Jasmine, seeming to understand.

As they wait in a long line at the traffic lights by the college Jade says, 'That man, at the funeral ...'

'Yes.'

'Mum must have known he'd be there. Do you think she really wanted you to meet him like that?'

'I presume so.'

'I wonder why. I mean, you'd think she would have warned you. Did she?'

Jasmine laughs, a little bitterly. 'No! I wouldn't have gone, if I'd known.'

'And how did it feel?'

Jasmine considers. 'I didn't feel anything. It's like you just told Carmel. Some things we don't choose, they happen to us and they aren't our responsibility.'

'But *he* chose. He should take responsibility for *you*.'

601

The lights turn green and Jasmine at last gets through and on to the main road. 'I'm sure,' she says, as she accelerates away, 'that's what Mum was hoping.'

'Ah.' Light dawns in Jade's understanding. 'Then you don't think ..?'

'No, I don't think it was about *me* at all.' Jasmine says.

Large houses and fields speed by. Jade opens the window. 'Have you ever missed your father?'

'I used to think I did, but I know now that I was just missing love; not especially a father's love.'

'I just wanted someone to be in charge and make things right,' Jade offers. 'Mum never seemed able to.'

'Fathers can't always, either. But it's what every child wants, deep down.' Jasmine slows and begins to indicate. To the right Bridge House basks in its grounds. Mrs Fairlie's funereal tributes have been laid on the terrace to be visible from the dining room window. They are a sad, inadequate remembrance of the former resident. Beyond Bridge House is the old stone bridge over the river, and the farmhouse.

'I think we must all be children, deep down,' Jade says. 'It's *still* what I want.'

Jasmine pulls the car into the drive and turns off the engine.

'I don't know what it is,' she says, turning to Jade, 'but something has happened to us. We've never talked like this in the past, have we?'

Jade is winding up her window. 'It's better though, isn't it?'

Jasmine nods. 'Oh yes. Did it start with Mikey?'

'I think so. His dip in the river washed all the crap away, somehow.' There is much more that Jade could say, but the feeling that putting it into words might jinx it, or—worse—might reveal it in a ludicrous light, makes her leave it unsaid, even here, even now.

Jasmine grimaces, 'It all washed onto Skinner's mother, poor thing.'

'Is that what she said?'

'No, actually, she said it was all right. It was over at last, she said.'

'There you are, then.'

There are two strange cars parked in the lane outside the farmhouse. Richard's is in the driveway. As the door yields to Jasmine's key a gale of masculine laughter roars from the kitchen to meet them. The hall is an assault course of abandoned school bags and lunch boxes. They pick their way across it. Jasmine glances into the lounge on her way past. Mikey and Lilly are eating chicken nuggets and chips from trays. They grin at her with mouths full of minced beak.

'That's a treat!' Jasmine says wryly. She is not a fan of convenience foods.

'Richard took us to the supermarket and said we could pick anything we wanted,' Lilly says, through semi-masticated mechanically-extracted poultry sinew. 'A main course and a *treat*.'

'Lucky children. What did you pick?'

'Lilly chose these nuggets and a chocolate muffin,' Mikey reports. 'I wanted a bag of crisps and a can of shandy but Richard said crisps aren't a main course and so we *negotiated* ...' he pauses, giving them time to be impressed with his new word, 'so I got these and *two* cans of shandy. But one's for another day.'

Lilly folds her arms, frowns and turns the corners of her mouth down. 'No fair,' she huffs, 'I should've got *two* muffins.' The effect of her protest is marred by the comedic smear of tomato ketchup around her mouth.

The girls laugh. 'Learn to *negotiate* Lilly!'

Richard emerges from the kitchen and pulls the door closed behind him. He is flushed and ebullient, kissing Jasmine with rapture.

'Just a minute,' she protests, struggling out of his arms and taking up a position of mock outrage. 'Where's *my* treat?'

Richard waggles his eyebrows. 'See me later,' he says with a lewd wink.

'Looks to me that Mikey's not the only one drinking shandy!' Jade observes, beginning to pick up the things from the floor.

'Shrewd woman!' Richard cries with delight. He turns to Jasmine again, twirling her round in a circle. He speaks quietly, quickly, with barely suppressed excitement 'Darling! You'll never guess what's happened! Who do you think is in that kitchen?' He cocks his head towards the door behind him.

'I don't know! Sounds like a crowd ...'

'It *is* a crowd,' he agrees, 'a very select and important one and they all have something in common.'

'What is it Richard? I can't guess!'

'They all work for Pickering's Light Engineering!'

Jasmine stares at him. 'Is Mr Pickering in the kitchen? He was at the funeral today, too. How odd. Why is he here?'

'Oh baby, can't you guess? He's given me my old job back!' Richard is ecstatic.

'Your old job? Oh but darling that's *wonderful!* How come? I mean, what about ...'

'The new chap didn't quite fit the bill. He's still on the team but the august responsibilities of Sales Manager went to his head and he sort of lost it.'

'Lost his head?'

'Nearly, I gather. But isn't it just *great?* Come on in and have some wine, and you can tell me about the funeral, and how Carmel is, and join in the party.' He flings the door of the kitchen open then, and ushers them both inside.

'Wine for my lady and her beautiful sister!' he cries, striding over to the fridge.

John Pickering is lounging against the kitchen worktop, smiling broadly. He still wears his funeral suit but the tie is in his pocket and his shirt collar is open. There's a can of lager in his hand. He has the satisfied look of a man dispensing largesse with a liberal hand. Matt and another man are seated at the table. Matt wears his newly bought work clothes; smart trousers and a shirt. The collar is a little too large for his neck, which shows white between the newly cropped line of his red hair and the tide mark of his summer tan.

At the girls' entrance both men push their chairs back and stand up. The other man is taller than Matt, five or six years older, broader, with curly hair and shy eyes. He smiles at Jade. She smiles back.

'Hello Ryan,' she says.

JENNIFER'S HOUSE IS quiet and immaculately tidy. It is all gleaming glass and pristine white leather, the pale carpet is a spotless expanse, the kitchen work surfaces are bare of clutter. She has worked all day at it and sits at last as evening draws nigh with a glass of chardonnay in her hand while her Marks and Spencer's dinner for one heats through in the perfectly clean oven.

She ought to feel satisfied. She has attained just that glossy-magazine standard of bright, spare opulence. Her ornaments are few but tastefully chosen; her Lladró figurines, white as albumen, three ethnic bowls, a slab of slate, layers of iridescent mineral nuggets in a tall, slender crystal vase. Likewise her pictures are daubs and scribbles, supposed to be very good of their kind, their artists quite the thing. But they mean nothing to her, there is no association. It is not as though she chose them to remind her of a specific time or place. They represent no memory or person. She had chosen them with a shrewd eye to affect—purely to make a statement—from a warehouse full of similar artefacts. There is no emotional connection at all; no history, no narrative, no heart. And now she gazes around her she realises that the house is impersonal and cold, almost institutional. It is what she had thought she wanted, but now she has sloughed off the clinging vines that had felt so constricting she finds that her struggles have left her alone, unsupported and friendless.

It was something, she thinks now, to have been needed, after all.

Michael has gone. She does not know it for a fact but nonetheless she feels it is true. She has seen him a few times, busking in the town, hanging out at the refuge in Bridge Street, and, one day, sitting on the grass verge of the by-pass cradling an injured bird. She had pulled over into the next lay-by and walked back on the grass verge to where he sat. She had to stop and brace herself against the hot waft of passing lorries, close her eyes against the grit and fumes.

'It's been hit by a car,' he had said, holding his tiny, trembling burden up for her inspection. He had neither greeted her nor expressed any surprise or gladness at seeing her. Snowy—lying patiently at his side—had shown more pleasure, waving his feathered tail amongst the tall grass and vivid buttercups.

'Are you all right Michael?' she had asked, hunkering down at his side.

'It'll die soon,' he had replied.

'Where are you going?'

He had looked at her as though she had asked a question either too inane or too profound for reply. The traffic roared past them. She could feel its metallic heat, and the warmth emanating from the asphalt.

'There will be money, Michael, when everything's sorted out. Not a great deal, but enough to get you a place, somewhere cosy where you could settle. Would you like that?'

A convoy of touring motorbikes had passed them, gleaming and powerful, their riders anonymous in expensive leathers and capacious helmets. Michael had lifted his hand in greeting and they had waved oversized gauntleted hands in response.

'Do you know them?' she had asked.

'They're kindred,' he had replied cryptically.

The bird in his hand had gone still. Only its feathers were lifted by the swirling turbulence of traffic-torn air. Its eye was suddenly blank and dull. Michael had lifted his hand to his mouth and blown a gentle breath over the tiny, fragile body.

'What are you doing?'

'Setting its spirit free.' His eyes had followed something dancing in the space above his hand, flitting from side to side, swooping and diving through the dusty, irradiated air.

'Can you *see* it?' she had asked, squinting against the glare.

'Can't *you*?' he had replied, turning towards her.

The timer on the oven begins to ping and she lifts her meal out and spoons it onto a plate. She has set the table, as always, with a napkin and a glass of water. The patio doors are open to the last rays of evening sunshine. Everything outside is golden and bright; the annuals she has planted are coming on splendidly, filling the borders with colour. But somehow the light doesn't seem able to permeate the house. A monochrome filter blocks the summer hues and all that enters is a cold luminescence that falls on the pale furniture and smoky glass, the neutral carpet and the hard, cold artefacts. It emphasises all their uncompromising lines with a chilly touch. It reminds her of a mortuary, or a crypt. Glancing down at the cutlery in her hands she imagines herself in the role of mortician, standing over the cadaver of her marriage, her family. But then, with a sigh, she lays the utensils down and pushes her plate away.

'You're not the coroner,' she says aloud, into the empty house. 'You're the corpse.'

She goes upstairs, to a remote drawer in the corner of an inaccessible cupboard at the back of an unused room, and comes down with a box. She clears the mantel of its soulless, artistic ornaments and places there instead an old brass key dish and a shiny glazed squirrel with his slotted log, and two of the china dishes from her mother's dressing table. She places two photograph frames on the coffee table, removing the picture of herself and Kenny and replacing it with the wedding shot of her parents, solemn outside a country church. The other is a black and white studio shot of Michael. Finally, from the bottom of the box, she lifts the patchwork quilt and flings it over the back of the sofa where it settles into soft folds and exudes the evocative odour of old dog and fresh vegetables and mother and home.

It is getting dark. Soon she must put on the lights and draw the blinds. But for now she sits against the familiar patches of paisley and gingham and thinks, 'This is who I am.'

HE DRIVES HER a long way out of the town, along roads she has never travelled before, through villages unknown. The road snakes past fields and farms, through woods, over an unmanned level crossing and the hump-backed bridge of a canal. The day is very fine, dappled with sunshine. The sweet cottages with their burgeoning gardens, the glimpses of mirror-river, the grazing cattle and trundling tractors all seem to Jade like pictures off an old fashioned chocolate box.

'I can't believe you've never been up to the Ridge,' Ryan says, changing gear and taking a steep hill at a lick.

'I might have been, I suppose. But I don't remember it.'

'We came all the time, on school trips, and Mum and Dad would bring us up on Boxing Day, too. We'd bring sledges if it was snowy.'

'Families have different traditions for Boxing Day,' Jade says dryly. 'We generally spent the day snatching one another's toys and cheating at *Cluedo,* and arguing.'

He doesn't laugh. It is one of the things she likes about him. He sees through her facetiousness. 'That can't have been much fun,' he says.

Jade has never been courted as Ryan is courting her. He is as reticent and respectful as the hero of a 1940s classic. They have been to the cinema and out for a meal. On both occasions he had picked her up at home and driven her back again. There has been enough physical contact for her to be sure that he doesn't find her repulsive. He takes her hand when they cross the road, and helps her into her jacket, and opens the door and ushers her through with a hand to her back or shoulder. But he has not kissed her yet. She wonders if it is because of her connection with Richard. It would be foolhardy, she supposes, to jump the boss' sister-in-law too precipitately. His consideration and restraint have made her feel like an entirely different person, a far cry from the easy, inebriated grope she has been in the past. And far from making her feel that she must fill the gap between them with flirtatious advances or gambits designed to arouse and inflame, she is tempering her behaviour to his. She is letting things develop naturally and allowing him to set the pace.

Presently the landscape becomes more rugged and they are driving across heathery moorland. It is purple and pink and brown and green, pocked with black peat pits and white sheep. It slopes up to a ridge in the middle distance where tiny specs of people can be seen labouring up the narrow, twisting path. On the summit of the ridge is a square, castellated tower. The sky, arching overhead, is Wedgewood blue enamelled with perfect clouds.

'What's that?' Jade asks, pointing.

Just then they pull off the road into a rough square of car-park. 'It's the Cage; it's a folly,' Ryan tells her. And then, sensing that she doesn't know what he means, 'A folly is a building that serves no purpose at all but was just built because the land owner wanted it, for the view, or to prove he could afford it. The Cage has no windows or doors and no roof. It's just empty and useless. But it looks good, doesn't it, up there on the ridge?' He swivels round in his seat and points through the rear window. 'There's the house, down there, see? From those windows you can see there's a view along an avenue of lime trees that leads your eye up to the Cage.'

In the hollow behind them she can see a massive grey construction of myriad windows and sloping roofs, towers and turrets, pillars and porticoes.

'Who lives there?' she gasps.

'No one, now. We'll go afterwards, if you like. You can look inside and there's a gift shop and a café.'

He has forewarned her to bring sensible shoes and plenty of layers. When they climb out of the car the glorious sun is belied by a brisk, penetrating wind. She zips up her fleece and wriggles her hands up the sleeves against the cold. Ryan slips his arms into the straps of a back-pack.

'Come on,' he says. He holds out his hand. It is warm.

They follow a narrow track through the heather across the moor. Above them birds wheel and cry to the empty sky. The wind in the brittle, brushy heather makes an incessant rattling, rasping sound.

They don't talk much. Their proximity, the twin tramp of their feet on the path, the syncopation of their breathing, is communion enough for now. After a while they come to a high dry stone wall with an elaborate wooden stile over it. He helps her up first. From the top she looks back the way they have come. The car is a small reflective shard in the landscape. There isn't another solitary person in view but the two of them, alone on the vast, tufty moor. It stretches to the rim of the horizon in every direction, a topography of possibilities, of hopeful travel and happy arrivals. It buoys her up, the openness, the freedom, the promise of it.

'Why did you ...' she begins, 'why did you follow me that night?' She looks down on him from her higher step. The wind in her hair is giving it a life of its own. She tries to smooth it but it is a hopeless case. The cold is making her skin pink and her eyes bright. She shines down on him while she waits for his answer.

'I was ... I thought you might ...' he begins, his eyes not quite meeting hers. Then he gathers himself. 'You can't stand there looking as you do and expect me to answer such stupid questions,' he says. 'Now get on over the stile, woman.'

Beyond the wall, downhill to the left, there are woods. The heather gives way to bracken as they follow the path to the right, across the slope. Young trees have been protected with wire netting.

'The deer damage them,' Ryan explains, although she hasn't asked any question. 'We might see some.' It is more sheltered here and Jade begins to feel warm. She unzips her jacket a little. They walk for about half an hour, following a path that sometimes seems as random and wandering as an animal track and is in fact littered with rabbit and sheep droppings. It is easy walking, keeping broadly across the slope, but gently descending into a slight groin that dissects the hill. Presently he stops still and says, 'Listen!' She tilts her head, hears wind in the bracken and birds overhead and, distantly, the musical note of water.

'A stream?' she says.

'Yes! We're almost there.'

They are standing in the fold of the hill. In the downhill direction the land falls away quite steeply from their feet. The bracken is sparser here, replaced by a bright green spongy turf, bristling with marsh grass and occasionally treacherous with protruding buttresses of shale that could turn an ankle. Ryan wanders a little away from her, off the path, testing the ground. Then, with a cry, he calls her to him. She makes her tentative way. He has crossed a steep, slippery, crumbled shale pavement. At his feet, from nowhere, from nothing, a small stream spouts and cascades in experimental runnels down the hillside. They are hardly more than trickles, bluish and clear on the shale, too weak even to erode the turf. They find their way past stones and resolutely sprouting foliage, meandering, following the way of least resistance. As it falls the water gathers more to itself, a kind of natural magnetism, so that within twenty or thirty yards what has started as little more than a leak has become recognisable as a stream.

Ryan stands with his stoutly booted feet on either side of the seeping font. 'You know that river,' he says, 'the one that goes across that playing field near your house, past the factory, through the town and out past Richard's house ... The one Mikey fell into?'

'Yes.'

'This is the beginning of it, the source. Isn't it amazing? Come on over.'

Jade hesitates. 'It looks slippery.' She is only wearing trainers, with no ankle support, and they leak. She looks across at the spring; such small, inauspicious beginnings. 'How do you know? I didn't even know it was the same river!'

He smiles a little coyly. 'We studied it at school,' he admits. 'We came up here on field trips. It's a bit pathetic really. I am hoping to impress you with my best GCSE geography!'

'I'm easily impressed,' she says with a laugh.

'Are you?' He is suddenly serious. He steps back across the shale, holds out his hands and pulls her towards him, across the fledgling watercourse. It is an easy step, after all. It is only a matter of believing that there is something on the other side worth making the leap for. All at once she is in a new territory. Everything has changed. She is so close to him she can feel the warmth of his breath. His head blocks out the sun. Something in her groin moves with a delicious squirm and melts like a dribble of warm wax.

'I don't think you have any idea how beautiful you are,' he says in a whisper, his mouth in her hair. 'I haven't been able to think about anything but you for a single minute since I first saw you.'

It is so humbling, to be loved. Coiled in our shells of unworthiness, it is easier to believe that we are loved because of the goodness and forbearance of the lover, than that we are inherently, intrinsically lovable. Jade can only think of the way she had looked that night, her inappropriate, borrowed clothing, the sprinks and smears of spaghetti sauce, her sullen frown. And later, of the bloodied feet, gashed head and helpless hysterics. She shows, in her narrowed, sceptical eye and with the slight, cynical tilt of her head, that she doubts.

He sweeps her doubt away—he sweeps her away—with his kiss.

Acknowledgements

I wrote this book between 2007 and 2010 although I had had an embryonic idea of it for a long time before that. It was written between the UK and the US and I have Lois to thank, once again, for the use of her shady and comfortable porch in Doylestown PA where the extreme heat of the summer I spent there was a marvellous inspiration for the baking drought that forms the backdrop to the stories.

Sometime in 2008, I think, I visited an exhibition called 'Palimpsest' at the Kraal Centre, St Joseph's MI. The artist had re-used his canvasses, over-laying old sketches with new ones in such a way that the two informed, illuminated and enhanced each other. It was an idea that caught my imagination and the stories began to over-lay each other in my mind. As I wrote, my characters, settings and time-frames started to over-lap and develop associations I hadn't initially planned.

I'd like to thank my readers, who gave me helpful encouragement and insightful suggestions; Barbara, Sharon, Jo, Abby and Tim, who suffered me to read the manuscript aloud to him. My particular thanks go to Pauline Summerhayes, AE Walnofer and Sallianne Hines who all read the revised manuscript with great care and offered such helpful feedback.

Thank you to Mum (who declared herself 'gobsmacked' by the book— I didn't even know she had the word in her vocabulary) and Dad. It is a source of sorrow to me that my Dad got to the end of his story before I got to the end of mine: he never did find out how things turned out. His death wove itself into the fabric of the final draft.

Thank you to Tim, whose love, encouragement and steadfast support is a daily blessing. Dreams do come true.

Thank you so much for reading this book. As a self-published writer I don't have the backing of a marketing department behind me. I rely on my readers to spread the word about my books. If you have enjoyed this book please consider returning to the platform where you bought it to leave a short review along with your star rating. This means a great deal to me and helps other readers decide whether to give my book a try.

Please connect with me via my website at www.allie-cresswell.com or via Facebook.

Tall Chimneys

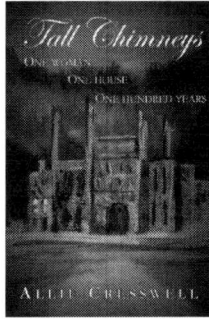

Winner of the prestigious One Stop Fiction Five Star Book Award and Silver Medallist in the Readers' Favourite Competition.

Considered a troublesome burden, Evelyn Talbot is banished by her family to their remote country house. Tall Chimneys is hidden in a damp and gloomy hollow. It is outmoded and inconvenient but Evelyn is determined to save it from the fate of so many stately homes at the time - abandonment or demolition.

Occasional echoes of tumult in the wider world reach their sequestered backwater - the strident cries of political extremists, a furore of royal scandal, rumblings of the European war machine. But their isolated spot seems largely untouched. At times life is hard - little more than survival. At times it feels enchanted, almost outside of time itself. The woman and the house shore each other up - until love comes calling, threatening to pull them asunder.

Her desertion will spell its demise, but saving Tall Chimneys could mean sacrificing her hope for happiness, even sacrificing herself.

A century later, a distant relative crosses the globe to find the house of his ancestors. What he finds in the strange depression of the moor could change the course of his life forever.

Also available as an audiobook

Relative Strangers

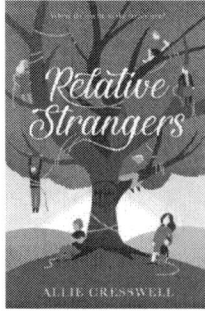

The McKay family gathers for a week-long holiday at a rambling old house to celebrate the fiftieth wedding anniversary of Robert and Mary. In recent years only funerals and sudden, severe illnesses have been able to draw them together and as they gather in the splendid rooms of Hunting Manor, their differences are soon uncomfortably apparent.

For all their history, their traditions, the connective strands of DNA, they are relative strangers.

There are truths unspoken, but the question emerges: how much truth can a family really stand?

The old, the young, the disaffected and the dispossessed, relatives both estranged and deranged struggle to find a hand-hold amongst the branches of the family tree.

What, they ask themselves, does it really *mean* to be 'family'?

Also available as an audiobook.

The Hoarder's Widow

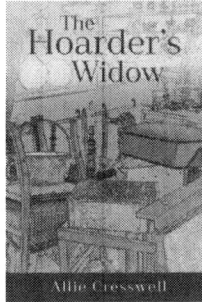

Suddenly-widowed Maisie sets out to clear her late husband's collection; wonky furniture and balding rugs, bolts of material for upholstery projects he never got round to, other people's junk brought home from car boot sales and rescued from the tip. The hoard is endless, stacked into every room in the house, teetering in piles along the landing and forming a scree up the stairs. It is all part of Clifford's waste-not way of thinking in which everything, no matter how broken or obscure, can be re-cycled or re-purposed into something useful or, if kept long enough, will one day be valuable. He had believed in his vision as ardently as any mystic in his holy revelation but now, without the clear projection of his vision to light them up for her as what they *would be*, they appear to Maisie more grimly than ever as what they *are*: junk.

As Maisie disassembles his stash she is forced to confront the issues that drove her husband to squirrel away other people's trash; after all, she knows virtually nothing about his life before they met. Finally, in the last bastion of his accumulation, she discovers the key to his hoarding and understands—much too late—the man she married.

Then, with empty rooms in a house that is too big for her, she must ask herself: what next?

The Widow's Mite

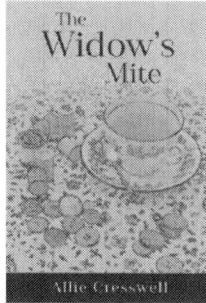

Minnie Price married late in life. Now she is widowed. And starving. No one suspects this respectable church-goer can barely keep body and soul together. Why would they, while she resides in the magnificent home she shared with Peter?

Her friends and neighbours are oblivious to her plight and her adult step-children have their own reasons to make things worse rather than better. But she is thrown a lifeline when an associate of her late husband arrives with news of an investment about which her step-children know nothing.

Can she release the funds before she finds herself homeless and destitute?

Fans of 'The Hoarder's Widow' will enjoy this sequel, but it reads equally well as a standalone.

Printed in Great Britain
by Amazon

68925307R00369